D0251539

NO LONGER PROPERTY OF
THE SEATTLE PUBLIC LIBRARY

THE

RIGHTFUL

QUEEN

ALSO BY ISABELLE STEIGER

The Empire's Ghost

THE
RIGHTFUL
QUEEN

Book Two of the Paths of Lantistyne

———————— ⚜ ————————

ISABELLE STEIGER

ST. MARTIN'S
PRESS
NEW YORK

This is a work of fiction. All of the characters, organizations, and events portrayed in this novel are either products of the author's imagination or are used fictitiously.

First published in the United States by St. Martin's Press, an imprint of St. Martin's Publishing Group

THE RIGHTFUL QUEEN. Copyright © 2020 by Isabelle Steiger. All rights reserved. Printed in the United States of America. For information, address St. Martin's Press, 120 Broadway, New York, NY 10271.

www.stmartins.com

The Library of Congress Cataloging-in-Publication Data is available upon request.

ISBN 978-1-250-08850-5 (hardcover)
ISBN 978-1-250-08851-2 (ebook)

Our books may be purchased in bulk for promotional, educational, or business use. Please contact your local bookseller or the Macmillan Corporate and Premium Sales Department at 1-800-221-7945, extension 5442, or by email at MacmillanSpecialMarkets@macmillan.com.

First Edition: 2020

10 9 8 7 6 5 4 3 2 1

Dramatis Personae

ADORA AVESTRI: Second child of Jotun Avestri and Maribel Hahrenraith. Self-styled princess regent of Issamira.

ALESSA: Kelken IV's older half-sister. Illegitimate.

AMALI SELRESHE: Wife of Dahren Selreshe and mother to Jocelyn. A skilled archer and hero of the war against Gerde Selte of Hallarnon.

ANDREW RYKER: The rentholder of White Eagle Roost, one of the largest castles in Esthrades.

ARIANROD MARGRAINE: Marquise of Esthrades. A powerful mage, though she strives to keep that hidden.

AZEL: A young Issamiri guardsman who often accompanies Hephestion.

BENWICK: A veteran guardsman at Stonespire Hall.

BRADDOCK: A Hallern army deserter and former mercenary. Companion to Morgan Imrick.

CADFAEL: A former arena fighter and soldier of King Eira's. Bears a scar on his face from a near-fatal wound inflicted by Talis. Brother to Rhia.

CAIUS MARGRAINE: Arianrod's father and the previous marquis of Esthrades. Died of illness.

CERISE: Marceline's older half-sister. A grocer's apprentice.

DAHREN SELRESHE: One of the foremost lords of Issamira. Husband of Amali and father to Jocelyn.

DAVEN MARGRAINE THE SIXTH: Direct ancestor of Arianrod Margraine. Allied with Talia Avestri against the Elesthenian Empire.

DAVEN MARGRAINE THE ELEVENTH: Arianrod's grandfather and a former marquis of Esthrades.

DEINOL: Bastard-born bandit. Partners with Lucius. Friend of Morgan, Roger, and Seth.

DENTON "DENT" HALLEY: Guardsman serving Arianrod Margraine. Her longtime favorite and confidant.

DIRK: One of Kelken IV's most trusted retainers. Has attended Kel personally for many years, and often takes a more casual tone with him.

EDITH SELWYN: Administrator of Lanvaldis for Imperator Elgar. A common-born scholar.

EIRA BRIONEL: King of Lanvaldis. Killed by Shinsei in the conquest of Araveil. Never married or sired children.

EIRNWIN: Advisor to Kelken III and Kelken IV.

ELGAR: Imperator of Hallarnon, Aurnis, and Lanvaldis. A mage skilled in enchantments.

ELIN MARGRAINE: Born Elin Vandrith. A noblewoman of Lanvaldis. Mother to Arianrod Margraine. Died in childbirth.

GERDE SELTE: Tyrannical grand duchess of Hallarnon, fond of torture and bloodshed. Died of illness. Succeeded by Norverian.

GHILAN: Former arena fighter. Currently serving Edith Selwyn of Lanvaldis.

GRAVIS INGRET: Captain of the guard at Stonespire Hall under both Arianrod Margraine and her father, Caius.

GREGG: Guardsman at Stonespire Hall. Famously stolid and incurious.

HAYNE: One of Kelken IV's most trusted retainers. Protected him from an assassination attempt in his early childhood.

HEPHESTION AVESTRI: Youngest child of Jotun Avestri and Maribel Hahrenraith. Prince of Issamira. Called "Feste" by his family.

HERREN: One of Kelken IV's most trusted retainers. Killed during the journey from Second Hearth to Mist's Edge.

HYWEL MARKHAM: Younger brother of Laen Markham and legitimized nephew of King Eira.

ILYN HOLM: Young guardswoman protecting Laen and Hywel.

IRJAN FIRESTARTER: A folk hero in Issamiri history. The first of many such heroes to bear that name.

IRJAN TAL: A ranger on the Gods' Curse. Assisted Morgan and Braddock in their crossing.

IRUZU SERENIN: Former king of Aurnis. Grandfather to Ryo. Reinstituted the rank of *shinrian* that had been outlawed by his grandmother, but decreed that it should no longer be awarded solely to men.

ITHAN VANDRITH: A Lanvaldian nobleman. The youngest son of a youngest son. A skilled swordsman. Cousin to Arianrod Margraine.

JILL BRIDGER: Guardswoman patrolling the city of Stonespire. Recruited by and protégée of Denton Halley.

JOCELYN SELRESHE: An Issamiri noblewoman from a distinguished family. Suitor to Hephestion.

JOTUN AVESTRI: Previous king of Issamira. Father to Landon, Adora, and Hephestion. Fatally injured when his horse threw him during a celebratory procession.

KELKEN RAYL III: Previous king of Reglay and father to Kelken IV. Assassinated by Shinsei.

KELKEN RAYL IV: Current king of Reglay. A boy of eleven. Can walk with the assistance of crutches, but only for brief periods and with difficulty.

LAEN MARKHAM: Legitimized nephew of King Eira and current heir to the throne of Lanvaldis.

LANDON AVESTRI: Oldest child of Jotun Avestri and Maribel Hahrenraith. Crown prince of Issamira. Long missing, and suspected dead by many.

LARS EURIG: An Esthradian rentholder in league with Andrew Ryker.

LIRIEN ARVEL: A wandering peasant from southwestern Hallarnon.

LUCIUS AQUILA: A *shinrian* who fled Aurnis after its conquest and currently lives in Valyanrend. Works as a bandit alongside Deinol.

MARCELINE: A bastard child, orphan, and skilled pickpocket living in Valyanrend's Sheath Alleys. Raised by Tom Kratchet.

MARIBEL AVESTRI: Born Maribel Hahrenraith. Wife of Jotun Avestri. Officially retains the title of queen pending the coronation of her daughter, Adora.

MIKEN: A *wardrenfell*: a human who is not born a mage, but who comes to be inhabited by stray magic that is powerful but almost always limited in scope. Possessed control over earth. Accidentally tortured to death by Elgar's men.

MORGAN IMRICK: Owner and proprietor of the Dragon's Head tavern in Valyanrend's Sheath Alleys. Friend of Roger, Deinol, and Lucius, companion to Braddock, and Seth's employer.

MOUSE: Sobriquet of Zackary Smith, the leader of the largest resistance group in Valyanrend. Nominally an apprentice smith.

NAISHE: An archer, hunter, and member of Mouse's resistance. Of Akozuchen descent, through both parents.

NASSER KADIFE: An old friend of Braddock's. A mercenary and talented archer.

NATHANIEL WYLES: Former captain of the guard in Valyanrend. Killed by Arianrod's magic when he sought to take her captive.

NORVERIAN: Gerde Selte's favorite companion and immediate successor. Incompetent and wasteful. Killed and replaced by Elgar.

QUENTIN GARDENER: Captain of the guard at Valyanrend's Citadel.

RASK: A member of Valyanrend's resistance and its most talented swordsman.

RHIA: Cadfael's sister and a refugee from Lanvaldis. Serving Adora as captain of the guard in Eldren Cael.

RITSU HANAE: A young Aurnian swordsman. Compelled by Elgar's magic to believe he is Shinsei, an unquestioning and indefatigable servant of the imperator. Possessed of an enchanted sword that increases his physical abilities but also perpetuates his loss of memory.

ROGER HALFEN: An exceptional swindler and thief, from a long line of famous swindlers and thieves. Friend of Morgan, Lucius, Deinol, and Seth. Half-unwilling mentor to Marceline.

RYAM OSWHENT: Varalen's young son, and Elgar's hostage to assure his father's compliance. Afflicted with the great wasting illness.

RYO SERENIN: Prince of Aurnis. A *shinrian* whose swordplay equaled that of any in his royal guard.

SEBASTIAN: Ritsu's closest friend. His fate has been hidden from Ritsu's memory.

SEREN ALMASY: Arianrod Margraine's bodyguard. A fighter of formidable skill who specializes in knives. Born in Esthrades, but spent half her life in the Sahaian Empire.

SETH: Morgan's kitchen boy. Killed trying to help an injured Seren.

SHINSEI: see *Ritsu Hanae*

SIX-FINGERED PECK: A seller of medicines at Valyanrend's Night Market. Loosely entangled with the resistance.

TALIA AVESTRI: Issamira's Rebel Queen and founder of House Avestri. Drove the Elesthenian Empire out of Issamira.

TALIA PARNELL: Member of Valyanrend's resistance. Reports to Rask.

TALIS: A *wardrenfell* with control over wind. A peasant from the mountains of southeastern Lanvaldis.

TOM KRATCHET: A thief and information broker. Raised Marceline after the death of her mother.

VARALEN OSWHENT: Elgar's chief strategist, unwillingly recruited. Rose to prominence after advising King Eira's soldiers during their war with Caius Margraine.

VERRANE: Nurse and caretaker to Caius and Arianrod Margraine.

VESPAS HAHRENRAITH: Younger brother of Maribel Avestri. A former general of great renown, and the current lord of Shallowsend.

VOLTEST: A *wardrenfell* with control over fire. An Aurnian scholar who was held in captivity after Aurnis's fall.

WREN FLETCHER: Mouse's childhood friend and subordinate in Valyanrend's resistance. A skilled fletcher.

ZACKARY SMITH: see *Mouse*

ZARA SHING: Esthradian healer of Sahaian descent. Educated in the medical arts in Sahai.

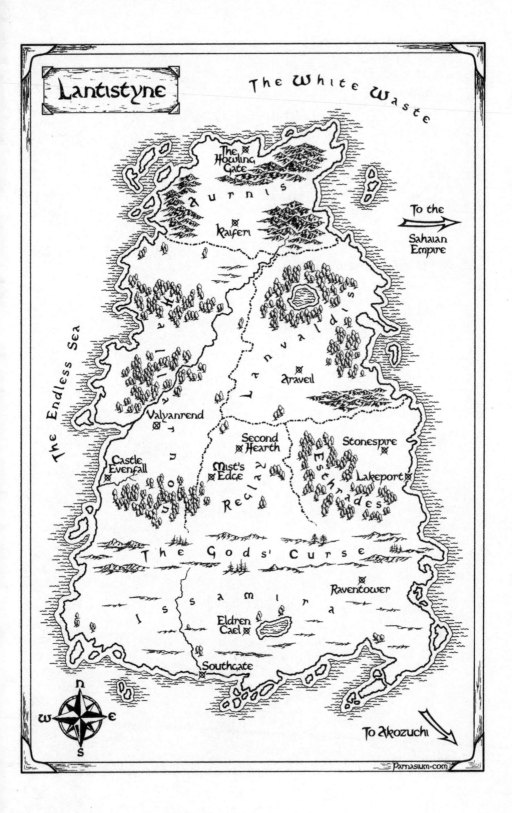

THE

RIGHTFUL

QUEEN

CHAPTER ONE

Lanvaldis

THERE WERE TIMES when Talis would see his face in her mind's eye—his face as it had been, before she had changed it. It was strange, and more than a little annoying. She was not one to take any note of faces, least of all those of people she'd killed.

Still, his persisted. She had never learned his name, but his face was clear in her memory. The perfectly proportioned nose, the high cheekbones, the elegant jaw—and those eyes, blue and blue and blue, no matter how much light or shadow fell on them. It was a face with all the outward markers of beauty, but it had never fooled her, not even from the first. She had seen past it to the emptiness behind his eyes, the way his gaze fell on her without interest or empathy. To him she was no different from the grass they stood on or the sky overhead: an inanimate background to whatever world he lived in.

But not at the end. He had seen her, truly seen her, at the end. Perhaps that was what kept bothering her about him. It was unfair, she had thought even then. He was a man who had intended her only ill, who would have subdued her if he could have. It was unfair of him to look so lost at the end, like an innocent child.

Things were less than ideal in many ways. The wind was picking up, worrying at the edges of her consciousness with its vague whistle. It prickled at the back of her neck, made the skin of her arms clammy and cold. She had too much of Voltest's influence with her today, making her irritable and on edge, too quick to startle, too quick to take offense. She could feel it lurking there, that anger, biding its time like a hunter in the brush. All it needed was a target.

Damn that man and his stupid face! She still couldn't tell whether the persistence of that memory was the cause of this skittish anxiety or a result of it, but still it lingered, floating behind her eyelids as she picked her way forward in the deepening dusk.

If I trip because of him, she thought, *I'd kill him twice.*

The path wound around the side of what could only be charitably called a mountain; the terrain was rocky and treacherous, but the summit was fairly low, only twenty or thirty feet above her. She'd walked it countless times before: it led south, through Cutter's Vale, which was usually the most deserted crossing between Lanvaldis (she wouldn't call it Hallarnon, whatever the maps said) and Esthrades. Though the overcast sky and the fading light made for poor visibility, she could just make out the vale far below to her left, a brief reprieve of flat land before you had to walk up into the hills again. There seemed to be more people passing through than usual, though Talis couldn't think why.

She had been born and raised in Lanvaldis, and though she would never have called herself King Eira's most loyal subject, she had an attachment to this country—stubborn and possessive more than affectionate, but there it was. It burned her to know her country had fallen under Elgar's sway, that, despite their power, she and Voltest had not been able to stall his plans to their satisfaction. Worse, the hesitation that had plagued Elgar after the Lanvaldian war seemed finally to have left him: Voltest was certain he would move imminently to conquer Reglay, and Voltest's information was never wrong. That left only Esthrades and Issamira free and clear of him, so to Esthrades Talis went. Perhaps there, in a country ruled by a rumored sorceress, she would find something more promising.

She was able to overtake most of the travelers in her way, silent stragglers fighting their way onward in ones and twos. But when she tried to pass a particularly weary-looking one, a slender boy struggling with a heavy satchel, she realized he was actually the slowest member of a group of three. The other two fanned outward, making it difficult for her to get past them, and she swallowed her irritation. She knew she wasn't really angry at *them*.

Their leader, a blond fellow who looked about eighteen or nineteen, called back to the boy with the satchel—a year or two younger than he was, with a long braid of hair so pale it was almost white. "You all right, Hywel? We're almost to the border."

The boy was breathing hard, but he drew himself up bravely. "I'm all right. Like you said, not long now."

"We'll make camp once we're well across. But let me know if you need me to take a few more of them. I doubt her ladyship will care who—"

He shut his mouth when the only woman in the group jerked her head hard at Talis, and then all three of them were looking at her. The woman's brown hair was cut short in back, but her bangs had been swept to either side and allowed to grow nearly to her chin. She tugged on them with one hand as she addressed the leader: "Seems she's trying to get past." Her point wasn't politeness, of course, but a desire to get Talis out of their midst.

The leader laughed. "You're in quite a hurry."

He hadn't meant it to sound condescending, Talis told herself, soothing the fire in the pit of her stomach. "There's nowhere I need to be. I simply walk quickly." She brushed past them, heading down the slope—and stopped, because she could finally make out the reason for the clogged foot traffic through the vale. There were soldiers down there, clad in the crestless blue-black that marked them out as Imperator Elgar's men. The travelers ahead of them had been slowed down by the soldiers' importunement, and they'd clustered up as they waited to pass through.

The group of three drew abreast of her again, and then they stopped, too. *"Fuck,"* the woman muttered, echoing Talis's thoughts perfectly.

Their leader had caught his breath, but he set his shoulders confidently. "It'll be all right. We've come so far, and after this it's easy."

"We could still turn back," the woman said.

"And go where? If there are soldiers even here, they're probably being pretty thorough. We have to cross somewhere."

Talis didn't precisely have to cross anywhere: her plans had not been so definite that she couldn't turn around, or seek out Voltest again. But she had decided to go to Esthrades, and she saw no reason to change her mind simply because a group of annoying soldiers had gathered. She was no stranger to unpleasant emotions: she knew anger well, and bitterness, and sadness in a thousand varieties. But she had stopped needing to feel fear years ago. Or, at least, she had stopped needing to be afraid of other people.

She left the others in an indecisive huddle and walked down the slope, falling in behind a tall man carrying a heavy pack and an adolescent boy who was probably his son. She waited while the soldiers asked the two of them question after question—their names, their hometown, what their route had been thus far and what it would be henceforward. By the time they were finally allowed to pass, she had fully prepared herself to withstand her own interrogation, forcing the echoes of Voltest's anger into the furthest recesses of her mind. But the closest soldier took one look at her and waved her through, without so much as a word.

"Just like that?" Talis couldn't help asking.

"Just like that," he agreed. "Unless there are any crimes you'd like to confess?"

If she'd cared to, she could have confessed enough crimes to drive that smug expression off his face. She ran through a silent inventory: unlawful destruction of property; theft, if you defined it loosely; sedition, definitely—any discerning judge would probably go as far as treason. And then there were all the murders, of course.

"Nothing at the moment," she told the soldier sweetly, and brushed past him when he stepped aside.

That might have been it, on a different day, and she couldn't have said why it wasn't. Perhaps it was that the wind kept getting stronger, tugging fretfully at her hair. Perhaps it was that after so long without human company, getting pulled into something even briefly couldn't help but stir her curiosity. But whatever the reason, just as she was about to leave the border crossing behind, Talis turned around to take one last look at the group that had been behind her.

She was just in time to see the soldiers leading them off into the trees.

Talis almost kept walking. But though she could ignore the little group, she couldn't bring herself to ignore the soldiers. They were Elgar's men, and if they had taken these people, no doubt they perceived some advantage would come to their master because of it. To question them, to imprison them, even merely to kill them, might bring Elgar some measure of satisfaction when he heard of it.

She couldn't allow that.

She let herself sigh once, because she just *knew* this was going to become a headache of outrageous proportions. And then she made sure no one was looking, and turned off the road into the trees.

Walking quietly was easy; the wind was howling by then, much louder than any noise she made among the fallen leaves. She stopped when the three of them came into view, surrounded by half a dozen soldiers. She didn't think it was meant to be an execution: one of the soldiers was in the process of tying the leader's arms behind his back, and though the others had all drawn their swords they seemed content merely to hold the other two in place. *They* both carried swords at the hip as well, and they seemed to be debating whether it was worth reaching for them—though the boy with the braid was shaking so badly he'd probably drop his getting it out of the sheath. She should step in before any sort of fight could break out—that would just be more chaos that she didn't need.

The problem was, if Talis used too much unnecessary violence, she'd have to worry about more than Voltest: *she* would dig her claws in. She knew how it went by now: distaste building up, clinging to her like tar, until before long she was too upset to continue, bile rising in the back of her throat.

Unless, of course, the violence became *necessary* violence.

"So this is what you were looking for?" she asked the assembled guards. She didn't even have to raise her voice; the wind carried her words straight to them. "I can't say I was overly impressed with them myself, but no doubt you have your reasons."

They shifted only half their attention her way, wary of taking their eyes off the group. "What's your business here?" one of them asked—he couldn't keep the confusion out of his voice, and Talis couldn't blame him.

"I'm still figuring that out, to be honest," she said. "But this is what I *can* tell you: I need you all to drop your weapons, immediately, and entrust your prisoners there to my keeping. If you do that, I promise I'll allow you to return to your comrades at the crossing."

They just stared at her.

"If you don't put your weapons down, however," Talis continued, "you're all going to die. I don't mean *probably,* I mean you will all absolutely, inevitably perish if you try to fight me. You'll die before you can even reach me." She folded her arms. "It's your decision. But whatever else happens, you can't say I didn't tell you the truth."

Even the group of three was staring at her now, but Talis had no eyes for them, only for the soldiers. They were all still standing there, frozen. "Make up your minds," she told them. "Put your weapons down, or try to hit me."

It probably couldn't have been helped, even if she'd been truly earnest about trying to dissuade them. She knew what she must look like to them: a single woman, unarmed, of unremarkable height and build. She knew their pride would demand that they not turn tail and run in the face of an unsupported bluff. She saw them nod at each other, determining which one of them would make a move toward her. And she saw him move—warily, not at a run, but he wouldn't have reached her even if he had sprinted.

She couldn't even really say it was a pity; if she was honest with herself, she preferred it this way. But she was fighting for her life now, and that meant she should be able to do as she liked without any interference.

So she let the wind go.

The man who had started to move toward her was flung backward and off his feet; he crashed into a tree, and there was a piercing crack as it shuddered from the impact, as his bones splintered. Of the five behind, the three closest were caught up as well: two merely hit the ground hard, but the third was ripped apart, an arm and a leg sundered from his torso completely. The last two were running toward her, and Talis took a moment to grudgingly admire their bravery before she caught them up, lifting them higher and higher until she could drop them screaming to the earth and let it do the rest.

Two left. One was just staring, shaking, but the other tightened his grip on his sword, sighted determinedly down its blade at her. Talis suddenly remembered that man doing the same thing, that brilliant sword of his catching the morning light, and she lashed out angrily, letting the wind carve a line down the soldier's arm. It tore through leather and skin, blood welling up in the cut.

The soldier barely had time to wince before she cut him again, carving out gashes in his thigh, his shoulder, between his ribs. She sliced across his forehead, cut both ankles down to the bone. And when he fell to his knees, defeated, she drew one last line across his throat.

A noise drew her attention; the last man had dropped his sword. He backed away from it, hands outstretched. "I'm sorry," he said, "I'm so sorry, I didn't know. Please, I—I'll go. I promise I'll go, and never bother you—I swear . . ."

Talis considered it. The corners of her mind were pulling frantically in opposite directions, but she'd been expecting that. Though the tension gave her a hell of a headache, she was able to carve out enough of a space in the middle to gather her own thoughts—or at least the thoughts she was fairly certain were hers. She hadn't said there was any time limit on the offer to lay their weapons down, had she? Perhaps it had been unrealistic to ask them to surrender without any proof. And it wasn't as if she had to fear that he wouldn't keep his word—what did it really matter?

For the first time since she'd faced them, she unfolded her arms, letting them drop to her sides. "All right," she said. "If you'll just leave this lot alone—"

She was interrupted by the sliding sound of wet metal, and a bloody sword-point burst out of the man's throat. It was withdrawn by the woman with the short brown hair, who had stabbed him from behind. She stepped away from him as he fell, and wiped her sword on the bottom of her trouser leg.

The unexpected shock of having her wishes disobeyed stunned Talis for a moment, and then her anger spiked. "What the hell do you think you're doing?" she snapped at the woman. "I told him he could leave!"

"Well, I couldn't let him," the woman said. "He would've told all his friends back there. He might've had as many as fifty men after us."

"I could've killed fifty! I could've killed *hundreds*!"

The woman shrugged, but her eyes were hard. "Then say instead that I preferred to kill one, rather than to have to watch you kill hundreds."

"You preferred? *You* preferred?" The rage was like falling, flailing ineffectually for a handhold and finding nothing. She drew a slash across the fingers of the woman's hand, deep enough to make her drop the sword; the bitch was lucky Talis hadn't sliced them clean off. She hissed through her teeth, and clutched the wounded hand as the blood welled up. "I'm not here to *work* with you," Talis said. "I'm not here to *help*. I only wanted to get rid of them, and if you interfere with me again I'll—"

The woman was inching toward her sword, but the leader stopped her with a gesture, cutting the air, his palm out flat. "Ilyn, enough. Fighting her would be useless." He stared at Talis. "What do you want from us, then?"

"That depends," Talis said. "Who are you, and why did you come this way?"

The leader fell silent, staring at his boots. Neither of the others made any move to speak.

"I don't intend to ask you again," Talis said. "And you had better tell me the truth. I promise you, the only thing I'm better at than killing people is holding a grudge, and your friend over there has gotten me halfway to a new one already."

Still the young man said nothing, his face frozen in a scowl of indecision. And then, unexpectedly, the boy with the braid stepped forward. "I'm going to tell her, Laen," he said. Then, to her, "What I'm going to say is true, but . . . it may sound unbelievable."

"I can tear people into pieces with my mind," Talis said. "Try me."

The boy nodded. "I was born Hywel Markham," he said. "This is my brother, Laen. We were approached, sometime before the war with Hallarnon started . . . well, we were approached by the king. By King Eira, I mean."

Talis frowned; King Eira, though long dead, was a prime example of just how long-lived her grudges could be. But she said only, "Continue."

Hywel swallowed. "The king came to our home—in secret, without any of his men. He told us that we were his kin. Our mother was born a bastard, and never knew her father. But Eira knew him, because it was his father, too."

"Eira had kept it to himself, to protect him and our mother both," Laen continued. "But he didn't have an heir, and he was old, and there was a war on. He didn't know what was going to happen to him. So he legitimized our mother, and gave her the papers to prove it—so his line would continue, even if he died."

Shit. A king could legitimize a bastard, true, but it was such a contentious practice it didn't happen often. Still, if she'd been Eira, she would have done the same thing—create a thorn in her enemy's side that would prick him even after she was gone. "So you're telling me your mother's the next in line. Your mother's the rightful queen of Lanvaldis?"

The brothers looked at each other. "Well . . . not exactly," Hywel said. "She *was* the rightful queen, but she's . . . gone now."

Talis stared incredulously at Laen. "So it's you. *You're* what we have? You or Elgar?"

He reddened. "Look, you asked us to tell you, and we told you! What more do you want?"

"You've only told me half," Talis corrected him. "What is the rightful king of Lanvaldis doing *here*?"

Laen stood up straight. "We did things Mother's way when she was alive. She thought it would only get us all killed to press her claim, so we kept it quiet. But after she died . . . we just couldn't stand it anymore, hiding away while Elgar's people did what they liked. We talked it over, and, well . . ."

Talis rolled her eyes. "You decided to pursue your throne—purely out of the love of justice and the goodness of your heart, I'm sure."

He scowled. "Look, if it'd been someone else, I'd fight for their right instead! I'd fight for Hywel, or anyone, just as long as they're not Elgar! We have to throw him out. We have to take Lanvaldis back." He paused, and took a breath. "So that's what we're doing here. Eira—our uncle—told some select members of his guard the truth before he died, and we were able to make contact with them. They got a letter to Arianrod Margraine for us, and she agreed to help—at a price, but that's about what you'd expect, right? There were more guards with us when we set out for the border, but Elgar's people must have gotten wind of something. We were attacked, and the rest of them . . . they secured our escape. Ilyn's the only one left."

Talis looked at the woman with new eyes, and saw that she was hardly any older than her charges. She must have been the greenest member, the runt, sent off with the lordlings more to protect her than so she could protect them.

"You mentioned a price," she said.

Laen tapped his pack. "We're each carrying three *very* thick books, pilfered from the royal archives in Araveil. The price the marquise demanded, in exchange for her help. And yes, she did specify the titles. It was hell to get ahold of them, I'll tell you that."

"So you're taking them to Stonespire Hall."

"That's right."

"And after that?"

"I don't know," Laen said. "That depends on what kind of help the marquise is willing to offer. It may be she merely shelters us until we figure out how to return, or she may have a plan to help us fight Elgar's people in Lanvaldis. They do say she's very clever."

Talis didn't doubt it, but her mind was already elsewhere—she had run out of questions to ask them, and now she had to make a choice. But headache though it would certainly be, if she was honest with herself, she had to admit she already knew what it was.

They certainly seemed pathetic enough. But even if all they did was fail and die, the failing and the dying would still take time. Time that she and Voltest could use.

"There's something you should know," she said to the brothers. "I hated your uncle."

Laen merely stared at her. But Hywel asked, "Why?"

"He found out about me. He had . . . plans. Needless to say, they didn't quite go as he intended."

Hywel bowed his head. "Then the fault is his, and we can only apologize for it."

Laen hesitated longer, but he finally nodded. "Aye, Hywel's right. It was his fault, not yours. And not ours, either."

"Even if it had been," Talis said, "you're in luck. There's one person I hate more than your uncle—one person I hate more than anyone. And that's Elgar."

"And . . . why do you hate Elgar?" Hywel asked—more hesitantly, as if he sensed this was a more painful subject.

"He had plans, too," Talis said. "But I wasn't the one he found." When the rest of them said nothing, she turned away, waving a hand in the direction of the road. "Come on. I'll protect you until you get to Stonespire. Least I can do to help Elgar's plans go awry."

She waited to see if they would protest, but none were forthcoming. Then, right as she was about to start walking, Hywel asked, "Ah . . . I hope you won't find it impertinent, but could I possibly ask you to heal Ilyn's fingers? It'll be difficult for her to hold her sword like this, and I'm sure it's painful."

Talis glanced at Ilyn, who was cradling her newly bound-up hand in the other. She merely glared back, and Talis turned to Hywel. "I can't heal," she said.

Hywel looked confused. "You can't? But I thought mages could do that."

Mages. All four of them had thought they were mages, at first. They'd heard the stories, of course—that magic was something the chosen few had from birth. But they'd just thought that it had been dormant in them somehow, that a sudden shock had unleashed it. How else could they possibly explain it?

But Voltest was the most learned of them all, and Voltest had told them the truth. *I've done as much research as I could,* he had said. *There's no denying it—there are too many discrepancies between our experience and that of mages, even the most unusual ones. We are something else. But I promise you, I will find out what.*

"Perhaps mages can," she said to Hywel, "but I can't. She'll just have to care for it in the ordinary way." She finally started walking. "Are you coming?"

As they fell in behind her, Talis put a hand to her neck, tracing the end of the silver chain that held the pendant beneath her shirt. It had been the four of them, that day.

It would never be the four of them again.

Chapter Two

Reglay

Lucius Aquila, if that was indeed his real name, was proving to be so annoyingly nosy and so impossibly persistent that Cadfael was beginning to regret they hadn't killed each other. Short of drawing his weapon again, he had no idea how to get the man to leave: threats had always been a crucial staple of his conversational repertoire, but attempting to use them on someone who'd just fought him to a draw would only make him look pathetic. "Look," he finally said, "I probably can't stop you from following me if you've set your mind to it. But there has to be something more worthwhile for you to do than this."

"Who said I was following you?" Lucius shrugged, the movement shifting his long hair over his shoulder. "Maybe we're just going in the same direction."

Struggling through a forest with only the barest idea of a path to guide them? Not likely. "You don't even know where I'm headed."

"Aye, but you don't know where *I'm* headed, do you?"

"I know you want me to ask you," Cadfael said, "so just go ahead and tell me."

Lucius tapped his fingers against the hilt of his sword. "Well. I suppose I don't have a *precise* destination. As I told you, I'm looking for my friends. They will *probably* be in Esthrades—unless the person *they're* looking for has left Esthrades, in which case they will probably be on her trail, wherever that leads."

"Then you'd do better to just follow this woman, wouldn't you?" Cadfael asked, in spite of himself. "If you find her, your friends will find you."

Lucius smiled. "No, because I'd really rather not find her—it will be best if none of us do. That's the surest way for us to stay alive."

"Does she have some grudge against you?"

"No, they're the ones with the grudge, she's just a better fighter. By a great deal, I fear." He tilted his head. "You ask a lot of questions for someone who wasn't interested in talking."

Cadfael gave a self-deprecating laugh. "Searching for people and getting revenge are two of my interests. I don't have many, so I've got to indulge the few I do possess."

"Oh? And who are you searching for?"

Well, and why not tell him, really? What would it matter? "He calls himself Shinsei. One of your people, if the rumors are true."

Lucius stiffened. "The man called Shinsei may be Aurnian in appearance, but he betrayed his people forever the day he joined Elgar's army. He is no countryman of mine."

"But was he born in Aurnis?" Cadfael asked. "Did anyone know of him, before he joined Elgar?"

"I couldn't say. But I knew all the greatest swordsmen in Aurnis, and I can promise you he was not among them. If he ever lived there, he kept his skills to himself."

"You knew *all* the greatest swordsmen in Aurnis? Surely not."

Lucius laughed. "You doubt me? Aurnis is a small country, and we prize our warriors highly. The queen's *kaishinrian*—her royal guard—were the greatest to be found at the time they were chosen, but they served her for twenty-five years, and could not help but grow somewhat rustier in that time. It was her son's *kaishinrian* who were the best warriors in Aurnis when I lived there." There had been fond remembrance in his face, but it faded, leaving only the sense of loss. "They died protecting their prince, as was their purpose. And no swordsman who could not defeat them could possibly deserve to be called godlike."

"But you must have held your own against them," Cadfael said. "If not more than that."

Lucius's expression slammed abruptly shut. "I'll ask you not to dishonor the dead by claiming I could be their equal."

"Come on. I'm sure you challenged them all at least once—it's clear that skill is important to you, or you wouldn't still be talking to me just because we had a rather strenuous duel. After seeing you fight, I can't believe there's anyone who could have outclassed you so completely."

Lucius hesitated, as if turning several answers over in his mind. Well, if he was determined to lie, it wasn't as if Cadfael really cared. But finally Lucius said, "I sparred with all of them, many times. And defeated them all at least once, though I also lost to all of them—often rather frequently. But it would take more than that to make me their equal."

"No," Cadfael said. "That's all it takes, trust me. The rest of it is . . . gloss. It just falls away."

Lucius's mouth remained a thin line, but his sadness showed through in his eyes; Cadfael could tell he wanted to argue, but not whether he actually believed whatever he wanted to say. Cadfael had known so many people who *spoke* of high ideals, not hypocritically but because they believed speaking of them could change the world enough to make them true.

But not Rhia. His sister had always believed everything she said, even the most naïve, tenderhearted sentiment. That just made it so much worse.

Perhaps he had revealed something in his own expression, because he realized Lucius was watching him closely. But he only said, "Well. Perhaps it is better if we keep our own counsel on that point."

"You'll hear no argument from me," Cadfael said.

Lucius hesitated again, then ventured, "So . . . is it bad form of me to ask whether you actually know where Shinsei is?"

"It is if you want to take his death from me," Cadfael said. "But no, I don't know where he is, not exactly. For a famous figure, he's remarkably elusive. And I can't pursue him while he's in Valyanrend—I hear he never leaves the Citadel if he isn't off on one of Elgar's orders."

"Yes, that's true," Lucius said. He smiled grimly. "It's a shame. If I weren't on more pressing business, I'd be tempted to offer you my assistance. But a man I consider my closest friend is about to drag an innocent boy into the notice of one of Arianrod Margraine's more dangerous retainers, and I can only imagine what an incident he'll make of it if I don't get to him first."

Leave it, Cadfael told himself. *It's none of your concern. It means nothing to you.* But his mouth said, "What? *Which* of Arianrod Margraine's retainers?"

Lucius looked at him curiously. "I doubt you've heard of her."

"I don't think you want to wager on that," Cadfael said. "It's a long story, but I happened to meet Arianrod Margraine not too long ago, along with a handful of her retainers. There was only one woman among them."

"Ah," Lucius said. "Copper hair, surpassingly flat demeanor, fondness for edged weapons?" He must have seen the answer in Cadfael's face, for he didn't wait to hear it. "So she really *does* work for the marquise. We suspected, but . . . it's good to know for sure, I suppose."

Cadfael was only half listening. Seren Almasy had helped him, of course. She had held him back from striking Elgar at Mist's Edge, an act that doubtless would have gotten him killed if he'd been rash enough to complete it. He hadn't forgotten, and would never have attempted to deny it. It simply wasn't the kind of thing he cared about, usually. He felt no urge or obligation to repay debts, and preferred to keep himself out of other people's business whenever possible.

But he knew, without having to consider it for a single moment, what Rhia would want him to do.

While on the road with the boy who had turned out to be King Kelken, Cadfael had said vengeance was all he could offer Rhia, that it was impossible for him to devote his life to living the way she would have. But that wasn't quite true, was it? He knew his sister as well as he had ever known anyone, and she had never tried to hide what she believed. He might not have been able to feel the convictions she had felt, but he could, at least, take the actions she would have taken.

"Look," he said to Lucius, "I'd really rather not have to fight you again. So . . . how invested are you in killing Seren Almasy? Because it so happens I'd prefer that she live."

If he had surprised Lucius, the other man recovered quickly from it. "Actually, I'd prefer that as well. It's my friend's intentions I'm not sure of. I can't picture him giving himself over so entirely to vengeance, but he was very angry the last time I saw him. I know I can make him see sense; I just have to get to him."

Rhia would have hated the idea of Cadfael's vengeance; he had known that from the start. It would have been one thing to kill Shinsei as a villain on the battlefield, a butcher of the innocent—that was something she would understand. But to chase him merely out of anger and hate, to murder him solely because he had taken Cadfael's sister away from him . . . she would never have wanted him to throw his life away on such a thing. He knew that, but it had never changed his conviction to see his revenge through. He'd have to apologize to her later, if any afterward existed in death.

But though he was too angry to give up on his revenge, he could delay it. He didn't even have a lead on Shinsei anyway—the man could be back at the Citadel already for all he knew. And he had this uncomfortable feeling about Seren, the same one he had about Kelken and his sister: the feeling of caring, in some small way, about what would happen to them, no matter how much he didn't want to. Was it because she had reminded him of himself?

"Oh, fine," he said to Lucius. "I'll help you, all right? At the very least, Seren

THE RIGHTFUL QUEEN   13

seems to be a great help to Arianrod Margraine, and Arianrod Margraine is trying to defeat Elgar. We both hate him, yes?"

"Yes," Lucius said firmly.

"Right. And then . . . we'll keep your friend from bloodying himself, however it would have turned out. Is that acceptable?"

"More than," Lucius said. He smiled. "I owe you for this."

Cadfael scowled. "I don't need you to owe me. Keeping that sword out of my face will be thanks enough."

Chapter Three

Issamira

IT WAS A merry band that marched back to Ibb's Rest, a glowing Prince Hephestion at their head. His soldiers clustered around him, laughing and shouting and jostling one another, holding their torches high to light the way back. Morgan, Braddock, and Nasser had fallen into step right behind the thickest cluster of people, where there was path to spare and it was less likely they would get in anyone's way. Nasser was still absently stroking his newly recovered bow, humming softly to himself. Even Braddock seemed satisfied, and well he might: any way you looked at it, their victory had been splendidly won.

Morgan glanced back over her shoulder, to where Hephestion's young captain was walking with the only two Issamiri soldiers who'd suffered wounds more serious than cuts and bruises. Neither wound was life-threatening, and both soldiers could walk unaided, but still the captain insisted on being the last in their train, keeping watch as they walked. One of the wounded soldiers, a young man with a hastily bandaged gash in his arm, asked her, "Do you think the bandits had reinforcements lying in wait, Captain?"

She smiled sheepishly. "No, I don't really. The prince planned this well—I suspect we cleaned them all up. I just want to be sure: the visibility is so poor out here." Her smile faded. "Will you be all right?"

He waggled the injured arm at her. "Would've preferred to get off clean, but it'll mend. Bound to be a talented healer at Ibb's Rest."

"Aye, I imagine so." She caught Morgan looking at her, and smiled again—it seemed to be her natural state no less than her prince's. "Thank you again for your help, miss. We had hoped not to involve any civilians in this, but your aid was most welcome."

"Eh," Morgan said, jerking her thumb at Nasser and Braddock, "it's these two you want to thank, not me. All I did was tag along after them."

"That still took courage," the girl said, nodding firmly as if that settled the matter.

Up ahead, Hephestion and the foremost soldiers had reached Ibb's Rest, but the prince stopped before the door, turning to scan the crowd. "Rhia, don't skulk about back there! You shone as bright as ever on the battlefield, and now you'll be flattered and celebrated accordingly. That's an order."

She grinned at him. "Flattery looks better on you, my lord, and you are more schooled in the ways of celebration than I could ever hope to be."

"Nonsense, I'll make an apt student of you yet. Have I not sworn it?" With a laughing gesture to his men, he indicated that they should go in ahead of him, and he waited for Rhia to approach.

But as the soldiers began to file inside, Morgan noticed something curious: many of them paused on the threshold, making some one-handed gesture before they crossed it. When their party reached the doorway, Morgan hung back so Rhia could pass her and join her liege, and she saw Hephestion make the same gesture: one hand raised, fingers pressed together and pointing upward, palm sideways, thumb out and pointed toward him. At his heels, Rhia hesitated, then didn't quite mimic him: she lifted and lowered her hand so rapidly it was as if she'd waved at the doorway before entering it.

Morgan cleared her throat to get their attention. "I apologize, but I have not been long in Issamira. Is this a southern custom? Do we neglect our manners by not following suit?"

For a moment the prince looked utterly confused, but then he laughed, making the gesture again more slowly. "Oh, this? It's such a habit I scarcely notice it. Ibb's Rest is a traveler's haven—sacred places in Issamira. Traditionally one pauses for a moment of prayer, but in these busy times merely the gesture is deemed sufficient— one-handed for us, of course, to pay the blood price."

"The blood price?" Morgan asked.

He bowed his head. "My sister tells me the Ninists held that bastards are impure by their very nature. But our priests teach us that every babe is born innocent, and no crime can blacken a soul beyond all redemption—though murder, as the foulest, demands a price. Thus anyone who has ever taken a life must pray one-handed, so as not to offend the gods by offering them a hand stained with blood. Of course, in practice most people kill with both hands, but it's meant to be a metaphor, I suppose."

At her side, Braddock shifted uncomfortably. "Does that mean we should . . . ?"

Hephestion shrugged. "It's as you like." Then, grinning mischievously at his captain, "You could even follow Rhia's lead and split the difference."

She ducked her head. "It just seems impolite not to . . . but then on the other hand it's not something *I* believe, so I don't want to act as if . . . well . . ."

Hephestion left her to it; it seemed like something he had heard many times before. "We don't have short memories in Issamira," he said to Morgan and the others. "The Ninists spent centuries trying to compel our consciences; we didn't fight so hard for our freedom just to turn around and do the same to other people. The Rebel Queen, from whom the house of Avestri is descended, decreed when she took the throne that all in Issamira may worship as they wish—or not worship at all—so long as they keep the peace. Just do whatever you think best—I promise you, no one here will care."

Even though he'd said that, the three of them still hesitated, until finally Nasser nodded, held up a hand the way Hephestion had, and ducked through the doorway.

Braddock glanced her way, and shrugged. "Why not?"

That was fine with Morgan, but it seemed from what Hephestion had said that the gesture for her would be different. She lifted both hands instead, pressing them together so they mirrored each other.

"Huh," Nasser said. "I'm a bit surprised." Braddock's lack of reaction said that he wasn't, even though it wasn't something they'd talked about.

"Oh well," she said. "I guess it's just never been necessary, that's all." But she wondered if that had been part of the gesture's purpose, in whatever long-distant era it had first been created: that you could not pray in public, even as a stranger, without revealing whether you had killed or not.

The common room of Ibb's Rest was packed and deafening, most of the soldiers well on their way to a drunken haze. But they clustered eagerly around their prince and his captain, enveloping the two of them in cheers and hearty thumps on the shoulder in a matter of moments.

Watching them, Morgan couldn't help smiling a little. "How strange. Can you imagine if anyone in Valyanrend were ever so happy to see Elgar or his captains?"

Braddock nodded. "They've earned their soldiers' trust, that's clear."

"And so young, too," Nasser said. "That is no small feat." He grinned. "Well, I think we've more than earned a drink of our own, given our contributions to the victory. Shall I fetch something for you, ox?"

"No, I'll come with you. Morgan?"

"Later, perhaps," she said. "But you go ahead."

When they moved off, she turned her gaze to Hephestion and Rhia again, only to see the captain gradually weave her way out from the throng, moving toward the far corner. There were several buckets resting on a table in the back—filled with water, Morgan realized, as Rhia dunked a tankard in. She emptied it in several gulps, then filled it again, sipping at it more slowly.

Morgan saw her opening, and approached the table. The girl intrigued her, for reasons she couldn't precisely name. Perhaps it was that her youth, her slight stature, and that golden hair all reminded her of Seth. Perhaps it was merely that she looked out of place.

"You aren't drinking?" she asked.

The girl shook her head. "Carelessness doesn't look good in a captain."

"No one could accuse you of that," Morgan said. "Even your prince is celebrating."

Rhia smiled. "As he should be. He fought hard for this plan, and it unfolded just as he predicted." But then she bit her lip, worry creasing her brow. "I just wonder if . . ."

"What?" Morgan asked, sensing that Rhia had half forgotten she was there.

She winced. "Oh, it's just . . . I was thinking about . . . what I'm going to say to the queen."

The queen. Morgan thought back to Irjan Tal, the ranger who had guided her and Braddock across the wasteland of the Gods' Curse. He had told them there were dark rumors of a civil war brewing, Issamiri citizens surreptitiously choosing sides between Hephestion and his sister. But Irjan had also said that the laws of succession were clear, and that he could not imagine the prince trying to dispute them. Looking at him now, Morgan couldn't help agreeing—if Hephestion truly possessed such treacherous depths, he had masked them flawlessly. And she couldn't imagine a would-be usurper trooping out to quash some bandits in a remote corner of the country so far from the capital.

But perhaps his sister saw things differently, or might worry that his success tonight would weaken her own position. And that, in turn, might make things more difficult for the captain, who after all reported to the queen, not Hephestion. "Are you worried she may begrudge her brother too great a victory?" she asked Rhia.

Though her smiles had been swift and sincere, the girl's scowl was no slower and no less intense. "Her Grace would never. Why would you even suggest such a thing?"

The girl could certainly be deadly if she chose—Morgan had seen that for herself during the battle. And yet she wasn't at all frightened by Rhia's anger. There were no threats hidden behind her words—just the truth of her feelings, plainly expressed.

So Morgan tried to answer the question in the same fashion. "Crossing the Curse, we heard there was unrest between the two of them. That's all. I had never met your prince until tonight, and his sister not at all—I've no cause to make any great judgments about them."

Rhia's expression clouded, though it did dampen her anger. "People like to gossip too much. They may live here, but they don't know Her Grace or the prince any more than you do—they just *think* they do." She twitched her shoulders uncomfortably. "It's not that I can't understand it—it's natural to think that rulers only care about ruling, and powerful people about becoming more powerful. That's what *my* king was like, back in Lanvaldis. He didn't care about his people, not truly." By then her eyes were so sad Morgan regretted bringing it up, but her gaze softened as it crossed the room to rest on Hephestion. "You don't have to believe me. But I can tell you that they're different—both of them."

Morgan looked over at the prince, too, caught in a dense knot of revelers, sharing in their laughter. "I can't even help liking him, and I've known him for an hour."

As if he felt the attention, Hephestion turned in their direction, waving at them in mock displeasure. "Rhia, what are you doing? I order you to come here and celebrate with me. I promise no foes are going to come charging through that door just because you take your eyes off it for a second."

Rhia smiled apologetically at Morgan and crossed the room to join him. He flung an arm around her neck and mussed up her hair, as if she were a younger sibling instead of a retainer. Having no further reason to stay in the corner, Morgan went to rejoin Braddock and Nasser, who had never truly left the revelry.

Braddock nodded at her as she sat down next to him. "I was just talking to Nas about our next move. I figure you and I should try to contact Roger in Valyanrend, at least—see what's going on back home."

"That makes sense," Morgan agreed. "We can't just keep drifting around forever—we don't have the coin. I've used up more of my savings than I'd like as it is, and I doubt you're faring much better."

She was about to ask Nasser what he planned to do, but before she could, she felt a presence at her shoulder. "Sorry," Prince Hephestion said. "None of my business, probably, but did I just hear you say you needed coin?"

Morgan tried to read his expression, wondering why he had asked. "We aren't beggars, Your Grace," she said at last. "Just trying to plot the best course for our travels. Did you have a suggestion?"

He ran a hand through his hair. "Well, more like a suggestion regarding the scarcity of your coin. And I'm not *Your Grace*—if you truly love titles, *my lord* is customary in Issamira for princes out of the direct line of succession."

Morgan remembered that Rhia had called him that as well. "Forgive me, my lord. In Hallarnon we have an imperator, and before that we had a lord protector, and a grand duchess—every title you could think of, and many more you couldn't. But we have not had a king in centuries."

"It's no real difference to me—though I suppose that's easy for me to say. What I meant to ask was . . . you lot helped us out, and you didn't have to. That tells me that you're capable, and you have a sense of what's right. There's something my sister needs done—something she wanted me to send some of the soldiers to do, once we'd finished here. But it's not a task any Issamiri soldier really *likes* to do, and picking a few of them for it makes it seem like a punishment. So if I sent the three of you instead . . . it'd take an unpleasant decision off my hands, and put some coin in yours."

Morgan exchanged a look with Braddock and Nasser. "Whatever you may think, my lord, we're really not the types to go looking for any more trouble than comes our way naturally. Whatever this task is, if your soldiers don't like it . . . what makes you think we'll like it any better?"

The prince inched himself into a spare seat across from them. "I suppose I didn't make the offer in the best way—I didn't mean to suggest the task is something dangerous, or even truly unpleasant. Have you heard of Raventower?"

"I have," Nasser spoke up. "A castle to the east of here, many centuries old."

Hephestion nodded. "Raventower is most famous, in our history, as the place from which our imperial overlords sought to put down our rebellions. The Ninists, and even before that, in the days of the First Empire . . . every time we rose up in an attempt at freedom, they would send some talented lord or favorite general to Raventower, to oversee our destruction." He scowled. "They always succeeded, of course. Time and time again, until the Rebel Queen's victory."

Morgan swiped Braddock's tankard and took a swig; he raised an eyebrow, but didn't comment. "So you're saying Raventower is an unpleasant place for your people?"

"For many of us, yes. My sister says there were many who wanted to pull the castle down, after Talia Avestri's victory. But she forbade it. Perhaps she thought there was a greater victory to be had in making it ours, or perhaps it was simply too useful to destroy. All I can say is that I have been to Raventower, and I doubt I will ever feel at home there."

Morgan glanced at Braddock and Nasser, but they seemed content to let her speak. "If we went to this castle, what would we have to do there?"

Hephestion laughed. "Hardly anything, once you arrive. The trouble is getting there in the first place. You said you were from Valyanrend, right? It would mean you wouldn't be getting home for some time. As your friend said, Raventower is east of here—the opposite of the way you'd need to go to get back."

"But that's not all?" Morgan asked.

He scratched the back of his neck. "Well. That's the other reason sending you might be better than sending my soldiers. Adora couldn't just send a messenger—as tonight's events will have told you, our roads are not always so safe as we could wish. You lot can defend yourselves, clearly, but you may not even have to. Bandits would suspect soldiers going to Raventower at this time of year to be carrying something of value, but you could glide by unnoticed."

"And this thing of value—"

"Would not be of value to you," Hephestion said. "They're writs, from my sister to Captain Fayder of Raventower. They tell the captain how much coin and how many soldiers she is granted use of in the coming months, among other things. And they're made out to her specifically, if you were curious."

Morgan didn't blame the prince for a bit of caution; they had only just met, after all. But she was so used to Sheath, where all the thieves that were her neighbors knew she was honest and scoffed at her for it, that she was actually surprised anyone thought she was capable of dishonest dealing.

No doubt her laughter confused Hephestion, but that was all right. "Sorry," she said. "We're not so desperate as to try to take them, especially since you'd apparently be paying us." Swallowing the rest of her laughter, she reached for Braddock's tankard again.

The prince brightened; this was territory he understood. "Right. Since it *might* be dangerous, and since it's so far out of your way, and since you'll have to pay expenses there and back . . . how does ten in gold sound for the three of you?"

Morgan choked on her drink.

Chapter Four

Valyanrend

THE DAY THE war against Reglay began, Roger was, for the most part, inside, sulking. He found out later that there had been soldiers parading through the streets in Valyanrend's richer and more populous districts, a bit of trumpeting to go along with the recited declarations, but Sheath Alleys hadn't gotten so much as a single herald. It was just as well. Nobody in Sheath wanted to see soldiers or heralds anyway.

He'd spent the morning hours in the tunnels, retracing his steps to the place where the ruby had shattered and trying to make his way from there. Trouble was, without the ruby to guide him, he had no way of knowing which passages would lead him closer to . . . whatever had made it glow like that. And that turned the tunnels into a proper maze. He'd found several new openings into different places in the city, any of which he would've counted a decent find a handful of days earlier, but now they just felt like cheap consolations. He was on the trail of something so much bigger.

He'd made sure to mark all the pathways he'd traveled, both in the tunnels themselves and on the map he was slowly but steadily making of them. He tried to tell himself that there could only be a finite number of passages in the place, and if he kept going he'd have to stumble onto what he was looking for eventually. But the thought failed to cheer him up any.

The empty Dragon's Head wasn't very cheerful, either, but Roger liked the space as much as he liked the admittedly slim hope that one of his absent friends might just come strolling through the tavern door one day. Morgan and Braddock had sent word that they were going off on an errand for one of Braddock's old friends in Issamira, and he'd heard nothing at all from Deinol and Seth, or from Lucius since he'd first left in search of them. Roger felt certain that Lucius would have tried to contact him if he'd found the other two, so that meant either he was still looking or he'd run into trouble of his own. None of the possibilities were reassuring.

And now they were apparently going to be fighting again. It would be fine for Roger—he was no soldier, and there'd be fewer of them to lay down the law if they were off fighting in the east—but somehow it made him feel sick to his stomach all the same, just as it had with Lanvaldis. He really needed to stop caring so much about things that were too big for him.

And on that note, *naturally,* Tom bloody Kratchet burst through the door.

This was notable primarily because Tom never came to the Dragon's Head himself—practically never went anywhere himself, if he could get Marceline to go instead. It was notable secondarily because he was probably looking for Roger, and that meant a complex and heinous inconvenience was about to unfold, right here in front of him.

"Listen," Roger said, in a perfunctory effort to forestall the incumbent calamity, "this is really absolutely not the correct day for—"

"*Halfen!*" Tom shouted, and oh, wonderful, he was already at the boiling rage part without even any need to work himself up to it.

Roger rubbed at his face. "What can you possibly want with me now, Tom? Haven't had a bet with you in months, haven't tried to sell you something in months—last transaction we had I paid you, in fact. And don't you try to tell me those coins were false, because you know damn well—"

"The girl's missing," Tom said—quietly, but with no less anger.

Roger blinked at him. "Beg pardon?"

"The girl," Tom repeated. "Marceline. She didn't come back."

Sweet fucking gods, he did *not* have time for this. "The monkey didn't come back to where? *From* where?"

"To mine, of course," Tom said. "Where else has she slept for near on ten years? And *from* where is what you're going to find out."

"Gods' sakes, Tom, it's not as if you're used to keeping a falcon's eyes on her— even I know you let the girl run where she will. Who's to say she's in any trouble just on account of spending a night out? She's young, but no fool."

"Aye, no fool," Tom agreed. "But she's been stirred up these past weeks—agitated, and like to take risks. Wasn't long ago she was asking me questions that raised more than a little concern, about business I thought she knew to stay away from. And why? Because of you, Halfen."

"I'm sorry," Roger said, "I must have heard you wrong. I thought I just heard you say that your monkey was any concern of mine, or that I would ever care to influence—"

Tom had been a fine pickpocket in his day, but he'd left off the practice in the past couple of years. It was true that Marceline brought in plenty on her own, but the rumor was that Tom's hands weren't what they used to be. But when Tom strode forward, seized Roger by the hair, and slammed the side of his face into the counter, Roger was eminently displeased to conclude that the rumors were shit.

Tom bent his head down close to Roger's. "It's important to me that you don't hear me wrong, Halfen, so I'll say it again. My girl is missing, having recently gone in search of rumors about our city's paltry excuse for a resistance. She did this because *you* were vaunting about your own abilities and putting the idea into her head that she had to stumble on a secret of her own in order to prove herself to you. So this is what's going to happen. You're going to help me locate her, because as much as it pains me to admit it, you'll probably have better luck at it than I will. And if we run into any difficulties getting her back, you help sort them out to the best of your silver-tongued ability. You do that, and we're square. She comes back on her own, and we're square." He took a deep breath. "She *don't* come back, and you better run very far, very fast, because I mean not to let you have any peace for the rest of your miserable life. Let me know if any of that was unclear to you."

Roger groaned. "I only wish it was."

Tom shoved him down harder. "You haven't told me if we have an understanding or not."

"Fuck!" Roger winced. "Gods, *fine*! Just get off!" When Tom finally released him, he sprang back, putting a good several feet between them. "Damn it, I knew that monkey would get me in trouble one day. Why don't you tell me what little you surely know, and we'll both see how bad this day can possibly get."

NO ONE EVER said that thieves were brave, no matter how many times they risked their lives. When they pulled off heists deemed impossible by the common crowd, they were cowards and connivers, merely because they used their heads instead of their swords. But warriors and heroes could keep their bravery, Tom had always said. Thieves had something better. Thieves had *skill*. Where others dredged up the courage to face death, thieves had the wits to turn upwind. That was the surest way to survive—understand the situation better than whoever wanted to kill you did.

Marceline took a deep breath. Understanding the situation, in the case of this so-called resistance, meant first understanding who was most likely to kill her. There were four of them in the room with her, and she gave them a quick once-over. The one who had first put the knife to her back in the street, a tanned young woman with short dark hair, had seemed pitying from the start, and she looked to be the youngest of the lot: about nineteen or twenty, while the others were probably several years older. But the sallow, scowling man who had been with her—Rask, they called him—seemed to have some authority over her, and he'd said capturing Marceline had been his idea to start with, so he'd hardly want to let her go.

They had come upon the other woman, Naishe, on the way to see their leader, and she was more difficult to read. She clearly disapproved of what Rask had done—or, at the very least, at his having done it on his own initiative—but now that the thing *was* done, it didn't mean she would be Marceline's friend. And as for this Mouse, their famed leader of the beautiful eyes, what member of a secret resistance group just *told* you who he was?

Mouse was relaxed, grinning, waiting to see what she would do. What Marceline properly wanted to do was roll her eyes, but she didn't want to risk making any of them mad. It was probably better to let him talk about himself, so she asked, "You really are him, then? The leader of Valyanrend's resistance?"

He spread his hands. "By popular agreement only. We don't try to compel anyone here—what would be the point of our existence if we did?"

The younger woman nodded approvingly at that, but Naishe said dryly, "Perhaps you might explain then, Mouse, how this child came to be here? *Her* presence seems to have been compulsory, given that I saw Rask and Talia dragging her inside."

The younger woman, who must have been Talia, had the good grace to look uncomfortable. "I never knew she was a child till I saw her, Naishe. But Rask said to bring her in anyway."

"And Rask, I expect, knew full well how young she was." Naishe turned her eyes to Mouse next, a silent question.

He sighed. "No, I didn't know, either. Rask never mentioned her age in his report."

"And you didn't think to ask."

"No, I didn't. That was neglectful of me, I admit." He turned to Rask, with that same engaging smile. "You've been unusually quiet, Rask. I'm sure you have an opinion on this matter."

"Aye, I do," Rask said. "The same I had from the beginning. Question her. Find out what she knows, and why she was looking for us—for *you,* particularly. I never said to do her any harm, but Naishe would twist this whole affair to spite me, as she so loves to do."

Naishe had been settling her half-strung bow in the corner as Rask spoke, but she spared an idle glance over her shoulder at him. "I have never done a single thing with your reaction in mind, Rask."

Talia giggled—and then saw Rask's face, and fell quickly silent.

Mouse was smiling, but since he had been smiling before, Marceline couldn't tell whose side, if any, he had taken in the argument. "And you—Monkey, was it? What would you have us know of you?"

"Not *Monkey*," Marceline snapped, before she could stop herself. "It's not supposed to be a *name*, it's just a thing people say."

"But you don't want to tell us your name."

"I certainly don't. I don't want to have any more to do with you than I have to, to be honest."

He laughed. "Then why spend so much time and effort in search of me? You were so resourceful in tracking me down, and now that you've finally found me, you just want to leave again? Even you must find that peculiar."

Marceline considered it, choosing her words carefully. They had all fastened onto her youth, which would normally irk her, but if it would help get her out of here she didn't mind using it. So she just told him the truth—a truth she would never have admitted to under normal circumstances, because it was too childish. "I wanted to see if you were real."

She saw the glint in his eyes—for better or worse, she'd intrigued him. "If *I* was real? You mean if the resistance was?"

"That, too. But you were the one I heard about. I didn't know any of the others."

"There," Rask snapped. "If we're in a position where children can hear about us as fairy stories, we're in a damn load of trouble, Mouse."

"I don't think she's just any child, though," Talia said.

The other three turned to her in surprise—she was clearly the lowest-ranked in the group hierarchy. Naishe asked, "What makes you say that?"

"Well, I was just thinking about everything Rask said. She was able to move about the city remarkably freely, and to spend a lot of time spying on us, or trying to. That suggests she doesn't have a conventional apprenticeship—she'd be missed if she kept running out on it over and over again. And if she lives with her parents instead, they must be quite lenient with her to let her frolic about on this kind of quest."

"Hmm." Mouse tapped his lip, then looked back at Marceline. "What do you say? Has she hit on it?"

"Well enough," Marceline said.

"So you have no parents, and you aren't an apprentice?"

"Not yet." She couldn't tell them she'd primarily been looking for the resistance to have something to impress Roger, so she could be *his* apprentice. That kind of apprenticeship certainly wasn't conventional, but she doubted these people would be pleased to hear about it.

"Then how is it," Mouse asked, "that you came to hear about me in the first place? Rumors of a resistance have always been plentiful—there were rumors before we ever actually existed, so we don't mind about them too much. But to find anyone who could discover I'm leading it is . . . unusual. And potentially troubling."

It was troubling for Marceline, too, because she couldn't tell them Tom was the one who'd found out. That would've meant explaining who Tom was, and where he was. Maybe Marceline wasn't brave, any more than any other thief, but she wasn't about to betray Tom to save her own skin, even if she were certain telling them the truth *would* save her. So she shook her head at Mouse. "You can ask, but I can't tell you."

Mouse didn't seem bothered by that, just curious. "Why not?"

"Because . . . because I owe the person who told me, and I'm not about to give him up. He's no threat to you—he doesn't even care about you, he only told me because I insisted. He didn't know your name—I learned that later, when I asked around your neighborhood. And I heard it isn't your real name."

Mouse shrugged. "It's what people call me, so it seems real enough to me. What *did* this friend of yours say about me?"

That was probably all right to admit to. "That you lived in Iron's Den, and that you were . . . that you liked to read a lot, and were famous for it. A . . . peasant historian, he said."

For a moment Mouse looked startled, and then he laughed loudly, delightedly, clutching his stomach. "Well, I'm sorry you don't want me to meet him! No one I know has ever called me a historian—only a daydreamer or a layabout. I myself would only say I *aspire* to be one—it's hard for a truant blacksmith's apprentice to get his hands on many books, after all."

Rask was scowling again. "Mouse, her associate knew where you lived! Who else among us might he know about—or what actions, or what connections? You've got to take these things seriously!"

"And so I do," Mouse said calmly. "I take everything seriously, Rask—I simply do so in my own way." He looked back at Marceline. "Here's what I think: our friend Rask, despite his own seriousness, is reading you entirely the wrong way. He worries that your investigation signifies either how widely rumors of us have spread, or else that we are being persecuted by some person or group that has taken a special interest in us. But you said, on the contrary, that your specialist in rumors was someone who knew about us, but didn't *care* about us. That would normally be very peculiar—why expend such effort to gain knowledge that's meaningless to you? Unless, of course, knowledge itself is your trade, or part of it. That leads me to two guesses."

"The Night Market," Talia said—and then looked guilty, no doubt realizing that Mouse had wanted to unveil the end of his speculation himself.

He sighed. "Yes, that's one of them, but probably the less likely of the two. We know the Night Market well—even have a fairly regular trade with some members of it. If you were the child or apprentice of one of their merchants, no doubt they could have arranged something less . . . roundabout to satisfy your curiosity. No, I'm going to go ahead and wager all on my second guess: that the most captious set of ne'er-do-wells on the continent has finally deigned to lower their haughty noses just a touch, and we've drawn the attention of Sheath Alleys at last."

Despite it all, Marceline couldn't help but feel a touch of pride at the effect those two words carried: there was power just in naming the place that had raised her, to those who truly knew what power was. Its effect on all the listeners was stark: Talia drew forward in curious fascination, but Rask and Naishe, for the very first time, had exactly the same reaction. They were stunned, in the first instant, and then deeply displeased, mouths set like stone beneath their narrowed eyes.

Naishe spoke first, turning the full force of her glare on Marceline, even though her words were for Mouse. "So you're saying this is a *thief*." She spat the word so harshly that Marceline wanted to step back, but she forced herself to hold her ground.

Mouse looked as amused as ever. "It's possible. Not all Sheathers are thieves, of course, but most are crooked in some way, and I know how you hate that."

"*Are* you, then?" Naishe asked Marceline. "You seem to have some pride. If you want to deserve it, tell us truly what you are."

"Oh, I see," Marceline said. "So you'll just be announcing that you're a member of the resistance in the middle of the noonday street, will you?" She didn't wait for an answer, but directed her next question at Mouse. "Supposing I am, what would you do?"

Mouse grinned. "Supposing you *were* . . . I suppose I'd have to tell you a thief is just what I've been looking for."

CHAPTER FIVE

Stonespire

IT HAD BEEN fifteen years since Seren had last been awoken with a kick to the ribs, but that didn't mean some mornings weren't worse than others. She started into consciousness flinching, seized with sudden panic as she felt the sun on her face and struggled to guess at the time. But then she recovered herself, slowed her breathing, took stock of her surroundings. She was inside Stonespire Hall, alone. All her knives were where they ought to be. She was not starving, merely a bit peckish after her long sleep. And she was no child, but a woman grown, long past needing to fear an assault from an old crone.

Seren could remember her face so clearly, even after all this time: long and thin, with sharp gray eyes and a tiny pointed nose. She had seemed so tall to Seren back then, so solid, as immoveable as a tree and just as sympathetic. There couldn't have been that much strength in her body, not really, yet Seren could well remember the pain of her blows, how she knew to hit hard enough to hurt yet not hard enough to debilitate. After all, if she'd crippled the orphans in her care, they would have been no use to her.

"And what have you done?" Seren could still hear it sometimes, in her dreams and in the waking dreams that could come on without warning. *"I wear myself out giving shelter to so many, and do you put in even the smallest bit of effort to pay me back? Do you think kindness is something that's just going to be given to you, on and on for your whole life long, no matter how ungrateful you are in return?"*

I'm not her creature anymore, she reminded herself, as she always did when this happened. *I became stronger than her long ago.*

She straightened up, and devoted her full attention to the noise that had woken her in the first place: discordant shouting, apparently from several different voices at once. Seren ran a rough hand through her hair, checked her knives one more time, and ventured out into the halls of Stonespire.

She learned the extent of the problem soon enough, and from there it wasn't hard to grasp a solution. Dent, the guardsman Arianrod trusted most, was nowhere to be found; Verrane, her old nurse, deserved a rest; and Seren suspected she was the best suited of the three of them for the task anyway, so she headed for the spire stairs herself. However, on the way she caught sight of the very source of the problem, and figured she could save time by confronting it that way. But when she actually tried . . .

The culprit was a skinny, freckled seventeen-year-old, just recently employed as a chambermaid at Stonespire Hall. She was carrying a heavy bundle of cloth, and she clutched it to her chest with a shriek as Seren approached her, backing against the nearest wall.

Well, on reflection Dent would perhaps have been better at this part. "That's quite enough of that," Seren said. "You'll come with me—"

"No, please!" The girl looked like she was about to weep. Who on earth got this worked up over a simple mistake? "It was an accident, I swear it! Her ladyship understands that, doesn't she?"

"I expect she doesn't care," Seren said honestly. "This isn't the first time this has happened, and it won't be the last. I'll take care of it, if you'll just hand me that—"

But the girl cringed back in terror as Seren tried to pry the bundle from her grip. "Don't hurt me," she said hoarsely. "Please don't—"

Under normal circumstances, Seren would have been unsettled but fine. But the dream was still fresh in her head, and the memory pierced through her before she could suppress it: *Don't hit me, please, I'm sorry, I'm sorry—*

"*Stop* that," she snapped, gripping the girl by both shoulders and shoving her hard into the wall. It was too hard. Her voice had been too loud. She shook her head fiercely, reaching for stillness, for the memory of where and who she was.

The girl was trembling in her grip, but she was quiet; no doubt she was too terrified to make any further noise. That . . . wasn't how Seren had wanted to handle this, but she supposed it couldn't be helped now. "Listen," she said, forcing any emotion from her voice, "just calm down, all right? No one's going to hurt you. You were right, it was just a mistake. All I want is to fix it, same as you."

The girl's lip quivered. "But . . . she looked so angry."

Seren sighed, releasing her grip on the girl's shoulders. "Well, you shouldn't have stared. I'm quite certain someone told you that you weren't to stare."

"I never meant to, Miss Almasy, but I didn't think they'd look like *that*. There were . . . so many of them." She shuddered again. "And she just looked at me like . . . like she was going to breathe fire on me. They say she can do that, you know."

"That's ridiculous," Seren said. The idea that Arianrod could breathe fire wasn't ridiculous—for all Seren knew, she really could. But it was ridiculous to think that she'd set a chambermaid on fire, by any method, for so trivial an error. Seren hoped the girl couldn't tell the difference. "I told you, no one's going to harm you."

The girl had calmed down, but she still squinted suspiciously at Seren. "But then why are you here, Miss Almasy?"

"Because someone has to fetch the marquise out of the godsdamned bath," Seren said, with every shred of patience she still possessed. "Now will you *give me that,* please?"

The girl looked down at the bundle of linens she was still clutching tight— that she'd been clutching when she ran out of the bath, and had been distractedly carrying around ever since. She looked back up at Seren . . . and back down again. "Oh," she said. *"Oh."*

Seren let out a breath, and her stored tension with it, her shoulders shifting back down. "Yes. *That.* I trust we understand each other now?"

Stonespire Hall was on the smaller side for a castle, but the first Daven Margraine had apparently placed a high value on cleanliness—he'd spared no expense in the bath's construction. It was an eight-foot square two and a half feet deep and tiled over in marble, though the rest of the floor was stone. And sitting in one corner of it, flicking ripples into the water with her fingers and otherwise doing what even Seren, with every scrap of loyalty she possessed, had to admit was sulking, was the lady of Stonespire herself.

She turned to look over her shoulder as Seren entered, and immediately smacked her palm against her forehead. "Oh, *honestly*. They had to go *this* far up the chain of competence before they found someone who could resolve this?"

"I'm afraid so," Seren said, setting the bundle down at the edge of the bath and searching through it for the largest of the cloths. "It seems the girl was quite high-strung. She believed that you'd sent me to administer . . . some gruesome punishment or other."

"For running off with my linens? Does she think we have nothing better to do?" She shook her head. "Sometimes I think you forget how terrifying most of Stonespire finds you—you do have a reputation as the deadliest person in my employ, you know."

Seren smiled. "Not at all. Acting as if you don't understand how terrifying you are is an excellent way to appear *more* terrifying—I shouldn't have to tell you that."

It was unusual for Arianrod *not* to be smiling, so Seren was relieved when she laughed. But then she held out the cloth, and Arianrod rose from the bath to take it, and suddenly the tension was back: Arianrod buried her fingers in the cloth, squeezing hard, but she didn't pull it toward her. She just stood there gripping it, staring down at the water.

Seren knew what it was, all too well. Under normal circumstances, if a chambermaid had run off with her linens, Arianrod would have walked all the way back to her chambers stark naked if necessary, rather than wait to be fetched out. (Gravis and Verrane would have gone into conniptions, of course, but that was hardly an incentive for her *not* to do it, though the resulting hour-long lecture on propriety might have been.) But that confidence had been stolen from her. She might have cared nothing for propriety, but she cared too much to give half the castle's occupants the opportunity to gawk at her scars. And she knew that, and knew that Seren knew it, and the indignity of it burned her, humiliated her, as so few things were capable of doing.

Seren knew all this, but what could she say that would make it better? That the scars didn't matter? How could she of all people say that, when she knew what they represented?

She was still struggling with herself when Arianrod spoke. "It's hardly the first time I've been stared at, obviously. It's been many years, and I've mostly gotten used to it—the temptation to look at something you aren't supposed to. I've gotten used to people's urge to tell me I'm still *beautiful,* as if *that's* what it was all about. But that girl just seemed to lose herself so completely—just standing there with her mouth half open like I was . . . gods, I don't even know what. Something deformed."

There was a question there, Seren knew. But she didn't need Arianrod to tell her it wasn't a question of beauty—that would have been easy to answer. As a purely physical matter, she'd given the scars less than half a thought. But the question wasn't *do they make me look ugly,* it was *do they make me look weak? Do they make me look like a victim?*

Seren drew in a breath, choosing her words with as much care as she could. "She's a sheltered girl, my lady. I suspect it was the idea of the cruelty behind the scars that appalled her, rather than their physical appearance, or anything about you specifically."

Arianrod's grip on the cloth hanging between them had eased as Seren spoke, and when she fell silent Arianrod finally pulled it from her grip, drying herself off with a briskness that seemed meant to make up for her earlier hesitation. But when she spoke the words were deliberate: "Do you remember where all your scars came from?"

Answering *that* question was easy as breathing. "Of course. I have to. I couldn't correct them if I forgot them."

Arianrod looked up in the middle of rubbing her face. "What does that mean?"

"It's what my teacher used to say. Every scar is a mistake. If I forget where they came from, I forget the lessons that came with them. How can I learn from them then?"

Arianrod frowned. "A mistake, eh? I suppose that's fair enough."

"A mistake," Seren amended, "but not a failure. A scar was a stalemate, he used to say." It was easy to recall Gan Senrian's face, even easier than that of the old woman: thick black hair always fashionably styled, a capricious mouth that could turn on an instant, twinkling dark eyes that always seemed to smile, and thus had always served to keep his true thoughts hidden. She could remember his words just as easily, and she stumbled only a little, just a slight pause while she decided what language to use. Gan had originally spoken to her in Sahaian, a language she knew Arianrod understood very well, but in the end Seren decided to take the time to translate the words into Lantian. "That you bear a scar means you made a mistake, but that you *live* to bear it means your enemy made one, too. So it represents a warning to both of you, against making the same mistake twice."

She'd spoken longer than she meant to, but Arianrod seemed to be considering her words. Seren was surprised at what she actually said: "That teacher of yours is one of the only people you've ever spoken positively about. Was he that important to you?"

Seren shook her head. "He chose me. He trained me. I'll always be grateful to him for that, but gratitude is all I owe him. In fact, I . . . don't hope to see him again. It will probably be safer for both of us if we stay a continent apart—I was a weapon to him, once, and he must know he will never hold me as such again."

"A weapon?" Arianrod repeated. "Does that make you a weapon to me now?"

This was the kind of question that should have been easy but wasn't, because

Seren could never understand why Arianrod was displeased with the answers. "If that is what you require of me," she said, and even though it was both obedient and sincere, she wasn't truly surprised to see Arianrod frown. What more loyal answer could she have given? What more could she have offered? "Why does that answer offend you?" she asked, surprised at herself for daring.

Perhaps Arianrod was surprised, too; whatever the cause, she was silent for several moments. She'd stopped what she was doing. "It doesn't *offend* me. I merely find it a . . . tiresome metaphor. People aren't weapons. And I vastly prefer it that way, though perhaps you disagree." She smiled wryly. "I find most traditional weapons boring, but perhaps that's because I've never been able to get them to do what I wish." She pulled a robe from the pile of laundry. "The thing I require of you, more than anything else, is that you not bore me. It's not something you normally have difficulty with, so don't spoil it by being stubborn about this."

"About what?" Seren asked, confused.

Arianrod knotted the robe tightly. "About this weapon business. About this debt business. About your need to put all these . . . frames around everything—frames that don't fit and are of no use. You and I came to an arrangement. It's an *arrangement,* and nothing else. We made it for the sake of our mutual benefit, and we took precautions against the day when it is no longer for that benefit, at which point it will cease to exist. And, I hope, it will leave neither of us the worse for it."

It was ridiculous, and frustrating. She could never say what she meant to say. Either she didn't know the right words, or they drew too close to things she knew Arianrod didn't care about. But still Seren persisted, because she couldn't seem to give this up, no matter how hard she tried.

Arianrod didn't wait for her answer. She brushed past her, padding damply out of the bath and leaving Seren in her wake.

GRAVIS INGRET WAS, at that moment, engaged in a negotiation he had made countless times over the nearly thirty years he had served in the Stonespire guard—a negotiation that always inevitably ended the same way. A message had reached him at dawn that Healer Zara Shing had returned to Stonespire, and that she would be coming to the hall to deliver her requests for supplies—and to examine the marquise, if Lady Margraine would allow it. Zara had been edging out of her prime even when Gravis was a young man, and must have been past seventy now, but it hadn't slowed her down any; she would not allow her body to do something so inconvenient as dying without her express permission.

Every time Zara returned to the city, Gravis exhorted her to stay in it, and every time it was her pleasure to rebuff him. He had been doing this since Lord Caius was alive—Lord Caius had used to do it himself, but Gravis was never in danger of losing his temper with her, so he had become the better choice. But Lady Margraine had never shown any interest in the argument, a nonchalance Gravis found strange. She was usually sensitive to potential advantages, and Zara certainly provided one.

Zara Shing was a proper healer, not a midwife or an herbalist or a swindling peddler. Her ancestors had come from Sahai, and the relatives she still had there had sponsored her journey back across the sea to learn the medical arts. It was said that Akozuchi produced the most miraculous healers, since its people's experiments in agricultural breeding had produced rare cures for many an illness deemed fatal. But the Sahaian medical academies taught their students the most about the human body itself: they cut up corpses in huge numbers, foregoing the sanctity of the dead in order to better aid the living.

There were many such healers in Sahai, but precious few in all of Lantistyne, even in the great cities. That was why Zara had returned at all, to spread her skills where they were most needed. But it was also why she refused to remain at the hall, to be employed as healer to the Margraines—she insisted on making a circuit of Stonespire and the surrounding villages, tending to those in need before moving on. It was a wide net, and there were many who slipped through it, as Zara could not know in advance where her help would be needed most. But it was how she preferred to do things, and no one alive had yet found a way to keep her from *that*.

There was a strange wrinkle to their script this time: Zara wasn't any more receptive, but she seemed actually interested in speaking with him. "Have you been advised by your soldiers in the city?" she asked, cutting into the middle of his latest entreaty.

"Have they advised me about what?" Gravis asked. "Surely nothing to do with you, as you don't tell them anything. If you wanted to leave your route with—"

"This isn't about me," Zara said. "It's about you, and your people, and what they're doing and not doing. When was the last time you left Stonespire?"

"The city, or the hall?"

"Either."

"I was in the city yesterday, and left its walls within the last fortnight. Why?"

"You found nothing amiss on your travels?"

"Well . . . I don't know," Gravis said. "What would be amiss? There were some troubles, as there always are, but I found nothing that alarmed me more than usual, no."

"Then I have to—" Zara started, and stopped. Lady Margraine had entered the room.

For some reason Gravis did not care to know, she was pinching water from the ends of her hair. But she straightened when she saw the healer, just a bit of tension entering the set of her shoulders. It was a response Gravis knew, just as he knew its cause: the scars on her back might have come from wounds inflicted by her father, but it was Zara who had truly sculpted them, since hers were the hands that had sewn them up all those years ago.

To Lady Margraine, at least, Zara awarded the barest inclination of her head, which was more than Lord Caius had ever received. "Your ladyship," she said, extending a sheet of parchment covered in writing on both sides. "My request for supplies, as usual."

"As usual," Lady Margraine echoed, taking the parchment. Lord Caius had always studied Zara's requests carefully, but the marquise barely spent ten seconds on each side. "This all seems in order. Will you require any members of the guard to help transport it?"

Zara shook her head. "That Jill Bridger already volunteered her assistance down in the city, your ladyship."

Lady Margraine nodded her approval. "Well, if Bridger's on it I doubt we'll need to give any more instructions on the matter."

"I have another concern." Zara stood very straight, and even though she was shorter than Lady Margraine, and even though she kept her chin level, she somehow managed to meet her eyes anyway. "I've traveled quite a ways, and seen more than one thing that didn't sit well with me."

Lady Margraine smiled. "Well, we can't have that. Do you plan on sharing this dire news with me?"

"You know Lars Eurig, I am certain?" Every word was sharp and hard, painfully precise.

By contrast, Lady Margraine's words came easily. "I could hardly fail to know him, though I don't get any pleasure out of it. He's one of my stupider rentholders."

"He is more than stupid," Zara said. "I passed through his lands on my way back south to Stonespire. You could probably tell me what I encountered there, but you won't, so I will tell you. His tenants were maimed, in unusual numbers. Lamed, or missing fingers or ears or toes. It seems there are unsavory characters about, who like to use peasants for their sport."

"Indeed," Lady Margraine said. Her expression hadn't moved a hair. "Those are certainly unpleasant tidings."

"Lars Eurig is building a new tower, for which he is taking donations, as he is not allowed to raise rents," Zara said. "I was told that, peculiarly, it is only those tenants who have refused to donate who seem to have come under the ire of these marauders."

"What an intriguing coincidence."

"It is nothing of the sort."

"So you have said."

"And that is your answer, is it?" Zara snapped. "That is as far as you care?"

"As far as I care?" Lady Margraine flipped her hand over, staring at her nails. "That's rather more imprecise than I'd expect from you, Zara. What I am prepared to *do* is a much more relevant issue, as you well know. And the answer to *that* is not anything I care to share with a roving healer, no matter how talented she may be. You perform valuable services for my people—entirely at my expense, I might add—but you are not one of my advisors, and have no business telling me how I should administer my lands."

"I know the suffering I have seen," Zara said. "And I know that you could stop it, and will not."

"You know that I could stop it and *am* not," Lady Margraine corrected her. "As to what I *will* do, even your splendidly educated mind knows nothing."

Zara muttered something under her breath that sounded like gibberish to Gravis—Sahaian, no doubt.

"I can understand that, you know," Lady Margraine said.

Before Zara could say anything else, the sound of a very familiar loping gait echoed down the length of the hall, and they all turned to see Jill Bridger's enormous boots closing the distance like something out of legend, bringing her to the throne in a matter of moments.

Height-wise, she was built like a spear, though that image did nothing to convey the breadth of her shoulders. She'd never quite managed to fully fill out the space demarcated by those two dimensions, and as a result she looked as if her body had been overstretched; you could almost imagine that she would lie flat, like a piece of paper. She certainly looked awkward, until you saw her chasing or fighting someone, at which point she looked like someone you wanted in the guard immediately. That had apparently been Dent's line of reasoning when he had shown up, more than fifteen years ago now, with a shopkeeper's adolescent daughter in a dress that had been let out at the hem more times than it could take.

Gods knew Gravis had always looked askance at the presence of women in the guard, but he could hardly have missed that his view was not a popular one, and Bridger was far from the only woman to flout it. Dent adored her, and so did most of her fellows in the city, and Gravis felt there was no point in arguing about it. She had become a fixture to him, like mortar in the walls.

"Guardswoman Bridger reporting, your ladyship, from down in the city," she said, bowing her long body in what seemed an impossible maneuver.

That was what she always said. And, as always, Lady Margraine raised an eyebrow and replied, "Yes, Bridger, I know who you are. Go on."

"Healer Shing contacted me this morning, your ladyship, that I might arrange for the transport of several heavier items she requires for her duties among the populace." Bridger seemed to notice Zara for the first time. "Ah. She's probably told you that by now."

"Indeed," Lady Margraine said. "You may do as she says. Was that all?"

Bridger swept a critical eye over Gravis, and it was not lost on him that she had to look down slightly to do it. She had always treated him with respect, and he had endeavored to do the same, but there was no love lost between them. She must have known that she owed all her opportunities to Dent, and that Gravis had opposed them in the beginning. Then, too, she was among the soldiers—far from a majority, but still significant—who believed Dent, not Gravis, should have been captain of the guard. "Not at the moment, your ladyship," was all she said.

"Then please, help the healer on her way."

As she spoke, Bridger turned to Zara, but Gravis kept looking at Lady Margraine for just a moment longer.

He saw her go suddenly still, staring at the far end of the hall. She had such an odd look on her face, like she couldn't believe what she was seeing, but when Gravis tried to follow her line of sight nothing struck him as out of the ordinary. Since it was the day the throne rested from judgments, they were doing a lot of resupplying, so the great hall was less ordered than normal, but that *was* normal. There was Benwick helping carry a barrel of salted mackerel, and that crate was probably bandages . . . he looked back at the marquise, who had barely twitched. What on earth was she staring at?

She leaned forward slightly, craning her neck. And then suddenly her eyes went wide, and without a word or gesture to anyone, she made her way down the throne's steps and started walking purposefully toward the entrance of the hall.

Gravis trailed after her, trying to walk slowly so as not to frighten anyone, but he was frantically scanning the crowd in front of him, looking for anything that could possibly be a cause for alarm. The only people with weapons he could see were her own guards. No one was running; no one was shouting. But the farther she went the faster she walked, as if in some ever-increasing state of emergency, though her expression remained composed.

It was inevitable that others in the hall would start to notice, and Bridger was unsurprisingly first, silently tracking Gravis and Lady Margraine with her eyes before inching her way toward them—easy to close the distance with a stride as long as hers, even if she wasn't running. And then Zara was moving, faster, approaching Gravis, craning her neck to see.

Lady Margraine had neared the hall doors now, and Gravis wondered if she was going to leave the castle entirely on this chase. But her steps turned to the side, not straight on toward the doorway, and then Gravis could finally see what she must be heading for. Not because the man in question seemed in any way troubling, but simply because he was the only thing present in that particular patch of space.

To Gravis he seemed unremarkable in every way. He could have been any peasant or day laborer or untrained messenger; he was five or ten years older than Lady

Margraine, slightly freckled, average height. He definitely seemed tired: he shuf-
fled a bit when he walked, though he still moved with a determination and purpose
that ruled out drunkenness. His head was tilted to the side, as if he strained to hear
something, and both eyes were blinking rapidly. His left hand swung at his side as
he walked, but his right was clenched into a fist.

As Lady Margraine approached him, he caught sight of her, and turned his steps
in her direction. As they came within arm's reach, Bridger broke into her full loping gait, enough to bring her closer than Gravis had managed. "Your ladyship—"

"Bridger, stand down!" the marquise barked, and Bridger stopped so abruptly
she nearly fell over. If anyone in the hall hadn't been looking at the marquise, they
certainly were now—she never used such a tone of voice.

Zara was hurrying toward them, but still too far away. Gravis himself was
afraid to move, after how the marquise had reacted to Bridger. But Lady Margraine herself simply completed the last couple of strides between her and the shuf-
fling man, and stopped.

"Are you Arianrod Margraine?" he asked, in a voice so soft that Gravis could
barely hear it.

"I am," she said, with not a hint of dryness or facetiousness. "You have something for me, I suppose."

He nodded slowly, but he did not speak again. She extended her hand to him,
palm up, but when he extended his own and made as if to pass something to her,
she shook her head slightly, dropping her palm so it sat below his still-clenched
fist. He looked puzzled, but obligingly turned his hand over and opened it. Something small and dark dropped into the air.

Lady Margraine went from stillness to urgent movement in the space of a blink.
She caught the object out of the air in a swiping sideways motion, closing her fist
around it and moving her arm out and back at the same time, so that before Gravis
knew what had happened she had already put her entire body between the strange
man and the object she was holding away from both of them, at the end of her
outstretched arm.

The man blinked again, just once, and put a hand to his head. He took a half-step
back, and looked around the room. Lady Margraine's entire body was tense, every
muscle in her arm strained tight, bones standing out on the back of her hand. And
then, as they all watched in disbelief, something sparked like lightning from between her clenched fingers, arcing through the air along her arm.

It was like the jaws of some animal, Gravis thought, as he watched it grow. The
long sparks, painfully bright, seemed to rend the very space they occupied; they
curved out from her fist and seemed to be trying to curve back in toward her arm,
as if to sink teeth into her flesh. Her arm was trembling in the charged air.

Zara finally reached them, passing Gravis by and approaching Bridger's position on her way to Lady Margraine's side. "Zara," the marquise said in a low voice, "keep your distance."

Zara was still walking, eyes on the space between Lady Margraine and the strange man, who was watching the sparks in as much confusion as the rest of them. "This man could have suffered some injury; he must be examined. And you yourself—"

As Zara passed Bridger, Lady Margraine gritted her teeth. Zara's robes became tangled around her legs, and she tripped; Gravis started to make what would have been a useless movement toward her, but luckily Bridger was closer and faster, and caught Zara before she could fall forward.

The sparks surged higher, growing thicker and brighter; they left garish after-images in Gravis's vision. Lady Margraine staggered back from the rest of them, carefully taking one step after another. When she reached the wall, she swept the tapestry back from it with her free hand, and struck her closed fist into the exposed wood.

For a moment nothing happened; in the next, that horrible light flickered and died, disappearing as if it had never been. The tension in Lady Margraine's out-stretched arm slackened, but she did not unclench her fist, and it was another few seconds before she removed her hand from the wall and stepped away from it. The hall was so silent that Gravis could hear the sound of her breathing clearly, quick and heavy. She moved her left hand across her forehead, putting a stray lock of hair back behind her ear. Then she looked around at them all—all staring at her, dumb-founded to a man. Gravis couldn't blame them; no one else knew even as much as he did, and he was shocked enough.

Lady Margraine smiled, and at first Gravis thought it was a little weak, but then he realized it was from the unaccustomed effort she was making *not* to be intimi-dating. "It's all right," she said, releasing her fist and displaying her open palm. "It appears I broke it."

Gravis stared at the object, which was, indeed, in two pieces. It was, or had been, a small, pointed stone, about the size and shape of an arrowhead. But though she might well have snapped it in half when she struck the wall, he was certain she hadn't truly broken it with any physical force.

It was clear that no one else knew what to say. "Your ladyship . . . what was that?" Benwick finally asked.

She gave a weary shrug. "Nothing good. And brought to me quite deliberately, it seems. *Not* by him, I think," she added hastily, when Benwick rounded on the man who had handed the object to her in the first place.

Gravis had nearly forgotten about him, but now he looked as lost as the rest of them, if not more so. He cringed away from the sudden attention. "I . . . this is . . ." He wrung his hands. "Esthrades, isn't it?"

"It is," the marquise said calmly. "Where might you be from?"

"I'm from . . . ah . . ." He winced. "From the coast . . ."

"What, near Lakeport?" Gravis asked, but that just made the man look even more anxious.

"No . . . from the . . . from the western coast . . . sir?"

Zara had had time to free herself from Bridger's arms by that point, and naturally had come right up to the marquise and the stranger without any sense of caution. Lady Margraine extended the hand with the stone to her. "I suppose you'd like to see it?"

Zara snatched up one of the halves, turning it over before her face, staring at it from all angles. "I expect you'll find," the marquise said almost lazily, "that it isn't very remarkable. But I'd like it back when you're done."

"Why?" Zara snapped. "If it's so unremarkable?"

"I never said it was unremarkable," the marquise said. "I said I expected you would find it so."

Zara shook the stone in her fist. "What was this? What did you do? You can't just pass this off as if nothing happened! For all we know, everyone in this hall was just in danger!"

The marquise's mouth twisted, a rare departure from her usual smirk. "Zara, had you touched that stone earlier, as you so clearly intended, you would be dead now. I certainly would never expect gratitude from you, but I'd at least hoped to avoid a lecture."

"Yes, it does seem my intentions were thwarted," Zara said, handing the stone back as if it were a dead leech. "Very curious that I tripped like that."

"Was it?" the marquise snapped. "I should think it the natural result of trying to move at speed while being as old as the hills." She made as if to turn back to the strange man, who Gravis agreed was a much more pressing concern. But before she could speak again, Almasy bounded into the hall.

"I thought . . . there was some sort of commotion about," she said awkwardly, when she saw them all just standing there. "Is everything all right?"

The marquise threw up her hands. "Well, thank the gods at least *you* weren't here for this! If I wanted you not to interfere I should've had to fling you halfway back to Sahai!" She pointed at the doorway. "Everyone except Gravis, stop gawking and return to your business. We've got to question this man, and we can hardly be expected to do it with an entire gallery of onlookers."

CHAPTER SIX

Mist's Edge

WHEN ELGAR'S DECLARATION of war arrived at Mist's Edge, Kelken Rayl was where he usually spent his waking hours: in the library, trying once more to decipher whatever elusive clue Arianrod Margraine had left for him in chapters seven and twelve of *King Arvard and His Campaigns*.

He'd already gotten Alessa, Eirnwin, and Hayne to help him tear through the library for any other books on Arvard, not that they had helped any. (Dirk had no patience for scanning spines, and his letters were shaky enough anyway, so everyone felt he was better employed elsewhere.) But Kel had suspected from the beginning that learning more about Arvard wouldn't help—Lady Margraine hadn't suggested he research Arvard, she had told him specifically to read those two chapters. And he doubted she'd intended to mislead him—if she didn't want him to know this secret, she need never have given him any hints in the first place.

But how were chapters seven and twelve even connected? Seven was mostly about Arvard himself: he had apparently studied many disciplines beyond just swordplay and strategy. History and agriculture, horsemanship and husbandry, painting and architecture, even poetry—the young king had learned them all. He had traveled all over Lantistyne while his father ruled, and conversed with countless scholars. Which was good for him, Kel supposed, but what did all that have to do with *him*?

And chapter twelve was more about Mist's Edge itself than it was Arvard—it highlighted the troops he'd brought to occupy the castle and the alterations he had made to it, including the inconveniences that sometimes resulted from those alterations. Kel had spent hours over it with pen and parchment, trying to sketch a map of the designs the book mentioned and compare it with the plans of Mist's Edge as he knew it, but that exercise had failed to tell him anything conclusive, either: he'd hoped there'd be something in the book that didn't match up with the reality, but that didn't seem to be the case.

He was brushing the end of the quill idly across the page, chasing away imaginary dust, when his sister coughed quietly from beside him—not a real cough, just one that announced her presence. It implied, too, that she had not come for a pleasant reason. He turned to face her, propping his cheek on his elbow. "What is it? You can tell me."

Alessa held out a roll of parchment. "This came for you. It's from . . . ah . . . the imperator."

"From Elgar? We can probably guess what it is, then." Elgar had made it quite clear what would happen if Kel refused to surrender Reglay to him. *As soon as I have marched,* he had said, *that will be the end of it.* He made a show of slitting the wax, unrolled the parchment, read it, rolled it back up. "Well," he said, "at least the man doesn't waste words."

"Then it's . . . ?" Lessa couldn't bring herself to finish the sentence.

"He's gifted us with his opinion that Reglay is, in actual fact, a truant province of the former empire, and thus under the rightful jurisdiction of Hallarnon. Terrible oversight on our part, it seems." That wrung a chuckle out of her, nervous but grateful. "Does Eirnwin know of this?"

"That a letter arrived from Elgar? Yes, I sent Hayne to tell him. I expect he'll make his way to us as soon as the news reaches him."

Kel sighed. "Well, if we're quick, perhaps we can come up with something at least a little intelligent to say before he gets here. Want to help me?"

Lessa bit her lip. "Eirnwin knows more about military strategy than either of us; he wasn't your father's most trusted advisor for nothing. I doubt we'll be able to offer any new insights there."

"But I'm the one who still has to make every decision," Kel said. "I expect the first will be . . . whether we stay here, or try to move somewhere else before the fighting starts."

Lessa nodded. "As to that, the main advantage and disadvantage are easy to see: this is, by far, the largest, strongest, and most defensible castle in Reglay, but it's also so far to the west that it's practically on Hallarnon's doorstep. If we stayed farther east, we could make Elgar fight much longer to actually reach us, but once he did we'd be in a poorer position."

Kel tapped his fingers on the desk, glaring at the closed book. "If any castle on the continent can withstand a siege, it's Mist's Edge. It was built for that purpose. No expense was spared in the initial construction, and I've just been reading about how Arvard reinforced it, with all this knowledge of architecture behind . . . him." He frowned. Something about that sentence was striking him oddly, but before he could tell Lessa about it, Eirnwin burst in, robes fluttering.

"Your Grace," he said, "I've only just heard. Do you wish me to—"

Kel held up a hand. "Hold a moment, Eirnwin. I have to finish . . . pondering something."

Eirnwin could hardly be blamed for his confusion, but Kel didn't want to risk dislodging whatever had taken root in his thoughts by explaining further. He repeated his last sentence in his mind, trying to find what bothered him about it.

True, Arvard wasn't an architect by trade, but he *had* studied architecture— extensively, if the book could be believed. And everything he had added to Mist's Edge worked just as he'd intended: the western tower gave a better vantage and was less drafty, the barracks made more efficient use of space, he'd repaired the outer wall—

Wait. He'd repaired the outer wall, except for a sizable chunk of it on the east side, which he'd had to rebuild when his efforts had collapsed it. An amateur's mistake, perhaps, but everything else had come off so flawlessly that this one oversight stood out. And though Kel had read the book three times, he couldn't recall a satisfactory explanation for *why* the wall had collapsed—"it was weak," perhaps, but then why so much weaker than the rest of the structure?

He reached across the desk, searching for the clumsy map he had made. "Eirnwin, what's by the east outer wall? Is anyone quartered there?"

"I . . . don't believe so, Your Grace. There are certainly no living accommodations in that area. It's mostly a bunch of storerooms, but items are all jumbled up inside them, out of any kind of order. I know I say I find this castle confusing in general, but *those* rooms make the rest of it look downright straightforward."

That settled it, then. If a large portion of the east wall had collapsed, Arvard would have been able to rebuild it as he saw fit, relying much less on what had already been put in place by his ancestors—and the master architect had created a chaotic mess? He must've wanted to discourage anyone from examining that area too closely. And if he had collapsed the wall on purpose, as a pretext so even his own subordinates wouldn't know what he intended to build there . . .

"Fetch Dirk and Hayne," he told Eirnwin. "We've got to go down there, right away."

Eirnwin blinked. "But . . . the letter, Your Grace?"

"And *then* the letter," Kel promised. "But this first."

IT TOOK THEM the better part of two hours to find anything at all. Eirnwin hadn't been exaggerating about the illogic of the storerooms: they found moth-eaten linens; bent swords; three kegs of an absolutely awful mixture that purported to be beer; two halves of different books with no relation whatsoever; a purse that contained twenty pieces of silver, four coppers, and a thimble; ten entire crates that just seemed to hold rope; a wardrobe full of infants' clothes; a wooden flute that wouldn't sound a note.

None of that deterred Kel in the slightest; it only made him more certain. "I doubt the trick is going to be in anything stored here," he told the others from just inside the doorway. "The clutter is meant to hide something more essential—foundational, I expect. I know we can't clear it *all* out, but try to look for something that could . . . mask something else."

He did feel guilty that he wasn't able to help search, but the floors of these storerooms were littered with so much detritus that wading through them on crutches was just asking to take a fall. Even Lessa had insisted on being right in the thick of the commotion, despite the copious amounts of dust they were all kicking up.

"You think we ought to clear out a space on the floor?" Dirk called. "See if anything's loose?"

"Ideally," Kel said, "but there's just too much there. Where would we move it to make the room?"

"I think we're looking for some sort of signifier," Lessa said, squinting at what Kel first thought was an ancient helmet, but that on closer inspection turned out to be a ruptured pot. "If Arvard hid something here, he had to be able to find it again. So it'd have to be something hard to dislodge from a specific place—something heavy, or unwieldy. Otherwise he'd risk someone moving it while cleaning or looking for something else."

"That makes sense," Kel said. "If he wanted to keep it a secret, he couldn't very well tell anyone not to move the—"

They were interrupted by an alarming crash, and whipped their heads around to see that Hayne, halfway along the opposite wall, had attempted to pull what turned out to be a rake from the pile of fishing nets that had obscured it, only to have the shaft come loose in her hand. The sudden loss of equilibrium had sent her staggering into some detached shelving, and the unnervingly heavy-looking brass candelabrum at the top, having already toppled over, was about to clear the shelving entirely and land on Hayne's head.

Before Kel could so much as shout a warning, Hayne twisted her body to the side, hurled the rake shaft like a javelin at the far corner, and angled her torso upward in time to catch the candelabrum in her now-free hand. She exhaled deeply, the tension leaving her body with her breath, and placed the candelabrum on a much lower shelf. "Your Grace," she said, "I'm beginning to think these rooms are hazardous by design."

Hayne's reflexes weren't exactly surprising to Kel; he'd had firsthand experience of how quickly she could react when he was seven years old, and she'd been the only guard in the banquet hall fast enough to get between him and an assassin's blade. No one had thought her very remarkable until that point, but Kel's father had honored her greatly afterward—not least because, lacking time to get her sword into the perfect position, Hayne had allowed the enemy knife to skate past it and into the meat of her arm, leaving a long scar that stretched nearly to her elbow. He'd seen that cut up close; he'd been less than a foot from her the moment it was made. It certainly wasn't a pleasant memory, but it was imperative that he not forget how much he owed her.

"What did you hit?" Alessa asked Hayne, breaking Kel out of his reverie. He turned to look at the corner where Hayne had thrown the rake shaft, recalling belatedly that there had been a metallic sound as it struck something. The only remote possibility was a tall, indistinct shape near the corner, half in the shadow of the crates piled next to it.

Alessa picked her way around an irreparably slashed armchair and a stack of mismatched curtains to the far corner, where a sheet had been thrown over something tall and lumpy. Facing it, she hesitated for a moment, then seized the sheet in both hands and tore it free, coughing at the resulting cloud of dust.

She had revealed a statue cast in bronze—once, perhaps, it had been a warm and golden color, but now the sickly green of it turned Kel's stomach. The figure, human-sized, was difficult to see, for it was covered in a cloak that whipped about its body in an unseen wind, tangling in the air and obscuring its face. It stood tall as an adult, but beyond that its age or sex were impossible to determine. The cloak had fallen into its eyes, but its cheeks and chin were visible, its mouth grimly set. Grimmer still, there was a manacle fastened about one upraised wrist, a short length of chain trailing from it—it ended abruptly, as if broken off.

"An escaped prisoner?" Kel offered, more to break the silence than anything else. He carefully made his way over to the statue, standing beside Lessa. This close, if he looked into the depths of its hood, he could almost fancy he saw an eye carved there, staring out of the dark.

Alessa prodded the statue's base with her foot, then crouched down. "There's something written here." She rubbed at the graven letters. *"Depiction of Irein, artist and era unknown."*

Eirnwin had joined them by then. "Tsk. One should never deface an artifact, even for the sake of recordkeeping. This must have been pillaged by amateurs. Perhaps, though I hate to say it, by one of His Grace's ancestors. The Rayls were soldiers before they were kings."

"Who was Irein?" Alessa asked. "Surely someone important, if there were statues carved in their likeness?"

"That's safe to say, but I've never heard of any historical personage with that name," Eirnwin said. "I've never known *anyone* by that name, in fact, past or present."

Kel leaned on one crutch, and tapped the other against the bronze. "Leaving that aside, this has to be our signifier. It's too heavy to shuffle about without purpose, and it looks important but not too obvious." To Hayne and Dirk, he said, "What do you think? Can this be moved? Should we get help?"

"Let us try it first," Hayne said. She and Dirk had to clear out a small space next to the statue before they could even attempt to move it, but once they did they were able to slide it a little ways across the floor without straining themselves. And when they were done, Kel saw exactly what he'd expected to see: a metal ring hiding in a cut-out groove in the floor, so that the panel surrounding it could be pulled up. There was another floor below.

"I knew it," Kel said. "Arvard collapsed that wall on purpose, and he did it so he could build this—and so he could hide that he was building it."

"Best to let us take a peek at it first, Your Grace," Dirk said, giving the metal ring a tug. He ended up having to use both hands to pry up the panel, and then he stared down into dark and empty space. "There's a ladder—it's not too far down to the floor, but the room's bigger than I can see in this light."

"We've got to explore it," Kel said.

"Your guards are perfectly capable of doing that, Your Grace," Eirnwin said. "You know there's no way you could climb down that ladder on your own."

It wasn't precisely true that there was no way. It was *possible* that Kel could've made it all the way down the ladder; it just wasn't worth the day's span of swelling and pain that would undoubtedly result even in the best of circumstances. "I concede that, but I still think I should—"

"Eh, that's not so, Your Grace," Dirk objected. "This ladder's not so tall. If I went ahead and stood on the bottom, and Hayne or somebody helped you down from above, I could catch you in my arms with hardly a rung in between us, and set you on the ground that way. They could pass the crutches down afterward."

"Even if you *could* manage that without hurting him, that isn't the point," Eirnwin said. "Whatever's down there, I think it's clear that it's been sealed off for generations. We've no idea what Arvard sought to conceal in this place, or how long he intended it to keep, or what state it might be in now. Letting His Grace go through without making a thorough investigation first is simply out of the question."

"Eirnwin," Kel said, tapping his crown, "would you say you're familiar with this thing on my head?"

Eirnwin smiled ruefully. "Alas, Your Grace, I must admit it. I seem to recall I was the one who placed it there."

"That sounds about right," Kel agreed. "It's not very comfortable—I can't say I'd recommend it on its own merits. But I *am* certain that confining my head in one of these things means I can explore as many strange secret rooms in my own castle as I please, and you can't actually forbid me from doing it."

Lessa chuckled behind her hand. Eirnwin bowed his head, but he still wore the same smile. "I am nothing if not your obedient servant, Your Grace. Let us plunge into this hellhole forthwith."

"Right," Dirk said, "so just pass His Grace down and let's—"

"*After* you get a damned light down there, you idiot!" Eirnwin finished, but he was laughing. "I understand we're short on time, but that doesn't mean you have to throw your own king down some hole in the ground without calling for a torch first! Honestly!"

IN THE END, Kel, Lessa, and Eirnwin all went with Dirk. Dirk's plan was a good one, and they got Kel to the floor beneath with minimal fuss. Hayne, who had passed him down, stayed up top to make sure the entrance remained clear, and the rest of them trooped after Eirnwin, who held the torch.

A tunnel lay at the bottom of the ladder, extending perhaps fifty feet before it widened out, dead-ending in a much larger room. The flickering torchlight revealed a line of barrels, each as high as Kel's nose, made of thick dark wood and banded twice with iron. They stretched off down the tunnel, each one placed directly after the last. They continued like that until the tunnel widened out, at which point they were stacked in one corner of it, numerous but out of the way.

"Supplies?" Kel asked Eirnwin.

"It's possible. Perhaps King Arvard sought to build a secret storeroom, as a last resort in case of a siege?"

Alessa sniffed the air, and coughed. "Do you smell that?"

"What?" Eirnwin asked. "I think my nose is clogged from the damp."

"It's sweet," Alessa said, and walked over to one of the barrels. She tried to lift the lid, but it seemed to be on fairly tight. She didn't give up, though, just dug her heels in and did her best to pry it up. Dirk approached to help, but she waved him away. Kel took a deep inhale, and finally got a faint whiff, more like sugar than perfume. It wasn't a smell he recognized.

Alessa started back as the lid finally and abruptly came loose. She peered into the depths of the barrel, sniffed again, and froze in place, still holding the lid in her hand. "You two might want to have a look in here," she said. "Eirnwin, I'm not sure, but if I'm right, and they're all like this—no, um, you'll want to pass the torch to Dirk."

That could hardly have failed to draw their attention, and they made their way over, Kel much more slowly than Eirnwin—the rough, uneven floor was wreaking havoc on his legs. But he made it, and peered over the edge of the barrel, careful his head didn't knock into Eirnwin's. With the lid off, the smell was *much* stronger: a strange, unappetizing sweetness that felt like it was coating the inside of his nose.

There was a silence, and then the hiss of indrawn breath, and then Eirnwin took several giant steps back.

"Dirk," he said, voice strained, "please pass me that torch back, pick up His Grace, and transport him out of here immediately. Take the crutches as well—*don't* drop them."

"What?" Kel asked, looking from Lessa to Eirnwin and back again. "What is it?"

"We'll discuss it upstairs," Eirnwin said. "Dirk, *please.*"

Eirnwin looked so utterly grave that even Kel, who would normally have protested letting Dirk pick him up like a baby, felt it best to submit without fuss, and they trooped back out of the passage and up the ladder, coming face-to-face with a surprised Hayne. Eirnwin shut the trapdoor firmly behind them—he'd probably have moved the statue back over it, too, if he'd been strong enough.

Kel certainly felt he was owed an explanation after all that, but before he could even draw in a breath to ask, another soldier barged into the storeroom. "Forgive me for interrupting, Your Grace," she said, "but a message has arrived, and they told me to make sure you'd heard of it."

"The one from Imperator Elgar?" Kel asked. "Yes, I was informed by one of your fellows a few hours ago. I've already read—"

But the guard shook her head. "Not that one, Your Grace. A letter's come from Arianrod Margraine."

CHAPTER SEVEN

Eldren Cael

THEY MADE GOOD time back to Eldren Cael—no doubt the prince was eager to share the details of his victory with the rest of his family. Rhia still felt a pang of dislocation every time she entered the city: in Araveil streets came in all different lengths and shapes, from long and serpentine to abrupt and bone-straight, but the actual widths of the streets did not vary much. In Eldren Cael, on the other hand, you had avenues wide enough to fit ten mounted riders abreast, and hidden backstreets so narrow one person practically had to slip through sideways. In Araveil the buildings were all of haphazard heights, but in Eldren Cael they were short around the outer walls, tending to get gradually taller the closer you got to the palace in the south. Yet still the palace towered over everything around it, its pale sandstone walls spreading wider than three avenues. Its smooth planes were sharply defined, impressively precise for so large a structure. It had been intimidating to Rhia at first, but now the sight of it only cheered her. Once again, she had helped Hephestion return safely home to his family.

The prince's mother met them in the great hall—word of their arrival must have reached her beforehand. Since her daughter had yet to hold an official coronation, Queen Maribel could still lay claim to that title, and Rhia did not doubt that she intended to make use of it until the final instant it was available to her.

"My son," she said. "From far have you come again."

"The same, yet different!" Hephestion called back, his exuberance taking any solemnity out of the traditional greeting. "What an undertaking it was, Mother—it came off just as I said, Rhia will tell you. Not a single soldier lost, and we went through them like a whirlwind! The *shock* we gave them . . . well, you can imagine." He ducked his head, suddenly self-conscious. Rhia had yet to figure out how they did it, but Hephestion's mother and sister both possessed the ability, through nothing more than polite and silent listening, to make you come to the conclusion that you had irrevocably embarrassed yourself, and poor Hephestion was affected by it more frequently than most. "The point, of course, is that we succeeded. As much as we could have hoped to, and more."

Rhia thought Queen Maribel was beautiful, though she doubted the queen would thank her for it if she said so. Indeed, the expression the queen customarily presented her—mouth pinched, brows closed stormily over her amber eyes—seemed designed to encourage the opposite view. She never spoke to Rhia directly, and usually waited to speak about her until Adora was present. Now she spared Rhia barely an instant, devoting all her attention to her son. "News of your exploits precedes you, Hephestion. By all accounts, you handled yourself splendidly."

Though Queen Maribel was beautiful, that wasn't to say she and Hephestion looked much alike. The queen was straight-haired and thin-shouldered, though she somehow seemed to take up more space by the sheer weight of her presence. She looked even less like her daughter—apparently it was Prince Landon who had most closely resembled her, though only Hephestion had her eyes. And she certainly never blushed, as Hephestion was doing now. "Oh, well, *somebody* handled it, that's the important thing. And Rhia's help was invaluable, as always." Looking around them, he missed his mother's pronounced lack of enthusiasm for that final statement. "Where's Adora? She didn't come down with you?"

Queen Maribel sighed, but her face was fond. "Your sister hasn't been able to tear herself away from her translation of Lisianthus all morning; it seems she's in the middle of a particularly difficult passage. But she promised she would join us shortly."

Hephestion huffed a little, but Rhia knew he wasn't really put out. On the contrary, it pleased him to know he had been out and active while his sister had remained at study. "I guess that's typical for her. Even now, as surprising as that is. Not that it's my place to advise her, but I should think the entirety of a queen's duties cannot possibly reside solely within the walls of her castle, no?"

"She is hardly lax in her duties," his mother said, "and you know what joy she derives from study. But perhaps you could attempt to make her see your point, if you thought it would be well taken."

"To make me see what?" a light voice asked, and suddenly Adora was among them.

Her hair was darker than her brother's, black as ink even in full sunlight. It would fall just as it wished, no matter what she did, and as a result it always looked as if she had just run a particularly challenging race. Her eyes were darker than Hephestion's, too, wide and expressive, reflecting her emotions much more deeply than her small and composed mouth. The eyes were the things your own eyes were most drawn to when you looked at her, and Rhia had come to learn that they had two primary attitudes. Often Adora blinked them owlishly, almost dazedly, as if against a bright light or after long and concentrated staring at something else. But then, just as you started wondering if she were paying any attention at all, her eyes would narrow sharply, gleaming bright, in a look of such keen intensity that even the boldest or most confident person would have trouble meeting it directly. There was never any warning, before she looked like that—as many others had found, to their great discomfort.

Of course her beauty could not approach Hephestion's; his handsomeness was not given even to one person in a thousand. Even her mother, perhaps, had fairer features and a more elegant bearing. Yet there were few faces Rhia had ever seen that she liked better than the queen's. It was a face that would only ever bear its anger solemnly and with dignity; its features would never twist in fury or warp into a sneer. And it could never be cruel, not in any extremity or under any duress.

Hephestion and their mother stared at her, some worry or unease passing over them before either spoke. In the end Hephestion was first: "Oh, you didn't . . . come in at a good time. We weren't trying to insult you, we just—"

"Of course not," the queen agreed, with a gentle smile. "But you can hardly say you wish me to understand something and expect me not to be curious. I am sure it is something *I* would wish to understand as well, if I only knew what it was."

Hephestion tugged miserably at his hair. "Well. It's only, Adora, that when Mother said you were at your Lisianthus again, I was concerned. Your realm is large, and yet you seem content to occupy no more of it than a tower room, most of the time."

Adora never bothered with hurrying to a response; she considered another's words for as long as she needed to before speaking, turning them over in her mind. "I'm sure there is some truth to that—Father was always sending Landon around the country, after all. Yet while he did so, Father himself was wont to stay at Eldren Cael. Perhaps, since you are *my* heir, it is only fitting that you should be able to range our lands more freely than I can."

"I . . . suppose," Hephestion mumbled.

"And you, Mother? Did you have more to add?"

Queen Maribel shook her head. "I don't, at the moment."

"Well enough, then." She smiled again, less muted this time. "I'm glad to have you and Rhia back, Feste—not least under such favorable conditions. You did well. Were there any complications I should know about?"

"None," Hephestion said, as Rhia fixed her eyes on the ground. "A fine bit of business all around. Now that we've sprung this sort of trap once, I don't know if we'll be able to do it again, otherwise I'd say there's a lot more good we could do. But I'm certainly satisfied with what we've already done."

"As am I," Adora said. "Rhia, would you walk with me awhile? Now that you're free to take up your usual duties again, there are a few things I wish to tell you."

Rhia bowed. "Of course, Your Grace."

Hephestion clapped her on the back. "Your work's never done, eh? I'm going to get myself as much of a feast as I can pilfer from the kitchens without consequence. Come up and join me, if you're able."

"If I am able, my lord," Rhia agreed, before they went their separate ways, Rhia following Adora out of the hall.

The queen said nothing for some time, simply letting Rhia follow her as they climbed floor upon floor to the battlements. There were soldiers on guard near the door from the north central tower, but the queen merely nodded to them and strode past, waiting until she and Rhia paced along an unoccupied stretch of rampart, a hot wind ruffling their hair. Then she said, "Why don't you tell me whatever it is Hephestion neglected to mention."

Rhia froze. Of course Adora would have seen through her, and Adora was the one she served; she knew she was bound to answer truthfully. But that didn't mean she felt no guilt about going against Hephestion's wishes, either. He was the one who had insisted Rhia dine with him at the palace as thanks for helping him fight off bandits in the street; without his kindness, she would never have met Adora at all, and she certainly wouldn't be employed as captain of the guard.

"It's all right," the queen said. "Whatever it is, I promise I won't irritate him with it."

"It's only . . . his wound, though mostly healed, was still giving him . . . some trouble. He didn't come to any harm in the fighting, only participated in it somewhat less than he would have liked. Everything else was just as he said."

Thankfully, Adora didn't look distressed, or even particularly surprised. "This recklessness in him is troubling, but you aren't to blame. Of course you would not go against his wishes, and no one can get him to listen to reason when he has decided otherwise. Were I to give you the authority to take stricter measures with him, I believe we would cause more problems than we solved."

"Yes," Rhia said. "I believe that as well, Your Grace."

"In that case," the queen said, "I shall neglect to bring it up with him, and trust instead that you will continue to keep a watchful eye on his recovery."

Rhia bowed. "I will not allow him to come to harm, Your Grace."

"Well, you'll do your best, at least. My brother is full of surprises." The queen brushed the curls out of her face—they flopped back down immediately—and looked out over the ramparts at the city far below. "You won't have an easy time of it here, either, I'm afraid. I had hoped we might make some progress on the Red

Crows while you were gone, to present you with good news upon your return, but I fear they have only grown bolder, and caused yet more harm."

The Red Crows were the most brazen of Issamira's many street gangs, robbing even children, the elderly, and the infirm, and not caring how many they killed to do it. Rhia and Hephestion had worked with the rest of Eldren Cael's guardsmen to kill or capture many of them, but it seemed they were always recruiting more. "Do you think we should not have left the city?"

"On the contrary." The queen smiled to reassure her. "The group you and Hephestion tracked down in the north would surely have grown even more severe than the Crows, given time."

Rhia felt the tension in her body relax. "That is good to hear. I did feel . . . that we were able to accomplish something worthwhile."

The queen's smile had grown slightly sad. "This must still be strange to you, though. I suspect you did not suffer from such bandits in Araveil, did you?"

"There are bandits everywhere," Rhia said, "but it is true that the gangs I've had to deal with here would be considered uncommonly large and well-organized, had I encountered them in Lanvaldis."

The queen nodded; she'd clearly expected that answer. "It is a tragic effect of Issamira's history, I'm afraid. For centuries we fought against the might of empire, even after all our cities and fortresses had been conquered; our people rose up again and again, even if they were only a hundred, fifty, a dozen strong. One cannot properly enumerate the Issamiri rebellions in any history book, for *someone* among us was always in rebellion, even if they stood alone. In small groups, we had to learn a new way to fight—to give a dozen men the strength of a hundred. We learned to appear out of nowhere, through a dust storm or in the dead of night, strike them like lightning, and then disappear to half a hundred hiding places. Even the Rebel Queen fought that way in the beginning, until the day Eldren Cael opened its doors to her, and the rebellion burst out of the shadows at last.

"But when the war was won, and Talia Avestri became Issamira's queen in earnest, there were those who were still displeased. There were those who believed true freedom for Issamira meant an end to kings and queens forever, and they turned against her after she accepted a crown. There were those who believed true freedom meant the ability to do whatever they pleased, and who sought only to promote anarchy. And there were those who had never joined the rebellion out of any sense of idealism, but only for the opportunity it gave them to kill and pillage as they pleased. These people took the tactics they had learned to fight the Ninists, and turned them against our own people. And, alas, those tactics proved just as effective, and remain so to this day. I wouldn't be surprised if there were members of the Red Crows, or any other bandit gangs, who could trace their lineage back to those who once fought for the Rebel Queen, or those who first turned against her."

Rhia was quiet, thinking on the enormity of that distant past. Her people, too, had been crushed by the Ninists, centuries ago. The ancestors of those who today were called Lanvalds had resided in a country called Selindwyr—a place never again to be found on any map, but that had covered present-day Aurnis and beyond. Selindwyr had been the last country in Lantistyne to resist being subsumed into the empire of Elesthene, and its people had fought the Ninists for generations. But in the end, after decades of fighting, they, too, had been broken.

The crimes inflicted upon the defeated people of Selindwyr by the invading Elesthenian army remained unequaled in the continent's history for cruelty and mercilessness. Entire cities were destroyed—the bare bones of many of them could still be found in Aurnis, and there were others the Aurnians had rebuilt. Children and civilians were slaughtered in huge numbers. There was no question of surrender—by that point, the Elesthenians had long since killed anyone with the authority to surrender. They simply inflicted suffering until they were confident all who remained alive no longer possessed the strength to fight back. And it had worked. While the Issamiri launched rebellion after rebellion, the people of Selindwyr—those who were left—had remained listless and hopeless, as if their very souls had been stolen. In a way, perhaps they had been.

The queen's gaze had been captured by something above their heads, and she kept tilting her chin upward as they retraced their steps along the ramparts. When they reached the door to the castle interior, she paused before the soldiers standing guard beside it. "Excuse me," she said, "what route do you customarily take during your watch?"

The guards looked at each other, and the one on the left quickly lowered her eyes. She was young, and her companion looked twenty or thirty years older, so perhaps she sought to yield in the face of greater experience. Yet even the man looked confused. "What route, Your Grace? We're charged with guarding the door. We always have been."

"So you don't move from this spot?" She took his silence as an affirmative. "It occurs to me that, hedged in by the tower and the wall like this, soldiers standing this close to the door lack the vantage down into the city that they might have if they moved even ten or fifteen yards down the wall."

"Down into the city?" the man repeated. "How does greater vantage of the city help us better guard the door, Your Grace?"

The queen's smile was one Rhia knew well—it was an attempt to take the sting out of her next words. "To be literal, sir, your task is indeed to guard this one particular door. But in general, your task is to secure this entire castle and those who dwell within it—with the help of many of your fellows, of course. I merely point out that, if only one of the two of you were to move ten yards down the wall, you would be able to guard the door and keep watch over the city at once. The *door,* perhaps, would be no better guarded, but certainly no worse; the *castle,* however, would see its security improved."

The female guard finally spoke up, with a wary glance at her companion. "It . . . does make sense. I'm happy to do it—you wouldn't have to move at all."

He cut the air in a dismissive gesture. "There's two on the door for a reason. You'd *want* two, if someone tried to come through who shouldn't be. There's lookouts at the *top* of the towers. Vantage into the city is *their* job."

"But you can't actually see the top of the tower while you're in its shadow like this," the queen said. "Let's say, for the sake of argument, that something happened to the lookouts at the top. From the position I've indicated, you'd be able to see that something was wrong; from here, you know nothing—including the fact that you now have no eyes on the city. As for needing two guards at the doorway, *this* door opens outward. If you remain positioned like this, it is not inconceivable that some potential foe might throw the door open, using it to bludgeon your companion here, and taking you by surprise while she is stunned. If she were on the wall, not only would she be out of the reach of any swinging doors, it would take her only a matter of moments to return to your side, should you need it."

It was all Rhia could do not to smirk at the man; surely he had no rejoinder for *that.* Even his companion seemed to regard the matter as settled. "Then I'll . . . I'll just move along the wall, Your Grace, like you said."

The man scowled, and opened his mouth as if to call her back. But Rhia fixed him with her fiercest glare, and between that and the way the queen was just mildly standing there, waiting to embarrass him further, he no doubt realized the foolhardiness of trying to correct her. Instead, he pointedly looked over her shoulder, withdrawing from the conversation.

"That will be all, then," the queen said sadly. "Thank you for your time." He barely inclined his head, still without looking at her, and Rhia gritted her teeth. She would have been more than content to reprimand him for such disrespect, but she knew that would only make Adora unhappier.

There were many who behaved this way around the queen. She had a mind that was ever working to solve problems, chipping away at them somewhere in the background even while she was primarily occupied elsewhere. She was full of suggestions in every direction: how this process could be made more efficient, how that task could be carried out more safely. People *should* have been glad to receive her advice, but Rhia knew not all of them were. Adora was not proud, and only sought to help people do their jobs better. And so they disliked her, for such people did not truly want to hear how they could do their jobs better. They wanted to hear that they were doing an excellent job already.

"Well, come along, Rhia," the queen said, once they were through the doorway and back inside. "I'm sure you're hungry, and I quite distracted myself out of a midday meal. We can put off weightier thoughts until our stomachs are heavier than our minds."

CHAPTER EIGHT

Stonespire

GRAVIS BARELY HAD time to swallow his breakfast before Zara was after him again, and that was all the proof he needed to know that the bad business of the day before wasn't yet concluded. He'd known Zara for more than twenty-five years, and when had she ever wanted the barest shred of his support?

"I know you heard it, too," she insisted, all but tugging at his arm. "The marquise said she'd have to send Seren Almasy *back* to Sahai."

"But, healer, you yourself spent many years in Sahai before you returned here, so it's not as if no one's ever done it before, or as if it *must* be a terrible thing if one does."

"You have long known the purpose of those years across the sea, Gravis. But do you think Seren Almasy ever studied the healing arts?"

"If so, she must've been the worst student they'd ever seen," Gravis said.

"In fact, I was roundly considered an excellent student," Almasy said, her calm words punctuated by the crunch of teeth into something hard, and Gravis nearly leaped out of his skin. She sat at the long table beside them, continuing to bite off pieces of blood apple; at least she wasn't cutting it with that damned knife today. "But not at the healing arts." She inclined her head to Zara. "You surprise me, healer. I had come to believe you preferred a direct approach. If you had any questions for me, you could simply have asked."

"Then answer," Zara demanded. "Are you or are you not one of the Inxia Morain?"

The words meant nothing to Gravis, and did not startle Almasy. She took a large bite of her apple, chewed and swallowed, looked Zara in the eye, and said, "No. I am not."

"There," Zara snapped, striking the table with the flat of her hand. "Why should I ask you, if you're only going to lie?"

"It is no lie," Almasy said. "According to the strictures of the Inxia Morain themselves, I have no right to name myself among their number. Had you asked whether I ever *was* a member of the Inxia Morain . . . I must admit even their many rules are not entirely clear on that point. But there may have been some slight window of time during which that description was not inappropriate."

Gravis passed a hand over his face. "I don't suppose either of you would deign to tell me what you're talking about?"

Zara gestured angrily at Almasy. "I have never *seen* her work, but there are many villages where you can hear tales of it. It has long concerned me, because skills such as hers must *come* from somewhere—you don't simply improvise your way to them. But finally she has admitted it. The Inxia Morain! When I was in the imperial capital, there were none more feared than the Inxia Morain."

Almasy laughed. "Their leaders would be thrilled to hear you say so. They work dreadfully hard to make sure that remains true. If only you could have been privy to one of their more anxious meetings about it."

Gravis had a singularly unhappy suspicion as to where this conversation was going. "And the Inxia Morain are . . . ?"

"It's Sahaian, obviously," Almasy said. "A *morain* is simply what we might call a guild. As for *Inxia,* that's a bit harder. I'm prepared to let the healer correct me, but . . . the Last Guild? The Final Guild? Something like that."

"The translation is irrelevant," Zara snapped. "They are no more nor less than the most exalted guild of assassins in the entire Sahaian Empire—or, as they would boast, in the entire world."

Gravis stared at Almasy. She did not look guilty, or even evasive. She might even have been smiling, just the tiniest bit. "So this entire time," he said, as calmly as he could, "this *entire* time, despite all your countless protestations to the contrary, you have been an assassin?"

Damn it, Almasy *was* smiling. He couldn't remember the last time he'd seen her reveal even this much enjoyment at anything. "Gravis, you're not listening. I'm not an assassin. I was *trained* by assassins. I never took a single contract—as I have always said, I *don't* kill for coin. I wanted the skills, not the lifestyle."

"That cannot be," Zara said. "They would have killed you for making off with their secrets in such a fashion."

Almasy shrugged. "Perhaps some of them attempted to. I've never encountered any, however—I would guess that my old teacher took care of any members with those intentions before they even had the chance to cross the sea. It seems like something he would do."

"Why would he spend so much effort on you?" Zara asked.

"For the sake of the look on your face right now, healer. The Inxia Morain do not truly deal in death; they deal in fear. That is their lifeblood, their currency— without it, they could not survive. If you lived in the Sahaian capital, you must have known where their guildhouse was—there's a sign over the bloody door. Yet assassins are against imperial law—though mercenaries aren't, a distinction I found strange. The Inxia Morain have an unspoken arrangement with Sahai's sitting emperor or empress: no member of the guild shall ever try to kill the current ruler, or anyone in their direct line of succession. In return, no sitting ruler shall try to destroy the guild. This arrangement came under threat only twice: the empress who intended to send her guards to the guildhouse in the morning found her firstborn child's body laid across the threshold of her chambers, and the order never came. And the heir of the only guild-assassinated emperor found her father's killer strung up before the palace, a hundred stab wounds in his body and a note of apology pinned to his breast. No other emperor or empress has ever been assassinated, and none made an enemy of the guild—even Empress Taienzi, who supposedly dared just about everything else, left the Inxia Morain in peace."

Her expression returned to its customary solemnity. "Everyone in the imperial city—indeed, everyone in the empire—is touched in some way by knowledge of the Inxia Morain, that belief that they can always find you, always destroy you, if that is their desire. But as you see, healer, almost no one in Lantistyne has even heard of them. Because your average Sahaian citizen considers this continent little more than a pathetic backwater—a useful trading partner, but no place for an imperial citizen to actually *live*—you'd be hard-pressed to find a guild assassin who would lower themselves to carry out business here. *That* is why my teacher was only too happy to have me return to the country of my birth—wherever I went, he knew the rumor of my skills would go with me, and of my skills' origin. And perhaps even Lantians would begin to fear the residents of a guildhouse across the sea."

Zara's face was still tense with anger, but she seemed more subdued—almost chastised, Gravis would have said, if it were possible for Zara to feel such a thing. "Then these assassins are more sinister than even I had guessed."

"Their skills in combat and subterfuge are extraordinary," Almasy said. "But they are mortal, and they die like mortals. Beyond that, they have only the power those who fear them allow them to have." She took a last bite of her apple. "As I said, I do not believe any of them will venture across the sea—not to kill me, or for any other reason. And unless you truly run afoul of her ladyship, you have nothing to fear from me."

"IT'S NOT DANGEROUS anymore, you know," Arianrod said, idly spinning the two fragments of rock on the surface of her desk. "I really did break it. It's just regular stone now."

Seren took a couple steps closer, staring at the broken object dubiously. She hadn't been there to see whatever it had done, but the reports she'd heard were not reassuring. "Is it like that thing you had me retrieve? A . . . *wardrenholt*?"

"Good guess, but no," Arianrod said. "It's just a rock that had a couple enchantments on it." She caught herself. "I shouldn't say that as if the thing were easy to make. It shows quite a bit of skill, I must admit."

Seren leaned against the one corner of the desk that wasn't piled high with books and papers. "You'll have to explain that if you want me to understand it."

Arianrod sat back in her chair, twirling a lock of hair around her finger. "Say you want to get through a locked door, and you don't have the key. How do you do it?"

This was surely some test again, but Seren tried to think it through dutifully. "Are there windows?"

Arianrod grinned. "And my father would have tried to break the door down, and someone else would've picked the lock, or found out who had the key and stolen it from them, or who knows what else. Watching someone try to solve the problem tells you as much about the way their mind works as it does about the problem. Magic's like that, only instead of one locked door your problem is the whole world. If *you* wanted to kill someone, Seren, no doubt you'd have many ways to go about it, but they'd all be related to physical realities: blades, bludgeons, poisons, and so forth. When a mage wants to kill someone, the limits are set by their own imagination." She picked up one half of the stone and turned it over. "This was a double blunder for Elgar—once over because it failed to kill me, and twice over because I can use it to figure out how he thinks."

"You're sure Elgar is responsible for this?" Seren asked.

"Well, I suppose I can't be *positive,* but I know he's a mage, and I know he'd like to kill me, and I know, after talking to the fellow who brought me this little present, that he picked it up while on a trip to Valyanrend, so . . . a compelling theory does present itself."

"That man brought it to you without knowing what it was?"

"He was very confused," Arianrod said. "He'd never been to Esthrades before, but upon leaving Valyanrend he saw a glimmer by the side of the road and stopped to pick it up. He wasn't sure what the object was, and yet it seemed absolutely essential that he deliver it to me—he couldn't tell us why. It continued to seem essential over many weeks, no matter how many mishaps he encountered—do you know his horse threw him when he'd gotten halfway, and he broke his wrist and had to stay in bed recovering in a nearby village? And yet the whole time they were urging bed rest, he kept thinking, *I've got to get this to Esthrades.* Such a persistent thought—how strange that it evaporated the instant he dropped the object into my hand."

She placed the fragment back on the desk. "That's probably all the information I'm going to get, so next I ask myself, *How did Elgar set this up?* I've got to try to think about it the way he thought about it. And what I've come up with is: two separate but interrelated enchantments. And that's *difficult.*" Before Seren could even ask, she said, "According to the books I've read from when magic was plentiful, an *enchantment* was what they called any spell centered on an object that had a constant or conditional effect. I can't imagine Elgar needed fewer than two: one to plant that very persistent suggestion in the mind of whoever picked up the stone, and one to unleash the spell that was meant to kill me. He puts both enchantments on this stone and leaves it outside Valyanrend for any traveler to pick up."

"He just left it?" Seren asked. "That doesn't seem very wise."

Arianrod grinned. "Seren, I'm surprised at you. It is one of the most common laws of human existence that, should a shiny object exist somewhere in the world, *someone* is going to pick it up."

"But it's *not* shiny," Seren pointed out.

"Not anymore," Arianrod said, "but *that* enchantment is a very easy one. Still, you bring up a good point: no fewer than *three* enchantments. One: *this will gleam until picked up,* most likely. Two: *once picked up, this will compel its holder not to release it until he has handed it to the ruler of Esthrades,* or thereabouts. And three: *once handed over, this will* . . . release whatever spell that was, but the basic idea is *kill.* Three enchantments on one object, and they all worked damned well. That compulsion lasted for *weeks.*" She frowned. "As for the substance of the compulsion, however, I'd say it's a little weak. It's a very simple thought—someone more skilled at manipulating minds could have tried to make sure he wouldn't shuffle slowly into the great hall and give me several minutes to see him coming."

"And also . . . I agree he probably used three, but why did he need three?" Seren asked. "Why not simply use the last one, give the thing to one of his soldiers, and ask the soldier to deliver it to you?"

"True! You're quite good at this." She tapped her fingers against the edge of her desk. "I'd imagine it's the same reason he sent those prisoners you told me about after the *wardrenholt*—he didn't use his soldiers then, either. I don't think he trusts them. I don't think he trusts anyone at all, if I had to guess."

Seren found herself brought up short—Arianrod knew almost nothing about *those prisoners,* and couldn't have meant anything by bringing them up. But Seren had finally almost been able to shake off what had happened with them, only to be suddenly shocked into remembering it. She wondered if Lucius had come after the others, if he knew what had happened to Seth. And there were those two they'd left behind in the Citadel . . . they'd have to be told, too, if they ever got out of that dungeon.

Arianrod marked her silence, but said nothing about it. "In the end, I can draw three useful conclusions about Elgar's way of thinking: one, he's extremely talented with enchantments; two, he's less talented at controlling minds, though he definitely seems interested in it; and three, he'd much rather entrust as much as possible to magic than rely on the skills or loyalty of his own people." She grinned. "Pity he doesn't try to kill me every day, eh? I'd have him fully deciphered within a week. Not that I expect that—this attempt must have been old. If he'd tried to set it up after returning from Mist's Edge, it wouldn't have arrived here yet, and it wouldn't have made sense to try, since he was already making that attempt to take me captive with his fifty-three men. My guess is our friend took so long to reach me that Elgar thought his experiment had failed outright. Which only works to our advantage—the more Elgar doubts himself, the better."

Seren hardly felt so sanguine about the whole affair; she hadn't seen the stone at work, but that just made it worse. Her imagination was free to conjure whatever images it wished, digging beneath Arianrod's cavalier attitude to wonder how close she had truly come to death. She stared at the broken pieces. "How did you know that breaking the stone would ruin the enchantment? Is that a common condition of these things?"

Arianrod shook her head. "If someone who wasn't a mage had broken it, I don't know what would've happened—probably nothing good. Physically breaking it wasn't the point. You remember how I said spells have to make sense to the one who casts them? Normally I consider myself decently creative, but I was a bit distracted by the certain death closing in on my arm, so I jumped at something simple. Broken things don't work anymore—a child could see that logic. Simple logic is easy to believe, so the spell worked even though I was distracted."

"So . . . breaking the stone broke the enchantment because you believed it would?"

"Is that really surprising?" Arianrod asked. "Magic is primarily an ability of the mind, after all. Imagination, and conviction. What can you dream up, and how deep is your faith in those dreams? These are the things that make a mage."

"But you can't become a mage just by thinking you are one," Seren said.

Arianrod sighed. "That's true. And neither can I eliminate the physical dangers of casting magic by thinking them away. Human beings are mortal, so I suppose even something as theoretically infinite as magic develops limits when housed in a mortal shell."

Though Arianrod seemed to have fully recovered from the weakness that had gripped her after she disposed of Elgar's soldiers, Seren could not shake off the memory of it as easily. She could set herself between Arianrod and any external threat, but this . . . "Did you suffer any . . . aftereffects this time? From breaking Elgar's enchantments?"

Arianrod smirked at her. "Does it look like it? A few moments of light-headedness, that's all." She resettled herself in her chair, brushing her hands across the books on her desk. "I ought to learn from Elgar, though. Giving some serious thought to enchanting could be just what I need to solve another little problem I was having, and his failures might be just as instructive as his successes. A series of enchantments, with one inciting condition leading to the next . . . but the conditions themselves could use some work. Still, it's promising."

"The enchantments," Seren asked, "but not how he got that man to carry out his will?"

Arianrod waved a dismissive hand at her. "No, that sort of spell is a waste of time. It's important to read about such cases in order to know how best to recognize and guard against them, but beyond that? Useless."

"It's useless to control people's thoughts? I'm not saying it's something I'd ever wish I could do, but if we're judging it on usefulness alone—"

"If we're judging it on usefulness alone it's still worthless," Arianrod said, as if they were discussing a topic so simple it was boring. "You've done many things that I wished—including things that would've been impossible for me to accomplish without you. I could say the same of Dent, or Bridger, or, gods, even Gravis. I didn't have to use magic on any of you for that. But do you really think Elgar's exploration into that field and his mounting paranoia are unrelated? The more you rely on a trick like that, the less you're capable of judging people accurately, until *anyone* who isn't under your control seems like a risk. And controlling minds is *hard,* which means it's also exhausting, which means it's detrimental to keep up for too long—too much effort for a poisoned reward. I prefer to simply employ the correct people."

It was strange. Everything Arianrod said made sense, and yet it somehow wasn't what Seren would've expected. "So you're saying you trust all those people?"

"Trusting *everyone* who serves me would be foolish, of course," Arianrod said. "But I trust Dent and Bridger. I think Gravis is an irredeemable ass, but I trust him to be loyal. I even trust Zara, in a manner of speaking—that her desire to help people above all else is sincere, and thus that she has no desire to involve herself in politics as long as there are patients to see. In fact, Seren, I would say I trust far more people than you do, so perhaps that is why you're so surprised."

"And me," Seren said, heart suddenly in her throat. "You don't trust me?"

Arianrod did not smile. Her mouth tightened, and her gaze sharpened, and for several heavy moments she said nothing at all. Then: "I believe that your desire to help me is genuine. Whether that's the same as trusting you is something you'll have to decide for yourself."

Though it was a disappointing answer, Seren tried to tell herself it was not as bad as it might have been. "So then . . . what would it take for you to trust me the way you trust Dent and Bridger?"

Arianrod laughed shortly. "Dent and Bridger are far less complicated than you are."

"I . . . don't think I'm all that complicated," Seren said.

Arianrod leaned back in her chair with a sigh. "And *that,* Seren, is precisely the sort of thing that makes it so difficult for me to give you the answer you wish."

CHAPTER NINE

Eldren Cael

CRYING TO HEAV'N, *they shattered the thick night,* Adora wrote, and immediately crossed it out. No. Dreadful. If she truly needed to try to pass *heaven* off as one syllable, she might as well throw the whole project over. She tried again: *Their prayers pierced the quiet of the night.* No. The last half was weak, and *prayers* wasn't really two syllables, either, was it? She liked *their voices broke night's stillness, stretching to far shores,* so of course it didn't remotely *pretend* to be in meter, and she had already used *voices* in the preceding line!

Adora forced herself to take a deep breath, leaning back in her chair to distance herself from the words on the parchment as much as to stretch her cramped spine. Allowing herself to get irritated would just ruin her concentration. Now. Read the line as Lisianthus wrote it, and think about the most important thing to preserve in the translation. Meter, obviously, but what about the *meaning*?

The trouble was that *waves of voices pierced the night,* the most literal translation, sounded inert and awkward in modern Lantian, besides being the wrong number of syllables. *Their cries pierced the night, like waves on far shores?* It might have been metrically sound, but it still felt lifeless. *Cries* was a good substitute for *voices,* though; it gave her one more syllable to work with. *Their cries . . .* something something something . . . *far shores.* Waves, something about waves . . . waves couldn't pierce, but they could break, right? *Waves breaking on far shores?* Or . . .

Adora picked up her pen again, and scribbled in another line. And then she rewrote the whole passage together, mouthing the words to herself:

And armies ranged the starry mountains o'er,
spears stretched toward the endless vault of sky.
A sea of hopeful voices, raised as one,
their cries, like waves, crashed down on night's far shores.

It still sounded so much more beautiful in Old Lantian. But at least it was a start.

Pulling the well-worn ribbon down to mark her place, she brushed her fingers over the cover: the tiny wrinkles in the leather, the gilt filigree. The title, at the center of the swirling patterns of gold: *Nortren Varstat e Valen,* or *A Tale of the Northern War,* by the great Old Lantian poet Valter Lisianthus. It was one of the things

Adora loved about Old Lantian that the word for tale or story, *valen,* and the word for world, *valyan,* were so similar, as if to say that a story was a little world of its own. Arianrod said it was just coincidence, of course, but what else could you expect from her? Arianrod had read *Nortren Varstat* once, most likely just to show that she could, and had pronounced Lisianthus's scholarship to be ludicrously negligent. He'd probably made at least half of it up, she said, which even Adora had to admit was . . . very likely.

Though she and Arianrod corresponded frequently, they hadn't seen each other for more than three years, since before their fathers had died. Adora could still picture her sitting in the empty chair in this very room. She had been a small child, but she had shot up in their adolescence, and her stiff posture had given way to draping herself over chairs, legs stretched out and one arm thrown over the back, those long fingers seeming to reach for something even in repose.

She could almost miss those old arguments now. It had been much easier to disagree with Arianrod about poetry, and Adora had been far more certain that she was right.

The letter lay at the edge of her desk, forbidding as a thrown gauntlet. Adora was half surprised it wasn't smoking. *Adora,* it said, in her looping, irregular hand, *I should, under normal circumstances, have no scruple against lending you the copy of Gorrin you requested. I found the tome in question dreadfully dull and vastly inferior to almost all extant research on the Valerian succession, yet you should have it for all that, if you truly desired it. Yet I can no longer in good faith loan you books of which I have only one copy, because I fear they may become lost forever in the chaos that will inevitably ensue if Issamira continues without a ruler. You are running out of chances, Adora. It is a miracle you have had even so many already. And all the misfortune that will arise from your cowardice will not be yours to bear alone. If you and Issamira fall, you make the coming wars needlessly harder for everyone on this continent who still believes Elgar can be defeated. I advise you to think on that, if you cannot be bothered to think on common sense.*

Not, perhaps, a disastrous letter from an ordinary person. But Arianrod could keep her good humor through all kinds of adversity; so many lines of evident irritability, from her, were the equivalent of a good bout of screaming from anyone else. Diplomatic relations were not, at the moment, going well.

After so many years, she and Arianrod argued like old foes who had met on every battlefield; they knew each other's rhetorical tricks as well as they knew their own, and so tended to eschew flashier methods in favor of simple, direct engagement. Adora would have answered her frankness with frankness, if she could have—she owed Arianrod that much. But Arianrod understood sentimentality the way geese understood the moon, and scrupulousness only slightly better. And so there was no point—was there?—for Adora to unburden the depths of her heart, and explain why she could not possibly take Landon's place while his fate remained uncertain. The chance, even the slightest chance, that he could return to find her seated upon his throne . . . how could she ever make up for such a betrayal? If she could truly believe, as Feste did, that Landon was dead, then the moral choice would be clear. But while things remained like this . . .

When their father was alive, he and Landon had been inseparable. He could always think of more he wanted to teach Landon, more places and people he wanted to visit, more books to read and stories to tell. Adora had never begrudged Landon their father's attention: he would be a ruler, and it was only right that he receive a ruler's education. But left to herself in his wake, she had done only as she pleased. She abhorred violence, so she had refused to learn the sword. She was shy by nature, so she had avoided most balls and court functions. She loved to read, so she had ransacked Eldren Cael's library for whatever it could give her: histories, yes, and tomes on political theory and military strategy, but also tales, songs, epic poems, works of historical speculation that were more fiction than fact, myths from foreign lands . . . they had provided her with countless hours of enjoyment, but they did not tell her how to govern. *She* had never received a ruler's education— how then was it possible that she could be a ruler?

She stared half angrily down at her translated lines. This was what she had wanted to be her legacy: though *Nortren Varstet* had been summarized in modern Lantian before, or a particularly wrenching passage explicated here and there, it had never been fully translated. If it turned out that her people required much more of her than a sense of the beauty these words possessed in their original language, it was her duty to give it. But how could she reconcile her duty to her people with her duty to her brother?

Whatever her family might think, she had vastly curtailed the time she spent working at Lisianthus, and it was time to put it aside until nightfall. She dragged the customary comb through her unrepentant hair several times, to dubious effect, and made her way down from her tower room. She'd intended to go right to breakfast, but she crossed paths with her mother at the base of the tower, a look on her face that suggested Adora was not going to get out of the ensuing conversation easily.

Adora opened her mouth, but before she could even think of the right thing to say, Rhia came barreling around the corner, stopping so short lest she knock Queen Maribel over that she nearly overcorrected herself into the opposite wall. "Oh! Your, ah, Your Graces. I beg your pardons. I only needed a moment for your permission, Your Grace." This last was directed at Adora, who was honestly glad of the distraction.

"It's no trouble, Rhia. What is it you wish to do?"

"It's what the prince wishes, Your Grace," Rhia said, trying her best to avoid Adora's mother's eyes. "It was my custom to attend him whenever he took the morning air with Lady Selreshe. But this morning he informed me that . . ." Adora had no doubt that the ensuing pause was so that Rhia could frantically rephrase Feste's actual words into something that could be repeated in front of their mother. ". . . that he did not see the usefulness of such an action, and that I would be better served down in the city, since he and I had so recently been away from it."

"He is well protected while he remains in the palace," Adora said, "and you must have many reports to hear and duties to resume. I agree that remaining in the city until afternoon would be a prudent use of your time. Was that all?"

Rhia bowed. "I believe so, Your Grace. Was there anything else you required of me?"

"Not to my knowledge," Adora said, though she couldn't help smiling a little. "However, the day is young. I know how to reach you, should anything occur to me."

Rhia nodded, and was soon speeding back down the stairs again. Her mother looked after Rhia's departing back, lips pursing in that disapproving little frown she always gave. "Well, she's certainly eager to please, isn't she?"

"Not . . . really," Adora said. "I believe it's more that she's eager to do what she believes is right. As we all should be," she added firmly.

Her mother raised an eyebrow. "Did you expect me to find fault with that? I could hardly oppose such a fine platitude."

An expertly placed barb—Uncle liked to say his sister was the greatest archer the world had ever seen, though she'd never held a bow. But Adora had to play games enough with the rest of the court, and was too weary to play them with her own mother. So she responded with only the truth: "I never expected anyone could oppose Rhia, and yet you do."

"That is more praise than she deserves," her mother said calmly. "And that, in truth, is the greatest fault I find with her: that you and Feste shower her with rewards she has not earned. She is younger even than he is, and untested in matters of consequence. She wields a sword well, and she does not lack for courage, but that does not make her destined to stand on the world's stage."

"Eldren Cael is not the world," Adora said, "and yet I must stand on its stage. As must Hephestion, and as did Landon, and Father before us. We did not even have to show swordsmanship or bravery to receive such prominence; all we had to do was be born to the right people."

Her mother bowed her head. "If you feel you are ill-suited for that task, the greatest share of blame surely lies with me and your father. I fear this has all been too hard on you, darling."

She had said *too hard on you*, not *too hard for you*, but Adora couldn't help hearing the ghost of the other sentiment behind the words, and wondered who had truly put it there. "It can be no harder on me than it was on Father," she said. "It is the same burden, and he always bore it gracefully. I can do no less.

"We should all be eager to do what we believe is right," she said again, not because she thought her mother disagreed with the sentiment, but because she wanted her to know how deeply Adora herself believed it, and how determined she was to devote herself to it.

"Adora." Her mother stopped, and faced her. "Is this what you truly want?"

"Of course," Adora said.

"Can you look me in the eye and say that?"

Adora did, wondering what words would best help her mother understand. "What I truly want is to help our people. To better their lives. And—wonder of wonders—I have been given more power toward that end than anyone else in our kingdom. To fail to use that power—to squander it, or bemoan the fact that I possess it at all—would be a betrayal of our people, and thus a betrayal of the principles I hold most dear."

"Duty is not desire," her mother said, for once with more melancholy than force.

"It *need* not be," Adora insisted, "but it *can* be. For me it is, beyond any other thing."

Her mother looked at her with such sadness, and Adora wanted to shout, *What? What is it? How do I keep disappointing you?* But she did not say anything, and neither did her mother, and the silence between them grew taut and heavy and insurmountable.

IN ARAVEIL, THE neighborhoods were largely demarcated by the wealth of their inhabitants. There were the sprawling manses of the fabulously rich, the turrets and picture windows and rose gardens surrounded by walls and gates and high iron fences; there were the crumbling, peeling husks, slumped as if huddling together for warmth, that were the refuge of old aristocratic families that had fallen on hard times; there were the bright and bustling lanes around merchants' houses, where everything was new and busy and potentially for sale, and there was always a place ready and waiting where you could discuss it over drinks. And there were places like where Rhia had lived with her father and brother, rows of similar single-story houses occupied by people who had snatched themselves out of the jaws of poverty but could still hear it panting an uncomfortable distance behind.

In Eldren Cael, as far as she had been able to tell, neighborhoods were determined more than anything by what their inhabitants did. So you had broad and sunny Haveren Street and all the little lanes curling out from it, where you could find grand shops stuffed with ball gowns of silk and satin and velvet butting up against tiny rooms where poor tailors made repairs for a handful of coppers. You had Estriver Square, where world-renowned actors came to put on *The Crossing at Midnight* or *The Tragedy of Wynfryd Mac Emmon* at the Knave, Quillspoint, or Silverbell theaters, while two streets away apprentice players performed dramas their friends had finished six weeks ago, free for all comers. And in one of Rhia's favorite parts of the city, Allespont Street, you could find an assortment of taverns, banquet halls, groceries, streetside food stands, and other eateries that were so dizzyingly diverse you could stay there for weeks and never see the same dish twice. Here, little more than a slender doorway between a Valyanrend-style banquet hall and a seller of expensive spirits, was the place Rhia preferred to take her breakfast, and she could spare twenty minutes for that this morning. She slipped through, waiting for her eyes to adjust to the dimmer light. "Morning, Yorben. Is the usual all right?"

Yorben was fifty-five or sixty, a potbellied man whose laugh was even louder than his ordinary speaking voice. "Enough baked eggs for someone twice your size? Won't be a minute."

Finding baked eggs in Eldren Cael wasn't easy. Livestock was not as common in Issamira as it was elsewhere on the continent: as Adora had explained to her, in Issamira's hotter and more arid past, arable land had been scarcer, and the people of those days could not afford to share their crops and water with all manner of beasts. But as the climate grew milder and trade with other nations increased, chickens became quite popular, and pigs to a lesser extent. (There were also more horses for the wealthy, but those were for riding, not eating.) Still, though you could now find plenty of eggs and pork in Issamira, milk and cheese were not popular, and Rhia couldn't remember seeing a single cow in all of Eldren Cael. There was no need for sheep, either, since it was too hot to wear wool. But the only *proper* way to make baked eggs required cheese *and* cream, so she'd had to search until she found Yorben. He, like many in the city, kept chickens, but he was the first one Rhia had encountered who also kept a goat.

The first time Cadfael had tried to make her baked eggs, he had been eleven, and Rhia had only been five. Their father had been away for several days, and he'd been trying to cheer her up by treating her to one of her favorites. All he managed to do that first time was burn his fingers, but he kept trying over the following weeks. The second time he burned the fingers on his other hand, and the third, fourth, and fifth times he burned the eggs, but on the sixth try he had done it, and several years later he was already better at it than anyone Rhia knew. It was a funny thing: he had only started trying to make them because he knew she liked them, but then she liked them more because he had tried so hard to make them for her, until she couldn't have said which of them was happier about it. But baked eggs were still the best way to start a morning, because it was one of the only times she could think about her brother and feel happier than she was sad.

Yorben served the eggs piping hot right out of the skillet, and for a while he seemed content to watch her eat. Then he said, "Hope it's not an imposition, Captain, but do you remember that boy Jost?"

Jost was only a year or two younger than Rhia, a skinny butcher's apprentice who was vaguely acquainted with Yorben. Rhia hadn't realized they knew each other when she first met Jost—she had stepped in to defend him from an assault, not by any bandits or other criminals, but simply by a couple of other young men who believed they could get away with it. With Adora's permission, she had fined the young men for public disturbance and assault of the citizenry; after that, it seemed the beatings had stopped, and she hadn't had the occasion to speak with Jost since.

"Of course I remember him," she said to Yorben. "Is he in some trouble again?"

Yorben scratched the back of his neck. "As to that, I can't say for sure—I'm no confidant of his. But I do know he came here looking for you. He knows you like to eat here, and he said he needed your help with something."

"Then it probably is trouble," Rhia said, dragging her spoon through the cream to get at the crunchy bits stuck to the skillet. "You don't need the captain of the guard's help to write love poetry or spend an unexpected windfall."

"He didn't seem frightened, though," Yorben said. "Nervous, certainly, though that boy's always nervous about something. But not frightened. He said he'd be waiting with some friends of his—they're camped out on the northwest side of the lake. If they stay there for too long someone'll run 'em off, but Jost said they'd be there through the week, and to ask you to meet him there if you showed up before then."

"Hmm. Well, now I'm confused. He can't be in too much distress if he's out enjoying himself with his friends. But then why come to me?" She polished off the last scrap of her breakfast, and left Yorben's coin on the table. "I've got a few more places in the city I have to check on first, but if I get done in time I'll head out to the lake. If he is in trouble, I've got to see what I can do."

The rest of her patrol through Eldren Cael went well enough: with the Red Crows still on the loose, having *no* major incidents while she and the prince were gone was too much to hope for, but the rest of the city guard had performed admirably in containing the fights that had broken out. It was a long walk to the northwest side of the lake from the city proper, but Rhia had time, and she wanted to see what was bothering Jost sooner rather than later.

Lake Rovere lay only a short walk outside Eldren Cael's walls—understandable, given that it was the city's only source of fresh water. Adora said that every generation or so there was a proposal to build a wall around the lake itself, enclosing it within the city in the case of a siege. But too many logistical problems remained unsolved—not least that the construction, which would take decades given the lake's size, ran the risk of polluting the water, accomplishing the very thing it was meant to protect against.

Rhia admitted to being fond of the lake as it was, a grassy basin formed by a gentle slope up to a hill and then back down to the water, surrounded by few trees but many flowers. All were free to drink from the lake, or to carry water away from it to use in their homes, but swimming in it was forbidden—as, of course, was throwing anything into it. But even though it was not far away, fewer citizens made their way out here than had in earlier times. In recent years, a system of pipes had allowed water to be pumped into great cisterns within the city's walls, making for a much shorter journey. But water was sacred to the Issamiri, and some preferred to see it in all its majesty, the lake stretching so far to the east that you couldn't see its far shores from the near side.

It would be easy to find Jost and his friends: if they were out in the open, they'd be visible from the ridge of the hill, and if they were under the cover of trees, there were only so many trees to choose from. Rhia came upon their tent under a half-dozen scraggly elms, an unlit firepit before it. Jost poked his head out of the opening when she called his name, the rest of him quickly scrambling after.

He looked much as she remembered him from so many weeks ago: he'd cut his hair a little shorter, and he'd taken to wearing a sword these days, but his anxious manner was the same. "Captain!" he said, somewhat louder than was necessary. "Oh. I wasn't sure you'd be coming." He looked down the hill to the north, where there were a couple other young men drinking from the lake. He waved to them, and finally got their attention. As they straightened up and started walking back toward Jost and Rhia, she got a better look at them: one had a face similar to Jost's atop a body that was taller and heavier, and the third, the tallest of the lot, was red-haired and lighter-skinned. They were both wearing swords, too, but they seemed more at ease with them than Jost was. "Your friends?" Rhia asked.

Jost grinned crookedly. "Well, my cousin, and my cousin's friend from Hallarnon. I'll introduce you when they get close enough."

"You're going to introduce the reason you wanted me to meet you here as well, I hope."

"Yes. Of course." He made as if to wring his hands, then stopped and forced them back to his sides. "You have to understand, Captain, I really am grateful to you. For all that . . . business before. Things would've been a lot worse without your help, and I know it. I don't want you to think I don't know it."

"I don't think that," Rhia assured him. "But you don't owe me anything, either."

He shook his head forcefully. "No, I do. I never expected any of this to happen. It's not the way I wanted it."

He looked back at his two companions, who had almost reached them. "What are you talking so much about?" the tall Hallern asked, more irritated than confused.

Jost hung his head. "I'm sorry, Captain. I promise you, I truly am."

Rhia was no longer the girl of barely seventeen who had fled the invasion of

Araveil, who had the will to fight but had never taken a life before. In the years since, she had been in countless battles, many of which had ended in death for her opponents. Despite what she knew many people thought of her, she was familiar with the concept of foul play—if she hadn't been, she wouldn't be alive right now. So she didn't waste time on being shocked, or saddened, because that would get her killed. In the handful of instants before Jost drew his sword, before his companions reached them, she had to decide what to do.

She and Jost had one thing in common—this wasn't the way she wanted it, either. He was clearly unhappy about this—perhaps he had been forced into it—and she wanted to spare his life if she could. But she did not want to fight three men at once, so she needed to incapacitate him. Perhaps someone else could have punched or otherwise struck him hard enough to do the job, but Rhia had no talent for fisticuffs, only for swordplay. Before she started carrying a weapon, she had lost every fight she'd ever been in. So she did the only thing she could think of: she outdrew Jost—she was naturally swift, and wielding a *tsunshin* made it even easier—and sliced into his leg, making him stagger back and fall to his knees. The wound was bleeding significantly, but if she could subdue his friends in time she could get him to a healer before his life was in danger.

After seeing Jost go down so quickly, the other two were wary of her—they had never seen her fight, after all, and most who had were a bit shocked the first time—but she could see from their grimly set faces that they weren't thinking of running. Jost's cousin inched over to her side, trying to get himself into the gap between her and Jost, but the Hallern came straight for her, no hesitation evident in his movements. She blocked his first strike easily, and they traded a couple more blows before he put a foot wrong. When she leaned into the next parry, he stumbled on the uneven ground, and she used the opening to slice across the front of his body, deep enough to kill him in moments.

She turned back to Jost's cousin, still slightly crouched a few yards from her side—but before she could do anything more, a pair of arms wrapped themselves around her legs. It was Jost, who had crawled across the grass to reach her. "Now!" he yelled to his cousin. "Hit her now!"

Jost wouldn't have been an exemplar of strength on his best day, and his wound had made him even weaker, so Rhia was able to break free of his hold right before his cousin reached them. She stepped back and sideways, but had no time to get her sword in any kind of position before the man struck, tearing into her stomach. Rhia staggered, shocked by the pain, by the sudden severity of the situation, but she forced herself to recover. There was no time for shock, wound or no wound.

It was bleeding hard, but it wasn't quite the wound Jost's cousin had hoped he'd get in, and he made a fatal mistake. His wariness had served him well thus far, but now he hesitated, trying to judge how badly Rhia was hurt, whether he should press his attack or retreat again, and left himself open in his indecision. Rhia's body screamed at her, but the movements were second nature, and somehow she was able to force herself through the slash, though it felt as if she were tearing herself in half to do it. The man fell before he had time to realize what had happened.

She staggered over to Jost, who still hadn't managed to regain his feet, though he was fumbling to draw his sword. He looked up at her as she approached, but didn't stop trying. She could almost admire his determination to see this through, if it didn't sadden her so much. "I *am* sorry, Captain," he panted, slowly getting the sword free. "But it was so much money . . . so much . . ."

She drew her sword across his throat, in the hope that he would die quickly and without pain. She had wanted to save him, but she was much more grievously hurt than he had been, and she knew if she passed out from blood loss he would have killed her.

She stared down at the three bodies, still not fully understanding what had happened. What quarrel had they had with her? Someone had . . . paid them, or else promised to? Who? Why? *It was so much money,* Jost had said. The words echoed in her head: *so much money . . . so much . . .* But money was spent on important matters. Who would pay so much for her alone? It was so hard to . . . think of . . .

She hardly knew what she did after that. She might have lost consciousness, or flickered in and out of it for the space of several heartbeats. But when she could remember herself she was stumbling sideways, one hand pressed to her stomach. Where was her sword? She should have sheathed it after . . . but no, of course, it was in her other hand. She tried to put it away, but her arm wouldn't move the way she wanted it to. She was so dizzy. She felt so far away from herself. Where was she going? There was so much blood on her hand.

She heard a sound, and lifted her eyes to see the lake, sloshing almost at her feet. She shouldn't . . . bleed in the lake. She should get help, she thought, but then her knees buckled and she fell onto them, hard, the impact jarring her whole body. She was still holding the sword. It was all she had left of them—of her father and Cadfael both. She couldn't let go of it, no matter what.

She rolled onto her side, curled into a ball in the grass. She was bleeding so much. She didn't know what to do.

She might have cried out, or perhaps that was only in her mind. But she slipped into blackness.

Chapter Ten

Eldren Cael

"Best to keep a closer eye on your swordswoman, Your Grace," Jocelyn said, twirling the piece she'd just taken between her fingers. The carved face of the tiny horseman somehow managed to look distressed even at this distance.

Adora glanced down at the board. Brilliant. She was down to one horseman and no archers, her mage was stranded in a remote corner, and she'd just landed her swordswoman in quite the bit of trouble. "Thank you," she said, as dispassionately as she could. "I was just thinking that myself."

Feste, sprawled on a low couch at their side, sat up to toss his newest olive pit into the bowl on the nearby table and took the opportunity to glance at the board. "Come on, sister, you've got to put up a better fight than that."

"I'm certainly trying," Adora said, tactfully refraining from mentioning that she was only out here at all because Feste had desperately required company that wasn't Lady Jocelyn Selreshe. Apparently he could be noble enough to leave *Rhia* free to attend her duties, but he didn't seem to feel Adora deserved the same courtesy. Well, it would get her mother to stop complaining that she was being impolitic by ignoring Jocelyn—for a few hours, anyway.

Jocelyn smiled at Hephestion. It was no flirtatious simper, despite her position as his most persistent suitor. Instead, it was the same smile she gave everyone: a beautiful smile, because she was undeniably a beautiful woman, but one that had always unnerved Adora. It seemed to suggest that you were at the root of a terribly amusing joke, and just hadn't realized it yet. "I'd be careful of placing any wagers just yet, my lord. Your sister may have me yet, despite her . . . disadvantages thus far."

"Well, I'm glad one of us thinks so," Adora said, staring at the board again. There was no point in being too aggressive with Jocelyn's mage so far forward. She inched one of her pikemen closer to the dividing line, but didn't cross it.

"Now I've got you worried," Jocelyn said, moving one of her riders forward in a blatant taunt. She'd hardly looked at the board. "Reverse check in two."

"It's my check this time, yes?"

"That's right, Your Grace."

Feste laughed. "Really, Jocelyn, it's damned lucky you know how to play sesquigon—or else it's lucky that Adora knows. Mother always loses her patience about halfway through a match, and I hate the damned game. Adora tried to teach

Rhia how to play once—and, I believe, nearly made her ill. I don't know who else you two would have to play with, if not each other."

"I can well believe sesquigon and the captain disagreed with each other," Jocelyn said, the little touch of added smugness grating on the inside of Adora's skull. She could rarely resist an opportunity to make a snide remark, especially if Rhia—or Adora herself—was its intended target.

"It's a rare mind that's cast for sesquigon," Adora said—an old saying, and one she knew Jocelyn knew well. Sesquigon was incredibly unpopular among the common people, for entirely understandable reasons; even Adora, one of the few people who genuinely enjoyed the game, had to admit that whoever had invented it must have been an ass of the highest order. Sesquigon was difficult to learn, completely unintuitive, full of dozens of rules that seemed to have been instituted just to make it more complicated, and impossible to play to completion in under an hour's time. If, for some unfathomable reason, you wanted to be good at it, you had to start by learning the movement ranges and permitted maneuvers for a dozen different types of pieces, the frankly bizarre conditions for victory and defeat, and the times at which you had to throw everything you'd already learned out the window and play by an entirely different set of rules. This last might or might not be coming up, depending on how the reverse check went.

Just in case, Adora adjusted her swordswoman: an entirely wasted move if they wound up in reverse, but she couldn't take that chance. Jocelyn hummed under her breath, taking a few seconds longer to deliberate this time but ultimately just using her mage to nab another of Adora's foot soldiers. "Reverse check," she said, handing the token over to Adora.

The token was anything that had two sides and that, when flipped, had an equal chance of landing on either side. One side was always colored, the other blank. Some people used flat stones with a dab of paint on one side, but this set had been in the Avestri family for generations, and used a token of silver with a dark R engraved on the non-blank side. That was the side Adora ended up staring at after she flipped the coin. "All right," she said, laying it on the table so everyone could see. "Officially in reverse."

Reversal lasted a dozen moves, and got its name because it meant you took all the rules about permitted maneuvers and flipped them the other way. Under normal rules, a pikeman was able to remove a rider from the board, but the opposite was invalid; under reverse rules, rider could take pikeman, but not the other way around. Normally mages were the most powerful pieces on the board, and could only be taken by an archer or a correctly positioned foot soldier, but in reverse they had their movement range drastically reduced, and you could remove a mage with a king or queen. (Unlike some other games, kings and queens referred to the same type of piece, simply called "rulers" in some books in order to avoid confusion.

This particular set had a king on one side and a queen on the other—Jocelyn had left Adora the queen, for an obvious joke.)

Moving her swordswoman *had* been a waste, then. Better and better. Feste reached for another handful of olives. "You know, Jocelyn, Mother and Father were both taught sesquigon by tutors growing up, but they didn't care for it until they met. They *loved* to challenge each other. They were so prideful about it that if one of them had a particularly crushing loss there'd be utter silence at dinner." He flicked a pit into the bowl. "Landon kept at it more than I did, but he lost interest once Adora started thrashing him all the time."

"I enjoyed it more, that's all," Adora protested. "It's easy to be better at something when you put in more effort." Feste rolled his eyes, but she ignored him.

"And have you found any opponents who gave you difficulty, Your Grace?" Jocelyn asked. "Besides me, of course."

"Only two," Adora said. "Uncle, and . . . a childhood friend." It was perhaps strange to refer to her that way, but Feste got in a sour mood whenever Arianrod Margraine's name was mentioned. "But I haven't gotten the chance to play against either of them in some time. Uncle is always either at home or wandering about somewhere near the Curse, and I haven't seen that friend in years." When was the last time she and Arianrod had played? It was before Caius Margraine had taken ill, but he had been away from Stonespire for the duration of Adora's visit. Arianrod had never been to Issamira, and would never have been permitted to go while her father was alive; every time they had ever seen each other, Adora had been the one to go to Esthrades. Though Arianrod had read books about every city in the known world, she was forced to imagine what it was like to live within them. So Adora had talked about summer festivals, plays at the Knave, grand dinners at the palace or whatever new culinary experiment she and Feste had picked up at a food stall. And they had played six games of sesquigon, the game Arianrod preferred above all others. Adora had only managed to win two, but Arianrod had said she was the only one worth playing. "Even when you lose," she had said, "you never make it easy." And somehow, even when she had lost, Adora hadn't been bothered by it the way she was bothered now.

That was the difference, she thought. Jocelyn played to win. Arianrod wanted to win, but she played for the sake of the game.

The first half of their time in reverse proved brutal for her. Perhaps Adora was nervous, but she couldn't seem to play to her usual standards. She'd think she had a good strategy in hand, only to be blindsided by a countermeasure that was all too obvious in hindsight.

There were only six moves left in reverse when her mother entered the courtyard, passing beneath the shade of the awning. Jocelyn looked up, her elbow jostling the board—the pieces rattled a bit, but thankfully none moved out of place. And as

Adora recovered from her brief startlement, she saw the board in a new light: there was a way she could win, but she had to pull it off before reversal ended. Her move, Jocelyn's move, her move, Jocelyn's move, and then her move had to decide it. But it was possible.

"Here you all are," her mother said, settling into an empty chair near Feste. "Ah. Sesquigon again, I see."

Jocelyn smiled. "Your daughter is the only one both able and willing to oblige me, Your Grace, so I have to make use of her while I can." *Make use of me is right,* Adora thought, but didn't let herself be distracted from the board. She moved her swordswoman back, undoing the move she had made before they entered reversal. Now the piece was back within range of Jocelyn's mage, but since they were playing by reverse rules it was the mage that was threatened this time.

"Unfortunately," her mother was saying, "I lost my taste for this game a long time ago. I expect it was for the same reason as my eldest son: too many humiliating defeats at the hands of a younger sibling."

"The prince was just telling me about that, in fact," Jocelyn said, glancing at the board. To Adora, she said, "Not quite, Your Grace," and moved her king over the line to take Adora's swordswoman. Turning her attention back to Queen Maribel, she continued, "Her Grace seemed to disagree, however."

"I'm not surprised." She looked at the board, keeping any thoughts from showing on her face with that elegant but expressionless mask she had perfected for so long. "It is Adora's custom to devalue her own abilities. She seems to be giving you a decent challenge for all that, though."

Jocelyn laughed. "The fact that you can see that so easily proves your own facility with the game, I should think."

That's fine, Adora thought, taking hold of her sole remaining horseman. *While the two of you get along so well, I'm going to win this game.* She moved the piece as far forward as she could—not far enough to actually take Jocelyn's king, but in position to do it on the next move.

"You've really thrown caution to the winds, haven't you?" Jocelyn said, scooping up the horseman even with her mage's reduced range. "Back to standard in . . . oh."

"Seems I wasn't the only one," Adora said, using her queen to knock over Jocelyn's mage and planting it in the newly empty space. "That's the game, I think." There was more than one way to win sesquigon, but one involved taking your opponent's mage while their ruler was on your half of the board.

Jocelyn raised her hands in surrender, but Adora hadn't missed the extra purse to her mouth. "So it is. An excellent performance, Your Grace." She started putting her pieces back in the box. "But I suppose we've sufficiently bored your brother already."

There were so many possible retorts to that that Adora had to bite her lip to keep from giving voice to one of them. "Then I shall leave him to you," she said, doing her best to ignore Feste's look of panic and betrayal. "I'm afraid I can't waste any more time at leisure today."

IT WAS AN ache that woke Rhia, but not the pain from her wound. It was the feeling, deep within her chest, that something had been ripped away from her—like hearing, on the day she returned to Araveil, that her brother had died of his injuries, and realizing that she would never see him again. This was some similar echo, but far, far distant—a loss that was older than her bones, and that would remain long after they had crumbled away.

Then she *remembered* her wound, and all other considerations were forgotten. She sat bolt upright, frantically feeling at her stomach for the tear in her clothing, trying to see how bad—

She stopped, and sat back on the grass, leaning so that she could lift her shirt and have a clear view of her abdomen. The shirt itself was soaked with blood, ruined by it, and there were a few large smears that had transferred to her stomach. But there wasn't so much as a scratch marring her skin.

For several moments she kept patting at her stomach, as if a wound of that size were something she could have overlooked. She couldn't possibly have dreamed the injury—look at all this blood! But if she wasn't wounded now . . . could the wound have disappeared? But that was impossible, too.

A sudden memory ground her thoughts to a halt. Impossible? No, not quite. Hadn't she seen just the opposite of this all those years ago, to her greatest sorrow?

By the time he returned to Araveil, Cadfael had been weak from blood loss. After he had reported to the king, Eira had let him return home, and sent his best healer to tend to him. But it was no use. The wound carved itself into his face again and again, as if an invisible blade stalked her brother from day to day, unwilling to let him heal. Impossible as it had seemed, Rhia could hardly doubt what she had seen with her own eyes—or the horrible consequences.

But Cadfael had been cursed—he'd admitted that himself. Talking had tired him, but he had been able to tell Rhia that King Eira had sent him to capture some kind of sorceress, and this was how she had punished him. Did that mean Rhia had been . . . blessed? When? By whom? She had certainly not been tracking any sorceresses, and as far as she could tell, she was quite alone here.

But whatever else had happened, this was magic. It had to be. What else made sense?

She finally stopped patting her stomach, and frowned, staring down at her hand. It was wet, though not with blood—that seemed to have all dried. Water? Oh no, the lake!

Of all the things one was not permitted to put into Eldren Cael's reservoir, blood was obviously high on the list. Rhia jumped to her feet, fought off a wave of dizziness, and walked the yard or two to the water's edge. That already seemed odd—even if her arm had been fully extended while she was unconscious, it shouldn't have been able to stretch all the way to the lake. She stared into the water; she couldn't see anything, but that was hardly conclusive. She'd have to report this to the queen, along with all the rest. And what an unbelievable report it would make: Jost's attack, the mysterious person or group who had paid him such an enticing sum, her disappearing wound—

Her hand flew to her empty scabbard, and yet another shock ran through her. Where was her sword? She seemed to recall that she hadn't sheathed it before losing consciousness . . . she'd been holding it, hadn't she?

She turned around, and easily found it several feet away from where she'd lain, though she still could have sworn she'd been clutching it when she lost consciousness. The grass and dirt were disturbed around it, as if it had been kicked or had otherwise skidded across the ground. She picked it up, tested it briefly, but found the blade undamaged. Yet another strange thing. What could this all mean?

Just to make sure this day didn't have any more surprises for her, she returned to Jost's campsite, half wondering if the bodies had disappeared, or if she'd find the three of them restored to health as she had been. But Jost and his companions were just where she had left them—lifeless all, and with all the wounds that she remembered. Rhia didn't know whether to be relieved by that or disappointed.

"THANK YOU FOR telling me," Adora said first, because it was worth saying. Even for a person as straightforward as Rhia, divulging all this couldn't have been easy. "I hardly know what to make of it myself."

"But you believe me," Rhia said. She'd changed her clothes, but brought Adora the blood-soaked shirt as evidence of her story. "You believe that it all happened as I said?"

"I could hardly do otherwise," Adora assured her. "And . . . I have to apologize. It's possible that your increased visibility as captain helped make you a target."

Rhia shook her head. "I doubt my position had much to do with it. And even if it did, I wouldn't regret it for that reason. But . . . do you think it's possible? That magic could have made my wounds disappear?"

"That's a difficult question. I mean, to say it's difficult is an understatement." The question of magic in general was one Adora had never wanted to think about, because the ramifications were so monumental. But Rhia had given her an honest confession, and deserved an honest answer. "It's clear that magic was commonplace once. All I have read confirms that. And if such a thing could be possible once, it would surely be foolhardy to say it could never exist again. But as for specific evidence . . ." She tugged at her hair. "It's unclear what the limitations of magic were in the past, and what they might be today. As far as I'm concerned, it's not entirely clear that magic has come back in the first place."

"No, it has," Rhia said, looking fixedly at the ground. "That I know for sure."

Adora raised an eyebrow. "For some other reason than what happened to you today?"

"Yes. Because . . . of what happened to my brother."

The reason for Rhia's tension instantly became clear. It caused her great pain to talk about her brother, as Adora and Feste had both learned, and she preferred to avoid it whenever possible. As a result, Adora knew precious little about him: that he was older (she did not even know by how much), that he had helped her learn the sword, that he was notably skilled with it himself, that he had taken care of her when their father was away. That he had had her current weapon forged for her, out of a sword that had once been their father's. Perhaps a half dozen very minor details. Certainly not enough to have a vivid idea of him as a human being.

She said nothing, and waited for Rhia to finish. "My brother died of a wound inflicted on him by a sorceress, a cursed wound that cut open every stitch and bandage applied to it. I saw this with my own eyes. And our king, Eira . . . he knew of this woman, too. He was shocked by what had happened to my brother, but not by her or her magic."

Adora winced. "No, he wouldn't have been."

"What makes you say that?"

"I . . ." Adora took a deep breath. "Rhia, you mustn't speak of this to anyone, but I will tell you because of what you told me—and for the sake of your brother. Before my father died, he had . . . a pact of sorts with your king and the former king of Reglay, the previous Kelken. Eira had some sort of proof that Father and Kelken believed—proof that those who could wield magic existed on this continent. They agreed to locate these people together, to try to use them to fight Imperator Elgar. But that's all I know about it. My father only discussed it with Landon, and it made Landon furious—he demanded that my father withdraw from this agreement, and it was only through his complaints to me that I know even this much. I suppose Father died before he could decide whether to obey Landon, though."

Rhia hesitated. "Your brother . . . he had already disappeared when your father died?"

"We don't know that for sure," Adora had to admit. "He wasn't in Eldren Cael when Father died, but he wasn't supposed to be—he was ranging the Curse, as Father wished. And Father's death was . . . very sudden." It had been so absurd. Jotun Avestri had won every battle he had ever commanded himself, had never sustained more than minor cuts in all his years at war . . . and then to die in such a meaningless way! He had always been popular with the people, and whenever he left or returned to Eldren Cael they came out in droves to see him, lining the wide avenues where he proceeded with his men. He had been going to leave the city that day, but he never reached its gates. His horse had thrown a shoe the day before, and he had accepted a substitute, a magnificent but ill-fated steed that had not been prepared to face a large and passionate crowd. It had panicked, and all its impressive size and strength had only served to throw her father that much harder from the saddle. He broke his back, and died delirious in his bed. She could still remember his last words. *Landon,* he had said, though she sat right beside him. *I cannot see. Where is Landon?*

"We sent messengers to fetch Landon as soon as Father died," she told Rhia. "They found the rest of his scouting party on the Curse, all dead—a bandit raid, by all the evidence. It's possible they didn't even know the crown prince was among those they attacked. But his body was not there. And we have never seen hide nor hair of him, living or dead, ever since."

Chapter Eleven

Valyanrend

WHEN CAPTAIN GARDENER came to fetch him, Varalen Oswhent was watching his son read a book.

It was one of the few ways Ryam had to enjoy himself. He could still walk, in a slow limping way, but it was dangerous for one with his illness to exert himself physically. Other cases had been known to have their hearts fail from running too fast, fighting too hard, going for too long without rest. He could not play with other children his age; he was only nine, and ones so young, no matter how you might urge them to be careful, did not truly understand death, and could not believe they were capable of causing another permanent harm.

His mother had already gone ahead of him; it was not uncommon, Varalen had later read, for one or both parents of a child with the great wasting illness to suffer from some minor form of it—no paralysis or muscle decay, but a lifelong weakness, a tendency to become ill easily, death at an early age. In the Sahaian Empire, where it had been researched most extensively, these symptoms were often recognized early, and their sufferers warned what might happen if they were to try to have children. But in Lantistyne, the illness almost always came as a shock: confusion, panic, then denial. Varalen had been through all three. He had started his research as a way to find hope, and by the time he had realized he would find none, he knew enough to make his despair that much worse.

Yet Imperator Elgar claimed he could cure it. It would have been impossible, of course, by any conventional method, but by now Varalen knew just how unconventional Elgar's methods truly were. To be a true mage, without any games or tricks, was something Varalen had always thought impossible, yet Elgar had proved it to him beyond a doubt.

"You don't seem to like the book today," Ryam said quietly, looking up. "I have other ones, if you want."

"No, it's not that," Varalen said, reaching out to touch the boy's hair—never a firm pat, never a crushing hug. It was all too easy to tip the failing balance of his health, and better to overestimate than the reverse. "I just have too many things to think about." He resettled the blanket around Ryam's shoulders. "Are you cold?"

"Only a little." He brushed his fingertips over the words on the page. "What are you thinking about?"

How could he answer that in any remotely truthful fashion? He didn't wish to lie to his own son, but the realities of his illness and of Varalen's role in the war were both too complex and damning to foist on so young a child. "The imperator wants many things from me," he said at last. "Complicated things. I like to think I'm clever, but even I find it all a challenge. Like . . . a puzzle to solve, only I have to keep all the pieces in my head."

He had believed he'd found the perfect plan to capture Arianrod Margraine, but she had thwarted it—because she, too, was a mage, Elgar had insisted. They had every reason to believe the war in Reglay would be a success, but then they would have to deal with Esthrades next, and whatever powers its marquise possessed. Then, if they somehow emerged victorious a second time, they would have to take Issamira to the south—the largest of the three by far, with the most formidable military.

Though he had been Elgar's chief strategist for years now, his master's success or failure had never occupied his every waking moment as it did now. He had never borne the man any personal love—but if he helped Elgar complete his empire, the imperator would heal his son. It was Ryam's only possible hope.

"That does sound complicated," Ryam said loyally. "But you'll do it. *I* know you're clever." He tried to turn the page, and frowned when his fingers shook. Varalen held his breath, but in the next instant the page had turned and Ryam was reading again.

He heard the door open, then the clearing of a throat, and forced himself to look into the honest face of Quentin Gardener, captain of the guard in Elgar's Citadel. It was almost worse that it was him: he clearly understood what he had to do, and regretted doing it, and that knowing sympathy in his eyes was just another wound. "My lord," he said, "His Eminence has summoned us."

It was to be expected, but that didn't mean Varalen had been looking forward to it. "Who will be watching my son?"

Quentin bowed his head. "My people. I can have them wait inside the room or out of it, whatever you prefer."

Ryam was not allowed to leave the Citadel, or to be left alone within it, because he was a hostage Elgar was keeping to ensure Varalen's compliance. Still, Quentin had always been as respectful and solicitous as his position permitted him to be. "Thank you," Varalen said. "I'll let my son decide whether he wishes to have company."

Ryam shrugged, a weary, stiff movement. "If they want to read, they can come inside."

Quentin smiled. "I'll be sure to ask them."

They settled on one guard within the room and one without, and then Varalen followed Quentin down the Citadel corridors to Elgar and his maps. He had them spread out over that large table as usual, and was standing up to pore over them, but he seemed calm, almost pleased. He looked up when they entered, smoothing a hand along the edge of the table. "Gather your things, Varalen. We leave for the front in two days."

Varalen wasn't taken aback so much as stunned to his core. "We're—what? Which front? Who's *we*?"

Elgar smiled sardonically at Quentin. "My strategist. Eloquent and perspicacious as always." To Varalen, he said, "You, I, and a select number of my very best soldiers will be crossing the border into Reglay, of course. Much of the army is already there, or will be there before us, but they await my order to move."

"Your Eminence . . . you and I both? Conquering Reglay will hardly be the undertaking that Lanvaldis was three years ago, and you accomplished the latter before I ever came to you. I would venture to say that even your presence alone is more than the campaign requi—"

"The conquest of Lanvaldis," Elgar interrupted, "was a nuisance and a mess—it took far longer than expected, and created far too many problems. I hardly wish for that campaign to be repeated. Our presence at Mist's Edge will ensure the siege goes well. If it proves to be as easy as we expect, we shall not be away long, and if complications arise, we shall be there to correct them."

It seemed to Varalen that Valyanrend itself was in a more turbulent position than Mist's Edge, war or no war. Kelken, the boy king, did not have the resources or the manpower to make the siege of Mist's Edge an overly complicated matter, so it just came down to reducing the time and the casualties on their side. "Your Eminence, I understand what you're saying, but I remain concerned about this city.

The unrest within Valyanrend's walls is rising. If some conflict should break out in our absence, even a minor one, who will have the authority to act in our stead? And will they be prepared to do so?"

Elgar stroked his beard, nodding slowly. "I presume you have some thoughts to that end?"

"I do. Your former captain of Valyanrend's city guard, the recently deceased Nathaniel Wyles, was a man who never sought to use subtlety if he could use violence instead. Rather than bring the dissident elements in this city to heel, he only fanned their flames—those brave enough to stand up in the face of hardship will only stiffen their resolve when they see how bad things can truly get. It reminds them what they're fighting for." He nodded at Quentin. "Captain Gardener here, while only trusted with the Citadel itself thus far, has proven both capable and moderate. Moderation, I think, is what Valyanrend needs most right now. Many who might be tempted to side with the rebels simply want to live their accustomed lives without incident; if they find they are able to do that under your rule, their desire for change will be snuffed out. You know Quentin's loyalty, and many of the common people know his integrity. He makes an ideal bridge between you and them. So give Quentin charge of the city, and let him appoint his most trusted subordinate to take his place here at the Citadel. When we return from Mist's Edge, you can always have him resume his former post, if you decide you prefer him there. But if a crisis should occur in Valyanrend, and you and I cannot be present, I would trust Quentin to handle it over any other."

Elgar paced halfway around the table, looking from Quentin to Varalen and back again. "And you, Quentin? What is your opinion on all of this?"

The captain scratched his side-whiskers, clearly uncomfortable with all the attention. "Well, I wish I'd known beforehand that Lord Oswhent intended to make such a suggestion, Your Eminence. As for the task itself . . . if it is your wish that I apply myself to it, I will do so. I agree with Lord Oswhent that moderation, at this time, would be a great boon to the people of this city . . . but, as he says, moderation has always been my way."

Elgar tapped his chin, and Varalen stayed silent; he'd made his argument as best he could, and there was no point in further entreaty. At last, Elgar said, "You will personally write reports to me at the front, to keep me apprised of all happenings and all potential happenings in this city. I will expect one every fortnight."

Quentin bowed his head. "Of course, Your Eminence."

"Then I give you leave to return to your subordinates, select one of them to assume your position, and brief them on what will be required. And I thank you for the quality of your service thus far."

Quentin bowed with his whole body this time, and then he left. Varalen managed not to sigh in relief. He knew Quentin would make sure his subordinates knew all that Ryam required in Varalen's absence, but he resolved to have another word with him before departing anyway.

To Elgar, he said, "I feel safer leaving him in charge, Your Eminence. Are there any other matters I should attend to before we leave?"

"Not precisely," Elgar said, "but there is one more thing I must tell you—and a set of instructions pursuant to it. Shinsei will be accompanying us to Mist's Edge, and given that you are not accustomed to being in close quarters with him, I need your assurance that you will not attempt to interfere with him in any way."

There were few people on the continent Varalen would have been happier to stay farther away from than Commander Shinsei, whose rumored madness and rumored martial proficiency made a terrifying combination. "Indeed, Your Eminence, far from wishing to interfere with him, I should be only too glad not to have any opportunity even to observe the weather with him."

"That may not be possible, given the demands and uncertainties of travel," Elgar said. "Here is what I need you to understand. A man like you loves to talk—and, I believe, talks all the more when nervous. Shinsei is not a man who loves to talk. Even subjects that may seem innocuous to you—food, literature, family—may trouble and displease him greatly. Therefore, you will keep your conversations with him confined to only what is absolutely necessary. Is that clear?"

Varalen laughed nervously. "I should hardly wish to trouble and displease the commander, Your Eminence. If he does not wish to speak to me, I will certainly not endeavor to speak to him if I can do otherwise."

Elgar finally nodded, and Varalen felt as if some oppressive weight had been lifted. "Then that will be all. You will gather your things, and if you have any requirements for the journey that are not currently in your possession, you will submit them to me by the end of the day. We have no time to waste."

CHAPTER TWELVE

Valyanrend

IT WAS STRANGE for a prisoner to say, but Marceline had stopped feeling anxious days ago, and was honestly quite content with her situation.

Now that she understood what the resistance members wanted from her, she hardly bothered being afraid of them. Mouse was the leader in more than just name: the past few days had made it clear that, while Naishe and Rask might disagree with him, their respect for his authority held. And Mouse wanted to let her go, in exchange for a favor that was so simple it had been all Marceline could do not to burst out laughing when he'd proposed it.

He could have been lying, obviously, but she knew he wasn't. It was a thief's responsibility to know how to read people quickly and well, and she'd seen the gleam in Mouse's eyes when he talked about Sheath. Far from making an enemy of her and her kind, he wanted to make friends.

It was a hopeless endeavor, of course; no one in Sheath had ever been moved by high ideals. But Mouse believed in it, and his belief would keep her alive. As to the rest, her own skills would be more than enough.

Since Mouse was the one watching her today, the morning was livelier than usual. Naishe was a stoic warden, never saying more than she deemed necessary, and Rask was even worse than that, keeping his conversation to either insults or stony silence. That girl Talia had seemed like a talker, but she wasn't trusted with a turn of her own. But Mouse liked to talk, too, and now that they were finally alone together, perhaps she could get him to answer a question that had bothered her since the day they met.

"Hey," she said, after swallowing her last bite of toast, "do you remember what you said when I first came here? That . . . it wasn't strange for a monkey to be looking for a mouse, or something like that. What was that about?"

"Oh," he said, with a sheepish laugh. "You remembered that, did you? I'd just finished this book about the Four Wars of Sahai. There was something there about a monkey and a mouse, so I thought it was a funny coincidence. That's all, really. I didn't mean to offend you."

"You didn't offend me," Marceline said. "But since you mentioned it, you ought to explain."

He sat back on the cushions. "It was about this clan leader from Inkei—you know, that country all the way to the east of Sahai. When the Inkeii rebelled against the Sahaians, he became a general, but in his youth he was just the head of a tiny clan on the western edge of Inkei. And back then people started calling him the Monkey—not literally, they called him the Inkish word for monkey, it was a play on his clan name. Apparently they called him that because he was very ugly—bowlegged, with hair all over. But he always had a reputation for cleverness, and he married a woman as clever as he was.

"Trouble was, this woman was beautiful as well as clever, and her hand had been much sought after. Her spurned suitors were furious at being passed over for the Monkey, so they sought a way to ridicule her. It seems they latched onto the fact that she was short and her voice was a bit squeaky, and she became the Mouse—a fit bride for a monkey, perhaps, but not for any self-respecting man. Does that answer your question?"

"Well . . . more or less." She fidgeted for a bit, but eventually gave in and asked, "So what happened to them?"

"To the Monkey and the Mouse? Quite a lot, actually. As I said, he became a general during the Four Wars, but even before that, when Inkei was still a mess of clans fighting to unify under one banner, he and his wife were wise enough to throw their lot in with the winning side early on. They were rewarded with land and riches when Inkei unified, and great political influence in the peace that followed the resolution of the Four Wars. Their children were brilliant and wise, and, one advantageous marriage later, their grandchildren grew up to rule the whole country. So while they were certainly laughed at during the early years of their marriage, I'm certain they were the ones laughing in the end."

"Good," Marceline said. "They deserved to laugh, after all that." A sudden thought struck her, and she blushed. "Look here, they *don't* call me a monkey because I'm ugly, all right?"

"Of course not," Mouse said, as if the thought had never occurred to him. "And I never had a squeaky voice, either. But I *was* small, when I was a boy. That's why they used to mock me by calling me Mouse."

"So you *don't* like the name?" Marceline asked.

He smiled. "Back then, I hated it. I'm not small anymore, so I could've left it behind. But I decided to take it for myself instead."

Before Marceline could ask why the hell he'd want to do that, the door banged open, and Naishe barged in. "No more of that, Mouse. It's time to take her out, not tell her stories."

He held up his hands. "As you say. Just trying to pass the time. Do you want me to come help you?"

"I wonder how much help you'd be," she said, as if to herself. "No, better not bother. No point in drawing attention to yourself."

Marceline looked out the window. "We're going out *now*? It'll be dawn soon."

"Right, and the Night Market will be nearing its end," Naishe said. "A perfect opportunity. Come along."

Marceline squinted from one of them to the other. "The fellow you want me to rob's at the Night Market?"

"The one *he* wants you to rob is at the Night Market," Naishe said. "I, as you'll recall, was outvoted." Then, to Mouse: "Expect us back within the hour, if this one doesn't cause any trouble."

Marceline wasn't given an opportunity to cause trouble, as Naishe kept a hand clamped around her wrist as often as she could without seeming suspicious. She had longer legs and more confidence in where she was going, so Marceline had to struggle to keep up. "I'm not going to run," she complained, rubbing her elbow with her free hand.

"Of course you are," Naishe said. "Why wouldn't you?"

"Because I don't *need* to. If I ran, that'd be like saying I didn't believe I could do it."

"*Or* it would be saying that you didn't intend to use your talents for the likes of us, just because we demanded it," Naishe said. Well, fair point. Marceline gave up, letting her arm relax in Naishe's grip.

"I don't mind all that much," she said, just to be clear. "Whether you admit it or not, you *are* causing trouble, and using the shadows and low places to your advantage. And your group seems to be good at it, if you've gotten this far. I can respect that."

Naishe said nothing, but Marceline hadn't expected her to do otherwise.

The Night Market was familiar to her by now, though she still couldn't help getting a little caught up in the bustle and excitement of it all—for the first few minutes, anyway, before Naishe dampened her enthusiasm by bringing her to an all *too* familiar merchant.

Six-Fingered Peck stood behind his stall of bottles and jars, and at least he didn't look any happier to see Marceline and Naishe than Marceline was to see him. "What on earth do you think you're about, girl?" he muttered to Naishe, as soon as they came close enough. "I didn't give you that information so you could use it to find *another* way to cause trouble for me."

With a sinking feeling that quickly turned to outrage, Marceline realized she could guess what information he meant. "I can't believe it. This is all *your* fault? You're the one who told this lot I was asking after them?"

Peck grinned at her, completely unabashed. "You did a decent job of getting the information you were after, I'll give you that. I was impressed, especially given your youth. But you're clearly new at this. I understand you must be used to being ignored and passed over, but it's always dangerous to assume you will remain so. You were so focused on what *you* wanted to know that you never thought anyone else would want to know about you."

Marceline scowled. "*And* you told me you had cut all ties with this lot."

That wore out his grin a little bit. "Believe me, I wish I could. But this one in particular is . . . very determined."

"Nonsense," Naishe said, flashing a cynical grin of her own—probably the kind of expression a hawk would give a rabbit. "Peck and I are practically old friends at this point." She leaned down so she could speak more quietly to Marceline. "We'll talk with him while we wait for our man to show. I'll point him out to you."

"Is it safe for us to be seen with Peck?" Marceline whispered back. "He was already being watched as a potential contact of the . . . you know. And it seems like he *is,* more or less."

Naishe shook her head. "That danger has passed—for the present, at least. The one Peck was seen in conversation with wasn't me, and none of Elgar's men will mark two of our descent doing business together."

"And me?" Marceline asked. "I'm hardly of any Akozuchen descent."

"No, but you're a child," Naishe said. "It's suspicious to just stand about, anyway. I can keep a lookout and do some business at the same time." She gestured at Peck's wares, which Marceline remembered were supposedly medicines. "You should watch. Knowledge of herbalism is a boon to anyone."

Marceline rolled her eyes. "Right." She barely knew what herbalism was—making plants into useful things, more or less. At least Naishe had finally let go of her wrist. She leaned against the side of Peck's stall, idly watching the crowd while Naishe listed what she wanted from him. But when Peck tried to push a jar of something forward, Naishe waved him off—and tapped Marceline hard on the top of the head.

"Pay attention," she said. "What I'm about to teach you could save your life." But then her face softened and grew wistful, and she suddenly looked much younger. "You know, that's what my mother told me, too—about many things, but always about medicine." She pointed to the jars. "This, when it contains what it claims to, is called rashenot. Ra-she-not. Made only in Akozuchi, but exported to every continent in the known world. Do you know what it does?"

"Of course not," Marceline muttered, curious in spite of herself. "That's why I'm still listening to you."

"Well, thank heavens for that." Naishe picked up one of the jars, brandishing it before Marceline's face. "A skilled healer may stitch and bandage a wound that would otherwise be fatal, saving an injured person from bleeding to death. And yet a single scratch has the power to kill, should the cut happen to fester. That is what rashenot is for. Applied to a cut, or the hands and instruments of a healer going about her work, it helps protect against infection."

"Oh," Marceline said. That did sound useful, she had to admit. "But if it can do that, shouldn't more people be buying it? I mean, you could sell it everywhere, not just at some obscure stall at the Night Market."

Naishe glared at Peck. "There is demand for rashenot in every city in the world, and the Akozuchen can only produce and export so much. So even a merchant with connections, like our friend Peck, will receive only a precious few jars at a time. But that is no good way to make money, is it? So they play their little tricks." She removed the lid of the jar she held, and took a deep sniff. "This, for example, is lamp oil."

Marceline was shocked, and then angry at herself for being shocked. She'd grown up with all sorts of swindlers, hadn't she? Perhaps she was just surprised to encounter one she didn't already know from Sheath. "So the whole business is a sham?"

"Not the *whole* business," Naishe said, prying the lid off another jar. "There're a few real ones in here. The trick is finding one." She sniffed again. "More lamp

oil." And again. "Hmm . . . melted butter, I think." And again. "Some sort of perfume . . . pleasant, but useless."

When she sniffed the next one, her face tensed. "Peck. This is anguis."

"*Lesser* anguis," he muttered. "It's a small jar, it won't do much—"

"You'll be giving it to me," Naishe said sternly. "And you'll not receive a copper for it. I'll pay you fairly for the rashenot, but this is an outrage."

He scowled. "How far will you go to ruin my business?"

"It's because of me you still have one. And if I find you with a jar of anguis
again, I'll empty it over your stall. We'll see how harmless you think it is then."
She set that jar to the side and reached for the next one. "Ah. And here we are."

She grabbed Marceline's shoulder with her free hand, shoving the open jar under her nose. "There," she said. "*This* is rashenot. You will not be able to tell by the
color, but you can tell by the smell."

She certainly could. The jar's contents were acrid and bitter, so strong that she
felt as if the liquid had gone up her nose. It was all she could do not to cough.
"Gods, that's awful!"

"But it's the real thing," Naishe said. "No tricks here. My mother taught me,
when we used to take her rounds together while Father was away."

Despite the stench, Marceline took another deep inhale, trying to commit it to
memory. "What happened to your mother?" she asked.

Naishe blinked at the question. "I . . . can't really say that anything 'happened'
to her. She was a healer in southern Hallarnon when I was a child, and she's a healer
in southern Hallarnon now. She has a customary route through the villages down
there, and it would take quite a bit to keep her from it. Why, what happened to your
mother?"

Marceline squirmed; when Naishe put it like that, it was as if Marceline had
wanted her to ask the question. "Well, she died, but a long time ago," she said, as
breezily as she could. "I barely even remember. I just thought . . . I didn't understand that you meant that *you* left, and she stayed the same."

Naishe held her gaze steadily. "So you live with your father?"

"*No,*" Marceline snapped, before she could help it. "He was a royal ass, and
anyway he's dead, too." He also might not even have been her father, but Naishe
didn't need to know that.

"You can't tell me you've been living on your own," Naishe said. "You're far
too young for that."

"I'm fifteen, and I'm not going to tell you who I live with," Marceline reminded
her. "That's the deal, isn't it?"

Naishe nodded, but she didn't look happy about it. It was odd—whenever
she started thinking about how Marceline was a child, she seemed to forget how
she felt about Marceline as a thief. To get her off the subject, Marceline poked at

the other jar, the one that had contained . . . anguis? "What's in this one, then? It's dangerous?"

Naishe pushed the jar out of her reach. "You don't need to know about this one."

"And I thought you were so keen to teach me. How can I avoid it if I don't know what it is?"

"Make sure you smell it, if you really want to avoid it." She pried off the lid and held it much more carefully in front of Marceline's face. It smelled strange, but not as bad as the rashenot: vaguely sweet, but not at all like flowers. Like some kind of sap or syrup, perhaps, though the liquid itself flowed as easily as water when Naishe sloshed it around slightly as she returned it to the table.

"The point with anguis is the color," Naishe said. "Like this, this lighter yellow, almost golden color? That's lesser anguis. If you soak your feet in it you can reduce gout, and it's good for blisters, too. The problem is it's also highly flammable—a single spark will do it. Even more dangerous is *greater* anguis, which smells like this except stronger, and is a darker color, more like amber. You should not ever encounter greater anguis—it's extremely rare. But if by some fell chance you do, you must get as far away as you can, as quickly as you can."

"Why?"

"Because I told you so, and I know much more about such things than you. I will not tell a thief such a secret; you can believe me, or not." She glared at Peck. "Had I found this man with greater anguis—"

"You wouldn't have," Peck said, "because if I'd had a jar of *greater* fucking anguis I wouldn't have needed to pass it off as rashenot. I'd sell it for a tidy fortune and be well rid of your—"

"Quiet," Naishe said, seizing Marceline by the arm and leaning close. "Our man's finally arrived. Try to look as casually as you can, but he's off to your left. Bareheaded, with a bushy brown beard. Wearing Elgar's blue-black."

When Marceline got a look at him, he was moving about at the edge of the ring of stalls. He was slightly flabby but not hugely fat, and his clothes weren't too tight, which was helpful. No armor to speak of, which was also a boon. Slow walker. Not very shifty. He'd have made a good mark even if she weren't already planning to rob him.

"I can do for him just fine," she said to Naishe. "There's still some crowds here; all I need is for him to get close enough to one and I can have it for you straight-away."

Naishe shook her head. "We decided you weren't to steal it tonight, remember?"

"*You* lot said that," Marceline agreed, "but looking at him now, I can't see the point of waiting. I can have it for you in a minute flat."

"We haven't prepared."

"*I'm* always prepared. I robbed two fellows on the way here, and that was with you grabbing one of my hands."

"*What?*" Naishe stared at her own hand, as if it had been burned. "When? What did you take?"

"Just some odds and ends." Marceline pulled out a silver brooch set with a tiny diamond and a burnished copper figurine of a bird. "Pretty, right?"

Naishe made to snatch them from her hands, but Marceline pulled them away. "Look, don't get angry. This is what you *wanted* me to do. I only nabbed these because I knew you didn't believe I could do it. But I can get the key off your man just as easy, I promise."

Peck chuckled softly. "Now you see what a handful she is. I'm just glad she's your problem now, and not mine."

"*I'm* still your problem," Naishe muttered, but it was clear her heart wasn't in it. She sighed, resting her fingertips against her temple. "I will tell Mouse what you've said, and what I saw you do—or *didn't* see you do, to be precise. I will recommend to him that we let you try sooner rather than later, and that your instructions be followed. And then I will recommend that we have no more to do with you, as I think that would be best for all of us. What do you have to say to that?"

Marceline beamed. "I'd say that's just about perfect."

CHAPTER THIRTEEN

Esthrades

"IF WE KEEP a good pace, and nothing happens on the road," Cadfael said, poking at the fire with a stick, "we'll be in Stonespire by early morning, day after tomorrow."

"Have you been this way before?" Lucius asked.

"Close enough. You've never been to Stonespire?"

"This is my first time in Esthrades at all, actually. After Aurnis fell, I went southwest. I wandered about in northern Hallarnon, but I made it to Valyanrend before too long, and I stayed there. So no, I hadn't been to the east at all before this."

"Lucky for you to run into me, then," Cadfael said, with only a little bitterness. Lucius had proved not nearly as talkative or intrusive as he'd feared; he still asked more questions than Cadfael wanted to answer, but he seemed not to mind when he was met with silence, and he handled his share of sitting watches and tending fires. He couldn't cook worth a damn, but Cadfael could, and either way, most of the stuff you could buy at these little Esthradian villages you could eat raw, like berries or hard cheese. The strawberries and raspberries were better up north in Lanvaldis, but he'd never had anything to equal an Esthradian blueberry.

"Stonespire's nowhere near the size of Valyanrend, but it's still a major city," he said. "Have you thought about how you're going to find your friend?"

"I have, though I've yet to find a plan that truly satisfies me." Lucius pulled his sword free of its sheath, squinting at the blade in the firelight. "He'll be looking for Seren Almasy, so getting on her trail will likely put me on his as well."

"But Seren will be up at the hall," Cadfael said.

"The best defended place in the city," Lucius said. "I know. Deinol wouldn't just walk in there, especially not with Seth accompanying him." He looked up. "Is there something wrong with my sword?"

Cadfael had been watching the play of firelight against the blade as he turned it, and perhaps memories had turned his face more sour than usual. "Not that I can see," he said. "It's just . . . been a long time since I've seen a *tsunshin*. My sister used to favor them, so there was a time when they were commonplace to me."

Lucius could hardly have missed the past tense. "Has she changed her mind since?"

Cadfael laughed bitterly. "Perhaps she would if she could. She's dead."

"Ah," Lucius said. His sadness looked so strangely genuine, though he'd never known Rhia at all. "When?"

"The fight in Araveil, when Elgar's soldiers were invading. Three years ago. They hadn't surrounded the city, and many people were fleeing through the northern gate. I made her promise to join them, but . . . I suppose it was a promise she couldn't keep. She got drawn into a fight with . . ." He swallowed hard, choking on the rest of it.

But Lucius understood. "Shinsei. Of course." He hesitated. "Is that when you got that scar?"

Cadfael shook his head. "I had it already by then—or I had the wound, at least. It's why I wasn't out there protecting her in the first place."

Lucius was quiet for a moment. Then, apparently satisfied with his inspection of his sword, he sheathed it again. "If you don't mind . . ."

Cadfael waved at him. "Ugh, go ahead and ask, if it's bothering you so much."

Lucius nodded, but his question wasn't what Cadfael had been expecting. "How is it your sister came to wield a *tsunshin*? It doesn't seem you ever lived in Aurnis, but there are no schools I know of outside it that could have taught her."

"Rhia taught herself, at first," Cadfael said. "Not the *tsunshin,* I mean—she started with rapiers, then sabers after that. She just picked up a sword one day, and wanted to use it, and even though Father always encouraged it, even he didn't exactly *teach* her. She just had an aptitude for it. The *tsunshin* came when a man who wielded one passed through our neighborhood, and offered lessons in the style as a way to earn his living. When she saw what he could do . . . he wasn't a *shinrian,* and

I'm sure you would have deemed him mediocre, but it was all she could talk about. She begged me to let her learn from him."

"I've no doubt she made her teacher proud," Lucius said.

Cadfael snorted. "Not at first, she didn't. He refused my coin—said the way of the *tsunshin* wasn't a path for women to walk, and that wasn't the way it was done in his country."

"Blatantly untrue," Lucius said firmly.

"So I found out. *I* didn't care about any *tsunshin* or *shinrian* or any of that, but I cared about making her happy. So I did my research, and I came back to him. I told him that I knew women had been allowed to become *shinrian* since the time of the current queen's father, and her son had appointed the very first woman to his royal guard. And if Aurnian royalty had thought it fit to allow women to follow the path of the *tsunshin* to its very highest peak, surely Rhia could walk it just a little." He sighed. "The fellow still complained that she didn't have a *tsunshin* of her own, but we had an . . . old sword lying around, so I went to the blacksmith and had it reforged. That finally satisfied him. He decided to move on eventually, but by then she knew enough of the style to use it."

Lucius smiled, but something about his eyes suggested his mind had gone somewhere far away. "You know, as it happened . . . I knew that woman. I knew her . . . fairly well, all told."

Cadfael blinked. "You knew which woman? I'm quite certain you didn't know my sister."

"No, I meant . . . you said you reminded this man that Prince Ryo appointed the first female *kaishinrian* Aurnis had ever had. That's correct, and . . . in fact . . . I knew the woman you mean."

Rhia would have been desperately curious, but all Cadfael could manage was, "Oh." Still, for his sister's sake, he continued, "An admirable sort, was she?"

"She was," Lucius said gravely. "Honorable. Loyal. Unfathomably brave—I think I envied that the most. And kind, even when she didn't have to be—which, of course, is the only true kindness."

That sounded like something Rhia would have said, too. "So what happened?" he asked. "What made this prince of yours decide to appoint her?"

Lucius leaned back on his hands, stretching his legs out away from the fire. "There was this place just outside Kaiferi that we used to call the Dueling Hill: a place of challenge, where any aspiring *shinrian* could declare their readiness to take on one of the order for the right to win the title. But in practice, many challenges went unanswered, the established *shinrian* too cowardly to accept a fight they thought they might lose. Rana was in the opposite school from me, but in that school she was considered the most promising student. As I held similar prominence in mine, we had sparred together more than a few times. She was truly everything a master of the first school should be—and every *shinrian* in Kaiferi had heard tell of it. Worse, she was a woman, and despite King Iruzu's decree so many years ago, many *shinrian* still believed women had no place in the order, and that it would shame them to lose to one."

"So no one would challenge her?" Cadfael asked. "Pitiful."

"No one would challenge her at *first,* but a *shinrian* did eventually step forward. Gao was new to the title himself, and among the newly minted *shinrian* he was considered the one to watch. He gave the others quite a thorough berating. Called them cowards, said they were a dishonor to the whole order—"

"If he felt so strongly about it, why did it take *him* so long to come forward?" Cadfael asked.

Lucius held up a hand. "For the same reason she refused him, when he finally got around to formally accepting her challenge: he was drunk, and she told him as much." He laughed. "Gao was drunk when he had his own duel—it was the only way he got anyone to agree to fight him, and he still won. Passed out directly afterward, I heard—he couldn't even remember the duel the next day. When the witness confirmed it he laughed so hard he couldn't stand up. Still, Rana's honor wouldn't allow her to accept an opponent who was in any way impaired, so they had to have their match the following day."

"And she won, I suppose."

Lucius gave the warmest smile he had yet. "Actually, she lost six times. And each time she challenged him again, for the following sunrise. Each day, too, the voices urging Gao to stop accepting grew more fervent. They feared, of course, that she might actually win, and so they could not have hoped to convince him. He did not view losing to her as something to be feared.

"On the seventh day . . . well, you can guess what happened. And once Prince Ryo heard the story, he wasted no time in offering them both a place amongst his *kaishinrian.*"

Cadfael frowned. "Was that wise?"

"Perhaps not. But it was the right decision, all the same." His smile faded. "Well. It was the right decision for him."

"But not for them?" Cadfael asked.

Lucius faltered. "Perhaps . . . perhaps it was, in a way. When Gao was appointed *kaishinrian,* he swore off drink that instant—it was all right for *him,* he said, but the prince's sworn protector couldn't afford to be in a stupor on the job, and his job was never done. That was a good thing, because I don't know that Gao's body could have lasted much longer, the way he was going. And becoming *kaishinrian* was what Rana had always dreamed of. After going through all that together, the two of them had forged a friendship no one could have torn asunder, and they protected each other as fiercely as they ever protected Ryo. Perhaps there are some who would not find that honorable, but I did. And I envied them above all others."

Cadfael sighed. "I can't say I ever fought a duel I truly loved—for me the sword has never been anything more than a way to earn a living."

"Perhaps that is the wiser path, after all," Lucius said. "As much as I admired their nobility, I could wish they'd had a little less of it, if it meant they would live in Aurnis still."

Chapter Fourteen

Eldren Cael

CHASING CRIMINALS WAS perhaps not the most restful way to spend a morning, but after all the strange happenings Rhia had to puzzle over of late, it was downright relaxing.

The days immediately following Jost's attempt on her life had been quiet, with no retribution, no second attempt, or, indeed, any important news at all. Rhia could not believe that Yorben had knowingly been a part of Jost's plot, and found nothing suspicious about his assurances to the contrary, but that also meant he could offer little insight into Jost's possible benefactor. The queen had also promised to find out whatever she could, but those inquiries would doubtless take time to bear fruit.

In the midst of all that, news on the Red Crows' movements had been a blessed return to normalcy. The queen had a number of members of the guard who presented themselves as ordinary citizens in order to dig up rumors, and one of them had figured out that the Crows planned to raid a trading center off the aptly named Serpentine Lane. Rhia and Hephestion had immediately set to devising a plan to box the Crows in once the raid began and capture as many as they could, but they'd known from the start that it would be tricky with so many potential exits off the street.

The initial counterattack had gone well, with over two dozen Crows either killed or captured. But when they realized the raid was doomed to failure, a smaller group had thrown everything into an escape, and had managed to break past the guards blocking the entrance to one of the side streets. Rhia and Hephestion hadn't had time for more than a glance at each other and a shout to all available guards to pursue before they took off after the fleeing bandits.

Rhia was small, but she was fast, and it wasn't long before she was pulling ahead of the rest of them, even Hephestion. She hadn't intended to leave them behind, but she couldn't afford to slow down; if one of the Crows encountered civilian resistance to his escape, there was no telling what he might do. Worse, the fleeing group seemed to have split off in different directions. Rhia encountered two together, tripped one up and sent him flying headfirst into the cobblestones, rendered one of the other's legs useless with a well-placed sword slash, and left them in the street for the pursuing guards to tie up; there was a third well ahead, and she didn't want him to gain any more ground on her.

She managed to follow him through half a dozen sharp turns, over a one-story roof, and through an elbow-skinningly narrow side street, only to come onto a wider straightaway with three possible exits and no sign of her quarry. She was hurrying down the lane, wondering anxiously which way she ought to turn, when she heard voices.

One rang clear as a bell, its syllables enunciated with great and deliberate precision, though it might have been trembling slightly. "Take care," it said. "The city guard is flooding these streets—you increase your chances of being caught every moment you delay. These are only children. Leave them in peace, and do right by yourself as much as them."

That was trouble if Rhia had ever heard it, and she sprinted in that direction. A deep voice answered the original speaker, and Rhia could clearly make out the derision in the tone. "You're in my way as much as they are. These gutter rats will tell anything for coin. D'you think I'm going to have my face tattled to the guard for the sake of three coppers and a crust of bread?"

Rhia finally rounded the corner, and took the whole scene in at once: four children, none older than ten, were crouched at the end of an alleyway, and in front of them was a young woman, pale as a foreigner, with her arms spread out in front of her. Facing her was a man whose identity Rhia did not need to guess at; the cloth tied around his forearm, black with a crudely embroidered bird in red thread, did that for her. She understood his problem immediately, if not his morals: the cloth covering the lower half of his face had been torn loose in his escape, and the scar cutting through his lips was certainly memorable.

She stepped out in front of the woman, hand on her sword hilt. "Right, there you are. Threatening children is despicable even for a Crow, but your group's previous crimes alone are more than enough to commit you to the queen's prison. The guard will arrive here in force any moment now. You will surrender yourself immediately, or else I will have to . . ." She sighed, and drew her sword in time to block her assailant. She hadn't actually thought he would surrender, but she had to *try*, didn't she?

He wasn't the worst opponent she'd ever fought, but Rhia had an excellent history of winning fights with even odds, and she parried his blows lazily, hoping to convince him he was outclassed. "You're all alone here," she insisted. "You can't possibly think you're going to kill me. If you would just—" But no, the rat made a desperate lunge past her and started to sprint toward the children—looking for hostages, no doubt. Rhia couldn't even really feel bad about catching him in the side of the throat before he'd gotten halfway. They never seemed to think she knew how to run.

She loosened her grip on the sword, resting her hands on her knees for a moment. "Are you lot all right?" she asked, squinting over her shoulder at the children. They seemed unharmed, and not even thoroughly frightened. Children who lived on these streets had probably seen quite a bit.

"They're fine," the woman said, approaching at the edge of Rhia's vision. "They may not thank you for protecting them, but perhaps you'll allow me to do it on their behalf. I didn't quite know what to think when I first saw you, but it seems you do know how to use that thing after all."

As soon as she was certain that no one was hurt, Rhia had been preoccupied with making sure her sword was clean before she slipped it back into its sheath. So when she stood up and looked into the woman's face, she was truly looking at her for the first time.

She had seen fine gentlewomen enough in Araveil, and although she had clearly noticed the difference between herself and them, it had never bothered her, or made her feel she ought to be any different than she was. It was as if they were two separate species, each occupying its natural and distinct place.

But the woman who stood before her now, clad in a faded green dress with a badly worn hemline, was so lovely that Rhia felt instantly embarrassed, as if she wasn't worthy to stand in the same space. The woman smiled at her, and it was equal parts grace, mischief, and something else, something rarer and more secret than the rest. It was a smile that laughed at you, though not unkindly—it made you feel its owner would laugh at herself just as easily, if you could only discover the trick of making her.

Rhia finished sheathing the sword, and took a respectful step back. "I wouldn't have allowed him to take hostages—I just wanted to give him a chance. I'm sorry if I alarmed you."

"No," the woman said. Her brown hair was woven into a single braid, long enough to hang down to her back, and it shook slightly with her movements. "I understand. I wanted to give him a chance, too." They were both silent for a moment, and then she extended her hand. "Glad to meet you, and even more so for the help. That was impressive."

Rhia was struck by a strange feeling, as if there was some memory she was trying to recall—not that she had ever met this particular woman before, but that the woman reminded her of someone else. But who could that be? Could you really meet such a person and forget about them so easily?

She shook her head to chase the feeling off, and her gaze fell on the children. "Do you know this lot?"

"I met them three minutes before you did," the woman said. "I think they live around here. I just happened to be near them when that man came charging through."

"She came to talk to him," the littlest girl said, nodding sagely at the Crow's body. "She told him he had to leave us alone."

The woman looked almost embarrassed. "'Twasn't—er, *it* wasn't quite as heroic as all that. I talked quite a bit at him, but when it comes to fighting I'm quite defenseless, so if you hadn't stepped in . . ."

"I'm glad I could be here, then," Rhia said, finally remembering to take the still-extended hand. They shook so solemnly it made them both laugh afterward, and then she added, "I'm Rhia."

"Just Rhia?" the woman asked, with another one of those arch looks.

Rhia rubbed at the back of her neck. "Most of the time."

Thankfully, the woman didn't ask her what she meant by that—perhaps she guessed it was a sticky subject. "Lirien Arvel," she said, and it took Rhia a moment to realize she was saying her own name.

"That's very pretty," she said, and then immediately wondered if it hadn't been a stupid thing to say.

Lirien Arvel only smiled. "Do you think so? My parents were very proud of it. There weren't many people where I come from whose families even *had* surnames."

"And where is it you're from?" Rhia asked.

"I'm absolutely certain you've never heard of it," Lirien said, "and you won't find it on any map. 'Tis called—" She frowned. *"It,"* she muttered under her breath. *"It."* To Rhia, she continued, "It is called Sundercliff, most likely because that's what the waves have done to it over the years. A very small village, and a *very* sleepy one. About as different from Eldren Cael as a field mouse is from a mountain lion."

"It's close to the sea, then?" Rhia asked, wondering if she could guess the village's whereabouts before she had to be told.

"Mm, close enough. There was a time when I walked to the base of the cliffs nearly every day—I knew those paths like the back of my hand."

There was no shortage of cliffs to be found nearly everywhere on the coastline, but that didn't mean she couldn't narrow things down. "I'm guessing it wasn't the eastern sea," she said, "as the more impressive cliffs border the Endless." She held up a hand before Lirien could tell her, and was rewarded with a laugh. "Was it the Hallern coast? South of the capital?"

Lirien's eyebrows rose. "That's quite specific."

"So's that habit of yours," Rhia said, "the one you seem to dislike so much. Plenty of dialects in rural Hallarnon, but *'tis* and *'twas* are in the southwest only. Near the sea, like you said."

Lirien shook her head, laughing again. "Such a simple word, *it*. You'd think I wouldn't have so much trouble remembering to use it, but the old habits slip out now and again. Shall I take it that you've been to my corner of Hallarnon?"

"Not me," Rhia said. "It's my father who went there—he told us plenty of stories of the places and people he encountered on his travels. I've been to more than a few places between leaving Araveil and coming here, but never to Hallarnon."

"You're from Araveil, then? That's a beautiful city."

"You've been there as well?" Rhia asked, not bothering to hide her surprise. "You're quite a traveler."

"I am that, yes. I don't have a home to return to—it's surprising how free that can make you feel."

"Did something happen to your village?" Rhia asked.

"Hm? Oh, no, it's still standing same as always—as far as I know, at least. I just don't have a home there anymore."

Even Rhia knew enough not to pursue that one. "Do you have a home here, then?"

Lirien shrugged. "Like you said, I'm a traveler. Folk like us don't need to put down roots." She tilted her head, as if trying to observe Rhia better. "To tell the truth, I took you for one yourself."

Rhia winced; she had been able to call herself a traveler for a long time, but now . . . "Well, that's . . . complicated. I used to move around a lot more, but I've been . . . stuck here for a while."

Lirien's smile turned mischievous again. "That sounds inconvenient. And here I thought"—she glanced down at the dead Crow—"you were skilled at removing impediments."

"I'm good at removing everything you can use a sword on," Rhia said, laughing in spite of herself, though it was too true to be really funny, "but when it comes to anything else—"

They were interrupted by the rapid patter of many footsteps, and the clink of metal. "Rhia, you idiot, there you are," Prince Hephestion said, and she whirled reflexively, even though she knew it was him. A couple of his guards stood behind him, but it seemed like they were the only ones who'd been able to keep up. He spared the Crow an appreciative glance. "Well, it seems like you were certainly having fun without me. You're damned efficient, I'll give you that. I just wish that every once in a while you'd *wait* when your lord commanded it."

Rhia inclined her head. "We can both only hope that I will one day master such an ability, my lord."

Hephestion's gaze drifted out to the children—and snapped up to Lirien Arvel, who was looking at him uncertainly. The look that unfolded on *his* face was no mystery—if Rhia had seen it once she'd seen it a hundred times. It generally meant that she was going to spend the next several weeks hearing embarrassing confidences, being asked for her opinion on such impossible subjects as how attractive another woman found him or what sort of gift would delight her most, and inevitably getting in the middle of a row when the queen pulled him aside and informed him, yet again, that it was not the duty of the captain of the guard to assist him in his romantic affairs.

He smiled at Lirien—that gleaming, perfectly dimpled smile that could make his lovers swoon at twenty paces. "I beg your pardon, miss. Was this rogue causing trouble for you as well?"

Lirien Arvel did not swoon, but what she did do was somewhat harder to pin down. Her lips twitched, as if she might smile back at him, but her beautiful eyes, which had been so bright and merry just a moment ago, were suddenly guarded and opaque. "This fellow? He was properly after the children, to be honest. I just happened to be here, and then . . ." She looked to Rhia. "It's this woman who saved all of us."

Hephestion grinned at Rhia, as fond as ever. "Yes, Rhia does have a particular talent for being in the right place at the right time. I've reaped the benefits of that myself."

Lirien looked from him to Rhia and back again, clearly trying to put something together. Finally, she said to Hephestion, "I beg your pardon, it seems you are—someone of importance, but I don't know . . ."

"Oh, of course!" He bowed, sweeping and graceful. "I am Hephestion, prince of Issamira. At your service, in any way I can be."

Something flashed across Lirien's face and disappeared, too quickly for Rhia to catch it. "Of course, I—I truly apologize, but I am a stranger here, and . . ."

Hephestion laughed. "I daresay there are many who've lived in Eldren Cael all their lives who wouldn't know me by sight alone. Please don't trouble yourself over it."

Keeping her eyes angled toward the ground, Lirien addressed her next question to Rhia. "And you know him—his lordship?"

Rhia opened her mouth, but Hephestion was quicker. "I should say she does," he said. "Rhia is our captain of the guard."

Lirien was already looking at her, and Rhia caught the flickers this time: disbelief, clearly, and then what might have been panic. "The—the *captain*?" She shook her head. "It seems I've been—very impolite—I had no idea—"

"You couldn't have had," Rhia said. "Even I don't believe I'm the captain most days. There's really no need for—"

But Lirien had already bowed to them both, and stood back up again as if uncertain whether she'd need to run. Hephestion had years of experience with this sort of reaction, however, and gently took her hand in both of his. "Miss, Rhia and I were in the midst of chasing down these scoundrels. That is our duty—we don't wish any reverence just for doing it. We are only sorry it took us so long to get here. Let that be the last word on it."

Though some tension remained in Lirien's face, she straightened herself back to her full height, and let her hand rest in Hephestion's. "If you wish for no thanks, my lord, I shall not offer any. But I am glad of your presence here all the same." She smoothed down her dress. "I hope you'll forgive my saying so, my lady, but you look very young. Have you served in this position long?"

Rhia felt her jaw clench, and tried to relax. It was as if she was being treated like a noble, of all things, and that prospect could only fill her with bitterness. But she wanted to speak for herself, before Hephestion could speak for her again. "I'm only the captain," she said, in the hope that Lirien would cease her *my lady*ing. "And no, I haven't. I still have much to learn, I'm sure, but I'm honored by my lord's faith in me."

Hephestion grabbed her shoulder playfully. "Rhia's not quite so young as she looks—fully twenty already, if she's to be believed, though I wouldn't blame you for doubting it." He finally, thank the gods, remembered the children, who'd been staring at him curiously. "Oh, damn it, we shouldn't let them stay here when a man's been killed, I should've . . ." He trailed off, letting go of Rhia, and crouched before the children, whispering to them earnestly. Hephestion had a way with children that Rhia had never seen equaled, and she didn't doubt that in half a minute more they would tell him anything he wished to know.

Lirien stepped to her side. "So that was what you meant," she murmured, too softly for anyone else to overhear. "About being tied up in a single place. I don't imagine the captain of the guard of Eldren Cael can leave it very easily."

Rhia felt suddenly guilty, as if she shouldn't have said that to Lirien in the first place. "That's true, but . . . there are people I can help with this position that I couldn't otherwise."

"Your prince not least among them, I suspect." Rhia said nothing to that; she wasn't sure what response would be appropriate. "Well, perhaps you'll forgive me for saying so, my lady, but I doubt we three have seen the last of one another."

Knowing the prince as she did, Rhia could only agree.

CHAPTER FIFTEEN

Reglay

"IT LOOKS LIKE we're making good time," Elgar said, pulling his head back from the carriage window. "We crossed the border just after midday, we'll be well into Reglay by dusk, and then it's only another day or so to Mist's Edge."

"Most of your soldiers should have already arrived there, if we're meant to be bringing up the rear," Varalen said. "What orders have you given them?"

"They'll only have arrived there if they met with no trouble on the road,"

Elgar reminded him. "And they are merely to dig in and prepare for the siege. They may communicate with Kelken and his people, but have no authority to meet any demands or set any terms without my approval."

That made sense. Elgar and Varalen already knew that Kelken the Fourth was slippery, despite his youth. Varalen wouldn't have trusted any of his subordinates to bargain with the boy king, either. Nor did he imagine Kelken was entirely out of tricks to play, even with so much set against him.

In the last set of reports they'd received before leaving Valyanrend, there had been one particularly odd detail: while Kelken had apparently sent several hundred of his men west from Second Hearth, he hadn't arrayed them on the border, and he hadn't sent them to bolster his forces inside Mist's Edge—the two most sensible things Varalen could think for him to do, unless he planned to abandon the fortress altogether and make his last stand in a different castle. But he hadn't let any of his men *out* of Mist's Edge, either, so a full-scale flight couldn't be in order. If it were any other young boy, Varalen would have put it down to an incompetent blunder, but he remembered Kelken too vividly for that. Whatever he was, he was no incompetent.

At least Elgar had consented to forgo horses for himself and Varalen this time. Carriages like this one, with glass windows built into the frame, were rare and expensive in Lantistyne, though Varalen had heard they were more commonplace in Sahai, where they had originated. It wasn't especially comfortable, but it was infinitely better than sitting on a horse, or in some rickety cart. Elgar might possibly have preferred the horse, though; he'd been restive since they set out. As for Commander Shinsei, he was thankfully not within the carriage, but had been placed on the seat beside the driver. Having spent more time in Shinsei's company over the past several days than he had in the year preceding them, Varalen could safely say the man made him as uncomfortable as anyone he had ever met.

Elgar was looking back at him. "The boy will have prepared something," he said quietly. "There wasn't even a token force at the border."

"I agree it's strange, Your Eminence, but he must know lining the border would be a waste. It would spread his men too thin, we'd cut through them too easily, and he'd have so many fewer with which to defend Mist's Edge."

"Yet one would think he'd at least try to use them to direct our path."

Varalen shrugged helplessly. "It is what I would do, but . . ."

The carriage bounced over a rock, and they both paused to resettle themselves after the jolt. "I can't believe you enjoy this," Elgar said, scowling. "Being shoved into a box like an object to be delivered. And these windows hardly give me a clear view of anything."

"*Enjoy,* Your Eminence, would be a gross misrepresentation of my feelings on the matter. I will, however, remind you that this box is much b——" He was inter-rupted by a sound alarmingly close to his ear, as of something burying itself at great speed into the carriage wall. He heard several more thrum through the air, and then the first shouts. "There we are, the greatest benefit of riding in a box. Arrows will hit the box first."

Elgar ignored him, too preoccupied with peering out the window to try to locate the source of the shots. "Halt!" he yelled, banging on the front wall of the carriage with his fist.

The driver obeyed him, and he rather adroitly kicked the back door open and swung himself out, putting the bulk of the carriage between him and the incoming second volley. "Shinsei, to me! Men, form up and find the enemy!"

In the midst of the ensuing commotion, Varalen tried to decide what to do. He was extremely averse to being shot, but he couldn't tell if he was likelier to suffer that fate by going outside to help or by hiding in here and hoping they wouldn't be overrun without him. And Elgar was out there, he reminded himself. He couldn't allow anything to happen to Elgar.

He took a deep breath, and pushed himself out of the carriage.

There was a handful of Reglian swordsmen—ten? a dozen?—but they had more than twice that. The graver threat was the archers. Varalen watched the vol-leys from beside Elgar, and noted a bit of good news—with greater numbers, you could have one set of archers loose while the other nocked a new set of arrows, but there didn't seem to be enough people for that here. Not only was there a noticeable arrow-free gap while they all reached for their quivers, they were already falling out of step with one another, the quicker ones firing early. How many arrows did he see fly in a single volley? Five? Eight? More?

Making a rash decision before he had time to think better of it, he waited for a break in the fire, climbed onto the carriage roof, and leaped from it into the lower branches of a nearby tree. He slammed into the trunk so hard he nearly winded himself, but he kept his feet on the branch, swallowed his grunt of pain, and clam-bered up. He had almost no experience with trees, but he'd grown up poor in Valyanrend with a lack of reputable guardians; he knew how to climb.

On the ground below, Shinsei was tearing into the enemy swordsmen with such unrestrained ferocity that Varalen shuddered, watching another limb go fly-ing. Elgar hadn't drawn a weapon yet, but he was watching the field carefully, shouting commands every so often. "What are you doing?" he snapped at Varalen.

"One moment!" Varalen shouted back, climbing up another level. There. He couldn't be sure there wasn't an additional archer or two hidden from his view by a tree, but the point was to decipher their general formation. It was just as he'd thought.

"They haven't surrounded us!" he yelled down to Elgar. "There's only a single line, nothing behind! We can break through!"

Elgar looked immediately to Shinsei. "Shinsei, press forward and break the line! Drag those archers out into the open! The rest of you, keep those swordsmen off him!"

Off of a battlefield, Varalen had only ever seen Shinsei move in an aimless shuffle, but he launched himself at the archers as if he'd been shot from a bow himself. Dodging a haphazard shot, he finally reached one, grabbing him by the hair and dragging him forward several steps before hacking his head off. The others moved to close the gap and step forward, surrounding Shinsei, who must have seemed like the greatest threat. But they exposed their whole formation, which must now have been clearly visible even to those on the ground.

Varalen saw Elgar brace himself against the carriage, knuckles whitening as he gripped the side. And then he heard the sound as the whole row of bowstrings snapped, the recoil from the drawn-back string so sharp that it whipped a red line across the nearest archer's face.

"Charge them!" Elgar yelled. He stumbled a little in place, but seemed no worse off than that. With their bows destroyed, the archers were useless, and even the swordsmen hesitated, confused when no more arrows arced over their heads. Shinsei tore into them like a wolf into meat, and the other soldiers followed him in force, cutting down the swordsmen and pursuing the fleeing archers into the woods.

Varalen carefully slipped back onto the carriage roof, taking Elgar's offered hand down to solid ground again. *He had to see them,* he thought. *He had to see the archers before he could snap their strings.* That had to be it, right? Why else would Elgar have waited for the archers to cross his line of sight?

"What was that you said?" Elgar asked him, as the sounds of fighting faded in the distance. "About why Kelken wouldn't bother to attack us out here? He'd spread his men too thin, we'd cut through them too easily?"

"And they were, and we did," Varalen pointed out. "We lost . . . four by my count, and as many more wounded. They're about to lose every one of their number."

"True," Elgar said. "As a stratagem, this is . . . not what I had come to expect from Kelken. What was he thinking?"

"I doubt it was an assassination attempt," Varalen said, more to himself than Elgar. "He would've gambled more soldiers. And while the carriage certainly makes you more conspicuous than you would be otherwise, his men couldn't have known for sure you'd be in it—or even that you intended to leave Valyanrend."

"Not even all my subordinates know I'm approaching the front," Elgar agreed.

"I think the Reglian soldiers believed they were just attacking any random group of Hallerns."

"Right, as if they were just supposed to launch an assault on anyone passing through here." A thought struck him. "If that's the case, the soldiers you sent ahead of our party may have run into a similar group, or groups. We should reconvene with them as soon as possible and hear what they have to say."

Elgar nodded. "And if they have encountered Kelken's men, what then?"

"I wish I knew." Varalen shook his head. "They barely killed any of our number—they're spending their own lives for negligible effect. It's a useless delay. It doesn't make sense!"

"Yet I believe there *is* sense behind it," Elgar said.

"So do I," Varalen said. "That's why I don't like it."

Chapter Sixteen

Stonespire

WHEN THE MARGRAINES sat in judgment, it was their custom to address the most severe issues first, and there was a general hierarchy in place to direct the order of cases. Thus, for example, punishments for crimes always came before accusations of crimes, which came before grievances in which the supposed wrongdoing was still within the boundaries of the law. This hierarchy only worked in cases in which members of the guard had been directly involved—it would have been too difficult to try to sort all the common people by severity of grievance, so they were placed after the guards and allowed an audience in the order in which they'd arrived. Of course, Arianrod herself was free to make changes to the order as she saw fit, to give primacy to especially respected personages, and today there were two: Andrew Ryker, rentholder of White Eagle Roost, and a man who claimed to be a Lanvaldian envoy. The Lanvald should, perhaps, have been heard first, given that the issues he had to discuss concerned two nations instead of one, but he cheerfully declared that he was content to wait. This was doubtless true, as waiting in line with the other complainants would allow him to observe how Arianrod conducted herself during these judgments, so he could better prepare himself to make whatever case he had to make before her. Arianrod had no intention of giving such an advantage away so easily, so the envoy was ushered, with all politeness, to a private chamber where he could rest himself after such a surely fatiguing journey. And since Arianrod set Gravis to watch over him, Seren wasn't concerned that the envoy would be able to glean any new information through conversation, even if he'd been the wiliest fellow this side of the eastern sea.

That left Andrew Ryker, a slim, sandy-haired man in his late twenties; it seemed he had recently inherited his position from his father. His bow to Arianrod was respectful enough, though there was a rigidity in his expression that suggested a man used to getting his way. "My lady," he said, "we of White Eagle Roost have meticulously kept the throne's stated rates of rent, for every year since those rents were first instituted by your honored ancestors. I come to you secure in the knowledge that my ledgers will bear me out on that score. But that is also to say that those very rents have remained rigid for generations—subject to careful review and amendment, yes, but even you must admit they have hardly changed over the many decades since their inception. I do not say such laws are unjust, and I mean no disrespect against your sovereignty. I merely ask for the recognition that times change, and needs differ. White Eagle Roost is one of the largest castles in Esthrades, and the most respected. In acknowledgment of this, and of our loyal service, I ask that you allow us to raise the rents an additional ten percent above their current rate."

Though he cloaked himself in humility, Andrew Ryker must have known the audacity of what he was asking. No rentholder had ever been given special dispensation to raise rents, not since a standard rate had been instituted by the sixth Daven on the advice of his daughter. Seren could not imagine Arianrod had any intention of granting his request.

For several moments there was silence, as Ryker waited and Arianrod smiled at him expectantly. When it became clear he was not going to say more, her expression melted into surprise—entirely disingenuous surprise, Seren would have guessed. "Yes, and? I assume you prepared *some* argument as to why I should grant your request? You can't have expected I'd simply acquiesce without so much as a single question."

Ryker had more likely expected her to *refuse* without so much as a single question, and he lost his stride, confused by her mild lack of reaction. "Wh—Surely I don't have to explain to you the difference between my White Eagle Roost and a sorry wreck like Dutton's Skyhaven."

Arianrod laughed. "Well, that's hardly a question it's to my advantage to answer—you could be referring to any number of things. Your seat has more windows. It's closer to the western border than the northern. It certainly doesn't smell of pig, at least."

"My lady," Ryker said, "taking only the size of the castle itself into account, White Eagle Roost is even larger than your Stonespire Hall. It has a hundred rooms, including its own library, and was once, as you know, the seat of proper lords. Indeed, should you care to visit it yourself, you should find it in no way a descent from your accustomed standards; everything from the food to the bed linens is of the highest quality. And yet you would have me on an equal footing with rentholders who keep 'castles' of a dozen rooms, who sleep on the coarsest wool and dine on thrice-salted meat at every meal? A child could see that we ought not even be compared."

"While I certainly hope to possess at least the intellectual capacity of the average child," Arianrod said, "I must confess that I have failed to grasp how anything you have said relates to the topic at hand. We were discussing rates of rent, yes?"

"Yes, of course," Ryker said, "which is why—"

"But *you* don't pay rent, Andrew," Arianrod said, as if she hadn't even noticed he was speaking. "Your tenants do. How does all this majesty manifest itself in *their* lives? Do you allow them to room in those fine apartments of yours, and provide silken sheets for their own beds? Do you serve them venison from your own table? Or is the sole benefit they derive from your increased stature simply the privilege of knowing that the master they serve sleeps on silk and dines on venison?" She smiled. "I should say, if you were serving a hundred mouths venison every evening, it's a wonder you didn't ask me for a rent increase ages ago. But somehow I doubt that's the issue here. What I'm hearing is that you have many nice things, and would enjoy some additional coin to help ensure you continue to have nice things. While I sympathize, that remains your problem, not mine—and, more to the point, not your tenants'."

Ryker forced his words out through lips pressed tightly together. "So, in brief, you mean not to grant my request."

"I certainly mean to wait until I am presented with sound arguments before I consider it," Arianrod said. "If you have been hiding any, by all means produce them now."

But Ryker had nothing more to say, and he knew it. He could not even express his anger with any dignity, as everyone in the hall had borne witness to the exchange and knew that he had failed to make his argument convincingly. As he finally left, Seren saw him trying not to clench his fists. Best to keep an eye on that one, she thought.

Though Arianrod kept both her eyes on Ryker until he had disappeared from sight, she did not seem bothered by his manner; if anything, Seren thought she had expected it, or was possibly even pleased by it. But she certainly didn't dwell on it: it was now time for the Lanvald's audience, and Arianrod sent more of her guards to fetch him back into the great hall.

The Lanvaldian emissary was one of the tallest men Seren had ever seen—not *the* tallest, since she had had the misfortune to behold Caius Margraine. But the Lanvald must surely have approached that stature, in musculature as well as height. He had even brought his own warhammer, a formidably heavy-looking thing, but contentedly left it with the guards at the hall gate when they insisted. His short hair was that brown-blond color so common in his country, his eyes wide-set and a watery blue.

Seren was, perhaps, already predisposed to dislike him, but that impression was quintupled when he opened his mouth.

"Your Grace," he said, with a careless bow in Arianrod's direction, "I am called Ghilan, and I have the pleasure to be the somewhat less than humble servant of Administrator Selwyn, currently governing our province of Lanvaldis on Imperator Elgar's behalf. She has sent me in the hope that we might conclude a trifling bit of business that is doubtless unpleasant for both of us, and that I am sure we both wish to be rid of as soon as possible."

Arianrod tapped her cheek. "Hmm. Administrator Selwyn, is it? I believe I have some vague knowledge of her, though I don't think we've ever met in person. What business can she possibly have with me?"

He grinned widely. "I'm certain someone as clever and capable as you has heard all about it, Your Grace. We've a young runaway in Lanvaldis—a scrawny commoner, no more—who's been stirring up trouble claiming to be the trueborn kin of King Eira, and the rightful heir to his throne. Nonsense a dozen different ways, but he's made many of our citizens uneasy, so the administrator wished to summon him to the castle and examine the truth of his claims. But wouldn't you know it, the little rat fled Araveil rather than be exposed as the swindler he is! The administrator and I were happy to consider ourselves well rid of him, but for the absurd accusations that she'd ordered our young man done away with in secret. So, very well, she sends me to turn him up and prove he's alive and as slippery a bastard as ever. But what do we hear but that he's fled into *your* country for refuge! With the result that here I stand before you, hoping with great optimism that you will assist us in rectifying a situation that's been so very trying for all concerned."

"I see," Arianrod said. "Well, far be it from me to cast doubt on any of your claims. I shall simply dwell on the relevant issue at hand—you wish to find this boy for your own purposes, and believe he currently resides in my country. But my country, while certainly smaller than your province of Lanvaldis, is still too large to be searched in a day, or even in several days. Did you happen to have any additional clues as to where this boy might be?"

The man rubbed his huge hands together. He affected a look of discomfort, but the merry glint in his eyes was undimmed. "That's just it, Your Grace—the unpleasantest bit of the unpleasantness that's fallen over both our lands. While I personally would never dream of impugning Your Grace's honor or sincerity, I am but the administrator's servant, and the administrator has received word that it is in your very castle that the accursed youth has claimed refuge. So, you see, this is an investigation as well as a diplomatic meeting."

"Your youth certainly isn't here," said Arianrod, with a slight laugh, "but I hardly expect that to be the end of it."

He bowed. "Indeed not, Your Grace. I must ask leave to search this place for him."

Arianrod shrugged. "Well, sir, it seems we're at something of an impasse. Whether this boy is a prince or a fugitive, he is not within the confines of this hall. I would, under different circumstances, be perfectly content to let you search the hall to confirm that fact, because I know you would not find him. However, the woman who employs you likewise serves a man who is my enemy, and you can't imagine that I intend to allow one of my enemy's servants free rein of my home."

He smiled. "You and the imperator are not currently at war, Your Grace."

"Oh, what a relief! I'm sure there's no way he could possibly intend me any ill, then." When he raised his hands helplessly, she continued, "As I said: an impasse."

"I grieve to hear it," the man said, "but I cannot say I do not understand it, or that I truly believe I have the right to force your hand in this. And if I remain in your country, even if I am outside your hall, to search for this boy, will I be . . . bothered by your people?"

"That depends on what you attempt to do while you remain in my country," Arianrod said. "I'm certain anyone who attempted to go where common citizens are not permitted, or who demonstrated behavior that might reasonably be attributed to a spy, would not find his stay here especially pleasant."

The man bowed. "I understand you completely, and remain thankful for your lenience. I do hope you won't take any of this personally." As he straightened again, he grinned at her, like a schoolboy pleased in advance by the trivial mischief he was about to cause. "If I didn't have a job to do, you'd find me only too pleased to linger in your company. You're just the sort of woman I like the look of, and that you know it only makes you more appealing."

Arianrod smiled at him. "What a curiously irrelevant statement. Will that be all?"

"Aye, Your Grace. That's all my business," the man said, his glee subdued not a whit.

"I'm glad to hear it. Then . . . Seren, since you're here, perhaps you will escort him from the hall?"

Seren nodded, and Ghilan made no objections. He followed her from the hall quietly enough, until they were outside the castle. But then he stopped, turning to regard her with another of his wide grins. "I've heard about you. Deadliest of all her servants, or so they say."

Seren said nothing to that, because she did not care to confirm or dispute his words.

But he didn't move on, just kept holding eye contact. It was irritating. "The administrator's gotten curious about you of late. She likes information, and Elgar had a lot of it to provide about you after Mist's Edge. Where you gutted one of his men, apparently."

Seren had killed that particular man as part of a staged duel to the death arranged by Elgar himself, against Arianrod's disinclination. But again she said nothing to this man, because she did not care if he knew it.

"They don't know anything else, you know," he said. "Where you came from, where you learned to fight. They'd certainly love to find out." He shrugged. "Not me, though. That's all far outside of my particular interest in you."

Seren said nothing. Her hands were restless at her sides.

He chuckled. "Gods, but you sustain that expression well. I'd hoped to at least get you a little curious."

"I have no business with you," Seren said, because he clearly wasn't going to leave until she said *something*, "and yours with her ladyship is concluded. Have you forgotten the way out? The gate is right in front of you."

"My interest in you," he continued, as if she hadn't spoken, "has nothing to do with where you learned to fight, or who taught you. All I care about is how good you are." He made an elaborate show of catching himself, and added, "At fighting, of course. I've certainly been known to seek an even more intimate acquaintance with women, but you're simply too far from my preferred type. I hope you won't take offense at that—you're certainly not ugly. That hair is quite lovely, and rather unusual. But you just don't have enough up here to make it really worth my while." He waved a hand over his chest. "I've never seen the point of a woman with no tits, you know? Seems like a waste."

"I fail to see the point of a man who's breathing, and have even less use for a man who talks too much," Seren said. "But *I* did not presume you cared to know my opinion."

He laughed. "Damned if that isn't the truth! You're right, that was careless of me, and I owe you an apology. I should have said I've never seen the point of a woman with no tits who can't fight, and you can certainly fight. How many people have you killed, would you say?"

Seren stared at him. "Did you expect me to keep count?"

"Oh, just an estimate would have been fine, but I know it's high enough. I can tell just by looking at you. I love a good fight, and as I've gotten better over the years it's been harder and harder to find one. And I'm not afraid of death, I promise you that. If you were willing, I'd take you on right now—just let me fetch my hammer from those guards that confiscated it and I'd be for you in an instant."

"If I ever decide to kill you," Seren said, "I won't wait for you to fetch the hammer."

He actually looked hurt. "Now that's hardly fair. What kind of challenge could you hope to get out of that?"

"I think you possess some misconceptions about me," Seren said. "I don't enjoy fights, and I don't need them to be challenging. In fact, I prefer winning them by a comfortable margin."

"Come on, that's nonsense. No one devotes that much time to getting that good at something they don't enjoy."

Seren considered it. "I enjoy destroying things that threaten me," she said. "Fighting is simply the means."

He shrugged. "I'd still like to take you on, but the administrator told me to cause as little trouble as possible, and it's not worth getting her put out over it when I can still find a decent fight or two back home. When King Eira was alive you had the arena—the old man loved blood sport, and he was prepared to offer substantial coin to get fellows to sign up to fight to the death. I had some fun there, though they made me use an ax instead of the hammer—they wanted spectacle, and they said the hammer ended things too soon. Never got to fight the most famous champion—fellow younger than me, though maybe about the same age as you. Just some bastard boy from the poor districts when he started, but he was gorgeous, so you had all these tenderhearted noblewomen who hated the sport but turned out anyway to see him. I thought if I kept winning I'd get to fight him eventually, but before I could the king plucked him right out of the arena and made a soldier of him—wanted him for higher things, I suppose. Araveil's ladies were heartbroken." He sighed. "Administrator Selwyn can take or leave blood sport, but since she's not willing to pay anybody any money to do it, the arena's all but dried up now. It's a shame."

"Says her loyal servant."

He grinned. "Oh, don't misunderstand. On the whole my situation's vastly improved with her. The administrator's taken much more notice of me than King Eira ever did—and even if he had, he was just some old man. The administrator's just as clever and *much* better looking—and she's not opposed to going a round with me as long as I stick to the limits of my job. Oh, and *there* I don't mean fighting, of course." He tilted his head at the hall behind him. "What about yours? She let you fuck her? She definitely seems like the picky sort, but not so frigid she can't enjoy a bit of fun."

For the first couple of seconds, Seren was too angry to say anything at all; she dug her nails into her palms in an effort to still the violent shaking in her hands. The man laughed loudly. "There, I knew I could do it! Finally made you angry, eh? Though I guess it doesn't go far toward answering my question: does it make you angry because she does or because she doesn't?"

"I am giving you one minute to go out that gate and never speak to me again," Seren said. "After that, I will cut you into five distinct pieces."

That made him laugh even louder, so that even the guards on the gate turned to look at them. "Don't worry, I've had my fun. But I'm sure we'll meet again, one way or another. Don't forget, Ghilan's the name, should my reputation ever precede me. It's been a pleasure, Seren Almasy."

He finally left, whistling to himself, and Seren retreated to the hall, in a fouler mood than she could remember being in a very long time.

GAN SENRIAN HAD been the first to ever warn her about her hands. She had known him . . . how many hours at that point? Three? Five? It was just the sort of man he was, to pick up on such a minor detail right away.

When she had first arrived at the guildhouse of the Inxia Morain, she couldn't have been much older than ten and had not known a word of Sahaian. She had been directed to Gan by accident, or fate; he was, if not the only member of the guild fully fluent in Lantian, at least the only one who would admit to being so.

He had questioned her for a long time, but his questions had been strange—and, to her mind, not about fighting at all. But when he had asked her why she wanted to learn his art, she could answer easily. "I've always been afraid, and I hate it. But as long as I stay weak, I'll never be able to stop. So I want to be stronger than anyone. If anyone tries to hurt me, I want to be able to kill them, no matter who they are." She couldn't look directly at his face. "Are you going to say that's a stupid reason?"

"Not at all," he said. "Fear is very unpleasant. It's perfectly understandable to want to be rid of unpleasant things. I only want to be frank with you. Sometimes, when we are able to push aside one fear, it simply makes room for another to take its place. The lonely man fears that he will never be loved, but finding a lover does not free him—instead he fears that she will stop loving him, or that something will happen to her. Strength—power—works in a similar way. Do you see?"

Seren wasn't sure yet whether she saw or not. "What are you afraid of?" she asked.

He had smiled, that smile that reached his opaque eyes. "Irrelevance." He paused, pursing his lips. "Hmm. The word sounds rather beautiful in your language. How dreadful to think that something so ugly could ever sound beautiful."

He laughed a moment, but greater solemnity replaced it. "Here is a more difficult question." He tilted his chin, emphasizing how he had to look down to meet her eyes. "Even given your age, you are scrawny and small. With proper nourishment, you will grow more, and age and training will make you stronger. But you will still be shorter and lighter than most of the men you will ever fight. However hard you train, you will never beat them in contests of strength. Yet you tell me you wish to be the strongest. How do you expect to accomplish this?"

Seren hesitated, and finally glowered at him. "You look like you have an answer, so why don't you just tell me?"

"The answer," Gan said, pressing his palms together, "is to think about your desire in a different way. What you really want, you see, is to be the *best*—to be the strongest by virtue of skill, not brawn. You think you will learn strength here, but what you will really learn is discipline, patience, technique—above all, *precision*. These are the things that will let you walk the way of the sword. But if you ever hope to be truly great, first you must throw away your anger."

That was the last kind of bargain she'd been expecting. "What are you talking about?"

"Anger is a double-edged sword," Gan said. "Whom it cuts depends on who wields it. For some, anger is a steadying force, a spur to action: it banishes their doubts, steadies their aim, gives them an energy and power that is more than physical strength alone. But for some people—and you are one of them—anger is only weakness.

"You have a . . ." He frowned. "I seem to have forgotten the word I want. What do you call a . . . a habit that is more than a habit? A habit that reveals character?"

Seren stared at him blankly.

"Damn. I *liked* that word in your language, too. I liked it because in your language it is also a word for speaking—it is a gesture that speaks, and so renders words unnecessary." Quick as a blink, he struck her cheek with the back of his hand—not nearly as hard as he doubtlessly could have, but hard enough to sting.

Seren recoiled, fighting down the shock and panic only with great effort. The worst part of being hit was she didn't just have to worry about the pain of it; sometimes, in the first moments afterward, it was difficult to remember where she was, and who was hitting her, and whether she was powerless to stop it or not. But she recovered herself, and glared at Gan furiously. "*Don't* hit me! What the hell did you do that for?"

"Ah, now I remember." He grabbed her hand, but loosely, so she could still feel how it trembled in his. "It is a *tell,* that makes your hands twitch in accordance with your rage. *This* is how your anger makes you weak. Do you understand now? Do you think these shaking hands will ever strike with precision?"

They certainly weren't at the moment. Seren gave up on practicing, throwing the knife into the ankle-high grass of the orchard and sitting down beside it, closing her eyes. These mistakes were becoming more frequent, which was unacceptable. In these times of heightened danger, it was more important than ever to retain complete control of herself. It was downright shameful that Ghilan had been able to play upon her emotions so well; thank the gods Gan hadn't been here to see it. She put her hands flat on the grass, and breathed deeply in and out, and tried to let go of anything that wasn't useful.

She heard footsteps behind her, but she could already tell it was Arianrod, so she turned slightly, opening one eye. "My lady?"

Arianrod moved to stand in her line of sight, so she no longer had to strain her neck. "Dent said you were in a huff, and that's such a novelty that I simply had to witness it. I think he was afraid of disturbing you, even to take his watch."

Seren opened her other eye. "Should I leave?"

"I don't mind. It's not as if any breach of security is going to occur with you here." She prodded the discarded knife with the toe of her boot. "So what happened?"

She would never have thought of concealing the truth from Arianrod, but that didn't mean she enjoyed telling her. "That Lanvald insisted on making a fuss on his way out. He'd heard about me, I guess, and wanted to see if he could make me angry—possibly as a way of coaxing me into a fight, I don't know. He was . . . disrespectful of you, for all the flattery he spewed to your face."

"Disrespectful? Gods, how shall I survive?" Arianrod clapped a hand to her heart. "To think that a servant should be obsequious in the presence of a ruler and gloatingly arrogant behind her back! I'm quite certain this has never happened before."

Seren was sure she must have looked sheepish, but she knew Arianrod wasn't trying to imply that she had acted wrongly, only that the whole affair wasn't worth any distemper. "I just . . . I don't like it when people misunderstand me. Especially when it's only for the sake of dragging me down to their level."

Arianrod bent to pick up the knife, examining it with idle curiosity. "Seren, do you know why I enjoy life so much more than you do?"

Seren couldn't help but smile at that. "I can think of a thousand reasons, my lady."

Arianrod laughed without any irony—the laugh of someone who hadn't been expecting to laugh at all. "I'm sure that's true, but I was referring to one reason in particular. I don't pay attention to the opinions of stupid people. Given how little you seem to want to bother with people at all, it amazes me how you fret over things they might have to say. If someone has an incorrect opinion of you, it only means you'll have the advantage when they misjudge you. Beyond that, it's just so much noise." She reached up to the nearest branch, pulling a blood apple down from the tree. "Want one? I'm starving."

She said it so casually, but Seren could still hardly believe it was a privilege allowed to her. Only ruling Margraines and their immediate family were supposed to be permitted to eat from the blood apple trees. Of course, since Arianrod was the only Margraine left, Seren didn't have to worry about cutting into her supply, but that didn't stop the disbelief. She remembered the first time Arianrod had offered her one of those apples, almost two years ago now—the smug look on her face, as if making a challenge.

It still felt like a challenge to take the apple from her, no matter how many Seren had plucked for herself.

CHAPTER SEVENTEEN

Valyanrend

THE NIGHT THEY finally decided to let her work was the first time she'd seen the lot of them together since they first apprehended her: Mouse, Rask, Naishe, and even Talia, who seemed to have wormed her way into the gathering despite her lower rank. She had also brought the food, and brightened when Marceline complimented it: perhaps she was the contact through which the resistance acquired it? It was delicious, nuts and cheese wrapped in thin slices of smoked pork and covered in honey, and at first Marceline was so preoccupied with eating it that she didn't notice their group had a new member; he hadn't spoken a word. But as Talia sat apart with her and the others formed a rough circle for a quiet discussion, she saw that on Mouse's far side was another young man, whose brown hair, desperately in need of a trim, had fallen into his face, leaving only one eye visible, a somewhat darker brown.

Mouse finally looked up from the little circle, speaking to her directly. "All right, here's what we've decided. Our anonymous friend, called the monkey, will go to the market with us. If our fellow shows again, the theft happens tonight. If not, we return every night until he does. Understood?"

"And *then* you release me," Marceline piped up. "According to your promise."

Mouse inclined his head. "Just so." He turned to his little circle again. "Any objections?"

"Not to that in particular," Rask said, "but I did have another bit of business I wished to discuss, now that we're all gathered here. Our lieutenant friend I mentioned, the drunk. There's no doubt he has something, and patrols are light in the Fades. He shouldn't have more than a handful of other guards with him at any one time; if you let me take my full number, we can overpower them easily. I just need your word."

The young man at Mouse's other side spoke up—though hardly so, as he had a very soft voice. "You don't have enough information yet, Rask. Going now would be impetuous, and put the others at risk. If you wait a few days, I can—"

"What?" Rask snapped. "Dither about? Make your arrows in the corner?"

The young man recoiled a little, but kept speaking. "No, I meant I know where he gets his supplies. If I watch him, learn his habits, perhaps I'll find a safer way to—"

"We can't attack him when he's at the shops, you idiot. It'd be no use even if you knew his whole blasted schedule."

"Still your tongue for once, Rask, and hear him out to the end," Naishe said. "He has as much right to speak as you do—he has been at Mouse's side longer than any of us."

Rask flushed angrily, but when Mouse made no move to defend him, he fell silent as she had recommended. The young man blushed a little, too, at all the attention. He brushed his hair out of his eyes before he answered, and for a moment Marceline thought she'd gotten their color wrong. But then she realized: only the left eye was brown, the right a muddy green. "I just mean," he said, "that I think your plan is too impulsive. Even if you didn't lose any of our own, you'd end up killing any guards your man was with, if not the man himself. Elgar won't ignore something like that. And we aren't ready for him to take so much notice of us, not yet."

"He's not wrong," Mouse said mildly.

"Seconded," Naishe added.

Rask scowled deeply, but he must have known he wasn't going to get what he wanted. "Fine. Then, no objections."

"No objections," Naishe echoed.

"None here," the young man said.

Mouse clapped his hands together. "Good. Then let's get started. Rask, you and I will leave first and make sure there aren't any surprises waiting for us. Naishe, you and Wren follow with our monkey friend."

"Talia, you're with me," Rask said. Marceline thought the girl looked a little disappointed.

After the other three left, silence fell over the rest of them. Marceline wasn't sure how long they were going to wait before following, but she *was* sure it would be Naishe who made the decision. But before that could happen, the young man named Wren unexpectedly spoke up again.

"Thanks," he said to Naishe. "For stepping in to defend me back there."

But Naishe's expression stayed as stern as ever. "You don't need to apologize to anyone, and you don't need to thank me. You are as much one of us as anyone could be—you ought to remember that as well."

"I . . . I know," he said, ducking his head. "I'll do better next time."

"The problem is not your value, Wren, only your own estimation of it. Your idea was a good one. But if you can't give voice to your good ideas, we are all the poorer for it." She smiled slightly. "I know all too well that forcing any measured proposition past Rask is like kicking a donkey, but it's a burden we all must bear if we are to keep guiding Mouse in the right direction."

He was still looking at the floor. "Oh, well, when it comes to Z—to Mouse, I don't know if it's fair to say I help guide him. He's always had so many ideas on his own."

Naishe gave a skeptical click of her tongue. "Mouse has a whole garden of ideas, that's for sure. He's just not very good at plucking the weeds."

Wren laughed, and then caught himself, and then looked guilty, but at least he was finally meeting Naishe's eyes; Marceline felt more anxious just looking at him. He seemed to finally take notice of her, and stuck out his hand awkwardly. "We . . . haven't met before. I'm Wren Fletcher."

"Is that a nickname, too?" Marceline asked, shaking his hand.

He looked confused. "No, that's my real name."

"We've put enough distance between our groups now," Naishe said abruptly, easing the door open. "Let's get going. I'm excited for the moment this one will no longer be my problem."

She swept out the door without waiting for them. Without her, Wren looked around for a moment as if he wasn't sure what to do. He blew all the air out of his lungs in a noisy sigh, like a snorting horse, and brushed the unkempt bangs back from his face.

"Are you going to be all right tonight?" he asked her gently, meeting her eyes this time.

She grinned at him. "All right? I'm going to be brilliant."

AFTER SIGHTING THE mark, the biggest trouble was making sure the others kept their distance while she approached him. There were quite a few furious glares back and forth before she was finally satisfied with the arrangement, and then she spent a little time milling through the crowd aimlessly, drawing closer to him in haphazard spirals. He stopped to haggle at one of the stalls, and they all seemed so surprised that she didn't even attempt to approach him then. Amateurs. *Anyone* would imagine they could be robbed while their attention was focused on something else; the point was to rob him when he thought it was impossible. So she waited until he wasn't doing anything more complicated than walking, and picked a little throng that was just right: a bunch of people, but not so densely packed she'd have to shove to reach him. She got close to him, and as *he* tried to brush past a young couple, she made her move. Just for good measure, once she was sure she was clear she tripped the man next to him, so they banged into each other and started growling, and slipped clean away in the confusion.

She gave the signal to Mouse, and the lot of them trooped back to the meeting house—only idiots would have showed their spoils in the open street. But as soon as the door had shut behind them, Rask turned on her. "Did you really do it? I barely saw you touch him."

"Aye, that's the point, idiot. If you'd seen me do it from that far away, I wouldn't be very good at it, would I?" She grinned. "Tell your leader to check in his pockets."

Mouse did so, and pulled out the key she'd stolen. "Damn, monkey, you're no thief. You're a bloody sorceress!"

"Make sure she didn't steal anything while she was in there," Naishe said.

"Oh, I did." She held up a silver coin between two fingers.

Mouse laughed. "You can keep it. This is worth much more than that to us."

But Marceline had more on her mind than the coin. "So you'll keep your word now, right? I'm free to go, and you won't trouble me again?"

They all fell silent, which wasn't the best possible response, and looked to Mouse. But Mouse just laughed again. "Why does everyone look so serious? A promise is a promise. If we seek to show ourselves as better than the tyrant who oppresses us, we must at the very least honor the bargains we make."

There were several exhales as the tension in the room dissipated; only Rask looked a little disappointed. "It's a shame we'll be out her skills, but I see your point."

"At first you wanted to kill me, and now you want to keep me," Marceline said. "How curious."

He snorted. "I never said I wanted to kill you, even back then. And if you want me to admit you're more skilled than I thought, fine. I was wrong. Happy?"

"Well enough. What do you need that key for, anyway?"

"That's not your concern," Naishe said, rolling her eyes at Mouse. "Though I'm sure he's about to tell you anyway."

Mouse grinned. "To tell you the whole plan would be unwise, of course. But we've had our eye on something big for a while, and this has gotten us a lot closer."

"It'd practically get us *there,* if only you could climb the Precipitate," Talia sighed.

Marceline really should have just kept her mouth shut. Roger and Tom would have kept their mouths shut. But that statement was so absurdly, blatantly, inescapably false that the words were out before she could stop them. "Can't climb the Precipitate? But of course you can."

Just like that, the whole room was looking at her again.

Rask spoke first, of course. "Climb nearly a hundred feet of wet stone? The Precipitate's slicker than a demon's bitch."

"You're speaking to a *child*," Naishe said, as if even she hadn't realized she could be this disappointed in him.

Marceline figured she should step in. "I didn't say it was easy, I just said it was possible. I've climbed it three times myself. Almost fell the first time, and I've known others who did fall, but none who died from it. Still, it's been known to happen."

"How is it that there are so many people trying to climb the Precipitate?" Naishe asked.

"It's a thieves' secret—or at least it's supposed to be. The ones who do it are mostly children, so not old enough to be proper thieves yet. Some particular one of them learns the trick from a relative, or an apprentice from their master, and shows the others how it's done. Then they make a game of it." She grinned. "If none of you ever heard about it, that tells me something else. None of you grew up on the streets. If you'd been an orphan like me, or a child running mischief for their elders, you'd already know."

Rask rubbed his face. "Mouse, if she really does know, she's got to show us."

"I don't *have* to do anything," Marceline said. "Not anymore. That's over with."

"It's over with when we say it is."

"Your leader already said it," Marceline pointed out.

"I did," Mouse agreed. "I did, and a leader who can't keep his word is worthless. So we will not compel you to help us." He crossed to her, and bowed deeply. "But I will ask you—entreat you, if you like—to give us your help. I'm not sure we could find anyone else to teach us, if you won't. And I believe learning the Precipitate's secret would be the best way to further our plans."

Marceline considered it. She still didn't want to join any damn resistance, but if they *did* manage to bloody Elgar's nose, she'd get a good laugh out of it. If showing them how to do this one thing helped in that regard, why not do it? But she didn't want them to think they could count on her for whatever they pleased, either.

"The first thing I'm going to do is go home," she finally said. "*Without* being followed, thank you very much. And if I'm allowed to go about my business in peace, it *may* be that I decide to come back here. But it has to be my choice."

Mouse bowed his head. "Well said. So it does." He smiled. "And so, I hope, it will be."

MARCELINE HAD BEEN in the full glow of her triumph when she'd finally returned to Sheath, but after dropping in at Tom's only to find it deserted and tromping through half the neighborhood in search of him, the luster was starting to wear off. She'd hardly expected the old man to embrace her and thank the gods for her return, but she'd at least expected him to notice she was gone. It wasn't clear that he'd done even that much. Well, so much for loyalty. He couldn't count on *her* to notice the day he finally dropped dead, which probably wasn't long in coming.

By the time she trudged over to the Dragon's Head, she wasn't looking for Tom anymore; the Dragon's Head was Roger's haunt, these days, and Roger and Tom, when not actively finagling something out of each other, tried to stay as far apart as possible. So, just like the old saying, that was where she finally found him: sitting at the bar, deep in conversation with Roger, of all people. He roused himself with an effort when he heard the door open—then saw her, and froze.

"What's all this?" she asked. "When did you two start having evening chats?"

Tom was still staring helplessly, so Roger answered. "Since you made yourself scarce, monkey, and your old man dragged me into the search against my bloody will. He was *so* damned sure you'd been apprehended by our nascent resistance, and wouldn't hear any of my assurances to the contrary. Maybe *you* can tell him where you've gotten yourself to for all this time—and make sure to tell him not to be so dramatic while you're at it."

While Roger was speaking, Tom had stared, blinked, stared some more, gotten to his feet, stared, taken several steps toward her, put out a hand, pulled it back, and finally rested it on her shoulder, as if touching something extremely delicate. In the same amount of time, Marceline had gotten what she believed was a serviceable grasp of the situation, and had realized just how much fun she was about to have. She let herself smile vaguely—no smirking yet, just a little enigmatic tug at the lips—and said, "Oh, I was apprehended by the resistance. More or less, anyway."

Tom's hand tightened on her shoulder, and Roger's carefully crafted look of put-upon weariness faded. "What do you mean?" he asked. "You were captured by the resistance, but you're standing here now? What did you do, annoy them so much they let you go?"

Now it was time to grin wide, to let him see how the taunt breezed right by her. She knew how wrong he was, and he was about to know, too. "Actually, their leader wanted me to stay on for longer. It was fun for a while—you wouldn't *believe* the food they have their hands on there—but I didn't want to get any more tangled up in that business than I was already, so I decided it was time to go."

Gods, but she wanted to remember the look on Roger's face for the rest of her life. If she could have, she'd have commissioned a portrait of it. But he swallowed whatever incredulous outburst he almost made, and tried his best to be scornful. "You're lying, monkey."

Marceline twitched one shoulder carelessly—not the one Tom was holding, because she didn't want him to think she was putting him off. "You know I'm not, but you can believe what you like."

Tom finally spoke, as if drawing the words out from deep within himself. "Didn't . . . hurt you, did they?"

Marceline shook her head. "They debated about it, but only at first. I made myself too interesting to them—and a little young, for good measure." She caught herself. "Oh, but I never said anything about you, Tom, or anyone else in Sheath. They tried to get it out of me, but I didn't let a single word slip. You're safe."

Tom was staring at her again, moving his hand so he could face her properly. "Girl," he said sternly, "you're a thief. If throwing me over was what you needed to do, you ought to've done it. Sentimentality will get you killed in this business."

She rolled her eyes. "*Or* I could've not thrown you over *and* not gotten killed, which is what I actually did, because I'm a good thief as well as clever. And you could've just said thank you."

Tom grinned. "You've proven yourself clever, I'll give you that."

She grinned back. "Were you really holed up in here with Roger trying to *rescue* me? Have a little more faith, old man."

CHAPTER EIGHTEEN

Eldren Cael

THERE WERE MANY tales—in Issamiri folklore, yes, but also in so many other cultures, whether on the Lantian continent or across the sea—about the treacherous guest. There would be some stranger with a fair face and an amiable demeanor, humble, grateful, inoffensive in every way. They would be invited inside, whatever *inside* meant in this particular tale: within the walls of a city or castle, through the doorway of a great manor house or a humble cottage. And once the stranger was ensconced there, strange and ill-fated things would start to happen. Cities fell to riot and ruin, brothers turned on one another, sudden plagues felled entire households. And when the damage was done, and the remaining survivors looked round or the too-late rescuers arrived at the scene, the mysterious stranger would be gone.

It wasn't a story Adora liked, most of the time. It was fine as an extended metaphor, the stranger as Death or Discord or Greed or any of half a hundred other personifications. But taken more literally, it was a story about fear of the outsider, about how people we don't know, people who aren't like us, can never be trusted, no matter their outward seeming. It had always been, to her, a story that marked a prejudice to be overcome, rather than any lesson to be learned.

And yet she could not deny that she wished her brother had never crossed paths with Lirien Arvel in the first place.

Feste's infatuations were nothing new, of course. Their father, once he realized all the anger and disapproval he could muster had no effect, chose to ignore his son altogether. Landon had offered only a few mild words of lecturing every so often, and their mother was primarily concerned that none of Feste's paramours caused a scandal or aspired to his hand. As for Adora, she knew that the best way to deal with her brother was to understand how he worked. His desire for many a woman had been cured after a single night with her, and even his most stubborn liaisons had lasted less than three turns of the moon. If you had the misfortune to be a royal prince with a pitiful amount of self-control, it was a mercy if you possessed an attention span to match.

Lirien clearly hadn't slept with him yet, though she could not possibly be un-aware of his intentions by now. She might have been circumspect, or undecided, or simply uninterested in Feste. She seemed to have almost no money and only a satchel's worth of belongings, so perhaps she merely sought to enjoy food and lodg-ing she could never have dreamed of affording otherwise; Adora wouldn't have blamed her for that in the slightest. And yet. And yet, and yet, and yet.

Something had bothered her about Lirien Arvel from the very beginning, something that grew stronger with every day she remained at the palace. It was the feeling of something that was not what it appeared to be, of an argument that seemed to make sense, but fell apart upon closer inspection. It was the feeling those gracious hosts must have felt in the old tales, when they looked into the eyes of their oh-so-amiable new guest and felt a chill they could not explain.

Today Feste had insisted they all tour the gardens together, and though the gods knew Adora had more pressing matters to attend to, she had allowed herself to be dragged along for the hour anyway. Lirien was mild and polite, if occasion-ally a little arch; Hephestion was cheerful and energetic, urging her on to see this or that specimen. Rhia seemed at odds with herself; it was her nature to be happy, especially when those around her were happy, too, but since Lirien's arrival she had been tense and fidgety, biting off the ends of her sentences prematurely, reluctant to be drawn into any sort of merriment. And Jocelyn watched Lirien as closely as Adora did; this was now her primary rival for Hephestion's attention, after all.

"What do you think?" Feste asked. "We must have at least a few varieties here you've never seen before. You probably got more weeds than anything in the coun-try, no?"

Adora had thought that Rhia's eyes were green, but Lirien's seemed to take that color to its highest possible zenith, as if all other greens would forever be dimmer in comparison. Her emotions flashed so quickly through those eyes that they were often difficult to detect; though she smiled at Hephestion, her eyes had seemed irri-tated, just for a moment. "We did not properly have any gardens in my village, no. It rains very often there, so hardy flowers thrive in the wild, but any more fragile beauties will just wind up drowned. It made more sense to let nature decide, and show us whatever she thought best."

Hephestion opened his mouth to reply, but before he could, Lirien took several rapid strides past him, to where Rhia was about to pull a flower toward her so she could inhale its scent. Her long braid snapped out behind her as she moved, and it drew Feste's eye like an iridescent snake. "Not like that, my lady," she said, brushing Rhia's palm aside with the back of her hand. "If you touch a blue star's petals even slightly, it'll shut itself right up, and leave nothing for the bees. Take hold of it lower down on the stem, but don't pinch." She demonstrated, coaxing the flower forward with only the gentlest guidance from her thumb and forefinger. "See?"

Rhia flushed down to her ears, as if Lirien had told her she'd just committed some grave insult. "Oh. Sorry, I don't . . . have much experience with flowers."

"You make a fair point about the bees," Jocelyn said, as if stifling a yawn. "I have been used to regard flowers as meaningless decoration, but I suppose there are creatures that depend even on them."

Lirien made no response; she rarely did, when Jocelyn spoke, though she conversed with the rest of them freely. Yet Adora sensed that this, at least, was not meanness or provocation, merely uncertainty as to how to proceed.

She knew that to most Hallerns, a "noble" was a creature as mythical and archaic as a dragon, a monstrous, avaricious beast possessed of unimaginable power. It was understandable: nobles had ruined Hallarnon long before it ever became known by that name. Valyanrend, the capital of the Elesthenian Empire, had been crammed to bursting with aristocrats of all stripes—many had castles of their own somewhere, but left them to their captains or stewards or knights, choosing instead to take a manor house in the city they believed to be the center of the world. And within the walls of that city, a noble could get away with almost anything. As for the seven nobles who made up the Council, they could get away with literally anything, since they alone determined Elesthene's laws. They had squeezed the common people until rebellion was all but inevitable, and after that rebellion was over, the residents of the newly formed country of Hallarnon were left with the entirely understandable desire to never behold a noble ever again. Unfortunately, though they succeeded in keeping the aristocracy from growing back, tyranny in Hallarnon flourished all the same, no matter what those tyrants called themselves.

But the other countries formed from the ashes of Elesthene had their own ways of doing things, and in Issamira and Lanvaldis the aristocracy remained, although almost none of the old aristocratic families did. In Esthrades, the sixth Daven Margraine had stripped the titles from every noble family in the country save his own, and in Reglay the former imperial general Kelken Rayl had crowned himself a king without seeing any need for additional lords. Lirien seemed well traveled in every country on the continent, but it was highly likely she'd never spoken to a noble at all before this.

And then, also, Jocelyn was Jocelyn. Adora could hardly blame anyone for not knowing what to say to her, noble or not.

"For a while, it was popular for ladies in Eldren Cael to wear flowers in their hair at balls, sometimes in quite elaborate arrangements," Feste was saying. "I thought it was lovely, but it seems to have fallen out of favor recently."

"I must confess I'm glad to hear it, my lord," Lirien said. "It sounds to me like a waste of healthy flowers." She smiled as innocently as you please, but there was that darker gleam in her too-green eyes again. She turned to Rhia. "And you, my lady? I suppose you must have attended many balls by now. Did you dance with flowers in your hair like all the rest?"

"No," Rhia snapped—a shocking loss of temper coming from her. But she caught herself immediately. "I mean—forgive me. I attend balls only when Her Grace or my lord require my presence to help ensure their safety. And I don't know how to dance. So . . . no."

"I did offer to teach her," Feste said, "but it wasn't an idea she took kindly to, I'm afraid."

"Should you like me to wear a gown as well?" Rhia said stiffly. "How would I run in it if you were attacked?"

"Military officers of whatever gender have been accustomed to attend balls in uniform, for precisely that reason," Feste said, smiling, "but have it your way, I suppose." To Lirien, he said, "I hope *you* don't hate balls, at least? Your presence would certainly much improve one."

"I love to dance, and I love music, and I find large gatherings invigorating," she said. "But I don't know that I've ever been to what *you* would call a ball, my lord. I have neither the gown nor the uniform for it."

Feste saw the obvious opportunity and pounced on it. "If that's all you're worried about, I would be more than happy to assist you in acquiring a gown that would suit you."

Lirien winced. "My lord, 'tis—er, it's generous, to be sure, and out of all proportion to my station, but I can't possibly accept such a—"

"Of course you can," Feste said. "I can well afford to bestow it—and I offer it without any obligation on your part, of course."

She shook her head. "It isn't that, my lord. I merely fear that I shan't be able to manage such a heavy and impractical thing on the road. That which I wear now perhaps seems shabby to your eyes, but it is sturdier than it looks, and has seen me through many a day of rough traveling. But I could not wear such finery as you mean through mud or brambles or across streams, so I should be forced to carry it along with all my other possessions. And I fear it should be heavier than all the rest put together. So as much as it pains me to say so, accepting such a thing is quite out of the question."

Adora rolled her eyes. *Ill-struck, brother.* Feste knew it, too, and for several moments he was rendered speechless—no common occurrence, to be sure.

Lirien Arvel smiled that smile of hers, impeccably beautiful but with that hint of something discordant in it. "I understand that you meant it as a kindness, my lord. That is why I attempted to thank you in the same way, and to avoid any rudeness. But when your kindness becomes burdensome for others to accept, were it not truly kinder to abstain from it?"

Jocelyn laughed as if the whole thing had been staged for her particular amusement. "Even if you were not so attached to wading through mud, Miss Arvel, you would perhaps find our fashions too heavy for you in this heat. You seem to be suffering enough even in that threadbare thing you love so much."

"Suffering?" Lirien asked. "I hardly feel the heat at all."

"Your face tells a different story," Jocelyn said. "You appear to be sweating quite severely."

Lirien's hand snapped up to her forehead as if Jocelyn had told her there was something foul there. Indeed, when she wiped her brow, her fingers came away wet; Adora could see, now that she was looking for it, that strands of hair had escaped Lirien's braid and were plastered to her forehead. She looked at her hand, and then at Jocelyn, as if there had been some threat concealed in Jocelyn's words. "Ah. It seems . . . I didn't realize . . ."

"If she's not feeling well," Adora said, loath to miss a perfect opportunity, "let us disperse for today. Rhia and I, at least, have duties of our own. Let your guest rest herself for at least the afternoon, Feste. Jocelyn, with me, if you please."

She had expected Jocelyn to be irritated, but she hardly waited for the others to pass out of earshot before saying, "I wanted to speak to you myself, Your Grace. Can it be you share my concerns about that woman?"

"I am certainly concerned," Adora said, "that you should have no ill intentions toward a guest of my family's, as you are one yourself. My mother may have called you here, but I am the one who allows you to stay."

"Oh?" Jocelyn said. "I thought only the queen could ask me to leave. Though we give you some nice titles in conversation out of courtesy, without a coronation you are still a princess, are you not?"

"If I need to be," Adora said, "you will find me queen enough for your purposes."

"Indeed? I find that unwise." She shrugged. "It seems to me that one should be very clear, at all times, as to whether one is a queen or not. Being a queen only sometimes is not possible in this world, even for one as exalted as yourself."

THE PRINCE MUST have hoped he would be able to be alone with Lirien after their return from the gardens, but after his sister left, his mother stepped in. She insisted that he had been neglectful of Lady Jocelyn, and demanded he accompany her for the rest of the afternoon to make up for it. She also insisted that Rhia escort Lirien back to the chambers Hephestion had given her—no doubt to get rid of both people she disliked at a single stroke.

At first Lirien had merely kept wiping her brow, but when Rhia had asked if she was all right, she had brushed the question aside impatiently. After that, Rhia had thought it best not to say anything, but Lirien broke the silence. "I fear I made you some slight earlier, my lady, which I regret. It was not my intention."

It made Rhia so sad to hear this frozen politeness from her. "It's *Captain*," she said, "or Rhia, or nothing. I am *not* a lady, nor ever will be. It's like you said before—if you're trying to be polite, that's not how it feels to me."

Lirien bowed her head. "A deserved admonishment. I apologize. I do wonder, though . . . I have known those who hated nobles, and I wouldn't have blamed them, but I don't get that feeling from you. Yet you hate the thought of *being* noble, if I don't miss my guess. It's curious. It seems we are opposites in that regard."

"Because . . . you *do* want to be a noble?" Rhia asked. "Really?"

Lirien laughed. "No, of course not. I meant that I dislike being thought of as common and poor, while you dislike the opposite. Is it truly so distasteful to be thought rich and finely blooded?"

"I've never been either of those things," Rhia said, "so to me it is, yes."

"Yet you don't give your name," Lirien said.

Her surname, Rhia knew she meant. "I don't. I . . . can't. I don't truly have a right to it, not under the law."

"Ah," Lirien said, with barely a delay. "So that's the reason. Not a lord, but a lord's bastard."

Those words hurt to hear, but she couldn't help but be impressed that Lirien had guessed so quickly. "You're nearly right, but wrong about two things. A lady's bastard, not a lord's. And the name I wish I could take isn't hers."

Lirien still looked curious, but thankfully did not question her further. "I do still think it is a pity you never learned to dance."

"I don't." Rhia laughed. "I've never wanted to. The day my father asked me if I wished to learn, my brother laughed so hard he—" She stopped. This happened sometimes: a memory of him would slip into her head so easily that for a moment it was as if he were alive again. And then she would remember, and feel that pain as if it were new.

"Your brother?" Lirien asked.

Rhia shook her head firmly. "He died. Forgive me. I did not mean to speak of him."

"I should not have spoken of him, either," Lirien said. "I didn't know."

But thinking about Cadfael's death made her think of her own miraculous survival, and how it might have been possible. Lirien had traveled even more widely than she had, she thought. Lirien might know.

Before she could think better of it, she stammered, "Can I ask you something else?"

Lirien smiled at her with that trace of mischief, and for a moment it was like when they had first met. "You can certainly try."

Rhia took a deep breath. "Do you think . . . that magic exists? Now, in the present, I mean. Do you think it could be possible?"

Lirien gave a surprised laugh. "Is that all? Of course magic exists, my l—sorry. Captain."

Rhia was so surprised herself that she would have forgiven the title. "But . . . just like that? How can you be sure?"

"Because I've seen it for myself. Many a time, by now." She shrugged. "I wouldn't say so to just anyone, and especially not to your royals. It's just the thing someone like them would think someone like me was wrong about, because common means simple, and simple means gullible. But I promise you, there can be no mistake. It's real."

"So what have you seen?"

"You won't repeat any of this to them?"

"You have my word," Rhia said.

Lirien leaned in close, lowering her voice. "I've seen a woman fly—not very high, I admit, but unmistakably, and in an open field, where there could be no ropes or wires about. I met a man who could look into the flames of an ordinary hearth fire and see what was happening leagues away, and a boy shorter than you who could move any stone. There was even one small village where a healer brought a young man back from the brink of death, though the villagers didn't thank her for it. And a score of other things, too, but I think you get the point."

"What about . . ." She swallowed the lump that had risen in her throat. "Have you ever seen a wound that wouldn't heal? That made itself anew, over and over again?"

Lirien looked as solemn as she had ever seen her. "Aye. 'Twas . . . damn it. *It* was a horrible thing to behold, but I did see it, once. How is it *you* came to see it?"

"My brother," Rhia said, throat dry. "That's . . . how he died."

Lirien started, as if she were seeing Rhia in a new light. "Ah. Then I would imagine that the thought of magic in the world brings you no joy."

"Why?" Rhia asked. "If he'd been killed by a sword, would I hate all swords, or all people who carry them?"

"But did you not ask me such a thing because you wanted to find out who killed your brother?"

Rhia shook her head. "My brother said, when they fought . . . that he was the one in the wrong. And even if he hadn't been, killing her wouldn't bring him back to life again. I just wanted to understand what happened to him." *And what happened to me,* she thought, but felt suddenly shy about revealing that much. If Lirien heard that story, she'd no doubt think Rhia made a terrible captain of the guard. "I wonder why more people don't know about it, if there really are that many people with magic out there."

"I think you're underestimating my penchant for travel, Captain," Lirien said. "As a fraction of people I met on my journeys in total, those who could use magic made up a very small number indeed. As for why they stay hidden . . . I have never met a person whose magic brought them happiness. That, it seems, is even rarer than a woman who can fly."

CHAPTER NINETEEN

Mist's Edge

IF VARALEN HAD thought it unsettling to be housed within Mist's Edge, it was hardly any better to be camped outside its walls, watching that mass of gloomy gray stone fade in and out of the fog night after night. Even on days when it didn't rain, the mist hung a layer of dampness over everything, a chill that no clothing or blankets could fully keep out. Elgar alone seemed unbothered, but for all Varalen knew, magic could prevent you from feeling the cold, too.

It had been a long time since he'd been in a proper military encampment, and he'd never actually been at a proper siege. Before Elgar had "recruited" him, he'd been serving one of King Eira's commanders in the east—a position he'd fallen into quite accidentally. He had learned much on those campaigns, but you could bet your last copper Caius Margraine would never be found on the defensive end of a siege. He'd read countless books about them, but books couldn't fully take the place of experience.

For the moment, they were camping out of the range of the archers on Mist's Edge's walls, waiting for Elgar's men to finish the ladders they were assembling. Elgar had instructed them not to bother with building more dramatic siege equipment—a ram in particular wouldn't be worth the time it would take to build. Mist's Edge's front entrance was one of its most impressive aspects, a thick metal sheet of a door with a portcullis behind. It'd be a hell of a ram that could shatter *that,* but they didn't need one. Or they shouldn't, if the information they'd gathered was correct.

"If it were me," he said to Elgar, as they ate bread and cold salt pork in his tent,

"I would've pulled more men in there before my enemies had a chance to surround me. And he *did* have the time for that."

Between them lay their first communication from Kelken, a letter they had received this morning. When they had first arrived, the inhabitants of Mist's Edge had refused to have anything to do with them, and would not open the gate even for a banner of peace. (Not that Varalen blamed them for that, knowing Elgar as he did.) But finally, after several days, the Reglians had agreed to lift the metal door for as long as it took to pass a message through the portcullis. *Further negotiation is pointless,* Kelken wrote. *You have made your desires clear; the only thing that has changed since we last spoke is that I have made up my mind as well. I will not surrender. I will hold out here to the last. If Reglay is to become yours, I and this castle must fall first.*

It was certainly a firmer tone from the boy, Varalen supposed. But it would have been a more impressive holding-out to the last if he'd brought more men to it.

"He had time to bring the men," Elgar said, "but not the supplies. He wants to keep us out here as long as possible, and he can't do that if his men are eating each other in a fortnight."

"Are we waiting a fortnight?" Varalen asked.

"I don't know yet," Elgar said. "I'm certain that, with a mind like yours, you have already seen the problem."

The problem, in brief, was that Elgar was fighting too many wars. The people of Hallarnon had been enthusiastic about the Aurnian war, and even more so about the Lanvaldian one, after they had seen how easily the former was won. But the Lanvaldian war had required more men and dragged on for longer than anticipated, and the two wars together had resulted in a significant number of Hallern casualties. Elgar could certainly impress people into his army, from Hallarnon as well as the territories he had conquered, but those soldiers would hardly be as reliable as those who had joined up willingly. Given all that, it was in their best interests not to wager the lives of their soldiers too readily. Elgar's forces still greatly outnumbered Reglay's, and in an ordinary situation they could simply send the men over the walls when the ladders were finished and bury the Reglians under the weight of superior numbers. But could they afford those casualties here when they still had Esthrades and eventually Issamira to work their way through?

Elgar started writing his reply to Kelken, bracing the parchment awkwardly against the bunch of crates they were using as a table. "I'm going to tell him that for as long as he stays in there, I'll take it that he *has* surrendered—he's surrendered his people to me. Let's see how much he still cares about them."

"It's true," Varalen said slowly; this was a distasteful possibility, but it was a war, after all. "Nowhere else in Reglay is as well guarded as Mist's Edge. You could pick off civilians as you like."

Elgar shook his head. "Not civilians. Massacres like that might move Kelken's heart, but they'll also make sure his people hate us, and remain the more loyal to him for it. Instead we'll send groups to subdue other key locations in Reglay—Second Hearth, for example. If they attempt to fight, we'll fight, but with their soldiers only; if they surrender, we won't harm them. If we occupy enough of the country, we can almost forget about Mist's Edge, or give the appearance of it: we give them a government and laws, we start keeping the peace—all things Kelken can't do anymore, because he's stuck in there. At that point, we'll already have conquered the country in every way that matters—and where was their king while we were doing it? Instead of some hero making a principled last stand, it becomes easier to see him as a scared little boy. And who wants a scared little boy for their king?" He finished the parchment, rolled it up, and poked his head out of the tent to call a messenger to pass it through the gate.

Varalen was impressed, though he didn't want to admit it. "That . . . does sound best. We just have to make sure to keep enough men camped out here that they can't find some way to make contact with the rest of Reglay."

"Of course. They don't have birds in there, do they?"

"The message-carrying kind? I doubt it. A few pigeons at best—there's not a parchment hawk in all of Reglay, I'd bet on it. Those birds are so scarce now they're practically extinct."

"I've heard Maribel Avestri's brother personally keeps half a dozen of them," Elgar said, raising an eyebrow.

"Perhaps he has three, Your Eminence—that'd be a tenth of the Lantian population right there. And he only has that many because he was willing to spend more time and coin on it than anyone else on the continent. The point is that Kelken doesn't have any, and even the queen's brother hasn't trained one to fly to Mist's Edge."

Elgar looked out of the tent flap and through the trees, squinting at the fortress in the distance. "You've already said that if you were Kelken you'd do all manner of things differently. But that doesn't help us with this particular problem. If you were Kelken, and you were doing things just this way . . . what reason could you possibly have for it?"

"As to that," Varalen said, "I do have a theory. But I want to wait and see how he responds to your missive first."

They didn't have long to wait; Varalen was half surprised the ink wasn't still wet when the reply was placed before them. *I expected such a response*, it said. *What I do now, I do for my people, whether or not they will ever understand, or ever forgive me. I know this in my heart, and I am resolved. You will not move me, no matter what atrocity you commit.*

"*I am resolved*," Elgar repeated. "I don't believe he's bluffing."

"No," Varalen agreed. "He could hardly have made his tone clearer."

Elgar laid the letter on the table. "So does this strengthen or weaken your theory?"

"The former," Varalen said. "You and I both met the boy. He is possibly the least prideful monarch I have ever beheld. He can't truly believe that what is best for his people is for him to preserve his own life as long as possible, whatever the cost to them. So if he is determined to stay in that castle no matter what, it has nothing to do with protecting his own life. There must be some other reason. And we're the only other reason I can think of. This army itself, I mean."

He waited for objections, but Elgar merely said, "Go on."

"As long as he stays here," Varalen said, "we have to keep an army watching over him—to prevent him from escaping, or from communicating with the outside world. His true goal is to keep this army in this spot as long as possible. And perhaps you as well, though he could not know for sure you'd put yourself in charge of the siege. I'd guess Kelken is waiting for something to happen, and is trying to keep us here in order to buy more time for that event, whatever it is. Assistance from Lady Margraine, perhaps? You said she was . . . like you. Could she do something or give him something that would enable him to defeat us?"

"To defeat us outright? To win the entire war?" Elgar shook his head. "She could devise all manner of hypothetical weapons he might use, but even the brightest mages of old struggled to defeat entire armies at a blow, and she and I are nowhere near that level."

"Then I can't say what it could be," Varalen said. "But I do believe he is waiting for something."

"So your advice would be to conclude the siege as soon as possible?"

"I'm not sure," Varalen admitted. "That's the other thing. The tone of these letters is . . . defiant. In a way, it's like he's daring you to attack him. If I'm wrong, and what he really wants is to tempt you to precipitate action . . . I suppose I'd recommend taking the middle road. Let's not wait forever, but let's gather more information before we rush over those walls."

Elgar nodded. "A sound plan. I shall make but one amendment—I won't be waiting here at all. If what he wants is either to keep me waiting here or bait me into going in there to get him, it's best for me to do neither. Instead, I will personally oversee what I told you we should do before—the taking of Second Hearth and other strategic locations in Reglay. I will leave the command here to you. Ideally, you will wait to give the order to commence an assault until such time as we have agreed, together, that it is the correct decision. But should you detect some emergency and decide that you cannot wait to get word from me, you have my permission to charge the castle."

Varalen had never in his life been given command of an army this size, but he had to admit that what Elgar was saying made sense. If Kelken really did have some great plan in motion, the best thing for Elgar to do would be to move around—the king could not update or refine any orders he might have given to his men outside, and the less Elgar remained in one place, the more difficult it would be for them to execute some prepared gambit.

He took a deep breath, and reminded himself of the person he was doing all of this for. "As you command, Your Eminence."

CHAPTER TWENTY

Stonespire

"AND HERE YOU are," Talis said. "I'm not sure that I particularly needed to be here, given how little trouble you actually ended up finding, but none of you can say I didn't do as much as I promised."

"I think we needed you," Hywel said quietly. "You took care of those soldiers halfway down all by yourself."

Talis rolled her eyes. "There were two of them. You couldn't have handled *two* without me?" But then she considered the combined assets of their little group: Laen was an entirely average swordsman, Ilyn seemed talented but was still nursing those bandaged fingers, and Hywel himself didn't look like he could cut through a sheet of parchment. They had needed her, hadn't they?

"I'm relieved," Ilyn said grudgingly—she and Talis had more or less made their peace on the road. "Those men would've reported to Ghilan, and the farther *he* is from us, the better."

Talis didn't know who this Ghilan was, and she didn't care. No matter how strong a warrior might be, she could cut him down from thirty yards away. From that distance, they all looked the same. "So you're going, right? Then go."

Laen immediately balked. "You said you'd take us to Stonespire."

Talis spread her arms out to either side. "And here we are."

"To the *hall,* I meant."

"It's on a bloody hill. We can see it from here."

"Knowing how to get there was never the problem," Ilyn said. "If Ghilan's still skulking about in Esthrades, he could've laid a trap for us somewhere in this city. We're so close, anyway. It won't be an extra hour of your time."

"He's really that clever?" Talis asked.

"*He* isn't," Laen said. "But Administrator Selwyn is, and she's the one he serves." Even Talis could hardly fail to know about Edith Selwyn. After the fall of

Lanvaldis, Elgar had spent some time in Araveil, waiting to make sure no further threats arose and personally announcing the new laws Lanvalds would be expected to follow as citizens of his empire in the making. But he couldn't stay in Lanvaldis forever, and when he left he appointed Edith Selwyn to take charge in his stead—a fairly wealthy woman, and even better educated, but still common-born. Talis was sure the nobles were seething—they were just doing it behind closed doors these days, she supposed. Administrator Selwyn did not have a reputation for leniency.

"All right," she said. "You have a point—it's hardly farther than I've gone already. I'll deposit you right in Arianrod Margraine's lap, if I have to."

"THIS DOESN'T ACTUALLY look like a plan to me," Cadfael said. "I'm sure it's logical to ask at taverns, but it took us the better part of the morning to do half a dozen, which only leaves . . . what, a hundred left? More? And what if they're moving around? What if they aren't even here?"

"Yes," Lucius said. "I know."

"So what are you going to do? You have to have a better idea than this."

He sighed. "Perhaps . . . perhaps, after all, it would be better to ask Seren directly."

"What for? If your friend's already found a way to get to her, we're probably too late, and if he hasn't, she won't know any more than we do."

"That's not necessarily true," Lucius said. "She knows this city much better than we do, and even if she doesn't already know Deinol and Seth are here, she might know a better way to go about finding them, or have resources she can use to that end—especially if she's as close to the marquise as you say."

"But why would she help you?" Cadfael asked.

Lucius smiled. "Because I want the same thing she does—to keep Deinol as far away from her as possible. She didn't strike me as an especially bloodthirsty person; if I explain that I'm looking for the two of them in order to keep them from bothering her, I think she'll accept that."

It was strange to describe someone with Seren Almasy's set of skills as not especially bloodthirsty, but Cadfael found he agreed. "Well, I don't mind coming with you to the hall. Perhaps Seren will speak to me, even if she won't to you."

Lucius laughed. "Did the two of you get along that well?"

"We never tried to kill each other, so I suppose she's at least fonder of me than of your friend. Come on. Once the day's judgments are over, the hall will close up for the night. Let's get there before then, if we're going at all."

Lucius nodded, and they fell into step. You didn't need to have been to Stonespire before to find the hall, as it towered over every other building and was visible from most places in the city. But Cadfael toyed with the specific route they took, turning here and there, trying to remember which streets formed the straightest line to the castle.

He looked up, just at the right moment.

There was a stubby, narrow cross street that connected two wider lanes, and he happened to glance down it for the scant few moments in which she was framed by its walls, walking ahead of a small crowd down the opposite way. There was just an instant of blankness, before his mind put all the different impressions of her together: messy, brown-blond hair; a face of sharp angles; short legs and thin shoulders and those colorless eyes. He thought she would just keep walking, but then she suddenly stopped, brushing a mass of curls out of her face. And perhaps that movement revealed something in her peripheral vision, for she turned her head sharply to the side—and wound up looking directly into his face.

They stared, for a moment—Cadfael couldn't move, and she did not. And then she dropped her hand, turned on her heel, and dashed off down the street.

"WAIT!" TALIS HEARD him shout from somewhere behind her. She had started running on instinct, before she'd had time to think about it. But now that she *did* have time to think about it, she hardly felt inclined to stop. She had no wish to talk to a man who still seemed determined to bother her despite the fact that she must at least have *nearly* killed him. She couldn't repeat that performance now, though, not in the open street. She had no scruples against attacking anyone who seemed dangerous, but she didn't want to make herself notorious, and there were too many potential witnesses about.

He didn't call out again, but every glance she risked over her shoulder showed him following behind. She couldn't tell whether he was gaining on her.

If he did catch up with her, what could he do? Even if he still bore the same sword from their last meeting, or another like it, she could put enough distance between them that he wouldn't be able to use it, or else cause a disturbance that couldn't easily be traced back to her. It wasn't any sense of danger to herself that made her reluctant to face him. As loath as she was to admit it, this flight had its origins in the fact that he lived at all, and the part she had played in that outcome.

Well, then.

She waited until they had turned into a deserted side street, to minimize those who might overhear. Then she suddenly whirled to face him, and achieved her objective when he drew back in surprise, confusion settling over his features. For pure physical reality, those features were largely as Talis had remembered them: that perfect nose, those deceptively blue eyes. But the scar somehow changed them, as if it had warped the skin around it, or as if it somehow caused light and shadow to strike his features differently. The result was a face that looked thinner, hollower, more severe. She had not really succeeded in making him less handsome, but he at least looked less approachable, and she supposed that was something.

"Why the hell won't you stop bothering me?" she asked.

He was panting, and he rested his hands on his knees. He did bear the same sword as he had that day, but he had not drawn it. "I have to . . . ask you something."

"Why?"

"Because I . . . because it's important."

Asking him why again would get them nowhere, so Talis chose a different word. "What?"

At least he took her meaning, and simply asked his question. "That day. When you cut me like this. Did you mean to kill me?"

Of course he would pick the question Talis least wanted to answer. "What if I said yes?"

"Then why am I still alive?" he burst out—angrily, it seemed to her. "What's stopping you from trying it again, and seeing it through this time? We both know I'm no match for you. If I annoy you, it's no trouble at all for you to be rid of me."

When she said nothing, his eyes narrowed. "That was it, wasn't it? The true nature of your curse?"

"I can honestly say I have no idea what you're talking about."

He drew an impatient finger down his scar. "This wound. The curse you laid on me. It opened itself, over and over again. No matter what I did, no matter how I fought for my life, it bled me dry, little by little. But as soon as I stopped fighting—as soon as I no longer cared what happened to me—that was when it healed. It stopped tearing itself open, and the stitches finally held, and now the scar looks like it could have come from any ordinary blade. Was that by your design? That it should kill me only as long as I didn't want to die?"

She could simply say yes, and let him think her that capable and that merciless, but she found she didn't want to. Telling him the whole truth would be troublesome, but she could at least tell him part of the truth. She wanted him to know what she had and hadn't done.

"It's not a curse," she said. "I don't even know what a curse properly is. I can make cuts out of the air, just by thinking about it, and I can make it so they don't heal, like what happened to you. That's what I did—and I'm not sorry for it, given what you were trying to do to me at the time. But a wound that heals or doesn't heal depending on how you're feeling? I don't know how to do anything like that. If it ended up healing, that had nothing to do with me."

He slumped a little, as if disappointed, though Talis couldn't imagine why. Was it that he had wanted to think of her as that much of a monster—as some kind of architect of his suffering? The thought made her almost as angry as she had been that day. "Look," she said, "I never asked you to come after me. I gave you a chance to leave. And when you made that impossible, I didn't do any more than I had to in order to be rid of you. So if you want to think that I devised a special curse *just for you,* go ahead, but I'd never—"

"No," he said. "Whatever you might have decided to do to me back then— even if you had cursed me as I thought—I could make no argument against it. I deserved no mercy from you."

"Wonderful," Talis said. "Glad to hear we agree on that point, at least. Surely, if you deserve none of my mercy, you also deserve none of my time, so you can't possibly object to leaving me in peace."

"How am I disturbing your peace?" he asked, as if he really didn't understand.

"You chased me down in the street!"

He at least had the good grace to look embarrassed, and Talis could honestly say it was her favorite expression of his thus far. She had hated that empty look he'd worn back then, as if he didn't even acknowledge her existence, but the despair had been almost worse. She'd never seen him smile, but it probably would have irritated her, because he probably would have looked handsome doing it and she'd be reminded, again, that any gods who existed in this world had no concept of fairness. But for one with his features to stand there awkwardly, half guilty and half mortified . . . she could almost tolerate him like this. Almost.

"Well," he said, after several moments of silence. "I understand, now, how that must have looked, especially given our . . . history. But I never meant you any harm— I'm sure I could never have caused you any harm, even if I had meant it. I just wanted to know what really happened to me. If you didn't intend for your . . . spell?—if it didn't break or wear off because you designed it that way, why did it?"

"It's not as if I know all the reasons why something like that might happen." That wasn't precisely a lie. She didn't feel guilty about it, either; when he had thought he could overpower her easily, he had hardly been inclined to show her any mercy. Now he seemed to believe there was nothing at all he could do to hurt her, and she had absolutely no intention of correcting him. "But I assure you it's quite gone. If there were any traces of the spell left, I'd be able to sense it."

Why did he still look so disappointed? But no, it was more than that—it was more than the scar on his face that had changed him, more than the passing of a handful of years. There was this absence of any kind of relief that he had been spared, as if what he'd really wanted was for her to either tell him the spell would still kill him eventually, or cast it again to make sure of it. *Don't ask,* she told herself. *Don't give him the satisfaction of your curiosity.* But the look on his face was so chillingly familiar—not from that day in the frozen meadow, but from a day long before she had ever met him, a day when she had stood alone and looked down at the world. And there was a small, aching part of her, made not of curiosity but of selfishness, that wanted, needed, to know what could make a person look like that.

"You weren't like this last time," she said. "You had fire in you. You tried to fight at first, even when you had no chance. What changed?"

"Back then," he said hoarsely, "I needed to do all I could to survive. There was someone I wanted to protect." He winced, trying to draw the next words out, and finally hung his head. "She died."

Talis clenched her fist, refusing to reach for the pendant around her neck. She hadn't been close to the boy who'd made it for her, not truly. It was that obnoxious woman he got along with best, but even he and Voltest had talked easily together. Yet all three of them had felt that the boy was their responsibility, that it was their job to protect him. Perhaps they had known, even then, that however much power he might come to possess, he would never truly be able to protect himself.

"Once there was someone I thought I ought to protect," she said. "Someone who was bad at protecting himself, but who I still thought . . . belonged in the world."

He smiled, for the first time. But it was poisoned with sadness, and though it didn't irritate her, Talis found she didn't like it at all. "Yes. Something like that. Although with me it was even more selfish. She belonged in the world, in the wider world, but I still would have kept her from it, to keep her safe. And to keep her with me. Because I never felt I belonged anywhere, but she seemed to think I belonged where she was."

"What happened to her?" Talis asked, trying and failing to imagine the kind of person a man like him would care about so much.

He scowled—not as satisfying as the embarrassment, but hardly as irritating as the emptiness. "Elgar happened to her. Or . . . Elgar's men, rather."

Talis's stomach twisted, but at the same time she wanted to laugh. "They must have a talent for it. That's what happened to the boy I used to know, too."

CHAPTER TWENTY-ONE

Stonespire

GRAVIS HAD KNOWN Arianrod Margraine all her life, and flattered himself that it took a great deal, from her, to surprise him anymore. He had long known her to be unpredictable, to be capricious, to be remote, and to be utterly disinclined to explain herself a whit more than was necessary. Yet when faced with her newest request, even he was stunned.

Lady Margraine had asked for three things. First: rocks. But not just *any* rocks, oh no. "Take care with the size and shape," she had said, as if there were nothing odd about the request. "Big enough to fit in one hand just right—a nice heft to them, but not a strain to lift. Not *so* round that they go rolling about uncontrollably, but maybe round*ish,* so they'd have a good arc if you threw them. And none that look as if they're about to split or that have any little fragments that might fall off."

"And . . . how many of these do you require?" Gravis had asked, trying to keep a neutral expression.

She shrugged. "You can bring as many as you like. I don't really know how many I'll have the time or the energy to use. Perhaps . . . as many as three or four people would be able to comfortably carry with them, if they also had to carry supplies?"

Second: rags. "I'd prefer not to have to cut up anything actually useful or valuable in this enterprise," the marquise had said, "but it is absolutely essential that I receive cloths without any holes in them, or that look as if they might easily tear. They must be at least large enough to securely wrap a human fist without any danger of even a single bit of exposed skin, but if they're much larger it's all right, as we can just trim them."

The third thing, mercifully, wasn't strange in itself: merely a few sacks. To hold the rocks and rags, Gravis could only assume. "And what will be the result of all this?" he had asked.

She hadn't even looked up. "Gravis, what on earth makes you think that's any of your business?"

She'd wanted the whole lot left in her study, and as soon as the day's judgments were concluded, she had retreated there alone, barely opening the door to take dinner. No one had heard any noise from within the room, but though the specifics were beyond him, Gravis was certain she was using the objects in some sort of spell.

As far as he knew, only he and Almasy knew about Lady Margraine's abilities. After what she had done the day that unknowing assassin arrived, there must be those who suspected something—Zara chief among them, he'd bet—but no one else had any definite proof. To the rest of the hall, her actions must have seemed eccentric, but not only did Lady Margraine herself have a history of eccentric actions that later proved beneficial, the entire Margraine line had built a reputation on it. He doubted anyone but him even thought to wonder about the items.

He was saved an evening of stewing over it, because Benwick came hurrying to fetch him before he could retire to his quarters. "Captain Ingret, sir, a moment. We've got strangers at the gate."

"It's past time for guests or petitioners," Gravis said. "They must know that."

"They do, sir, but they claim to've come late on purpose, to avoid the crowds. They claim their arrival is a matter of great secrecy, but that her ladyship is expecting them. They say she can confirm this herself, but they're willing to show proof to anyone with sufficient authority."

"And an ordinary guardsman isn't authority enough for them?" Gravis asked. "Haughty visitors, these. But I'll speak with them."

There were three of them, barely out of childhood; they looked like Lanvalds. The one with the long braid probably looked younger than he actually was, but the other two had short hair, as if they wanted to look older. They all wore swords, but from the way they carried themselves, he guessed the girl best knew how to use hers.

"I am Gravis Ingret, captain of the guard in this city," he said, hoping that would satisfy their need for authority.

"We're supposed to meet with Her Grace, sir," the boy with the braid said. If he called her *Her Grace*, he was definitely a foreigner. "My brother carries a letter from her, written in her own hand. She wished us to come here, and has promised us her aid."

That seemed . . . generous of her. "Who are you, that she would extend you such an offer?"

"We'd prefer not to say that out here, sir."

Gravis exchanged a look with Benwick. "Well, give me this letter."

It was undoubtedly in her hand. "'*If* you should come to Stonespire . . . such aid in your troubles as I can provide . . . I will demand in exchange that you surrender the tomes to me permanently.'" That certainly sounded a lot more like her. "Where are these tomes, then?"

The older boy shifted the pack he carried. "We've brought everything she asked for."

Gravis folded the letter, and let his hand drop to his side. "Benwick, you stay here. I'll ask her ladyship, but I suspect all is as they say."

Indeed it was, and their guests were finally invited in. Lady Margraine met them in the great hall, though she was visibly tired—so she *had* been casting spells. "I'm glad to see you made it in one piece," she said to the older boy. "We had quite the uncharming visit from your administrator's lackey; you barely missed him. I was able to tell him quite truthfully that you weren't here, though I doubt he believed me." She yawned. "Gravis, I suppose I can trust you to get them settled in the appropriate chambers? You may consider them deserving of the highest courtesy." To the group, she added, "Let us dine together tomorrow, and discuss our current situation. In the meantime, ask Gravis for whatever you require. Oh, and leave the books with him, too; he can put them in the library."

It was hardly a miserly offering, but it seemed to leave the elder young man dissatisfied. "I would prefer to meet with you immediately," he said, chin high, with what he no doubt hoped was a steely expression. "Regarding the aid you promised me. You never provided specifics, and I wish to make sure of them as soon as possible."

The girl seemed loyally oblivious, but the boy with the braid knew his brother had misstepped, if his wince was any indication. Lady Margraine saw it, too, and turned to him. "Hywel, was it?"

The boy bowed; Gravis thought his shoulders shook slightly. "That's right, Your Grace."

"Perhaps, by the time we meet tomorrow, you will have instructed your brother more fully as to the position he occupies, and the appropriate behaviors pertaining to it." She swept past them without another word. The elder brother made as if to follow her, but Hywel caught his sleeve, beseeching him with a wounded look that even Gravis would've found hard to resist. The boy pulled his arm free, but he stayed where he was.

Gravis led the youths to their rooms, staring straight ahead so the brothers had some semblance of privacy for their grumbling. "There's no benefit to brashness here, Laen," he heard Hywel say. "Do you think you impressed her? Do you think she's more inclined, now, to give you what you want?"

"No one on this earth's going to just *give* you what you want," Laen said.

"She's certainly given us more than nothing. Sheltering us here can't come without risk, and whatever aid she provides, it'll be something she might otherwise have used for herself. Showing gratitude doesn't make you look weak, it makes you look like you understand your situation. All you have now is your claim. That's not nothing, but it's not enough."

"It's *our* claim," Laen said, but that was hardly an argument.

Gravis took that opportunity to cut them off, because they had arrived at what passed for the guest wing—not very large, as for a castle Stonespire Hall could not boast immense size, but they had enough rooms to spare, at least. "I hope this will do for you at present. If I can bring you anything, please let me know at once."

"Dinner?" Laen asked hopefully, suddenly looking much younger. "We haven't had much to eat today."

Gravis held back a smile. "I shall see what the kitchens can do."

SEREN DIDN'T OFTEN leave Stonespire Hall so late at night, but Arianrod had sent her down to the city to fetch Bridger, who was more or less the most significant of her guardsmen outside the hall itself. Supposedly, she had taken the place of Dent, who had been just as well-loved in the city but had been reassigned to the hall guard when Arianrod was young. Seren had no quarrel with Dent or Bridger—on the contrary, she supposed she owed them a certain amount of respect, given the former's efforts to protect Arianrod and the latter's to clean up the city. And Bridger had never seemed suspicious of her, the way some of the other guardsmen were.

She hadn't spent more than a decade with the Inxia Morain to *not* know when she was being followed, but she didn't immediately recognize the follower. She waited before confronting him, leaving the hall a good distance behind. But when she finally turned and strode up to the shadow in question, she wasn't at all prepared for who it belonged to.

"Seren," Lucius Aquila said calmly. "I see you remember me."

Seren didn't think he was going to assault her in the middle of the street, but she readied herself anyway.

"I mean you no harm," he said, palms up in front of him. "I didn't come here in anger, and I don't care about the stone you stole. If anything, you did me a favor by keeping it away from Elgar. I hope it *is* magic, and I hope your mistress incinerates his black heart with it. All I want is to find them, and bring them back alive. And though I've no desire to quarrel, I *will* say that, given how you used us on the road, merely telling me what you know is far less than I might have asked of you."

He was a professed bandit and thief, a fighter and murderer of no common skill, and yet Seren did not doubt for a moment that he spoke the truth. She had known from the beginning that, for whatever reason, he was someone who did not wish to kill if he could solve a problem by any other method. If there was anger in him, he had found a way to bury it far deeper than she'd ever imagined. Seren could almost be envious, if she wasn't certain he paid the price somewhere else, in a far less pleasant way.

"You mean Deinol and Seth," she said, heart sinking. How could she tell him that what he wanted was impossible now?

"So you *have* seen them." He paused, painfully tentative. "Did you and Deinol . . . fight? Did you . . . ?"

"I didn't harm them," she said. "Don't misunderstand me—I *would* have, had I needed to. But that . . . was ultimately unnecessary."

Lucius sighed in relief, and she wanted to urge him not to, to find some way to make him aware, beforehand, of the grief that was lying before him, obscure but close enough to touch. How was it that she should be the one to tell him, she who had never had to convey such sadness to anyone?

He must have seen something in her face, for he grew still again. "I sense you have not told me all you know."

"It shouldn't be me," Seren said, furious to find herself stammering. "You can't . . . you shouldn't . . . hear such a thing from me."

Lucius's face was calm in a way she had never been able to make her own: not the erasure of all emotion, but merely a measured amount of it, as if he could confine himself to feeling only as much as he wished. "I have received grave news before, Seren. I've had my world shattered. Whatever you have to say, though I may grieve, it will not break me."

Even so, she could not look at him as she spoke. "Whatever your friend originally wanted with me, it was ruined. We were both caught in the middle of . . . well, it was an attempt on my life, I suppose. And the boy . . . in a misguided wish . . . he wanted to help . . ." She shook her head. "He *did* help. But . . ."

She couldn't say any more, and raised her head, hoping Lucius had understood her meaning. His expression was still veiled, his lips pressed together. "And Deinol?" he asked.

"He was alive when I left him," she said. "But I don't know what became of him after that."

"Could you venture a guess?"

Seren hesitated. "If he lives at all, and he has not returned home, I believe he is here. He's not used to forests, to village life—I doubt he could survive in it. There's Lakeport, of course, but I don't know why he'd go there when Stonespire is so much closer. If you want a list of taverns and inns I'd check first, I can give you that much. But I won't help you look, so don't ask. He and I . . . it would be better for both of us if we did not meet again."

Lucius opened his mouth, but it was someone else's voice Seren heard: "Good evening, Miss Almasy," came the mild and deferential tones of Jill Bridger, her looming shape casting a large shadow over Seren and Lucius. "Are you perhaps being inconvenienced?"

Bridger was possibly the only person on earth who knew Seren reasonably well and yet could still imagine that someone inconveniencing her would keep breathing long enough to continue at it for any length of time. Perhaps Seren could have felt touched by it, if things were different. "It's all right, Bridger," she said. "I'm about to send him on his way. But it's good I ran into you—her ladyship actually sent me down to fetch you. There are matters pertaining to the security of the city that she wishes to discuss in person."

Bridger stood attentively straighter. "I shall report to her right away. Unless you require anything else?" She still looked curiously at Lucius.

"I don't," Seren said. "Thank you. Good night."

After Bridger had vanished down the street, she braced herself for Lucius to try to change her mind, but he did not. "I suppose you lied," he said instead—amiably, as if they were friends having a chat. "About many things, of course, but this especially."

Not many *things,* Seren thought, but she only said, "This?"

He waved a hand at the city all around them. "You said that you had no loyalty to Esthrades, yet you're in service to its *ruler.* You're a more loyal Esthradian than most of the people living here."

"I'm *not,*" she snarled, taking even him aback with the force of it. "I was *born* in this city. No one knows better than I do what misery lay hidden in the grimy and low places of this hellhole, and I would *never* devote myself to defending *that.*"

He recovered his composure damnably quickly. "Lay?" he repeated. "Not *lies*?" His sharpness was really getting annoying.

"I would never say people aren't still miserable here," she said. "But it is no longer the way it was when I was a child." She took a deep breath, looking away from him, and made a decision. "Do you know what a flesh-monger is?"

"I've never heard that term, no."

Seren paused, giving herself time to reconsider. But no, she still wanted to tell him. "They sell children. Well—not always children. But almost always."

Lucius shook his head. "You can't sell children."

She laughed against the ache in her chest. "Of course you can. You can sell anything people will buy. And I promise you, there are people who will buy children."

He was still shaking his head. "No person can ever be property. It's against every law in every country in the world."

"And yet such transactions take place in every country in the world—even in Valyanrend. Even in *Aurnis*. And certainly in this city, where I have seen them with my own eyes."

She'd lost control of her hands again, but she could hardly have expected otherwise. "Who can say how many flesh-mongers thrived in this city when I was young? Dozens, with hundreds of confederates willing to supply them with children, and who can say how many buyers? That's how it works, you understand—you buy impoverished or unwanted children, and then you sell them again, for much more, once you prove that they're obedient—once you've made sure of it. To particularly disreputable brothels, or else to more . . . private individuals."

She'd intended to shock him, of course, but Lucius looked even more upset than she had expected. "Here, perhaps," he croaked. "I've never been here, so I don't know . . . but not in Kaiferi. Nothing like that could ever have happened in Kaiferi. If anyone had known, we would never have . . . ." It was as if he considered it his own responsibility to stop such a thing, his personal failure if it had flourished without his knowing. She wondered if he had always been a thief; he really didn't seem cut out for it, did he?

His next words were so soft she could scarcely hear them. "Did you say all that because you . . . ?"

"No," Seren said. "It was . . . a near thing. But the sale never took place."

"But then . . . you said that it *used* to be like that. When you were young. Is it not any longer?"

"It would be overly optimistic to assume no child is ever mistreated in Stonespire," Seren said. "But the rotten system was torn out by the roots." She nodded up at the castle. "It was that woman who just passed us, Bridger—when Lady Margraine came to the throne, she chose a group of guardsmen to find and apprehend the flesh-mongers, and Bridger volunteered to lead it. She was more successful than

I could ever have believed. By the time I returned to this city, the operations I knew from my youth were razed to nothing. They have orphanages in those neighborhoods now. The throne pays for them."

"So you agreed to work for the marquise not because she rules Esthrades, but because of what she did to help children in your former position?"

"No, not . . . not exactly." That question again. People seemed so fascinated by that question. She knew Lucius's curiosity was neither cynical nor crude, but still . . . the truth was it had become difficult to think about, even in her own mind. It was so mixed up, so much more complicated than it had once seemed, and that wasn't something she wanted to share with anyone. But the reason why this had all started, all those years ago . . . that she could still remember clearly. That, in its way, was still true. "For a more personal reason. For a more personal favor. And because she is . . . someone I wanted to be like. Someone I . . . admired."

"Ah," Lucius said quietly. "That I understand."

"I don't think you do."

"I think you might be surprised." His mask dropped enough to let some deeper sadness glimmer in his eyes, but she knew it was hopeless to guess at where it came from. If he'd wanted to tell her, he already would have.

"I'll leave it be, then," Seren said. "Can you possibly need anything else from me?"

Lucius brushed his hair out of his face, and smiled his composed smile. "That list of taverns you mentioned," he said, "would be perfect."

THE TAVERN WAS crowded, and the crowd made it hot. The air was stale, and smelled of wine-soaked breathing. There were pockets of loud conversation, groups laughing and singing together, but around the edges of that merriment there were outsiders shrinking away. He was still shocked to find himself among the latter. He had loved to laugh, before. He had hated to be alone.

The ale was cheap, and so bitter Morgan would never have condescended to sell it, but he'd had so many tankards of it at this point that he couldn't taste it anymore, or much of anything else. It didn't really matter; he wasn't drinking it for the taste.

He leaned over the bar, resting his head in his hands. He was sure he couldn't stand without swaying. Someone jostled his arm, and he looked up into the face of a tall Aurnian man, one eye, or what was left of it, covered by a dark leather patch, the strap cutting across his high forehead. In a place as close as this, with so many drunkards and would-be drunkards about, a physical altercation with a man who looked like that was usually enough to start a fight, and Deinol attempted to slump slightly less, though all that happened was his arms flopped on the bar like fish. But the tall man backed off, a mild expression in his one remaining eye. "Sorry," he said, and Deinol only then realized he was carrying several tankards at once.

"'S all right," he mumbled.

He watched the man over his shoulder, and saw him join two other Aurnians at the end of the bar, just a couple seats from Deinol himself. There was a man seated in the stool at the very end, and a woman standing beside him as if she was too restless to sit—not quite pacing, but not standing still. She had short black hair, and a sword at her left side—all three of them did, now that he looked. *Tsunshin*. Just thinking the word made his heart ache. He'd only ever seen one of those before, and might not ever see it again. Or if he *did* see it again, that might even be worse.

Damn it. Wasn't heavy drinking supposed to make you forget about things like this? If not, what was it good for?

The tall man set one of the tankards down in front of the seated man, who took hold of it without a word. Then he much more clumsily passed another to the woman, reaching all the way across her body so he could put it into her left hand. Which was odd, because she wore the *tsunshin* on her left side, and Lucius had said you always wore it on your non-dominant side. Deinol looked down, hardly knowing what he was expecting to see in place of her right hand—a stump? a wood or metal imitation?—but it was just a hand hanging there, made out of flesh and with all the fingers intact. He couldn't see what they were drinking.

He rested his head on the table while they conferred in low voices, taking a gulp of ale every time he remembered it was there. He had to ration it out. Only so much coin left.

He was able to hear the Aurnians better after the bar-goers seated between them got up and left, but it was hard for him to follow. They were wondering whether to leave or stay where they were, a question Deinol had asked himself many times since coming to Stonespire. The answer was always the same: if he did leave, where would he go?

The two standing ones did most of the talking, but it was clear their seated companion was listening intently; his dark eyes had an intense, burning look to them, as if he didn't know how to do anything halfway. "Lanvaldis does present an opportunity," he said softly; Deinol could not have said he mumbled, because every word was enunciated precisely. "It's been relatively stable for years. Now, for the first time, that's on the brink of change."

"Not quite," the tall man said. "There's a spark of unrest, to be sure, but we know all too well those sparks don't always catch."

"Well, staying here will be useless," his companion said, bringing the tankard to his lips. "There won't be any fighting here for some time. And if there is, it'll be because Reglay and Lanvaldis have already been brought under control."

"Only a matter of time, where Reglay is concerned," the tall man said.

"Which is why we should move to the place where we might actually be able to make a difference."

The other two were silent, until the woman said, "We could always go farther north. We could go back to—"

"No," the seated man said harshly. "There's nothing to work loose back there. Elgar has them too firmly under his heel. It's not the right time."

"When will it be, Kaihen?" she asked. "It'll all be for nothing if we can't—"

"I know," he said. "I will never give up on Aurnis. But the indignity of our loss . . . the extent of our loss . . . if we want to do more than die honorably, we must be careful. Though it burns me as much as it does you."

Perhaps his reprimand struck her especially hard; when she spoke again, her eyes were on the floor. "I didn't mean to act as if—"

"I know what you meant. You don't need to apologize, or make excuses for yourself. I haven't forgotten what you sacrificed."

That made all three of them fall silent, and Deinol slumped all the way forward, letting his cheek hit the wood of the countertop. He listened to his own breathing, and tried to let everything else fade into so much indistinct noise. Why did they have to be so serious? Nobody came to a place like this to be serious.

The next thing he knew, someone was slapping his shoulder—the man behind the bar, who wasn't Morgan. Of course he wasn't Morgan. "Hey, you can't sleep here. You want a room for the night, you've got to find somewhere else, and pay for it."

"Aye, just an accident," Deinol muttered, pushing his hand away. "Not . . . easy to sleep around here."

The Aurnians were still in their corner, in murmured conversation, their heads pressed close together. Fighting in Lanvaldis, eh? Must be nice to believe you could keep the cause alive, even after all these years—it was more optimism than Lucius had ever shown. But maybe that just proved how foolhardy it was, he thought, trying to rub the bleariness out of his eyes.

Chapter Twenty-two

Stonespire

SEREN RETURNED TO Stonespire Hall with heavy steps. She had tried to do what she could for Lucius, but seeing him had made her feel as if she'd been dragged back to the day Seth died—or as if part of her had been stuck there since it happened, unable to reach the present.

She went to report to Arianrod more for the sake of seeing her than anything else. Arianrod was in her study, as she had been for most of the day. Beside her on the floor were two piles of rocks. In the larger one, the stones were simply stacked in a heap, but in a cloth sack there were about half a dozen, each tightly wrapped in its own length of cloth. It was some sort of enchantment, Seren didn't doubt, but she was far less interested in the specifics than in the weariness in Arianrod's face. She was leaning half-slumped against the back of her chair, but she turned her head when Seren entered, if only to frown.

"Did something happen?" she asked. "Bridger said she thought some stranger was bothering you—an Aurnian, not anyone she knew."

Seren hesitated. She would never have lied to Arianrod, but she hardly wanted to have to explain that whole mess with Seth, and she doubted Arianrod would find it of interest anyway. "I know him—not well, but we've had some dealings in the past. He hadn't been to Stonespire before, and when our paths crossed he took the opportunity to ask for my help with something."

"Well, that's vague," Arianrod said.

Seren winced. "There's . . . not much to tell, my lady. He's searching taverns for a friend of his—who may not even be here in the first place."

Arianrod's face twisted, as if she'd been going to say one thing and then abruptly decided on something else. "I suppose we can dismiss the matter if you wish. You obviously found Bridger as I asked, but was there anything else you had to tell me?"

"Not at the moment, my lady. Will you be continuing with that?" She glanced at the rocks.

Arianrod sighed. "Not tonight. I'm not used to this enchanting business—I hate to say it, but I suspect Elgar could have done all this much more easily. It's more tiring than I'd expected."

Seren had never ceased feeling uneasy after witnessing the intensity of Arianrod's exhaustion in the aftermath of Elgar's attack, so the less Arianrod was pushing herself in this regard, the happier she'd be. "Shall I bring you anything else?"

"That won't be necessary. I was thinking of retiring for the evening anyway."

"Shall I accompany you, then?"

Arianrod yawned. "Probably be best if you did. I doubt you could find a chambermaid in the entire hall who's still awake, and I hardly want to rouse one just so she can sleepwalk her way through fumbling at my laces."

Seren climbed the stairs at her side, trying to judge how severe her exhaustion was, but what she found set her mostly at ease. Arianrod wasn't moving very slowly or carefully, and color seemed to be returning to her face rather than leaving it. The steep stairs caused her no trouble, and by the time she reached her bedroom near the top of the spire, she was smiling.

The room couldn't be all that large, because at this height there was only the spire, which wasn't very wide even at its base. Arianrod kept most of her books and papers in her study, and in here there was only a much smaller desk wedged into a corner; most of the room was taken up by the bed and the clothes. The window looked out onto the orchard, as almost all the spire's windows did, and a large rug covered most of the floor to ease the chill on bare feet.

Arianrod shut the door behind Seren and kicked off her shoes, then turned so Seren could get at her laces. As a child with the old woman, she had only owned one set of clothes—if such was even the proper name for what they were—and she would never have dreamed of letting them out of her grasp; she'd never have seen them again. During her years with the guild, she had been provided with as many sets of clothing as she wanted, but she had chosen only simple and practical things, nothing that required another's help to put on; such a thing would have been a dangerous weakness. She wasn't completely unfamiliar with those who could be naked in front of other people as if it were a matter of course. But she still wasn't fully at ease with nobles' peculiar custom of actually allowing near-strangers to dress and undress you, a practice that would probably always seem to Seren to be terribly unsafe.

She did have to admit that all potential assailants were unlikely: Verrane, who'd taken care of Arianrod and her father before her; a select group of chambermaids, none of whom had ever struck Seren as particularly dexterous or cunning; and, occasionally, Seren herself. While Arianrod evidently didn't care much about her own safety, she *did* care about being stared at, and any new servant who couldn't drag her eyes away from the scars in time would not get a second chance to perform her office.

It wasn't that Seren never found herself tempted to stare, but it was only in the way you might insist on examining a wound on someone you cared for, pushing their covering hands away: to make sure you knew the full extent of the damage, and to assure yourself it would be all right. To make sure there wasn't something you'd left undone that might help take their pain away.

But her eyes were not drawn there tonight; the worst she did was struggle with the laces a bit. Arianrod chuckled. "Truth be told, you're about as deft at this as a sleepy chambermaid. I'd have expected more graceful work from someone with your training."

"Someone with my training would find it more expedient to cut the laces, my lady," Seren said. "You would find me quite deft at that, but I don't think you'd thank me." She dropped her hands, then remembered herself, and held the edges of the dress so Arianrod could step out of it. "There, you're done."

"Much obliged." She could do the rest of it herself, and Seren took the two strides to the window to give her privacy. The tops of the apple trees were below their heads from up here, an indistinct mass of leaves. "It's going to be a bit chaotic here with the arrival of our Lanvaldian friends, I don't doubt," Arianrod said, amidst the rustle of fabric. "But I'm expecting at least one more guest, and I want to keep them here until he arrives. I won't even have to fabricate an excuse, since enchanting the rest of that pile should take quite some time. Watch the Lanvalds carefully, of course, but don't worry too much—they're not truly adept with blades *or* subterfuge."

Seren would make sure of that, but she only said, "I will watch them, my lady. Would you prefer me to guard your door tonight?"

Arianrod laughed. "Seren, do you know the last time a Margraine was killed in this room?"

"Never," Seren guessed.

"Never," Arianrod repeated, and she seemed pleased at the answer. "How did you know? Have you been reading history?"

Sensing a cessation of movement, Seren looked back over her shoulder to see Arianrod leaning against her bed, having put the dress away and changed into a light linen shift. "I didn't *know*. But the blood apples would ruin a poisoning approach, the hall's well-positioned and impossible to reach by scaling the hillside, and the spire's the easiest part of it to defend, especially the higher up you go—this is the loftiest perch in the whole city by a wide margin. If you could get inside the castle and wanted to kill a Margraine, it'd be much easier to do it during some event in the great hall—while the ruling Margraine was seated in judgment, or at a ball or banquet."

"Spoken like a true professional. But then you must know that guarding the door, while charmingly thorough, is rather overdoing it."

"I leave that to your own judgment," Seren said. "I'm prepared to do whatever is required of me."

"Well, I promise I won't require anything of you until the morning, at least." Seren waited, and sure enough, there were the five words she had hoped for: "But stay, if you like."

Seren stayed—precisely where she was, and very still. "Yes," she said. She didn't know if Arianrod actually needed her to say it, or if her continued presence was good enough. But she always said it, because she wanted to.

Arianrod relaxed a little, leaning back on her hands, as if she'd put off something heavier than the dress. "I thought I'd caused a little trouble for you, the other day—by talking about Sahai in front of Zara. I hadn't expected you to tell her so much about it—and Gravis, too."

Seren inched slightly closer, trying to feel out whatever invisible boundaries remained. "It didn't matter to me. It was never really a secret, I just didn't want to act like my past was anyone's for the asking."

"Well, I'm pleased every time Gravis learns something is none of his business—a lesson he can never learn too often, as far as I'm concerned." She smiled. She smiled so often, and Seren had spent so much time trying to parse the differences between them, to find some way to guess at her thoughts. It was not that some smiles were true and others false, but that Arianrod could find humor in things others could not: adversity, discourtesy, the unexpected—even in things that would have caused others fear. Perhaps in sadness, too, though if Seren had ever actually seen Arianrod sad, she did not know what it looked like. "You look so uncomfortable," Arianrod said, and perhaps that smile had a bit of a challenge in it?

"No," Seren said, truthfully, though she cursed her shoulders for tensing up as if trying to make her a liar. "It's not that, I just . . ." She just what? She was just so terrified of making a mistake? She just wanted, far too much and far too inappropriately, when she knew all too well it was not for her to demand anything of Arianrod?

She could find nothing to say that was both true and suitable, so she said nothing. She dropped to one knee at Arianrod's feet, so Arianrod didn't have to look up at her from the bed. She brought Arianrod's hand to her mouth and kissed it, and hoped that she would take it not as a liberty, but as permission.

Arianrod pulled her hand free, but before Seren even had time to wonder if she'd overstepped, Arianrod had curled both hands into the cloth at Seren's shoulders, and pulled her forward so they could kiss.

Once it started it was always easier. The first few times had been more difficult, because Arianrod had seemed uncertain about what she wanted—and so Seren, who wanted to please her, had been at a loss as well. But now Arianrod reached for her with confidence, and Seren could just react to being touched: return the kisses that were given to her, press into Arianrod's hands. She waited for Arianrod to divest her of her own clothes before she ventured to grasp the hem of that shift, but Arianrod let it go easily, and then Seren was free to slide her hands up Arianrod's sides, one hand skirting quickly and carefully across the stripes of too-smooth skin upon her back to tangle in her long pale hair.

Arianrod kissed her throat, and Seren did not flinch, even when her lips touched those places where the blood beat dangerously close to the skin, where life could be so easily snuffed out. Arianrod slipped a hand between her legs, and Seren closed her eyes, giving herself over to not just the pleasure but the peace of it: the feeling that, for once, she need not do or be anything but precisely as she wished.

It was perfect, for a time. It was always perfect, save that it always ended. And in the world outside this room, Arianrod did not always say what she wanted, and Seren did not always know how to give it to her.

She wished she could feel content, but the same old worries were already creeping back into her heart. For how much longer would she be able to do this? Because she did not know what Arianrod had seen in her to begin with, she had no way of knowing how long this might last, or who might replace her. Or even if Arianrod would just grow bored, and pronounce the experiment over. She did so hate to be bored.

She was currently looking as pleasantly worn out as Seren wished she could be, but then she rolled to the side and glared at the candle on her desk. It went out, as did the one on the windowsill nearest her bed, leaving only moonlight to illuminate the room.

Seren started, then caught herself—of course Arianrod could do that—and Arianrod laughed. "It's a lot more fun now that I don't have to hide these things."

"It's impressive," Seren admitted, "but it's going to make it a lot more difficult for me to get back out of here. You might have waited for me to get my clothes on, at least."

"I thought you trained to move efficiently in low light? If not, you should probably start practicing." She yawned. "Or you can sleep here, if you'd rather not move. It's certainly not a small bed."

It wasn't that Seren had never slept there before, but the other times had all been inadvertent—she had fallen asleep without meaning to, and Arianrod had either done same or else hadn't felt the need to wake her. But to do it purposely felt presumptuous, and she didn't want Arianrod to think that she did not take her duties seriously, or that she felt entitled to anything of hers. "It seems . . . careless, at a time when strangers are within the hall, to sleep when you also—"

"You've got to sleep sometime." Arianrod stretched her arms above her head. "And when I'm awake I'm also going to be requiring things of you, you know."

Seren bent her head. "I can sleep as well downstairs."

"Then go downstairs," Arianrod said, shrugging deeper into her blankets. "Good night."

That must have been that, as far as she was concerned, because she closed her eyes, and, when Seren did not move, made no attempt to question her continued presence. They stayed like that until Arianrod's breathing evened out, and her face lay smoothed by slumber: devoid of any smile, but with a softness that was not cold.

Was it not, Seren wondered, a mark of great trust to sleep in someone's presence, untroubled by what they might do? Or did it just mean that Arianrod felt Seren was beneath her concern?

She wondered if it would be so impossible, after all, to simply curl up beside her—not touching, just *there*. Or could she even just remain here, unsleeping, and watch over her? She almost always felt ill at ease in the presence of other people—they were unknown variables, and it would have been imprudent to let her guard down completely for even the weakest of them—but Arianrod's presence had the opposite effect. She was possessed of such force of will that it seemed impossible anyone should ever outmatch or outwit her, and if she had decided that she preferred you alive, it felt like she would keep any ill from befalling you, either. Seren had felt that from their very first meeting—but their first meeting also served as a reminder that Arianrod had vulnerabilities of her own, and Seren's job was still necessary.

She sat there for a long time, an indistinct shape among indistinct shapes in the gloom. And then, finally, she slid her feet noiselessly to the ground, dressed quickly in the darkness, and slipped out of the room.

CHAPTER TWENTY-THREE

Esthrades

THE FIRST TIME Cadfael had ever seen her had been in the early winter, in that godsforsaken meadow, the grass all frozen and brittle, unmelted by the weak sunlight of early evening. The first person he had asked, in the village's tiny tavern, had declared her, without a moment's hesitation, to be the one King Eira had sent him to find. A strange woman, with no people, who walked the frozen forest at dawn and dusk. A woman who was said to stir up restless spirits, or even darker things—who was not, clearly, *one of us.*

To him she had seemed entirely unremarkable, dressed like any peasant, with golden-brown ringlets and eyes so faded they seemed almost colorless. She had a stern face, with an unyielding jaw, but she lacked the musculature of a fighter, and she carried no weapons that Cadfael could see. He had never believed in restless spirits, and as for darker things, it seemed to him that men's souls were twisted enough for any enterprise, without the need to bring myths into it.

It was shocking to him now, but he could not remember what he had said to her at first—that he had come from the king, no doubt, and that she was wanted at the castle. But beyond that? Had he said anything at all, or just the bare minimum to excuse what he was about to do?

The truth was, he'd spared her barely a thought. He had been distressed the whole length of that journey, because he and Rhia hadn't made up when he had left her. It had been the worst fight they had ever had, because Rhia hated things she saw as dishonorable, and she hated being lied to, and finding out he had done both at once had driven her into a fury he'd only ever seen directed at other people before. The only *reason* he'd lied to her was because he knew she wouldn't understand: participating in the arena's blood sport might have seemed like the action of a callow murderer, but it wasn't as if Eira had ever forced anyone to compete. If you wagered your own life for coin and lost, that was your own fault, wasn't it? And if, as Eira and the arena managers realized how popular a fighter he was with the people of Araveil, they had started selecting his opponents more carefully, that wasn't his fault, either.

But he knew Rhia wouldn't see it that way; she believed what she believed, and that was that. So he'd told her he only participated in the nonlethal contests, and since he had strictly forbidden her from getting within a mile of the arena, she had no way of knowing the purses he brought home were far too fat to have come from anything but death.

It had worked well, for a couple years, but it also meant that the deception was doubly bad for being a deception in the first place, and triply bad for how long it had lasted. The ironic thing was he'd stopped his arena bouts by that point; he'd already come directly into Eira's employ. But that hadn't made any difference to her, and she'd *still* been sulking when he'd told her he couldn't delay his departure any longer. That sulk had been far more vivid to him than any expression on the woman's face, but only at first.

The first thing he remembered was something *she* said, because he hadn't been expecting it: "How do you intend to ensure I come with you?"

"His Grace's orders permit me to use whatever force is required to bring you before him," Cadfael said.

"Is that right? Well, you're free to use as much force as you can. I will use as much resistance as I wish." She said that with a certain amount of relish, like a cat imagining the struggles of a mouse.

"It is late now," Cadfael said, "and I would not wish to travel any more until the morning, with you or without you. But I will return here at daybreak. If there is anything you have left undone, any good-byes you wish to speak, see to it before that time. And I would not suggest running away—I will find you, and the result will be the same."

The woman's eyes were hard as flint, and almost its color. "I never had any intention of running away. If you seek me tomorrow morning, you will find me here, just as I am now."

"Good," Cadfael said.

"It will not be, for you, if you come here tomorrow," she replied. "Since you have offered me a day's courtesy, I will offer you the same: leave me in peace, and be on your way. If you do this, I will consider that no quarrel exists between us, and I will not pursue you. But if you come for me tomorrow, it will be too late. I will show no mercy, even if you beg for your life."

But how, back then, could he have understood her power? When he returned to the meadow the following morning, he found her standing there, just as she had promised. A gust of wind rustled the blades of grass between them, carving a momentary swath through the meadow, and she raised her eyes to his. "How unfortunate that you could not see sense."

Cadfael shook his head. "On what basis should I have believed your warnings? I am a skilled warrior, and you are none at all."

"That is true," she said. "If I were merely a warrior, you might have stood a chance."

He sighed. "Well, hurry up and try your best, then. His Grace awaits our return."

"Ah yes," she said. "Your king. I must confess that his behavior has puzzled me."

"I don't know what he wants with you, either," Cadfael said. "I would tell you if I knew."

"No, it's not that." She turned her head slightly, looking past him and out across the meadow. "I know exactly what he wants with me. That part is no mystery at all."

The wind snapped around the trees at the edges of the meadow, and they swayed with a great cracking of branches and whispering of dead leaves. Then the gusts broke past them, and tore their way through the meadow, making Cadfael sway on his feet a little as their ferocity caught him off guard. The chill made his face sting, as if trying to rub his skin raw. But the skin of his arms prickled from something more than cold—the sense of some wrongness in the air around them, something that was not as it should be.

"Why send only one man?" she asked. "In *your* instance it is not so very remarkable; you have made it clear you know nothing of the true circumstances in which you find yourself. But your king must have known what you would face—or had some idea, at least—and still he chose to send you alone. It perplexed me yesterday, but I believe I have finally hit upon it. Your king *knew,* but he did not truly understand. He dreams, in some vague and insubstantial way, of power, but he cannot allow himself to contemplate the idea that that power could be beyond his ability to subdue—could be *so* great as to be frightening, even to one who wears a crown."

She smiled then, and it *was* the smile of a cat, or of some larger and more menacing predator. "If, by some miracle, you should survive this, you can tell your king his mistake was sending one man. To subdue me, he should have sent an army."

A shrill screaming filled the air—the call of a hundred birds, as they rose from the gale-tossed trees all around the meadow and fled screeching into the distance, beating their tiny wings as best they could. And then even that noise faded, as the wind snatched all other noise away before it could reach him, and only its screaming filled his ears.

He had been afraid, in some distant way. But more than that, he had felt like one in a dream. He had drawn his sword, because what else was there to do? But though he held it aloft, he did not know what to cut with it. The blade somehow seemed to provide the smallest bit of a break in the gale, but it was blowing so fiercely that each step toward her took every ounce of his strength. He'd never reach her.

"I told you I would not show you any mercy," she said, and the wind carried her words right to his ears. "You and your master think only of yourselves—of how you can use us and take from us, as if we hadn't lost enough already! Where were you when we suffered? Where were you when we were defenseless? But as soon as we find a smattering of power, here you come like a vulture to pick us clean! I won't endure it!" It was the rage in her eyes that finally dispelled the fog of incredulity from his mind. No dream could have been so vivid as that.

He had felt the implacability of that rage, the unfathomable gulf between her power and his, and for the first time in his life, he had known not just defeat, but the despair that comes with it—the despair he had seen in the eyes of so many arena combatants when they realized they could not best him. He wanted to live. He wanted to see Rhia again. But he knew she would not spare him. He knew what it was to feel no need for mercy in your heart.

Past the point of hope, but in rage at his own impotence, he flung the sword away and spread his arms wide. "Put an end to it, then!" he yelled. She flinched in surprise, and he could see the sadness in her eyes that was even deeper than the anger, the sadness that never changed. "If you want my life, then take it! Just take it! Take—"

He felt a sharp sting on his forehead, and at first he thought something had been kicked up by the wind and struck him. But when he pressed his hand to the sore spot, it came away wet with blood, and he could feel it now, flowing past his nose and dripping from his chin.

"There," she said, cold and expressionless. "Consider that what I owe you. Survive it, if you can."

And she had left.

IT WASN'T THE same meadow, of course. This was Esthrades, for one thing, and it was summer instead of winter. There were more birches flashing their silver bark from between the trees surrounding them, and the grass was longer and wilder, even so close to the city of Stonespire. When he was young, his father had told him stories of how all of Esthrades had been a forest once, many centuries before it had ever been called by that name, and the grass yearned upward as if it could remember that time, and wished to bring it back again.

She was quiet by Cadfael's side, but she had remained there. He felt as if they were bound together by some precarious spell, that could snap at any moment, and he was torn between wanting to prolong it as much as he could and wanting to make the most of it while it lasted. What question had he most wanted to ask her? In the end, he said, "Will you give me your name? I never had it of you before."

"You never asked it of me before," she said, with her customary sharpness. "And I never had yours, either."

"It's Cadfael. I'd offer you the surname as well, but I have two, and can claim neither."

"Which is to say you have none," she said, but she seemed amused. "Nor do I, though I'm not bastard born. Talis is my name."

It helped, somehow, to finally have something to call her, after all this time. It made him feel more at ease. "Where are you—"

"That's far too hasty," she interrupted. "The next question is mine to ask."

He laughed. "Conversation with you seems to be a series of hard bargains."

"It is a fitting way to converse with you," she said. "Now. What do you want of me, truly? I explained to you what happened, and yet you're still here, so it must be more than that."

He searched for a way to say what he could barely communicate to himself. "I suppose . . . to say it as simply as possible . . . I want either a reason to live, or a reason to die."

She scoffed, but her eyes were troubled. "I can't imagine you'd ask the person who tried to kill you why you should live. And if you want to die, you don't need my help."

"I don't *want* to die," Cadfael said. "I'm just . . . finding it difficult to live."

He expected her to make some retort to that, but she did not. She was silent, and that troubled look did not fade.

"Some people are born with one purpose in life," he said. "If they are kept from that purpose, their soul sickens within them. I belonged with my family. My purpose was to protect them, and I have failed it irrevocably. Now I don't know what to do. I feel that, if I am alive, I should use that life for something. I feel that if I am to walk into death knowingly, I should do it for some reason. And yet I have found no reason, for one or the other. I have been chasing the man who killed my sister, even though I know she would not wish me to. But you . . . he is someone who wronged me, but you are someone I wronged. If you killed me, it would be your right. And if you wished me to live, but sought recompense for the wrongs done you in some other way . . . I would prefer to live for that reason. I would feel closer to my sister that way."

She folded her arms. "So you just seek to use me."

"Yes," he admitted, "but it's not as if I'm not giving you the opportunity to use me, too."

She brooded over it for a time, arms still folded. "The truth is, I know nothing of how to balance scales. You seem to think I have a sense of justice that you lack, but that isn't really true. I've killed people, too, and I can't swear it was always with good reason. So I can't clean your conscience for you. I'm not capable of it, and, moreover, I have no interest in it."

"Well," Cadfael said, "to be fair, I don't have much of a conscience in the first place."

"You have something," she said, unsmiling. "Whatever it is that can keep a broken man whole enough to keep looking for *reasons*." She tapped her foot, and unfolded her arms, and he knew she wasn't done, so he waited. "Were you ever told that old fable? Of that princess of the Selindwyri who came to these very forests in search of her brother, and pledged herself to the service of a sorceress?"

His father had told that story many times. "To serve her for a year's time, in exchange for one wish? That was it, wasn't it?"

"Things can work that way in tales," she said, "but you and I can hardly waste a year. Yet, like that sorceress, my . . . companion and I have things our magic makes it more difficult to do—things that might come easier to one with no magic at all. You might help us with that—it's not a purpose, but it's something to do."

"But what is it specifically?" Cadfael asked.

She shook her head. "I can't tell you without his permission. There were four of us, once—we were born strangers, but our gifts drew us together. One of us was killed, and one of us ran away, and . . . I don't wish to lose the only one I have left. And he has grown very, very mistrustful of late—not to say he kept his heart wide open to begin with. If I can draw him out, you might learn much and more about this world—things scarcely another soul could tell you. Is that purpose enough?"

Cadfael inclined his head to show his gratitude, and when he raised it, he found he was smiling, just a little. "My sister would call it an adventure," he said.

CHAPTER TWENTY-FOUR

Valyanrend

EVEN THIS LATE in the evening, you could still hear the song of the anvils in Iron's Den.

Even without the noise of the hammers, you'd know you passed a smithy from every blast of heat that wafted from a forge. But Iron's Den wasn't all about metal, despite its name: you could get any weapon made or refined there, and many methods of defense as well. Naishe paused to inhale the scent of leather from a nearby tanner's—she much preferred that to iron and soot—but she wasn't here to buy anything today. A lucky thing, as the shops were closing.

She stopped in front of the two-story wooden building—bedrooms above the shop, kitchen in the back—with a many-times-repainted sign proclaiming it Fletcher and Son. She knew it didn't refer to Wren and his father—the Fletchers had been fletchers for generations, with the occasional daughter making an appearance, but it so happened the two current Fletchers fit the name perfectly. She rapped at the doorpost like usual, and then stepped away, so anyone looking out the windows would have a clear view of her.

After a couple minutes, Wren's father came out, a big, hearty man always eager to laugh. He was wiping his forehead with a rag, and then switched to wiping his hands. "Good to see you, Naishe. Forgive the boy; he'll be down in only a few moments more. Wanted to finish the lot."

"Good evening, Mr. Fletcher," she said. "I can wait."

"It's my fault, really," he said, throwing the rag over one shoulder. "Lot of orders lately. I've been needing his help more than usual. Appreciate you putting up with the lateness."

She wasn't certain why Wren's father took this tone with only her, as if his son were something he had to apologize for, when she well knew he thought the world of Wren. "Wren works as hard as anyone I know," she said. "I'm the one who's calling him away from it."

Wren's father opened his mouth, but before he could speak, Wren burst through the door, throwing his shoulder into it and hurrying into the space between Naishe and his father as if to protect one or both of them from the other. "Sorry, sorry, everyone," he said, slightly breathless, "I'm done now, thanks for waiting. The rest are in the back, Father, and you promised to let me off until tomorrow noontime, right?"

His father slapped him on the back. "Consider it a promise kept. You've done careful work as always. I hardly feel like a master of my craft with you in the house."

"Oh, no, it's not like that," Wren said, the way he always did, and Naishe always had to resist the urge to tell him that his father clearly got more joy out of praising him than he would have hearing the whole city praise himself.

His father snapped the rag at him playfully. "Go on, then. You enjoy your leisure, and I'll enjoy mine, eh?"

They weren't going to enjoy any kind of leisure, but Wren's father didn't need to know that. As they started walking, Wren passed the bundle he was carrying to her. "Here you are. Sorry I couldn't have them ready when I said, but they're all there."

Twenty arrows, fletched with the silver-gray feathers common to Fletcher and Son. Though Wren and his father both made them, Naishe didn't doubt all of these had come from Wren himself. "Thanks. And don't worry. I wouldn't ask for them if they weren't the best, and you won't even let me pay you."

Wren ducked his head. "Well, we're both part of the same cause. It wouldn't seem right."

She laughed. "Have it your way. Everything else all right at home?"

"Sure, it's all normal. My parents are as energetic as ever, and whatever they think I'm doing, it can't be what I'm actually doing, because they don't seem concerned in the least."

Naishe was still waiting for a reply from her mother after finally telling her what she was actually doing, and she wasn't entirely sure that hadn't been a mistake. It had felt wrong to keep lying to her, and she *had* always said you had to follow your own principles in life, but if Father got his nose in it . . .

"What are Za— I mean, Mouse's orders?" Wren asked.

She tucked the arrows under her arm. "He's at the hideout, with that Sheather girl and Rask—and maybe Talia, too, if she could manage it. Even though I cautioned him against it, he's going to answer a bunch of her questions, as recompense for her help with the Precipitate problem." She gave him a rueful smile. "Honestly, you don't *have* to be there. More than anything, I came to fetch you because I wanted to talk to you away from the others."

"Well, if we don't have to be there, they won't care if we're late," Wren said. "We could . . . take the long way round."

She knew what he was really asking. "Why not?"

They turned their steps north, and Naishe said, "What do you think of Mouse's continued confidence in the thief?"

Wren rubbed the side of his face. "Well, as to that, Mouse has always had a fascination with Sheath, even when we were boys. But he's also not an idiot, and he does have a certain effect on people. They tend to do the things he wants. . . . As you and I could both attest."

"But our goals align with his," Naishe said. "We have solid principles he could appeal to. What does this girl have?"

"I suppose it's something of the opposite effect, isn't it?" Wren asked. "Mouse has a fascination with Sheath, and she has a fascination with . . . not *our* resistance exactly, but the *idea* of a resistance, don't you think? Otherwise she'd never have gotten involved with us to start with. I don't think it's anything like what Rask believed—that she was some sort of spy. She seems all wrong for that."

Naishe agreed with him there—the girl had the ambitions of a thief only, and had shown no concern for the greater balance of power in their city. But that was just what made her think she couldn't be counted on. She might show some passing interest, but it would only last until she felt herself to be in danger—which would be inevitable, if she kept associating with them.

She stopped at the next street corner, and looked at Wren. Normally it was calming to take these walks with him, even their silences companionable and undemanding. But she felt some unaccustomed tension, something unsaid between them—that must have come from him, because Naishe could not think of anything she herself wanted to say.

She batted the hair away from his right eye. "You ought to cut that. I don't know how you can see anything."

"That's what the other eye is for," he said, with a self-deprecating smile.

She knew as well as he did that he kept the hair long to keep from having his mismatched eyes remarked upon. She had not known him in his childhood, but perhaps the sting of mockery from others was not something he could easily forget. He seemed like that kind of person to her; there was a delicateness to him that suggested even slight disapproval could leave a lasting impression, like clay that would bear the prints of too-careless fingers.

She could tell him that it was silly to care about the eye, but there would be no point. What mattered was what he thought about it, not what she did.

They were silent again after that, but she thought the tension had eased a bit—until an enormous shadow fell over them, blotting out the light of the moon.

The longest, widest, and deepest river on the continent, the Viander had its origin in a great spring high up in the mountains of southern Aurnis. From there, it cut a swath across northern and central Hallarnon, unfordable at any point, even on horseback. It finally poured over the cliffs to the west and into the Endless Sea, which dwarfed even its vastness.

It did make sense that the largest river in Lantistyne should be used to nourish the largest city in Lantistyne, but for one problem: the Viander was leagues to the north, far too distant to transport water to the city for daily use. Or it would have been, under normal circumstances.

Just as there were no written records of Valyanrend's construction, so there were no records of the building of the great aqueduct that ran down the hillside south of the Viander and over Valyanrend's walls, finally ending abruptly in a cascade of falling water that filled the great underground cistern and from thence made its meandering way to many smaller cisterns, fountains, and man-made pools. Supposedly, in the language of the first Lantians, the aqueduct was called the Arkhe Laeshet, and perhaps those who lived in its shadow in the villages between Valyanrend and the river still called it that. But Valyanrenders only had one name for the jutting bridge of stone and its waterfall: the Precipitate.

"She really climbed this thing?" Wren asked, resting his hand against one of the massive stone pillars that supported the aqueduct. Though the Precipitate had no leaks, even after so many centuries, the falling water still misted the air in great clouds, condensing on the pillars so that there was scarcely a dry spot to be found.

"I saw it myself," Naishe had to admit.

"How did she do it?"

"The holes." She took his hand and moved it, pressing it to another pillar, the one the monkey had showed them earlier. The rock was pitted with small holes along its side, large enough to use for a finger- or toe-hold. "Anyone climbing it would have to take off their shoes. But it can be done."

"Anyone?" Wren repeated. "Did you decide who *is* going to climb it?"

Naishe hesitated. "We did."

He covered his hidden eye with his hand, as if it hurt him. "They're making you do it, aren't they?"

"They aren't *making* me. I argued for the job—Rask would've taken it if I'd said otherwise. But think about it: archery, strength, nimbleness, stealth—all originally honed from hunting, but they'll serve me as well in this. No one else can boast all four."

He bit his lip. "I'm half surprised Mouse didn't volunteer."

"He considered it," Naishe said, "but Rask and I overruled him. This job is one of great responsibility and great danger, which was doubtless why he thought he ought to take it. But it's also one that requires physical strength and fighting prowess, so we convinced him I was better suited. He can't afford to die in the attempt."

"And neither can you," said Wren, as if trying to extract a promise from her. "So you won't."

Naishe did not smile, because she knew a smile would not comfort him. Instead, she looked at him seriously, letting him see her resolve. "So I won't," she told him.

"CLIMBING THE PRECIPITATE *is* a clever way to get atop the outer walls, I'll grant you that," Marceline said, around bites of bread and cheese. "And there are guard posts there, I suppose."

"There's one post in particular that we can ensure will be lightly guarded," Rask said. Though Mouse had spoken animatedly, he had to force all of his words out; he clearly didn't like sharing their plans with her. "The right person could slip in and out without alerting anyone."

Marceline scoffed. "What, are you afraid to fight guards?"

She was so used to Rask's prideful scowl that she'd been expecting it. But all he did was laugh, without saying anything at all.

Mouse laughed, too, but he also explained. "Of course you wouldn't know, but

Rask is our best swordsman—best in the resistance, to be sure, but even measured against all others, he's fairly remarkable."

Marceline stared at Rask. "He doesn't look it."

"And you don't look like much of anything, runt," Rask snapped, "but that doesn't make you any less of a damned magician with other people's coin, does it?"

"I haven't been learning for all that long," Talia piped up, "but they tell me I'm not bad, either."

"You're not bad because *I'm* training you. But you've quite a ways to go yet, and it'd do you better to remember it."

"To answer your question, monkey," Mouse said, "we don't wish to fight guards because the people of Valyanrend are not our enemies. Not the people who wish Elgar gone but lack the means or the courage to do anything about it, not the people who have not yet chosen a side, and not even the people who serve Elgar out of desperation, or out of a mistaken belief that he will do more good for our country than harm. The only people, besides Elgar himself, that we are setting ourselves against are those heartless creatures who serve Elgar as a means to satisfy their taste for power or for butchery. We have killed some of *them* before, and would again. But we do not wish to murder his servants indiscriminately and tell ourselves that we are liberating the very people whose lives we have stolen."

Marceline frowned. "You're never going to defeat Elgar if you won't fight his men. Your only other option would be to assassinate him, and good luck with that."

Mouse shook his head. "That's not the kind of fight we're waging, or the kind of victory we want."

"Then what kind of victory do you want?"

He smiled. "We have no wish to divide this city into factions, to pull Elgar and his supporters down only to take their places. That is a very old story in Valyanrend, and one that rarely ends well. We would kill Elgar if we could, but only because we believe his continued rule will make a peaceful life in this country impossible. What we *want* is for everyone else in this country to realize that, too."

Marceline understood that he was telling her all this as a mark of confidence, so she tried not to sound too skeptical from the start. "Most people already understand that Elgar's a warmonger. Most wouldn't claim he's a man of virtue. But the way I understand it, he's not as bad as the ones we had before."

"Not as bad for whom?" Mouse asked. "Would the Aurnians and Lanvalds agree, do you think?"

Marceline wrinkled her nose. "I won't argue with you there, but . . . you have *met* people, right? They care about what's better for *them,* not for foreigners."

"But Elgar won't be better for them—for us, any of us, all Hallerns. That's what we have to prove to them." He folded his hands. "Elgar's been able to wage his wars without much of a peep from most Hallerns, because the only civilians getting killed and losing their land have been foreigners, and the only soldiers killed or injured were those who volunteered for the job. But we're on our third war now, with doubtless more to follow. Volunteers aren't infinite, and you can bet they'll dry up something fierce when Elgar moves on Issamira. No Hallern alive wants to fight on or through the Gods' Curse, and even once you make it through, the disadvantages keep piling up: the Issamiri army is known to be formidable, the Issamiri treasury is known to be equally so, and, most compelling of all, they thoroughly trounced us last time, when Gerde Selte tried it. You've proven you're clever, monkey, so you tell me: what do you think Elgar's going to do when he decides it's time to move on Issamira and his people say no?"

Marceline had to admit to a chill at that prospect. "You're saying he won't accept it, that much is clear. But what else can he do?"

"What he can do," Mouse said, "what he *will* do, is resort to a draft. He'll start in the more remote villages, then in the poorer districts here in the capital— mustn't ruffle the feathers of the rich until he absolutely has to, after all. He'll say he's cleaning up the country: taking poor fellows, orphan boys just old enough, men apprehended for minor crimes. But the more he needs, the more he'll find a reason to take. He might set his eyes on folk like me and Wren: Iron's Den apprentices, familiar with the materials of warfare, if not the fighting of it. If he hears of Rask's skills, he might try to take him, too—or even Naishe, if he decides to extend his reach to women. And your Sheath won't be spared, I'm sure of that."

Marceline felt cold all over now, but she tried to think it through rationally. "They'll leave us alone," she insisted. "They always leave us alone. We're too much for them to chew on. There are those where I'm from that, if you caged them, could make you regret it in a hundred little ways, and a few big ones. They know that. They'll leave us alone."

Rask snorted. "Good for you. Haven't you explained enough, Mouse? It's obvious she doesn't really care."

"There are many people in this city who'll be harder to convince than she is," Mouse said, "and yet we must convince them. Knowing that, how can I stop here?"

"Without proof, you're wasting your breath. Why else would Naishe be willing to risk her neck climbing that damned aqueduct?"

Marceline caught her breath. "Proof?"

"Proof," Mouse repeated. "That's what we've been searching for. And now, we believe we're about to find it."

ONCE THE DUST had settled, things between him and Tom had shaken out about even. True, Tom had battered him unfairly and demanded help that turned out not to be needed, but he'd also been right, in the main, about what had happened to his monkey in the first place. *She* looked brighter and more cheerful than ever these days, smug with her new sense of self-importance and full of secrets not even he knew. She knew he wanted to know, and she knew he'd never give her the satisfaction of asking, and both things pleased her enough to make her downright jolly nearly every time she saw him. But her old man left him alone, or was at least prepared to let the two of them go back to their mutual resentment and occasional payments for unavoidable services rendered.

And now, with man and monkey alike no longer breathing down his neck, Roger was free to return to his map. Without the ruby, he chose passages blindly, but at least he'd never found a dead end, or a passage with no apparent meaning: they all eventually led to the surface. He'd yet to find one that went to Goldhalls, the richest district in the city—Lucius and Deinol would certainly have a use for that one— and though he'd found two going to the Glassway, where the city's most talented artisans resided and thus where the most expensive works of art were created, they were both too exposed to be of much use.

But what he really wanted to find was whatever had made the ruby react so violently, and he sensed it was within the tunnels themselves, not in the out- side world. He was of a divided mind: half of him thought it would have to be dangerous, and half of him fretted that, without the gemstone to guide him, he wouldn't even notice it. It had reacted to that emerald pendant, after all, which he had yet to wring even an instant of interest out of. But it had reacted only slightly. If the emerald was its definition of *a little bit,* what would *a scale-breaking amount* look like?

As he turned the corner, the torchlight illuminated a dark shadow on the wall, and Roger flinched back, muffling a shout in his throat. Two tense heartbeats later, his mind had resolved the object into a metal brazier mounted on the rock wall, and he took several deep breaths, trying to make himself relax. He was clearly still on edge after that incident with the ruby.

But here was an unusual find—he couldn't recall having ever seen a brazier in the tunnels before, and he'd seen a great deal of them by now. Was it so travelers down this way could be sure to see something important, or so they could have both hands free and see at the same time?

After he ventured several more feet down that branch of the tunnel, he caught sight of a second brazier ahead of him, on the same side of the wall as the first. All right, so whatever he was supposed to see should be—

—between them, where there was a heavy wooden door set back into the tun- nel wall. He'd certainly never seen one of those down here. And wouldn't you know it, it was locked. Goodness, what was he to do?

The lock was ancient, and not just in terms of the metal used for its construction:

it was of so rudimentary a design that Roger wouldn't have been surprised if it was the first damned lock ever invented. He could have tripped it with a bent twig.

After retrieving his torch from the brazier, he returned his hand to the door handle and took a deep breath. He hadn't grown up listening to Gran's stories for nothing. This was a secret room in a secret tunnel that was part of an entire winding maze of secret tunnels under a city so ancient its construction had been lost to time. There could, conceivably, be just about *anything* behind this door. It was not at all naïve or idiotic to imagine there could be some great treasure stored here: mountains of gold, ancient artifacts, the weapons of kings, the hoard of some great thief's most famous plunder. *Or* it could be something terrifying. Skeletons. Monstrous rats. Some heinous creation of blades and spikes that would come careening at his face the instant he opened the door. Tax records. Or, of course, it could simply be disappointing: he could swing the door open, revealing only yet another tunnel, and another leg of this seemingly endless maze.

Well, he'd invested too much time and effort in this to be turned aside by a little mortal danger . . . right? Hope for the best, prepare for the worst, that was the proper attitude for a Halfen. He tightened his fingers around the handle, turned, pulled, braced himself to run, and *really* hoped it wasn't the thing with the spikes.

The first thing that happened was a cloud of dust whirling into his face, kicked up by the rapid swing of the door opening outward. He coughed, wiped his free hand across his face, noticed a faint rustling sound from ahead of him, and lifted his torch high. And then he lifted it higher, and took several steps forward until he was standing in the middle of the small room.

"Ah," he said. "Of course. *Books.*"

If nothing else, he had to admire the room's resourceful use of space; there wasn't enough standing room for three fully grown adults to occupy it together, but there were books stacked on all sides, arranged into carefully neat and balanced towers, shelved in recesses carved into the stone. There wasn't a single one that didn't look ancient, and there were several he would've been afraid to touch, lest they disintegrate under his fingers. There were heavy tomes bound in wood and slender journals bound in leather, rolled-up scrolls stored carefully in racks, and some stacks of parchment without any binding at all, weighted down with a stone on top. A tiny wooden desk just managed to fit in the corner on his right, with an uncomfortable-looking chair pushed in. There were books stacked even on one corner of the desk's limited space, with a dusty quill resting on the opposite side next to an ancient candlestick that still contained about half a candle. And in the center of the desk, kept in place by another small stone, was a single sheet of parchment, full of small, neat writing. Roger brought the torch closer, and bent his head to read.

If you find this, have mercy.

If you find this, think well.

I cannot say, o future's child, what lessons you will have been taught, what jailers may have raised you in what spider's-thread prisons of the mind. I dare not hope that you may know the Paths, but I pray they give you something to cling to beyond blind obedience, beyond acceptance and tractability. Already I hear such things boomed out over the heads of an adoring crowd by the Ninists' vile Speaker, such things repeated by tutors to the children given to their care. But I know that, however deep the tendrils of men's minds reach into the darkness, just so far they stretch toward the light. There will be some, in any age, in any time, who will incline to goodness as to destiny, though whole mountains stand in their way. If you have ever wished to be among such a number, I beg you to take care with what you find here.

To preserve this collection, many have given their lives. Think, I implore you, on what that truly means. If you destroy these tomes, so too will you destroy the work, the passion, the final hope of those who may have died centuries before you were born—who died martyrs, their only peace the belief that these hidden truths might be saved and one day brought to light by one who shared even the smallest shred of their bravery.

If you have ever loved to know and to learn, there is so much here for you. There may be things your time has forgotten entirely—truths the Ninists believed they had succeeded in purging from the world forever. We have saved research notes whose authors were whipped in public for blasphemy, ancient tales and songs that were outlawed because they did not teach a lesson the Ninists wanted people to learn. Historical figures who defied the great powers of their time and were too successful at it had their biographies smudged, or tainted, or erased altogether—but we have not forgotten. We have them for you here, as they were meant to be. And, of course, the books of magic: that great possibility that lived in this world once, and may never live in it again.

Take these books, with our blessing. Read them. Learn from them. Bring them home. Give them away. Only do not destroy them, not when they have come so far—not when they mean so much. Remember the dangers of ignorance. Remember that deceit is a weapon that will always turn itself back on the wielder. These books contain the truth—a rare and precious thing in my time, and perhaps in yours as well. And we who have worked so hard merely wish the truth to live forever.

There was no signature, or closing of any kind. Roger straightened, and looked around the crowded room. There was a tight, tangled feeling in his chest he couldn't put a name to. If he was sad, then why? The books had survived. The anonymous writer's wishes had come true.

Perhaps, it was the idea of someone who loved something so much, and who was so powerless to protect it, that all they could do was beg strangers to let it live.

He carefully lifted the candlestick to the torch until the wick caught, and then he put it back down on the desk and put the torch in the brazier. Returning to the room, he raised the candlestick and examined the options before him.

There were so many to choose from that he hardly knew what to do, but he wanted to see *something* of this ancient scribe's treasure trove, and eventually he pulled free a delicate volume bound in red goatskin. But when he opened it, half holding his breath, he gritted his teeth in frustration. Instead of the letters he knew, the well-worn pages were covered with all manner of foreign shapes, in incredible varieties. If this was a language, it had far more than twenty-six letters in it, and most of them looked fairly complicated to draw. Whatever truth was contained in these pages, he couldn't discover it.

But the scribe had written in letters he knew, even if the sentences themselves sounded a little stilted and hoary to his ears. That meant there had to be some books here that he could understand. He brought the candlestick close to the shelves, shielding the paper from the open flame with one hand, and squinted at the rows of spines. Some books had no titles, and some were in those strange shapes. Others he could read but not understand, and must have been in foreign but less arcane languages. And, yes, there were those he could read.

A lot of it was dry research—probably terribly interesting to someone well versed in these particular subjects, but Roger knew he was hardly the reader for it. Stories and folktales, as the scribe had said—even tales for children—and piles upon piles of history. The rise and fall of the first empire; the history of Selindwyr; Issamiri kings and queens and heroes; a huge tome detailing every law ever enacted by every Sahaian emperor or empress since the country's founding; a timeline of Akozuchen advancements in agriculture, cross-breeding, and medicine. There were more specialized biographies as well: this famous pirate captain, that clan warrior from the eastern forests in the days before Esthrades's founding, a handful of notable mages. Roger reached for *The Life and Legacy of the Outlaw Bael Giffe,* but before he could pull it down, he reminded himself that it was late already, and he couldn't bring any of these back with him to Sheath. He couldn't chance anyone seeing the tome and wondering where he'd gotten it. But he could come back another day. And he'd keep the candlestick; it provided much more flexibility than the torch. He really should've invested in one to start with.

He tapped the edge of the desk, brushing his thumb against the aged parchment with the unknown scribe's final message. "I'm not going to destroy them," he said, "so you can rest easy. I'm not one for this tendrils-to-the-light business, and I'm sure there are many better you'd have preferred to find your treasure, but I won't destroy them. Will probably sell a fair bit, though, eventually. There's got to be a few collectors out there who would pay in blood and flesh to get their hands on these."

He was going to leave, but he stopped in the doorway, and turned back one last time. "If it helps at all, we won, you know. Or at least . . . they lost. They're gone, and we're still here. So . . . I hope that's something."

CHAPTER TWENTY-FIVE

Eldren Cael

ONLY A SLIGHT breeze ruffled the edge of the awning over their table, but Adora felt an unseasonable chill blow over her nevertheless. She was eager to be gone, yet fretful over what might happen without her. Earlier in the morning, while she had studied reports from half a dozen different military outposts, composed polite demurrals to marriage offers from three noble families, spent an hour meeting with a team of craftsmen regarding the expensive, tedious, and wholly necessary matter of large-scale repairs to the city's oldest bathhouses and proposals for the more effective conveyance of water to drinking fountains, and puzzled, yet again, over the traditional layout of palace guard rotations, Hephestion had led an excursion down to the lake, solely in the hope that it might impress Lirien. Then he insisted the lot of them take lunch together in the courtyard, in an absolutely transparent ploy to foist Jocelyn off on Adora after the meal. Worse, when Rhia had come from the city in search of her, Adora had made the mistake of asking her to join them. For whatever reason, Lirien seemed determined to put Rhia between herself and Hephestion whenever possible, which only served to make him annoyed and Rhia miserable.

"The lake really is beautiful," Lirien said, determinedly ignoring the sour mood of every other person at the table. "I grew up with an ocean, so I thought I wouldn't be very impressed, but it's lovely every time I see it." She looked around at the rest of them. "I've heard that most residents of Eldren Cael cannot swim. Is that true?"

"Not as much as is famed," Hephestion said. "It's just that the lake is the only body of water anywhere nearby that's deep enough to swim in, and we aren't allowed to. But I often visited my uncle at Shallowsend as a boy, so I can proudly say I can swim quite well. I suppose you must have, too, with your ocean right there?"

"I am the best swimmer I know," Lirien said, so calmly it didn't even seem like a boast.

Feste laughed. "So confident! I'd certainly be glad to race you, if you like."

"There is a great difference between rivers and the sea, my lord," she said.

Adora couldn't swim at all until recently—although she and Landon had explored far and wide together, their journeys had never called upon them to cross water by any other method than a bridge. But the moment Rhia had learned how uncommon swimming was among urban Issamiri, she had all but begged Adora to let her teach her. *If swimming is not common in this area, that is all the more reason Your Grace should learn,* she had said. *If some assailant should push you into a river or lake, you must be able to save yourself.* "I know how," she told Lirien, "but I confess I don't do it often. As Feste said, it is not possible here."

"It would be possible if we went to Shallowsend," Hephestion said. "Uncle's not often there these days, but he'd let me use the castle anyway. It's practically on the riverbank."

Adora could hardly think of a more disastrous proposal. He'd clearly intended the invitation for Lirien alone, and without Adora or their mother there, he would be free to act on every single inadvisable, impulsive, lust-soaked idea that flitted into his head. He might as easily marry Lirien as promise her the moon.

She did not know what Lirien herself thought of the plan; her face was wreathed in a gentle smile, and for once her brilliant eyes gave no clues. "I'm sure that such a journey is hardly necessary, my lord. It is one thing to be your guest here, but to be the entire reason we visited your uncle . . . it is more attention than I am comfortable with." A sensible reply, if she meant it.

"Nonsense," Hephestion said, predictably. "It's no trouble at all—"

"It would be trouble, Feste, for almost everyone concerned," Adora interrupted. "For Uncle, for Mother, for me, and even for Lirien herself. You may not be the king, but you are my heir, and it is not seemly for my heir to frolic about chasing his own pleasure at such a momentous time."

Feste scowled. "Well, that's a change, isn't it? When I want to help, I'm ushered away like a child, but when I want to chase my own ends, I'm suddenly indispensable."

"That's hardly true," Adora said quietly, when what she really wanted was to shout at him for such a poor showing in the midst of company. "I have never wished to burden you with duties. I well know your generosity and openheartedness, and have always wished you to display those qualities in their best light. But what you propose now is selfish, and I believe you know it."

She felt the tension between them stretched taut, and the misery on Rhia's face proved she felt it, too. But Lirien said cheerfully, "If it was only for the sake of a little swimming contest, my lord, then I hope you'll set your mind at ease about it. In the absence of any actual race, you're free to think what you like about your own abilities and mine, which, I assure you, is a far pleasanter outcome than you might have had. But if you're so eager to prove yourself competitively, we have a beautiful city at our fingertips, and a splendid palace all around us. Surely you can think of something that doesn't require us to travel to Shallowsend?"

"I . . . don't know that you and I have many other abilities in common," Feste said, distracted for the moment. "I'm told I sing well, though you'll never see me awarded the cloves and cinnamon."

A pound of cloves and a pound of cinnamon were the highest traditional reward any Issamiri noble house could offer a bard of uncommon distinction, but Adora doubted Lirien knew it. She hid her confusion well, though, and merely said, "I can whistle gamely, my lord, but I cannot sing, though I've loved music since I was small. It has been one of the great pleasures of travel, to hear so many different songs."

"Then I have been remiss in not having more played for you," Feste said, "but we can hardly use that for a competition. Are you fond of games of chance?"

She smiled. "I have almost no coin to speak of, my lord, and it would not be very ladylike to bet anything else."

He rubbed at his face. "Well, the only other thing I'm much for is swordplay."

"Oh, are you?" she asked. "I've never so much as owned a sword, but perhaps you might show me your skills anyway? I saw your captain's when we met, and can vouch that she is more than she appears, but—"

Feste leaped to his feet. "A fine idea! A good spar is just what we need to get our blood up after such an indolent afternoon. Come on, Rhia, what do you say?"

Rhia looked as if she would rather choke down sand. "My lord, you wish for me to fight you?"

"Not a *fight,* we'll just use practice swords. Wood only, no sharp edges to speak of. It's been ages since we've had a decent spar—you know it as well as I do."

It *had* been ages, because there was absolutely no point to any contest of arms between those two. Rhia shook her head fiercely. "My lord, my job is to protect you, not to cause you harm. Even in jest, I don't think it would be wise to stage such a contest."

"Can there truly be such danger in it?" Lirien asked innocently. "I thought sparring with wooden swords was customary. Surely those weapons would not be used if serious accidents were common?"

Rhia flushed, though Adora could not tell if it was from anger or embarrassment. "You don't seem to have much familiarity with the practice, so perhaps you should not be so eager to urge it forward. Swordsmanship is not a game, and I am . . . uncomfortable when it is made to feel so. Training is one thing, but I would not fight for pride any more than for money."

Adora didn't like the sudden look of calculation in Hephestion's eyes. "I've hit upon it," he said. "You and I, Rhia, have no reason to fight on our own. But I *do* have a quarrel with my sister."

Adora knew her brother too well not to immediately see where this was going. "This Shallowsend business, I assume?"

"Precisely. We cannot agree as to the merits of such a journey. Now, if you were Landon"—a carefully unkind barb, and beneath him—"we could simply have it out between us. But there is no honor in challenging someone who never learned the sword. So let me challenge your champion instead."

"If I were Landon," Adora said, as composed as she could be, "we would still not hold such a duel, because he would find this as unseemly and embarrassing as I do."

He scowled. "Well, you know the fastest way to silence me about it. Do you take issue with Rhia's skills? I'll let you pick any member of your guard that you prefer."

No, Rhia would be the best choice for this. She would die before she threw a match, even against a prince of the realm. It was a concession Adora didn't wish to make, but it *would* be the quickest way to silence him. She could not imagine that Rhia would lose, and then Feste would have only himself to blame.

She tightened her jaw, and met her brother's eyes. "If you are so set upon this, then let it be as you wish. But if you lose, I wish the right to extract my own favor from you."

"What sort of favor?" he asked warily.

"I haven't decided yet," Adora admitted. "But it won't be cruel or unreasonable— surely you know me better than that."

He thought about it another moment, then nodded. "I accept those terms."

She sighed. "Then let us call for the guards."

Poor Rhia stood there biting her lip, twisting herself about as if she could catch sight of some way to get out of this. It wasn't that Adora didn't feel sorry for her; Rhia certainly didn't deserve to be caught in the middle of their quarrel. But Feste wouldn't blame her for acting as his opponent, or why would he have suggested her himself?

Still, she had to ask. "Rhia, will you agree to this duel in my stead?"

Rhia looked down. "If Your Grace commands it, then I must."

That was hardly enthusiastic consent, but Adora would take what she could get. "And so I do."

Rhia nodded, and unbuckled her sword belt, placing it almost tenderly to one side of the courtyard, far out of the way of what would become the dueling ground. And out of the corner of her eye, Adora saw Lirien slide a hand across her mouth, just a bit too slowly to hide the smile that had crossed her face.

The group of soldiers who brought the sparring swords and helped draw the circle lingered, and Adora didn't command them to disperse; let them see the out-come of the match, if they wished. She still couldn't believe Feste looked so confi-dent, until Jocelyn leaned over to her and whispered, "I wonder how this one will turn out, Your Grace."

Adora stared at her. "Can you possibly think the outcome in doubt?"

"If they used live steel," Jocelyn said, biting down with relish on one of the pre-cious few almonds remaining in the bowl, "I would have a clear favorite to wager on. But your captain loves that northern sword of hers, which comes with its own set of movements. There is no way for her to approximate such movements with one of our wooden practice swords—the shape is completely different."

Gods, she was right. No doubt the same thing had occurred to Hephestion; small wonder he believed he had a chance.

Sure enough, from the moment Rhia and Hephestion first faced each other, you could see the awkwardness in the way Rhia held the wooden sword. Adora held her breath before proceeding, hoping she hadn't made a grave mistake in agreeing to this duel in the first place. But when she asked both combatants if they were ready, Rhia's nod was as firm and confident as Feste's, and Adora decided to trust in her. "Begin."

Adora knew Hephestion was a talented swordsman, and would never have begrudged him that praise. But Rhia fought as if it came as naturally to her as breathing—as if she were just letting her sword do what it wanted to do. In anyone else, that lack of discipline would have spelled disaster, but Rhia was like some minstrel who, carried away by music in the midst of a song she knew by heart, would stray entirely from the sequence of prescribed notes and create something new and wondrous on the spot. It was only after watching her for some time that Adora had begun to catch those movements she must have practiced endlessly—the initial draw-and-downstroke of the *tsunshin* from its sheath, or the way her arm snapped out, just now, to block Feste's lunge at her shoulder—but so many others seemed the inspiration of the instant: the way she stepped to the side and wrapped her free hand around the hilt, angling the sword on a diagonal as she moved in to block again, would have produced an entirely different result if she had done it with the curved blade of a *tsunshin,* yet she seemed to have predicted it exactly. She wasn't as aggressive offensively as Adora was used to seeing her, and perhaps that was her only concession to the unfamiliar weapon.

Her brother was using his superior strength as best he could, trying to put enough of his weight behind his swings to bear down on Rhia and keep her on the defensive. He finally caught her off balance; she stumbled, and though she didn't go down, the knee of one leg bent almost to the ground. When she tried to push back up off that foot, she found the heavy weight of another of Feste's swings above her.

Rhia snapped the leg she couldn't lift out sideways in a kick that probably couldn't have pushed Feste off balance, but that startled him back just far enough to let her maneuver out from beneath his sword. The diversion clearly irritated him—he must've thought he had her—and his next swing was intemperate, easily blocked with that reflex-quick movement of her arm. Her next strike was too fast for him, and fell hard upon his shoulder with an unmistakable *thwack*.

"There," Rhia said, struggling slightly for breath. "If this had been a real sword, you'd be—"

The rest of her sentence was cut off when their swords collided again. "My lord," she said, "this is not very sporting of you."

"Nonsense!" he insisted. "It's not over until one of us lands a fatal blow. It's common dueling procedure."

That wasn't exactly a lie; the rules were variable, and Adora ought to have settled them with her brother before the match began; now he was free to claim he had believed they were whatever he wished, and she could not gainsay him. When Rhia risked a glance at her to confirm Hephestion's words, all she could do was shrug helplessly.

"Something of a mistake there, Your Grace," Jocelyn said cheerfully.

"Quite," Adora muttered.

Knowing now that she couldn't hope to stop Feste just by successfully striking him with the sword, Rhia became more cautious, saving her strength for the moment when he would truly leave himself open. Feste, on the other hand, increased in recklessness, sometimes batting away her strikes with his shoulder or the side of his arm when he was too slow to meet the block with his sword, heedless of the bruises he'd no doubt have tomorrow. It was irritating Rhia, Adora could tell; this wasn't the honorable way to approach a duel, and she must have felt that she was being used.

Then Hephestion let her next strike sweep along the length of his arm as he stepped forward, trying to pull the sword from her hand. That couldn't possibly have been an acceptable dueling tactic, but before Adora could say anything, Rhia moved with merciless speed, striking the back of Hephestion's sword hand with all her strength.

Had the sword fallen wrongly, she could have broken his fingers, but Rhia had doubtless judged that the time for civility was over. Hephestion's face said he knew what was happening but was powerless to stop it: he could neither hold back his yelp of pain nor keep his battered fingers from opening, letting his sword fall to the ground.

Rhia did not hesitate, but stepped up and pointed her sword straight out, the tip an inch from his throat. "This must surely be the match, my lord."

Feste hesitated for barely a moment before he lunged. He would have used the opening to grab for her sword, but her arm flailed—it must have been instinct—and the sword caught him on the side of the head. Rhia pulled up short in panic, Feste shouted as he prepared to charge again—

And Adora got to her feet, because that was more than enough. "*Hephestion.* Your duel is concluded. Stand down."

He stopped in place, but gazed at her mockingly, brushing his sweat-dampened hair out of his eyes. "Oh, what, is that an order?"

"Does it need to be?" she asked, praying he would leave it there, that he would just leave all of this and go back to his accustomed self.

They stood there in silence, a tangled web of emotions between them. Feste was defiantly abashed; like a gambler who cannot keep from throwing good money after bad, he must have known that each maneuver only added to his shame. Rhia, as ever, was most preoccupied with the fear that she might have done something wrong, and guilt kept her from meeting anyone's eyes. And Adora felt angry, and sick of all this, and ashamed that she had not been able to stop any of it from taking place. Father, Landon—either one would have been able to sweep all this aside with a wave of his hand, without letting any of it stain him. But Adora did not know how to do that without resorting to draconian commands—the tyrant's way, was it not? How to deal with such obstinacy while still remaining as compassionate and gentle as she believed a queen should be?

Finally, Feste laughed—a strange laugh, full of so much bitterness, such a rare thing coming from him. "With me you want to be the queen, sister. Only with me." He took several strides away from his fallen sword, leaving it on the ground where he had dropped it, and opened his hands wide. "Well, never let it be said that I, of all people, do not know how to concede a defeat."

He spared one last glance for the table, where Lirien avoided his gaze and Jocelyn met everyone's with exuberant smugness. Then he turned to stalk away, and Adora decided to let him: some time apart might be what they all needed just now. Rhia turned the other way, looking to Adora with a question in her eyes. But then her face changed, and she broke into a run.

Adora didn't have time to understand. When she looked around, all she could make out was a body in motion before Rhia stepped between them, and there was the dull sound of an impact, something striking wood. Then she saw what had happened, and drew back in shock: one of the guards who had stood by and watched during the duel was standing in front of Rhia, furious determination on his face. He had drawn his sword, and Rhia had lifted her wooden one to meet it, and the two blades were locked together, mere feet from where Adora stood. The strike had been meant not for Rhia but for her.

Rhia had just fought a hard duel with an unaccustomed weapon, and she was breathing hard, covered in sweat already; her arms trembled as she tried to hold the sword steady. She had met the guard's stroke as solidly as any of Hephestion's, but this was live steel; it had buried itself in the wooden sword, nearly cleaving through it.

Though Adora knew Rhia's strength well, that body had never seemed so small and vulnerable before, those shaking arms the only thing keeping that deadly steel away from their flesh. Rhia gritted her teeth, trying to plant her feet firmly, but then the guard swung again, and this time he cut the practice sword in half. She knew him, Adora realized; it was the man whose position on the wall she had altered not so long ago. She recognized the fact, but did not know what to do with it; could what had happened then possibly have anything to do with what was happening now?

Then, of all people, Lirien got to her feet, pulling the cloth from the table with a loud crash that made Jocelyn pull back in shock. But before she could do whatever she meant to do with it, the guard lashed out with an elbow, striking Lirien hard in the center of the chest. She went sprawling, with a strangled gasp as all the air went out of her, and the guard turned back to Rhia and Adora. Rhia had only a stubby piece of the broken sword, but still she set her stance with the same determination.

Through the white haze of her panic, Adora cast about frantically for what she could do. The table and whatever harmlessly diverting objects lay around it were too far away to reach, she couldn't throw herself at him without going through Rhia, there were no weapons nearby, and even if there were—

Her thoughts were shattered by a loud crack, and their assailant staggered; it was only when Feste repeated the motion a second time that Adora realized he'd picked up his own sparring sword and brought it down against the back of the guard's skull. "What the hell are you doing?" he shouted. "Put that sword up! Get away from my sister!"

Despite his battering, the man moved forward again, and Hephestion swung the practice sword at him a third time, so fiercely that it broke upon impact—as did the guard's cheekbone, Adora suspected. He barely kept his footing, and this time his face changed, as if his view of the situation had somehow altered. He adjusted his grip on his sword, angling it inward instead of outward.

"No!" Adora, Rhia, and Feste all shouted at once, but they were too late. Almost casually, the guard swung the blade of his sword up and passed it across his throat, blood spattering Hephestion's clothes as his corpse fell forward.

For several moments they all stood there, stunned. Hephestion moved first, stepping closer to Adora's side. His expression was tentative, regretful, concerned. "Sister. Are you hurt?"

"I'm fine," Adora said, though that was only true of her physical state. She looked around, but there was no one else to take guidance from. It was for her to decide what must happen next. "Rhia," she said first. "Please help Lirien to a healer—and with whatever else she may require. After that, you are to rest, whether or not you believe it necessary." Neither Lirien nor Rhia objected, and as they were leaving, Adora turned to the rest of the guard. "If any of you know anything about this man that you think relevant, I ask that you tell me. If there is some grievance against me among your ranks, I should like to think we can resolve it with less drastic measures than an assassination."

"That's just it, Your Grace!" someone burst out, unable to contain herself any longer, and Adora recognized the dead guard's young partner. "I know he was rude to you on the wall before, and he grumbled about it after, that I admit. But after three days doing it your way, he relented—he told me it was better, and that you had a good head for these things. So I can't believe it was pettiness, Your Grace. I don't know what it *could* be, but it wasn't that."

Well, there went the only tenuous motive she could have ascribed to his actions. "You didn't notice anything unusual about his behavior?"

The young woman shook her head. "Nothing, Your Grace. I was the one who convinced him to come out here at all. I thought it would be grand to see the duel, but it took some persuading to get him to abandon his lunch to come with me. He seemed just the same as any other day—even right up until he charged Your Grace, I never would have said that he could do it."

Adora looked to Hephestion, only to find her confusion mirrored on his face. Jocelyn, too, was drawn and serious, almost weary, with not a trace of playfulness about her. "I think you and Jocelyn should withdraw to someplace more secure," her brother said at last, turning to the guards that remained. "I'll get this business sorted as best I can, shall I? But don't go too long without me or Rhia at your side. It's a damnable business to be stingy with your trust, but we have no choice now, do we?"

LIRIEN HAD MADE half-hearted protests about seeing a healer, and the verdict had borne her out: she had no injuries to speak of, not even any visible bruising as yet. But she did not protest Rhia's escorting her back to her chambers, though she did not seem thankful for it, either. After such a trying, terrifying situation, it was Rhia's instinct to huddle close to other people, to remind herself that she and they were alive. But Lirien seemed to have withdrawn inside herself, as if she were a city that had barred its gates. Her face was expressionless, and she looked straight ahead without seeming to focus on anything in particular. Her hands hung slack at her sides.

Rhia wanted to say something, even if it was useless. "I'm . . . sorry you were involved in all that."

"It's not your fault," Lirien said—not kindly, not irritably, just as if stating a fact that should have been obvious.

"Were you frightened?"

"No."

"Are you still hurting?"

"No." She pressed a hand to the place where the guard had struck her, as if she'd forgotten about it.

"I was frightened," Rhia admitted. "I should never have left my sword so far away. Thank the gods the prince was there. If it had only been me, I . . . I don't think I could have protected the queen."

"You did all you could have done, given the circumstances," Lirien said. "Some things are beyond anyone's strength. There's no point in berating yourself about it."

Rhia shook her head. "It's my job to keep Her Grace from harm."

"Then perhaps you should reexamine your ability to perform that job." The words hung heavy in the air between them, but Lirien did not look shocked or abashed; she had not spoken impulsively. "Sorry," she said, after some moments of silence, but she did not sound sorry; she sounded flat, matter-of-fact. "Do you think that a cruel thing to say?"

"I know cruelty was not your intent," Rhia said. "I know you are only being honest."

"Honesty can cut, just like any blade," Lirien said. "I'm aware of that."

"Yet if you would risk wounding me with it, you must have your reasons."

"I'm trying to understand something," Lirien said. "You've played the part of a servant decently well so far. But your life's ambition is not to be a servant, is it? Not even to a queen, however much honor there might be in it?"

"You're right," Rhia admitted. "Though I am grateful for the position, I never wished to be a captain. There are times when I have felt caged by it. I *believe* in what the queen is trying to do, in a way I never thought to believe in a ruler. More than that, she and her brother helped me when I had nothing, and now they are in danger. If I left them now . . . it would not be right. But perhaps there will come a day when things will be different. Perhaps then I might—" She stopped. Lirien was sweating again, but as if from illness rather than heat; there was an unnatural brightness to her eye, a pallor to her skin. "Are you feeling unwell?"

"I'll be all right. I just . . . what I meant to say . . ." She mopped at her forehead, brushing the hair away from it. "I feel . . . that we are similar. Do you not feel the same?"

Rhia wished she could say yes, but it would not be the truth. "On the contrary, I've always felt that you and I are very different." She hastened to add, "I don't mean that as an insult. I wish that I could be more like you."

Lirien smiled bitterly. "You would not say that if you knew me better." She took a deep breath, resting her forehead on her fingertips. "Will you answer me one question? It's very important."

"Of course," Rhia said.

Lirien lifted her head, and met Rhia's eyes. "If I were to tell your prince that I wish to leave his castle, and never to see him more so long as I live, would this be permitted to me?"

Rhia was shocked by the question. "Wh—but—of course he would. I know he must have shown himself poorly today, but he is hardly such a villain as to keep you here against your will."

Lirien smiled with an archness that was harder and sharper than mere mischief. "You have not properly listened to the question, Captain. I told you it was important, so, if you would, please make sure you understand me clearly. If I wished to remove myself from Prince Hephestion's presence forever, would he permit the granting of that wish at the moment it was made? Would I not be beseeched to change my mind? Would I be subjected to no bargaining, no protestations of his feelings or his hopes? Would he believe my own feelings are immutable, and truly never seek to find me again?"

Rhia bit her lip. "He might be more dismayed or more . . . reluctant than you would like," she said haltingly, "but never to the point of anything wicked. He is a kind person—a good person. I am utterly sure of that."

Lirien sighed. "Unlike you heroic types, I am not in the business of deciding whether people are good or bad—merely of deciding what *I* were best to do, in order to achieve the results I desire. Do you think I am a beautiful woman, Captain?"

She clearly was not fishing for compliments, so Rhia tried to answer in the same tone. "I do."

"I do as well—in fact, I am certain of it. It may seem arrogant to declare such a thing, but it is actually quite necessary to my survival. Had I remained in Sundercliff, I could very well have remained ignorant that I was a beautiful woman—the rest of them would have greatly preferred it, to be sure. And were I rich or powerful, I could likewise adopt a modesty others would find charming. But I am a beautiful woman with no money, no position, no people, no one to speak for me or intervene on my behalf. And this means it is crucial, at all times and in all places, for me to know and remember that I am a beautiful woman. Do you understand my meaning?"

Rhia swallowed hard. "I do," she said again.

Lirien's face softened. "That's why I said we were alike, you know. People look at you, too, and see something they wish to possess—not beauty but ability, a rare talent for the weapon you have chosen. So you, like me, must understand what that means for you. You must not allow others to take from you until you have nothing left."

They had reached her door long ago, but she had made no move to enter until this moment, putting one hand out to turn the knob. "Do you think I am hopelessly foolish?" Rhia asked. She had not meant to, but she didn't want to leave things that way, as if Lirien had decided she was beyond saving.

Lirien smiled, and this one wasn't sharp at all, only full of melancholy. "I think, Rhia, that if more people were fools after your fashion, this world would be a much more beautiful place."

CHAPTER TWENTY-SIX

Issamira

AFTER HEARING PRINCE Hephestion's description of Raventower, Morgan had been expecting to see a huge fortress. But the castle she and Braddock came to was modest in size, a simple square of stone walls around the eponymous tower. It was only that tower that was truly impressive: tall and dark, it reminded Morgan of a needle, jutting starkly up from the earth and casting its long, thin shadow over them. It was easy to imagine some imperial general looking out of its topmost window in centuries gone by, preparing to subdue the Issamiri people yet again.

Despite their best attempts, they had arrived without Nasser; he had refused Hephestion's offer, claiming he had business back in the west that could not be put off any longer. It must have been a matter of truly great import for him to ignore so much gold, but he would not even tell Braddock what it was, so they had been forced to let him go.

The prince had given them a letter explaining the reason for their presence here; the soldier at the gate read it over without complaint and ushered them inside, only relief crossing his face. "Captain Feyder'll be mighty pleased to get these. She's been fretting over them for days."

Captain Feyder turned out to be a broad-shouldered, well-muscled woman of about thirty-five, who looked over the writs with a practiced air. "Aye, that's what Her Grace promised. Very good. I'll have the other half of your payment drawn off as soon as I sign these, when I send the first batch of requisitions down."

"Much obliged," Morgan said. The captain nodded, but didn't speak again, engaged in signing each sheet of parchment, occasionally making a stray mark or two in addition.

Braddock had strolled over to the window; the captain's office was only about halfway up the tower, but it still provided an impressive view. "You been stationed here long?"

"Five years," the captain said, with a slight laugh. "I've gotten used to it."

"What's up above us?"

"Archives, mostly—surprising amount for a fortress that was always intended for military function. I guess one of the old generals had a fondness for research." She cast her eyes up at the ceiling. "And the top floors are the primary officer's quarters, though I don't spend much time there. Not a viewpoint I really want to share."

"Don't blame you for that," Braddock said. "I suppose you don't see that much fighting here anymore?"

"We don't, thank the gods. Up until a few years ago, we had to be prepared to march north across the border at a moment's notice—King Jotun and the former marquis of Esthrades hated each other, and the king wanted to be prepared in case Caius ever tried to bite at the border the way he did with Lanvaldis in the north. But it never happened, and after the marquis died the order relaxed."

Braddock seemed intrigued by that. "I'd heard Caius's daughter was the more fearsome of the two."

Captain Feyder shrugged. "I've heard the same, but Queen Adora—"

She broke off when one of her subordinates burst into the room, glancing over his shoulder every so often as he spoke. "Er, Captain, I've been sent up from the yard—it's, ah, Lord Hahrenraith. Lord Hahrenraith is here."

The captain rolled her eyes. "So see to him. Extend our hospitality. I'm busy here, and he has no jurisdiction at Raventower."

"But Captain, he asked to see you specifically—"

"That can't be necessary. Tell his lordship that I cannot possibly be spared, as I am in the midst of—"

"In the midst of giving other guests a much warmer welcome, I see," came a smooth voice, and Feyder's young subordinate nearly jumped out of his skin. The man who'd come up behind him was approaching fifty, though there was surprisingly little gray in his black hair and small pointed beard. In his youth he must have been very handsome indeed, but enough of that beauty still remained that he could hardly complain. His eyes were light brown, a familiar warmth in their depths tempered by a glittering keenness. "I'm wounded, Captain."

Unlike the other soldier, Captain Feyder did not seem intimidated, merely put upon. "My lord, these guests have legitimate—"

The man made a pained noise, as if she'd struck him. "Captain, please! What have I ever done to you? The other title, if you care for my pride at all."

The captain curled her fingers around the edge of the table. "My lord, you retired from the generalship years ago. That title is no longer appropriate."

"Bah, nonsense! A man forged by war can never truly retire from it. Or a woman, either, I suspect. You'll learn that well enough if they ever try to force *you* out of service—which I don't see you very eager to leave, by the way."

The captain smiled. "Perhaps if *I* had my own castle to return to, I'd be more amenable to the idea."

The lord barked out a laugh. "The damn castle is the problem! It's the only reason Maribel was able to convince Jotun to force me out."

"I'm grieving for you, my lord." He gave her such a wounded look that she sighed. "All right. I'm grieving for you, *sir*."

"Thank you, Captain. You're a noble soul." As she rolled her eyes, he passed his own over Morgan and Braddock. "Ah! But I must beg your pardons. Guests of the captain's, I believe? I hope I didn't inconvenience you."

"It's no trouble, my—ah, sir," Morgan said, before Braddock could volunteer anything less tactful. "I'm afraid we were the ones taking up the captain's time with idle chatter before you arrived."

"Oh, she's well used to idle chatter; I make sure to visit her as often as I can." He swept them a low bow. "Vespas Hahrenraith, sometime general of the Issamiri army and currently the extremely reluctant lord of Shallowsend."

Morgan did not know his name or his castle's, but that meant nothing; her knowledge of Issamiri aristocracy was far from comprehensive. "Morgan Imrick, sir, sometime tavern keeper back in Hallarnon. This is Braddock, my . . . companion." Braddock inclined his head, but seemed content to leave the talking to her. Good.

Lord Vespas's eyes lit up. "Hallarnon? Not many travel to Raventower from over that way. What brings you so far from home, Miss Imrick?"

"Morgan, please," she said, "and we only sought to be simple travelers at first, until fate crossed our path with a prince of the realm. He paid us to make a delivery for him, and so we went east."

"A prince? You mean Hephestion?" Lord Vespas laughed. "How like the boy to drag bystanders into his affairs! I pray you will forgive him any imposition."

"Oh, no," Morgan said, embarrassed, "truly I think he mostly sought to help us on our way, sir. The pay he offered was . . . too generous."

His lordship's eyes were warm—and, Morgan noticed, oddly like the prince's. "That is like him, too. He has always been kind, if sometimes clumsy at it."

"Do you know him well, sir?" Morgan asked.

"I should say so! The boy happens to be my nephew." Morgan must have started, for he held up a hand. "Forgive me, I should have mentioned it earlier. It is how I came to inherit Shallowsend in the first place."

"I'm not sure I follow you," Morgan said.

"Ah, of course—you Hallerns have not had proper nobles for many a day and year. I cannot speak to every nation—though my young niece no doubt could—but in Issamira even one of noble blood may not hold two separate titles at once. To prevent succession squabbles, I suppose. My sister, Maribel, grew up the heir to Shallowsend, but she was required to give up that title in order to wed Jotun Avestri and become queen. It was a fine deal for *her,* of course, and our parents were doubly thrilled: their daughter would give them royal grandchildren, and their son, whom they previously feared doomed to a life of itinerant fighting and carousing, would now become the lord of their own castle one day. Alas, the son himself had been rather looking forward to the itinerant fighting and carousing, and has not a single blessed idea of what to do with a castle. My steward has only to say the word *linens* and my mind positively *recoils*." He caught himself, with a sheepish laugh. "Forgive me, I must sound a proper ass about this. I would've been only too delighted to give up my claim to the place and let Jotun or his heirs bestow it on some deserving servant of the crown, but Maribel would skin me alive. She never cared to serve in the army, but I promise she is the more dangerous of the two of us. She can make a man's soul depart his body with a single well-placed glare. I usually require a sword to produce the same effect."

Captain Feyder shook her head. "He's dangerous enough, though he doesn't look it. He rode with King Jotun himself, fought at his side, and won fame second only to the king's."

"And then was forced out of the army because my sister felt it was keeping me from my lordly responsibilities." He paced to the window and looked north over the horizon, to where the Gods' Curse lay. "I am seen as a meddler, in a time of supposed peace," he said slowly. "But this is no true peace. Lantistyne is as out of sorts as ever it was, and the problem has long passed from the realm of peaceful correction." He looked at Morgan. "Have you spent much time in Valyanrend, Miss Imrick?"

If he was going to keep calling her that, it was doubtless intentional, and Morgan did not correct him again. She said only, "I live there."

"Ah. And you are still young—can you possibly remember much of when Gerde Selte reigned?"

"I do," Morgan said. "Or at least, I remember what it was like in my part of the city. I never met Gerde Selte, or knew anyone who had. There was certainly a fear laid over everything, in the back of people's minds. It was only too clear that our ruler needed no reason for even the most violent actions, beyond her own amusement. But we were so low . . . I don't think any of us truly believed, deep down, that we'd ever be important enough to gain her notice. So we just went about our lives as best we could, as we would have if she hadn't been sitting up there in the Citadel burning and leeching and strangling people. That's what I remember, anyway. Does that answer your question?"

"And more," Lord Vespas said. "You have my thanks, and my apologies. But here, in this country, I think we regarded Gerde Selte as some sort of demon. As you say, she needed no reason for bloodshed, and she had destroyed all her political rivals with a cunning and ingenuity that were even more impressive in someone as demented as she was. Hallarnon's army was strong, and she seemed to know how to lead it. Jotun was a young king then, in age as well as experience; his mother had only recently died. He knew he had to fight her off, and he offered me a position at his side more because I was his wife's brother than for any other reason. We had no idea whether we were going to win. We didn't dare think about it. We just focused on what we had to do in the moment, and then what we had to do next, until suddenly we found we had not just won the war, we had beaten her back behind her borders so soundly she would never try to bloody us again." He shook his head, but Morgan caught him smiling slightly, as if at a fond memory. "My countrymen look at your Imperator Elgar now, and they see no demon, just an ordinary man. And why would you fear a mere man, when you have fought a demon and emerged victorious? But they are mistaken. Gerde Selte never succeeded in conquering another sovereign state. Elgar has conquered two, and is about to make it three." He looked back at Captain Feyder. "And so you see, Captain, the truth is that matters are far more dire today than they were when I was young."

"Your brilliance in that war is well-known, sir," the captain said. "But even Gerde Selte didn't exhaust her armies attacking every other country in Lantistyne first, the way Elgar is doing. If he does finally turn his gaze here, what shape will his army be in?"

"That won't matter to him," Lord Vespas said. He asked Morgan, with a grim smile, "Will it, Miss Imrick?"

She stiffened. "I don't know him personally, sir."

"I didn't mean to imply you did. But you must know more *of* him than the captain here, surely?"

Morgan had certainly spent some time in the man's dungeons, but his lordship didn't need to know that. "He seems to be a determined man, sir. He will have what he wants, and cares little for the means used to obtain it." He was willing to use Lucius and Deinol to retrieve that artifact for him, after all, even though that hadn't worked out very well for him.

"As I said," Lord Vespas told the captain.

She shrugged. "Reality is reality, sir, and cannot be changed by a man's outlook or opinions. If Elgar won't care that his army is ragged when he sends it against ours, I hope he won't care when he loses, either."

"Even Gerde Selte cared about that, and she was far madder than he is. No, Captain. He has a plan." He chuckled softly. "I know what you think of me. I'm the man who's only got a hammer, and all I can do is swing away. But I am no bloodthirsty warmonger. I know how to use a sword, yes, and I am proud of my skill. But I would gladly hang it up forever, leave it to gather dust on some wall, if I only knew the country I love would be safe without it."

"If it should ever not be safe," the captain said, "you know my sword would be first alongside yours, sir. But it is no virtue in a soldier to fight when she is not called, and it is only your niece who can call me."

"Indeed." Vespas sighed. "Poor Adora. If only Jotun had lived a few more years, he could have taken care of this for her, and left her to be a queen of peace. She was born for that."

"I thought she was born second," Braddock muttered, and Morgan resisted the urge to elbow him in the ribs.

But Vespas Hahrenraith did not look offended. "She was born to do great things," he said, "and against that destiny, birth order matters little. Fate has certainly worked things out in her favor, or else . . . *someone* has." He tapped his fingers against his thigh. "Captain. You are under no obligation to tell me, of course, but . . . Esthrades remains quiet? Even through this turmoil in Reglay?"

"Esthrades remains a ways away from Raventower," she said, "but from what I have heard, and what I can say to civilians, no large-scale conflicts have taken place there yet. There was a rumor some time ago that Elgar had sent men to try to take the marquise captive in her own castle, but I haven't been able to confirm it; it's possible the attempt never actually occurred, or was only poorly conceived from the start."

"It would be like Elgar to try to get at her through such roundabout means," Lord Vespas said. "I never had cause to meet that girl, but Jotun always said she was brilliant, and now Adora says the same. And even if not . . . it certainly would keep him from exhausting his armies. Which brings me to my next question." He addressed himself to Morgan and Braddock—still smiling, not visibly tense, and yet she could tell he was readying himself for something. "What, precisely, are the two of you doing here?"

"Delivering a message, and supposedly getting quite a bit of coin in exchange," Braddock said. "Pretty sure we mentioned that."

"Of course, but that's not what I meant. That's why you're at *Raventower,* but it doesn't explain what you were doing in Issamira when you first encountered my nephew. Who is, unfortunately, much kinder than he is sharp, even if that is unkind of an uncle to say."

Morgan exchanged a glance with Braddock, and then looked at Captain Feyder. "As he says, we aren't familiar with nobility. What obligation are we under to answer his questions?"

"None," the captain said, with a brevity that surprised even Morgan.

Lord Vespas sighed. "I suppose that means I can't get you to ask them for me, can I?"

"Sir," she said, "consider my position. I have indulged you many times, out of respect for your former rank and service. But to accuse these people of—"

"My gods, I'm not accusing them," he said. "It's far too premature for that. I simply asked why they were here."

"We were here because a friend asked us to be here," Morgan said. "But more than that, I don't think he or I want to say."

"Didn't even want to say that much," Braddock muttered.

"And you intend to go back home to Valyanrend?"

She had said they lived there, hadn't she? Damn it. "Yes, of course."

"*When* do you intend to go back there?"

"I . . . don't know," Morgan said. "We might go now, if nothing happens that would make it . . . inconvenient."

"Such as?"

"I don't wish to say, sir."

He beamed at the captain. "You see? To *me,* all that sounds suspicious."

"So they're spies, are they? Who just happened to cross paths with your nephew?"

"Again, I didn't say that. But since you brought up the possibility . . ."

"They didn't break the seals on the writs."

"But I found them in conversation with you, and who knows how long they talked to Hephestion, or what they got out of him?"

"They didn't get anything not available to the public out of *me,*" the captain said. "I'm not an idiot."

"No, you're just more trusting than I am. And younger, which may not be coincidental."

"We don't have any evidence on which to hold them."

"Which doesn't mean we should simply let them leave before we have a chance to find out more."

"That's enough," Captain Feyder said, getting to her feet. "I don't want to have to do this to you, my lord, but you are no longer an officer. You are a private citizen at a military fortress, which means not only do I outrank you, you have no authority here whatsoever. You are not permitted to give orders to my men or anyone else, save your own retainers, and your retainers must yield to my soldiers. If you attempt to detain these people in flagrant disregard of these considerations, you leave me no choice but to clap the lot of you in irons and leave it to your niece to sort things out."

Lord Vespas smiled, unperturbed. That didn't make Morgan feel very confident about what was about to happen. "An excellent summation of our current position, Captain. I am glad we all know where we stand."

The captain glared at him suspiciously. "Does that mean you'll allow these people to leave?"

"As you say, Captain, I lack the authority to detain anyone in a military fortress. But I assume our guests will eventually decide to leave it, presumably to return home." He shrugged. "*Outside* of a military fortress, I remain one of the most prominent nobles in the country—not by my own choice, of course, but there you have it—and either the brother or uncle of the queen, depending on which queen you're talking about. If, outside of a military fortress, I were to find these people suspicious, it would not be at all odd or unusual for me to have my retainers detain them and bring them to Eldren Cael to await my niece's judgment. Now, I'll be the first to boast of Adora's kindness and sense of justice, so if these people are innocent, or even if there is no way to prove them guilty, I am certain she will insist on my sending them on their way. But it would still be . . . very inconvenient, yes? To be brought so far out of their way by people who will guard them very closely, and then to have to wait to be acquitted by a very busy monarch . . . who knows how much time they might waste?"

"All right," Morgan said, because he was obviously truly addressing her and Braddock, "let's hear the counteroffer, then."

He laughed. "I knew instantly that you were a woman of good sense, Miss Imrick. The counteroffer, as you so charmingly put it, is as follows: the two of you accompany me back to my seat at Shallowsend. I can point it out to you on a map if you would like to judge for yourself, but I can assure you it will not take you one single step away from the route you would take to return to Valyanrend anyway. You will be my guests, not my prisoners, and treated with all the respect that implies—and I will pay all the expenses of our travel myself. I will also, of course, not interfere with or confiscate the just reward you are about to receive from the captain. If, by the time we reach Shallowsend, I have failed to find any proof that you are spies, we will part ways, and you will be free to make the remainder of the journey to Valyanrend with my best wishes. And if you are not spies, I cannot possibly find any proof that you are, can I?"

"Famous last words," Morgan said grimly.

He bowed his head, accepting that. "Believe me, I know how hard it must be for you to trust me. But I have no desire to harm innocent people, and I am not so paranoid that I wish to see every shadow in chains. All I know of you now is that you are clever and perceptive, you hail from the city of Valyanrend, and you travel with a strong protector. There may very well be no more to it than that. But in these dangerous times, I would sleep better if I could be sure."

Morgan looked to Braddock, who nodded slightly—a sign that he would trust her decision. "So. Travel the way we would've gone anyway, only at reduced expense, so long as we endure your company? Is that right?"

"Indeed, though I flatter myself that my company is not something to be endured."

Morgan might have sounded nonchalant, but she didn't love either of her current options. The man clearly knew how to bargain, and on the face of it, his offer was a good one. But on the road with him, the captain would not be there to intercede, and there was no way she and Braddock would be able to fight their way through the sea of Lord Vespas's retainers alone, if it turned out they had to. On the other hand, while she didn't quite trust his lordship, she trusted the captain, and the captain clearly both knew him well and found it inconceivable that he would detain strangers on the road for any especially foul purpose.

She met Lord Vespas's eyes. "It's a deal, so long as we're clear about the benefits of being a guest; I expect to hold you to that. If I must travel with an aristocrat, I intend to travel *like* an aristocrat."

She was watching him closely for any sign of anger, but all he did was laugh. "I would have done that much anyway, but I'm happy to swear to it, if that will help convince you." To Braddock, he said, "And you, sir? Are we in agreement?"

"She told you," Braddock growled.

He grinned at the captain. "There, you see? We managed to avoid any dramatics or ugliness in your fortress, which is how I always prefer to go about things. I simply make it more difficult and annoying for people to *not* do what I want than it is for them to do what I want."

"I'll keep that in mind," Morgan said. "I'd be happy to learn the trick of it myself, I'll tell you that much."

CHAPTER TWENTY-SEVEN

Stonespire

"YOU MAY GO," Lady Margraine said. But then, as if reconsidering, she added, "Do you know anything of Zara's whereabouts?"

"She's still in the city," Gravis said. "I think she was setting bones today—fellow pitched off a roof and broke both his legs—but she said she'd be staying longer. More illness than she expected to see. She'll be brewing her medicines, administering them personally. After that's done, she may go out to the surrounding villages again, but for no longer than a few weeks before she returns, to judge the effects of her cures."

"Hm." Lady Margraine tapped a finger against her lips. "And none of that would have anything to do with an increased desire to keep an eye on me, would it?"

Gravis shrugged. "I have never had any talent for understanding that woman."

"Oh, she's easy to understand. It's getting her to listen that's the difficult part."

"And yet I don't think," Gravis ventured, "that in this case . . . that she was wrong to bring the matter of Eurig's actions before you."

"She wasn't, from her point of view," the marquise said.

"And what is your point of view?" Gravis asked.

She stood up, and Gravis thought she would walk down the steps before the throne and leave the great hall, ending the conversation there. The time for complainants to approach had passed, and she had been looking more worn out since her work with the stones began. But again she seemed to reconsider, and sat back down. "When any group of people unite in a common cause, they take on one another's weaknesses as well as one another's strengths," she said. "Eurig's weaknesses far outnumber his strengths, so I need him to remain part of his particular group as long as possible, to help bring down those members who are more cunning than he is." She twirled a lock of hair around her finger. "Just as I need Andrew Ryker to remain, to bring down those who are humbler and more cautious than he is."

"Well, they're both rentholders," Gravis said, "but I don't think that's the sort of group you mean."

"They're conspirators," she said, surprising him with the forthrightness of her answer. "I've been onto them for some time. They want to get rid of me, and believe a continent-wide upheaval is the perfect stage for it—that I'll be too busy with Elgar to deal with them. Of course, if they *did* overthrow me they'd be conquered by Elgar in the next instant, but this sort of person never thinks about such things. They see much less than someone like Zara—not even a single move ahead, just a vague idea of how much better they'd be at the game."

"Then . . . you know Lars Eurig and Andrew Ryker are guilty of treason, and you're just going to let them stay in their positions?"

"Until they slip up, and reveal the other members to me," the marquise said calmly. "Which they will undoubtedly do, given enough time."

Gravis frowned. "You rule this country. If anyone has a duty to uphold the law, it's you. To just let this continue, while you're certain of it—"

"And that kind of thinking is why you'll never be any good at this. If I pluck these two now, the rest will hide. I need to get them all at a stroke."

"Zara seems to think Eurig's hired swords will hurt more of his tenants if you wait."

"She did think that," the marquise said. "She happens to be mistaken."

"They *won't* hurt more of his tenants?"

"Indeed. *Those* hired swords won't, anyway. Seren had killed the lot of them before Zara ever got to Stonespire." She rested the back of her hand on the arm of the throne. "I do understand that having a set of principles, and keeping to them, is difficult. I understand that doing it takes strength—strength of character and will, not just strength of arms. But it doesn't necessarily follow that keeping to your principles is going to do anyone any good. It can even be worse, sometimes—it can make you overlook the most vital things. As my father did."

"Your father," Gravis repeated, a low growl in the back of his throat. "A man you know I admired, and to whom I owe much."

"A man whose failures outweighed his successes," she said, ever merciless. "My father wanted to be a just ruler, I do not dispute that. He believed that, as marquis, it was his responsibility to teach his people virtue. That was a mistake."

Gravis recoiled, as if she'd struck him. "How on earth could it be a mistake?"

"Take the stealing, for example. The act of theft ran counter to my father's conception of virtue, so he sought to curb it by executing thieves. How well would you say that worked, Gravis? Did it teach our people virtue?"

"You know it did not," Gravis said.

"Indeed. And why not?"

"Because they could not . . . it was not . . . a suitable deterrent. Even that, the greatest punishment he could offer, was not enough."

She sighed. "This is going to be harder than I'd thought. Let me assist you a bit. Why is it that people steal?"

Gravis scowled. "Because their desire for personal gain outweighs their desire to do good."

She sliced a hand through the air impatiently. "No. Useless. Try again, and this time act like you're actually trying to solve a problem, and not just looking for a way to reaffirm your own moral superiority. In every society, in every time, has there been precisely the same proportion of thieves to honest men? If people steal more often in some times and places than others, there must be a reason for it, right?"

Of course that followed, but Gravis could not figure out what she wanted him to say. In the end, he folded his arms and muttered, "I give up. Tell me the answer."

"The answer is that it's a stupid question. It's so ridiculously broad it cannot possibly be answered. People steal for as many reasons as they lie or cheat or fight or kill. That is one of the problems with principles, that they make you believe impossible questions have easy answers." She folded her hands in her lap. "If we're going to get anywhere, we've got to get more specific. Let's start with the children. My father executed many children for stealing food—so many that his own guards began to desert him, because they could not bear to apprehend such young and desperate thieves, knowing what would happen to them. Why do children steal food? Even you should be able to answer that one, Gravis."

He felt like a child himself, but he answered anyway. "Because they're hungry, I expect."

"Well, why aren't they being fed?"

"For . . . two reasons," Gravis said, wary of answering too quickly. "Either their parents and guardians lack the coin to feed them, or their parents and guardians are dead, and thus are incapable of feeding them."

"Good. Either they're impoverished, or they're orphans, or both. Let's start with the latter cause. Why are there orphans?"

Gravis started to answer, stopped, considered. "That's another stupid question."

"Good! It certainly is. Let's refine it: at the time of my father's disastrous law, why were there *more* orphans in Stonespire than there were, say, a decade previously?"

Gravis knew the answer to that one, though it hurt his heart. "Because . . . because of the war. Because their parents died in the war."

"Precisely. So. My father wages a fruitless war with King Eira over a few hundred acres of bare rock that no one else in Esthrades has ever given a thought to. His soldiers die in this war, and their orphans multiply. The orphans, without guardians to provide for them, start to starve, and in their desperation they steal. My father blames them for this, and answers them with executions. I have never claimed any moral rectitude, but even I know hypocrisy when I see it."

"But hypocrisy was never his intention," Gravis said. "He didn't understand—"

"Exactly. He didn't understand, because he never cared to try. He sought to stop all the things he didn't like from happening, but possessed not the barest shred of curiosity as to *why* they were happening. And he moved ever farther from his dream of a virtuous society. So it is when you attempt to decide how things ought to be without first understanding how things are. You act against yourself, and never even realize it."

"Your father," Gravis said again, but not fiercely this time; it was a plea, or as close to one as he could come. "Answer me . . . one thing about your father."

She sighed. "I didn't kill him, Gravis. Not even with magic. Do you really still doubt that?"

He shook his head. "No, I know you did him no harm. But with the abilities you have . . . could you have saved him, if you'd wished to?"

She leaned back against the throne, tilting her chin so her gaze lifted above his head. "No," she said, finally. "I couldn't have."

"Do you know that for sure? I thought that, in ages past, great mages had the ability to cure illnesses."

She laughed. "Indeed, in ages past even *decent* mages could cure illnesses. But this is a different age, and I am a different mage. And, more specifically, I know I couldn't have because I tried." His shock must have shown on his face, for she added, "It wasn't out of pity—you know me better than that. I just . . . wanted to see if I could do it. It felt like I *should* have been able to do it—like it made sense, which is all I usually need for a spell. But when I tried it, nothing happened. The only thing I accomplished was wearing myself out."

Gravis spoke slowly. "Then it must have been because you didn't truly want to save him."

"You're an expert on magic now, are you?" She stood up, leaning against the arm of the throne for a moment. "You might be right. But then again, I have truly wished to cast a spell before, and have still been unable to."

There was a clatter of footsteps on stone, and Benwick entered the room. "Oh, your ladyship, you're still down here. There are people at the gate asking for you. Again."

"In such tumultuous times, Benwick, we must expect more guests than usual. And these, unless I miss my guess, will be much more welcome." She nodded to him. "Well, come along, Gravis. We might need your help."

Gravis was glad to go, to satisfy his curiosity. He was doubly shocked by what he saw—both that she could be so pleased at their arrival, and that their arrival was possible at all. Three people stood before them, and two he definitely remembered. The boy had put off his crown, but could hardly have put away his crutches, and even without them, Gravis well remembered his face, the solemnity of a much older man resting like a weight upon the features of a child. His sister, too, Gravis remembered, the bastard with the golden hair. The other woman was taller, dark-haired, clearly well used to the sword that hung at her side. Gravis thought he recalled her from Mist's Edge, but he could not be certain.

"I'm pleased you could make it, Kelken," the marquise said. "I was starting to think you had decided not to come."

"I apologize for our lateness. The blame for that must be laid at my feet . . ." He smiled, sudden and wry, at the joke he had not intended to make. ". . . such as they are. Travel is difficult for me, no matter how I try to go about it. And I came, my lady, because of the letter that you wrote me. If it was meant in earnest, I could hardly have done otherwise."

KEL LIKED HER study. He would have imagined something cold and austere like his father's, full of heavy stone, with books and papers arranged into meticulously neat piles. He had liked the sight of Stonespire in general, the way all that wood spread out from the stone tower, expanding and protecting it, the inverse of the apple trees ringed by their high walls. The study was more of the same, stone lightened by the wood, the rugs, the windows, so you felt like you could breathe. And the books and papers, while not truly chaotic, were not meticulously arranged;

they bore the marks of a mind constantly in motion, always taking up one thing and another, like a great beast that forever hungers, imagining its next meal even as it eats the present one. He wanted to have a room like that, one day.

He could hardly believe they had succeeded in making it here at all. Hayne had come with them to carry Kel if necessary, as assistance if Lessa had one of her coughing fits, and to keep her safe from what would happen at Mist's Edge, but none of them fooled themselves into believing she would be steel enough if trouble should befall them. But they had passed unremarked—slow, because of Kel, but unremarked.

Arianrod Margraine offered him her chair, and leaned against the desk as he got himself settled. "You still seem hesitant," she said. "I had hoped your presence here signified an end to that. Are you not resolved?"

Resolved—that was what he had told Elgar he was, in one of the many letters he had written and left for Eirnwin to use, to help support the ruse that he was still there. "You wrote in your letter that this war had more need of me than of my country. I decided to trust you. The only end I could see was dying as the beaten king of Reglay, and if there is more than that . . . you must tell me what it is. I hope I have at least enough resolve to meet it."

"Then I'll explain, and you can decide for yourself if it is something you can do." She picked up a great rolled map, and cleared a space on her desk so she could spread it out. The continent of Lantistyne, naturally. Arianrod pointed to Reglay in the center. "Here is your country: the smallest on the continent, and surrounded on all sides. Hallarnon, Lanvaldis, Esthrades, Issamira—you share borders with all, and any taken alone would be more powerful than you. And yet you have lasted so long unconquered for precisely this reason—because no one could move against you without encouraging their neighbors to try to break off a piece for themselves as well, and all wished you to remain as a buffer between them. Elgar has upset that balance. With Lanvaldis in his grasp, the strategic value of Reglay has been reduced to almost nothing. Holding it would not be worth the effort it would take—recapturing Mist's Edge will certainly be a pain if we end up having to do it, but it may prove unnecessary."

"You needn't worry even about Mist's Edge," Kel told her. "I . . . took measures before I left that will make recapturing it a moot point." That had been the hardest decision of all—harder than deciding to leave in the first place, harder than agreeing with Eirnwin and Dirk that they couldn't come with him. But, strategically, it had been the right decision. King Arvard had known that he could never leave such a formidable fortress in the hands of his enemies; if he had not, there would have been no secret room beneath Mist's Edge, and all of this might never have happened.

Arianrod looked curious, but did not ask him what he meant. Instead, she turned her attention back to the map. "Your advisor must have taught you history, Kelken. Do you remember how Elesthene was defeated?"

"There were . . . many factors," Kel said, trying to recall Eirnwin's lectures. "So much wealth had become concentrated in the hands of so few that the economy was no longer sustainable . . . confidence in the nobility had been on the wane for some time, and plummeted after the schism within the Council . . . the Ninists lost control of their message, or else of their Speaker . . . Did you want me to keep going?"

She smiled. "A good answer, but that's not what I meant. Militarily, do you remember how Elesthene was defeated?"

Kel leaned forward and swept his hand over the map. "It started down here. Talia Avestri's rebellion took back Eldren Cael for the Issamiri. She joined forces with your ancestor, the sixth Daven Margraine—and Councilors Radcliffe and Trevelyan, later. So they had the south and a bit of the east, and tried to push their army toward Valyanrend from there. Valyanrend was the seat of Elesthene's power, just as it is the seat of Elgar's."

"And now perhaps you see where I'm going," she said. "The coalition fought well, but it was difficult for them to make headway—until one of Radcliffe and Trevelyan's many brilliant ideas came to fruition." She tapped the northeast. "The descendants of the Selindwyri, crushed by Elesthene for so long, could yet be stirred to rebellion—and no one frightened the leadership in Valyanrend more, for they could remember how many generations the kingdom of Selindwyr stood firm before it fell. They sent a huge portion of their army east, to crush this rebellion with all the mercilessness they showed the last time—"

"Giving Queen Talia and Lord Daven the opportunity to break through in the west, and bring the fighting to the walls of Valyanrend itself," Kel finished. "But then the people of Valyanrend rebelled. Sebastian Valens killed Lord Darrow, his former master, the rest of the Councilors surrendered to the people, and the Ninist leaders were assassinated. And Talia Avestri turned back, rather than crush an already broken city."

"Just so." She tapped that same spot in the northeast again. "Elgar is trying to re-create Elesthene, and we can try to re-create the manner of Elesthene's loss—or at least part of it. Three elements are crucial: a strong offensive from the south, chaos and disorder in the east, and rebellion from within Valyanrend's walls. Elgar will not be able to survive all three, no more than the Councilors of old could."

"That makes sense," Kel said, "but what do I have to do with any of those things?"

"Nothing, so far. But many things are about to change—to be set in motion— all across the continent. The more important thing is who you *are*, Kelken."

Kel frowned. "Well, being a king isn't nothing, but it seems to me you have one here already." He had briefly spoken with King Eira's heir over dinner, an older boy who had seemed kind enough, despite a somewhat awkward and blustery nature. Of his younger brother, he remembered most vividly that the young man had tried to slink into a far corner of the room, only to smile apologetically when he found Alessa already there. The guardswoman, Ilyn, had seemed awestruck by Hayne.

"There are altogether too many kings and princes running around lost for my liking, I'll give you that," Arianrod said. "And one queen who's lost only to herself. She's the one who could help us most of all, if she only had a mind to. But don't hold your breath."

Something about the way she said it gave Kel pause. "Do you know Adora well?"

Arianrod snorted. "Know her? She's been borrowing my books since we were eight years old. Always takes entirely too long to return them, too."

"And what is she like?" Kel asked. He'd been curious about Queen Adora since the letter she'd sent him back at Mist's Edge. *May the crown rest lightly on your brow all the days that you wear it, and may those days be long.* "Do you like her?"

Arianrod had to consider her answer. "Adora is . . . well, she's no fool, that's undeniable. And she's interesting, when she's not actively trying to be otherwise."

"But she won't help us?"

"She won't help us *now*," Arianrod said. "But if I know her, and I do, she will move after one of two things happens: Elgar declares war on Esthrades directly, or Issamira experiences a true crisis."

Kel sighed. "Wonderful. So she'll only help us if things are already looking dreadful."

"I'm glad you understand." She gave him a dry smirk. "That's the first problem, and the most severe—her hesitation is harming our chances of a strong offensive in the south. But as to the other two things we require—chaos in the east, rebellion in Valyanrend—things are looking much brighter. It is Laen, of course, who provides the seed of the chaos we want to sow."

"He's necessary," Kel agreed. "When King Eira was believed to have no successor, even the richest, most powerful nobles who hated Elgar had nowhere to focus their dreams of resistance. With an heir of the blood to unite behind, the situation is vastly different."

"Exactly. So many of them were simply waiting for the opportunity."

"And yet . . ." Kel wondered how best to say it. "Laen is . . . untried. He was not raised as a prince, and most of these nobles will not have ever met him. Can he truly be enough for them?"

She raised an eyebrow. "Do you know anything about Edith Selwyn?"

"The woman who governs in Lanvaldis? No, I don't know anything worth reporting."

"She was an academic before Elgar conquered Lanvaldis—wrote a couple interesting treatises and many more mediocre ones. Politics, history, magic. She is qualified, I suppose, as much as anyone Elgar was likely to choose could be—she's obviously never governed before, but she seems to be doing an efficient job of it. Which is part of the problem. The other part is her blood. Hundreds of years ago, a Richard Selwyn moved to Valyanrend, made an immense fortune, and bought a noble title. You may remember his daughter from your history books: Cecelia Selwyn."

Kel did indeed remember a long-ago lesson with Eirnwin. "Ah. Vespasian Darrow's wife."

"That's the one. The Darrows, of course, had no issue, and so the noble house of Selwyn ended there, a mere generation after it had begun. But the Selwyns who remained in the east—in what would become Lanvaldis—survived, though they were not nobility themselves."

Kel laughed. "I think I'm starting to see. Elgar couldn't have chosen a more perfect insult to the Lanvaldian nobility if he'd designed her specifically for the purpose. She's good at her job despite having no experience at her job, her blood is simultaneously beneath theirs and of a historical significance theirs will never have, and it's a Hallern peasant-turned-emperor who's allowed her to cut ahead of them in line. I suppose they'd be willing to put a monkey on the throne if it meant getting her off it."

"A monkey of noble blood, but yes." She grinned. "And to be fair, Administrator Selwyn is good at her job only from Elgar's perspective. If you actually live in Lanvaldis, and prefer not to be tortured or executed, not to have your land and assets confiscated at her whim, and not to have your correspondence pored over by strangers . . . she is perhaps not as fine as you could wish."

"So between the nobles who hate her for petty reasons and the nobles—and other citizens—who hate her for legitimate reasons, she's made a lot of enemies. If enough of them unite against her—presumably under Laen—Selwyn will have to get reinforcements from Hallarnon to stop Lanvaldis from breaking away from Elgar's empire. Which just leaves rebellion in Valyanrend. What are our chances of that?"

"Well, there's already a resistance in Valyanrend—a wily and persistent one, if the stories are true. And they have plenty of coin for the present, so it may just be a matter of time."

"How do you know that?" Kel asked.

"Primarily through the spies and other contacts of the Lanvaldian nobility; they're able to spend their resources in that area more discreetly than I could. Some of them are financing this rebellion directly."

"All right, so where do I fit into all of this? Since the situation in Issamira is the only one that doesn't seem to be proceeding more or less smoothly, I assume that's the one you want my help with?"

"No, actually," she said. "I won't prevent you from going to Issamira if that is what you wish, but I don't think it would be the best use for you. I want you to accompany Laen and his brother back to Lanvaldis."

Kel blinked at her. "You want me, not yet a man grown and incapable of carrying myself anywhere without crutches, to go to Lanvaldis and attempt to assist them in throwing out their Hallern conquerors by force? I do think I have *some* skills, but I can't fight, and I don't have a mind for battle any more than I do a body for it. What use can you possibly think I will serve over there?"

"Legitimacy, for one thing," she said. "Laen's claim runs through his mother, a bastard legitimized in secret—you could hardly blame anyone for being skeptical. But no one could ever doubt you are the rightful king of Reglay, and your support for him may help convince others. But the most important reason I want you to go with Laen is as an example."

"An example of a king?" Kel asked. "He won't take kindly to that. He's half again as old as I am."

"And you still intimidate him, for all that," she said. "Come on, Kelken. You spent your whole life being what he has only recently become: a prince of the realm. You were raised from birth to be king; you were always aware that it was your destiny, and those around you did their best to prepare you for the role. But who prepared Laen for anything?"

"And if I don't wish to go with him?" Kel asked. "Is that truly the best thing you could think of for me to do—worth leaving all my people at Mist's Edge?"

"Well, at Mist's Edge all you were going to do was die, so if I'd asked you here to sweep my floors you'd still, strictly speaking, be more useful here than there," she said, as serenely as ever. "Kelken, you are a guest, not a prisoner. If you would rather try to persuade Adora, I will not stand in your way. Though I still say what I said to you at Mist's Edge: if she continues like this, some crisis is going to befall her country, and you don't want to be there when that happens. I can't say precisely what form it will take, but I know the nature of power, and I know she is not truly filling that throne. Someone else will, however they can."

May the crown rest lightly on your brow, she had written, and he had been certain that was something she had never felt. "Does she hate the idea of being queen that much?"

"No, I don't believe so," Arianrod said. "But Adora has always been a coward."

Kel frowned. "Plenty of cowards have thoroughly enjoyed the chance to sit a throne."

"No, I don't mean a coward like you're thinking," she said. "If some god should descend from above and say to Adora, *Cut off your hand to save your people,* she could do such a thing easily. She has *that* kind of bravery. But if there is no god to tell her anything, and the choice that falls to her instead is *Trouble your heart to save your people* . . . Well, she was raised the second child. I suppose I should say that no one ever taught her how to make such a decision. *You* seem to have learned it already, if what you said about Mist's Edge is true, and you're only eleven."

"I . . . didn't really leave Mist's Edge to save my people," Kel admitted quietly. "I expect that as many of them will die as would have if I'd stayed. I know Dirk will die for certain, because he was the one who volunteered to . . . to do what must be done, if Elgar's men should breach Mist's Edge's walls. If he dies before he can do it, there are others who have sworn to take his place—others I could not save." He had known Dirk as a prankster, a simple, merry fellow, who scorned sophistication in favor of openness. But the solemnity he had shown, the ease with which he had put himself forward to face certain death . . . it was as if Kel had never truly known him at all, and now he never would. "Eirnwin may live, but I had to leave him there—he pointed out, correctly, that Elgar's strategist, that Varalen Oswhent, is too clever. If he doesn't see me *or* any of the people closest to me make an appearance, he will certainly guess that it's because we aren't truly there. And the rest of my people . . . we could not empty Mist's Edge as much as we might have. We could not let Oswhent guess what we planned, and we could not risk that some spy might let it slip, so only half a dozen people at Mist's Edge even know what will happen there. I have troubled my heart, that is certain. But that alone won't save my people. I chose to save myself, so that I might help save this entire continent from the designs of a tyrant. In the face of that, even Reglay is a small piece—no matter how dear it might be to me." He looked back up at her. "And you? I suppose such decisions have always come easily to you?"

She shook her head. "I could not say, truly, that I have ever made such a decision."

"You must have. You've been moving pieces around the board much more skillfully, and for far longer, than the rest of us."

"There can be no doubt of that," she replied. "But it seems my heart does not wound so easily as others' do." She turned back to the map. "Was there anything else you wished to discuss with me?"

He hesitated over whether he should say the last thing, whether it would make him seem childish. But she prized correctness, didn't she? If she'd said something wrong, he imagined she'd wish to know about it.

"I don't mean to make a point of it, but I'm twelve now," he said. "I had my birthday while we were on the road."

Surprisingly, she did not laugh—he would not have blamed her if she had. She wore that wry smile, but he did not think she meant to mock him. "May you have your thirteenth in happier times."

Chapter Twenty-eight

Eldren Cael

THE SUN HAD only just risen when Adora and her mother stepped onto the roof, and the early-morning heat was still mild, even at this time of year. The palace was full of painstakingly smooth, flat planes, and very few curves, and the roof was no exception; the towers rising all around them were square, and the expanse of stone before them was flat and wide all the way to the wall, with plenty of room to walk.

"There are few things so urgent that they could not have waited an hour or two," her mother said, but she did not seem angry, or even especially tired. "May I venture to guess that it was not speed that led you to set our discussion at this time and place, but rather a wish for privacy?"

"You're right, of course," Adora said. "I wished to reduce the possibility that anyone would intervene." Jocelyn especially, but she did not say that. "This conversation has become unavoidable, and perhaps you have already guessed what it contains, but I still hope you will hear me out." She had decided on the words she would use the night before, so there was no need to search for them. "You may think," she began, "that I have scorned the lessons you have tried to teach me, preferring Father's and Landon's and Uncle's to your own. This has not been so. I understand that even the most amiable face must be pored over with all care, to grasp the heart that lies beneath it. I understand the need for fruitful alliances, and the immense importance of marriage for those in our position. Indeed, I flatter myself that I have thought as seriously about these things as you have—I have merely reached different conclusions as to what were best to be done."

She hesitated, but her mother didn't interrupt her, and she chose to take that as a good sign. "I don't wish to marry yet, Mother. Not while things are so uncertain. Not while I am so uncertain of myself. And then, because of Hephestion, I am not the last of my line. We might well see him married first—but never to Jocelyn Selreshe. I don't wish to anger her family—I know Dahren and Amali Selreshe are powerful, and we owe them much. But she is not . . . I will have no alliance with her, now or ever." She took a deep breath. "And now you must tell me where you fall in this: on her side, or on mine."

Her mother rolled her eyes. "There's no need to be so dramatic about it—I would never pick a side opposite my own child, and Jocelyn Selreshe is certainly not my child. If you wish to dismiss her, your position gives you that right."

"Let's make a deal, then," Adora said. "We'll get rid of Jocelyn, and we'll also get rid of—"

"You'd get rid of that captain of yours, if you truly wished to please me," her mother said.

Adora's heart felt heavy. "No, Mother, I can't do that. We need her now more than ever. There are times I feel I can't set a foot down in all of Eldren Cael without treading on a viper. Rhia is the only person, outside of my own family, that I truly trust. Had you been there when I was attacked, you would have seen her merit with your own eyes."

Her mother's face pinched, though she was, as ever, a master at controlling it, and did not scowl as a less disciplined person would have. "Whom do you propose to dismiss, then, if not her?"

"We'll get rid of all Hephestion's suitors," Adora said. "We will wash our hands of Jocelyn Selreshe and Lirien Arvel both—and I am confident our house will be the more serene because of it."

That gave her mother pause. "I admit I have never trusted that Arvel woman. But Hephestion would never allow it—wherever we sent her, you know as well as I he'd go chasing after her, the more determined for the adversity we placed in his way."

"But Feste owes me a favor," Adora said. "That was the only good thing to come out of that ridiculous contest—he won't go back on his word. We'll dismiss his suitors, and I'll find *something* worthwhile for him to do, somewhere else. So he won't be able to chase after her, not until he's done paying back what he owes me."

"You don't think he'll still try to find her?"

Adora shrugged. "I personally think it's more likely he'll become infatuated with someone else within a week of his arrival, no matter where he ends up going. But if I'm wrong, I suppose we can deal with it then."

THE HEAT WAS beginning to pick up, and Rhia stole anxious glances at Lirien whenever she thought she could get away with it, searching for traces of the apparent fever that had plagued her the day before. Lirien had seemed sluggish all morning, her eyes going hazy every so often, but she wasn't sweating or pale yet, and she spoke to Rhia readily enough.

The market around Allespont Street was always busy, but they'd gotten to it ahead of peak hours, and the food stalls didn't seem to be sold out of anything yet. Rhia had asked Lirien to pick what she'd like to eat, and fortunately the bashi stalls always kept a large supply on hand, due to how popular the stuff was.

Bashi looked like thicker, elongated rice, but Adora had told her that rice was actually a type of seed, while bashi was made out of water and flour. If stored correctly, it took years to spoil, and it was so versatile you could prepare it with almost anything. In this particular dish, the bashi had been simmered in oil and onions and flavored with pepper and chunks of meat: a heavy dish for a hot day, but Rhia couldn't deny how good it tasted. Since they'd have to give the bowls and spoons back when they were done, they hadn't gone far, sitting atop a low garden wall near the side of the road.

"I certainly hope she's taking proper advantage of my absence to do as she wishes," Lirien mused between bites. "I'd hate to think she bought me such a satisfying meal and got nothing out of it." She meant Adora, of course; Lirien was no fool, and knew that if Adora was keeping her from the castle and everyone else in it, it was in accordance with some plan. "Were you at least able to patch things up with your prince?"

"I . . . well . . . for the most part, I suppose," Rhia stammered. Hephestion had been contrite, that was true—or at least he had apologized—but at the same time he had tried to insist his actions were understandable, though Rhia could not understand them. He had seemed to want to be close with her again, and at the same time to hold her at arm's length. "His behavior of late has confused me, I confess. But I don't think he bears me any grudge."

They were silent for a while, eating and watching the crowds around them. Rhia was still thinking about the things Hephestion had said, and wondering which of the two of them was truly being unreasonable. And whatever Lirien was thinking of, Rhia was no closer to knowing it than she had ever been.

"Have you ever . . . been in love?" Rhia asked.

Lirien glanced over at her and smiled. "That's not something you're supposed to ask a lady, is it? Not that I am one, but . . . well."

"Does that mean you think it's a childish question?"

"It means I haven't any answer that you'll like. What made you ask it?"

Rhia shrugged, but she knew the matter wouldn't be dislodged that easily. "It was something Hephes—my lord told me. He said I had never been in love, and that was why I couldn't . . . understand him."

"Oh?" Lirien asked. "And is that true?"

"That I've never been in love?" Rhia blushed. "Probably."

Lirien laughed. "See, you don't want to answer it, either."

"No, it's not—I mean, I *suppose* I haven't. I don't know what people mean by it. There are all the songs and stories, of course, and I like them as much as anyone, but I've never felt like they were about anything that could happen to me."

"Well, poor little you. They say life is empty without love, especially when you're young." She scraped a final spoonful out of her bowl. "As for me . . . perhaps I have been in love many times, and perhaps I never have, and never will be. I have *thought* I was, more than once, but whatever it was at first, whatever excitement I felt . . . I could never catch hold of it, to find out if it was really there. And eventually I realized that I find people easy to like, but very hard to love." She smiled, a deeper melancholy behind the easy self-deprecation. "You see? I told you you wouldn't like it."

Rhia didn't know what to say. It was true that she didn't like hearing those words—they made her so sad, for reasons she couldn't fully explain. Finally, she said, "In a way, it seems a dangerous thing to me, wanting to be in love. It seems like wishing to be destroyed. My parents ruined both their lives because of it—she couldn't compromise enough to be with him, but she couldn't break with him, either, and her death left an emptiness in him even my brother and I could never heal. Even at best, it just seems like . . . like a distraction from all the more important and fulfilling things you could be doing."

Lirien laughed. "I understand you there. I've always thought it's much better to have fun for a while and then go your separate ways. When people get too attached, it always causes problems. Once you get some experience, you'll learn that very quickly."

That wasn't what Rhia had meant at all, but before she could say so, Lirien held up her empty bowl. "I suppose the queen can't have us back yet?"

"Not yet," Rhia said, grateful for the reprieve. "She said until the afternoon at least."

"Then I suppose we'll be taking a walk. What about to Estriver? We probably can't spend the time on a whole play, but maybe we'll find a bard—I've always been partial to a good ballad."

Rhia had no objections to that, and they were soon on their way. She knew Lirien might easily have teased her, but she obligingly let the subject stay buried. "If all this ends up meaning you can finally leave," Rhia asked, "where would you go next?" She hesitated. "Are you all right?"

Lirien was sweating again, hair sticking to her forehead. She brushed it away angrily. "I'm fine. I'll be . . . fine in just a bit."

"Perhaps you should choose a colder climate," Rhia offered.

"No, I . . . I barely even feel the cold, so what's the point?" She laughed, but it sounded strange. She squeezed into the series of alleyways that were the quickest way to Estriver, and Rhia hastened to keep close to her, in case she should grow suddenly worse. "I've always wanted to see the Howling Gate, you know. But I can't go north just now."

"Why not?" Rhia asked.

"There are people I . . . don't want to see there." How could she move so quickly when she seemed so unwell? She put a hand to her head. "Oh, you should . . . leave me alone . . . for a while."

"That's just what I shouldn't do," Rhia said, though she didn't insist on closing the gap when Lirien tried to back away from her. "What if you can't get back on your own?"

"No, it wouldn't be . . . that. It's not that kind of sickness. It's just—"

Rhia felt something brush by her, and turned, too slow, to see what it was. By then the man had already reached out, and pulled Lirien's hunched form close to him. He had already drawn his sword, and he lifted it high, resting the blade against Lirien's throat.

Rhia reached for her own sword, but the man pulled Lirien even closer to him. "Don't do that!" he snapped. "Don't make me harm her!"

He wasn't wearing the armband of the Crows, and he wasn't anyone Rhia recognized, whose goals or grudges she might be able to understand. He looked unremarkable—shabbily dressed, but not in rags. He was shaking slightly, but she didn't think he was frightened, or bluffing.

"Who are you?" she said. "What do you want?"

"Who I am doesn't matter. I want the sword. Give me the sword, and I'll let her go."

Rhia's hand darted toward the hilt instinctively, but the man shouted again, "Don't!" She stopped, holding her hands up, and he relaxed slightly. "Unbuckle it, and slide it over to me. *Don't* draw it. I *will* cut her throat." Rhia realized why he was shaking. It was because Lirien was shaking, and he didn't want to cut her by accident. But Lirien didn't seem afraid, either; if anything, she seemed almost angry.

"Why do you want my sword so much that you're willing to kill for it?" she asked, trying to buy time so she could figure out what to do.

He laughed hoarsely. "If you knew how much it was worth, you'd sell it yourself. For that sword . . . for that one sword . . ."

It was so much money, Jost had said. Was that why he and his companions had attacked her? Had it not been an attempted assassination at all, but an attempted theft instead?

If someone was offering a reward for vardrath steel, that made a certain amount of sense; it *was* incredibly rare, and it was possible that rumors of her having a sword made of the stuff could have spread. But something struck her as odd about the way the man had talked about the sword—as if the reward had been offered for Rhia's sword specifically, not just any one he could find, or anything made out of vardrath steel at all.

"I just want the money," the man insisted. "I don't care about her, or you. Give me the sword, and I'll let her go. I swear it."

Rhia considered her options. She knew she was fast, but she didn't think even she was fast enough to reach him before he slit Lirien's throat. And she believed he was telling the truth. There was no reason to doubt he wanted the money above all else, and if that was so, why risk the wrath of the throne and the guard by killing her? And that meant, as far as she could tell, that giving him the sword was the likeliest way to ensure she and Lirien got out of this alive.

"Don't be angry," Cadfael had said, the day he brought the swords home. "I know we said we wouldn't take his sword apart, but it's not what he wanted. He wanted to be able to protect us, even after he was gone—to help us protect ourselves. And that stubborn old man won't train you if you don't have a sword, so . . . I thought you should have a great one."

She wanted to fight to keep it—to die, if she had to. It had been given by their father, an inheritance to prove the blood ties the law wouldn't let them acknowledge. It had been shaped by Cadfael, the other half of his own. With the death of her family, it was the thing that meant the most to her in the whole world. But it wasn't worth a person's life.

"All right," she said, holding the scabbard steady with one hand while she reached to unbuckle it, fingers trembling against the metal. "I—"

When Lirien moved, at first Rhia thought she was trying to take the man off guard, to twist out of his grasp while he was distracted. There would have been no chance of that, but he made a noise of surprise and shifted his sword arm so he wouldn't slit her throat by accident. And Lirien moved her own arm into that space, and gripped the blade of his sword with her bare hand. He leaned into it instinctively, and then he and Rhia both flinched, shocked at how Lirien hadn't. She hadn't even blinked.

The blade was cutting into her hand, biting ever deeper into her flesh as she forced it away from her body. Blood was running freely down the metal, and even the would-be thief squirmed as it dripped onto his hand. But there was no sign of pain in Lirien's face, or even concern. "I don't have the patience to deal with this," she said to him. "Surely you of all people can appreciate how hard it is to be good all the time? I wasn't meant to play the maiden, but here we all are, and no one else is going to do it. But gods, you lot make it difficult to remember why I'm supposed to care what happens to you." She gave a disappointed sigh. "Perhaps I could grip this sword even harder, stare deep into your eyes, and tell you to abandon this foolish plan and run for your life. Perhaps you would even listen to me if I did. But I'm not going to. You can just die."

There was a soft crackling sound, like something brittle crunching underfoot. All three of them had gone very still, so Rhia didn't immediately see what was wrong. But when Lirien let go of the man's sword, he didn't move a hair. He stared and stared at her, unblinking, and Rhia realized that there was something wrong with his face. It was too still, and the color looked as if it was starting to turn. His eyes were glassy and dull.

She drew warily near him, and placed a hand on his arm. The first thing she noticed was that it was impossibly cold for this weather, and the second thing she noticed was that there was no give to it. It was unnaturally stiff, as if . . .

Lirien glanced at the bluish corpse the way you might look at a puddle by the roadside. "Ah," she said. "I suppose that was a bit . . . unsubtle. We can't just have him standing here like that." She lifted her intact hand, and jabbed him hard in the forehead; rigid as a board, his whole body toppled over, landing with an unnatural impact and a louder cracking noise. As Rhia watched, dampness began to seep into his clothes.

She turned to Lirien, but found the only thing she could say was, "Your . . . your hand."

It was just hanging there at her side, blood dripping from the deep cuts in her fingers and palm. It was barely holding itself together. But Lirien stared at it with utter calmness. "Oh, drat. Knew I forgot something." She shook her hand out hard, as if trying to dispel pins and needles; it was a blur in the air, and then it was still. Lirien spread it in front of her, palm up, fingers wiggling, as if she were checking the joints. Beneath the blood, it was entirely whole.

Lirien grinned at her. "There, see? Good as new."

"What . . ." Rhia swallowed hard, trying to gather her scattered wits. "What did you do?"

Lirien raised an eyebrow. "It can't be that hard to figure out, surely? Our friend there was *quite* frozen, though I'm letting him thaw out now, and the only other thing I did was fix my hand. You've seen magic before, right? So this should all practically be boring to you."

Rhia had no idea what to say or do. It was one thing to see aftereffects that made no sense—Cadfael's wound, or the absence of her own—but to see the world change so thoroughly in a single instant sent her mind reeling. "So you could always do that. You could have killed him—you could have killed any of us—whenever you liked?"

"Are you saying you can't kill people whenever you like?" Lirien asked. "Or are you saying it's the method that makes the difference?" Drops of water had gathered on her formerly injured hand, and she scrubbed at it idly with the uninjured one, the blood slowly coming off. She smiled at Rhia, a smile as beautiful as ever, but sharper now, colder, with a hint of something much more dangerous in it than simple mischief. "Oh dear, why do you look so distressed? Can it be it pleased you too much to have someone to protect? Now that you know I have wits and strength to spare, you find you don't like me quite so much as you thought?"

"No, that's not—I don't—" She did feel dismayed, but not at the knowledge that Lirien was powerful. "You were . . . different. How you are now, and how you were when we met." *I wanted to give him a chance, too,* Lirien had said, though

Rhia was only just now realizing what she had truly meant. "You were someone who cared. Was that a lie, too?"

"Oh, no, not at all," Lirien said. "I care a great deal—more than I should, probably. Just not at this moment. I can't right now, you see. And while I'm so refreshingly free of sentimentality, there's something we have to discuss. You're going to want to tell the Issamiri royals about this, but you won't."

Was that a threat? "I have to," Rhia said. "I serve Her Grace, and with your power—"

Lirien waved a hand at her words as if they were so many buzzing flies. "You aren't going to tell them, Rhia, because you *owe* me."

She closed the distance between them, reaching out with her newly restored hand, and Rhia tensed, knowing Lirien could kill her as easily as she had that man, and doubtless didn't even need to touch her to do it. But no magic followed in the wake of the gesture; Lirien merely pointed one finger, holding it an inch from Rhia's navel. "I think it was . . . just here, wasn't it?" Her finger slashed a line across Rhia's stomach. "Quite a bad wound—and now that I've seen you fight, I know it's not because you're untalented. You must not have been very careful, to mess things up so badly." She laughed. "Imagine my surprise when you appeared before me a second time! *Oh gods,* I thought, *this poor fool's going to get herself killed all over again.* And then you were so brilliant! So you see, I'd guessed that you were softhearted before we ever spoke a word."

Of course. Of course it had been her. Hadn't Rhia just seen her use the same spell on herself? "You found me by the lake," she said. "You healed me?"

"I certainly did. And believe me, you needed it. You're lucky I didn't delay my walk another ten minutes. I like being around water, and not just because it . . . gives me more options, so to speak."

"But why did you save me?" Rhia asked. "I wasn't even conscious. You couldn't have known anything about me."

"Because I could." She smiled. "Is that not enough for you? I liked your face. It seemed sad for you to die, and needless. So I saw to it that you did not. What skin was it off my back? And *because* you weren't conscious, I knew you couldn't tell anyone about me." She shrugged. "But no matter why I did it, the important thing is that I did it. I could have turned away and left you to die, but instead I saved you—a stranger, to whom I owed nothing. Are you really going to be so ungrateful as to give me away, exposing me to all the fear, hatred, and danger I have been so careful to avoid?"

She was right. Adora wouldn't harm Lirien just for being a mage, but she would hardly just let her go, either. She'd want to know all manner of things—how Lirien's powers worked, what her intentions with them were, whether she knew of any others like her. Who could say when or if she'd finally be satisfied, and Lirien could go free?

Then she thought of something else. "From the brink of death," she said. "You saved me from the brink of death."

Lirien stared at her blankly. "Yes, I just said that."

"You told me something before," Rhia said. "You said a healer saved someone from the brink of death, but she wasn't thanked for it. You said you can't return to the village that was once your home. The healer you talked about was you, wasn't it? This fear and hatred you've tried to avoid . . . it's not hypothetical to you. It's something you've experienced before."

Lirien laughed, but for the first time since she'd destroyed their attacker, Rhia thought she saw a hint of pain cross her face. "Ah yes, the witch of Sundercliff. Truly the most dangerous creature ever to imperil that sleepy town, to hear its people tell it. That boy . . . I was far out in the water; I didn't even see him until it was too late. The waves threw him against the shore, and there's no beach out there, only merciless rocks. His body was so mangled—he would never have survived without my magic. I didn't know what else to do. And for that . . . for that, I . . ." She winced, pressing a hand to her head, her eyes squeezing shut. She trembled for a moment, and when she opened them again, her expression had changed, all that blade-sharp cheerfulness wiped away.

"Oh," she said. "Well, I wouldn't have wanted to say all that in quite that way, but I suppose none of it's untrue." She massaged her temples with one hand. "Can we get away from here? I'll explain. I probably owe you that much. I just . . . want to do it somewhere else."

"OUR VILLAGE WAS small, and isolated, but it was right on the shores of the Endless Sea, on a cliffside far above the water. When I was a girl, I found a way to climb down the cliffs to the very edge of the water, where sea met stone. The path went so far down that at high tide certain parts of it would be submerged, but I never once got stuck, never slipped on the rocks no matter how wet the waves made them. I liked to stand there, in the shadow of the cliffs, and watch the sea. In front of me, where the path ended, the waves had eaten a great hole in the rock, and when they struck the cliffside they would break against it, sending these huge spurts of water high into the air. I loved to stand there even when the weather was foul, when everyone else wouldn't venture out of doors. The waves would swell, get pelted by the rain—all those millions of droplets striking the surface and disappearing. So I—I'd stand there and just . . . think about things. The sea, and how far it stretched, and whether anything lay on the other side of it, if there could really be some magical land lurking there like in the tales. The world, and how big it was, and how many things were in it—so much more than I could ever comprehend. I was such a silly little village girl, you know. I thought things must surely be going to happen to me—in a world where I could see such sights, surely grand things existed, and could happen even to someone like me.

"It was a day just like any other; the sea seemed calm as I walked the paths, and I was as surefooted upon the stone as ever. But then, as I neared the end of the stone path, a great wave rose up out of nowhere, a wall of water many times as high as I was tall. It surged from the sea and crashed against the cliffside, and when it returned to the ocean it dragged me with it.

"I was a strong swimmer even as a child, and I had braved the waters of the Endless Sea times beyond counting. But the current that drew me under that day was like none I had ever experienced before. There was water all around me, water all I had to breathe—the pain was so great I was sure I was dying. When I finally lost consciousness, I did not think I would ever gain it again."

She smiled faintly. "I was wrong, of course. The sea spat me back out, and I awoke on the same stone outcropping from which it had taken me. It was so strange, though—it must have taken such force for the waves to hurl me back atop the rocks. Enough to strike my head open, perhaps, or at least to leave me cut and bruised. But I did not have a single scratch—not so much as a tear in my clothes. And I did not awaken choking or spitting water, but as calmly as if from a long sleep.

"And after that I was . . . different."

"But no one else knew?" Rhia asked. "Until you got thrown out?"

"I wasn't so foolish as to say anything to anyone. I knew what they were, even back then. I only healed him because he would've died otherwise, and even he was horrified by it." She looked down, at some imaginary point Rhia couldn't see. "Not a single person spoke up in my defense. Not everyone condemned me, either, at least not openly. But if anyone felt sympathy for me, they kept it to themselves. Even my own parents were silent."

She rested her cheek on her hand. "I was still naïve back then. I had thought I was . . . if not precisely well loved, at least that I had no quarrel with anyone. But perhaps they had always sensed that I thought I was better than they were." She frowned. "No, that's not quite right. It wasn't that I thought *I* was better, it was that I *wanted* better. I wanted to travel the world, to see such marvelous and interesting things—palaces and cities, mountains and forests, other oceans than the one I knew. People who had done and seen and knew unbelievable things. The people of Sundercliff would never be enough for me, and they knew that. So they sent me on my way—to find that fascinating other world I was always dreaming of, and never to trouble theirs again." She sighed. "It's so easy to feel that you are stuck in a cage, until you're forced out of it. Then it just feels like being locked out, instead of locked in."

Rhia had wanted to see the world, too—you fairly well had to, to have adventures. But she hadn't wanted it under those circumstances, either—the conquest of her city, the destruction of her life with Cadfael. It became much easier to travel when you no longer had a home. "When you say you were different," she said slowly, "do you mean like the way you were after you killed that man? Is that . . . part of your magic?"

Lirien shook her head firmly. "It wasn't like that. In the beginning, it was like a dream. Even after I got thrown out, I was happy, because I knew I'd be able to do as I wished—to see the world. I could defend myself from any attacker, heal myself from any injury. As you might imagine, I'm quite good at catching fish—I don't even need to use a net. I knew which water was safe to drink, and could purify it if it wasn't. I knew all kinds of things about water: where it was, the quality of it, all the things it could do. Do you know how much water is in a human body? Do you know how much water is in the *air,* even when it isn't raining? I could feel all of it, and I could make it do whatever I wished."

She bowed her head. "But then I met *them.* At some point I'd started to feel them out there—I can't tell you how, I just *knew* that there were other people like me somewhere, and I started getting these vague ideas of where they were, whether they were closer or farther away from me. I decided to try to meet them, because I was curious—and because I thought they'd understand, I suppose. That was the worst mistake I ever made.

"It wasn't so bad, at first. I liked Voltest all right—that's not his real name, he started calling himself that after he got his powers. It's some word in Old Lantian; he used to be a scholar, before. He knew a lot of things, and was able to find out even more. He was the one who told us we weren't mages; he'd always doubted it, from the very beginning. Mages don't get their powers in that way, he said. Mages just *have* them. What we are was rarer even than that, but he found it. *Wardrenfell,* they were called, back when people still tried to learn about magic instead of just hiding it all away. Born ordinary people, who were affected by some kind of . . . well, he could tell you better than I could, but some magic that had gotten loose, and run wild in the air. Or in the water, in my case, I suppose? And the magic chose us in some way—though it's hard to say how, as disembodied magic can hardly be said to have a mind. Voltest said *wardrenfell* of the same type are bound up together—it's as if the magic that inhabits us is a bunch of broken-off pieces of the same whole. And that's why we stay aware of one another, even when we're far apart. *He* was prepared to leave it there, but Miken wasn't.

"Miken was the youngest of us—a boy of only fifteen when he died. He was from here—not Eldren Cael specifically, but a village not so far away. He thought that we were supposed to be together, that the magic had brought us together for that purpose. We tried to tolerate each other for his sake, but you can well believe I didn't get myself out of Sundercliff only to have another group of people placing responsibilities on me that I never asked for. And Talis hates other people, so the idea was poison to her to start with."

"Talis?" Rhia asked, and Lirien bit her lip.

"I'm sorry," she said. "There's no tactful way to say this. Talis is the one who killed your brother. I've known that, and I didn't tell you before, because I couldn't see a way to do it without telling you everything else. If it's any consolation, I've never liked her."

It was strange, to finally hear her name after all these years, when even Cadfael had not known it—to hear someone refer to her as an old acquaintance. But she could say to Lirien honestly, "That's all right. I told you, I never meant to seek vengeance. But I would like to hear the rest of your explanation—you don't have to tread carefully around mentions of her just for my sake."

Lirien relaxed a little. "Well, in the end the four of us compromised. We never had to worry about being apart, since it was so easy to find one another, so we divided our time between doing as we each pleased on our own and coming together every so often to humor Miken and share information. It was all right for a while, but then . . ." For the first time, her downcast eyes turned not just melancholy but truly sorrowful. "It wasn't just that Miken didn't appear when it was time to meet, it was that we couldn't feel anything from him, that we suddenly had no way of knowing where he was. Of course it occurred to us, even then, that this was because he was no longer of this world, but we had no way of confirming his death one way or the other. We gathered in the west, because that was the last place any of us could recall feeling his presence. It was winter, more than three years ago now . . . some weeks after Talis had her encounter with your brother, as I recall. And that made us even more nervous—we knew at least one king was looking for us, and there might very well be more.

"What water is to me, fire is to Voltest, and he'd been developing this way to see things in his flames. True things, things that really happened. He could build a fire in a place, and see what had occurred there—months earlier, or sometimes even years. But that didn't help us, because we didn't know the last place Miken had been. So Voltest tried to use the flames in a different way—to center them on a person instead of a place, and see what had befallen that person in the past. It took him some time, but . . . in the end, we were able to confirm Miken's death for ourselves. Beyond . . . beyond any doubt."

She fell silent for a while, gathering her composure. "That's when everything started going wrong. It makes sense, doesn't it? We were parts of a shattered whole.

Without Miken, there was no longer a balance between us. And our magic . . . changed. Instead of simply being able to sense one another, it was as if our minds became muddied, bleeding into each other. I don't just know where Voltest and Talis are—I feel some echo of what they feel. And what they feel is never anything good. They're different from me and Miken—they were hurt, badly, before we ever met, and they won't let the wound of his death heal, either. They want revenge, and when I'm near them, I can no longer tell whether the anger I feel is theirs or mine. They take advantage of it—when they're both in agreement on something, it takes all my strength of will to resist it, and sometimes . . . I can't."

Rhia slid her fingertips over the back of Lirien's hand, trying to offer sympathy without being presumptuous. Lirien didn't acknowledge the gesture, but didn't pull away, either. "It's getting worse," she said. "It's getting worse all the time. It's like our own minds are becoming labyrinths—like every time it's a little harder to find our way out. It's like the magic makes us ourselves, just *more*. Voltest was always short-tempered, Talis was always dour, but now anger and despair blot out everything else for them—or else she takes refuge in his anger to escape from her own sadness. And I wasn't meant for this—for the task of ensuring they don't go too far. I try to hold them back, but it doesn't always work the way I intend."

"But they can influence you, too," Rhia said. "Was that what happened when you killed that man?"

Lirien stiffened. "No. That was just me."

"I'm not trying to judge you," Rhia said. "But you really *were* different, for a while. You changed, and then you changed back. Didn't you?"

"It's like I said. We're becoming more ourselves—we're becoming ourselves too much. Voltest's true self is full of rage, and Talis's true self is full of grief, and mine . . . mine is devoid of those things. Mine is . . . happy." She gave a bitter smile. "That's the joke, do you see? There's this part of me—larger and larger lately—that's just enjoying herself. The way I was when I first started traveling, before I met any of them, when the world seemed like one giant opportunity waiting for me. It's this desire to just keep enjoying myself, and doing what I like, and to stop worrying about other people. That's *my* labyrinth. It might not sound so bad, and it isn't—for me. But if I ever became truly lost in there . . .'twould be very unfortunate for other people."

"I think I understand," Rhia said. "You aren't just fighting them, but yourself as well."

"So to speak."

"I can't even imagine. The strength of will—"

"Don't misunderstand who and what I am," Lirien said. "I have rarely lied to you outright, but it is true I have pretended to a more delicate disposition than I possess. Experience has taught me this is the best way to avoid confrontation, and

I *must* avoid confrontation, because there's no way to know for sure how I will react. But at no point have I ever aspired to a life of charity or heroism. I just wanted to be free; I wanted to do as I wished, and nothing more. I would've been quite happy if such a dreadful responsibility had never befallen me. It's exhausting, and it bores me, and I wish I could push it onto someone else. But there is no one else. That's all."

There was only one thing Rhia could think to say to that. "Is there anything I can do to help?"

"Don't tell anyone else about this," Lirien said. "And get me out of this city, with assurances that I won't be followed. I think you understand, now, that *I* was never afraid of Hephestion, but if he seeks to importune me and bargain with me, he may be the one with something to fear. I have no wish to do him harm, yet I may harm him all the same. And it is very easy for me to harm someone."

Rhia considered her options. "I'll talk to the queen. I won't reveal your secret, but I will ask her to grant your wish. I have never asked any favors of her, and I believe she trusts in my integrity. It may be I can get her to agree."

"So you'll keep my secret after all," Lirien said, not quite a question.

Rhia nodded. "I will."

"Why? Because of what I said before?"

"That I owe you?" Rhia shrugged. "Well, you weren't wrong. You did know me as well as you believed. To refuse to repay such a great favor would be . . . unforgivably churlish. And I don't believe keeping your secret from her will result in harm to the queen."

"It's really that simple?" Lirien asked.

"I'm told that I'm a simple person," Rhia said. "By those who are too kind to call me a fool, at least."

SINCE THE ATTEMPT on Adora's life, Feste had been, if not precisely chastised, at least conciliatory, and he did not protest when she summoned him. "I won't mince words with you," she said. "I need you to fulfill that favor you owe me, since Rhia won the duel."

He sighed. "I understand. And a prince, of all people, should keep his word. Let's hear this disagreeable task."

"Jocelyn Selreshe," Adora said, "must leave our city, and once again return to her family's home in the west."

For a moment Feste stared in disbelief, and then he started laughing. "And you expect me to refuse? Have you forgotten that I myself have yearned to be rid of her from the very first day she showed her face here?"

"As usual," Adora said, "you charge ahead without waiting to hear the rest.

I talked to Mother, and she agreed that Jocelyn should leave—but on two conditions, neither of which you will like. First, that we do all we can to appease Jocelyn, lest she return home with a tale of outrage and offense to tell her parents. And second . . . that we dismiss Lirien also—or else, if you will not, that I use my favor to part the two of you for a time. You know what strife our parents had with Landon, and how ill Mother would take another such quarrel."

Unlike Feste, Landon had seemed entirely uninterested in taking any kind of mistress . . . until he wasn't. Also unlike Feste, his passion for the woman who eventually caught his eye had endured, and he and Father had argued for months and months: Landon had not dared to defy Father so openly as to marry someone he deemed unworthy, but he refused to throw her over, either. It had seemed their quarrel would never end—until, more than a year after meeting her, and many months after he and Father had started feuding, Landon had abruptly parted ways with his mistress, and never spoke a word about her after that day. He'd apparently drowned his sorrows with a rash of uncharacteristically wanton behavior in the following weeks, but then even that abated, and he returned to his former disinterest. Adora had wanted to ask him, many times, if he had truly felt love for that woman, or desire that dried up, or merely a wish to spite Father, but she had never been brave enough. He'd get this look on his face if you so much as approached the subject, a look so sad and forbidding it forced you to turn aside.

To her surprise, Feste did not react with immediate outrage. His exuberance was considerably dimmed, but he kept his words cautious. "Just let me talk to her first, all right? If she must go, I don't want her to misunderstand me, or to think ill of any of us."

"I don't object to that," Adora said, "but first we must handle Jocelyn. As long as you act with courtesy, she has nothing true to complain about to her parents. This is how I see it: you choose a day to take Jocelyn aside, away from me and Mother, and explain why a marriage between you cannot ever come to pass— leaving out all the reasons that are personally insulting to her."

"I understand. We're laying the fault at my feet, yes? If it'll quit me of any obligations toward her, I'll pronounce myself the least, ill-fittingest man from here to the other side of the Endless Sea. And after I do that, I can talk to Lirien? And then I'll have fully acquitted myself for that embarrassing duel?"

"That's right," Adora said. "I won't ask anything more of you than that."

"Then I suppose I should count myself lucky that it's not any worse," her brother said.

Adora was inclined to agree. But because nothing could ever come off smoothly these days, she hadn't had that settled for an hour before Rhia, newly returned from the city, arrived to give her report. She hovered nervously at the door to the study before Adora asked her in, and that alone meant she had something more than routine to say. "Were we in the city for long enough, Your Grace?"

"You missed all the important conversations, so I suppose so," Adora said. "The only wrinkle is that I suspect Feste still thinks he can persuade Lirien to stay with him, but all that means is that he'll try and fail, right?"

She'd spoken lightheartedly, but a shadow passed over Rhia's face at the comment. "I don't think that would be wise, Your Grace."

"To let him make his suit to Lirien? Why not? You don't think she'll accept it, do you?"

"No," Rhia said. "I cannot imagine that she will."

"Then what's the harm in letting him try, if we know it'll be for nothing?"

Rhia squared her shoulders, and took a deep breath. "Your Grace. I have something to tell you—something I can't fully explain, even if you command me to. Lirien Arvel must be sent away from here. It is what she wishes, but even if it were not, if she remains here something terrible will happen. You must let her go, and you must prevent my lord the prince from going after her, at all costs. I can't tell you how I have come to this opinion, or why I am so certain of it; I can only ask you to trust me."

If Rhia had truly decided she could not share this information, then it was no use trying to persuade her; in matters of personal principle, she was ever immoveable. So Adora tried to piece together what she could. "And if I wished to speak with Lirien?"

Rhia bit her lip. "I would not recommend even that, Your Grace. Her path was never meant to cross ours, and it'll be better for everyone if we separate again. Even you have sensed that, I think; you've been so uneasy since she came here."

Adora could hardly deny that, though she wished she knew more about what specifically Rhia feared. She sighed. "Wonderful. Now I have to go back on the word I just gave to my brother, which is bound to reopen the quarrel I thought we were finally on the verge of closing."

"Does that mean you're going to listen to me?" Rhia asked.

"I don't think it would be wise of me to do anything else. I know you would not say such a thing unless you were completely certain. And I have long felt that there is . . . something strange at work here." She leaned forward. "But now we must plan even more carefully if we are to keep matters on their proper course. And you and I must keep some things hidden even from Hephestion, which is not what I would have wanted. But I believe it is the best way."

THERE WAS ONE thing more that happened that night, one that Adora could never have foreseen. She was preparing to go to sleep when a guard tore up the steps of her tower, waving a scrap of parchment received from a messenger who had arrived at the palace in no less haste. And when Adora looked at the unfolded paper, there before her was a name she had never expected to see again.

There can be no mistake, Your Grace. It was Prince Landon himself.

Chapter Twenty-nine

Esthrades

It was the first untroubled sleep Talis had had since she first started traveling with Cadfael, and that alone should have warned her. The gods never had anything good in store for her; if something fortuitous seemed to happen, it would only yield worse fortune later.

For all her misgivings about him, he hadn't done anything Talis could find suspicious, and she'd tried. He followed slightly behind her as they walked, but he never attempted to slip out of sight; he was naturally quiet, but responded easily when spoken to. She didn't know if he was trying to appeal to her on purpose, but she didn't think so; despite his looks, he seemed a man to whom the very idea of charm was utterly foreign. And he was surprisingly resourceful at cooking.

Still, their nights had been uneasy, because sleep was the only time at which he'd be able to overpower her. Cadfael declared himself entirely amenable to whatever arrangement she thought best, but left it to her to puzzle out what those arrangements might be. Her sense of caution warred with her sense of embarrassment, and in the beginning caution won. Which was how she ended up spending her first night in a tree. But the more nights passed in which he didn't do anything but sleep, the harder it became to believe he really had any furtive intentions toward her. She was starting to get downright careless, so perhaps, in a way, having another incident served her right.

She hadn't been up an hour when the discomfort started, a vague pain in her head combined with a sudden murkiness to her thoughts, that renewed sense that she was no longer the sole occupant of her own mind. Voltest's anger was a distracting heat at the far edge of her consciousness, but she was used to that by now; worse was the change in Lirien's thoughts, the usual serenity replaced by something more turbulent, like wracked indecision. Talis didn't care about anything that troubled Lirien, but she depended on that calmness as a last resort. And when the wind started whistling strong enough to tear leaves from the trees around them, she knew she wouldn't have it.

Beside her, Cadfael stopped uncertainly. "Are you doing that?" He already had to raise his voice to be heard.

How could she answer that? "Not on purpose, but it is . . . because of me. Can we keep walking? It'll get worse if we just stand here."

"All right." For a moment she thought he was going to offer her his arm, but he settled for matching his pace to hers, keeping a respectful space between them. As they moved through the trees, the incline grew steeper; the Lanvaldian mountains were far off, thank the gods, but still the land arched toward them, as if it was as stubbornly drawn to the past as she was.

"I'm . . . from there, you know," she mumbled to Cadfael; she hadn't meant to, but anything that could serve as a distraction would be helpful now.

He bent his head toward her. "What?"

"The mountains." She risked a look east, in their direction; she couldn't see anything but trees, of course, but she knew they were there. "That's where I'm from. That's where I was born."

"Not many people can say that." He kicked a loose rock out of the way before she could trip on it. "I hear there's not much up there."

"There's even less now," she said—too bitterly. It made her head throb, and the wind howled in response.

Cadfael noticed. "What do you mean by that?"

Damn it, this was going to be a bad one. "I think . . . I think maybe you should leave, and come back later. Just an hour at most—it'll all be fine by then. It's never lasted longer than that."

He didn't look convinced. "And what will happen if I stay?"

"You'll . . . get hurt, maybe."

"I don't care about that."

"I don't want you to see it. I don't care if you follow me after that, but I want you to get out of here before—"

There was a sudden crack, and they both jumped: a dead tree, leaning precariously against a more youthful trunk, had been caught in the rising gale, and crashed down to the forest floor in a spray of leaves. The wind blew them back toward her, and she raised a hand to shield her face—and stumbled under the weight of the rising pain, falling to her knees. The despair rose up, louder and more terrible than any storm, and smothered her.

For several moments she couldn't see, and then she realized she had shut her eyes reflexively, to protect them from the grit kicked up by the screaming winds. The trees creaked all around her, and she prayed there weren't any more about to topple over, because she couldn't stand up. She didn't know where Cadfael was; she couldn't feel his presence, and when she cracked her eyes open she could only tell he wasn't in front of her.

Then he touched her arm, a tentative brush of his fingers against her elbow. "If this is going to continue, we should get to higher ground," he shouted. "There's too much debris down here; we'll get hit by something."

"I can't stand up," she said—not as loudly, but the wind made sure he heard her. "I can't move from here."

Instead of protesting, he tried to sit down next to her. But that brought the sword too close, inches from her skin, and she shrank back. "Keep that away from me!" She hated the fear in her voice. There had been so many swords that day.

At first he didn't understand, but then he looked down, and must have realized what she meant. They stayed like that for several moments, as she clutched her head and he stared at her, unmoving. And then he unbuckled his sword belt, and pitched it off into the trees.

He took hold of her arm again, and tried to help pull her to her feet. But though she had flown in the air before, now she felt as heavy as lead, and he could not move her. Instead, he put one arm in front of her and the other above her head, as if that would really provide any protection if something heavy came toward them, and ducked his own head down, so it pressed against her shoulder.

She couldn't hear even the wind anymore. She shut her eyes again, and for some incalculable length of time it was as if she'd stopped existing in the present entirely, and could only relive the past. That was, perhaps, the bargain she'd made without realizing it: without this power, she could never have escaped that day alive, but it was this power that made sure she would be trapped there forever.

Then she could feel his presence again, and hear the wind, slackening. She took a deep breath of air, and the wind didn't snatch it away from her. She breathed, slowly and deeply, and finally she raised her head. "I think it's going to stop now," she said, because she couldn't promise him any more than that.

She tried to stand, but it was too soon, and when she stumbled he caught her arm. But this time she felt lighter, and he was able to hold her up. She brushed him off, but tried to do it gently, so he wouldn't think her entirely ungrateful.

"Is it all right if I go look for my sword?" he asked. "I know about where I threw it, but I hope it didn't get blown off somewhere."

"It wasn't," Talis assured him. "And yes, go on."

She was right, of course. He dug it out of the underbrush, dusting it off carefully before he buckled it back on. He did seem fond of the thing, though she had to admit he'd thrown it away readily enough. Did she have to thank him for that?

He closed the distance between them more hesitantly, though the wind had died down almost completely, just a few stray wisps hardly strong enough to ruffle their hair. "Are you still in pain?"

She tapped her forehead. "It usually wears itself out."

"That's not really an answer."

She sighed. "It doesn't hurt like it did, but it's still . . . *wrong*. It's always wrong. But there's nothing I know of that can fix that."

He frowned. "Was it like that when we fought? You seemed in control of it then."

"I *am* in control of it," she insisted. "I just . . . it makes me feel things, and then the wind responds to those things, because the wind is part of me. And back when we fought . . ." She tried to remember. "We would've just lost him, though we didn't know it for sure yet. Our powers would have been much more stable then." Off his look, she said, "When we lost Miken, I mean. The fourth of our number. Here, look." She reached under her shirt, and brought out the pendant with its tiny diamond. "He made these, one for each of us, and enchanted them himself. He liked to say the earth spoke to him, though of course that wasn't literally true. It told him where all kinds of treasures were hidden, and he was able to cast minor enchantments on the things he found. When we wear them, they enhance this natural ability we seem to have, to sense where the rest of us are. It's still not completely specific, but, for example . . ." She gripped the pendant in one fist, trying to concentrate. "I know that Voltest is north of us, and that he's much closer than Lirien, who is so far south she must be in Issamira. She's been in the same place for a while, which is unusual for her." She let the pendant drop. "That's why we had so much difficulty figuring out what had happened to Miken—someone must've removed the pendant before he was taken to Valyanrend's Citadel, which is where he died. I'm sure that if he'd died wearing it, we would have known instantly."

Cadfael was quiet for some time, no doubt wondering what he could get away with asking about someone who had died. "This boy. His connection to the earth was the same as yours to the wind?"

"More or less," Talis said. "Voltest's connection is to fire, and then I'm sure you can guess what Lirien's is. It suits her, too; I've told her that to her face, though she didn't like it. Water's such a capricious thing: cold or scalding, hard or liquid or intangible. It's always changing itself to suit the situation."

"I can guess how you feel about her, too, I think," Cadfael said, smiling slightly.

Talis huffed. "If everyone else liked her less, I'd be able to tolerate her more. Even *animals* like her, though you'd think a horse or a bird or a cat wouldn't care about human standards of beauty. But it's like they *know*." She clicked her tongue. "If I had that kind of beauty, I'd be able to make people like me, too."

Cadfael shrugged. "I don't know. In Araveil there seemed to be general agreement that I was handsome, but I can't think of many people there who liked me."

Talis surprised herself by laughing. "Well, you're different. If you devote yourself so thoroughly to being an ass, of course people are going to react accordingly."

"But I don't," he said. "I've never cared much whether people liked me, but I haven't tried to make them hate me any more than the reverse."

"Right, exactly. You don't need them, and you don't care if they know it. Even Lirien has a side like that, and when she lets it show, you can bet people hate it just as much. It's just that she knows how to wear a smiling face, and you don't. You can't expect your looks alone to do everything."

"So even you think I'm handsome." He didn't say it like he was gloating, though, just as if it was a new piece of information to puzzle over.

"I also think you're irritating," Talis reminded him.

He hesitated, his mind clearly gone somewhere else. "Can I ask you another question about that boy? Miken?"

"What is it?"

"He was the opposite of you, right? The air and the ground are opposed, if you think about it. So when he died . . . is that why things are so much worse for you now?"

Talis shook her head. "It's an interesting theory, but if that were so, Voltest and Lirien would still have their proper opposition, and they'd be fine. But Voltest isn't fine. In some ways, he's in an even worse state than I am. Even Lirien's been affected, though much less so. We're not two sets of two, we're one set of four. And we're not *opposed*. We were in balance, and now we're out of it."

"Then why isn't Lirien affected as much as the two of you?"

"That's one of the things Voltest is trying to figure out." She debated how much she should tell him. "He does have one theory—that it's because of how these abilities came to us in the first place. With him and me, it seemed to happen because we had great need of them. But the pattern doesn't hold. Lirien was out for a bloody walk, and Miken was *sleeping*. He took a nap in a meadow one afternoon, and dreamed that flowers started blooming all around him. And when he woke up, he could move boulders with his mind. I wish it had been that easy for me." She sighed. "Go on. I know you want to ask me."

He had enough grace to look embarrassed, at least. "It was something painful, wasn't it? That's why, when you said it makes you feel things . . ."

"Yes." The wind played with a drifting leaf, and they both held their breath. But nothing more severe happened, and Talis spoke again. "Voltest was a scholar. After Aurnis fell, the invading Hallerns kept him in his tower, making him do research for them. For a whole year he wasn't allowed to leave, and that's a long time for anger and resentment to grow. I don't imagine they treated him very well, either. Then one day one of his captors knocked over a candle, and with all that dry paper . . . before anyone had time to do anything, it was already out of control. Everyone else tried to flee, but Voltest ran *into* the flames, to try to save his books. And he didn't burn, or else . . . he said the fire burned him on the inside, instead of the outside. And then he could use it whenever he wanted, because it was part of him."

"I understand," Cadfael said, "but that wasn't really my question, either. Though I don't mean to say that you have to answer it."

She didn't have to, of course. But rather than keeping her mouth shut, she found she wanted to get it over with quickly, as if she could expel it and drive it away from her. "It was when my village was attacked. Not by anyone noteworthy, just by desperate men who had even less than we did and helped themselves to what was ours. Just about everyone I knew was killed. I was on the hillside when they came—if I'd been farther up I could have hidden from them entirely, but they saw me, and a couple chased me up the mountain. And I . . . when I was up there at the top, trying to get away from them, I . . ." She gritted her teeth. "I . . . fell. And the wind caught me. So that's why. I can do all these things, but only because of the worst day of my life—the day I lost everything else."

He opened his mouth, but she raised a hand to silence him. "Don't ask me about it, and don't say you're sorry. You asked, and I decided to tell you, but there's no way you could understand it. So don't try."

He shut his mouth, but almost immediately opened it again, with a different question. "Would you like to be free of it?"

"Of what?"

"Of . . . the wind, and all that comes with it."

Just thinking about it made her uneasy. "What kind of question is that? I'd be defenseless. How can I ever feel safe if I can't protect myself?"

He shrugged. "I suppose I feel much the same, even though the greatest swordsmen in our history still often died before their time. I just thought that I wouldn't want to have those powers myself, if they came at such a cost. I relive the worst moments of my life far too often already."

ALL THAT NIGHT, the dreams would not leave him.

Cadfael had been a vivid dreamer even as a boy; he had never sleepwalked, but had occasionally thrashed so violently in the grip of some nightmare that he flung himself from his bed. The dreams that night were all of Rhia, or of his father, or both of them. Cadfael's earliest memories were of his father, who had been, to that small boy, an entire world: protector, teacher, exemplar. A place to belong. It was only when he grew older that he understood how carefully his father had crafted that role for himself: bastard children were viewed by the world as unwanted, inconvenient, a shame and burden to their parents. So his father had raised his children twice as high, doted on them twice as fiercely, that they might never doubt his pride or his love.

He dreamed of a night twenty years ago, when his father came home with a mournful look upon his face and a tiny baby in his arms.

In reality they had spoken of many heavy things that night; his father had shared as much as a six-year-old boy could hope to understand. But though in the dream those hard words floated away, he saw the baby so vividly, sleeping on the table where they took their meals. He touched the back of her curled little hand with his finger—he could still remember doing that. "She's very tiny, Father," he said— skeptically, as if his father had brought back a weapon that was defective.

His father smiled down at the infant. "Aye. Born a bit too soon. But she'll be just fine, so long as we take good care of her. You'll help me with that, won't you?"

"Yes," Cadfael said, bowing his head, because it was a serious promise, and he wanted his father to know he meant it. He touched the baby's hand again, and her little forehead, and her little nose. She sure could sleep. "Hello," he said. "I'm your brother."

And then the dream changed, and she was no longer a sleeping infant but running toward him, weeping. He closed his arms around her reflexively, and she sobbed into his shoulder—in pain and terror, the way she'd never cried at nightmares. He realized there was blood on her fingers, and then that it wasn't hers, and then that she'd dropped her sword in the doorway. It was bloody, too. "I'm sorry!" she wailed, over and over. "I'm sorry, I'm sorry!"

He woke in pain, a tightness in his chest so strong he could barely breathe. It had felt so real. It was as if he had truly been comforting his sister just a moment ago, only to have her slip through his fingers like sand. It was as if he had been listening to her worries all over again, and still, after all this time, he felt the helplessness of being unable to understand the things that were most important to her.

He couldn't go back to sleep; he had to move, to clear his head. But he didn't want to wake Talis after she'd had such a trying day, and he didn't want her to wake up alone and think he'd deserted her in the night. He took his sword with him, but he left everything else, his little pack with the scant supplies he used when traveling, and hoped that would be enough to let her know that he'd return.

He was careful not to wander too far from their camp, lest he lose his way back. It must have been near dawn; the eastern sky was not yet pink, but it had grown light enough that he wasn't picking his way between the trees entirely blind.

A bastard child was an easy target for bullying, and when he was young Cadfael endured his share of it from the neighborhood children. But they loved to bully Rhia even more, not just because she was small, but because she had no sense of strategy or self-preservation: she never ran away, and she always got angry, and she always tried to fight back. For years she got into fights with whole groups of children, and never won a single one. Cadfael always patched her up afterward, but no matter how many bruises and scratches and skinned knuckles she got, she was always too stubborn to cry.

The first fight she ever won was her first fight with blades.

The boy was one of her most dedicated bullies, eager to show off his first sword. He'd probably just meant to wave the blade in her face to scare her, but the idiot ought to've known by then that Rhia didn't get scared, she got angry.

She had torn a huge gash in the boy's arm, stunning both of them. He had started screaming as the blood began to flow, and she had run for home, right into Cadfael's arms.

Cadfael took action immediately: he threatened the boy, and then he threatened the boy's parents, until he was certain that none of them would try to seek revenge. But when it came to Rhia's own feelings, he found himself at a loss.

"It's more of a good thing than a bad one, really," he had tried to tell her. "How many others have tried to brawl with you since then? Maybe now you'll finally have some peace."

"They're all afraid of me," she said glumly, looking even smaller than usual without the boundless energy that always seemed to make her take up more space.

"That's what I'm saying. That's what you *want*. If they understand that you can hurt them back, they won't try to hurt you in the first place." He shook his head. "If you didn't want to be able to fight them and win, why fight back at all? Surely you didn't just want to take a beating over and over?"

"Of course I wanted to win, just . . . now that I have, it's not like I thought it would be."

"Well, what did you think?"

She looked down. "I wanted them to understand that it was wrong. It was cruel to say those things about you and me and our parents. And it was cowardly to fight me in numbers just because I was small and ill-matched, and they knew they could get away with it. I thought that if I could beat them, I could make them understand that it was wrong. But all they understand is that I'm frightening. And now I can't fight them anymore, because if I'm stronger than they are . . . then I would be wrong." She put a hand to her forehead. "But if fighting when you're weak means you lose, and fighting when you're strong makes you a bully, then what should I do? How can I make them understand?"

And what could he have said to her, then or now? It had been years, and he was no closer to knowing. "I don't think anyone's ever going to understand that, Rhia," he had said to her then. "Even I don't understand it."

It was just at that moment, when he remembered the question she had asked—the question he couldn't answer. He saw a flicker in the corner of his eye, though he couldn't tell whether it was light or movement or something else. He whirled, already on his guard: what could have gotten so close to him in this forest, and made no sound?

"You disappoint me, boy."

For just an instant, one melancholy moment divorced from logic and time, he thought his father stood before him.

Even after he remembered, after he reminded himself what was and wasn't possible in this world, still the resemblance was uncanny. The man had his father's build, the height, the broad shoulders and muscled arms. The hair and stubble were the same, the same pale color, the same style, more gently windswept than truly unkempt. His father's eyes, that were Rhia's eyes, that slightly faded green.

But the man was not his father, and not only because his father was dead. The man's face was not his father's face, nor was it that of anyone Cadfael knew. And the expression that face wore . . . his father had never looked at him that way, with such harshness and disdain. For all his size and strength, he had always been gentle with his children, in words and gestures both. His father would never have called him a disappointment.

Cadfael put a hand on the hilt of his sword. "Who are you?" he asked.

The man laughed. It was not his father's laugh, loud and hearty—it was a scornful laugh, and it grated on his ears. "What is knowing that worth to you?"

"Nothing," Cadfael said. "But I am told honest men do not fear to give their names."

The man's lip curled in a scowl. "*You* may call me Yaelor—though I am no dog, to turn at the sound of my name. Nor need you introduce yourself to me; I know you all too well."

"Well, I don't know you at all," Cadfael said. "What is it you think you know of me?"

The man's face was stern, unyielding, still so prideful—it was always prideful, whatever other changes passed across it. "Much and more," he said. "Enough to know how little you have done with yourself these past few years. You shame yourself with this paltry existence. Strength has been given to you, but you use it to no purpose. You let selfishness and impotent anger rule your heart. Would those you claimed to love rejoice to see you now?"

Cadfael would have been less stunned and angrier if he could have understood where the man's knowledge was coming from. Was he some relative of his father's? Or could he possibly have anything to do with the Glendowers, his mother's people? He might almost have thought old Lord Glendower had sent the man to shame Cadfael into doing his bidding, now that Rhia was dead, but Lord Glendower was dead, too, and his father had no living family that he knew of.

Meeting Talis had certainly made him reconsider what was and wasn't possible, and while he did not yet suspect this man was like her, still he did not seem of common men. Cadfael drew his sword. "You have given me no reason to hold my tongue or my temper with you. You have given me no reason for trust. Now answer my questions clearly, or be driven from this place as one with ill intent. Who are you, and how do you know me?"

Cadfael was not short or small, yet the man made him feel so, looking down at him from his great height. But it was more than that: most excessively proud men revealed themselves as fools with the first three sentences they spoke, but this one had none of that foppish bluster. He wore his pride like something he had earned, like a truth that suffused his entire being—less like a king wore his crown than like a warrior wore his scars, the proof of his courage carved into his flesh.

"I have told you already," he said. "I am Yaelor, and I know you because you cannot hide from me as you can from your fellow men. Do you need to be coddled even now, after all you have seen? Are you still so fragile as to gape helplessly at the truths of this world, you who faced the wind itself and lived?"

Cadfael gave an uneasy laugh. "It seems you aren't lying about one thing. I'm starting to think there's nothing you don't know about me."

For the first time, the man seemed to choose his words carefully. "I know all you have done, but not what you will do."

"Are you a mage? Or . . . one of whatever Talis is?"

"No."

"But you aren't an ordinary man."

The man raised the haughty angle of his chin even farther. "I never claimed to be."

"What are you, then?"

"I am Yaelor," the man said again, which was really starting to get irritating. But then, as if relenting, he added, "That is the who, as well as the what. I can answer no more clearly than that."

"Well, you obviously came here to speak with me," Cadfael said, "so I hope you can be clearer about that, at least."

Again Yaelor seemed to be picking over his words. "I have come to convince you to do something. It is something that *must* be done, but even I don't know how to make you see that, when you care about so little."

"You can start by answering two questions," Cadfael said. "What is it, and why must I be the one to do it?"

"There is a life that you must save. Even now there is a plot in motion, a craven attempt to kill the queen of Issamira. I had thought it might be avoided, that the queen and those who serve her might either uncover the plot or foil it before it could truly begin. But that will not happen now. They have made too many mistakes. The plot will unfold as planned, and the queen will soon be in grave danger. And if she dies, the future will be bleak in this land for a very long time."

Cadfael could hardly believe what he was hearing, but this he understood. "You mean Elgar. If the queen dies, Elgar will have his Elesthene? Is that what you're saying?"

"I have told you that I do not know what will be," Yaelor said. "But I know what is. There are three heirs to the blood of Talia Avestri, but only one can do what must be done. Adora Avestri must live, and she must claim her throne. If she does not, I cannot see any way forward." He paused. "Your second question. You must be the one to do this, because . . . because I can ask no one else. You may not believe that, but it is the truth." He clenched his jaw. "I do not lie. Only cowards lie."

Cadfael almost smiled; that sounded like something Rhia would say. He found that he believed Yaelor's words, as strange as they were. "I took a king's orders once, and protected another for a brief time. But I wouldn't even know the first thing about how to foil this plot, or how to save the queen. How do you expect me to succeed?"

"If you go to Issamira," Yaelor said, "you must cross the Curse above Shallowsend, and follow the banks of the Sverin River southward. If you do this, I will appear to you once more. I will tell you all I can, and I hope and believe that will be enough. And you are better equipped than you think. Your father's sword, in the hands of one who knows how to wield it as you do . . . the queen's greatest foe should certainly fear such a thing." He sighed. "You don't care for others' struggles; I would know nothing about you if I did not know that. But you at least hate the one who calls himself Imperator Elgar, do you not? Does destroying this foul dream of his hold no satisfaction for you at all?"

"You know why I hate Elgar," Cadfael said. "You know, and you have the gall to mention it to me? If you truly know so much—"

"Don't," Yaelor said; he actually looked agitated. "I know what you wish to say. But you don't understand—"

"You want me to trust you!" Cadfael shouted at him. "You would have me believe in your judgment, in your aims; you would have me believe you have some wish to prevent tragedy. But, what, Rhia wasn't important enough for you to use all this knowledge of yours to help me protect her? I would have done anything you asked—I would have pulled the stars from the sky, if you had told me it would help make a world that she could live in. And instead you come to me *now*, after all this time? Now, when I am already ruined?"

He wouldn't have imagined it was possible, but at last Yaelor looked chastised, the brilliance of his self-possession dampened. His words came slowly, and Cadfael could tell he was making an effort to infuse them with sincerity. "I cannot give you the full answer to that, the truest answer. I cannot because I am not free to do whatever I wish in this world. I have made deals with those whose power equals my own; there is a balance we struck ages ago, a balance that must be kept, because we have borne witness to what happens when it is not. Even to say what I have said to you now, I strain at the boundaries of that balance. If I did not appear to you at the moment you would have wished, it is for that same reason—that it was not permitted to me.

"You think that you are ruined now, but I tell you it is not so. There is more within you; there is more you can become. What you must fear is not the ruin of the past, but the ruin that may be yet to come. You stand at a crossroads. If you do what I have said, you may find a truth greater than you have imagined possible. You may find paths open to you that you thought closed forever. But if you do not intervene to save this queen and her country, it may be that you one day discover the full consequences of your inaction. Should that day come, you will feel a grief unlike any you have ever felt before, pain to make all the pain of your past seem trivial. Then, and only then, will you become truly lost."

What could hurt Cadfael more than he'd been hurt already, when the people he loved most were so long dead? And yet to ignore such a dire warning seemed like running into a storm and daring the lightning to strike you.

Perhaps there was some middle ground. "You want me to believe you have this ability—to know things you shouldn't be able to know. Do you know where Shinsei is right now?"

"I do," Yaelor said, "but that knowledge is worth far less to you than you think."

"I'll decide what it's worth to me," Cadfael said. "And I'm trying to offer you a deal."

"Adora Avestri's life for the whereabouts of the man others call Shinsei?" Yaelor shook his head, but not in refusal. "Let me amend the bargain thus. If, when you have done what I require, Shinsei still lives, and you still wish to find him, I will ensure that you do. If you find that you no longer care, you may ask me for another favor instead."

"Even better. I'll not dispute those terms."

"Then you will do what I ask of you?" Yaelor said, searching his face for the answer.

Cadfael sighed. "I'll consider doing what you ask of me. I'm a bit busy right now. You should already know that, if you know so much."

Yaelor shook his head again. "This is not what you should be doing. The one possessed of the wind is in need of help; that is certainly true. But you cannot help her. Indeed, if chaos breaks out in Issamira, things may become worse for her as well."

"Because her comrade is there," Cadfael guessed. "This Lirien, who's supposedly as capricious as water. When the boy died, Talis's abilities started to bring her pain. If this woman dies, too . . ."

Yaelor said nothing, but the look in his eyes communicated much.

"Can anyone help her?" Cadfael asked. "You said I can't. Does that mean some-one else can? Or is there nothing that can be done for her at all?"

Again Yaelor chose his words carefully. "I have seen those like her before: those whom magic harms as much as it helps, whom it nourishes and feeds upon in equal measure. Some of them have surrendered utterly to madness, and died gruesome deaths. Others have lived long and fruitful lives, full of joy and purpose. As she is now . . . she stands at a crossroads, just as you do. Either fate is open to her. Neither is inevitable. But neither is impossible. I can say no more than that."

"All right," Cadfael said. "I understand, I suppose." Perhaps he could ask that question instead, he thought suddenly. Instead of Shinsei's whereabouts, he could ask what could be done for Talis. It wouldn't be betraying Rhia, as Rhia herself would have vastly preferred it—that he help someone rather than hurting someone else. But he pushed that thought away; in order to ask Yaelor anything at all, he'd have to save this queen first, and that would hardly be the struggle of an afternoon. "Wait, didn't you say there were others like you? If I do what you want, will they try to stop me?"

"I doubt they will try to stop you outright," Yaelor said, "though they may try to toy with you in their own way. Above all others, you must fear Amerei—that jealous trickster, who must see her claws pierce all before she is satisfied. It has long pleased her to try to lay claim to what is mine, and our feud has continued unabated since its beginning so long ago. Tethantys is as much an unscrupulous liar, but he seeks other prey, and tends to grow bored wherever his interest is not naturally strong. But Amerei will seek you simply because you are mine—because she wants everything, but she wants those things most of all that seem impossible for her to possess. And you . . . there is much of her in you already, more even than you know."

"And these others lie?" Cadfael asked. "You don't, but they do?"

"To lie is cowardly, and cowardice is against my nature," Yaelor said. "You cannot expect them to care about such things."

"So are you saying you don't want to be a coward? Or that you *can't* be one, even if you wished to?"

Yaelor gave him a look of such scornful offense that he took a step back. "Why would I ever *wish* to be a coward?"

He couldn't help laughing, though there was bitterness in it. "You really should've considered helping my sister. You would have loved her."

Yaelor stared at him, and in his face were the marks of a pain even more intense than his anger had been, a pain that was sincere and undeniable. "I have loved her," he said. "I love her still. So few have walked so far along the path, and borne themselves so well." He bowed his head. "You know her so well, and yet even you cannot know how much she would wish you to do as I have said."

Saving an imperiled queen from underhanded villainy? It was the kind of undertaking Rhia would have loved most. What a pity she was not the one to receive it. "I've said I'll think about it, and I'll think about it. Until then, let me talk to Talis on my own. I need to . . . work things out with her."

"It will all be according to your will," Yaelor said. "But time grows short."

Cadfael left him standing there, motionless, and walked back toward where he'd left Talis. But when he turned to look behind him, a dozen steps on, he wasn't truly surprised to find that Yaelor was gone.

Chapter Thirty

Mist's Edge

ELGAR AND HIS men returned to Mist's Edge with no more warning or fanfare than the thunder of their horses' hooves as they approached. Varalen had just come in from watching the wall again, and was in his tent writing down his newest observations when he heard the commotion. He stuck his head out in time to see the soldiers ride into camp. Could Elgar really not even have sent a messenger?

The imperator himself nearly leaped down from his horse, handing it off to the nearest man without a care. "I see you still haven't made a move on the castle," he said—a question, not an accusation.

Varalen handed him the parchment he'd been writing on. "I couldn't convince myself it was the right thing. The boy's playing a very curious game here. How go things in the rest of Reglay?"

"Second Hearth is ours," Elgar said, taking a seat without looking up from the parchment. "We had a few skirmishes outside it, but they all ended in surrender. We've been scrupulously merciful." He waved the paper at Varalen. "You'll have to explain this to me. Is this Kelken's curious game?"

"One would think," Varalen said, "that the boy either wants us to try to climb his walls and fetch him out, or he doesn't. If, as I originally thought, he wants to keep us here as long as possible, then any direct attack on our part would be disastrous for him. And yet I can't shake the impression that a direct attack is just what he wants."

"And this paper?" Elgar asked.

"My observations to that end. Every morning there's this one fellow who comes out on the wall—I think I recognize him from when we stayed at Mist's Edge at Kelken's invitation, one of the guards who stuck close to the king. Every morning I see him up there, peering down at the camp and deep in conversation with one of a handful of others, always one of the same three. I suspect their task is to judge how close we are to an attack, and in the event we do decide to scale the walls, I think there's something they're supposed to do."

He tapped the parchment. "I've been experimenting a bit. A couple times I ordered the men to make preparations, to ready the ladders as if we intended to use them that day. And I observed their reaction. There was quite a flurry of conversation, but ultimately the same thing always happened: that one man went into the tower above the east wall, right there, and didn't come out again for hours, until it was clear we weren't going to attack. He must have been preparing something for us."

"A trap he's trying to spring, perhaps."

"Right, whence springs my problem. Not only do I have to decide whether to attack or not, I have to decide whether my invaders should storm the eastern wall and tower in force immediately, in an effort to stop whatever they're trying to do over there, or whether I should instruct the men to give that area as wide a berth as possible." He set the parchment down. "But you've returned—unexpectedly, too. I assume this means you intend to take control of the army here again?"

"No," Elgar said. "That's what I originally came to talk to you about, actually. I'll be returning to Valyanrend."

Varalen sat back in surprise. "Returning? Why? It seems like you have things well in hand here."

"Which means my presence has become less necessary," Elgar said. "Quentin, however, does not have things well in hand back home." He waved away Varalen's protests. "I'm not blaming the man; without the honesty and thoroughness of his reports, I wouldn't be able to understand what's going on at all. It's simply that he's not properly equipped to deal with the matter, and I am."

"And might I ask what matter that is, Your Eminence?"

Elgar pursed his lips. "This resistance. They've grown too large, and too confident. There have been a couple of incidents—incidents Quentin doesn't understand, but I do. At this point, it's not enough to foil their plans—I need to crush them. I need to show anyone who would join them the hopelessness of that endeavor. And that's simply not something Quentin can do in my place."

"But you're confident you can?"

"I am. I've figured out what they're after, and . . ." He smiled slightly. "I've been preparing something that I've wanted to test for some time. This seems to be the perfect opportunity."

Whatever it was, Varalen was certain he didn't want to know about it. There was a far more pressing question to ask, anyway: "What does that mean for me, Your Eminence?"

"I still need to take this castle," Elgar said. "How you do it is up to you, but I need you here until then. I'm leaving you all the men I've stationed here, and half of those I took with me to eastern Reglay; I won't need them in Valyanrend." He paused. "And Shinsei, I think."

A chill ran down Varalen's spine. "Shinsei? Surely not. Will he even obey my orders? He does not seem to bear any loyalty toward anyone but you."

"That is so," Elgar said, "but he understands what a chain of command is. If I tell him that, while the both of you remain here, he's to follow your commands in my stead, he will do so."

"And we're all to stay here until the siege is concluded? No matter what?"

"Unless I send you word in the future saying otherwise," Elgar said. "But don't expect that. I need that boy dealt with, Varalen. We won't have enough men to move on Esthrades if we can't finish things here."

And he was anxious to conquer Esthrades, Varalen knew. He saw Arianrod Margraine as the greatest remaining threat to him, and who could say whether he wasn't right?

"I understand," he said.

"Good. I leave tomorrow at first light with the men I'm taking with me. When next I hear from you, I wish to hear that Kelken Rayl is in your custody, or dead."

CHAPTER THIRTY-ONE

Valyanrend

ROGER HAD TAKEN to using the old candlestick when he traversed the tunnels. He'd left some spare torches in the braziers on either side of the secret archive, in case more light was required, but he liked the maneuverability the candlestick allowed him, and perhaps after all this time exploring his eyes were adjusting to the dark.

He had spent some time investigating the archive, but it was so enormous that it was difficult to make much progress, or to find what and where the most valuable secrets were. He was often thwarted by another book in that strange language, or else in a language that wasn't strange but wasn't his own. Then there were the books that were trivial, or about subjects that didn't interest him. He'd skimmed quite a few books about famous thieves or outlaws, and those were entertaining—stirred up more than a few ideas in the back of his mind, too. The books on magic were

tantalizing but fruitless—he didn't have any himself, so reading about how someone might use it if they did have it depressed him after a while. And he'd tried to
read some history, but there was so much of it he hardly knew where to begin.

Eventually, he'd decided that the books weren't going anywhere, and he might
as well explore the tunnels again. Discovering the archive at all made him think he
was getting closer to something important; the archive itself probably wasn't what
had drawn the ruby's power, but he did think whatever it was was nearby.

He spent the next several days mapping out all the passages closest to the archive, but when he finally did find something, he literally stumbled into it. He'd
never found any steps in the tunnels before, only slopes, so he wasn't used to watching his feet, and nearly fell on his face as the floor went over a hump and then
dropped away. He swayed several steps forward before he'd fully recovered his
balance, and when he managed to look about him, he was already standing in the
room.

It was the largest room he had ever found in the tunnels, by a huge margin.
Walls and ceiling all fell away around him, so that for the first time the dimness felt
empty instead of stifling. Then he realized he could actually make out the walls and
ceiling, despite having only a single candle; it was lighter in here than it had any
right to be. It took him some time to figure out where the light was coming from:
all the way up there in the ceiling, he could just make out a tiny hole. As small as it
was, it must have bored incredibly deep to reach all the way to the surface.

There were braziers all along the walls, and standing upright on either side of
the only other thing in the room. Or, to be precise, the nine other things: nine
stone statues, arranged in a slight semicircle.

At first, without considering it carefully, he thought this was some underground Ninist vestry, so strongly did he associate the religion with the number.
But of course that couldn't be true. In any Ninist vestry, there were indeed nine
statues, but separated—seven above and two below, not nine all together. And
when he examined the statues in detail, they did not correspond to the Ninist figures he knew. The first one would have been easy to mistake for the Magician: a
smooth-faced figure with long hair, carrying books and scrolls in great armfuls.
But as Roger brought the candle close, he saw that this was a woman in her prime,
not a boy on the cusp of manhood. The second and third places would have gone to
the King and Queen, but the second figure, though finely dressed, clutched a crown
in his fist rather than wearing it on his head. Something about his expression and
posture made Roger doubt that crown belonged to him by rights. And the woman
on his other side wasn't wearing a crown at all; she was dressed like a common soldier, brandishing a broken sword and a shoddy wooden shield in a defensive stance.
Then came a somber, scholarly man, carrying a heavy book under one arm and a
set of scales in his hand; after him was a young mother, tenderly watching over the

sleeping infant she held in her arms. The next figure was an old man, dreadfully thin, dressed in rags and barefoot, with one hand extended as if to bestow a gift; on his palm rested a single crust of bread. On his far side a lutist played her instrument soundlessly; the next statue, of a young man with closed eyes and a serene expression, puzzled Roger for some time, until he noticed the man's arms were bound behind his back, and his bare feet rested upon kindling. A martyr?

That would have been unnerving enough, but the ninth statue was more unnerving still. A cloaked figure, of uncertain age and gender, only the nose and mouth visible beneath the shadow of its stone hood. It had a hand pressed to one side, and an arrow shaft sprouted from between its fingers. Yet it did not seem to be in its death throes; it was posed as if struggling on, feet firmly planted, upper body bent forward, toward whatever lay ahead. There were many more arrows at its feet, most of them broken.

These could not possibly be the Nine—or not the Ninists' Nine, at any rate. Did that mean Gran had been right? She'd told him many times that the Ninists had built their religion on the bones of another, older sect, devouring it in the process. Could these be the gods of that old religion? It had always struck Roger as odd that a monotheistic religion like Ninism had spent all its art and symbolism depicting nine humans, while there were virtually no depictions of their Lord of Heaven. But it made sense, if they were trying to get the number right in order to draw these other practitioners into their fold.

Yet the statues themselves were at odds with that theory. These didn't seem like statues of gods, or at least of anything that Roger might call a god. They all seemed preoccupied by things that were so essentially human. Why would a god need to bother with books? Why would a god need to fight with a sword? And surely gods couldn't starve or burn, or be wounded by any mortal arrow?

As Roger examined the statues in the light of the candle, he noticed something else. At the base of each statue, the pedestal upon which each figure rested, there were letters carved into the stone. He bent down to look, and swore. Every inscription was in that same bloody language, those ornate and incomprehensible symbols.

Setting the candlestick down on the ground in front of him, Roger pulled out a spare piece of parchment and a thin stick of charcoal. He made his way around the semicircle, doing his best to copy down each inscription. He didn't want to, but maybe he ought to give the list to Tom; might be he had some reference for it buried somewhere in those old books of his.

After he was done, he looked the statues over once more. They were as well carved as any Ninist statues he had ever seen; the expressions of the figures were all so vivid. The tenderness of the mother, the determination of the fighter, the resolve of the martyr . . . the sculptor had conveyed them perfectly. Roger found his eyes drawn to the statue of the man with the crown, so detailed it was chilling: he was gripping that crown so hard, you might well fear it would cut into his flesh. There was a wary tension in his stance, as if he feared that, even now, some attack might come from an unforeseen quarter, ready to snatch his prize away from him. And his face . . . what a face that was to behold. Whatever apprehension might still show in his posture, that face betrayed his triumph, lips frozen forever in the beginnings of a satisfied smile. And though his eyes were stone, it was so easy to imagine how they would gleam, reflecting the candlelight. . . .

Roger froze. Something had just occurred to him, staring so deeply at the statue's face. They must have been old, this lot—centuries old, or even millennia. And these tunnels must have been deserted; he'd been exploring them for weeks now, and never so much as heard another human soul.

And yet, however long these statues must have lain here in the dark, forgotten and unattended, they were not covered by a single speck of dust.

Those stone eyes, that he had examined so carelessly, now unsettled him: locked in an unseeing stare, and yet so expressive they could almost come to life. Nine figures, and seven pairs of staring eyes—the martyr's closed lids were a reprieve, but the cloaked figure was worst of all, the unanswerable mystery of what his eyes were like.

Roger found he'd backed away from them, holding the candlestick between his body and theirs. He fancied he felt a warmth in the air, not from the slender flame but all around him, as if a crowd pressed close, breathing down his neck.

You're panicking, he told himself. *You're dreaming things up.* Yet even as he tried to calm himself, he knew he had to get out of this room, and did not know when he would be able to return to it.

CHAPTER THIRTY-TWO

Stonespire

BECAUSE STONESPIRE HALL was on the small side for a monarch's castle, no room could be superfluous. The long table was rather large for a party of five, but there was no smaller dining room in the hall—they dragged even larger tables out to the great hall for feasts. At least the additional seats meant it was no trouble to accommodate anyone else who might happen to dine with them, as occasionally Ilyn or Captain Ingret did. But tonight it was just the five of them, a long oaken table, and yet another platter of fish.

"What is this one?" Prince Laen asked Arianrod, picking up tonight's specimen between two fingers as if that would tell him more about it.

"It's pickled mackerel," she told him, biting into her own with relish.

"Didn't we have that yesterday?"

"That was *smoked* mackerel." Evidently pleased with the piece she'd sampled, she heaped more onto her plate. "Tomorrow perhaps we will have herring."

"And will the herring be smoked or pickled?"

She shrugged. "It'll be salted, probably, but I'm no cook."

"You're doing this on purpose," Laen said.

"Feeding you? Yes, I admit that my deliberate intent in serving you dinner was that you should eat it."

Hywel, from the far corner of the table, cleared his throat. He and Lessa had taken to occupying that corner together, leaving Kel and Laen to huddle close to Arianrod. No doubt it was a concession to their superior rank, but Kel still didn't like having his sister so far away. "I think my brother is merely . . . confused by the abundance of fish, Your Grace. I understand Esthrades's coasts are the finest for fishing on the continent, but do you always eat this much of it?"

"Well, of course not," she said. "I was taught to serve fish to foreign guests, because it might be their only chance to eat it. But our forests are as abundant as our waters—if you wanted meat, you had only to say so."

Laen just seemed relieved she hadn't done it to offend him—that the reverse was true, in fact. Laen, Kel had realized, was always thinking Arianrod did things to offend him, even when that could not possibly be true. It had something to do with Arianrod, whose constant smirk always seemed to hint she was getting one over on you, but more to do with Laen himself, and his own deep sense of insecurity.

"I'll tell you what," Arianrod continued. "As recompense for serving you so poorly, allow me to offer you anything you please from my ancestors' extensive collection of spirits. We probably have anything you could name, and many more you can't."

Laen took that as a challenge, of course. "I've heard about Sahaian *sanghis,* but I've never had the chance to try any. What about that?"

Kel had never heard of whatever that was, but though Lessa and Hywel exchanged a worried look, Arianrod was untroubled. "A fine choice—we do a fantastic trade in the stuff. And we might as well celebrate, since I'm just about finished with the help I promised you."

Laen scowled. "Right. The help. Which doesn't consist of soldiers, coin, or anything at all from your armory, and yet is somehow worth my time."

"Because it is more valuable than those things, yes." She sighed. "When you act like this, it makes me concerned about giving it to you. It's very dangerous, and when I tell you it's dangerous I need you to take me seriously. I tried to put some safeguards in to protect you, but if you don't use it *precisely* as I've said, you won't be happy with the results."

"You said it was just a bit of dabbling, didn't you? That that was all I could expect? And it's still so dangerous?"

"Can I, ah, ask what you're talking about?" Kel asked. "Or is it a private matter?"

Laen shrugged. "It's not private to me. The lady told me she had learned how to manipulate small bits of magic, and she could create something with them to help me in the battles ahead. And that's hard enough to believe to begin with, wouldn't you say?"

"*Magic?*" Kel sputtered. "But aren't you trying to figure out how to bring it back? Did you really succeed already?"

The question had been meant for Arianrod, who raised an eyebrow at him. "I don't recall that we ever spoke of my aims regarding magic. Even so, you aren't wrong; it seems your powers of perception are to be commended. As for your second question, no. I have not yet succeeded. What I have managed to create for Laen now is only a fraction of what I could create, had I fulfilled my goals."

"But how did you do it? Could you teach someone else to do it?"

"I already asked that," Laen said. "But either it really can't be done, or she just doesn't want anyone else to know the secret."

She smiled serenely. "One of those two things, to be sure."

Kel probably wasn't going to get much more out of her, but before he could decide on a different approach, Seren Almasy entered the room. "My lady, they're a bit concerned in the kitchens that you should take dessert. They understand the demands of courtesy, but it has been some time, so . . ."

Arianrod didn't seem to find the wording of those sentences odd in the slightest, but Kel couldn't say the same. "By all means, let them bring it up if they're concerned. Oh, and while you're here, will you go to the cellar and fetch us a bottle of *sanghis*? Our young prince is curious."

"You won't like it," Seren said to Laen, but before he could question her, she had already bowed and left.

When the last course was served, Kel understood why Arianrod's servants had so wanted her to eat it: everyone else at the table was served a slice of truly delightful blueberry pie, but Arianrod was given a plate of baked apples and a tiny steel vial. Kel knew exactly what the apples were, but was intrigued to see her unscrew the top of the vial and dust them with reddish brown powder. "What is that?" he asked.

"Cinnamon. You've never had it before?"

"This is my first time seeing it in person. Is it very strong?" She'd been careful how much she added to her food.

"Not at all. It's sweet more than anything, and pairs remarkably well with apples. It's just very expensive, and harder to get than *sanghis*. It only grows in Issamira."

"If it's so rare, I'd like to try a bite of it," Laen said, and the horrified expression on Hywel's face made Kel feel instantly sorry for him.

But Arianrod didn't even look up from screwing the top back on the vial. "Certainly not. This was a gift from Adora, and I can't say when or if I'm going to get any more. She can't stand the stuff herself, but she knows how fond I am of it." She frowned. "It is irksome that I can't return the favor. Over the course of her visits north, she discovered a great love for the very blueberries you're all eating now. But any I sent would spoil before they ever reached Eldren Cael."

Before Laen could reply, Seren reappeared, carrying a tall, thin bottle of dark green glass and a half dozen tiny drinking cups, each one shaped like a smooth, oversized thimble. As she deposited the bottle and glasses in front of Arianrod, the marquise asked Laen, "You don't object if we share it, I hope?"

"Of course not," Laen said, "though if I know my brother, he will not venture to taste it."

Hywel put his hands out as if trying to push the bottle away from him. "Indeed, I'm only too happy to leave more for the rest of you."

"I don't think I had better, either," Kel said. "I'm still small, so the effects will be even worse for me."

Arianrod shrugged. "In that case, I suppose it falls to the two of us to—"

"Um," Alessa said, waving her hand slightly. "I'll have a single glass, if you don't mind. But just the one."

"So there is some courage to be had at this table after all! I'll give you the first one, then."

Arianrod filled one of the tiny glasses, then passed it around the table to Alessa, who sniffed it carefully and wrinkled her nose, but at least she hadn't coughed. She took the tiniest of sips from the little glass, and then she did cough, but only slightly. She licked her lips contemplatively, and sipped again. "Well, it's certainly strong, though I can't say much for the flavor."

Arianrod laughed. "Don't scare off our young prince before he even has a chance to try it." As she poured for Laen, she added, "Before anyone gets *too* drunk, though, we ought to finish discussing your departure. I shall, of course, be happy to provide you with food and supplies enough to get you back to Araveil."

Laen shocked Kel by not downing the little glass all in one go; he sipped at it as Lessa had, though not quite as cautiously. "But no soldiers."

"No soldiers," she agreed. "I need every one of those that I can get. However . . ." She glanced at Kel, who nodded. "The king and I were thinking that you might allow him to accompany you."

Laen's eyes narrowed. "Why should *he* want to go?"

"His Grace would do you a great honor to stand at your side," Hywel said beseechingly. "His support can only help us, Laen. No doubt he knows we need it."

"But he's . . . well, a boy," Laen said. "Are any of my allies or potential allies really going to listen to him?"

"Though this may seem incredible to you now," Arianrod said dryly, "to many of the people you will meet, there will not be so great a difference between Kelken's youth and yours. Certainly, when they see the way Kelken carries himself, that difference will appear even less."

Laen didn't like hearing that, though he settled for scowling and polishing off his drink. "And you, Kelken? What do you have to say about this?"

Kel tried to strike the appropriate tone: confident, but not overmuch, lest he touch off Laen's insecurity. "Though I am young, I spent years in the kind of study that wouldn't have been available to you. I know a great deal of history, politics, and etiquette, and I'm happy to put that knowledge at your disposal. Though it's no fault of yours, your Lanvaldian nobility has a reputation for being especially prickly, and I have . . . experience in that area you should find useful." He shrugged. "And when people try to accomplish great and difficult things, it's wise not to turn away help, wouldn't you say?"

Lessa beamed at him, and even Hywel gave him a grateful smile. Laen rubbed at his face, though Kel wasn't entirely sure it wasn't a reaction to the drink. "Well, when you put it that way . . . it is churlish to turn away help, and I can only be grateful that you'd be willing to put yourself in so much danger for my sake." He glanced at Lessa. "Would your sister be accompanying us as well?"

"We have discussed it, and she does not wish to be parted from me," Kel said. "I want her to decide her own fate, no matter the danger. She hasn't always had that ability."

Laen nodded vigorously. "I understand that all too well. My mother spent much of her life in a similar position."

"She was, in the end, able to live a life that brought her happiness," Hywel said quietly. "And sometimes I think her decisions were much wiser than our own. But she must have suffered through a great deal of pain, before Laen and I were ever born."

That's right, Kel thought. *Their mother was a bastard, too.*

"I promise I won't be a hindrance," Lessa said, "even if I can't fight."

"I can't really fight, either," Hywel said, with a sheepish smile, "so you can't possibly be more of a hindrance than I am already."

Laen raised his empty glass. "I, for one, am ready for a second round. Arianrod, I notice you haven't even had your first. I thought you were going to join me?"

"Ah, of course. I quite forgot about it." Arianrod filled her own glass—and then gulped it down in two swallows, setting it back atop the table with a satisfying clink. "There, now we're even. By all means, commence the second round."

She finished off her second glass as quickly as the first, and Laen glared at his own, as if it mocked him. He managed one big swallow, but coughed as it went down, thumping his chest. He finished in two smaller swallows, but he didn't look happy about it.

"Good enough," Arianrod said cheerfully. "Shall we have a third?"

"I will if you are," he croaked.

They each finished two more glasses, after which Laen looked halfway to collapsing and extremely red in the face, and Arianrod looked unchanged in any way. But before Laen could slide his glass over for another refilling, Hywel pleaded, "Laen, don't. What do you think you're trying to prove?"

"Not trying to prove anything," he mumbled. "If she can have it, why can't I have it?"

"Your brother's right," Alessa said. "Besides, I think the marquise . . ." She blushed. "I don't mean to be rude, but I think the marquise is cheating."

If Arianrod thought it was rude, she didn't show it; in fact, she looked delighted. "I suppose you could call it that. By all means, enlighten the rest of the table."

"I've read many books on medicine," Alessa said, haltingly now that so many eyes were on her. "There's a theory, originally Sahaian, that just about anything that can get you drunk . . . well, that it's poison. It's just that it's a poison that'll only kill you in very large doses, or over a very long period of time. Of course it's not a secret that drink can kill you, but most healers are still trying to fully understand why that is. But if it works, essentially, the way poison works . . ." She looked at Arianrod. "You *can't* get drunk, can you? If eating blood apples protects you from poison, it should also protect you from *sanghis*."

Arianrod clapped her hands. "See, Laen? She's proving her usefulness already."

"But then what about when we were at Mist's Edge?" Kel asked. "You told Elgar it was impossible to say whether or not the blood apples really worked!"

She gave a little sigh. "Kelken, please go over that sentence again until you understand why I might wish to do such a thing."

". . . Oh," Kel said. He did deserve that. "There's no reason to tell an enemy the truth, I suppose."

"And great reason to encourage our enemies to keep trying a method of assassination we know won't work. But, gods, the sixth Daven was poisoned *three times*. Do people think he was just extremely lucky?"

AFTER LAEN WAS put to bed, Kel and Arianrod retreated to her study—she with the rest of the bottle of *sanghis*, which she kept drinking like it was water. "You presented yourself well to him, I think," she told him.

"And you played quite the prank on him, which could only make me look better by comparison," Kel said. "But I do think he took my words well."

She leaned toward him. "Tell me honestly: what do you think of our Prince Laen?"

Kel had no intention of being dishonest, but it still took him some time to put his impressions into words. "I think he is what he appears to be, someone who is angry about the state his country has been plunged into and wants to do everything he can to fix it. He doesn't *dis*like the idea of being king, that's obvious, but I think what's more important to him is ridding his home of Elgar's influence, and letting someone more virtuous take over. So if he became king, I doubt he'd rule in ways that were intentionally cruel or unjust, or that he'd refuse all offers of advice, especially if they came from people he trusts already."

She smiled. "I don't doubt that's honest, but you seek to be honest without being negative. Let me hear all of it."

Kel sighed. "He acts before he thinks. That's the problem. He lets his emotions get the better of him." He winced. "Not that I can say I've never done that myself. But it's worse in Laen than in me, and it's what worries me about him most: that at some crucial moment, he could be swayed into making a dangerous decision, and it would destroy him. But even so . . . you're right. I can help him, and I want to try. He's certainly going to need it."

"You can start by helping him with this." Arianrod reached down and opened a sack resting beside her desk. She pulled out a roughly spherical object, wrapped in cheap cloth. "These will be my gift to him."

"What are they?" Kel asked.

"They're rocks wrapped in cloth. I can't say that's merely what they look like, because that is, truthfully, what they are. But they're also much more than that. There is magic dwelling within each one of these—magic I painstakingly put there."

"But you won't tell us how, I suppose."

She met his eyes in a rare moment of seriousness. "You may think what you wish, Kelken, and perhaps it will not even be so far from the truth. I neither owe nor desire to give Laen any explanations—anything I might tell him, he would merely misunderstand. But as for you . . . if we had more time, perhaps I would have more to say."

He ventured a smile. "Then I'll have to make sure I make it back here, so I'll be able to bother you about it. In the meantime, what do I need to know about these to help Laen?"

She extended it toward him, but in a way that suggested he was meant to look, not touch. "He should not unwrap them at all, unless he intends to use them. But if he insists upon doing so, he must remember: the bare rock cannot touch stone or metal. When he wants it to work, on the other hand, it *must* touch stone or metal— wood, cloth, or flesh will do nothing. But he should only try to use it when he's far enough away—that's why I made sure the rocks were small enough to throw. *Never* at close range, or he'll kill himself. And he'll probably want to try one out, either to make sure it works or just out of curiosity. Try to encourage him against this, if you can; these were very difficult to make, and I won't be sending him any more. I wouldn't want him to waste one only to find he had need of it later on."

"All right," Kel said. "So these are, I suppose, weapons that affect a wide area?"

"That's right."

"And they change from a harmless rock to a dangerous weapon when they touch stone or metal, which is why they're wrapped in cloth. You're right, that's exactly the kind of thing Laen will want to see for himself immediately. I'll do my best to make sure he doesn't. Am I allowed to ask how they work?"

"I can explain," she said, "but I doubt it will do very much to prepare you. Inside each of these rocks, I put a large amount of energy. They'll hold that energy within them indefinitely, until they touch stone or metal. When that happens, the energy will force itself out, shattering the stone in the process and repelling the shards outward. The magic itself isn't what's going to cause harm—what's going to cause harm is splinters of rock flying in all directions at an incredible rate of speed. They'll punch through armor and bone; they'll probably dent stone walls. I didn't make them as strong as I probably could have because I didn't want the shards to fly so far they'd risk hitting you no matter how far away you were when you threw them. But you *are* going to want to be far away. Once you start using them you should get a feel for the size of the area of impact, but until then you can't be too careful."

Kel tried to picture what would happen if he were struck by a piece of rock moving faster than any mortal hand could throw. He didn't like the result his imagination provided. "I'll make sure Laen takes the proper precautions. He has people waiting in Araveil to shelter and support him?"

"He does. A frankly impressive number, though of course it's more thanks to Selwyn than to Laen himself."

"Then I think we have a chance. Maybe even a good one." He sat back in his chair. "I should thank you for your help in all this, because I know Laen won't. And because Lessa and I might well be dead at Mist's Edge right now, if not for your invitation."

"Are you surprised that I offered help?" she asked.

"I'm not, actually," Kel said. "But Eirnwin was." Eirnwin who stayed behind. Eirnwin who might already be dead. He brushed the thought from his mind.

She smirked. "Because I am a cruel person?"

"You aren't," Kel said, "and even Eirnwin didn't think you were, just careless. But Lessa put it best: carelessness is foolish, and you would never let yourself be that."

"I do seem to keep underestimating your sister. You should tell her to speak up more." She brushed the hair out of her face. "As for you, it is no small thing to be a better judge of character at your age than an old man with a reputation for wisdom."

Kel shook his head. "Not about people in general. Just about you. Eirnwin understood my father better than I ever did, or could have. And I studied him my whole life." He rested his chin in his hand. "Can I ask you something?"

"I thought you were resolved." She grinned. "I hope you're not planning to be that timid with Laen on the road."

Fine, then. He would just ask. "Are you afraid of anything?"

"Didn't you just say I wouldn't let myself do anything foolish? Only fools fear nothing at all, Kelken."

"So what are you afraid of, then?"

"Losing, I suppose, but not in the way you probably think." She tapped her chin. "The most frightening thing I ever read was something that really happened. It was one of the largest groups of *wardrenfell* ever recorded—scholars guess they numbered around a hundred, though of course we'll never know for certain. The initial event put magic in the hands of those who had never possessed it before, with almost no restrictions, which is very unusual for *wardrenfell*. Instead, there was a price. Every time one of these *wardrenfell* cast a spell, they forgot something. It could be anything, big or small, essential or trivial, and there was no way to tell what it would be: one of them might slay an army and only forget what she ate for breakfast that morning, while another lit a candle and forgot his own name. The worst cases forgot so much that they no longer understood who they were or what was happening to them—some even went on rampages, flinging spells at anyone who tried to get near them, until their minds were little more than empty shells. I was much younger when I first read about it, but I remember thinking it was the most terrible thing I had ever heard."

"Ah," Kel said. "Well, that's like you."

She smiled again. "Is it?"

"To be forced to choose between magic and knowledge," Kel said. "That's what would be the most terrible thing for you, isn't it?"

She let her gaze drift about the room, not avoiding the question, just pondering something of her own. "It's not even really about that. The idea that you could lose knowledge so easily . . . that was fearsome to me. I always thought of knowledge as something to hoard, something you worked painstakingly to gather up and keep. And then, to learn how easily it could be wrested from you—something that took years to learn could be gone in an instant. And it isn't as if I didn't *know* that—even though I have quite an exceptional memory, I'm certain I've forgotten countless things over the years. Even things I might dearly wish to know, if I could only remember what they were. Perhaps that's the part of death I find worth fearing—the death of the mind, not the death of the body."

"But you aren't afraid of true death?" Kel asked.

The pause was even longer, as she grappled with the answer. "I'm not. Or, at least, I haven't been, most of the time. There was one time, when I was young . . ." She sighed. "Elgar blabbed all about it at Mist's Edge, so there's no sense in tiptoeing around it. It was when my father nearly killed me. At the time—before Dent found me, before I reached a healer—I thought I truly was dying. I thought there was nothing I could do. I can't say I ever feared death, before then, and I can't say for certain whether it was truly fear I felt. It was more like . . . sadness? Regret? The sense that I was so young, and there was so much I could have done, so much I had wanted to do, and now instead there would just be nothing. The bitter reality of that." She hesitated, just long enough to brush her hair out of her face again. "It was so long ago now . . . I can barely remember what I felt. But I wonder if, dying, I would feel that way again."

CHAPTER THIRTY-THREE

Eldren Cael

RHIA'S HEART HAD been in turmoil all day, but there was nothing for it. She would apologize to the prince later, as profusely as he wished, and mean every word. But for now she was the queen's captain, and the queen had ordered her to take Lirien Arvel from the city while they knew Hephestion was occupied—in keeping his promise to her, and entertaining Lady Jocelyn for an evening during which he would bid her farewell. She and Lirien made their way to the north gate in the light of sunset, keeping to less occupied areas and giving the entertainment districts a wide berth.

Lirien was oddly quiet; Rhia suspected she was ill again, or whatever the word was for what happened when the magic within her was in turmoil. "Would you feel better to have a horse?" she asked. "The queen has given me permission to pay for it."

Lirien laughed weakly. "I wouldn't feel better in the slightest, as I don't know how to ride. I should be fine on foot."

They took several more turns in silence, and it occurred to her that this would be her last chance to say anything to Lirien at all. After tonight, they most likely would never meet again.

"I hope—" she mumbled, but Lirien was already speaking.

"I was thinking—" She stopped, more uncertain than Rhia was used to seeing her. "Were you going to say something?"

"Nothing important. You go on."

Lirien rubbed at her arm. "I've just been thinking that . . . you should come with me. Or I don't mean *with me,* specifically—you can go wherever you like. But you should leave this city too—now, tonight. The way things are going, I don't think your life will be very long if you stay here. You are caught between too many different forces, all of them powerful. They will tear you apart."

It was so unexpected that Rhia didn't know what to say. She was touched that Lirien was worried about her future, but the idea of leaving seemed impossible, beyond what she had ever considered. "It's because I worry about this city's future that I should stay. The worse things get, the more Her Grace and the prince rely on my service. If things were easy here, perhaps . . . perhaps I would find it easy to leave." She hadn't meant to say that last bit, but realized as the words left her mouth that they were true. Lirien had reminded her of it once before—that she had wanted to travel the world. Once reawakened, it had become difficult to put that dream aside.

"Doing things because you think you *should* do them is no way to spend a life," Lirien said. "It's no way to even feel like you're alive—no way to be happy."

"I understand why you would feel that way," Rhia said. "But for me, doing the things I think I should do is the only way for me to be happy." She smiled sadly, remembering. "My brother couldn't understand it, either."

Lirien still looked troubled. "Now that Adora is gone—"

"She won't be gone for long," Rhia said. "Even if she wouldn't say what her journey is for, she did say it was unavoidable, and that she'd return to Eldren Cael as soon as possible. She is not the kind of person who gives her word frivolously."

Lirien bit her lip, as if words she knew she would regret were trying to force themselves out. When she finally spoke, her voice was very quiet. "There's one more thing. If this really is the last time we may see each other, there's something I have to ask you. I didn't ask before because I thought it might be impolite, or even cruel. But now I feel it would be crueler not to ask, and certainly more dishonest." She hesitated for the space of a breath, pulling herself together. "Are you absolutely certain your brother is dead?"

At first shock and regret scrambled her thoughts, but she did her best to force them down. If Lirien was asking this, there had to be a reason. "If you're asking if I ever saw his," she swallowed, "his body, I have to say I haven't. But this was right after the sack of Araveil—there were so many dead that they were piled into mass graves, and many citizens were never able to recover their loved ones' remains, or

give them any proper burial. And given that I wasn't there to speak for him . . ."
She trailed off. "What makes you ask that question?"

"It's Talis," Lirien said. "The one who cast the spell on him. I can't say I enjoy
knowing her, but I *do* know her. The more times Talis mentions something, the
more likely it is that it's bothering her, and the more times she insists something is
true, the more certain you can be that she fears the opposite. Given that, she talked
about your brother a conspicuous amount. She must have insisted half a dozen
times that even though she hadn't seen him die, he was definitely, *definitely* dead by
now—it was like she was trying to convince herself. So I . . . given what he means
to you, if there's some chance he escaped her spell . . ."

Rhia tried to consider the matter as if it had happened to a stranger. "I don't
know much about magic, but I saw his wound—it wasn't so severe that it could kill
someone on its own. If the magic wore off somehow, and the wound stayed stitched
up, he could almost certainly have recovered. But if he lived, what reason could
anyone have for telling me he was dead?"

"Who was it specifically who told you he was dead?" Lirien asked.

"It was our neighbor, though he didn't see the body, either—he had it from the
healer Eira sent to care for Cadfael. Apparently, the night Elgar's people reached
Araveil, someone caught sight of me, ah, doing something reckless and inadvisable.
I was supposed to be fleeing the city, but I caught this man of Elgar's who'd butch-
ered civilians . . . it's an embarrassing story, but I got away all right eventually.
But while I was stuck outside Araveil waiting for things to calm down, the story
was circulating, and it seems that, even wounded as he was, Cadfael tried to find
Elgar's soldiers to ask what had happened to me. I don't know if he ever heard the
story—our neighbor said he saw Cadfael stumble back home, but he was exhausted
and feverish, and the healer immediately shut him back up in his room. And . . .
it seems he never left it again. The healer confirmed his death—our neighbor was
clear on that. So either she lied to him, or he lied to me, and I can't think of any
logical reason for either."

"Just because you can't think of a reason, that doesn't mean no reason exists."

"That's certainly true," Rhia admitted. "But it's more than that. I believe that
Cadfael is dead, more than any other reason, because he has never tried to find me.
Even if there was some grand conspiracy—even if he were spirited away somewhere in his weakness, and I was told lies to cover up his disappearance—so long
as he lived, he would always come back for me. I don't say this out of some need
to be important to him; I would be so much happier to know he was still alive
somewhere, even if it meant he was willing to abandon me. But I know my brother
the way sailors know the stars. After our father's death, we were all we had. Even
his sword is the other half of mine. He's strong, resourceful, determined—not the

kind of person to be put off from something he's decided to do just because it's difficult. And he isn't like me. He has only ever done the things he wanted to do. If he decided to find me, he would find me, or die in earnest. But it's been three years."

Lirien didn't tell her she was being ridiculous, which was something. If anything, she seemed thoughtful. "Voltest," she said, "my other companion . . . I told you he can find people. Anyone whose face he has seen with his own eyes. But because the three of us are connected, sometimes he's capable of finding people he's never met, but that Talis or I have seen. In those cases, though, he needs to know the person's name, and Talis and I need to be physically connected to him.

"He offered several times to search for your brother, when Talis started telling stories of her fight with him. But though I think she might have been tempted, Talis had to tell him it was impossible, because she'd never learned Eira's soldier's name."

She took a deep breath. "If you come with me, we can find them. With the two of them together, and your brother's name, Voltest will be able to see him. You would know, without question, whether he is alive or dead. And I believe they will agree to do it. Talis will, at least; I know she's long been curious about his fate, no matter how she tries to hide it."

Even though Rhia had just said she was sure, though she truly believed she was sure, still that offer made something twist painfully within her chest. "I thought you were trying to avoid them. I thought being near them made your difficulties worse."

Lirien didn't back down. "If that is the only way to get you to leave this godsforsaken city while you can, I'm willing to risk it."

If it had been Cadfael instead of her, she knew what he would do. If he possessed even the smallest seed of doubt about her death, he would follow any lead, accept any offer, that would let him know the truth. Could she do less for him than he would have for her? Didn't she owe it to him to at least investigate this possibility?

But she owed Adora, too, and Adora was definitely alive. There was no way to chase this without leaving this city, where Adora needed her most; even if she sought to ask permission, Adora was gone from Eldren Cael, and Lirien could hardly be expected to wait for a message to reach her.

She looked up, and discovered she could see the city walls now; they would be at the gates in another minute. She was running out of time. "Lirien . . ."

But Lirien was no longer looking at her, attention caught by the familiar figure that slipped out of the shadows of a nearby cross street to confront them. Rhia stared in confusion, and more than a little alarm. "Lady Selreshe? What are you doing here?"

Jocelyn Selreshe looked slightly disheveled—only a wrinkle in her dress, a loose hair here and there, but in someone who put herself together so carefully, it was unusual. Rhia also thought she was moving with a bit less grace than was her wont, as if she had been injured, though she bore no visible traces of it.

"Ah, Captain." Jocelyn smiled, and that, at least, was the same as ever—that sneering, insincere smile. "Dutifully playing your part in matters far beyond your ken, as usual. How Adora lucked into the service of one so tireless, so faithful, and so beautifully dim, I will never know."

Rhia ignored that, as she had countless jibes before it. "Where is my lord? He was supposed to be with you."

Jocelyn waved a hand carelessly. "Oh, Hephestion and I have certainly been together. He had a great many things to say to me, as it happens. I'm glad the two of us have finally had the chance to discuss our feelings in full. But I had to leave him for just a moment; there's something I have to take care of here first."

Without warning, she lunged for Lirien's arm. Lirien shrank back, and Rhia stepped between them, careful not to touch Jocelyn, but making sure she and Lirien stayed separate.

"Even the peasant has you in obedience now, does she? But I have business with her, and I won't be put aside."

"I have no business with you," Lirien said softly; when Rhia glanced over her shoulder, she saw that sweat was starting to break out on her forehead again. "And I don't care to know what yours can possibly be, not at such a time. I'm leaving."

She made for the gates, not more than fifty feet away, but Jocelyn barked out a harsh command. "Stop there, sorceress! I have not given you leave."

Lirien turned, throwing up a hand before her face and snapping the palm outward, as if to brush away a fly that had flown at her. "What was that?" she asked—in more confusion than anger, Rhia thought.

"You heard me," Jocelyn said, with an icy smile. "I was watching you, the day of that little duel. I saw how you stirred up trouble between the prince and this useless excuse for a captain. I saw how you made such a show of pretending to help the queen, when I know you care no more for her than I do. And I thought it very strange, how no one could find any satisfactory motive for that guard's sudden attack upon Adora. How convenient that he killed himself before anyone could question him. But that's not what really happened, is it?" She took a long stride forward, and again Rhia hastened to put herself between them. "It was your spell that controlled him, wasn't it? It was your will he obeyed then, not his own!"

At first Lirien merely blinked at her, and then her eyes narrowed in outrage. "I can't do anything like that! And even if I could, I have no reason to wish the queen dead. Whatever you think you've figured out, you're mistaken."

"Lady Selreshe," Rhia said, before Jocelyn could begin another string of accusations, "this woman is about to leave Eldren Cael, and will not trouble you or the royal family again. I am escorting her to the gates on the queen's orders. You have no right to keep her from leaving, or to force her to answer any of your questions, and I will not permit you to do so. If you truly insist on pursuing these charges, you may bring them up with Her Grace when she returns." She turned her head slightly. "Lirien, you should be on your way. Staying here will only cause more trouble."

Lirien took a hesitant step toward the gate. "What about you?"

"I'll keep her from following you."

"You can try," Jocelyn said, lashing out with an elbow to try to push Rhia aside. Rhia caught her arm easily, but Jocelyn drove her shoulder so forcefully into Rhia's ribs that it knocked the breath out of her, and Jocelyn was able to slip free while she was stunned.

"Lady Selreshe," Rhia coughed, wondering in a panic if she'd have to draw her sword to put an end to this, "don't—"

But Jocelyn had already swept past her and grabbed Lirien's wrist, catching the end of her braid with her other hand and giving it a vicious tug. "I'm not going to let you flee. You *will* answer to me, witch."

Lirien's smile was just as cold, but much more strained. She was breathing hard. "You . . . really don't want to call me that. Let go of me at once, or I'll—"

"You'll do nothing, peasant, save confess your crimes." Rhia stepped toward them, but before she could get close enough, Jocelyn released Lirien's braid and struck her, not an open-handed slap but a closed fist. She'd quite obviously never thrown a punch before—she even gripped her thumb in her fingers—but she was not a weak woman, and the blow hit Lirien's cheekbone hard. The mark of it evaporated almost immediately, but Jocelyn drew her arm back to try again, and Lirien's eyes flashed—

Rhia put a hand out, to stop either or both of them, but was a moment too slow and an inch too far, and winced in expectation of either the second strike or Jocelyn's transformation into ice. But neither happened. Instead, Lirien screamed. It was a long, drawn out, horrible sound, the herald of unbearable and unrelenting pain. She screamed and screamed and screamed, and Jocelyn just stood there in perfect calmness, still holding Lirien's wrist in her hand.

Rhia laid both hands on Jocelyn's arm and pulled, but somehow she couldn't break her grip. "What are you doing? Lady Selreshe! Unhand her!"

Jocelyn shrugged. "As you wish, Captain." She opened her hand, and Lirien's legs gave out; she collapsed upon the cobbles with a painful impact, gasping for breath. Such unrestrained cries had brought a crowd running, including a member of the guard, and Jocelyn turned to him imperiously. "Fetch Prince Hephestion to deal with this matter. He shouldn't be too far from here. Use all haste." The man ran to obey her without question, and Rhia was angry enough to feel disappointed in him. But before she could say anything, Jocelyn had turned to her next. "Now. Captain. Drag this woman to her feet, and hold her until the prince arrives."

Rhia's response to that was to draw her sword. The hilt was strangely cold, and growing colder, though the night was mild. There was a strange buzzing in her ears, like an insect's whine, but perhaps that was just her anger playing tricks on her. "Lady Selreshe, guest or no, nobility or no, I am an inch away from arresting you. *What* have you done to her?"

Jocelyn scowled. "Put that sword away. Put it away *now*."

The chill was making Rhia's fingers start to go numb, but she didn't loosen her grip. "I'm afraid I must leave it drawn, my lady. Must I hold *you* until the prince arrives?"

Jocelyn still looked angry—angrier, even—but it was tempered by growing disbelief. "How are you doing that?"

"How am I doing what?" Gods, Jocelyn wasn't going to listen to a word Rhia said, was she? "Lirien, are you all right?"

Lirien was still gasping for breath, head bent and both hands braced against the cobblestones. "Y-You can't . . ." she managed to sputter, but Rhia couldn't tell if she was talking to her or Jocelyn. She lifted her head slightly, as if even so little took all her strength, and Rhia saw how drained of color her face was, how her lips trembled.

Her eyes finally focused on Jocelyn. "You can't," she said again, "you *can't* have. It's not—"

"Possible?" Jocelyn smiled. "What would an unlearned peasant know about what is and is not possible in this world?"

"Rhia, you have to stop her before . . ." Lirien swayed, fighting for breath. "She . . . she stole . . . she took . . ."

Rhia and Jocelyn both turned at the sound of a shout, and saw Hephestion running at full speed toward them, surrounded by a knot of guardsmen. "Jocelyn! Rhia?" He came to a confused stop, dropping to one knee by Lirien's side. "Lirien? Are you hurt?"

Jocelyn rolled her eyes. "Will everyone stop fretting over her? Stand up, Hephestion."

To Rhia's surprise, Hephestion sprang immediately back to his feet. "What's happened?"

Well, that wasn't the outrage Rhia had hoped for. "My lord," she said, "I'm not sure how exactly Miss Arvel was injured, but I am certain Lady Selreshe is responsible. She sought to importune Miss Arvel here—to make all manner of accusations against her—to bring violence against her person—"

"Violence?" Hephestion exclaimed. "Jocelyn, what is the meaning of this?"

Perhaps Jocelyn thought she might say what she pleased to a common captain, but Rhia would have expected that now, at least, she might look uneasy. Instead, she merely sighed. "Well, Captain, I did try. You can't say I didn't try." To Hephestion, she said, "I'm sorry to have to tell you this, dearest, but I'm afraid your captain is a traitor."

Just that, and nothing more. No evidence, no arguments. And yet, instead of asking for proof, instead of asking Rhia to defend herself—instead of laughing in Jocelyn's face—Hephestion looked somewhere between distressed and confused. "Oh. Are you . . . quite certain?"

"There can be no mistake," Jocelyn said. "I'm sure you wouldn't have wanted things to come to this, but she has left you no choice; you will have to have her brought to the dungeons straightaway."

Hephestion blanched. "Rhia, to the dungeons? How . . . unfortunate. I'm sure she must have had her reasons . . ."

"That remains to be seen," Jocelyn said smoothly; then, to the rest of the guards, "If you would? She can't be allowed to keep swinging that sword around, can she?"

"My lord," Rhia said, so at a loss she could hardly speak, "will you not ask me for my own account of this? Have you so little faith in me?"

For one moment, she felt sure he saw her clearly. He looked so sorrowful and abashed, and raised a hand as if to reach out to her. Then he noticed the other guardsmen's stares, and put the hand to his forehead. "Forgive me," he mumbled. "I'm . . . acting strange, aren't I? But my . . . my head hurts so, I can't—"

Jocelyn put her hand on Hephestion's arm—a gesture of comfort, but without any warmth in it. But before she could speak, Lirien coughed, raising herself up onto her knees but trembling too badly to stand. "So that's . . . how you had such an elaborate scheme to accuse me with. How you . . . knew so much. Because . . . it was you." She squeezed her eyes shut, but she seemed steadier, if still a shadow of her former self. "Rhia, you won't . . . be able to convince him. It isn't his fault."

Rhia was looking at the soldiers who had come running with Hephestion, but she only knew one of them by name, a young man called Azel who had been injured at Ibb's Rest. She doubted she could convince the lot of them to take Jocelyn prisoner if Hephestion didn't support the order. But if Lirien was right, and Jocelyn could use magic to affect him . . .

She knew her speed was her greatest asset in a fight, and she judged it well. Either Jocelyn couldn't cast a spell to stop her, or she couldn't cast it fast enough, but Rhia's sword cut the air perfectly, about to cleave through Jocelyn's torso—

And then she nearly fell trying to wrench it away, to keep the strike from touching Hephestion. He forced himself between her and Jocelyn. "Rhia, stop! What are you doing?"

"My lord, you don't know what she's done! You don't know the danger she poses to you!"

"She's right," Lirien said. "If you lot don't arrest her now . . . but I wonder if you even can."

"It's true his lordship has been acting strange." Azel turned to his companions for support. "You've seen it, haven't you? Ever since he spoke to Lady Selreshe this evening."

"The dungeons are plenty large enough for you, boy," Jocelyn said calmly. "Think well whose side you wish to be on, once the dust has settled."

Azel flinched, but set his jaw defiantly. "I've always been his lordship's man."

"Then please him by apprehending this traitor," Jocelyn snapped.

"The captain wouldn't—"

"Hephestion," Jocelyn interrupted. "Tell them what we wish."

The prince straightened, his hand falling from his head. "It's unfortunate, Azel, but it's as Jocelyn says. Rhia, drop your sword, or it will be taken from you."

There was no trust or affection in his eyes, though otherwise they were disconcertingly normal; it would have been easier if he had been entirely changed, like a sleepwalker or a man possessed. Rhia considered her options. Even if she could fight through Hephestion and his guards in order to get to Jocelyn, she'd be harming the very people she meant to protect. But if she gave up . . .

In the end, she couldn't drop the sword, and she couldn't strike. Even Azel helped the other guards restrain her so they could take it, guilt and misgiving in his eyes.

CHAPTER THIRTY-FOUR

Lanvaldis

THE WIND WAS biting this far north, even in summer. Talis rested atop a high rock, looking down from the hill into the ravine below. Beside and below her, Voltest stoked his fire, face intent.

Voltest had always liked the cold—not unusual for one born in Aurnis—but contrary to what she'd have expected, he only liked it more after he received his powers. He claimed the fire within him became unbearable when it was hot outside as well, but Talis had always felt most uncomfortable on still days, not breezy ones. And though Lirien claimed heat or cold were all the same to her, Talis had noticed she grew restless in dry weather, no matter how she tried to hide it.

"What are you looking for?" she asked—raising her voice a little, as Voltest could be a difficult man to reach.

"Nothing yet," he muttered. "I'm preparing myself." At least he seemed milder today, not wound up and ready to snap as he had been so often lately. "How much exactly did you tell this man about us?"

She shrugged. "More than you would have, I'm sure. Not everything. I told him our names, and about the balance. I told him it was getting worse." *I told him how this happened to us,* she couldn't say, because Voltest would certainly be angry at that. "Does it matter? He has no magic of his own. There's little he can do to us."

"I don't like the idea of that knowledge being out in the world. Who knows whom he might tell?"

Talis laughed. "I wouldn't worry about that. He's very much not a talkative sort."

"Except with you, it seems."

"Aye, well, I don't really understand that, either."

He did look up then, slightly. "Do you believe this story of his?"

"About why he had to leave? Who knows?" She fidgeted, leaning back on her hands. "It's certainly the strangest story I've ever heard, but that makes me more inclined to believe it, not less. Anyone should be able to come up with a more convincing lie than *that.* And he's also rude, so I imagine if he wanted to leave, he'd just leave, and not care what I thought."

"So you truly believe he's going to Issamira because a strange man told him its queen was in danger?" Voltest pressed his fingertips together, one eyebrow trembling in the perfect picture of judgmental nonjudgment. Perhaps his scholarly background was to blame, but whenever Voltest wasn't being angry, he was being pedantic instead. Or no, that wasn't right; Voltest was pedantic all the time. It was only that when he was angry his pedantry was the least of your problems.

Talis sighed. "If *you* told people you ran into a fire once to save some books, and no flame has ever been able to touch you since, would they believe you, or would they think you mad?" She considered it. "I suppose *he* might be mad. But I believe that he believes it. Or at least I think I do."

"I could look for him," Voltest offered. "He told you his name, so he'll appear in my flames now, if I search for him and you help me."

"That's all right," Talis said. "Even if you do see him heading toward Issamira, that doesn't necessarily mean he's going there for the reason he said." Inwardly, she wondered at her own reluctance. Was she afraid of seeing incontestable proof that he had lied to her? Or did she just not want to be seen to care about where he was and what he was doing? "What about this queen of Issamira? Wouldn't it be quicker just to look for her, and see whether she's in any danger? Aren't you curious about what this plot against her might be?" After Voltest had learned to center his visions on people, not just places, he had made the clever but unnerving decision to travel around Lantistyne, trying to look upon the faces of as many of its rulers as he could, that he might spy on them whenever he wished. The results had been mixed—by then Aurnis's rulers had been dead for a long time, and Eira had died before Voltest could reach him. He had seen Kelken the Third, but his crippled son was not used to traveling out of doors, so now that the father was dead Voltest no longer had eyes on Reglay. Curiously, though he had seen them both, he had difficulty getting either Elgar or Arianrod Margraine to show up in his flames, and even he couldn't say why. But Issamira had been a great success. Voltest had managed to behold not only Jotun Avestri, who had died soon after their encounter, but his wife, his daughter, and his younger son as well. Only the elder son, who had been gone from Eldren Cael and was soon reported missing, had escaped him.

Voltest smirked at her. "I was curious, yes. That's why I looked for her already. But if she's in any danger, I can't see it. She's not even in Eldren Cael at the moment; she's traveling with a small band of her soldiers, though I haven't been able to figure out why, or where they're going." He shrugged. "It doesn't really mean anything either way; your man said the plot against her was brewing, not that it had already been sprung, so who knows from what quarter it could arrive? I wonder if he knows she's no longer in Eldren Cael, though."

"He's not going to Eldren Cael anyway," Talis said. "He was supposed to go down some river . . ."

Voltest started. "Not the Sverin?"

"Aye, something like that. Why?"

He gazed back at his flames, brooding on them as Talis had seen him do so often. "That's . . . very strange. As far as I can tell, the queen is traveling *up* the Sverin."

"Huh," Talis said, absurdly relieved. "Maybe they really will run into each other. Who knows, maybe he'll even be able to do something." That made her recall something else she'd been avoiding, and she knew she'd feel sour about it later if she didn't ask. "By the way . . . there *is* someone I'd like you to look for, if you don't mind."

"I don't. You hardly ever ask. Who is it?" He held his hands up, letting the heat of the flames wash over them.

"His name is Laen," Talis said. "Laen . . . Markham, I think."

"And who is Laen Markham to you?"

"To me specifically, no one at all. But to Lanvaldis in general, it seems he is its king—or at least he's trying to be."

Voltest pinched the bridge of his nose, a familiar gesture that meant he was trying to keep his irritation from catching fire. "You discovered a plot to install a new king in Lanvaldis? Why did you not lead with *that,* instead of this nonsense about that soldier you didn't actually kill after three years of talking about it?"

Talis scowled, her own anger flaring up in response to his. "I'm mentioning it now. Don't act like you've been done some great harm because I kept it back for another twenty minutes. What do you care what happens in Lanvaldis, anyway?"

"We both care about what happens to Elgar. If Lanvaldis fights back, he will hardly be unaffected."

"Aye, and that's why I'm bloody telling you now, isn't it? Are you going to look for Laen Markham or aren't you?"

Voltest brusquely shoved a hand toward her; in situations where he had to rely on her or Lirien to see something in his flames, the physical contact focused his concentration. There was always a queasy feeling as his magic touched hers: two elements that were not meant to mix, brushing up against each other but refusing to truly combine.

Talis leaned forward, aiming her gaze at the fire but letting her eyes focus how they willed. Voltest said that he heard his visions, as well as seeing them, but he was the only one; all the rest of them had was sight, even with his help. But the images were usually clear, even if she constantly had to take care she didn't lean too far forward and scorch the end of her nose.

She saw a cart on a country road, drawn by a single horse. Laen's brother Hywel was sitting on the driver's seat, as gentle with the ambling horse as Talis would've expected. On either side of the cart walked Laen, Ilyn, and what looked like another guardswoman, who seemed to be enjoying the chance to stretch their legs. And within the cart itself, seated among the sacks of supplies, were two people Talis did not know: a girl about Hywel's age with golden hair, and a much younger boy, eleven or twelve. They were talking to each other, and occasionally to Hywel, though only the girl was looking at him; the boy kept his eyes on the road.

Talis squinted at the scene before her, searching for more clues. "Why the hell is he going *that* way?"

"Which way?" Voltest asked.

She pointed at the mountains on the cart's right side. "That's where my village was—far, far off in those mountains, but I'd know them anywhere. That means they're heading *north,* from Esthrades back to Lanvaldis."

"Well, I don't find it at all odd that the supposed king of Lanvaldis would be trying to get to Lanvaldis, and not anywhere else," Voltest said, with another of his superior looks.

"I still don't like it," Talis grumbled. "I didn't go to the trouble of rescuing him for him to just plunge back into danger again." Voltest released her hand, and the image in the flames disappeared. "What are you doing?"

"I accomplished your favor, as requested. Now I have my own task to fulfill."

"And what is that?"

"Lirien," he said shortly.

Talis scoffed. "Don't give her the satisfaction."

"It's not about what she wants." He looked up at her, frowning. "Have you really sensed nothing?"

"What do you mean?"

"The feeling I'm getting from Lirien is . . . odd. It has been for some time. You don't think so?"

Talis considered it. She usually tried to block Lirien out as much as possible, but . . . "There was something a bit strange a day or two ago—it was as if I lost her for a moment. It was like what happened when Miken . . . well, you remember. But it was only for a handful of instants."

"Precisely," Voltest said. "She was gone, and then she came back. But I don't think she came back the same. And since then, I haven't been able to see her."

Talis threw up her hands. "*You* might've just led with *that*. Of course *that's* concerning."

He shook his head. "I want you to concentrate. I want you to tell me if you sense something strange from her."

Talis grumbled to herself, but she did try. "It is somewhat muted," she admitted. "It's her power, the way I always feel it: the capriciousness of water. But it's like it's . . . not farther away, but perhaps as if there's something between me and it. As if the power is . . . contained."

"Surrounded, I would have said." Voltest extended his hands, and the flames leaped to caress his fingers, like the eager tongues of so many faithful dogs. "Caged." He glared at the fire, and it shrank a little, as if sorry to have displeased him. "Damn it! Why can't I see her?"

"When was the last time you could see her?" Talis asked.

"Days ago—I can't say exactly. I don't look in on her much, since she hates it so."

"Well, if you can't see her now, can you go backward? Can you see her at some earlier time?"

"I can try." Looking through both space and time at once was always difficult for Voltest, and he could only look backward, never forward. The farther back he went, the harder it was, but normally Talis and Lirien were the easiest people for him to find, so perhaps he'd turn up something. He glared and glared, and finally perked up. "There! Come and see. This feels like it's about three days ago. She was still in Eldren Cael then."

Talis moved to sit closer to him. The images were hazy, but she could definitely make out Lirien. "All right, now see how far forward you can go."

"I had figured that's where you were going with this, yes." He narrowed his eyes in concentration, and Talis saw the images start to blur, vanishing and reappearing, drifting across the flames like ripples across a pool of water. She couldn't make out any individual scene, though she did see flashes of Lirien's image. And then Voltest made a noise as if he'd been punched in the chest, and the vision resolved itself at last.

For some time the two of them just stared at it, unbelieving. But someone had to speak, so Talis did. "That woman, she . . . stole it? Can that really be what happened?"

"From what I could hear," Voltest murmured, "there can be no mistake."

"Then what we've been feeling since then . . . it isn't Lirien at all, is it? It's been that woman the whole time."

"She can only be a mage—a true mage," Voltest said. "She must have found some way to hold Lirien's power within her own."

"But that's impossible! Isn't it? I thought you said it wasn't possible!"

"I said," Voltest said slowly, as if he were trying to remember the words himself, "that my research indicated that a mage's power was part of them, and could not be removed. But I also said that we were not proper mages, and that the nature of a *wardrenfell*'s power has never been clearly understood."

"You said that it could never be undone!"

"I said I *doubted* that *we* would be able to undo it. A doubt that was, I admit, a bit presumptuous. I certainly have no idea how that mage was able to accomplish it."

Talis looked back at the empty flames. "And you can't see anything of Lirien after that moment?"

"No, but I might . . . huh." He stared, but he hadn't made Talis privy to whatever he was seeing. "Well, would you look at that? I can't see Lirien, but I can trace her power back to its new source."

"This mage? Even though you've never seen her in person?"

"Even though."

"Well, what's she doing?"

Voltest squinted. "I believe she's currently in the castle at Eldren Cael. She's . . . giving orders? This is odd. I know she can't be the queen; I've seen the queen's face before. Arrangements to announce a betrothal? But even if she were to marry the prince, he should be giving the orders, not her—he is the only Avestri in Eldren Cael now that his sister is . . ."

The two of them caught their breath at the same time. "It can't be," Voltest said.

"I can't believe it, either, but I think it is. A plot against the queen."

Voltest stood up, pacing away from his flames. "This must be stopped. What this woman has done—this is every bit as brazen as what was done to Miken. I can't find Lirien—I don't even know if she's still alive! We can't allow this to—"

"She's alive," Talis said firmly. If Voltest lost himself to anger now, she'd never be able to get him to focus. "This sense of her, it's more than raw power. It's still her essence, even if it's being controlled by someone else. I can't imagine that so much of her could remain in this world if she had left it."

Voltest looked condescendingly skeptical, but at least he looked less angry. "You have no basis to be certain of that."

"But you don't think I'm wrong, do you?"

He sighed. "I don't. But we must investigate this."

"Of course," Talis said. "We've got to kill this bloody mage, to start with."

"Indeed." He waved a hand, and the fire died to embers. "Even if she does have Lirien's power, the two of us together should make quick work of her."

"That's what would probably happen, aye," Talis said. "But I don't think we should do that."

She was prepared for him to round on her in anger, and did not flinch. "Did you not just *say*—"

"We've got to think about this more carefully," she said. "If Lirien isn't dead, she's almost certainly a prisoner. Prince Hephestion is possibly in danger as well—we don't know under what circumstances this betrothal has taken place—and I doubt our mage adversary intends Queen Adora to live for very long. No one would love the destruction of House Avestri more than Elgar, and if we charge into the palace throwing fire and wind—"

Voltest sliced an impatient hand through the air. "I follow you. All right. We must, of course, save Lirien, and we'll do all we can to keep the royal succession of Issamira intact. What do *you* suggest toward this end?"

"I suggest, actually, that the two of us pursue different ends, for the time being." She gestured at the spot he'd recently vacated. "You might want to sit down again. I expect we'll be planning for quite some time."

CHAPTER THIRTY-FIVE

Stonespire

IN THE HOUSE of the Inxia Morain, the windows were always kept unlatched. Not because no burglar would be insane enough to breach the sill, although that was true. But there were always children and adolescents training among the Inxia Morain, and children and adolescents had needs. There were other schools of assassins that tried to breed such impulses out of their charges, to make them something other than human. But the founders of the Inxia Morain had been wise, and had known what Seren, even in childhood, had always been aware of: if you wished to make the perfect killer, humanity already possessed all the ingredients you required.

And so no discipline governed the nights of the house's residents; the windows were wide, the sills broad, the neighboring rooftops within easy reach. Any brooding child could flit into the darkness and sulk alone, and any restless adolescent could sneak away to whatever brighter corner of the city they pleased. Though only fully anointed assassins of the Inxia Morain could accept contracts, those in training were free to loot the spoils from anyone they killed, and many of Seren's peers had loved to spend their evenings drinking and gambling away considerable sums, teasing her when she preferred to keep aloof. But she had still loved the freedom of those open windows and the world of rooftops beyond, secret roads that stretched to the inland port, to the Palace of Memory, to every market stall and tavern in the city, and even to the Palace of Seven Points where the emperor and his family dwelled, the only place in the whole city members of the Inxia Morain feared to tread. Not for anything that those within could do to them, but for the actions their own superiors might take against them, should they be suspected of trying to break the age-old trust that lay between the imperial family and their foremost guild of assassins.

It would take a true acrobat to navigate the roof of Stonespire Hall—two parts curved and rounded wood to one part smooth and slippery stone, the one wrapped around the other in a complex embrace. Seren had no desire to fall to her death, so she had never swung out of those windows, and had only ever entered and left the hall by its front doors. The roof would have been useless anyway: Stonespire was so much higher than anything else in the city that you could not leap from it to anywhere else. But it made her feel restless, some nights: the sense, in the back of her mind, that an accustomed avenue of escape was no longer open to her.

She turned sharply at the approaching footsteps, but relaxed when she saw their owner. "Dent. Were you looking for me?"

"Not in particular. I'm done for the evening. Just surprised to see you here at this time of night."

And not attending Arianrod, he meant. Seren had been left at loose ends for days now; whatever Arianrod was puzzling through at the moment, it was not a matter she felt Seren could help with.

He seemed to read her thoughts. "I believe, after sending all our guests on their way, her ladyship has turned her attention to our conspiring rentholders—a problem none of us could handle as well as she will. She knows them well, that Andrew Ryker in particular. When he was barely a man grown, he tried to court her—one of a flock of them that used to flutter about back then. With that great pride of his, I'd bet the rejection still stings him."

"Pride indeed, not to be deterred by all the rumors that she had no heart."

Dent shook his head. "Ridiculous. Everyone has a heart."

Seren pressed her lips together. "That's like you to say."

"You misunderstand me, Seren. I don't mean everyone possesses goodness, or empathy. Some hearts are naught but tarnish and rot, all the way to the core. But everyone has one. For better or worse."

"She wouldn't be pleased to hear you say that."

"I have told her so to her face, many times." Dent's smile was kind. "I'll always be grateful to you for the care you take on her behalf, Seren. But I am surprised that, after so long, you still treat her with a delicacy she would despise. It is your job to protect her from danger, but can you really think you have to protect her even from your true thoughts?"

Dent cared deeply for Arianrod, and seemed to bear Seren no less goodwill than he did her. So she told him the truth, though the words left her mouth a little unsteadily. "It's not . . . to protect her. Not truly. It's to protect me."

Dent tilted his head back, tapping his hands at his sides. "Ah."

Seren said nothing. What more was there to say?

"I don't suppose anyone could blame you for that," Dent said. "That kind of courage is difficult to come by. But even so . . . consider telling her of your concerns, at least. It may do you both good, even if you don't convince her."

He took his leave then, and set off for the city below, where he often spent his evenings these days. It did please Seren a bit, that he felt his liege to be safe in her care.

She had more than a few misgivings about intruding on Arianrod in her study, but after that conversation with Dent, she would have felt craven not to. At least Arianrod admitted her readily enough. "This has all been boring anyway. Did you need something?"

How to answer that? "No, but I . . . I'm still . . . worried about this business with the rentholders. About their conspiracy. I don't think we're addressing it as . . . robustly as we ought to. The ones we know are part of it—which in my case are Ryker and Eurig, though you may know of more—if you wished me to kill them, I could accomplish it easily. If not, you could at least have them arrested, search their correspondence for any coconspirators . . . There are many options."

Arianrod cocked her head. "Say I were to arrest them, then. On what evidence would I do such a thing?"

Seren blinked. "Do you need any?"

"As it happens, yes. I have to act on behalf of a country, and that means I can't ignore its laws. The laws can be whatever I please, of course, but once I've decided what they should be, I have to be seen to uphold them. If I make them only to disregard them when it's convenient, why should my people care what they are?" She leaned back in her chair. "Elgar remains the greater threat. If I didn't have to deal with him, I suppose I could root out these conspirators piecemeal. But I'm busy, so I'm going to do it all at once."

"But that plan relies on *them* to make a mistake."

"They will. You don't know those two like I do. I grew up with Andrew Ryker—he's intelligent enough, but he's never undertaken a task in his life without overestimating his ability at it. That includes the most boring fifteen minutes of *my* life during our adolescence, but I'll spare you the details of that story. Eurig is older, but that simply means I've known him for longer. There are certainly those who feign imbecility out of shrewdness, but . . . trust me. Lars Eurig is not one of them."

Seren knew Arianrod well enough to know she'd come to a firm decision on this. "I . . . apologize for my presumption, then."

But as seemed to happen more and more often, the very thing she said to smooth over the situation only made it worse. Arianrod frowned. "It wasn't presumption, and I don't require an apology. Especially because I well know I haven't convinced you any more than you've convinced me." She rubbed her knuckles against the side of her jaw, as if bothered by the tension in her own expression. "You never used to cringe before me like this. I did not take you for one to swallow opinions and dodge questions like a sycophantic courtier."

There was a question imbedded in those words as well, so Seren tried her best not to dodge this one. "It is harder . . . now that I care more what you think of my answers. What you think of me for giving them."

"Which is as much as to say I've made you worse by keeping you in such close company." She wrinkled her nose. "Is there no way you can possibly stop caring?"

What a question. It was the kind of question only Arianrod could ever ask—either because she really could make herself stop, or because she didn't know what caring was like in the first place. "Even if I could, I don't want to."

"Why? What good is it doing you? And if you say anything about *debts* again, I will absolutely throw you from this room."

Now Seren couldn't help asking a question, because she had puzzled and puzzled over it to no avail. "Why does my gratitude bother you so much?"

"It isn't *correct*," Arianrod insisted. "Things that are incorrect bother me. I know that I helped you once, but I didn't help you to help *you*. I had no way of knowing what would happen because of it, so I didn't think of it as taking a risk. And . . . things were different then. I was so young."

"So does that mean if you had it to do over again, you wouldn't make that choice?"

"What's the point of asking that? I'm never going to have it to do over again, so what does it matter?"

Even if Arianrod did regret it, Seren couldn't blame her. But still, the thought of it . . . "That's not an answer to my question, either."

"Then perhaps you shouldn't ask questions whose answers you don't truly wish to hear." Taking that as a dismissal, Seren turned away, but Arianrod stood up from her chair. She buried her fingers in the cloth between Seren's neck and shoulders, pulling her closer so her arms rested against Seren's chest. "This close, your knife is faster than any spell I could cast. And yet I do not shy away from you, though I know well what you could do to me if you wished it. *That* is trust. *That* is the respect you should seek, not any words I might say. What more would you have of me than that?"

What more? Nothing that it would be fair to ask for—nothing that could be freely given for the asking. "I . . . nothing. Nothing I can say."

But still Arianrod held her there. "You went to the Inxia Morain because you wanted strength. You passed all their trials, survived all the dangers they placed in your path. You could have stayed in Sahai forever; you could have amassed a fortune. But you didn't, because you didn't wish to be bound by even their rules. You wanted something difficult, and you *earned* it—how many people can say that? The only thing that's holding you back from climbing even higher is your own stubbornness."

Arianrod stared at her for a long moment, as if searching for something in her face. Finally she let her go, though Seren wished she hadn't. "I might as well be talking to myself." She sat back down, and leaned her temple against the tip of one finger—more resigned than thoughtful. "I wish to be alone. I think, whether or not you admit it, that you do as well."

DEINOL WAS ENTIRELY sober when his world was upended once more—which, in retrospect, was for the best, though it certainly didn't feel that way at the time. He'd drained so much of his coin that he had to use what was left for emergency purposes—to wit, buying the cheapest food possible. He was about to swallow his last bite of stale crust when a blur of color and motion slammed him off his stool, and he nearly choked on it.

He hit the floor hard, and the blur resolved into a tall shadow, the glint of steel, the fall of long dark hair. He'd known it was coming. It was why he hadn't just let the coin run out completely or drunk himself to death, perhaps—because he was destined to meet this further doom first. Or maybe he was just as stubborn a bastard as everyone always said.

"What do you think you're doing?" Oh, that voice hurt to hear. "Do you know how long I've been looking for you? Do you know all the places I've been?" Lucius was lighter than he was, but he still fastened his hands on Deinol's shoulders and hauled him bodily to his feet. "What are you playing at, taking your leisure in a place like this? Did you intend to just cut us all off, and never speak to us again?"

He hadn't given it the definite shape of an intention. But he had known that if he ever spoke to any of them again, he'd have to tell them, and he didn't know how he'd ever manage to do that. "No, I wasn't—it wasn't anything against you. I wish to the gods you'd been with me the whole time. Or . . . no. I wish I'd never left you to begin with."

Lucius's glare didn't soften. Deinol wasn't used to seeing him angry, but he couldn't say it wasn't warranted. "Where is Seth?"

"Lucius . . ." He'd intended to put it off any way he could, but the way Lucius was staring at him . . . there was no uncertainty or anxiousness in his expression. "You're looking at me like . . . like you already know."

"I do know." The words fell on him like a blade, like shards of ice working their way into his blood. "I still want you to say it to my face. You owe me that much."

He did, and more. That didn't mean he could do it. He gestured half-heartedly around the room, where they were already drawing looks. "Not here. Let's go outside."

They found a deserted alley far enough back from the main road that they wouldn't be disturbed. Before Lucius could ask him again, Deinol managed a question of his own. "How could you possibly have known? Did you . . ." He trailed off as the realization hit him. "It was Almasy, wasn't it? You found Almasy before you found me." Then Lucius really did know, and there was nowhere to run. Deinol spread his hands. "Lucius, you have to believe that I regret it more than anything. More than anything I've ever done."

"I do believe that," Lucius said. "But I still want you to tell me. In your own words."

It was that or fall to pieces entirely, Deinol supposed. He took a breath, trying to calm the racing of his heart long enough to put his thoughts in order. "At least I can say it wasn't because I chose something shameful, or driven by rage—I was actually trying to help. I was angry at Almasy, but there was nothing right about a group of disgruntled village louts plotting to ambush her. Seth . . . wanted to help her, too. And he did, much more than I ended up helping either of them. I got separated from them—I was trying to fight the attackers on my own, to draw them away from him, but there were more in the forest. I didn't get to him in time, and Almasy had been injured. I don't think he *meant* to trade his life for hers, but it was still brave. Almasy . . . it wasn't her fault. I think she would've saved him if she could have." His throat closed up, and he had to look away from Lucius until he could breathe again. "So I buried him, because I didn't know what else to do. And that's it. I don't know what else I can say."

"That's enough," Lucius said.

"Well, then *you* have to say something. What do you want me to do now?"

"Mostly I'd like you to come back to Sheath with me," Lucius said, as if it was obvious.

Could Deinol really have placated him so easily? "Why?" he asked.

"Because that's where we live? Unless you've fallen in love with Stonespire instead, but it doesn't look like it."

"But . . . does that mean . . . that you've forgiven me?"

"That's what it means," Lucius said.

He had spent so much time dreading this moment that it had seemed like the inevitable end of everything. He hadn't been able to imagine an afterward, and he didn't know what to do with it. "That can't be right. If you pity me so much—"

"Deinol, listen to me." Lucius gripped his shoulders again, but this time there was no anger in the gesture. "Now I know the whole story—what you did, and what you didn't do. So I can tell you with certainty that I once did something much, much worse. Something I suspect you'd never be capable of doing. It's a wrong I'll never be able to put right—a regret I'll take to my grave. That's why it was never my intention to judge you. I just wanted to hear the truth. And more than that, I wanted you to hear it. If you decide you want to move on from this— that you want to be part of the world again—first you have to understand what you did and didn't do."

It was impossible to hear something like that, especially about someone you cared about, and not be curious. But he didn't want to repay Lucius's kindness and forbearance by immediately demanding something of him—something that, had Lucius been willing to give it, he doubtless would have given already.

So he let it go. "All right," he said. "If that's what you want, I'll come back to Sheath with you. Although there might be . . . a problem." He winced. "How much coin do you have?"

"Not as much as I'd like to have," Lucius admitted. "But enough to get back, so long as we sleep outside more often than not and eat only what's necessary."

"Aye," Deinol said. "But I don't have that much. I don't have much at all, is what I'm trying to tell you."

"Ah," Lucius said. "That *would* be a problem. A problem I'm sure we could easily solve if we were back in Sheath, but here . . ."

"It's not unsolvable here, either," Deinol said. "I admit I've been spending most of my time in drunken self-pity, but I've been here longer than you, and I've heard more than nothing about . . . opportunities."

Lucius looked skeptical. "Even if you have, we don't know this city well enough to attempt something on the scale of our jobs in Valyanrend. And when it comes to smaller jobs—purse-snatching, tricks like Roger's—I know you don't have any more skill than I do."

"I grant you that, but there is a middle ground. We don't need a windfall, just enough to get us home. As long as we aren't greedy, we can manage it." Despite the potential risk, there was something comforting about talking to Lucius about things like this. It made him feel like the man he had been before Seth's death and the man he was now were still one and the same. "How about this: I'll tell you everything I've heard, and you tell me if we can put anything together that'll satisfy you. If not, we'll start weighing other options."

Lucius smiled. "I think I'll take that offer."

CHAPTER THIRTY-SIX

Issamira

AS A PROUD Valyanrender, Morgan hated the nobility on principle. Still, she had to admit they knew how to travel. Each night Lord Vespas and his servants turned a barren expanse into a majestic camp, sturdy tents erected around a cheery fire and stuffed with cushions and blankets. Some of his party were hunters, and killed or foraged their food as they traveled, but they still had all manner of nuts, tubers, spices, and a creation of flour and water called *bashi* that Morgan was really starting to grow attached to. She and Braddock were given their own tent every evening, and ate whatever Lord Vespas ate himself, usually at his side. As for their host and captor, he had yet to begin anything that could even generously be called an interrogation, and he hadn't limited their freedom in any way. Morgan was starting to believe she could take him at his word, but she also knew just how perilous that assumption could be.

Tonight they did have fresh meat: the hunters had felled some sort of wildcat that Morgan was very relieved not to have seen alive. Nights in Issamira could be surprisingly cool, so she was doubly grateful for the fire and the warm food. Even Lord Vespas always started drawing his cloak more tightly around himself once the sun went down.

He was a dangerously entertaining host, full of a seemingly endless supply of jokes and stories, ranging from old Issamiri myths to things that had befallen him and his family directly. His sister and her husband, the previous king, came vividly to life in his tales of them, as did dozens of old friends, fellow soldiers, foppish courtiers, villainous bandits . . . it seemed as if the man had met half the population of the world at one point or another. Even Braddock had started to relax around him, content to cast amiable doubt on some of his less credible stories.

"Twelve?" he said. "Come on. I'll give you four. *Maybe* five, if he really was a legend. No more."

Lord Vespas shook his head. "Alas, all our versions of the tale say it was twelve."

"Then why didn't *he* get the heroic title, instead of another one of your Irjans? All sorts of men have become kings, but I've never heard of any that slew twelve armed warriors by himself."

"There would have been many hundreds more than twelve deaths, if Irjan Pactmaker had failed to unite the clans," Lord Vespas said. "Our ancestors saw that as the greater glory."

"Eh, well, far be it from me to argue with the great glory of peace, but I think it's more likely they gave him the title and not his uncle because his uncle didn't bloody kill twelve bloody men."

"You're hardly going to change his mind by swearing about it," Morgan said, reaching for another slice of meat.

"The swearing conveys my great belief in the opinions I have expressed," Braddock said. "Wouldn't want his lordship to think I was doubting him in anything less than passionate earnest." He elbowed her gently. "What about our Irjan, eh? Probably deserved a heroic title just for the way he breezed us over the Curse. I've never seen anything like it."

"It was impressive," Morgan had to admit.

Lord Vespas laughed. "Yes, that's certainly the surest way to impress a northerner that I know of. Did you know that even when your people ruled over us, they still couldn't figure out how we did it? In the days of Elesthene, they made crossing points through great trial and labor, driving wooden posts into the ground in sight of one another so they could guide travelers' paths. After Talia Avestri unified Issamira, she had small bands of raiders sneak onto the Curse in the middle of the night, pull up a post here and there . . . just enough to ruin the pathway. And when the armies of the west came to try to subdue us, they found themselves stranded in the middle of the Curse, demoralized and disoriented—easy prey."

There was something about that story that bothered her, and it took Morgan a moment to place it. "In the middle of the night? You can cross without light? Even when we went, we were told to go in the morning, because they couldn't take anyone across at night." She frowned. "Or is it just that they wouldn't?"

Lord Vespas shrugged easily. "Well, taking charge of border crossings is not my role. Perhaps it's merely a charming story."

"Horseshit," Morgan said, making Braddock laugh. Lord Vespas looked as if he wanted to as well, though he merely touched his mouth with the tips of his fingers.

"Forgive my evasiveness," he said. "I have many secrets I must keep."

"I imagine you do," Morgan said. "And I'm not unfamiliar with that position myself, so I can hardly chastise you for it."

He raised an eyebrow. "You have many secrets to keep? How did that come about?"

She hadn't forgotten why they were traveling with him in the first place, and she considered her words carefully. "Did I already say I own a tavern? I've a reputation there for fair dealings, and I'm proud of it, but a lot of that comes of knowing which secrets to keep and which trouble to throw out of doors."

He laughed. "Yes, that does seem to be a requirement of the profession. I suppose I owe you some additional respect, then."

Morgan was about to ask why, but caught herself. "Because waypoints on a journey are sacred?"

"Just so." She didn't miss his pleased little smile. "As the proprietor of such a waypoint, you must have helped further countless journeys, knowing and unknowing."

She hadn't thought of it like that, and found she enjoyed it. But Braddock brought her out of her reverie. "Not mine. She messed that one right up. Got to her tavern and never left it. Or else . . . given where I am now, perhaps she lengthened my journey more than even I knew." He yawned, but forced it down. "Now, my lord, back to this matter of your Irjan and his man-killing uncle. Don't think I'll let you escape so easily. How is it they're all named Irjan, anyway? Is it some title given to a hero?"

"Not at all. It's mostly coincidence, with a bit of probability thrown in. After the first Irjan became a legend, people started naming their sons after him. Purely by chance, some of those Irjans became heroes as well, and the frequency of the name increased even further. By now it is probably the most popular name in all of Issamira—that or Talia, after our Rebel Queen, from whom Jotun and his children are descended."

"So who was the first Irjan, then?" Braddock asked. "The one who started it all?"

Lord Vespas answered without even having to think about it. "That would be Irjan Tal, immortalized in song and story—in one particular song, most famously—as Irjan Firestarter."

Morgan and Braddock exchanged a look. "Huh," she said. "Just like our guide."

"Your guide?" Lord Vespas asked.

"The one we were telling you about earlier, who took us over the Curse. His name was Irjan Tal as well."

Lord Vespas's eyebrows rose. "Indeed? I'd say it's quite the coincidence, but I suspect it was nothing of the sort."

"It must be bothersome for him," Braddock said. "Like being saddled with a destiny right from the beginning. Or is Tal a common name as well?"

"It isn't," Lord Vespas said. "A name chosen by fate indeed." He got to his feet, stretching with a polite yawn. "Perhaps you will excuse me for the evening? There are several letters I should write before I retire."

Morgan would have been content to let him go, but Braddock sidled up to him awkwardly, speaking in a low voice. "Er . . . to presume, my lord . . ."

Lord Vespas did not laugh, just stared at him carefully with his clever eyes. "You have my encouragement to say whatever you wish to me."

"Then . . ." He seemed to be purposely keeping his eyes fixed on a point just to the left of Lord Vespas's face. "I believe I saw you notice it. A man has been watching us all evening. A man not of our party. I have tried not to look his way, in case I spooked him, but he still sits at his post on that hill right over your left shoulder."

It took all Morgan's willpower not to look, but Lord Vespas remained calm. "I am aware of the man you mean. He passed through our midst earlier today, and exchanged hails with my guardsmen. He is in the service of a woman I know well, and asked if he might follow in our shadow, for security's sake. I told him he was welcome to dine with us as well, but he refused."

Braddock didn't seem reassured. "If he wanted to be safe, why not remain among us, especially if you extended the invitation? And that vantage . . . it's good for watching *us,* not watching the rest of his surroundings. Who is this woman he serves?"

"Amali Selreshe. A very old friend of mine, since the time of the war with Hallarnon. The best scout and archer we had, as valuable to Jotun as I was myself. I trust her as much as I trust anyone alive. But I'll keep an eye on him, if that will assuage your fears."

Braddock followed Morgan back to their tent readily enough; once inside, however, he couldn't resist a parting grumble. "I'd feel better if his lordship were more suspicious of that fellow than he is of us."

"The thing is . . ." Morgan tried to put the feeling she'd been having into words. "I *don't* think he suspects us, not really. Perhaps he's simply an excellent dissembler, but—"

Braddock snorted. "Why do all this if he thinks we're no concern of his?"

"I didn't say *no* concern. But I think it's more complicated than he's saying. Maybe he hopes to learn more about the state of Valyanrend from us?"

"It's possible." He flopped onto his back. "What a tale we'll have for the others when we get back, eh? *If* we get back."

"We'll get back," Morgan said, with all the confidence she could muster. "Do you think I'm going to die down here and leave my bar in Roger's hands?"

CHAPTER THIRTY-SEVEN

Stonespire

DEINOL LEANED BACK against the cold stone of the alley wall, trying not to make any restless movements. There was still a bit of foot traffic passing through the street ahead, and the thieves they were waiting for doubtless wouldn't make their move until it was completely deserted.

Back in Valyanrend, Deinol and Lucius were all too familiar with the varieties of the local guards—which was to say, they knew where to find three out of every five who had only half a heart for the task at hand, and were quick to turn tail to "fetch reinforcements" at the slightest sign of trouble. But the Stonespire patrols were foreign to them, and they couldn't afford the time it would take to learn. Instead, they had left it to the local thieves to understand the local guards.

It was a good enough plan that Deinol felt a bit guilty for intercepting it. It seemed that in Esthrades, after an especially lucrative haul, merchants paid a tax to the throne at the conclusion of the sale, rather than waiting till the end of the year. The building they were watching housed the most recent payments, which were carried up to the castle . . . every so often, he supposed. They were counting on their local friends to know enough not to rob the place when there was nothing in it.

There was only one guard outside the building, and the thieves melted out of the shadows and struck before he had time to make a single sound. One of them pulled his body around the corner of the building while the other picked the lock on the door, and once they'd disappeared inside Deinol nodded to Lucius across the way, confirming that they'd charge the men as soon as they came back out.

It went too well. The thieves scanned the street for running guardsmen without giving a thought to the presence of their own kind, and without surprise on their side their skill with blades proved greatly reduced. Deinol and Lucius took them both out without suffering a single scratch of their own, and when they removed the satchels from their targets' backs they found them pleasantly heavy with coin.

They walked away at a casual pace; they weren't being pursued, so running would only have served to draw more attention. But as they reached the corner, as they were about to turn off into the sequence of alleys they'd chosen for themselves beforehand, a crowd spilled out of the building they had just passed. A group of drinkers from a tavern, probably, judging from the laughter and ragged singing. Oblivious, the lot of them marched right toward Deinol and Lucius, who hurriedly drew away, making for the other side of the street.

But it was too late. The drinkers were close enough to see two things: the heavy bags slung over their shoulders, and the fresh blood on their clothes.

The man at the front of the crowd was somewhat horse-faced, with a long and slender neck but a robust frame. When the others backed away, fear in their eyes, this one man ran toward them, and only then did Deinol notice he wore a sword on his belt. This was about to get a bit more complicated, then.

"I've got him!" he told Lucius, and stepped forward to engage.

He'd thought it would be over quickly. He'd also assumed the man was drunk, which, if the precision of his strikes was anything to go by, did not seem to be the case. But Deinol was talented, too, and younger and stronger. When the man finally dropped his guard on the left side, Deinol lunged without hesitation. His blade tore through leather and cloth and met flesh, slicing a wide path from wrist to elbow, and the man cried out in pain, dropping his sword from weakened fingers and instinctively bringing his good hand up to try to staunch the flow of blood from the wound.

"Come on!" Deinol called to Lucius. "Looks like the rest of them scattered. Let's—"

Lucius's focus suddenly shifted, concern blossoming into alarm. "Look out!"

Deinol turned just in time; if he hadn't been able to parry that blow, it would have taken his head off. The newcomer was taller than he was, and was either freshly rested or just naturally formidable; he had to fend off three more of her strikes before he could even get a good look at her. Though she was broad-shouldered, and had her share of muscle, her limbs still somehow looked elongated and spindly, reminding him of some water-striding insect. She forced Deinol back from the wounded man, keeping him on an impenetrable defensive. As soon as she'd carved out enough space, she called, "Guardsman Halley, are you well?" It was only then that Deinol realized the truth: the man he'd just fought had been no concerned civilian, but a guardsman currently off his watch.

"I'll be fine!" the wounded man called back—quite the show of confidence, given the state of his arm. "I don't believe these two have any comrades. Don't fight to protect me, just subdue them!"

The woman hadn't taken her eyes off Deinol for that whole exchange, and he hadn't seen any openings in her stance, either. She was deceptively strong, even for such a tall woman, and she didn't seem to be tiring at all. He hated to admit any kind of incompetence, but guards were like rats, and they needed to get out of here before they drew the whole horde. "Lucius, I can't beat her! I need some help!"

Lucius obligingly interposed himself between them, but there was something wrong with the way he fought. He didn't take any initiative, just blocked the woman's strikes and kept her away from Deinol. Deinol knew he was faster than this, but he didn't seem tired, or wounded, just . . . reluctant? Did he know this woman?

When Lucius finally swung his blade high, Deinol thought he was going to cut the guardswoman's throat. When the blade connected with her temple instead, he was confused for a moment, but only for a moment. Lucius had intended to bludgeon her, not kill her; when she fell to her knees from his first strike, he aimed a second one, careful, nowhere near as forceful as he could have, and turned away.

"What are you doing?" Deinol asked.

"We don't need to kill her," Lucius insisted. "We've done enough. Let's just get out of here."

Deinol would have stopped to argue, but that was time and breath he needed to run. It took all his concentration to keep pace with Lucius even for several dozen feet, but before they could get much farther than that another guard came barreling down a side street toward them. Lucius barely slowed his stride; he lunged at the man, tearing his leg open, but Deinol could tell the stroke had been purposely mild, only meant to keep him from pursuing them. Even more guardsmen were running down the main thoroughfare; someone must have raised an alarm. Lucius turned to survey their options—and let out a cry of surprise as a large object launched itself at him, pinning him to the ground.

The object turned out to be the body of the guardswoman from earlier, who seemed thoroughly recovered from the knock she'd taken mere minutes ago. She kicked the sword from Lucius's hand and slung one long arm around his neck, pinning his lower body to the ground with the weight of hers. "Surrender yourselves," she said, the slight hitch in her breathing the only concession to her exertion. "You have attacked her ladyship's citizens and guardsmen. We will subdue you with lethal force if we must."

THE COMMOTION IN the great hall was so widespread it drew even Almasy's curiosity, though she hung back while Gravis moved to question the men at the head of the column. "Gregg, give me a report! What's the meaning of this?"

Gregg gave his usual obliging nod. "Thieves, Captain. Down in the city. Guardswoman Bridger rounded them up."

"It's the middle of the night," Gravis said. "Thievery is a minor crime; they're to be housed in a cell until tomorrow's judgment. Bridger knows this. What is she doing?"

Gregg shrugged. "There was blood spilled in the streets, Captain. The blood of her ladyship's guards, as well as civilians. Guardsman Bridger thought she would want to be told immediately."

Gravis caught his breath. "Do you know how many were attacked? Was anyone killed?"

"There have been five reported deaths so far, Captain, and Guardsman Halley was seriously wounded. Guardswoman Bridger is helping him to—"

"Dent? Is he here? How was he wounded?" Gravis was already wading through the crowd; if Dent was with Bridger, he could just look for her head inevitably poking above everyone else's.

Sure enough, he spotted her, and made his way to Dent's side; he had what looked like a bedsheet wrapped around his arm. "Dent, are you all right? Gregg says you apprehended some thieves."

"I'm fine," Dent said, for what was surely the dozenth time, "and it's Bridger who apprehended them, while I flopped about bleeding." He kept struggling with the sheet, and winced as his tugging aggravated the still-unseen wound. "Bridger, we have to make sure her ladyship—"

"Is that them?" Gravis asked, as two men came into view behind them, hands bound behind their backs. They were both young and dark-haired, though one's was much longer than the other's. The long-haired one looked calm, almost resigned, but the other was palpably nervous, eyes darting every which way.

"They're talented swordsmen," Bridger said, nodding toward the long-haired one. "That one especially. Strange, though."

"Why do you say that?"

"They seemed prepared to kill Guardsman Halley, but not me," Bridger said. "Those they attacked at the scene of their initial crime were all slain, but the rest received superficial wounds, designed to restrict movement rather than to kill." She glanced back at Dent. "Guardsman Halley, her ladyship is here. What would you have me do?"

Gravis looked up, and saw that it was true; Lady Margraine had entered the hall, calmly surveying the commotion. "Bridger, where are you? I'm told you have the heart of this tale."

Bridger hesitated a moment, still looking to Dent, but she must have realized there wasn't time to confer with him. She stepped forward, her stature easily drawing eyes. "Jill Bridger, from down in the city, your ladyship. Your pardons for disturbing your rest."

"Yes, I know who you are, and I don't care about my rest," the marquise said. "Just give me the point."

"Perhaps Guardsman Halley might assist me in the beginning of it," Bridger said, "but I am the one who ordered these two men brought before you." She indicated the culprits with a wave of her hand. "We found them in the middle of a robbery, and successfully apprehended them. But they fought back very strenuously, and blood was shed in the streets—even that of your guardsmen. In total, one guardsman, two clerks, and two other civilians we've yet to identify were slain, and two more guardsmen were injured. I myself was battered, but not badly hurt, and require no rest from duty. I have taken the liberty of calling Healer Shing to attend to the others."

Lady Margraine rubbed at her forehead. "What a mess. You did well to handle it as you have. Did—" Her sudden flinch confused Gravis, until he saw where she was looking. "Dent. You were wounded in this struggle? Let me see it."

Dent raised his uninjured arm beseechingly. "I have been fussed over by more than enough people, and like it as much as you would. The cut is painful, and deep, but I shall not lose the arm." He was clearly trying to show himself to be as strong and healthy as he could, but Gravis did not miss the marks of strain in his face, and was sure the marquise did not, either.

"You will go to Zara immediately, Dent. You will submit yourself to her, and do everything she tells you without fail."

"My lady, if you'll allow it, I would much prefer to be present for the—"

"That wasn't a request. I can have you carried, if you make it necessary."

He winced. "It won't be, please. Bridger can answer any questions in my stead." But it was still with palpable regret that he left the hall, and Lady Margraine did not turn away from him until he was fully out of view, as if she thought he'd try to escape somehow.

It was a more severe eye she turned back to the culprits. "You heard the guardswoman's report. Do you dispute any of it?"

The long-haired one opened his mouth, but the short-haired one was faster. "We didn't kill them," he blurted out. "I mean, we did, but only the ones who tried to steal it first, not the rest of them. We didn't even go in the building."

"Well, that illuminated almost nothing." She turned her attention to the long-haired one. "Perhaps you can translate for your associate?"

He bowed his head. "The two dead men your guards could not account for were the ones who originally devised the theft. They killed the guard, and any clerks within the building—as he said, we never entered it. We killed them when they emerged, and took the coin."

"I see. So you intend to argue you only slew criminals, not innocents or guards, and deserve leniency for that reason?"

"I intend to argue nothing, Your Grace. I merely sought to provide an accurate account of what we did and did not do."

There was no smirk upon her face, not even the barest hint of amusement. "So you came by knowledge of this attempted theft. And rather than report it, or try to stop it, you thought only of your own benefit. You stood by while these other criminals slew a member of my guard and as many people as they pleased within the building. And once you had relieved them of their coin, you wounded whatever members of my guard you needed to, in order to ensure your escape. Is this an accurate account of what you did and did not do, sir?"

Gods, but it looked like she'd actually hurt him. He kept his gaze trained on her feet. "It is."

"And the guards you wounded? I suppose you would have killed them, if it had been a choice between that and your lives?"

He swallowed hard. "I . . . suppose so."

"Well, if nothing else, you have provided me with a clear picture of the crimes committed tonight. This country has a history of dealing too harshly with theft, and I would not, under normal circumstances, risk reopening that wound. But while your theft might be answered with imprisonment or forced labor, your more violent crimes cannot be. For the pain you brought to my guardsmen, and for the lives of innocents that could have been saved by less selfish men, you will answer with your own lives." She brushed the hair out of her face. "Unless there is any further judgment required, that will be all. Bridger, I will leave it to you to—"

"No, wait! You can't!" Gravis knew whose voice that was, but his mind wouldn't let him believe what his ears were hearing. But sure enough, when he turned to look, his eyes showed him the same thing: Seren Almasy, suddenly caught in the gaze of the entire hall. There wasn't a face that didn't show surprise—even the thieves' themselves. Most people weren't used to hearing Almasy say anything at all, and no one in Stonespire had ever heard her say something in direct contradiction of Lady Margraine's pronouncements.

Gravis sought out *her* face most of all, and found it surprised like the rest. But not the surprise he would have imagined—not the surprise he felt himself. Hers was only slight, and fell away in an instant, replaced by the coldness he knew, though not the smile. "I can't?" she repeated, in that quiet voice that could inspire terror in an unlucky subject.

Even Almasy flinched from it; Gravis could not remember if it had ever been directed her way before. "That's not . . . I misspoke. I know, of course, that it is within your rights . . . fully within your rights . . . but please. Please, in this case . . . just in this case, please show mercy. Just not death. Any other punishment, save that one."

Gravis looked over the thieves with new care. How the hell were they connected to Almasy? They seemed as baffled by her reaction as he was—or at least the short-haired one did. The other made his emotions much harder to read.

Lady Margraine was standing very still, and he could not read her face, either. Was she angry? Bewildered? Anxious? He knew one thing only—she was not smiling. "What are these men to you?"

Almasy bowed her head. "To me . . . to me, nothing."

"Seren," Lady Margraine said, her voice slowly rising with each word, "while pardons may certainly be offered where appropriate, we are not in the habit of offering them for no reason. If you truly want to see mercy for these men, then *stop lying to me!*"

The words lashed the air, forceful and furious, and those closest to her took a step back, widening the circle around her. Lady Margraine herself seemed momentarily surprised by the reaction, as if she hadn't meant to speak so loudly, and her next words were in her normal tone. "Seren, this is not a simple case of theft, or of the helpless and destitute just trying to live another day. These men have taken lives, and allowed others to take more—they have borne arms even against those whose duty it is to carry out my justice. In that way, they have committed an offense against me, too."

"I know that," Almasy said, her eyes firmly cast down.

Lady Margraine's mouth twisted. "But it means nothing to you."

"Not nothing, but . . ." Almasy looked as poor as Gravis had ever seen her, but still struggled to speak. "I have to do what I can to defend them. There is no intimacy between us, yet I . . . I feel I owe it to them to beseech you on their behalf. I . . . can say no more than that."

"Speak plainly. You *could* say more, but you *will* not. You leave me only this to go on? Another one of your mysterious debts, perhaps?"

Almasy spread her hands helplessly. "I don't know how to argue that they *should* be spared, given what they have done. But I would do anything, anything you would accept, to grant them mercy."

Lady Margraine had gone so still that Gravis could not even detect the movement of her breathing. "Anything," she repeated—quietly, but with a firmness that let it carry the length of the hall. "You would do anything."

"Anything you wish of me. You need only name it."

Lady Margraine stayed where she was, as if frozen in the past. There was a crease in her brow, and her hands, hanging at her sides, trembled just a little, as if counting the seconds against the fabric of her dress.

She was uncertain, Gravis realized. She was trying to decide what to do.

Everyone else remained silent until she bestirred herself—he did not even hear a cough. At last she spoke, with nothing in her impenetrable calm to suggest she had not reached a firm conclusion. "Very well, then. If that is your decision, then out of respect for all you have done for me during your service, I will show mercy."

Almasy visibly relaxed. "Thank you, my lady."

"But these men are still criminals who have disturbed the peace of Stonespire, and I will not permit them the opportunity to try a second time," the marquise continued. "They are hereby exiled from this city forever, and will be apprehended and brought before me immediately should they ever be seen within its walls again. And should they ever commit another crime in Esthrades, in this city or out of it, I *will* have them executed." She looked to the men. "Do you understand these terms?"

The long-haired man bowed his head. "I do. They are more lenient than we deserve." His companion said nothing, but nodded hastily in assent.

"I can't help but agree," Lady Margraine said, "but I have already given my judgment a second time, and don't fancy revising it for a third. Is there any reason why you two cannot be gone from Stonespire this very night?"

"None that I know of, Your Grace, if we are not impeded by anyone."

"Then at least that much should be simple." She addressed the rest of the gathered crowd. "Anyone who has nothing of note to add—that is all of you, I hope—may please go immediately about their business. Bridger, you've seen these men fight; you will choose as many guards as you think necessary to escort them from the city."

Bridger nodded, the crowd already beginning to disperse around her, and Gravis started to leave as well, thinking the night's business over. But as Almasy edged away, presumably to return to her chambers, Lady Margraine said, "No, not you, Seren."

Almasy moved against the crowd of people, returning to the marquise's side. "Is there something else you require of me, my lady?"

"Not as such, no. I merely thought that since, no matter what your connection with these men truly is, *some* connection exists, you might wish to leave with them."

Almasy frowned. "I don't. Leave where?"

Lady Margraine shrugged. "The hall, at least, though you could easily leave the country or the continent as well, if it pleases you. That part is up to you."

It was Almasy's turn to grow still, and pale, her lips moving for several moments before a word came out. "Why?"

"I'm dismissing you," Lady Margraine said—calmly, but with no trace of amusement. "Your service is no longer of use to me, nor do I desire it. You promised me, when we first came to terms, that should I ever see cause to dismiss you, you would leave in peace, without any trouble to me and mine. I am exacting that promise from you now. Leave my hall, and do not return to it. That is all I require of you."

Gravis had never thought he would have cause to pity Seren Almasy, but gods, if he didn't feel it now. How many times had he and others accosted or insulted her in all manner of ways, without getting even a twitch of a reaction? And now it was as if her stoic expression had broken open, revealing the face of an entirely different woman. He could almost have thought she would burst into tears. "Is there . . . nothing I can do to change your mind? Is there no way I can possibly remain here—no other punishment you could exact?"

Again the marquise shrugged, but this time the gesture was heavy with resignation. "And in return you'd do what? Anything? It seems you've promised me anything thrice over. You insisted on being allowed into my service, you swore to do anything required of you . . . except, it seems, anything you don't like. Now, to save these thieves, you're prepared to do anything . . . except for all the things you don't like. So tell me, Seren: what precisely *are* you prepared to do? What is it that *you* would accept?"

Almasy stood there, trembling like a leaf in the wind, unable to make any reply. What could she have said, after all?

"That's what I thought," Lady Margraine said. "Well, Seren, the world is wide. I wish you happiness in some other part of it." And just like that, she moved aside, leaving Almasy still standing there helplessly. "Gravis, I am returning to my rest. Make sure she departs. Try not to gloat about it."

So she said, but she turned before she could leave the hall, looking back at Almasy with a challenge in her eyes. "Seren. Will you break even that promise? You so love to make them, but are you incapable of keeping even one?"

Almasy shrank back, and curled into herself, and bent her head, and went away.

AFTER THE CHAOS of their judgment, the rapid surge of dread and despair and shock and relief, the quiet of starlight and the sight of a distant forest under the moon felt somehow empty. Insufficient, rather than refreshing. That tall and fearsome guardswoman and her fellows hadn't bothered to escort them more than ten feet beyond the walls of Stonespire before leaving them, with a parting word for Almasy alone: "I hope to see you return someday, Miss Almasy."

Almasy herself had not moved from the spot. She was just standing there, eyes open but fixed on nothing in particular. Deinol would have been content to leave her there, but he didn't have to say one word to Lucius to know how well that would go. *He* was watching her with all the intensity of a bird of prey.

"Look," Deinol said. "We can't just stay like this forever. *Somebody's* got to say something."

Almasy didn't turn her head, or blink. "Seren," Lucius said, "what are you planning?"

Deinol had expected her to ignore the question, so he wasn't surprised when she did. But Lucius spoke again. "Seren. I have nowhere I must be, and can keep asking until you answer me."

"Then do that. Ask yourself hoarse, if it pleases you." Her voice sounded as if she'd already done that herself, but at least it was proof she hadn't become wholly unresponsive. "You have your freedom—more than I do, since you aren't barred from anywhere you wish to be. Why don't you tell me *your* plans?"

"I plan to accompany you," Lucius said. "But I'll need to know where you're going, and what you're going to do once you get there."

"You aren't going to do that," Almasy said. "Why won't you leave me be? Haven't I sacrificed enough for you?"

Deinol snorted. "It was quite the comfortable position you'd arranged for yourself, I don't doubt, but with your skills you'll never be short of work. If anything, I'd say things have improved for you now that you're free of her, if she's even half the headache she seem—"

He hadn't truly been paying that much attention to her, but even so the first punch seemed to come out of nowhere, grazing one nostril as it struck his cheekbone. The second was wilder, less disciplined, glancing off his ear. She would have gotten a third one in, but Lucius got his arms under hers, wrenching her hands behind her back and holding them there.

She was a good sight less deadly without a knife, and she could not break Lucius's hold. But as she struggled, Deinol got a good look at her face, and that struck him harder than her blows had. If a mere gaze had power, it would have been enough to burn him to ash.

"If that's how you feel, then why save us?" he asked. "You didn't have to. We'd never even have thought to ask you."

She stopped struggling, and sagged against Lucius's body. But her voice was no less vehement, a low and vicious snarl. "If it were only about *you,* I'd have plunged the knife into you myself. But it was . . . for him."

She hadn't even said a name, and still the word cut Deinol to the quick. More than anything, he felt guilt: that the loss of someone he had valued so highly could have slipped his mind even for a moment, while it had remained in hers.

"Seth," Lucius said quietly. He was probably the only one of the three of them capable of giving voice to that name. He relaxed his arms, and Almasy slipped out of his grasp, but she didn't try to distance herself from them.

"I'm not someone who sets much store by human kindness," she said. "But to stand there and do nothing while the people he loved most were put to death . . . that would be too cruel, even for me. I just . . . I couldn't do that to him."

"Did you know she would dismiss you for it?" Lucius asked.

Almasy shook her head. "*That* never occurred to me. Honestly, I thought she would execute you anyway, no matter what I said. What logical or legal reason could I have given her to spare you?" She sighed. "Even I don't really understand why she did it. If she was angry at my impertinence, why do as I asked?"

"I am grateful," Lucius said. "To you, even more than to her. But that doesn't mean I won't keep asking. What do you intend to do now?"

She groaned, but at least she didn't try to hit anyone. "Why does that matter to you?"

"You saved our lives, at considerable personal cost. I'm permitted to be concerned for you, if I choose to."

Almasy dragged a hand across her face. "At one time I would have said there was no longer any reason for me to remain in Esthrades, but now it would be useless to go anywhere else. There's a plot brewing in this country—the pathetic conspiracy of a handful of rentholders. They think they're going to . . . unseat her in some way, or else start a civil war, and have been trying to gather coin, fortify their domains—all sorts of arrangements to that end. I'm going to foil their plot, and destroy the participants."

Deinol frowned. "Do you think stopping this conspiracy is going to get her to take you on again?"

She shook her head. "I'm not doing it for that reason. It wouldn't work, in any case. She isn't one to be moved by sentimentality. I'm doing it because it's what I want to do."

"Then you won't turn down help," Lucius said. "Will you?"

Almasy hesitated. "You're offering in earnest? You will truly apply all your ability toward my cause?"

Lucius gave a slight bow. "I swear it by all the honor I once believed I possessed."

"Then follow me. We're wasting time, and I won't slow down for you."

She stalked off toward the distant trees. Lucius followed with a measured stride, and Deinol ran to catch up, with the uncomfortable feeling that he'd seen this scene unfold before. "You don't have to come," Lucius said—not a dismissal or a challenge, only a statement of fact.

"Like hell I don't. Haven't we had enough to do with her already?"

"That's what I said before *you* left. I can't say it now. This is something I have to do."

"What, help her foil this plot? You didn't even know about it a minute ago!"

"Not that. The specifics hardly matter." Lucius spoke softly, so Almasy couldn't overhear. "I need to make sure. If she does what she says she's going to do, then fine."

"And why wouldn't she?" Deinol asked. "What else do you think she's going to do?"

Lucius said nothing. He only brushed past Deinol to walk faster, keeping Almasy always a short distance away.

CHAPTER THIRTY-EIGHT

Issamira

ADORA HAD NEVER seen a horse die. She knew that they were slain even in times of peace, even with no cruelty or ill intent—when weakness, illness, or injury made their lives so painful that the blade was a mercy. She knew that in times far distant, when their need was great, her wandering ancestors had killed and eaten their horses, though the bond between them and the beasts that bore them on their journeys was no trivial thing. After that horse had given her father his fatal fall, the stablemasters had asked her if she wanted him slain, for being a creature of such grievous misfortune. But of course she had declined. How could the horse have known what he did?

She supposed she still could not say she had seen a horse die. But here were their corpses, a dozen frightful, distorted heaps, flies buzzing upon the drying blood. Adora swallowed hard. She had not eaten yet this morning, but she would need to, to keep her strength up, and it would have to stay down.

She would have felt more secure with Rhia by her side. But Rhia was needed in Eldren Cael, so it was to Olar Aronai she turned instead, a fixture of her father's personal guard for the last five years of his life and the most experienced of the twenty she had taken with her. "Can you explain this to me? What could anyone gain by killing our horses? And how could we possibly have failed to catch them at it?"

Olar pointed across his body, to the camp they'd made along the banks of the Sverin. "Not all our horses, Your Grace. Only those we tied farther out. The ones closest to the camp were spared. That suggests there are only a few of them; they were afraid to be caught in our midst."

She tried to keep her voice gentle, but firm. "Fair enough, but that does not address either of my questions."

He bowed his head. "They're questions I have as well, Your Grace. Killing our horses makes our pace slower, I suppose; they could be softening us up for a later, larger attack. But as to how we didn't catch them, I haven't any idea. Perhaps you might take a couple of the animals by surprise, but with so many . . . even this far away, the screams would have alerted those on watch, and woken up half the others."

They had woken Adora up, and Olar as well. But by the time they had joined the small crowd running toward the horses, the perpetrators had already managed to complete their business and flee. The two on watch, Vimmas and Irjan, had said they arrived in time only to put the last remaining horses in the group, cut but still thrashing about, out of their misery. Who could kill twelve horses with blades and get away so fast?

"Where is everyone now?" she asked, looking around the camp. "I count fifteen heads, and you're the sixteenth. We have two away." They'd given two scouts leave to take horses from their scant remaining supply to search for the hidden assailants in a wider berth around the camp, but Adora didn't really expect them to find anything. "Who does that leave?"

"Vimmas and Irjan. They went to go find some smaller river or creek in which to clean themselves. Ill luck to wash the blood of horses into the Sverin."

It was the widest and longest river in Issamira, and an important source of fresh water; Adora didn't know about ill luck, but she was still happy to keep any sort of blood out of it. "What do you think we should do when they return? Forge ahead as planned, or wait?"

Olar blinked at her. "That's up to you, Your Grace."

Right. Of course it was. Adora sighed. "I'm just asking for your opinion."

"Well, as to that . . . there's no strategic advantage to be gained by staying here. Better to go somewhere we can find more horses."

"If our search gets us close enough to Shallowsend, that won't be a problem," Adora said. "I'm sure Uncle will—"

The sound of hooves striking the earth made her look up. The scouts were returning at a slow trot—empty-handed, as expected. But there were Vimmas and Irjan, walking along behind them. Had they all decided to return together for some reason?

When she tried, afterward, to remember the sequence of events, to isolate the moment when she first felt something was wrong, Adora's mind played tricks on her. The whole scene was filled with dread in her memories, every glimpse of those men a sinister and portentous one. But in reality she had most likely been slow to alarm, as slow as the rest of them. There must have been a moment when they all realized that the scouts were gathering speed and would not stop, that Vimmas and Irjan were following with swords drawn. There must have been a moment when those relaxing in camp saw two of their comrades in their midst with weapons in hand, and understood, because nothing else was possible, what they meant to do with them.

There must have been a moment, but by then, blood was already being spilled.

When they first started to fight, even as some part of Adora's mind recoiled in horror, another said, *This is all right, dreadful, but not catastrophic, they can't possibly defeat you.* That was at the start, when fourteen soldiers had faced down only four on foot and two ahorse. But the fourteen were surprised, and none had drawn weapons; the number was halved almost immediately, guards trampled or cut down before their hands could reach a sword. Then the element of surprise was gone, but the damage had been done. Two more went down under hooves when her group's first act was to throw themselves at the horses before they could break through and trample her. They slashed the beasts in a cruelly ironic imitation of their traitorous comrades' actions of the night before, and dragged their riders down to death. But then it was five to four, five already battered from struggling with the horses— except for Olar, who had stayed back to shield her with his body.

"Your Grace, stay behind me," Olar said, as they both edged around the camp. Only a few horses were left tied up, and she knew he meant to get her on one of them.

Vimmas and Irjan didn't let them. When they spun away, Adora thought they meant to keep killing, but of course that wasn't necessary; all they had to do was cut the ropes, and the poor beasts bolted from the carnage, fleeing with a speed it was hopeless to wish for. Olar swore under his breath. "I'll protect you, Your Grace. If you think you see an opening, run. But judge carefully."

She didn't see an opening. All she saw was the continuing battle all around her, more lifeless bodies falling—now one of hers, now one of her sudden enemies'. "Olar, you have to help them."

"I know. Stay back."

The last remaining fighters turned and turned around her, the aggressors trying to push through to reach her, the others driving them back or to the side. But still blood spilled upon the banks, more and more with each moment, one wound begetting another. One strike, two, three, and suddenly there were three men left standing, Olar caught between a newly one-armed Vimmas and an Irjan stained with blood that was not his own.

Olar fought bravely, but it was over in the time it took Adora to run only to the river's edge. He fended off a weakened Vimmas, feinted toward Irjan, turned back and lopped Vimmas's head off, tried to correct back the other way again, blocked . . . but his riposte, misaimed, merely cut a sliver off Irjan's forearm. Irjan's sword stabbed in an upward diagonal, in through the gut and out the upper back. A killing stroke.

So close. So, so close. But Irjan's wound was trivial, not even enough to slow him. It was like that moment in the courtyard, seeing that man charging at her and knowing she had no way to fight him. Only Rhia and Hephestion weren't here to save her now; if she couldn't save herself, she was doomed.

Afraid of missing even the smallest detail, she almost missed the largest. But her eye fell upon the river itself, and stuck there. She could hear Rhia's voice in her mind, clear as day. *If swimming is not common in this area, that is all the more reason Your Grace should learn. If some assailant should push you into a river or lake, you must be able to save yourself.*

She didn't know if this man was from Eldren Cael. Even if he was, there was no guarantee he did not know how to swim. But if there was a chance . . . just a chance she was a better swimmer than he was . . .

At the time, with that sword closing in on her, it was the best she could do.

She used the time before he reached her to run alongside the bank, forcing him to draw close to chase her. And then, when he thought he had her cornered, as he prepared a swing that would've slit her throat, Adora spun around, ducked her head low, and charged with all her strength.

There was a rush of air and a dreadful whistling noise as the blade passed over her head, and then the impact jarred her whole body, her head crashing into his ribs, arms held close to her sides and fists striking his lower torso, the initial shove followed by all the weight of her body.

She felt it, the final tipping point as he lost equilibrium. He was forced to stumble backward or fall outright, but he stumbled out into empty space.

Adora was even more off balance than he was; she had known she wouldn't be able to disentangle herself from him after the impact. So she did all she could do, and fell into the Sverin right on top of him, the cold water closing over them both.

CADFAEL HAD NEVER been to Issamira before, but if he were forced to give an opinion on it, he would have said that it was very . . . flat. What hills he had passed were all mild, inviting slopes, with hardly an incline to be seen steep enough to make you sweat. More common were the kind of plains that seemed incomplete without a horse galloping across them full-tilt, overjoyed at so much unobstructed space. At least he couldn't possibly get lost; the Sverin was rather difficult to miss. The sound of it was oddly comforting, all that rushing just to make it to the southern sea. It was a place Cadfael had never seen, so how could he begrudge the river its hurry to reach it?

He lost track of the time as he walked, but the sun was high when he realized he was not alone. "I wish I was more surprised to see you," he said. "I don't like the idea that I'm getting used to this."

Yaelor looked precisely as he had the last time Cadfael had seen him— unnervingly so, as if he'd merely been painted onto the fabric of the world. "You must hurry," he said. "She is close, but things are moving quickly now."

"She's in danger?" Cadfael asked.

He bowed his head. "Still and always. You're going the right way, but you must hurry. She is alone."

Cadfael was prepared to run, but before he did, there was something he had to check. Quick as he could, he reached out, trying to close his fingers on Yaelor's arm. But he only felt empty air. Or perhaps it wasn't quite empty: a strange feeling passed through his body, less a physical sensation than a mental one. Something . . . familiar? Nostalgic?

"Aha," he said. "I thought so."

Yaelor said nothing.

"Are you a ghost? Is that why you look so much like my father?"

"No," Yaelor said firmly. "If I look like your father to you, boy, that is your fault, not mine. You're wasting time."

But Cadfael persisted. "Is this some sort of magic? Are you sending your image to me from somewhere else?"

Yaelor was taken aback by the question. "I . . . In a sense, I cannot say that is an inaccurate accusation. I am both here and not here. I am everywhere I need to be, but nowhere am I as you are."

"Are you human?" Cadfael asked. "*Were* you ever human, at any time?"

"That is a question it would take too long to answer. If you truly wish to know, ask me when you have accomplished the task I gave you."

He gritted his teeth. "Fine. How far away is she?"

"If you move quickly, your path should cross hers within an hour. As I said, she is alone."

"How far away are her pursuers?"

"Far. But they are not idle, and can do much damage from where they lie. It is not given to me to reveal their plot to you; you must do that for yourself, or else rely on her knowledge."

"And are you going to tell her what you told me? This business about the heirs of Talia Avestri and the fate of the continent and such?"

Yaelor's face grew stony. "Have you heard nothing I have said, boy? For me to speak such things to her is forbidden. For me to appear before her at all would be . . . unwise, I suspect."

"What? How on earth am I supposed to approach her, then? How is she going to trust me? She'll think I'm mad!"

"If you were to tell her the truth of how your path crossed hers," Yaelor said calmly, "then yes, I suppose she would think you mad. Perhaps you would do well to come up with an alternate explanation."

And just like that, he was gone, as if the problem he'd left for Cadfael were a trivial one. He was no silvertongue; he'd be lucky if this queen didn't run at the sight of him.

But he doubted Yaelor was bluffing, and that meant he was short on time. He didn't run, because that might affright her if she saw it, or make him look worse. But he walked as quickly as he reasonably could, keeping his eyes trained on the horizon.

SOMEHOW, SHE MANAGED to drag the body with her onto the riverbank.

The weight of it felt normal, the skin like human skin. If not for its hideous drowned face, it could almost have been sleeping. She forced herself to search it for any clues as to why the man it had been had done such a thing, but found only a handful of silver and copper coins, a stray flint but no striker, and a bit of lint. She stripped the corpse of its leathers anyway: they wouldn't fit well, but they were sturdier than the clothes she was wearing, and she would draw less attention in them than in something so obviously fine. Then she crawled several feet away and vomited into the bushes. When her stomach finally settled, the drying water leaving her skin clammy, she crawled back to the clothes, and told herself that she had to put them on, and then she had to decide what to do next.

But did she, truly? Or if she didn't, and just curled up here on the bank and shut her eyes and never moved again, would anyone in the world truly be the worse for it?

You are running out of chances, Adora. So Arianrod had written, and of course she had been right. But what sense was Adora supposed to make out of *this* disaster? What specific failure had led her to this point?

It was possible that the whole thing had been a ruse from the start—that someone had arranged for the sending of that letter to lure her away from Eldren Cael. Or the traitors could merely have used this journey as a staging ground for a plot they'd been waiting to set into motion for some time. But was the plot their own, or had they been acting on someone else's orders? It could have been Jocelyn, but would Jocelyn be so bold? And could she bribe or coerce so many guards into doing her bidding?

She stared at the cooling corpse. Her first murder. The irrevocable staining of her hand, a sullying from which no Issamiri could ever again be clean. *I'll never be able to pray two-handed again,* she thought, *not as long as I live.* For so long she had turned away from even the specter of that crime, eschewing battleground and practice field alike, while her brothers' hands fell away, while she had never known a time when her father and uncle did not lift a single palm to pray. Even Rhia, for all that goodness seemed to shine from her, was not free of that tarnishing, though she did not pray to any gods.

But in thinking of Rhia, in thinking of her father, Adora's blood ran cold. If Rhia had killed in the time she had spent in Eldren Cael, in whose service—on whose direct orders, more often than not—had that been? If Adora decided that the Red Crows or any other foe should be hunted down, could she alone escape the stain of it, just because her hand had not held the blade?

She looked at the dead man again, forcing herself to take all of him in. *I did not say that the river killed him; I pushed him with the intent that he should drown. If I can kill a man with water, why not with words?*

Her first murder must truly have been years ago, the first time those under her command had killed on account of those commands—and to think she couldn't remember when that was! What a shameful, hypocritical mistake, to think she could be queen, or princess, or regent, or whatever the hell she had thought she was, and avoid that burden!

Feste was back in Eldren Cael, still. The line of Talia Avestri would continue, with or without her. Would it matter if she never returned? If Feste believed Landon was dead without a body, if he had been able to move on, would he not do the same for her? He, at least, would never bother with a regency.

But no. Until she understood how this plot had been set into motion, she could not say how far it might stretch. If she was in danger, why not Feste, or even their mother? She needed to uncover its source, and for that she needed the resources available to a queen.

And even beyond that . . . there was a part of her that said running away in defeat would only be heaping one kind of failure atop another. She couldn't just say she had failed, and use that as an excuse to stop trying. That, more than anything else, would be beneath a queen.

She cringed as she did it, but she managed to pull the dead man's clothes on; they were still soaked through, and felt disgusting against her skin, but her own clothes were just as wet. He'd let go his sword, so she had no weapon to steal, but by some miracle her purse had not been washed away. Most importantly, she still had her ring, so she could prove her identity if need be.

She might not know exactly where she was, but she knew how to get where she needed to go next. Her brief trip downriver with the guard's body hadn't taken her very far, and from the banks of the Sverin, all she had to do was follow the river north to reach her uncle's castle of Shallowsend. She couldn't be certain she could trust any of his servants—why could there not be traitors among them, if there had been among her own? But she could always trust Uncle himself, and even if he were not at home—which, in all probability, he wasn't—she knew how to get a message to him without fail. With his help, Adora felt certain she could uncover the truth behind this plot.

Until then, it was a long walk to Shallowsend. Best to get started.

TRUE TO YAELOR'S word, Cadfael hadn't been walking for much longer than an hour when he saw . . . someone.

He hadn't been expecting someone of great beauty, or someone whose exceptional qualities shone forth in her face, or any similar nonsense out of a tale—it wasn't as if he'd never beheld a ruler, after all. But even so, he was caught off guard by the woman he saw, dressed in ill-fitting leathers. She did not look like someone who'd had a restful or pleasant day: her mass of black curls seemed to have lost a battle with both water and wind, and she kept tiredly brushing them back from her face as she walked, to no avail. She wasn't carrying any supplies that he could see, and no weapons, either. He could never have said whether she looked like a queen—far be it from him to say how a queen might look. But more than anything else, she looked like she could be anyone.

He slowed his pace as they drew closer together, trying to use the delay to come up with a plan. She probably *was* the queen, right? Yaelor had said that she was close, and that she was alone. If he'd needed to distinguish her any more clearly, he wouldn't have done so.

The woman had been looking off across the river, her dark eyes blinking lazily, like someone in a stupor. But she must have seen some part of him out of the corner of her eye, because her head snapped to the side, and that aimless stare narrowed to something so sudden and sharp that Cadfael took an involuntary step back. Was she suspicious of him already?

"Afternoon," he blurted out, stopping where he was.

She stopped, too, but angled her body as far away from him as she could, every muscle tensing to flee. "Good afternoon. Did you need something?"

"No, I . . ." He licked his dry lips, swallowing hard. "I thought maybe you did. You don't look like . . . I mean, no offense intended, but you seem to have been through something of an ordeal."

She glanced down at her clothes—that was a concession, at least. "An ordeal that's in the past now. I'm in no distress at the moment, though I'm grateful for your concern." She certainly didn't look it. "All I need is to continue on my way."

There was no point in asking if she wanted him to escort her; she clearly didn't, and it would just inflame her suspicions further. Well, fuck it, then. What other choice did he have? "I don't mean to alarm you," he said, trying to pitch his voice lower while still giving it enough strength to cross the distance between them, "but, you see . . . I know who you are. So I find it rather concerning that you're traveling in such a state."

She started, color draining from her face even in this heat, and nearly stumbled into the river. Cadfael resisted the urge to grin. This was her for certain.

"Who are you?" she asked, voice trembling slightly, though he heard steel in it, too. "How would you know me?"

Yaelor'd made the truth of that impossible, so Cadfael scrambled for a plausible lie. "You wouldn't know *me*, of course, Your Grace, but I've seen your face before."

"When?" she insisted. "Where?"

Damn. Cadfael wasn't very adept at telling lies; he had no moral objection to it, but he usually didn't need to. If there was an obstacle in his way, it was faster to just cut it down than to try to convince it the sky was green. "It was . . . far in the past now. Some public function—a parade? I wouldn't know the rest of your family, but you have a rather . . . memorable face. It stuck in my mind."

"I have been told that," the queen mused, and he knew he'd been right not to say anything about beauty. That stare looked like it could cut through flattery like a sword through flesh. "Where is it that you're from?"

She didn't care, she was likely just trying to catch him out. Best to stick to the truth, then. "I was raised in Araveil, Your Grace, but I've become something of a wanderer since our great misfortune three years ago."

"A Lanvald, then," she said, with an expression he couldn't place. "So I am not *your* queen."

"There isn't a ruler on this earth I'd claim as mine, not anymore," Cadfael said. "But I did recognize you, and . . . and your people speak well of you, and if you're in this state, I can only think something's gone very wrong. I couldn't just pass you by and not at least ask." He could have, easily, under normal circumstances, but he tried to infuse the words with the feeling Rhia would have brought to them.

The last thing he'd expected was for the queen to give a bitter laugh. "Do they speak well of me? In what far corner of the world did you hear such a thing, I wonder?"

Gods take it all, but this lying business was difficult. He couldn't let her see him stumble now, not when she was starting to talk to him. "Ah, some . . . some fellow where I took my rest just last night, was the most recent. Big man, big talker—he bothered me more than a little, to be honest. But I remember what he said clearly. 'There are three heirs to the blood of Talia Avestri,' he said, 'but only one can do what must be done.'"

She was still giving him that naked-blade stare, but she looked troubled, too, and something else he couldn't make out. "How strange. You're certain I'm the heir he meant?"

"There's no mistake about that, Your Grace. He made sure I knew it, whether I wanted to or not." He smiled—a true gamble, as he wasn't used to doing it, but he was feeling bolder now. "So, you see, I had to ask. Tell me truly, are you in some trouble?"

She took her bottom lip between her teeth, pacing a few steps along the bank. "I was," she finally admitted. "But it's past now."

"Are you sure of that, Your Grace?"

She made a frustrated little noise. "No, of course not. That's why I'm going somewhere I can try to *make* certain of it."

"And you're going alone?" He touched the sword at his belt. "I may only be one man, but I can use this well. If your need is as great as it seems, I'd be willing to escort you wherever it is you're going."

"For how much?" she asked.

"Oh no, I don't need anything," Cadfael answered—too damn quickly. *Idiot!* he screamed at himself. *That's the most suspicious thing you've said yet!*

The queen was backing away again; he doubted she could outrun him, but that wasn't a situation he wanted to get into. "Listen," he said, "I understand how this must look. I've no idea what you've been through, but it was clearly harrowing enough, and there's no good reason why you should trust me. If you can think of something that would assuage your fears, only name it and I'll perform it. I'll even surrender my sword to you—though if we do run into trouble, I think it'd be better if you gave it back, because I'm not sure you'd know how to use it." Again he thought of Rhia, the things she'd say in a situation like this—the things she'd *know* to be true. "If you've suffered some injustice or misfortune, it's the duty of anyone who can to help put it right. I'm sure I'm far from the best person for it, but I'm the one who's here. I'd like to give it a try, if you'll allow me."

For a long time she stared at him, and that gaze frightened him; if anyone could truly see into a man's soul, it'd look like that. And if she could do any part of that, and she judged that he didn't mean those grand words he spoke, he'd fail not just her, but Rhia, too. He might not have been able to believe the things his sister did, but he'd never want to make a mockery of them.

Then Adora's shoulders dipped, the release of a breath she'd been holding. "Our destination is Shallowsend, where my uncle has his seat," she announced. "I may need to leave for elsewhere after we reach it, but I'll not force you to follow me against your wishes."

Cadfael shrugged. "We'll see when we get there. I don't know of anyplace I need to be, and one's as good as another most days." He pointed the way he had come. "It's back north, your uncle's castle?"

She nodded.

"All right, then." He tapped his sword. "Should you like this as assurance?"

She tensed a little, but shook her head.

"Thank you," he said. "I know it can't have been easy to take me at my word. And . . . the sword means a great deal to me, so it's a comfort that I can wear it still."

The queen gave him another nod—and then, slight and careful but unmistakable, an actual smile. "I've decided to trust you," she said, as if that trust were a gift she'd bestowed upon him. "You . . . remind me of someone."

CHAPTER THIRTY-NINE

Mist's Edge

SHINSEI WAS THE first one over the wall. It was easy, because he was not afraid. Finally, after so long sitting helplessly in camp, mired in inaction while he waited for Lord Oswhent to come to a decision—finally he was doing what he was meant to do. He was furthering his master's goals, in this as in everything.

Lord Oswhent felt certain that the Reglians had some last line of defense, something hidden on the east side of Mist's Edge. So after a series of feints, intended to confuse and demoralize their enemy, he had finally ordered a true strike. They had to hit the fortress's east side first—destroy everything and everyone there, and then block it off to keep anyone else from entering, he had said. They had to keep the Reglians from using whatever it was they had. *If you can find it, fine. But take no chances.* Yes. That was simplest. That was best.

It was before dawn, but only just; Lord Oswhent had wanted it that way, so that the dark could still obscure them while surprise was on their side, but afterward they would have more light to see by. It had rained in the night, and that had worried him, but it had lessened to nothing but a damp mist in the air by the time they set up the ladders, and the stones weren't very slick. The Reglians had been going about relighting their exposed torches, but hadn't gotten to them all before the attack began. They'd given priority to the east side, though, and the blaze made Shinsei squint, but only for a moment.

The Reglians had been vigilant, but there weren't many of them. Shinsei charged without waiting, was already drawing blood before his fellow soldiers caught up to him, but it was clear they outnumbered their enemies handily. *Be careful,* Lord Oswhent had still said. *Do what you came to do, but don't take unnecessary risks.* Fair advice, but let others take it. His master wanted him to succeed, not to be careful.

They fought along the top of the wall first, pressing forward to north and south until they held the whole east side. Then Shinsei threw open the tower door, and led the charge down. They swept through the halls of Mist's Edge like a flood, washing away everything: when they had killed all those they saw, they broke down doors, tore apart rooms, always searching for the Reglians' prize. Finding nothing, they moved ever onward, trickling down and down as inexorably as the blood they spilled.

He had only a handful of comrades with him when he reached the bottom floor; the others had either stayed behind to keep the rest of the Reglians out, or were still searching the rooms upstairs. He waited for them to disperse before he took the direction no one else had chosen, checking the doors on one side of the corridor.

He went through two empty rooms before he found them: two soldiers hiding behind the third door, who jumped out at him when he opened it. He cut the man's head off and stabbed the woman in the gut, but by then another soldier had run over to the group from farther down the hall. Shinsei slashed at him carelessly, and ended up landing a cut down the leg that was good enough to immobilize him. No need to do more. He had to see what was in that room.

As he approached the doorway, he passed the two surviving guards—though the woman wouldn't stay that way for long. She slid down the wall, leaving a trail of blood behind her. "You've got to get up," she said to the other. "Get back to the outside. That wound . . . you can still . . ."

He shook his head, wetting his dry lips. "Dirk," he said—a name? "Is he . . . ?"

"Don't worry," Shinsei heard her say, as he passed out of sight. "He got down there. We pushed it back. They'll never . . . in time. You should . . ."

Shinsei scanned the room, looking for more of Kelken's guards. It was busy, jumbled, full of crates and sheets and rust and furniture, broken things and dusty things and things half-obscured in shadow. He didn't understand why the light fell so strangely, and then he did: one of the braziers, the one in the far corner, was missing a torch, and shadow grew there as if it could eat the light, hungry and waiting. Something prickled against his arms and the back of his neck, as if something breathed heavily, panting, too close.

He'd been about to turn to leave, to shrug the feeling off like a shirt that itched, when he saw it: a flicker—light, movement, *something*—in the far corner, in the darkness without a torch. The shape of a human body.

Shinsei lunged, swinging the sword with all his strength.

A noise: metal ringing sharply against metal. Pain shooting up his arm, vibrating in the bones of his fingers, in his shoulder, in his teeth. A convulsive movement: his hand spasming, fingers opening, sword sliding into empty air. Another noise, still harsh but softer, as it struck the floor.

Shinsei stared into the dark, reeling, uncomprehending, clutching his aching hand. What had happened? What did he hit? He ran to one of the other walls, snatched the torch free, waved it at the darkness as if he could frighten it away.

A shape emerged. Human, but not human, crusted in sickly green. A statue. Yet he had seen movement. Hadn't he?

The statue was cloaked and hooded, dragging broken chains. Shinsei stared into the void beneath that hood, and though a chill settled over his skin, he still felt that unnatural closeness, warm and stifling. Something brushed the back of his mind, a memory of another dark, stifling room, deep below the ground. Something bad had happened in that room. The worst thing, he was suddenly certain— the worst thing that had ever happened to him, had happened in that room. He put his hands out in front of him, as if the memory were flitting before his eyes and he could grasp it. But he'd forgotten he still held the torch, and it slipped from his clumsy fingers, fizzling out on the cold stone floor and engulfing the statue once more in darkness.

A voice whispered, *"Run."*

Shinsei ran. He ran faster than he had ever run in his life, back down the corridor past the dead or dying guards until he finally encountered the rest of the imperator's men. "Run!" he screamed at them. "Run!" But he couldn't wait to see if they'd obey. He had to keep moving. He had to get out of the dark altogether.

He pushed his body to its limits, desperate for just a glimpse of sunlight, a single breath of fresh air. And finally he was out, panting, stumbling into the courtyard. Soldiers surrounded him, asking concerned questions, but he pushed them away. He didn't know where he was going, just that he had to put as much space between him and that room as possible. He struggled toward the far western wall . . .

And then there was a noise that broke all other noise, a furious roar that rose up in smoke and fire and the tearing of stone.

Instantly the air was filled with the scent of charred flesh. Stone fountained into the air and fell upon the ground like rain, and where it struck it burst heads and shattered bones. There were bodies, too, or the warped ruins of them, scorched by flame and broken by overwhelming force, falling upon the ground, falling with the stone. The castle itself was attacking them, eating itself, eating everything.

And Shinsei screamed and screamed and then screamed louder because he couldn't hear himself, couldn't hear anything above the terrible sound of the world being ripped into pieces. He would have screamed until it killed him, but a block of stone hit the dirt of the courtyard so hard it bounced, and Shinsei flung up his arm but the stone kept going anyway, banging the nub of his wrist into his temple and blotting him out into inky darkness.

CHAPTER FORTY

Lanvaldis

THE STONES OF Faine Vlin did not reach high; they were scattered over the ground, and only the first floor of the castle remained—barely. The west wall's holes and crumbling mortar were plugged with rags and sacking, and the wood-and-stone bandaging that served for a new roof looked very precariously balanced. Kel felt a pang at the sight of it: Mist's Edge was likely a ruin now, too, because of his own actions.

"Faine Vlin may be in ruins, but Laen and I lived there for more than a month, and did not want for anything," Hywel told Kel and Lessa. "It's a more comfortable resting place than you'd think."

"Almost anything would be an improvement over the bottom of that cart," Kel said. He stretched his legs, trying to prepare them for the movement to come; he wanted to appear as strong as possible in front of Laen's comrades, whoever they turned out to be. "Do you truly expect to find anyone inside?"

"Absolutely," Laen said. "They promised to leave at least one of their number here to make contact with us."

"Presuming they have not run into any trouble," Hywel amended. "But I have known our allies to be quite resourceful, Your Grace."

Kel had tried many times to get Hywel to use his given name while they were on the road together—in public certain customs must be followed, but here, with only squirrels to bear witness, it seemed cumbersome and unnecessary. But the tractable Hywel had proved surprisingly stubborn on this point. "Which of them would it be?"

"I don't know. Perhaps a former member of Eira's guard; we certainly have enough of those to spare. Many of them remained loyal to us, not least because Administrator Selwyn threw most of them out and placed brutes like Ghilan above the rest."

"I thought you said your guards had been killed when Selwyn's men found you," Hayne said.

"Only those in that particular group, my lady. We have many more in reserve yet."

Hayne jerked her head at Alessa. "You save your *lady*s for her. I don't merit or require them." Lessa blushed, but though Kel personally thought Hywel could stuff his *lady*s altogether, he kept that to himself.

As they approached the spray of stones, Laen brushed aside a curtain of ruined cloth—a former banner, perhaps—and led the way through a low doorway. As Kel had expected after seeing it, what remained of Faine Vlin was beneath the earth, down a flight of shallow steps worn down from the passage of so many feet.

Beneath the tranquil surface was a cavernous chamber, filled with both sealed and empty barrels, half-full racks of swords and spears, bows leaning against the walls, tables piled with parchment, quill, and ink. There were doorways at the edges of the room—he couldn't tell how far down into the earth Faine Vlin might extend. And there was a single man, reclining in a chair in a manner that was somehow familiar, one long arm coiled around the back of it, his feet carelessly propped up on an empty expanse of table.

Both the Markham brothers started back in surprise, but Laen recovered first. "Lord Ithan! Can the captain truly have allowed you to remain here unattended?"

The man smiled, and sprang effortlessly to his feet. Though a man grown in truth, he was still young, with hair as pale as Lessa's. He wore a thin coat that would not have looked out of place on a common soldier, but the quality of the tunic under it was still evident, even beneath the dirt and grass stains. "They all argued up a storm, to be sure, but I insisted. Surely you are well enough acquainted with my stubbornness by now, Your Grace?"

"I'm glad of it," Laen said. "I had rather see you than the lot of them—save the captain, but of course he could not be spared."

"I am also glad to see you well, my lord," Hywel said, "but please allow me to introduce our newest allies, sent with all the recommendation your esteemed cousin could bestow." He bowed in Kel and Lessa's direction. "His Grace King Kelken the Fourth, and his natural sister, Alessa."

This Lord Ithan's friendly smile did not waver at either the sight of Kel's crutches or the word *natural*. Kel hugged one crutch in the crook of his arm so he could extend his hand far enough to allow the man to grasp it. "Well met indeed, my lord, but I'm afraid you have me at a disadvantage. Who is this cousin of yours?"

Lord Ithan shook his hand firmly. "My full name is Ithan Vandrith, Your Grace, and I have the honor to be first cousin to the marquise of Esthrades."

Kel understood immediately. Arianrod's mother was born Elin Vandrith, a noble of Lanvaldis, and would naturally still have family there. No wonder those blue-gray eyes were so familiar, though it was strange to see warmth behind them instead of coldness. "Ah, of course. But, though grateful, I'm surprised to see you here, Lord Ithan. Surely House Vandrith cannot openly support Laen's cause?"

"Oh, we can't. And, indeed, we aren't. I drew the lucky lot, you might say." He grinned sheepishly. "A bit of playacting. It was decided that I should run off—in a fit of rebellion, as it were. I am the youngest son of a youngest son—far out of the line of succession, and thus more easily risked. But I am the best swordsman in our family, and have borne this since I was eighteen."

He moved his hand, and Kel saw that it had rested on the hilt of a sword. Glimmering gold, it had been fashioned to look like a spray of feathers encircled the hand that held it. An opal adorned the pommel, its multicolored hues on full display even in the dim light.

Lord Ithan drew the sword, and a sigh went through the room. It was a beautiful blade, that could not be denied. But the sword Cadfael had treasured had gleamed just as bright, though the hilt was plain. "Vardrath steel?" Kel asked.

Ithan beamed. "Just so. Our house's most treasured possession, and my pride in particular. My flight from Araveil accomplished two things, you see—it allowed me to join this effort directly, and kept this sword out of Selwyn's grasp." Off Kel's blank look, he added, "She's officially confiscated it—more than one noble family has suffered a similar indignity since she came into power. So before her men could come for it, it became necessary for me to flee with my prize in the dead of night, unbeknownst to my poor relatives. I was always a rash and passionate boy, of course, but they *never* thought me capable of such an extreme act. They're *very* apologetic, but they simply have no idea where I might be found."

"Will Selwyn believe that?" Kel asked.

Ithan shrugged. "Probably not, but she can't prove that it is untrue. It does deny me my family's protection, but I accepted that. I'm a better fighter than I am a thinker, so it is best for me to be somewhere I can fight." He rubbed his hands together. "But tell me, my friends, what news from my cousin? What does Your

Grace plan to do next? The captain is not so far from here, with the largest part of our forces. I can easily lead you to them."

To Kel's surprise, Laen looked uncomfortable, rather than excited. "I'm eager to rejoin them, my lord, but unfortunately . . . there is one matter Hywel and I must attend to first."

Kel and Lessa exchanged a look. Whatever this matter was, the Markhams had not breathed a word of it at Stonespire, and Hywel was looking uncomfortable, too. "Hywel and I must return home," Laen said. "To our childhood home, where we lived with our parents. There is something we left there—something we must reclaim."

"What can possibly be that important?" Lord Ithan asked, giving voice to Kel's thoughts exactly. "Selwyn will surely be watching the place—if she has not burnt it to the ground already."

"She would not do such a thing," Hywel said. "She maintains that we are pretenders and charlatans. Destroying our property would only prove that she fears our claim. And though it pains me to say it, my lord, it is our claim that we must retrieve."

"Your *claim*?" Kel repeated. "The paper bearing King Eira's seal—the proof of your mother's legitimacy? You're telling us you don't have it? Why did you never mention this to Arianrod?"

"To avoid the same reaction from her that they're getting from you, I suspect," Lessa said, much calmer than Kel felt. She turned to Hywel. "It is possible, my lord, that such a paper may not be required—it is my understanding that the majority of the nobles here are eager to support you. If you did return to your home, how certain are you of finding what you seek there? Selwyn may not have burned the place, but she will undoubtedly have searched it."

"I am entirely certain," Hywel said, without hesitation. "Our father bore no other distinction, but he was a carpenter without peer. They can search as long as they like, but they will not find it. And to answer the question you were too kind to ask, we did not bear it with us on our flight from Lanvaldis because we feared capture. Selwyn would likely have left us alive, but the proof of our claim would have been destroyed."

"But now that we wish to fight back, we need it," Laen said. "Every convert we win because of it will be necessary."

Lord Ithan clicked his tongue. "Well, it's not ideal, but it's not impossible. Let me draft a report to—"

Hayne drew her sword, silencing him. "Did you hear that?"

Kel tilted his head. "What? I only hear the wind."

He had just enough time to notice the Markhams exchange a swift glance with Ilyn before a powerful gust poured down the upper stairway into the room, blowing quills and parchment from the tables, rattling the weapons in their racks, and nearly snatching Kel's crutches from his hands.

A woman stood at the top of the steps, wind billowing her clothes and blowing her loose hair about her face. "Laen Markham!" she shouted, her voice booming off the stone. "I know you and your brother are in here!" Her gaze fastened on Ilyn. "Oh, and you, too. Tell the rest of them I don't mean any harm."

"I could," Ilyn said, rubbing her knuckles. "*Do* you mean us harm?"

The woman rolled her eyes. "Of course I bloody don't. I'm not someone who likes to waste time, and it would definitely have been a waste to spend all that time protecting you only to kill you now." She rubbed at her face. "Gods, but I had a time finding you. I've been in this bloody forest for days, getting the wind to carry me the slightest scraps of sound. If I didn't know the area . . . And not a bit of gratitude from you, but I expected that. I didn't come here to be thanked."

"Ilyn," Kel said, "perhaps you'd like to explain this . . . situation to the rest of us in more detail?"

"I can do that myself," the woman said. "I know why you're gathered here, and I think I can guess what you're trying to do. I came here to tell you I'm going to help you do it."

Chapter Forty-one

Mist's Edge

THE ENTIRE EAST wall of Mist's Edge was a pile of rubble. Both the eastern and southeastern towers had collapsed, and the outer wall of the northeastern tower had been ripped off, exposing the interior to the open air. More rubble dotted the courtyard; some larger pieces had struck the walls on either side, but hadn't caused any damage more extensive than denting an arrow slit or slicing off the top edge of a stone. The castle itself wasn't destroyed, but its impenetrability was; Mist's Edge could still offer shelter, but it was no longer a fortress, and would be useless as a stronghold in any battle.

Varalen had obsessed for so long over whether Kelken wanted them to storm the castle or not; it had never occurred to him that the boy found both outcomes equally acceptable, because it had never occurred to him that the boy was not in his own castle. If the Hallern army spent months outside his walls doing nothing, fine; it kept them irrelevant. If they came in to get him, fine; his trap was intended to destroy as many of them as it could, leaving that many fewer to come chasing after him once the deception had been revealed. The one thing he didn't want them to do was the one thing Elgar had never permitted Varalen to do: leave the castle altogether. That was why it was necessary for them to believe Kelken and his sister were still within Mist's Edge's walls.

And that, of course, was why Kelken was willing to get so many of his men killed delaying the Hallerns' entry into Reglay: so he and the girl could leave the castle unobserved, and have a head start if the worst should happen and their ruse was discovered. That was why he was willing to exchange messages—all written beforehand, no doubt—but not to appear in person. And now matters had proceeded just as he had planned, and Varalen was left with the following: no king in his custody, a staggering number of casualties to his own forces, a castle that was now useless, a commander who seemed too disturbed to be anything but similarly useless, and the knowledge that he'd been played for a fool by a boy whose balls hadn't yet dropped.

It was good for Kelken that he wasn't here; if he had been, Varalen would've wrung his scrawny little neck. Instead, he had to settle for calling the old advisor before him. He was the only Reglian of any real authority who was both here and alive; Varalen doubted he would know everything, but he surely knew *something*.

Eirnwin, the man's name was; Varalen remembered that. He flinched as the soldiers flung him down at Varalen's feet. It was a little harder than they needed to, perhaps, but Varalen didn't correct them; the time for civility was over.

"I expect you're rather pleased with yourself, aren't you?" he said. "You played your part as decoy admirably, and you didn't even have to die in that pit of hellfire your king conjured. You must have known that was a possibility."

Eirnwin coughed. "At my age, how could I allow my place to be filled by someone younger?"

"How noble." Varalen spread his hands. "Where are the king and his sister?"

The old man smiled. "You aren't going to ask me about the explosion itself?"

No, he wasn't, first of all because that was yet another delaying tactic, and he wasn't stupid enough to fall for this one. But second of all, he wasn't going to ask because he already knew. The smell hung in the air for hours after the attack, a cloud of sickly sweet smoke like burnt sugar. Greater anguis, the highly combustible version of its merely flammable cousin. If he had more time, he'd want to know how the boy had managed to get enough of the stuff to do that much damage, since the Akozuchen had stopped making it generations ago. He doubted there was any of it left, wherever it had come from; you'd have to be a fool to cart something that dangerous around with you when any stray spark could set it off.

"If your liege hadn't put me at such a disadvantage, perhaps I'd be able to speak more leisurely with you," Varalen said. "But with my time have gone my patience and all my manners. Where are Kelken and his sister?"

Eirnwin bowed his head. "You don't truly expect me to tell you that."

"Well, it's that or allow my men to beat it out of you."

The threat had no visible effect on him; he'd surely expected it. "I can't stop them from trying."

Varalen wouldn't have stopped them, if he'd thought it would work. But torture was time-consuming and almost always worthless. He needed to get whatever clues he could from the old man's behavior. First, think: if *he* were Kelken, where would he go?

There was no way the boy was still in Reglay; he'd just blown up the safest place in it. If all he wanted was to keep himself away from Elgar, Issamira would be safest, but its succession problems made it a tempestuous place. Besides, the Avestri hadn't even sent a representative to Kelken's coronation; how could he be sure they would harbor him?

But then he remembered the coronation, and who *had* been there. They'd had enough time to conspire then, hadn't they, despite Elgar's best efforts? "Right," he said. "Of course. The marquise. But then what, I wonder?"

Eirnwin scoffed, but couldn't entirely hide his discomfort. "The king would have no reason to tell me his future plans. He must've known I'd fall into your hands, even if I lived."

Varalen grinned at him. "That's probably true, but he couldn't stop you from speculating. You wouldn't know it given my performance here, but I'm supposed to be rather clever. Let's see if I can speculate as well as you."

He could see the unease in the old man's eyes, though the rest of his face was calm. It suggested that he feared how easily guessed the true answer might be, to one of Varalen's intellect, and *that* suggested he already had all the information he needed. He just had to put it together. "All right, let's say your master's fled to Arianrod Margraine. What will happen after that will unfold not as Kelken wishes, but as *she* wishes. She's not known for her tender heart, so I doubt she sheltered him out of charity. She must have a use for him. Now, Kelken is a crippled boy, so no one would have any use for his physical abilities. It'll be his mind, his blood, or some combination of the two. She can use him as a rallying point, but to do that . . . Issamira wouldn't work, or Aurnis, but Lanvaldis—"

Eirnwin remained admirably stone-faced, but Varalen no longer needed him; he had already realized, to his mingled satisfaction and alarm, just what she would have sent the boy to do.

"What do you think?" he asked Eirnwin, as cheerfully as he could. "If I leave for Araveil now, will I catch them in time?"

He wasted none; the only concession he made to appearances was that he didn't sprint out of the room. Varalen himself did not normally have the command over Elgar's soldiers, so while he'd been put in charge, he had no rank within their hierarchy. The one with the highest rank here was, strictly speaking, Shinsei, but even if he hadn't been knocked unconscious during the attack and even less coherent than usual since waking, Varalen would never have gone to him. Instead, he found Commander Jevran, a man whose reports he'd long admired, but whom he'd never expected to see in person before this campaign.

"Jevran," he said, "I'm about to give the order to march to Lanvaldis, immediately. We'll take as many men as we can, all those who are well enough to make the journey—except for those who are absolutely necessary to guard the prisoners and attend the wounded here. I'm telling you first, so that you can ensure we move out as quickly and efficiently as possible."

He knew what Jevran's reaction would be, though he made sure to act as if his words were unremarkable. When the man balked, he looked exactly as Varalen had imagined. "My lord, to . . . to Lanvaldis? Lanvaldis has no relevance to our mission here. I'm as unhappy with its conclusion as you are, but that doesn't mean we can just pick a new one."

"On the contrary," Varalen said, "our mission has not ended. It will not end until Kelken Rayl is in my custody, or dead. To further that aim, I need all available soldiers to march with me to Lanvaldis, as soon as possible."

"Kelken has gone to Lanvaldis? How do you know?"

"A conversation with his advisor. Knowledge of history and tactics. It doesn't matter. I can explain the rest to you on the way. But we need to get these people moving."

"My lord," Jevran insisted, "His Eminence said we were to remain under your command only for the duration of the siege at Mist's Edge. Once the siege was concluded, we were all to return to Valyanrend immediately, unless he gave us further orders himself. I know events have not transpired here as you might have wished, but you don't have the authority to order us to go to Lanvaldis. We'd need to send a message back to Valyanrend—"

"We don't have *time* to send a bloody message back to bloody Valyanrend!" Varalen snapped. "I am telling you I know what the boy intends to do! If we sit on our asses waiting for Elgar's verdict, Lanvaldis will be in chaos before we even set out! We have to leave *now*, while we still have a chance of catching up to him."

Jevran looked genuinely torn. "I understand what you're saying, my lord, truly. But we simply don't have the authority—"

"Let me ask you what you'd prefer, Commander," Varalen said, through gritted teeth. "Would you like to return to Valyanrend now, an utter failure, with nothing to present His Eminence but a list of the men we lost besieging a ruined and empty castle? Or, when he next hears of you, would you like it to be through a message we sent behind us, informing him of our quick thinking in discerning a plot against him and our unflagging determination to use all our power and haste to thwart it? And when we *do* thwart it, which we can only do if we leave *now,* will he not name you a hero? Or would you prefer to be the one to tell him that I was *going* to send you to thwart it, but you wouldn't let me?"

Jevran clenched his jaw, freezing where he stood. He did not move a muscle as he debated with himself, but Varalen had seen the effect his words had on the man, and already knew what his answer would be. Finally, Jevran relaxed. "No one here could hope to be certain of convincing Commander Shinsei, my lord; if he is to come with us, you must accomplish that yourself. But I am with you, and so is every soldier under me."

Varalen inclined his head. "Thank you, Jevran. You may leave Shinsei to me."

He'd said so with confidence, but that was hardly how he felt. If Shinsei got it into his head to stay where he was—or, hell, to set off across the sea—there was nothing Varalen could do to stop him.

He and Jevran found Shinsei where all the rest of them had left him: sitting in his tent, staring at his empty hands. Varalen waited a respectful few moments, to see if he had anything he wished to say, but Shinsei hardly seemed to understand his presence. So Varalen stepped into the very center of his field of view, and raised his voice, trying to speak as clearly and simply as he could.

"Shinsei," he said, "we're leaving. We need to go to Lanvaldis with all haste, to put an end to a rebellion against His Eminence before it truly starts. Are you prepared?"

He wasn't at all sure what the man would do: Elgar had ordered his obedience during the siege in Reglay, but had said nothing of what would happen afterward. Shinsei was just odd enough to take that sort of thing literally.

He didn't look angry or affronted, at least; he just gazed at Varalen mournfully. "I need my sword," he said. The other soldiers had told Varalen he'd been saying that since he woke up, repeating it more often than he did any other thing, and saying very little else. As for the sword itself, no one could say for certain where it was, but it was most likely buried in the debris of Mist's Edge's east wall; no one had been able to find it anywhere else, and he hadn't been holding it when he'd run out into the courtyard and been struck down.

"You can have your pick of swords," Varalen said. "We certainly have enough to spare." To Jevran, he said, "Has no one replaced his sword?"

"We offered him half a dozen," the commander said. "But it seems he will have his own, or none."

It didn't make any sense to Varalen; from what he remembered, Shinsei's accustomed sword was an ugly thing, dull and unbalanced. Was it some sort of superstition? "Did you refuse the swords the others offered you?" he asked.

Shinsei looked back down at his hands. "It was kind of them to offer. But it won't do any good. I can't be useful to him without my sword."

"I'm sure that's not true," Varalen said. "You still know how to fight, don't you?"

To anyone else, the question would have been obvious and rhetorical, but Varalen cursed himself as soon as it left his mouth; of course Shinsei would ponder it like the sagest mystery. His eyes grew huge, staring and staring up at Varalen. "I don't," he said. "It's the sword that knows."

Gods, Varalen thought at first, *I don't have time for this nonsense.* But then he caught himself. He remembered who Elgar was, and what he was capable of. He remembered the unearthly way Shinsei dominated a battlefield, and how lost he seemed off of one. *Was* it possible? Could Elgar have forged some kind of connection between his commander and his sword, so that wielding it augmented his abilities?

He couldn't say it wasn't possible; he couldn't say anything wasn't possible, where Elgar was concerned. But a couple of logical wrinkles presented themselves right away. First, if you could increase a man's natural talents, why not start with someone who was naturally talented? Elgar had plenty of soldiers who could fight superbly without the use of any magic; why not give such a sword to them, instead of to someone who declared himself a weakling without it? And second, if you could make a sword that increased a man's talents, and you had an army and a continent to conquer, why only make one? Shinsei had been fighting for Elgar for years; surely that was enough time to recover from any strain he might have incurred from creating the first one?

It was a tantalizing question, but he had to press onward. "Shinsei," he said, "if you want to stay here, you can. But the rest of us are going to Lanvaldis, to help His Eminence. What will you do?"

"It'll . . . help him?" Shinsei asked. "It'll help him if I go?"

"We need every person we can spare," Varalen said.

Shinsei stood up, nodding sharply. "I'll do what I can, then. To help him. I'll go."

"I'm relieved to hear it," Varalen said. "Jevran, if you'd give your orders now?"

CHAPTER FORTY-TWO

Issamira

SHALLOWSEND DIDN'T QUITE live up to its name. Though it was nestled snugly in a bend of the Sverin, as if the river had sought to throw a protective arm in front of it, the shallows didn't precisely begin or end there as far as Cadfael could see. Perhaps the river was a little shallower here than it had been farther south, but on the whole he felt it was more poetry than accuracy.

But he couldn't deny that the castle itself was beautiful. Built of a pinkish sandstone that glowed rosily in the light of the setting sun, every part of it was ornately carved. The lower half would have been simply squat and square stone walls otherwise, but with the carvings every corner, plane, and edge was made of pleasing angles and curves. Above it all, dizzyingly tall towers stretched toward the sky like slender fingers, the tops blunt enough that you could stand on every roof.

"Shallowsend has been in my mother's family for generations," the queen said, as they stood by the parapet in the last light of evening. "Talia Avestri gave it to the Hahrenraiths as a reward for their valor and loyal service during the war."

Cadfael was still staring at the towers. He wondered how the queen would reply if he said, *There's a castle that's been in my mother's family for generations, too. My sister and I were born there, though we don't remember it.* Instead, he asked, "You lot were really so eager to have queens and nobles again, after all that business with Elesthene?"

"*Your* lot were just as eager, as I recall," she said, truthfully enough. "But we always intended it to be different. The nobility would be accountable to the people, and must tirelessly work for their benefit. And the queen must do so most of all."

"And you believe that, do you?" Cadfael asked. "You're going to be a servant of the people?"

The queen bowed her head, but she did not blush. "I am sure I have been much less than they deserve. I was not raised to rule, and . . . much of this is new to me. But that has always been my goal."

Though he had never spoken of such a thing with King Eira, Cadfael was certain the man would have found such an idea absurd, if not downright laughable. "I think there are many who would say . . . that such a thing is simply impossible."

He still had to stifle the urge to jump every time she narrowed her eyes at him. "It is more than possible. It is necessary. Without such a goal in mind, how could you even begin to govern?"

Cadfael wisely decided the question was above his ability to answer, and she did not compel him to. She seemed more at ease now that they'd reached the castle than she had been on the road—this must have been somewhat of a return to normalcy for her. Perhaps the presence of her uncle's guards and servants had something to do with it, too; at least several of them knew her personally, if the way they threw their arms around her when she first arrived was any indication. Cadfael had accepted the servants' thanks but refused their coin, settling instead on a hearty dinner at the queen's side. And now he supposed he had to wait for her to decide what to do next, and hope it didn't include dismissing him.

He heard a sudden rush of air, caught a moving blur out of the corner of his eye, and then there was a bird perched on the edge of the wall that was larger than a lapdog, regarding the two humans as calmly and regally as if they were servants arrayed for its pleasure. At first glance Cadfael thought its feathers were pure black, but as he drew closer he realized they were a deep brown, with hints of dark red where the light caught them. Before he could examine it further, the bird shrieked at him indignantly, spreading its majestic wings just enough to grant it some space. But it settled as Adora approached, and allowed her to ruffle its feathers gently. "There, there, Daya," she murmured. "He didn't know." To Cadfael, she said, "She's a parchment hawk—very rare these days, but peerless in carrying messages when they're properly trained. They're skittish around people they don't know well."

"She's as eager a worker as anyone could wish, Your Grace. Despite such a long journey, she flew up here faster than I could walk." They turned to see one of the servants who had attended them at dinner approaching along the wall. "I hope I wasn't interrupting."

"Not at all. Uncle only uses his birds in emergencies, or for matters of great secrecy. Did something happen?"

"We were hoping you could tell us, Your Grace. This letter was addressed to you." The man held out a slender roll of parchment closed with a heavy seal. "She brought it in late last night—beat some nasty fog to get here, too. I'm sure you can recognize your uncle's hand. It's good you came here when you did—we'd have sent it on to Eldren Cael this afternoon if you hadn't shown up first."

"Oh," the queen said. "Well, that's lucky, I suppose. It's been ages since Uncle has sent us anything through such a method." After thanking the man, she moved off to give herself some privacy, unrolling the parchment after struggling for a few moments to break the thick seal without a knife.

Her expression, before she bent her head over the parchment, betrayed nothing, not even curiosity. But as she read, a violent tremor ran down her arm, and her convulsing fingers crumpled one side of the letter in her fist. She stood there, breathing heavily, the fingers of her hand tightening and tightening as if she could grind the paper to dust.

"Bad news?" Cadfael asked.

She glanced up, startled, and he realized she had forgotten he was there. And then, as if nothing had happened, she turned to her uncle's servant.

"I apologize for the abruptness," she said, "but I'll have to ask you to ensure everything is made ready for my departure tomorrow at first light. I had hoped to stay here longer, but that simply won't be possible. When next you see my uncle, please tell him that I wish I could have waited for his return. I'm sure he'll understand."

After the man had left, she returned to the bird, who had remained perched patiently on the wall. At first she just stroked its feathers in silence, but then she said, "I have to go to the Gods' Curse. I can't take any servants with me—mine, my uncle's, it doesn't matter. But . . . perhaps you will come with me."

Cadfael nodded. "If it's that or leave you to go alone, I should definitely come."

She breathed out heavily—was that relief? "Thank you. Without you, discretion would compel me to do this all on my own, and given what has already befallen me, I cannot say how dangerous that might be. It was a true stroke of good fortune that brought our paths together."

If only you knew, Cadfael thought.

The queen stared at her hands, realizing one of them was still clenched into a fist around the letter. She thrust it at Cadfael. "I have other preparations I must make. Tear this up, please—burn it. I don't want to look at it."

Rhia would have torn the letter up without reading it; the very idea of reading it would never have occurred to her. But Cadfael was not Rhia. He disposed of the letter, all right, but first he unfolded it, scanning the brief message:

My dear,

I have recently made the acquaintance of a charming group of travelers who insist they were aided in their crossing by a talented young ranger known as Irjan Tal. They were quite certain of this point, so I don't believe there can be any mistake.

I considered what I ought to do for some time, and in the end I decided I had to let you know. I hope you understand.

I will take no other action as a result of this news, save on your direct orders. And I shall tell no other soul what I have heard, from this day until my last day. That, to me, seems to be best.

Ever devoted,
Your uncle

CHAPTER FORTY-THREE

Valyanrend

"YOU'LL FORGIVE THE unasked-for observation," a man's voice said, "but you appear to be trespassing. Or, at the very least, you appear to be contemplating it."

Marceline executed her about-face carefully—quick as if startled, not quick as if guilty. She stood at the side of the street, in the shadow of the warehouse wall, so she'd be harder to see clearly. Luckily for her, the man before her was not a guardsman, at least not openly.

He was a thin man, younger than Tom but older than Roger—late forties or early fifties, probably. He was dressed simply, though Marceline knew expensive tailoring when she saw it. His hair and beard were black, but the hair was graying above his ears. He carried two weapons, a sword and a knife hanging on his belt, but he didn't seem about to draw either.

Marceline wasn't nervous; she hadn't been caught doing anything obviously suspicious, and this was a public street. For all anyone could say, she'd just been passing through. "Excuse me, sir," she said. "I wasn't aware I was trespassing. Is this your warehouse?"

He smiled vaguely. "You could say that. I own a great deal of property in this city."

Must be nice, Marceline thought. "Well, I wish you continued good fortune, then."

"That's kind of you to say. More and more it seems I am surrounded by those who wish me the opposite." But his tone was calm, not bitter; Marceline doubted his ill-wishers truly bothered him. "Were you not hoping to see some of my good fortune for yourself?"

"Sorry?"

"This warehouse." He knocked against the wall. "You seemed rather curious about it."

She was, but only because Mouse and his fellows were. Though Naishe's mission had apparently come off flawlessly, she hadn't found any proof of Elgar's plans for a draft. But she *had* found papers pointing toward something of great value he was storing in a warehouse in Silkspoint, and, as thanks for her help, had warned Marceline to keep away from the area. If Marceline chose to investigate it instead, what business was it of anyone else's?

She gave the man her best impression of innocent puzzlement. "Is there something special in it? Oh, and you've chained the door and everything. I don't know how anyone could even get through when it's locked up that tightly."

"So you're saying you can't pick locks, then?"

In times like these, it was best just to do whatever Cerise would have done. "Sir," she said, puffing herself up indignantly the way she'd seen her sister do countless times, "I may not have been given the same good fortune as you, but if I had the means to dress myself up as prettily as one of *your* daughters, perhaps you'd be able to tell that my breeding and my morals are as fine as anyone's."

He laughed. "I don't have any daughters, but if I did I doubt their breeding or morals would be any grander than yours. Perhaps you'll accept my apology." He nodded at the warehouse. "And a bit of information, which is far more valuable than any apology. If you're used to traveling down this way, I wouldn't continue it."

"Not even to use the road?" Marceline asked.

"Not even that. Here." He put a careful hand against her back, pushing her out into the center of the street where the view was better. "You can go around this building fairly easily, but there are only three main roads out of this area that don't get snarled up in alleyways: west, north, and south. It's easy to patrol, and to defend, if you have to. And I have it on good authority that patrols will be increasing in the future."

That's what the orders Naishe found had said, too. "But aren't you happy about that, sir? It'll mean more protection for your belongings, won't it?"

"Indeed. But the guards of this city grow more on edge with every passing day. It's all these dissident elements lurking in Valyanrend, thinking they've grown strong just because they haven't been caught yet. But they will be. In the meantime, hanging about near groups of riled-up guards, as well-meaning as their intentions might be . . . I wouldn't advise it." He gave her a slight bow. "I hope that makes up for any rudeness you might have seen in me."

"Oh, that's all right, sir. It's nothing worse than I've heard before. I will be sorry about the road, though; it makes a nice shortcut up to Edgewise."

Once she was absolutely sure she'd left him behind and he wasn't trying to follow her, she reached into her pocket to examine the trinket she'd taken out of his when he'd pushed her into the street. It could hardly be called that; as far as she could tell, it was just a painted little rock, pale and slightly pointed, like an artisan had tried to carve an arrowhead from the wrong material. It didn't look at all valuable.

Well, the value wasn't the point, really. The victory had been meant for her pride, and in that she'd done rather well.

SHE WAS STILL bored, and she didn't feel like going back to Sheath, so she decided to loiter in Draven's Square instead. It was still light out, but stalls were already going up for the Night Market, the most enterprising merchants engaged in arranging their wares for display. Marceline flitted aimlessly through the rows of stalls, waiting for some obscure object to catch her attention. She didn't see Peck, which was lucky for him—after blabbing about her to the resistance, he deserved more than an earful from her.

She couldn't have said what drew her eyes to the two of them, out of all the people gathered in the square. They didn't look particularly strange, or particularly opulent, or even particularly dangerous. And yet, once her eye had happened to fall on them, it stuck there, somehow reluctant to draw away again. They were a man and a woman, walking slowly about the square as if they had no fixed destination, and merely wanted to take in the evening air.

The woman was mature, but not yet past her prime; there were a few threads of gray in her hair, but her face was only lightly lined. She was still strong and quick and bright, and her sharp eyes flicked from point to point with purpose and understanding. The man was younger, pale and dark-haired, with heavy circles under his eyes as if he'd gone many nights without sleep. But he did not seem distressed or discontent; he was grinning a wide, confident grin. There was something strange about that grin, though Marceline couldn't put her finger on what it was.

"At least you can always count on this old place," he was saying to the woman. "Always the rush of forward motion—the advancement of enterprise, no matter the cost! It's invigorating, don't you find?"

"It's busy," the woman said, though she did not seem irritated. "Too much haste. And the scent of greed is overripe."

"Nonsense! I've always found it makes the perfect spice." He beamed at a pair of hagglers as he passed by, but they paid him no attention. "The feeling of one's fortunes at stake doesn't just quicken the blood, it sharpens the mind. One day I'll get you to admit that."

"You've been waiting a very long time," the woman said. Her smile was a subtle thing, but strong, like a curling vine.

"And yet, though I've never lacked for time, I've always hated to wait. Curious, I admit." He cast a glance over the market—and, Marceline was sure, looked directly at her for the duration of a moment, though it felt longer. "Well?" he asked the woman. "What do you think?"

Her brow furrowed. "I don't think what I have to say will please you."

"That's never stopped you before."

"Well then, it isn't . . . clean. It's reckless, it lacks elegance, and I expect it will rouse anger among the others."

"The *others* have to deal with Amerei, next to whom even I have always seemed temperate and manageable. Besides, Yaelor and Irein have both taken actions of their own already, and much more dramatically than I propose to."

She shook her head. "It is given to Yaelor neither to threaten nor flatter, but to offer a choice to his incarnate, and leave it to his will. And none of us could ever hope to command Irein. But if you do what you intend, you will have to answer for it."

"So then I answer for it. It's hardly the worst thing that could happen."

"It may upset the balance," she warned.

"And what has the balance done for me, or any of us? Have your far-seeing eyes lost sight of your past glories, or of how ignominiously they were stolen from you?" But she wasn't going to change her mind, and he saw it. He sighed. "Do you intend to stop me?"

"You know I cannot stop you," she said. "But nor will I offer you pity in your grief, should you only cause yourself ruin."

"Well enough." When he brushed past her, it was with determination, or even defiance, as if he would do what he would do, and let fate and fortune try to catch him if they could. He stared across the distance between them, and extended his hand.

"My young friend," he called, and he could only be talking to her—his eyes were fastened on hers, unblinking. "Will you come speak with me awhile?"

Marceline looked around, fearful that his gesture had exposed her to the crowd's notice. But no one else was looking at her, or at them; no one seemed to care. So though she felt more than a twinge of apprehension, she crossed the square, and stood before him.

He smiled, and again she felt that there was something strange about it, though she could not think what. It did not seem threatening, or cruel—perhaps a bit smug, but she could tell he was trying to curb that impulse. "I thank you for your time. I hope I have not frightened you. I merely thought you might be able to help me with something."

Many a fair or foul enterprise had begun with those words. Marceline kept her expression closed. "What is it that troubles you, sir?"

He spread his hands wide. "I have been called many things, but it has always felt surpassingly strange to me to be called *sir*. My name is Tethantys, and this is my comrade Asariel." The woman clicked her tongue, as if to remind him that she had not given permission to be brought into this discussion. "I am, as it happens, on quite familiar terms with your friend Roger Halfen, though don't expect him to admit it. And in the course of our acquaintance, I have . . . well, I must confess that I have spied upon him, and discovered a rather fascinating secret."

"You'd have to get up damned early in the morning to get one over on Roger," Marceline said, impressed in spite of herself. "But I don't know what your dealings with him have to do with me."

"Nothing yet," he admitted. "But this secret presents . . . not precisely an opportunity, nothing as definite as that. It would have great potential, in the right hands. But those hands can't be mine, as much as I might like them to be. I have other associates, even less amiable than good Asariel here, and they would not look kindly on me, were I to interfere in matters they wish undisturbed."

"You know there're a *lot* of tricks that start out just like this, right?" Marceline asked.

He laughed. "The number of tricks I know would quite confound your young mind, I fear."

"Are you going to tell me next that half a dozen Sheathers have already tried to buy this information off you—offered outrageous sums!—but the one you *really* want to sell it to is me? The monkey, a slip of a girl who hasn't even been apprenticed yet?"

She thought he would laugh again, or at least smile ingratiatingly, but instead he looked suddenly serious; when he spoke his voice took on deeper tones. "No. I will share this secret with you, or with no one. No Sheather knows of it but Roger and I, and no more will, if you do not wish it."

His solemnity caught her off guard, and she stammered, "You . . . you know Sheath so well? I've never seen you there."

That, of all things, brought the smile back, and she found she could breathe easier with it there. "I have long regarded Sheath as something of a second home—or third or fourth or twelfth or twentieth, as it were—and flatter myself that I am well apprised of its citizens and their affairs. It seems to me that, though young, you show a certain promise. But I would like to see you become more than you are—and I sense that you want that as well.

"Here is my proposal, my young friend. If you wish it, I will tell you this secret of Roger Halfen's. I will demand no price of you—it is simply yours for the asking. If you do not wish to know it, I will not tell you, and I and my companion will be on our way. It is a choice you are free to make, of naught but your own will."

Something about that last bit unnerved her—the words, or else the hungry way his smile stretched as he said them. She went over it all again in her mind, trying to find some hidden catch. "This secret," she said slowly. "Is it true?"

He shrugged. "I wouldn't blame you for being skeptical. I cannot claim I don't lie when it suits me, after all. But Asariel never lies, so perhaps you might ask her if I speak the truth."

"What, not ever?" Marceline exclaimed, before she could help it.

"Not ever," the woman called Asariel said firmly—the first words she had spoken directly to Marceline. "It goes against my nature."

Marceline knew logically that it would be foolish to accept such a claim, and yet . . . "What do you say, then?"

The woman nodded. "In this," she said, "he means to speak the truth."

"There you are," Tethantys said. "If you can find any more potential loopholes, I will be happy to provide counter-assurances. But I am not actually trying to trick you."

Marceline thought more deeply on it than she ever would have believed—the chance to know a secret of Roger's, and to know it without *his* knowing, was delicious enough to jump at. But all her thief's senses told her to be wary of something that seemed too good to be true. Sad to say, but she would have felt more comfortable if Tethantys had asked her to pay. That would've made sense.

But in the end she said, "All right. Tell me." What danger could just knowing bring down on her, especially if it was something Roger knew already, and he was doing just fine?

Tethantys's smile was brilliant, and yet somehow still odd. He stepped closer to her, and leaned down to whisper right in her ear.

When he was finished, she stood there gaping at him. "Are you sure about this? He's really been hiding all that from us?"

"I assure you it is just as I have said. You're free to confirm it for yourself or not."

Marceline frowned. "All right, but now that I know, what is it you expect me to do?"

He was still grinning. "Oh no, *expecting* anything would ruin it. I simply want to see what you will do, whether or not it's what I expect."

"And what is it that you get out of all this?" she asked.

He leaned forward again, but not toward her ear; he faced her directly, a gleaming, almost feverish fire alight in his pale eyes. "When you contemplated my offer—when you decided to accept it—you felt it then, did you not? That spark of desire that let you dream of what could be, that urged you to set aside caution and fear for the sake of that promise of possibility?"

Marceline's voice died in her throat. It wasn't fear that she felt, exactly, but a sense of the strangeness of this encounter, a chill that stood her hair on end.

Perhaps Tethantys understood, because he drew back, with a cheerful shrug. "To me, that feeling is beyond price. If you feel differently, I suppose that can't be helped." He looked to his companion. "Well, Asariel? I suppose you will say I have done too much here already. Shall we be off?"

"In a few moments more," she said. "Let me have one more stroll through Ashencourt."

"Ashencourt?" Marceline asked. "What could possibly interest you down that old alley?"

Asariel smiled sadly. "Nothing now, but the memory of what used to be there, in happier times."

Ashencourt had been a cramped and dilapidated handful of backstreets for as long as Marceline could remember, and she had never heard anyone say it had once been anything else. "What used to be there?"

Asariel sighed, deep and portentous, the way a lover sighs when asked to describe their beloved. But she only said, "What a good question." Marceline waited for more, but there wasn't any.

Tethantys laughed at her confusion. "You've got to be careful with questions around Asariel." To her, he said, "You're finished, yes?"

"Well and truly."

"Well indeed." He smiled at Marceline. "Oh—one more thing. If you happen to run into a fellow calling himself Amerei, I'd be wary of him. He has a thousand faces, all of them fair, but he lies even more than I do, and has vanity enough to pull kingdoms to the ground. Good luck, my young friend."

They didn't look back at her again, but melted into the crowd, moving in the direction of Ashencourt. What *had* used to be there, that had so bewitched that woman's memory?

Then something struck her—a memory of her own, from the much more recent past, and part of what had seemed so strange. She thought back to that moment again, trying to make sure her mind wasn't playing tricks on her, but she was sure the sensations she remembered were accurate. When Tethantys had told her his secret, he had bent his head close to hers, as if to prevent anyone from overhearing him. But while she had heard his voice clearly, she had not felt his breath, though his lips had been right beside her ear.

Chapter Forty-four

Esthrades

DEINOL WAS LEARNING all kinds of things about forests he'd never wanted to know. As far as he was concerned, fires belonged beneath cookpots, wood belonged stacked in a neat little pile beside the hearth, any birds bigger than pigeons belonged on spits, wolves belonged under the skinner's knife, and wasps belonged precisely nowhere. Lucius was happy to have Almasy explain about this plant or that set of tracks, but all that information did was remind Deinol how long it had been since he'd been in Sheath, and how stupid he'd been to have left it in the first place.

He kept expecting Lucius to grow bored once he realized Almasy was doing exactly what she'd said, but instead he just got more wrapped up in this conspiracy: the list of names, the possible connections between all these rich people and their fancy estates. Deinol certainly didn't mind bringing types like that low, but the world was full of them, sprouting up as persistently as these damned weeds.

Almasy hadn't wanted to start with this Andrew Ryker fellow, because she and the marquise already knew he was part of it. The point was to find what *other* rentholders might be part of it. As to that, the three of them had spent long hours investigating the comings and goings on estate grounds during the day, and Almasy had left them behind to do some investigating of her own at night, the nature of which she didn't reveal. The result of all this, if Lucius and Almasy's mutterings over the fire of an evening were any indication, was that they'd found a couple individuals who seemed suspicious, but no one so far that they could prove was guilty.

And for whatever reason, that made Almasy want to come here, to the woods of this conniving asshole. "Does he own this entire damned forest?" Deinol asked, swatting a branch out of the way.

"No. No one would accept that—not the Margraines, and not the common people. He has until the standing stones to the south, and in the west until the meadow. It's . . . five square miles or so? He can hunt outside it, of course, but so can anybody else."

"Why wouldn't anyone accept more?" Lucius asked.

"Because the forest is important to us. You've possibly noticed that Esthrades has a lot of forest? We could clear it out, if we really wanted to—make more farmland. But we don't, because before Esthrades became Esthrades—before it was given to the Margraines, or subsumed into Elesthene—the people of the forest clans lived here. We're descended from them—you can still find the ruins of structures they built here and there, like the tower that forms the backbone of Stonespire Hall. The forest was important to them, and we remember that. It doesn't sit well for any one person to have too much of it."

"Come on," Deinol said. "You believe that?"

She gave him that crooked grin he was getting used to. "Do I believe I don't want a rich rentholder to have any more land than he's already got? Absolutely."

"You know what I mean. What's the forest going to do to you that's worse than just being itself? Make more wasps?" He shuddered. "Never mind, that would be enough for me."

She shrugged. "I was raised in Stonespire, and then . . . elsewhere. Preoccupied with the concerns of city life. But someone who was born out in some little village . . . like our captain of the guard. He could tell you stories of every single thing that's ever been said to live in these woods, real or imagined."

"Did you learn all this from him?" Deinol asked.

"No." Almasy went very still. "From her. She didn't believe in the things the captain did . . . sprites and demons and that sort of thing. But she did believe . . . that a person could get into the forest, and it could get into them."

Well, wasn't that a perfectly horrible thought? But then Lucius said, as if reading his mind, "The city can get into people, too. You know that as well as anyone."

"The city doesn't—shit!" Before he knew what was happening, Deinol was staring into a pair of large black eyes attached to an absolutely terrifying creature. He knew what a deer was, obviously, but it was one thing to see a head or two mounted on a wall and quite another to have the whole rack of antlers right in front of him, easily ten sharp points just at first glance.

"Just step back!" Almasy snapped, grabbing him by the arm and hauling him away from the creature. It didn't pursue, just stared at them, as if trying to decide what they were for. He could see the coiled strength in its flanks, betrayed even in subtle movement, and it held its head so proudly, as if all those antlers weighed nothing. Was any crown ever so heavy?

"Deinol, they only eat grass," Lucius said. "It's fine."

"That wouldn't save him if it were rutting," Almasy said. "But it's early for that yet. Just back away a little and wait for it to leave. It doesn't look angry."

She said that, but then all three of them held their breath, never taking their eyes from the stag. It evidently didn't feel the same way, because it paced off into the trees, bending its head every now and then to nip at the grass.

When Deinol sighed, the loosening of tension made him feel weak in the knees. "Well, thank the gods for—"

"Don't thank them yet," Almasy said, and he heard it: the sound of hoofbeats.

He'd been so shaken by the stag that at first he thought it was another deer, charging at them this time. Lucius grabbed his arm, but wherever he sought to drag him, he wasn't fast enough. Almasy, already halfway to cover, saw it, too, and cursed, doubling back to their side.

It was a horse that came galloping through the trees, its white flanks dripping with sweat. Astride it was a young man with sandy hair, digging his heels in impatiently. He stopped that when he saw them, though, pulling the horse up short. It was then Deinol saw the quiver upon his back, the bow clutched in one hand. A hunter.

"That's Andrew Ryker," Almasy muttered.

The man peered down at them, eyes narrowing. "Seren Almasy? What is the meaning of this? Stonespire is your accustomed haunt, not *my* land. Are you here on her orders?"

Yes, Deinol thought. *Just tell him yes, and he won't dare—*

"No," Almasy said. "I've been dismissed. I move only at my own leisure now."

Ryker let his eyes run down his bow, as if Deinol weren't already painfully aware of it. "Come now, no games. I did not take you for that kind of woman. If she sent you here, you must not be afraid to say so. That would make your business official, after all, and I could have no quarrel with your presence. I should hardly like to be embarrassed in front of her by going to complain, only to find you had her sanction after all."

"Again," Almasy said.

"Pardon?"

"You wouldn't like to be embarrassed in front of her again. Especially not so soon after the last time."

Ryker clutched the bow so tightly the color drained from his knuckles. "*If* you are not here on official business, Seren Almasy, then you are a trespasser at best. At worst, I might fear one with your . . . gifts . . . has gone feral without a master. And if you have been dismissed, I can deal with you as I please."

"If I have been dismissed," Almasy said, expressionless, "I am a common Esthradian citizen, under her ladyship's protection. So, legally speaking, I am still not yours to deal with as you please."

He smiled, a tight, miserly little smile. "If you're dead, who'll be left to tell her?"

Almasy shrugged, but she finally backed up a couple steps, muscles tensed in readiness just as the stag's had been. "If that's your game, I hope you're better at archery than you are at negotiating."

Ryker lunged for his quiver, but Almasy was already off, darting this way and that in a jagged pattern through the trees. Lucius put a hand on Deinol's arm. "Come on, move. We don't want to get caught up in this."

They started running, too, on a diagonal away from Almasy, but Deinol risked a glance over his shoulder at Ryker, who was putting away the arrow he'd drawn with a curse—too difficult a shot, most like. He was just daring to hope Almasy knew what she was doing, when the sound of hoofbeats announced the arrival of two additional riders, these as out of breath as their horses. "Master Andrew," the elder of the two of them said, "I know you had the stag in your sight, but I must beg you not to abandon—"

"Forget the stag!" Ryker snapped. "Your targets are those three in the woods! I want them brought to ground, by whatever means necessary!"

Very distinctly, he heard Lucius mutter, "Fuck."

After that, it was pure chaos.

Deinol had lived as a bandit for years, but a *city* bandit. He knew how to run, but his adversaries had always been runners, too. His feet carried him forward through the carpet of dead leaves as quickly as they ever had, but his strides were feeble compared to the horses' powerful gait. "Is this what you envisioned?" he shouted furiously at Almasy with the first breath he could spare; he wasn't going to die without at least attempting to have the last word.

"You'll be fine!" she shouted back, some distance ahead of him and to his right. "Just don't run in a straight line, and use the trees!"

The three of them were better at maneuvering than the riders were, but that was about all they had in their favor. And if the riders managed to herd them together, it was over. With that in mind, Deinol tried to go sideways as well as forward, running back and forth in an irregular pattern meant to separate him from Lucius. There was a *thunk* as an arrow buried itself in the tree trunk nearest him, and he looked back to see not Ryker but his third servant, this one younger, on a speckled pony.

Perhaps the man had chosen Deinol specifically to follow, or else he was just the slowest of the three of them, but the pony kept after him, no matter how he darted through the trees. He dodged around trunks, making sure to put them in the archer's line of sight; he changed direction as often as he could without closing the gap between them, but none of it seemed to do any good. And then, just as Deinol tore his way through a bush whose thorns gouged him even through his breeches, it happened again: a glimpse of huge black eyes, and the raw points of bone.

He didn't think; all thought had been driven out of his head, too far out of reach to grasp. He flung himself down upon the leaves, curled into a ball, hands over his head. This was it. He'd either be shot, or gored, or trampled from either direction—

A shadow fell over him, and he heard the pounding of hooves. Then an awful, drawn-out scream echoed through the forest, and it took Deinol a moment to realize he wasn't the one screaming. He wasn't, as improbable as it seemed, in any pain.

He lifted his head. The stag's charge had caught horse and rider just off-center; its antlers had scored a deep gouge in the horse's back, but had pierced its rider's flesh. As Deinol watched, it bore him still screaming to the ground, ramming its head down again until the noise stopped. It shook its antlers free of the body, the points wet with blood. They stared at each other, and Deinol waited helplessly for it to lower its head once more into a charge. But instead its ears flicked about, and it turned away, leaping over the bush he'd stumbled through and running off into the forest.

Deinol got to his feet, though his legs were still shaking. The archer's wounded pony was making shrill pained noises, and he moved toward it a few steps without thinking, as if he knew what to do for it. He turned slowly, trying to get a larger view of his immediate surroundings, to see who or what was nearby.

From somewhere behind him, he heard Lucius call, "Look out!"

Deinol at least had the presence of mind not to look for Lucius himself, but for whatever it was he saw. A flash of white and brown and sandy blond resolved itself into a figure. He was staring right at the point of the arrow nocked upon Andrew Ryker's bow, and was so suddenly overwhelmed by the hopelessness of getting out of the way that he didn't even try.

There was a hand on his forearm, a soft grunt as a hip rammed against his, and he was forced sideways and down, hearing the arrow strike something above the level of his eyes. He was safe. *Lucius,* he thought, looking up to thank him, but it was Almasy he saw beside him. Almasy, with an arrow sprouting from her left shoulder, held between the fingers of her right hand. The shaft rested against the edge of her knife.

Deinol couldn't speak, couldn't even stand up. He could see Lucius out of the corner of his eye, edging carefully toward them, though Ryker was in the way. Even Ryker was staring at Almasy in astonishment, as if he'd thought the arrow would pass through her, or bounce off harmlessly. And then he laughed, in a kind of hysterical relief. "Is that it?" he asked. "That's the strength of her prized butcher? She would've had the whole country cowering in fear of you, and you're just some dog after all."

He turned to call out to his guard, who'd stopped his horse where it was after Ryker struck Almasy. "When we return to the estate, I'll want messengers called immediately, and my scribe. I'll need drafts to Eurig and Cantor notifying them of the presence of this stray on my lands, and urging them to take caution. Ask Cantor to pass the message on to Claremont and Apglen."

The guard hesitated. "But surely not now, sir?"

"No, now you can help me finish this lot—even easier than that damned stag. If there's even a chance it's still—"

There was the noise of something slicing through the air, and the conversation abruptly ceased. In Ryker's case it was probably out of shock, but his guard literally could not have given him any answer, as there was now a knife buried in his throat. He slipped sideways off his horse, which fled, dragging his body behind it for a bit before his foot fell free of the stirrup.

Ryker's eyes darted all around the area, as if he thought some additional player would reveal themselves. But Deinol looked right at Almasy, and waited for Ryker to look there, too. She was hunched over, breathing hard, right hand still pressed against her shoulder. But the knife was gone from it.

She gave Ryker her crooked grin, only slightly shaky. "Call me a wolf, at least," she said. "Even a child knows an injured wolf can still bite." She directed her next words at Lucius: "You can kill him now. I have all I needed from him."

Lucius didn't hesitate. In the time it took for Ryker to fumble with his reins, Lucius had already stepped to the horse's side. Before Ryker could dig his heels in, he slung one arm around his stomach and fisted the other hand in his shirt, pulling him back and down. Once his feet were free, Ryker slid off his horse so smoothly that it backed away from them but didn't rear or bolt. It got a lot more skittish when Ryker started screaming, though.

At first it was for his guards to help him, after Lucius let him hit the ground and put a foot on his chest. Then he shouted that Almasy would pay for this, that the marquise hadn't sanctioned his death, but Almasy wasn't even looking at him at that point. The moment she'd seen that Lucius had him well in hand, she'd taken careful steps toward the body of the man she'd killed, taking her hand from her wounded shoulder to pull her knife out of his throat. She looked back at Lucius. "Do you want me to do it?"

"There's no need for you to strain yourself further," Lucius said, as calm as you please, and drew his sword now that he had both hands free. Still Ryker screamed, though it was almost wordless now, or maybe it was begging—and then Lucius's blade cut his throat, and the forest was suddenly silent.

CHAPTER FORTY-FIVE

The Gods' Curse

WHEN OUTSIDERS TRIED to guess how the Issamiri outriders were able to navigate the Curse with such facility, they almost always based their hypotheses around some sort of visual landmark others did not know to look for: specific dead trees or rock formations, changes in the color or consistency of the soil—even constellations, never mind the fact that guides regularly led people across during the day. But in truth, there were no reliable visual landmarks on the Curse. They could have been easily established—and had been, in the long ago days of the Ninists and their unimaginative chains of wooden posts. But the Issamiri leadership had never wanted to repeat that process, because as long as the secret to crossing the Curse remained a secret, they had the advantage against any invading army. And the secret was that crossing the Curse had nothing to do with your eyes at all.

The secret to crossing the Curse was in the wind.

It sounded simple, when you first heard it—and no doubt the first foreign powers who'd successfully bribed an Issamiri for that information had thought so, too. But in actuality, the shifts you needed to look for were so subtle, so vulnerable to change, that you couldn't be *told* how to do it—you had to *practice* doing it, with someone who knew by your side to tell you when you were doing it right, just as Adora had done with Landon years and years ago. And since the Issamiri kept a strict watch on the Curse, it was rather difficult to convince your informants to venture out there to practice with you: they'd be put to death for treason if they were caught at it.

It was not correct to say that the wind across the Curse always blew in one direction. The wind across the Curse acted like any wind anywhere: there were wild gusts, capricious twisting breezes, stifling calm spells, gentle, playful periods, and even dangerous dust storms. But all of that was simply a distraction. You had to let it wash over you, understand it, and discount it, searching always for what lay beneath it: a different, stranger sensation, a slight *pull* in the air, as if a small child tugged weakly but insistently at her clothes, her hair, the tips of her fingers. Adora closed her eyes, and behind her, Cadfael cleared his throat. "Is that . . . part of the process?"

"We don't explain the process to outsiders," Adora said. "Forgive my bluntness in saying so, but it is for the best. I promise that I know what I'm doing. This is a point of pride among the Issamiri—it doesn't mark our coming of age for nothing."

There, she'd found it, that eternal tug. This wind beneath the wind always pulled inward, from every direction on the Curse, to a single point: the Curse's very center. So as long as you knew the four points of the compass, you could cross easily: keep the wind at your back until you reached the halfway point, growing ever stronger the closer you got to the center; then, on the way out, keep that same wind trying to pull you back.

She spurred her horse forward, and was relieved to find that Cadfael walked his behind her without further protest. "So *everyone* in Issamira does this?"

"No," Adora said. "It's tradition, but not everyone thinks tradition is important. And you have to be taught to do it, a process that can take months—months spent away from home. Some Issamiri simply cannot afford to spend so much time away from their lives learning to do something that may not ever have any practical use. But the Avestri always at least attempt a coming of age crossing, because the Curse is so connected to our ancestor, the Rebel Queen. It's especially important for heirs to the throne to be good at it, to show the people we still possess the same mastery over the land that she did."

"Sorry," Cadfael said. "I'm not familiar with the Rebel Queen—I know she smashed the Elesthenians on the field, but not more than that. What mastery do you mean?"

"Oh," Adora said, but of course a foreigner wouldn't know. It was one of the most famous tales in all of Issamiri history, and any one of her countrymen would have been told a hundred times. "It was in the middle of the war against Elesthene, just after Talia Avestri had finally killed, captured, or thrown out all the empire soldiers in this country. She and her allies and subordinates held a great council for many days, trying to decide what to do next. There were many in her ranks who felt that their work was done, that now that Issamira itself was free, they could devote themselves to rebuilding and leave the rest of Elesthene to splinter into nothingness or shore itself up as it willed. But Talia Avestri and her staunchest supporters wished to continue the war on the other side of the Curse. They felt that Issamira could know no true peace until the empire was destroyed for good.

"The Rebel Queen was much loved, and her word had been as good as law in many other instances. But when one can either fight or celebrate, the latter choice must seem very tempting indeed. And then there were those who said their queen could not keep a neutral view of the conflict: while Elesthene still lived, Esthrades was vulnerable, and Talia Avestri's affair with the sixth Daven's son, Theodosius Margraine, had become public knowledge by that point."

She felt for the wind again, and adjusted her horse's direction accordingly. "In those days, the Gods' Curse was known to be expanding. Very, very slowly, but just large enough for the difference to be perceptible to the human eye from one morning to the next, if the appropriate instruments were used. There were many who argued that this was a more urgent threat than any that might have come from the remains of Elesthene: if they could not find a way to halt the Curse's progress, Issamira itself might one day be nothing more than a barren wasteland.

"It was that point that ultimately put an end to the deadlock. After three days of bickering, Talia Avestri commanded the attention of all, and announced her intentions: she herself would sit vigil on the very edge of the Curse, absorbed in the exercise of her resolve and the offering of prayers to the gods. And she would stop the Curse's expansion herself. Once she had brought such a thing to pass, there could be no doubt that she was chosen, and that it was with her that the brightest future of Issamira's people lay. And so she did."

She glanced over her shoulder to see Cadfael looking as shocked and skeptical as she'd expected. "That can't be right. It's just a story, isn't it? A myth, to explain the unexplainable, and immortalize a beloved queen."

"I admit it is unexplainable," Adora said. "I could never even guess how such a thing might have been accomplished. But it is no myth. There were hundreds of witnesses, perhaps thousands, to Talia Avestri's act. Many of these witnesses kept written accounts of what they saw that day, or passed them down orally to their descendants. They all agree: at sunrise, Talia Avestri rode out to the Curse and plunged her sword into the ground at its very edge, that all could mark where it had stood at that time, and could clearly see if it crept any farther. She spent the day riding upon the Curse, speaking to her people, purifying herself. And that night, at sundown, she sat before her sword, for a motionless vigil meant to last until the following dawn.

"There were countless eyes upon that sword, to ensure that it should not be moved—eyes of those loyal to the Rebel Queen, and those who were skeptical of her gifts. Countless eyes watched every moment of her vigil, and reported that she barely stirred to breathe. And countless eyes witnessed the truth, the following morning. Not only had the corruption of the land failed to pass the blade of Talia's sword, it had recoiled, ever so slightly, from touching that blade. And ever since that day . . ." Adora cleared her throat, making a slight adjustment. "The Curse has never again expanded. And though we who are her descendants don't understand how she accomplished such a miracle, still we try to prove to our people that the Avestri are masters of the Curse, and are not mastered by it."

"And you have no idea how she did it? Even after all this time, even the Avestri don't know?"

"Well," Adora said, "I'm sure you understand that even if I did know, I wouldn't be able to tell you. But I truly don't. The question obsessed my father, but his fascination brought him no closer to solving it. As for me, I am content to believe that it happened, and that it represents a duty the Avestri must never forsake. Though if the opportunity came to learn the secret . . ." She smiled at herself. "I must admit I would give much for it."

BY THE TIME they reached the third outpost, Cadfael had been given plenty of time to think it over, but he was still no closer to anything resembling a theory. When they'd reached the first one, on the south side of the Curse, she'd asked after this Irjan Tal, only to be directed west to a second. But there they were told he'd already left on a crossing, and they had to go north after him. Cadfael supposed he had to credit the queen's navigational abilities: when they reached the closest outpost on the other side, the woman they met told them Irjan Tal was indeed here. That meant Adora, like this experienced ranger, had made the shortest possible line between two outposts. Perhaps there was something to that rubbish about the Avestri having mastery of the land after all.

But still, Irjan Tal. What was the significance of that? The letter had contained no physical description, no background, just a name and a profession. Unless the bit about travelers giving him the information was some sort of prearranged code, he had no idea what her uncle had meant her to understand from so little. Irjan Tal himself, at least, was no code: the woman showed them where he was, leaning against the far side of the outpost wall, a man and a ranger and not a symbol for anything more abstract. He was unremarkable to Cadfael's eyes, about his own age and height, shaggy-haired, clean-shaven, not particularly tall or short or handsome or unhandsome. But after just one look at him, the queen took off at a run, leaving Cadfael behind as if she'd forgotten his existence.

Cadfael stayed where he was, because she didn't seem afraid, and he knew her for a cautious person. If she wasn't worried about this man, he probably wouldn't cause her harm. It never even occurred to him to think about the reverse, not until the queen's fist connected with Irjan Tal's face.

It wasn't a slap, or a theatrical strike, meant to shame more than wound. It was a true punch, full of pure fury and whatever physical force she could muster. Irjan Tal staggered a little, and Adora punched him with her other hand in the shoulder—weaker, but no less furious. By the third attempt, he'd caught both her hands, and Cadfael was already moving toward them, before any of the staring onlookers could do the same. The queen didn't wish to announce her identity, but that meant no one here would feel obligated to let her do as she pleased.

"Everything all right, Irjan?" the woman who had pointed him out asked, with an edge to her voice that conveyed all it needed to.

The man himself had only looked shocked for the duration of that first punch, and was now merely solemn and sad. "Please don't worry. I, ah, deserved that."

That didn't discourage the looks they were getting, just made them go from concerned to curious. Cadfael sidled up to the queen. "Is there anything you need me to do?"

She pulled her hands free, and Irjan let them go. "No. Thank you. I just need to speak to him." *Alone,* she didn't have to say.

Part of him still felt uneasy, what with all Yaelor's talk of how much danger Adora was in. But he could hardly keep a queen from doing what she thought she had to do. "You'll be all right with him?" he asked her.

"No," she said. "But he won't harm me."

THE CURSE WAS the right place for a conversation like this. The blasted land had never seemed as forbidding to Adora as it did to others, both because she knew she could navigate it and because even this expanse of dust had once been cowed by the will of an Issamiri. But now it seemed to mirror her spirits and her hopes, withered and barren. A reunion she had prayed for, but never like this.

She looked up at the man at her side. So different, and yet so much the same. He'd let his hair grow, and wore more dirt than finery, but he was not changed as she could have expected. He did not look weary or worn down or prematurely aged; he looked healthy and well, nothing more forbidding in his face than concern. In a way, that was almost worse—that living away from all of them, away from his duty, for so long had weighed so lightly on him.

Landon lived. For how many years had she longed to walk with him again? How many times had she imagined the joy she would feel, if they could only be reunited? And now, having him restored to her at last, what did she feel? Anger, more than anything, and that made her sick.

"How did you find out?" he asked quietly.

So you can hide yourself away better next time? Adora thought. "If you truly wished to hide, you should have chosen a better name, brother. Even Uncle knew it was you."

"Irjan?" he asked. "What better name was there? I know half a dozen fellow rangers alone who bear it."

"Not that. Your surname. Irjan Tal, the true name of Irjan Firestarter, your favorite. Irjan may be common, but Tal is beyond obscure. You remember the story, I'm sure: Irjan and his sister both changed their names upon marrying, and if there have been any Tals since, there is no record of them.

"But you made a worse mistake, brother. You forgot that nowhere in the ballad of Irjan Firestarter is his surname given, and that ballad is all the common people have to know him by. So the name you chose was one that rang false, but a false name only a learned man would know enough to steal. I could almost have hoped . . . that you wanted us to guess. But I suppose that is untrue."

"Uncle doesn't know anything about ballads," he insisted.

"Uncle knows only what I've told him about ballads," Adora corrected him. "I suppose that shows he listens to me more carefully than you do."

There was a silence, in which he looked abashed and Adora tried to decide whether she should tell him that was too harsh, that she was sorry. She didn't.

Landon struggled to speak. "Adora, I'm not sure what you want, but I want to help you. If you want me to talk—anything you want to know—or if you just want me to listen . . . Tell me what I should do."

I want you to return to Eldren Cael and sit your throne, Adora thought. *I want you to understand for yourself how obvious that is. I want you to tell me what I should do!* But she already knew, deep within her heart, that the time for that had passed. So instead she asked, "Why did you not return? Was your party truly attacked, or did you feign that somehow?"

"I would never have done that," Landon said. "The attack was real—a disaster on my part. I was distracted—I was supposed to be leading them, and instead I allowed us to be caught unawares. Our two groups destroyed each other. No one escaped unwounded, and no one but me survived those wounds in the end—on our side, at least. At first I didn't return because I couldn't; I was too injured to travel. I found shelter, but the people there didn't know who I was, and I was too ashamed to tell them—to admit my failure."

"And when you recovered?" Adora asked.

He sighed. "By that time, news of Father's death had reached me. I knew what would be asked of me when I returned. I almost wish . . . that it had not reached me, that I had come home all unknowing. If that had happened, I would never have been able to escape."

"Escape? Escape what?"

His hands balled into fists. "Adora, I was more than ashamed. I was afraid. I didn't know how I would face you all when I saw you again—my people and my family both. I would have to let it be known that the reason I failed to attend my own father's funeral was because I was too weak to keep those under my command from being slaughtered. That they died protecting me, and for no other reason."

He shook his head angrily. "No, that's not . . . that's true, but it's not the whole truth. I owe you that. I don't know if you noticed, but even before I left for the Curse back then, I was melancholy, and anxious, and not myself. That's why I was distracted on that ranging; for weeks I'd been turning things over and over in my head, losing sleep, unable to concentrate on my swordsmanship . . ."

Adora thought back to that time. "You did seem . . . different, but you and Father had had so many arguments. I thought you were just worn down by them."

"I was, but there was something worse." He threw his head back, drawing in a deep breath, and for a moment Adora thought there were tears in his eyes. "I can't do it, Adora. The one thing a king must be able to do—the smallest, most basic, most essential thing." He gave her an expectant look, as if he believed he'd presented her with a revelation, that she must now surely understand everything.

His words had made sense to her until this moment—a horrible kind of sense, but sense. This was . . . what was he talking about? He had been the perfect prince; she had seen that herself. Perhaps there were some things he could not do, but something so essential it could not be missed? "Landon, if this is some sort of riddle, I don't know the answer. You couldn't protect our people, or serve their interests? Your sense of judgment was impaired? I know that can't be true."

"No, you're still . . . your thinking is too complicated. It was when . . . it was back when I bore myself in a way that made Father angry with me. When I piled up indiscretion upon indiscretion, with no purpose, as he saw it, other than satisfying my own lusts. But I did have a purpose. I just couldn't tell him that."

"So you weren't just angry because he'd told you to end your affair."

"No, that was what started it! It was naïve, Adora, I admit that, but at the time I believed that if I got her with child, Father would relent—that he would never wish for the instability that would result from a royal bastard. But we were together for so long, and nothing happened. I just had to know. I had to know whether the defect lay with her or with me. And by now I'm all but certain of it, as certain as I could be."

Again he gave her that look, as if to say, *Now, surely, you must understand.* But as Adora looked at him, as she finally comprehended what he'd meant by *the most essential thing,* she could not even bring herself to feel pity.

"That's it?" she asked. "That's *it? That's* what grieved you so much you couldn't return to us? *That's* what made you think you couldn't be king?"

She could tell she had wounded him, but she didn't care. *How dare you care about this,* she wanted to say. *How dare you think* this *is more important than what you owe our people, or Father, or me.* A king had to bear so much on his shoulders, the dreams and fears and pain of his people as well as his own. If he allowed himself to become mired in his own problems, he would be lost. Couldn't one ask that they did not touch him as they did ordinary people?

"Do you think that the question of succession isn't important?" he asked. "After how much trouble it's caused both of us? You would have had to be my heir, Adora. You, or your children if I outlived you. If I had returned, and confessed the truth, your life would still have changed. You would have had to spend all of it waiting for that day—when I would die, and you would rule. If it would pass to you anyway, why should you not start now, rather than live your whole life in my shadow?"

As if she had not done that regardless. "Because it's your birthright! Because it's your responsibility!" She did not think she had ever been this angry. There was nothing liberating about it; it felt like it was choking her, shaking her in its fist like a doll. "It's too painful to be borne, Landon—that all this time, you were out here playing ranger when we needed you. That you would discard your most sacred duty as easily as a coat, just because it did not fit as you wished!"

Sorrow warred with anger in Landon's face. "I can't rescue you, Adora," he said—softly, but she heard the bite in it. "You've spoken so much of the responsibility we owe our people, but then what are you doing here? Why have you abandoned them in search of me? You wished to find me so desperately because you wanted me to take it all away from you, to tell you that the birthright and the responsibility are mine, and that you're free to spend every day reading poetry in your tower like you used to. But I can't do that for you. Say what you will, but I will die before I sit this kindgom's throne. That's what I'm trying to make you understand."

"How dare you," she said. "How dare you leave it all to me, when you know I'll *never*—"

I'll never be as good as you, she had been going to say. *I'll never be able to do what you could!* Yet even at the very heart of all this rage and sorrow, some part of her mind whispered, *Is that true?*

It was a paradox, wasn't it? If Landon was so impossibly far above her, how could her judgment ever surpass his? And yet she knew herself to be in the right. *If you lack the competence to determine how Issamira should be ruled, you have no business telling anyone else what to do about it. If you do know what must be done, why can you not simply do it yourself?*

Landon was of paramount importance to her, because she loved him. But that love, and that anger, and that regret, had nothing to do with her duty or her goals. She had been right, just minutes ago: a ruler could not afford to become mired in their own problems. She needed to give the people of Issamira a ruler who understood that.

She loved him, but she didn't need him. That was true, and now she couldn't unknow it. It drained the anger out of her as if from a puncture, but it didn't leave her feeling empty. For the first time in longer than she could remember, she felt unrestricted, and free.

She no longer needed to stand here arguing with him. "I—never mind that. This anger serves no purpose."

"Your anger is understandable—"

"Never *mind*," Adora snapped. "Let us conclude this calmly, and without regret. Let us say what must be said, and then no more."

If she could have known of this moment before living it, she would have thought that living it would break her. And it was true that the grief she felt was no trivial thing. It was the crumbling of an idol, but more than that, it was the loss of everything their relationship had ever contained, all the chances to live and grow together with someone she loved. But over all that sadness, she felt relief. For the first time in so long, she was certain of the right thing to do.

"Landon," she said, "we are of the blood of the Avestri. Before our bonds as a family, before the love and care we bear each other, we must always think of our people. So I will be as cold and as final with you as I must be, and that means I will ask you only once. Will you accept the crown? Will you be our king, as is your right?" She had to say more than that, she told herself. She had to use anything and everything that could possibly persuade him, this one last time. "If you say yes, I will do all I can to restore you to your throne. I will fight with you against your enemies; I will silence any who might dare to question your identity, or demand an explanation for your absence. I will serve you as well as I can, for as long as I can, with all the loyalty and skill I may possess." She held his eyes with hers, praying he would not doubt her sincerity or her resolve. "But I will ask you only once."

Landon's voice was quiet, but unmistakable. "I . . . cannot, now. I don't wish to disappoint you still further, but . . . I cannot."

She had known what he would say before she asked, yet even so his reply stung. But she swallowed that hurt, and moved on. "Very well. If you will not be my king, Landon, then I must be your queen. I must protect our people, and I will. But I cannot do that if Landon Avestri exists. So from this moment onward, he must cease to be."

She pointed north, off beyond the horizon. "You must leave Issamira forever— every inch of it, from the Curse to the southern sea. That means you cannot remain a guide here as you have been—you must make your home only in the northern lands henceforward. And you must remain Irjan Tal, or whatever else you choose, for the rest of your life. You must never reveal your true identity, for the sake of our kingdom. Surely you must see why this is necessary, lest you ever be used in a plot to undermine my right to the throne."

Her brother hesitated, but Adora's glare never wavered. At last, he bent his head. "I understand. I will do as you've said. I swear it."

She swallowed hard, doing her best to put the necessary steel into her voice. "If, at some point in the future, you should ever reconsider . . . if you should ever decide to reclaim your throne . . . I am afraid you will have to fight me for it. Issamira can only have one ruler, and its people deserve one who is wholly committed to that task, not one who flits in and out of it as it suits them." That much, at least, she had learned from Jocelyn.

"You don't have to worry about that," Landon said. "This is not something I would ever reconsider."

"Good." Her breath caught, just for a moment, before she said the rest. "And when I return to Eldren Cael, I will tell our people that you are dead. I will tell our family that you are dead. And to me you will be dead, from this day until the day we meet in some world beyond this one."

Landon shook his head, smiling a sad smile. "There is no world beyond this one, sister."

Her face did not soften. "Then, brother, we will never meet again."

"HE MUST'VE DONE *something* awful to you, though," Cadfael said, pulling his skillet off the fire and handing Adora her half of the bread. "You don't strike me as someone who gets angry like that often."

"I'm not someone who should get angry like that at all," she said, using the bread to scrape up a sample of his newest concoction. Whatever he'd added to the pork was definitely to its benefit. "It was . . . childish of me, and I regret it. But at least the matter is concluded. He made no attempt to justify himself, and was content to settle things according to my wishes."

At Cadfael's insistence, they had made camp for the night in a pitiful stand of trees just north of the border, rather than on the Curse itself. Adora couldn't blame him for his unease; it was natural for a northerner to feel safer when surrounded by trees, and uncomfortable in the middle of a vast plain, even one that wasn't as unnervingly still and dead as the Curse. They wouldn't lose much time, and could make the crossing faster in the morning when they were better rested.

"So what now, then?" he asked. "Back to your uncle's?"

"I'm not sure," she admitted. "My next step must be to root out the cause behind the attempt on my life, but how should I go about such a thing? My first thought was that my uncle's wisdom would be a great help, but I am uneasy at the thought of being away from Eldren Cael any longer than I have to. Perhaps I should return there first, and summon him to me." She finished her last bite of bread, and reached for another piece of meat, now sufficiently cool to pick up with her fingers. "If I returned to Eldren Cael, would you follow me?"

"Yes," Cadfael said, without hesitation. "Until this matter of treachery is concluded."

"That's quite a responsibility to undertake on behalf of a foreign queen," Adora said. "You still don't wish for a reward?"

He shrugged. "You aren't in much of a position to offer one now. When things have settled down, perhaps if—"

Suddenly, the fire went out.

It did not sputter, or smoke, or flicker: in the space of a moment, it was extinguished so utterly she could almost have imagined its existence. Adora looked all around her—pointlessly, as to her maladjusted eyes the darkness was near total—but it wasn't raining or windy, and there hadn't been anything nearby that could have affected the fire.

There was a rustling across from her, and Cadfael muttered, "Hey, did you—"

There was no time for either of them to say more. Some dark shape blurred its way between the trees, and before Adora could so much as throw up a hand, it had rammed into her with all its strength.

She was flat on her back, and there was something heavy pressing into her abdomen. And the fire suddenly flickered back to life.

But it wasn't the fire she and Cadfael had lit, she realized, as she blinked away the glare. It was burning around the hand of the man who had his knee on her stomach, his other hand at her throat—not trying to cut off her air, just warning her against moving. He was Aurnian, long-haired and disheveled, in a tattered red cloak. There was a grayish cast to his face, and it took Adora several moments to figure out why: it was smeared all over with soot, rubbed into the skin.

"Adora Avestri," he rumbled, voice deeper than his frame would seem to allow. "I have business with you."

CHAPTER FORTY-SIX

Near the Gods' Curse

"GET AWAY FROM her!" The fire she and Cadfael had lit abruptly rose up between them, keeping him from charging directly at the man holding her down. He edged around the blaze instead, sword already drawn.

The man in the red cloak held his burning hand threateningly close to Adora's face, but the heat of it felt oddly far off, barely brushing her skin. "Keep your distance."

"You keep those flames distant from her. If you want to fight, you can fight me; if you want to talk, there's no need for that."

The man in the cloak locked eyes with him, and Adora could tell that something passed between them, some recognition or agreement. "I wish to speak and be heeded," the man said, "but I don't mean to harm the queen. I will talk peacefully, but you will listen."

"You've certainly captured my attention," Adora said. "Can we convince you to get off me?"

"If he puts his sword away, and remains on the far side of that fire."

She nodded at Cadfael, and he complied, though he was scowling. The flames around the man's hand subsided, and he allowed Adora to get up. They gathered around the fire, and she rubbed the soreness out of her limbs, trying to use the movement to inch toward Cadfael as surreptitiously as possible. "I suppose you already know who I am, though I don't know how, or how you found us. What business do you claim with me, sir?"

The man shook his head. "No *sir*. I need no false politeness from your kind. Merely answer my questions truthfully. Do you or do you not claim responsibility for Issamira?"

She had not made it through the events of the previous day only to hesitate now. "I do."

"Then what have you to say in your defense? How could you have allowed this to happen?"

Adora could name more than one thing she blamed herself for having allowed to happen, but she had to find some way to get her bearings. She needed to know what he intended, not simply sit here docile and compliant. "Are you a citizen of my country, that you would accuse me thus?"

"I am not," he growled.

"Then who are you?"

"You may call me Voltest."

Ash in Old Lantian, so almost certainly not his real name. "And what right do you have to demand explanations of me, Voltest, when I hardly even know what you mean?"

His lips curled back from gritted teeth, and his whole body trembled. "Lirien Arvel," he forced out at last, and Adora couldn't hide her shock at hearing *that* name, of all things. "You have allowed her to be used in the worst possible fashion. She was a guest under your roof, and you were so careless as to abandon her to your usurper while you hid yourself away here?"

His entire statement was so odd that Adora could only stare, confusion dampening even her fear. "My usurper? Do you mean Hephestion? He would never take the throne from me, and I would never *abandon* it to him. As for the rest, you seem to have mistaken camping for hiding. I have every intention of returning to Eldren Cael as soon as possible."

He glared at her. "We both know your brother is of no consequence. Had you only kept the watch on that woman that you ought, many unfortunate events might have been avoided—including, unless I miss my guess, the attempt on your life?"

"How did you know about that? How could you know who was behind it?"

Voltest laughed. "You might as well ask how I knew you were here. The answer is the same."

An answer he was not ready to give, it seemed. But as long as he did not lay hands on her again, she could play his game a little longer. "I can only assume you are speaking of Jocelyn Selreshe, but she would have no claim to the throne even if she could kill my brother, too. It was clever of her to devise that plot on my life—if she was truly the one who devised it—but she would have to scheme much further than my life in order to steal my throne."

Voltest's lips spread in a sharp smile. It was a smile devoid of any warmth, or even mirth; it was the rictus grin of a corpse that stood unmoved in the face of others' misfortunes. "Can it be?" he asked. "Can it truly be you do not know?"

A possibility suggested itself to Adora's mind—something that could not be, yet that chilled her even to think. "Tell me," she whispered. "If you wish me to set everything right, I will, but you must tell me."

Voltest's words came slowly and deliberately, each one chosen with the greatest care and savored to the last drop. "In Eldren Cael, Your *Grace,* they say you have perished, the group that escorted you torn to shreds. But to temper this sad news, the palace sends it cheek by jowl with gladder tidings: a royal wedding, held with the utmost pomp and accompanied by all proper festivities, between His Grace Hephestion Avestri, and the Lady Jocelyn Selreshe."

Adora's voice died in her throat, and her breath nearly went with it. She had known it, somehow; it was impossible, and yet she had known it. "How?" she choked out. "Hephestion would never . . . he has never wished . . ."

"His wishes are irrelevant," Voltest said. "The only thing that matters in Eldren Cael now is what Jocelyn Selreshe wants, and she wants to be queen."

Cadfael spoke up from the other side of the fire; she had nearly forgotten him. "Who is this woman? Has she captured the queen's brother and this Lirien Arvel somehow?"

"I have seen her in my flames," Voltest said. "She is a mage of no common skill. She has captured Lirien's magic, and with it she has captured the prince's mind. He is her creature now, and cannot rebel against her will."

Adora pressed her hands against her eyes. "This—what you are saying is . . . even if any of it were possible, for you to know it . . . for you to have seen it . . ."

Again Voltest gave her that mocking smile. "Would you like to see it for yourself, Your Grace? Disbelief will not save you, so I will happily help relieve you of it." He pointed at the fire. "Look there, and tell me what you wish to see."

He was right. It was useless to say what was or was not possible; she had to find out the truth for herself. She fixed her eyes on the center of the flames. "Whatever you say she has done to my brother. Let me see that, if you can."

For the first few moments she saw nothing, but then an image took shape, frighteningly clear: her brother's bedroom, just as she remembered it. There were no colors in the image beyond that of the flames themselves, but it moved as fluidly as if it were taking place right in front of her. Feste and Jocelyn stood within the room; their lips moved as if they spoke, but Adora could hear no sound. "Do you know what they're saying?"

"She is telling him he must announce your death. He is resistant, but he always yields. I have seen this pattern play out many times."

Feste's face did seem . . . odd: confused, and vaguely upset, but also as if he were only halfway present. Jocelyn reached out to cup his cheek in her hand, and he trembled as if he would flinch away. But then he went still, and dropped his eyes submissively to the floor.

Adora felt herself shaking, and fought to keep steady. "Is this happening right now?"

"No," Voltest said, unmoved. "She is not with him now. I am showing you the last time she was. The image feels recent to me—a day old, perhaps."

"Let him see, too," Adora said, gesturing to Cadfael to join them. Voltest hesitated, but ultimately did not protest when Cadfael crossed to their side of the fire. "You can hear their words?"

"I can. If you could hear them, you would know instantly that she has warped his mind in some way. She offers no reasoning or logic for her pronouncements; she simply forces them on him until he agrees. Without the aid of magic, she could not possibly convince anyone with such a method."

Adora could hardly comprehend such a violation. Were these horrors truly possible, not just in some distant past but in present time?

Another thought struck her. "What about my mother? Is she still alive? Can you see her?"

"If she is alive, I can see her." He raised his hands toward the fire, and the image changed. And there was her mother, crumpled into a heap on the floor, sobbing bitter, unrestrained tears the like of which Adora had never seen from her. One shaking hand was raised in prayer, though she was too upset even to mouth any words through her tears. Adora wondered at first why her mother had lifted only one hand: she knew no more of combat than Adora did herself, and without any royal blood, she could not have ordered any of Eldren Cael's guards to kill on her behalf. But then she realized: *It is my life. She thinks that I am dead, and she holds herself responsible, for wishing to keep the viper so long within our midst that it could spread its poison freely.*

It was more than Adora could stand to see her composed and regal mother in such a state. "No, not—enough of that. Where is she now?"

"Jocelyn herself? We shall see." Again he raised his hands, and again the image changed—and when it settled, Adora felt a sick twist in her stomach.

RHIA STILL DIDN'T know why she wasn't dead.

Jocelyn had nothing but hatred and contempt for her; there could be no doubt of that. And whatever affection or trust the prince might ever have felt for her,

Jocelyn had somehow stolen that away, too. For all the time she had been down here, Hephestion had never been to see her, or sent any messages to her through his retainers. He had not even cared to have her questioned, which he would surely have done had he been in his right mind, even if he believed her a traitor. So though Rhia remained largely ignorant of what was happening in the world above the dungeons, she could be sure events moved forward according to Jocelyn's will alone. And yet . . . here she still was. She was allowed food and water, brought at the hands of her former comrades—some apologetic, some openly mistrustful. What use could Jocelyn still have for her?

She had not thought herself any closer to finding out, yet when footsteps broke the silence of the stone halls, it was not her evening meal she saw but Jocelyn herself—and, even stranger, she had Lirien in tow. Rhia had not dared to hope that Lirien still lived—her absence from the same cells that held Rhia had suggested Jocelyn had other plans for her—but she looked no worse in body, though considerably ailing in spirit. She lifted her head once, quickly, to catch Rhia's eyes, and then just as swiftly dropped it again.

Had this confrontation happened the first day Rhia spent down here, perhaps she would have tried to say something defiant. But she was beyond that now. She had to conserve her strength, for whenever it might be needed. So instead she asked only, "What do you want?"

"Ever the conversationalist, Captain," Jocelyn said, unlocking the door to Rhia's cell. Rhia was securely chained to the wall at all four limbs, and could barely turn her head at the approach, but Jocelyn moved to stand in front of her, so they were face-to-face. "And when I've taken the trouble to bring you such important news! It seems that Adora will not be returning to us. She met with a . . . tragic and unforeseeable end while on the road."

Rhia betrayed no reaction. "When? Where?"

Jocelyn shrugged. "At some point during her journey up the Sverin."

"Which is to say you don't know for sure. You believe she is dead because you planned for it, not because any confirmation of it reached you. Or am I wrong?"

"You aren't wrong," Lirien spoke up. "She stopped receiving messages from the queen's party. They haven't been spotted anywhere—it seems they've disappeared. That's all she knows."

It did Rhia good to hear her voice. Though her eyes had been trained on the floor, and worry was plain in her face, her voice was strong and clear—there was even a slightly mocking edge to it. That was not the voice of someone who had given up.

Jocelyn ground her teeth. "That merely means she is as likely alive as dead—and if she lives, she is without her retinue. I suppose she might run to her uncle, but

I'm having him taken care of. Without her last ally, what will that little mouse do? Plead with me to return what I have taken, for decency's sake?"

"You underestimate her," Rhia said.

"Oh, perhaps. At least if she finds the courage to return here, I can witness her death with my own eyes. But that is not what I came to discuss with you."

She stepped forward, tilting Rhia's chin toward her with two fingers, like a horse's whose teeth she intended to examine. "You're a simple creature; I understand that. But it is the very fact of your simplicity that has me so perplexed. How could *you*, of all people, defend yourself against me?"

Rhia stared at her. "If I could have defended myself against you, do you think I'd be here now?"

Jocelyn rolled her eyes. "I don't mean with your *sword*, you unimaginative little insect. You must have seen how I made your prince mine, with hardly a pinch of effort—mine beyond appeal or recovery. It's hardly the extent of what I've done, even without the aid of Lirien's magic. I once made a man eat his own fingers." She must have seen something in Rhia's face, for she took a step back, holding up her hands. "Oh, I had nothing against him. I just needed the practice. But I had never, in the course of all my experimentation, encountered a mind I could not move—except for Lirien's, of course, but she had magic of her own, so there's no mystery there. But *you*—you're about as magical as a stone, yet I cannot seem to make you obey even the most basic command. How on earth do you do it?"

Had Jocelyn attempted to sway her mind? Had that been every time she ever asked Rhia a question or gave her an order, or only some of those times? The very fact that she didn't know demonstrated how completely those attempts had failed, she supposed. But she didn't know the reason any more than Jocelyn did. "You said yourself I don't know anything about magic. If you can't explain it, what do you expect me to tell you?"

Jocelyn smiled, which surprised her; she was not one to accept being refused. "I confess I'm not as skilled as I might be in the reading of faces. Whenever it's been absolutely crucial for me to know the truth, I've always had the option of compelling someone to tell it. So this is quite new for me." She jerked Rhia's chin roughly upward, so they met each other's eyes. "If your mind could only have been *normal*, things would have been so much easier for both of us. All that loyalty you feel for Adora, the devotion, the excessive respect—I could divert it all in my direction more easily than snapping my fingers. I could induce you to believe that making me happy was the noblest and most exalted task you could ever perform. Or else, if all I needed to do was dispose of you, I could have turned you loose upon the people of this city like the brute you are, spurred to mindless slaughter until the rest of the guard brought you down."

Rhia couldn't help a shudder at the thought that she could be so easily turned from everything she had ever believed in. She didn't think Jocelyn was bluffing. If she tried to control Rhia again, would whatever had protected her before still hold?

"You don't like that idea, do you? I don't blame you; it would be quite the ignominious end for someone who aspired so pridefully to virtue. But unfortunately, since you already know I can't do it, it's useless to threaten you with it. And since I don't want to dispose of you until I've learned your secret, I've had to come up with a more creative use for you."

She produced a knife—not the most threatening object in Rhia's mind, especially given what she'd already seen Jocelyn do. "Do you know I've never actually drawn blood before?" Jocelyn asked. "It's amazing how bloodless you can be when you can simply persuade people to adopt the appropriate opinions. Besides, I'm given to understand torture is actually quite complicated. You've got to inflict enough pain to be effective, but you can't wholly disregard the well-being of your subject, either. Quite the delicate balance."

Rhia looked to Lirien, hoping for some hint as to what Jocelyn intended. But though Lirien's face showed apprehension and sorrow, Rhia could not read anything else in it.

Jocelyn's own face was a mockingly polite mask. "However, now that I've relieved Lirien of the gifts she did not deserve and was in the midst of shamefully squandering, I have a few new skills to test. Let's start cautiously, shall we? Just in case something goes wrong."

Before Rhia could speak a word, Jocelyn struck, burying the knife in her shoulder. Rhia was too startled to stifle her cry of pain, but perhaps she couldn't have even if she'd known it was coming. The pain was intense, unrelenting for the several moments Jocelyn stood twisting the knife. And then she pulled it out, and a moment later, the pain stopped as if it had never been.

Rhia craned her neck, trying to see what Jocelyn had done to her. She could see the blood still seeping into her shirt, but beneath the torn and stained fabric there was no cut.

It was like that day by the lake, she realized. Jocelyn had healed her, just as Lirien had back then.

"It's fascinating," Jocelyn said. "Lirien's magic allows me to expand the reach of my own powers, but it seems determined to flow down its own channels as well. It *wants* to heal—and, as you can see, it's quite adept at it. So it doesn't matter that I've no experience with torture: as long as I don't kill you instantly, I can keep you here with me as long as I like. For example, I couldn't normally do something like this—" She lunged forward again, with more confidence this time, and carved a gash into Rhia's abdomen. Against that pain, she couldn't keep her eyes open or her mouth clamped shut; her whole body seized up, recoiling from the intensity but finding nowhere to go, only a stone wall to batter her further. She felt like she couldn't breathe; when she forced her eyes back open, spots danced in front of them, blurring her vision. The wound was already healed, but she still couldn't stop shaking.

"So," Jocelyn said. "I suppose you *really* might not know how you shook off my spell, but there's no harm in asking again."

But she truly didn't know—and even if she did, revealing it would only consign her to worse fates. What choice did that leave her but to endure?

When Jocelyn saw that she was not going to speak, she aimed her next strike at Rhia's face. Again Rhia flinched with nowhere to go, closing her eyes as she felt the blade cut across her cheek. "I wonder what the limit to this kind of power is," Jocelyn mused. "If I cut out one of your eyes, could I put it back again?"

Rhia heard the grunt of an impact, and then a harsher collision, metal on stone. She opened her eyes just in time to see Lirien scoop the knife up from the floor and scramble back from Jocelyn, her arm held out in front of her.

"Oh, come now," Jocelyn said. "You're back to being ordinary again, remember? You must know you won't be able to hurt me with that."

"I don't need to hurt you," Lirien said. She raised the knife—and held it to her own throat. "What do you think will happen to my power if I die, Jocelyn? You must have thought about it—if you hadn't, I doubt I'd be alive right now. Do you think it'll still be there, after I'm gone? Or do you think it'll follow me, and disappear from this world? And if it does, how long do you think you'll be able to last, without it there to bolster your abilities?" She smiled grimly. "I know you fear that. I know because I've stood here blabbing on at you all this time, and you've done nothing, when it would have been the work of a moment to compel me to drop the knife. You're afraid that if you direct the smallest bit of my magic at me, even though I have none without what you've stolen, that it'll still come back to me—it'll stick to me just like you forced it to stick to you." She raised her chin, pressing her throat against the blade. "Come on, Jocelyn. Try it. See what happens."

In the silence that followed, Rhia blinked hard, trying to clear the fog from her vision so she could focus on Jocelyn's face. But it was frozen, unreadable.

"There," Lirien said, finally. "That's what I thought." She dropped her hand. "So leave her alone. *I* wasn't bluffing, and you can easily keep her imprisoned without hurting her further. You know she's never going to do what you want. Find some other way to satisfy your grudge against Adora."

Rhia's lips were cracked, her throat dry, but she managed to mumble, "Her grudge against . . . Adora?"

Lirien's face softened, pity replacing her defiance. "I don't know if this makes it better or worse for you, but you must know you're nothing to her. You're loyal to Adora, and Adora's out of her reach, so she hurts you instead. Like one child breaking another's favorite toy."

Jocelyn scowled, but did not argue with Lirien's words. Instead, she held out her hand. "You can give me that knife, or I can have half a dozen guards take it from you and break your fingers. I'll leave her alone, but even you must see that if you threaten to kill yourself for every inconvenience, you'll lose whatever bargaining power you may have."

Lirien hesitated, but finally held out the knife. Jocelyn took it from her—and slapped Lirien across the face with her free hand, so hard that her head snapped to the side.

Lirien started to laugh—a wild, belly-shaking laugh, echoing off the stone. She stretched her neck, and wiped her mouth with the back of her hand, though blood kept slowly seeping from her split lip. She flicked her tongue out to taste what was left. "Oh, that's *it*! I had almost forgotten!"

After everything else had passed her by, that was the first thing to visibly unnerve Jocelyn, and she took a step back. "Don't tell me you've succumbed to madness now."

"On the contrary. My mind hasn't been this clear in years." She thumbed at her lip again, smearing the blood slightly. "It's the pain, you see. I had forgotten . . . not what pain *feels* like, but . . . I had forgotten that it was important. Every cut or bruise I got started healing the instant it was inflicted; why *should* I have cared? But that was my mistake. I allowed my mind to become . . . clouded. I hadn't even realized how much, until you hollowed me out."

She grinned at Jocelyn. "Did you think to take only the benefits of my power, and avoid its curse? If my mind is clear now, yours must be growing cloudier by the day. The more you make use of your new gifts, the deeper they'll take hold. Soon you'll forget, too. And then you'll lose, just like I did. Wait and see."

"THAT'S ENOUGH," ADORA said. She pushed herself back from the fire, but she could still see the images, the satisfaction with which Jocelyn wielded that knife, the way Rhia's body spasmed helplessly against the chains. "I've told you I will do all I can to help you. But enough of this hideous display!"

"I am not causing any of this to happen," Voltest said. "I am merely showing you what is, within the boundaries of the realm you claim to rule. If you are displeased at what you see, it would be more correct to blame yourself."

She hardly needed *him* to tell her whose fault this was, when the knowledge burned fiercely enough within her own breast. "You can blame me all you like, just stop it! I've seen enough!" She swept her hand toward the flames, hardly caring if they burned her, just to erase that image—

A hand caught hers, trapping it in place. A hand that trembled, like a leaf in a strong wind. She looked back to see Cadfael as shaken as she felt—no. More. Much more, from the pallor of his face, his staring eyes, locked on Voltest as if he had forgotten she existed. "How dare you," he croaked. "What cruel trick is this? What impossible, lying—" He choked on his own words, bending his head as he labored to compose himself, and Adora managed to pull her hand from his weakened grasp, wondering why he should be so affected.

Voltest was as calm as ever, though his lip curled in scorn at Cadfael's outburst. At least he had finally ceased whatever power he had used on the fire, which flickered its accustomed color without any deeper meanings. "It is no *trick,* fool. It is my gift. How do you think I found you? My flames have never told a lie."

"But that's not *possible!*" Cadfael's head snapped wildly around, turning to Adora instead. "Your Grace, do you know that girl—that woman in the images he showed us? The one who was . . . the one who suffered?"

"I know her very well," Adora said. "That was Rhia, my captain of the guard in Eldren Cael."

It was clear the name upset him, but she didn't know what to make of it. Could he have known Rhia in her childhood? "But when did she—how did she—how did that happen?"

What an odd question. "Well, I'm the one who appointed her, of course, but my brother met her first. She had fled Elgar's sack of Araveil, and traveled the continent since, but beyond that I don't know much of her life. Is there something in particular you wish to know?"

He raised one arm, pressing his scarred flesh against the heel of his hand as if to keep the wound from opening again. "Fled," he muttered. "Fled? But then how could . . . ?" And then it was as if he'd been hit by a thunderclap. He dropped his hand, raised his head, balled both hands into fists. "That *bastard,*" he roared, half-rising to his knees. "That bastard *lied* to me!"

"We've been over this," Voltest said. "My flames do not—"

"Not *you,*" Cadfael snapped. "Elgar! Bloody Elgar! I spent all this time thinking she was dead, and it's because he lied to me! I should have killed him when I had the chance!"

He had seemed a man of so few feelings, who could get beyond dull irritation only with great effort. In a way, seeing such a towering rage take hold of him was unnerving. But in another way, it was as if she were watching a dead man come back to life. And then, caught by all the expressiveness, all the passion in his face, she really *looked* at him.

The two of them didn't truly look alike. They had different eyes, different hair, different noses, different builds. They had a different range of expressions, different ways of moving, of carrying themselves. But looking at him in the light of the fire, watching it trace his cheekbones and the line of his jaw, Adora could see the resemblance, slight but discernible, to a face she knew so well.

"Who are you?" she asked him. "Who are you really?"

He turned to her again, and she saw his body relax. "My name is Cadfael, like I told you. I am the natural son of Maia Glendower, onetime heir to Grayeaves, though she died before she could become its lady. My sister, Rhia, is her only other child. I would never have tried to hide my relationship to her, but I did not know you knew her. I thought . . ." His voice cracked. "I thought she had been killed three years ago."

"But this is . . . very strange," Adora said. "Rhia told us that *you* had been killed three years ago—that she survived Elgar's invasion and fled the city, only to learn of your death upon her return. And I know she did not lie, not only because such a deception is not in her nature, but because the grief it had caused her, and still caused her, was unmistakable."

Cadfael clapped one hand to his forehead, and then the other. "Of course! Damn it, I should've . . . We must've just missed each other." He shook his head, fingers buried in his hair. "I never would've done it if I'd thought she was alive. Or at least I'd have left a note or . . . It never even occurred to me that Elgar would have lied about her death. I still can't think what reason he could've had for it, unless he just wanted to be cruel."

Adora was still trying to follow all this. "Are you saying that your own death was a lie? You faked it?"

"It wasn't quite as elaborate as that," he said. "As far as everyone else knew, I was at death's door already. When I heard Rhia was dead, I didn't care what happened to me, but that was when I finally . . . well." For a moment he looked uncertain, but then he finished, "When I pulled through and recovered from my injury. No one was expecting it, and I didn't need to stay alive for anyone, or stay in Araveil. I thought, given the incoming regime, that it'd be dangerous to stay there after it became known that I'd been one of Eira's best men. So I asked the healer who treated me to say I was dead, if anyone asked. I didn't honestly think anyone *would* ask; I didn't have any friends or other relations to speak of. And it'd be easy enough for her to say so—there were mass graves all over the city from the fighting. No one would demand to see a body."

"So when Rhia came back," Adora finished, "she must've heard from this healer that you were dead. But why did you think *she* was dead? Did you really say that Elgar himself . . . ?"

Cadfael nodded darkly. "Aye, I had it from his own mouth. The night his soldiers attacked, I made Rhia promise to flee the city until things calmed down. But the next day there was this stir about our neighborhood—somebody'd seen her that night, staring down one of Elgar's butchers, but fled lest he get caught up in it. He hadn't seen the result."

He gritted his teeth. "I was wounded, weak, still bleeding. I thought I was dying. I didn't have anything to lose. I needed a stick to walk, but I blundered my way to some camp Elgar's men had set up in the center of the city. I yelled at them as loud as I could—demanded to know what had happened to her. It wasn't the sanest approach, I suppose, but I'd been bleeding for days and days. I wasn't in my best mind. Imagine my shock when Elgar himself showed his face." His scowl hardened. "That bloody demon. I can still see his smirk now. The most painful words I'd ever heard in my life, and he grinned the whole way through. His *Shinsei* had killed her, he told me—she thought she could stand up to him, and she paid the price. And like a fool, for three whole years I never questioned it. But what reason could he have had to lie? Was it truly just for cruelty's sake?"

"I don't know," Adora said, "but there can be no mistake. Rhia has been living with us in Eldren Cael for almost a year now, and she is very much alive."

Cadfael covered his face, breathing in and out behind his cupped hands. She couldn't tell if he sought to hide a rush of tears, if he needed time to adjust to this new revelation, or if he was simply weak with relief. But when he dropped his hands again, his eyes sought hers immediately, alight with a purpose she had never seen from him before, not even when he had argued so determinedly to accompany her when they had first met.

"Your Grace," he said, "I am for you. I will do whatever you require. I will protect your life—I will help you regain your throne—I will fight that woman for you, anything. Anything that is necessary. But we must save her. I cannot bear . . . to know she lives only to lose her again . . . to have such hope ripped away would ruin me. And if you know her, you must know she does not deserve to die at that woman's hands."

Adora thought again of the pain Rhia had endured. If Voltest had told the truth, and they had seen events as they were happening, then perhaps Rhia was still suffering at this very moment, in the palace Adora never should have left. No, Rhia did not deserve to die. Not at Jocelyn's hands, and not for Adora's sake.

She put her hand over Cadfael's, gripping his fist tightly in hers. "I told you that a queen must be the servant of her people. Citizen or not, your sister has risked her life on my behalf, many times. To abandon her now would be a betrayal of all I have been taught, all I have ever believed. I must regain my throne, and I must subdue Jocelyn, for my family and my people's sake. But saving Rhia must be part of that. Perhaps I could not be both a queen to her and a friend, but either way I must repay her loyalty."

Cadfael nodded firmly. "Then I will devote myself to that effort, from now until we have reached a satisfactory conclusion."

She released him, and turned to their interloper next. "And you, Voltest? Since you are so unhappy about this turn of events, will you lend us your aid to set it right? I should think you would have an easier time of it than any of us, given your power."

Voltest's lip curled. "How typical of a royal—always looking for others to do the unpleasant work for you. But unfortunately for you, Jocelyn Selreshe poses a problem I am ill equipped to solve. There is a possibility I could subdue her alone— and if I had Talis, the third of our number, at my side, I'd be certain of it. But it would be a bloody battle, and I imagine many casualties would result from it. Even worse, if we killed Jocelyn as she is now, I am not certain what would happen to Lirien's magic. Would it return to her body? Or would it die with its current host? If the latter . . . we lost one of our number before, and became unstable in mind and magic both. I cannot say what would happen if we were to lose two. I doubt it's a risk you'd wish to take, considering how strong we are."

Well, he wasn't wrong. "Are you saying you have another plan?" Adora asked.

"I am. What we must do is pull Lirien's magic from Jocelyn's body while she is still alive—it will both make killing Jocelyn much easier and ensure that Lirien's magic will not disappear, and can be returned to her."

"Can that be done?"

"Before Jocelyn pulled her little trick, I would have said no," Voltest admitted. "But she proved it was possible by accomplishing it. If *she* could steal the magic from Lirien, there is no reason why another mage should not be able to steal it from her. Provided the mage is powerful enough, of course. But Talis and I cannot do it—it must be a mage of the ordinary sort. And that means we need to find one." He looked down for the first time. "I acknowledge that this is no simple task."

A powerful mage, was it? Well, as soon as Jocelyn staged her coup, and as soon as the world of magic finally revealed itself to Adora, the rest of it had probably become inevitable. Better to get it over with sooner rather than later, though that didn't mean it would be easy.

"In fact," she said, "it is the simplest thing you have asked of me so far, though we must hurry. It'll take us out of our way, and we have no time to waste." She got to her feet. "I need to tell my uncle enough to keep him out of danger, but we'll be traveling away from Shallowsend . . . I'll have to write him a letter and send it back at the earliest opportunity. Voltest, you'll need to come with us—I don't trust myself to be able to fully explain what we require without your help."

"Wait," Voltest said. "When I first came to you, you met my tidings with disbelief. Now all of a sudden you're confident you know a mage?"

"Yes, that was an error on my part, I admit," Adora said, already orienting herself in a northeasterly direction. "But if mages exist in the present day in any significant form—and I am now convinced that they do—I have undoubtedly met at least one other. And I know I can get her to help with this." She started walking. "Are you two coming? Stonespire Hall is distant yet."

Voltest reluctantly fell into step with her. "What's at Stonespire Hall?"

"Its marquise, I should hope," Adora said.

CHAPTER FORTY-SEVEN

Esthrades

"I THINK IT'S time to discuss our options," Almasy said, her face pale in the light of the fire. "Or, well, mine, I suppose."

Deinol knew better than to glance at her shoulder; he'd seen it far too many times over the past several days. He knew what it looked like, even if he wished he didn't.

They'd found a village healer, someone who could remove the arrow and treat the wound it had left. But the wound wasn't healing; if anything, it was getting worse. He could tell the pain it caused Almasy was increasing by the day, just from the way she moved, her former effortless grace replaced more and more by clumsiness and exhaustion. Lucius helped her change the dressing each day, but instead of scabbing over, the wound only leaked more pus. Deinol did not like the way it smelled.

He was impressed by how calm she still seemed; he doubted whether, in her place, he could have done anything but panic. But he wondered what even she could do about this.

"The healer who treated you must not have been sufficiently skilled," Lucius said. "If we went somewhere else—"

"They'd tell me what I already know. I doubt it was the healer's fault. And healers can only be as strong as their medicines, after all." She winced, and rubbed her arm. "If this is an infection, and it gets into my blood . . . I know what will happen. If I were well, perhaps I could kill the conspirators Ryker revealed to us, but there is no time for that now. I must, at the least—I *must* ensure that those at Stonespire learn their names, so they can expose them."

She paused, bent her head, stared into the fire. When she looked at them again, she had pushed away her weariness; her gaze was determined, intent. "I cannot compel you to do as I wish. I can only ask you . . . help me return to Stonespire. If I become feverish . . . if I become weak . . . it may be I cannot finish the journey on my own. And if I die . . ." She gritted her teeth, but did not drop her eyes. "If I die, you must deliver those names to Stonespire in my stead. A messenger will not do—who knows what could happen to a messenger? Cantor, Claremont, Apglen. You must remember. You must bring those names to Stonespire."

"We were *exiled* from Stonespire, on pain of death!" Deinol hardly wanted to shout at someone in her condition, but he couldn't help himself. "We'll be executed if we go back there."

"No, they wouldn't—if you helped them, they would understand. She would understand. Or even if you didn't step foot inside the city, but told the guards upon the wall . . . used them to reach Bridger or Dent . . . I'm sure no harm would come to you. I swear it."

Deinol scoffed. "You said we would be fine in that forest with Ryker, too."

Still she held his eyes unflinchingly. "And so you are."

She didn't quite emphasize the third word, but he felt the sting of it anyway. He still hadn't thanked her for that. It wasn't that he was too proud; he just couldn't summon the words, knowing how insufficient they would be in the face of consequences like that.

"I cannot compel you to do as I wish," Almasy said again. "I have nothing of value I can offer you, save my weapons and my remaining coin—but if you wanted those, you could just wait for me to die and take them."

"We wouldn't do that." Lucius's voice was firm as iron, and Deinol didn't disagree. They were thieves, to be sure, but that . . .

"I wouldn't care if you did. You can have them. You can have anything you want from me. Just . . . please." It was like he was looking at a different person, the way sorrow and pain made that normally passionless face seem so much younger. He had never imagined that pleading was something she was capable of. "This is . . . my last wish. This is all I have left."

Gods, he hated this. He knew that he would never hear himself praised for bravery or virtue, but he wasn't a cruel person, was he? Though he had once dreamed of revenge against her, that dream had long since died. If he could wave his hand and will her injury away, he would have done it gladly. But as important as this was to her, what would it truly accomplish? What would he be risking his life for?

"I can't understand it," he said. "Your lady dismissed you. She made you no concern of hers. Isn't it foolish to sacrifice so much on her behalf, when she would never repay even half of what you suffered?"

"No, you—you have it all backward." She cradled her wounded arm, curling in on herself. "I'm the one who can never possibly equal what she sacrificed—what she gave me. She hates to hear it spoken of, but . . . when I was a child, she saved my life. Before I became what I am now, when I had nothing and was of no value to anyone. She intervened to save me from the cruelty her father called justice, and for that he . . ." She squeezed her arm tightly. "She suffered much more than this. She suffered, while my life became my own for the first time."

She looked up at them, and smiled her melancholy smile. "Fifteen years she gave me, since that day. Compared to that, what are three names?"

She is the only person who ever cared whether I lived or died, she had said to Deinol, so long ago now. But he didn't see how he could reconcile that with the coldness of the woman he had witnessed. "If she made the effort to save your life, she'd want you to spend whatever was left of it doing something for yourself, rather than for her. Or at the very least, she couldn't fault you for a bit of selfishness now."

Almasy was still smiling. "But it is selfish. I hated Esthrades when I was young. Because my entire life there had been suffering, I thought it had always been that way, and always would be. But she told me that the Margraines had been trying to improve this place for generations—that her father was just a blot upon their legacy. She told me that . . . that she would show me Esthrades as it was meant to be. I wanted so much to see it—the world that she would create. I wanted it more than . . . almost anything."

Lucius bit his lip, and looked down at his hands. "We can help you reach Stone-spire, at least. As long as you make it there, you can give the marquise the names yourself. If we end up having to make another choice . . . let's save that discussion for when it becomes necessary."

"But what if I'm too weak by then? I can't die not knowing if she'll be safe!"

"No one can promise you that, Seren," Lucius said, so sorrowfully Deinol's chest ached in sympathy. "The continent is in turmoil, and she's near the center of it. Even if she foils this plot, what of Elgar's plans for her? If you want to be sure of her safety, the only thing you can do is live, and see it for yourself."

"I wish I could," Almasy whispered. "I've tried so hard to live even this long. It always seemed like everything was set against me, from the very beginning."

Deinol understood that, to some extent. No one was inclined to be kind to a bastard, a whore's son, and as a child he'd often cursed the unfairness of it, that he had to suffer for something he couldn't control. Why were some children allowed to be born without that stain, and others afflicted with it for their entire lives?

"It's like Lucius said," he told her. "You try to stay alive, and we'll try to get you there."

IT WAS A strange day indeed when Lady Margraine was more irritated with Dent than she was with Gravis, but rather than feel relief, Gravis found he hated it. It had always been maddening the way those two would close ranks against him, but this new tension between them just made him anxious. Worse, he didn't know which one of them he agreed with. He'd always been suspicious of Almasy, and should have been glad to see her gone, but like this . . .

Every moment he had free and she was in private, there Dent was, pleading to have Almasy recalled. She'd taken to leaving her study to avoid him, but he always tracked her down. Gravis had hoped to come to the orchard for a little quiet, but of course, here they were, taking the early morning air before the marquise sat her throne for the day. She was sitting on the grass, leaning against the trunk of a tree, heedless of any remnants of the morning dew. Dent paced around her, gesticulating wildly with the one remaining arm that wasn't bound up in a sling.

"There comes a point," Lady Margraine said, "at which one can only imagine both sides have said whatever they can say on the matter, and the wise course of action becomes dropping the argument."

"No doubt," Dent said. "But I can't do that, my lady."

Gravis cleared his throat, so they wouldn't think he was trying to eavesdrop. They both looked his way, but didn't seem to consider his presence important enough to affect their argument. "Dent," the marquise said, "if you want to be concerned about Seren, that's up to you. But she's taken care of herself her whole life, through more adversity than any of us. She's one of the most competent people I have ever met. What exactly do you think is going to happen to her?"

Dent rubbed his forehead. "It's not a matter of that, my lady, it's . . . difficult to explain. Whatever anyone else may think, I know that you don't just govern according to your whims. I know you've always thought very carefully about the best way to do things, from making judgments to changing laws to any other thing. And I don't think . . . I mean, I *know* . . . that being dismissed is not what Seren deserves. It's . . ." He gave her a sad, helpless smile. "If I say it's unfair, that won't mean anything to you. But I can't truly tell you it's unwise. It concerns something other than wisdom."

"I have been unfair to her? That's what you're saying?" The answer was clear in his face. "Dent, we're in the middle of a crisis like few Esthrades has ever faced. Many of lesser intellect than mine would have run out of options already, and those left to me are few. I must, as you say, consider everything carefully, and under those circumstances, I must do away with things that are illogical and unpredictable. I must have no use for those who will not *be* useful. I *told* Seren that if she wanted to be among my retainers, I needed to be able to rely on her. And what has she done? If she's willing to overturn even a relatively routine judgment with no explanation, what else might she be capable of?"

Dent winced. "I'm sure that if you asked her to explain—"

"I have asked her to explain! I have asked her to explain a hundred things, a hundred times!" Again there was an instant when she seemed to realize how loud her voice had gotten, and to be surprised by it. When she spoke again, it was much softer. "Dent, it's not the punishment you seem to believe it is. I honestly think . . . that being away from me will improve her."

"I very much doubt that, my lady."

She did not answer that, and got to her feet. "I'm already late. Don't follow me all the way to the throne, please."

Dent stayed where he was, but as the marquise went back inside, she brushed by Bridger, going in the opposite direction. All of Bridger's shifts were down in the city, so she must have come here of her own accord, but the marquise did not look surprised to see her. "He's right there. Maybe you can do something with him."

And then she was gone. Bridger's loping strides brought her to Dent's side in an instant. "How is it, sir?"

He sighed. "The same."

"Dent," Gravis said, "don't be angry, but why do you care so much? I admit that I've never liked Almasy and you always have, but I had no idea she was this important to you."

"It isn't about my personal feelings for her," Dent said. "You and I are hardly old men, Gravis, but that doesn't mean we're going to live forever. Against our deaths, we must ensure that our lady will still be surrounded by the right people." He cast a significant look Bridger's way, but he hardly needed to; Gravis had long known the faith Dent placed in her. "I don't wish to flatter myself, but I have known her ladyship all her life, and I have understood her better than most. I understand that there is no need to try to make her other than she is. Seren, I feel, has always known that as well. She knows what her ladyship is trying to do, and believes in it as few ever have. That is why I wished to have her stay." He hesitated. "And Seren loves her. I don't know what it will be worth, but there's that."

CHAPTER FORTY-EIGHT

Lanvaldis

IT WAS A dark and cavernous room, deep underground. The damp air was cold and stifling, the frequent coughs from the shadows around him providing the only break in the heavy silence. Or no, not the only break: there it was, the sound of a body being dragged, dragged, dragged across the stone floor. The body had no movement of its own, and the men who carried it made no sound, not even a cough. But still he was frightened, because if another body had come out, that meant another person would have to go in. *Not me,* he thought. *Not yet.*

There were dozens of forms around him; most he did not know, or could not see well enough to recognize. And there, by his side, curled in on himself, was—

"Shinsei?" someone asked.

Shinsei remembered where he was. The covered wagon shuddered as it rolled over a stone, and he looked across the small space into the face of Lord Oswhent, who was watching him closely. "Were you dreaming?" he asked.

Had he been? "I don't know," Shinsei admitted. "I think I was . . . remembering something. Or trying to. The trouble is, I don't know if I'm remembering something that happened to me, or something that happened to someone else."

Lord Oswhent gave him that look he had seen so many times, from so many people: the look that said he wasn't making sense. "If it happened to someone else, how could you possibly remember it?"

That was a good point. People didn't normally remember things that hadn't happened to them, did they? "But you see," Shinsei said, "the thing I think I remember . . . I don't remember *how* it could have happened."

Lord Oswhent turned to the side, looking out of the open back of the wagon, and cast a disapproving eye over the struggling ranks of soldiers. They never moved as quickly as he wished. There weren't anywhere near enough horses for them all, and hardly any wagons or carts. He had decided to bring along those soldiers who were wounded lightly enough to recover by the time they reached Araveil—but that meant they could only go as fast as their slowest members. "Well, we clearly have time," he said, turning back to Shinsei. "Explain it to me. Perhaps I can help you figure it out."

Shinsei tried to remember the images, the sounds. "It was . . . a very big, very dark place. It was underground. There were many people around me, sitting. There were soldiers, but the soldiers were all standing or walking."

"Were you being held prisoner?"

". . . Oh." He tried to think. "I don't think we were allowed to leave, so I suppose we must have been. But that's the problem, do you see? I don't remember a time when I was held prisoner. I don't remember where that room was. And if it had happened to me, I would remember that much, right?"

Lord Oswhent shrugged. "Then it was probably a dream. Before you ran out into the yard, you were in the corridors of Mist's Edge, right? A dark cavern of sorts, where something frightening happened. You probably just had a dream that reflected the fear you felt back then."

Shinsei shook his head firmly. "No, you have it backward. The fear I felt in that room at Mist's Edge . . . I felt it *before* the explosion. I felt it because the dark and the damp and the silence made me remember that other time."

Lord Oswhent rubbed his chin, his brows drawing together. "Shinsei . . . did you truly run away just because of that?"

"No," Shinsei said. "It *was* that, but it was also because I heard a voice. It told me to run."

"And do you . . . often hear voices that tell you things?"

"Yes," Shinsei said. "I'm listening to yours right now."

Lord Oswhent clapped a hand over his mouth, though if he wanted to laugh, Shinsei didn't know why he felt he had to hide it. "Yes, well, that's . . . true, but not what I meant. Do you often hear voices that . . . that you don't know where they come from?"

"Oh," Shinsei said. "I understand now. No. That was the only time. And even then . . ." He hesitated. "This is going to sound strange."

"If it's something that *you* think is strange," Lord Oswhent said, "then I would absolutely love to hear it."

Shinsei touched the back of his neck, the shell of his ear. He had felt no breath there when the voice spoke, but he had sensed a presence all the same. "I felt that it was the statue that spoke to me."

"The statue?"

"It was in the room with me, before I ran. It was probably destroyed in the explosion. A person in a hooded cloak, dragging broken chains." He could remember clearly how it had looked in the torchlight. "I don't mean that the statue's lips moved, or even that I heard the voice coming from that direction. I just . . . when I heard the voice, I somehow felt it was the statue speaking."

Lord Oswhent made a soft noise; Shinsei couldn't tell whether it was a laugh or a groan. "Not so long ago, I would have told you quite confidently that such a thing was impossible. Now . . . I don't know." He tugged at his robes, his pale fingers standing out starkly against the red fabric. "Shinsei, did you mean what you said about your sword? Is it that one sword that gives you the ability to fight, and no other will do?"

"I'm not sure. But it seems that way."

"What does that mean?"

"My swordsmanship is perfect." Even now, the words were so easy to say, slipping from his mouth as if they wanted to come out. "That's a thought I've had for as long as I can remember." He winced, rubbing his head. "But I can also remember not being very good at swordplay at all. And that was when I had a different sword. But maybe those are someone else's memories, like being imprisoned in that dark room was."

Lord Oswhent rubbed his fingers over his chin, against his mouth. "Shinsei," he finally said, "I think it would be best if you didn't fight anymore, at least until we figure this out."

"But I want to help," Shinsei said.

"I know you do. But we'll find something for you to do that isn't fighting. It'll be important. I promise. But for your sake, as well as everyone else's, we need to be more certain about what you can and can't do before we put you on a battlefield again. Especially given how distressed you became last time. And . . . well, perhaps, in the meantime, you should do some more thinking about this other person whose memories you seem to have."

"I don't know," Shinsei said. "I don't think I like his memories very much."

"And do you like the memories *you* have?" Lord Oswhent asked.

Shinsei opened his mouth, and shut it again. Again he opened it, and again no words came out. The answer seemed so simple until he tried to say it, as if someone were pulling the words away from him. He stared and stared into Lord Oswhent's face, but he could not answer.

CHAPTER FORTY-NINE

Esthrades

IT STARTED WITH an apple.

That wasn't precisely true, of course; you could trace the thread of it back and back, to that very morning when the old woman had told Seren this was her last chance, and just what would happen if she couldn't be useful. You could trace it back to the evening the flesh-monger who called himself Malvan, who kept staring at her in the street, had come to whisper to the old woman about profits and losses and the slender girl with the pretty hair. Perhaps you could trace it back, finally, to the day her parents died or left or met whatever misfortune took her from their hands and left her for only the old woman to claim. But the final sequence of events, that took Seren from the worst thing that had ever happened to her to the best thing . . . that started with an apple.

It was a perfect specimen. Huge and delicately shaped, a red so crisp you could taste it, with just the slightest brush of green across the top like a remembered caress. It hung tantalizingly on the edge of the market stall, as if just a breath of wind from the right direction could send it toppling over the edge and into a waiting palm.

She could never have stolen it successfully, of course. She was the worst pickpocket of the old woman's flock, clumsy and timid and awkward. But she was so hungry and so desperate, and it was such a simple and beautiful thing. If she could just have a few bites of something so bright and clean, some dazed part of her said, surely she would find the strength to figure out what to do next, to keep the old woman from throwing her into Malvan's clutches. She just needed a tiny bit of sustenance, that was all.

The instant the stall's owner started shouting at her, she'd dropped the apple in fright. It had disappeared beneath pounding feet, its perfection trampled into dust.

She still remembered whipping around a corner and right into the path of a guard, a youngish man with a long face who looked as terrified as she felt. "Run!" he hissed, stepping aside. "Go!"

But there was no time. Two of his fellows picked that moment to round the corner, and one had grasped her by the arm before she could blink. "Well done, Halley," he said to the man with the long face. "Slippery little one, this."

The man stood where he was as if frozen. "A thief." Not a question.

The one holding Seren nodded. "Tried to nab an apple off a stall. It's like they just can't help themselves, eh?"

Mournfulness settled over his features. "No," he said softly. "I suppose they can't."

SHE COULD NEVER forget her first sight of the marquis on his throne—a tall, imposing man, thick and cold as the icicles that hang from tavern roofs in winter. His cheeks and jaw were furred with so much dark hair that it obscured his mouth, but she could still tell his expression was disapproving. There was no kindness in those small, narrowed eyes, not for her or for anyone else in the line of complainants that stretched before him.

A girl sat in a tall wooden chair at his right side. Seren would never know her own age precisely, but the girl looked no older than she was, no matter how impressive her bearing might be. She did not look like the marquis, but like him she felt cold. She looked cold, too, with the paleness of her skin, her hair, her eyes, as if she were covered by a thin sheen of snow. There was a book propped up on her lap, and she was bent slightly forward as she read. Seren couldn't tell if she had any conception of what was happening in the room.

Because Seren had been brought in by the guards in response to a crime, their party jumped the line of complainants, and she was shoved roughly before the marquis, sprawling to her knees. "Well?" he asked. "What has this one done?" His voice was loud; it seemed to reverberate from the walls.

One of the guards opened his mouth to speak, but the marquis cut him off. "Halley!" he barked. "Don't just stand there uselessly. Explain."

The long-faced guard bristled at the command in a way that was intimately familiar to Seren; he did not like this man, but lacked the power to oppose him. But then he looked at the girl serenely turning pages in her chair, and then down at Seren, and his face grew soft and mild again. "My lord. This . . . child. We received a report from a man down in the city. It seems this child . . . attempted to take an apple from his market stall." His head stayed bent. "It falls to us to ask you what you would do."

Caius Margraine stared down at her, unsympathetic and unimpressed. "If she was caught in the act of stealing, she is a thief. I do not tolerate thieves. What more is there to say?"

"She is . . . very young, my lord." The guard's words were meekly spoken, any anger or reproach carefully purged from them. "On this day . . . on a day that is meant for joy and celebration . . ."

"Do you think I don't know what day it is?" the marquis spat, envenomed. "What will one more day do for her? If she has committed such a crime while so young, it only speaks to a shockingly precocious aptitude for vice. You!" he snapped, and it took Seren a moment to realize he was speaking to her. "What do you have to say in your defense? How can you explain this crime?"

Seren knew it was not an honest question; he had already decided, in his own mind, what the answer was. And all she could feel in that moment was anger at the unfairness of it: he had condemned her to death, but she also had to explain herself to him?

Her words came out sharp and stiff. "What was I supposed to do?"

He scowled. "What?"

"What else," Seren repeated, louder, her hands trembling in the manacles, "was I supposed to do?"

"What *else*?" He leaned forward, his great hands curling into fists. "What *else*, but take what someone else has labored to sell, and leave nothing in return? What else, but scorn honest work for the sake of a reward you haven't earned? Gods, you people disgust me." He turned to the guards. "Take her away and have done with her."

They seized her arms, and the third guard turned his face away, squeezing his eyes shut in something like pain. If her rage could only have been given form then, it could have burned hot enough to obliterate them all, the old woman and Malvan and this hateful marquis and all his hundreds of guards. She would have burned them, destroyed them, torn them to pieces—she would have blotted out her whole world into nothing.

But she couldn't. She was just a weak little girl.

She heard a soft noise, and looked up to see that the marquis's daughter had snapped her book shut. She tucked it carefully between her thigh and the arm of her chair, and turned to the towering figure at her side. "I'll have my present now, Father," she said.

His bushy eyebrows drew together in confusion. "Arianrod?"

"My present," the girl repeated calmly. "You told me I could have whatever I wanted for my birthday. I wish for a pardon for this child." She said it as if she were not a child herself.

Seren was not naïve; she felt no sweet rush of hope at the girl's words. But she felt, at least, a loosening of despair. It was not over *yet*.

The marquis's surprise did not leave him. The mournful guard, too, was staring at the girl in astonishment. "Arianrod," the marquis finally said, "when I sit in judgment, it is not for me to decide matters according to my whims, but to carry out the law as best I can. Pardoning this thief would go against that duty. Do you not see why you should not ask me for such a thing, even if it is within my power?"

The girl gave him a scornful glare. "Pardons are part of the law, too, you idiot. Do you want a list of all the pardons our ancestors have issued over the centuries? We'd be here all day." She rolled her eyes. "You ought to be *thanking* me. No one's going to say how wise and just you are for doing this. If you let her go, they'll all be relieved. You have any number of reasons: her youth, my entreaty, a spirit of generosity because of the celebration we're about to have. But if you keep doing this, they'll hate you. How much harder do you think it's going to be to rule them when they hate you?"

The marquis's anger was heavy and oppressive, his massive fingers curling to his palms. Seren didn't know how the girl could face him without quaking. "If I grant you this," he said, "that will be *all. All,* do you understand? You will have nothing else—no trinkets from the marketplace, no new gowns, no banquet in the great hall. None of it."

"I should think a human life far more interesting than all that," the girl said, and Seren would always remember that—not *more important* but *more interesting*.

"Very well," the marquis said. "I will spare the life of this criminal, and you will go back upstairs and sit at your studies for the rest of the day, and woe betide the servant who so much as pulls a merry face in your direction. Are we agreed?"

The girl smiled, quick and cunning. "We are."

The marquis turned from his daughter and addressed his guards. "Escort the criminal to the dungeon."

Her expression faded, replaced by surprise and anger to equal his—perhaps they were related after all. "But you just said—"

"I did indeed," the marquis said. "And I will keep my promise; the child will live. But she is a criminal—she cannot be allowed to run free. She will spend the rest of her natural life in peace—and in a cell." He gestured to the guards. "Take her away."

The guards took hold of Seren's arms, hauling her to her feet, but she took no notice of them. She was watching the marquis's daughter, whose face showed the most intense fury. But there was no heat to it, no intimation of blind rage; it was the coldest emotion Seren had ever seen, like the creeping frost that kills. "You cheated," she said, softly, so dangerously. "You *cheated* me."

Her father smirked, his beard snarled about his twisting lips. "You had best learn to be more careful when you bargain with me, Arianrod."

Seren had heard the name several times by that point, but it was only then that it sank in. *Arianrod.* That was the name of the girl who had saved her life.

THERE FOLLOWED A time in which Seren believed she had merely traded the worst possible fate for the next to worst: a life sentence in the dungeons, to age and die without ever seeing the sun. She'd hung heavily in her chains, too numb and exhausted to cry. Even the rage was gone from her.

But she was not fated to remain in that state. Light footsteps echoed from heavy stone walls, and once against the marquis's daughter stood before her. Arianrod, Seren reminded herself; Arianrod was her name.

A ring of keys swung loosely from her finger as she peered through the bars. "Well, at least you're awake. You want to get out of here, don't you? Then be quiet and do what I say."

When she had unlocked Seren's cuffs, she stepped back, allowing herself a moment to look satisfied. "There. Now listen. Most of the hall's at my birthday feast—Father only set one man to guard you, and I put enough whisperwood sap in his stew to keep him asleep for hours. Speaking of food—here." Seren had been so distracted by the keys that she'd failed to notice Arianrod was carrying something on her back—a rather weighty satchel. She rummaged around in it, and pulled out a slightly squished roll of bread, which she unwrapped and handed to Seren. "There's more food in here, but *don't* eat any more yet. You don't look to be in a very good way, to state the obvious. You're probably starving. If you overeat now you could cause yourself a great deal of harm. So start with this, and let's walk."

The bread's awkward shape didn't matter. It was the softest, freshest thing she'd ever held in her hands; it melted so blissfully on her tongue she could have wept. Arianrod let her get a couple bites into it before starting to walk away, and Seren followed her, fearful of getting left behind.

She was so hungry that she'd already finished it by the time they started climbing the winding steps out of the dungeon. Arianrod's pace remained purposeful throughout the climb, but she hesitated on the upper threshold, and Seren could well understand why: there was no way they could possibly get away with this. With all the people in the castle, let alone in the city, they'd never be able to get Seren out unseen. Most likely they wouldn't even get ten yards.

Arianrod was muttering to herself. "Got to be an easier way than just doubling it, but even I can't be spotted leaving the castle or in the city. . . . Blanketing an area is too imprecise, and with so much at stake . . ." She tapped a finger against her lips. "But an area is *one* thing, that's the key, got to think of it as *one*—" She suddenly jabbed her hand downward, slicing through the air. "Hah! Obvious." But then she looked back at Seren, and something flickered across her face. Uncertainty?

Then it was gone, and before Seren could do anything, Arianrod reached back, and took Seren's hand in hers. Seren flinched, which just made Arianrod grip tighter. "Hey, pay attention. This is *very* important. You can't let go, no matter what happens. If you let go, there'll be nothing I can do for you. Do you understand me?"

Seren *didn't,* really, but she understood about not letting go, which was probably all Arianrod required. She nodded, and wrapped her fingers around Arianrod's hand. It was strange: she'd thought nobles were supposed to pride themselves on clean hands, but Arianrod's nail beds were dark, as if there was dirt caught under them.

"There," Arianrod said. "Can you still walk quickly like this? If we go too slowly I'll get tired." That last sentence didn't seem to make sense, but Seren decided it was wisest to ignore it.

She nodded again. "Does that mean you have a plan for getting past everyone?"

"Naturally. You just leave that to me." That grin was back, radiating confidence. Seren herself hardly felt confident, but she didn't want to make Arianrod angry by questioning her. So she just held tight to her hand, and followed her back into the heart of the castle.

With what she knew of Arianrod now, Seren could easily understand what had taken place, but her younger self had had no way to make sense of it. They walked through Stonespire Hall, passing any number of people: guards, servants, guests to the party that was now missing the reason for its existence. And . . . no one did anything. Sometimes Seren was sure some nearby person's eyes flicked right to the spot she and Arianrod occupied, but none of them reacted—not to betray they'd seen anything strange, nor even to incline their heads to their lord's heir. It couldn't be that everyone was so busy they truly didn't notice, but could they possibly be too afraid to question Arianrod about what she was doing or where she was going? Because it seemed almost as if they really couldn't . . . as if they really couldn't . . .

She made some involuntary sound, a pathetic whimper she tried immediately to suppress. "It doesn't matter if you make noise," Arianrod said, misinterpreting the source of Seren's fear; the chambermaid brushing past them with a stack of linens didn't even turn her head. "Just remember not to let go of my hand."

"How . . ." Seren's throat was dry. She tried again. "Why aren't they stopping us?"

"I don't want them to," Arianrod said.

"Then . . . are you doing this?"

Arianrod looked back at her, and grinned. It was the same smirk, with the same confidence as before. But that was the first time Seren could remember feeling truly awed by it—and, too, the first time she had begun to truly believe in it. "I can do anything," Arianrod said. "I can do anything I want."

An impossible statement, anyone else would have thought—and so Seren herself thought, later. But at the time, she scarcely questioned it. Someone like this, who seemed as if she had never been afraid of anything in her whole life . . . surely someone like this could find a way to achieve whatever she desired, no matter how unlikely it might seem to others.

And once she stopped being afraid, Seren found it wondrous, even strangely beautiful. They left the hall and descended the steps cut into the steep hill, and when they reached the streets Seren remembered, everyone just passed her by, without any cruel or suspicious or mercenary looks, without any shouts or threats. However she looked, whatever she said, it didn't matter. No one could get to her. No one even knew she was there to be gotten.

They made their careful way through the city, heading for the eastern gate. Arianrod was bursting with instructions, most of them related to things she'd put in the satchel, which Seren had already realized she was meant to take with her when she fled the city. Here was how much coin Arianrod had given her and how to hide it, here was how much the cloak and brooch were worth if she had to sell them, here were directions to Lakeport if she wished to go that far . . . it went on and on. Seren listened in silence, but finally she could hold back no longer. "Why are you helping me?"

Arianrod shrugged, though her nonchalance did not reach her pale and troubled eyes. "Call it a whim, if you like." She fell silent, and when she spoke again, she said something Seren would never have expected. "You know . . . you were right, before. When they brought you before my father."

"What do you mean?"

"You asked him what you were supposed to do, in order to not die. But you were right—that there was no answer. My father thinks you stole because you thought you could get away with it, or because you're just . . . bad, the way he thinks some people are. But that wasn't it, was it? You were hungry, and you had no money. You did it because you didn't know what else to do—because it was the only thing you *could* do. Right?"

Seren stared at her. It was so strange to hear her thinking all laid out, as if it were the simplest thing in the world. "That's right," she said.

"So the problem isn't anything to do with you—how you think or what you want or whether or not being good is important to you. None of that would have changed the outcome. The problem is in the way things are set up. And that means what happened isn't your fault. It's *his* fault."

It was freeing, in a way, to be told that, after so much time having been told the opposite. It felt as if it opened up a little more space inside her, made it easier to breathe. But it made her angry, too. If it really was the marquis's fault, then how dare he blame her for it? If it was really his fault, why wasn't he trying to fix it? "So it'll always be like this? I can't fix it, and he won't, and that's all there is?"

"Of course not." Arianrod smirked. "There's me. I'm going to fix it."

"And . . . are you so sure you can?"

"I'm sure. Because I already know what I have to do. Behind everything, everything that's ever happened, everything that ever *could* happen, there's . . . imagine a giant web stretched over the world, full of hundreds of thousands of threads connecting hundreds of thousands of things together. And even though those threads are invisible, they're controlling things all around us, all the time. So when something is going wrong, when something is *built* wrong, you can't fix it without knowing what it's connected to, why it happened, why it keeps happening." Her smile was so bright with confidence it almost hurt to look at. "I'm going to understand it all—how every thread connects to every other. And then I'm going to use that knowledge to build something that works. No matter how long it takes." She looked up at the sky, and then back at Seren's face. "What about you? What do you want to do?"

Awed by the enormity of the task Arianrod had set for herself, for a moment Seren couldn't think of anything important that she wanted. But then one desire burned in her, fueled by a cold certainty. It didn't matter how far away she got from the old woman, from Malvan, from Caius Margraine. Everywhere she went, there would be people just like them. There would be people who wanted to hurt her, to use her, to take things from her. And if they wanted to, they would, because she couldn't stop them.

"I'll buy a weapon," she said, wishing it were in her hands already. "Weapons. As many as I need. I'll train every day, every day until I'm strong, and even after that. I'll train until I'm stronger than anyone, and then if anyone tries to hurt me or make me do things, I'll kill them."

"Stronger than anyone, eh? I'd like to see that."

Seren found herself smiling at the thought, and she realized Arianrod was smiling, too, in a way that wasn't sharp or arrogant. She wasn't used to smiling, and especially not to smiling *with* someone, and for a moment she felt something better than just the absence of bad things, relief from fear or pain or anger. She felt as if she could really succeed. As if she'd be all right, one day.

Caught up and carried away by that feeling, she blurted out, "And someday—when I'm strong—let me pay you back for this. Let me do something for you."

But Arianrod had shattered that moment with a laugh. "You? Don't be stupid. What could you possibly do for me?"

Those words had inspired a pain Seren had never felt before, one she couldn't name and didn't know what to do with. But before she could say anything, as if in a strange kind of sympathy, Arianrod winced, catching her breath sharply. "I . . . think this is as far as I can go," she said. "I wanted to take you to the gate, but I still have to go all the way back by myself, and . . ."

Seren looked her over with concern. "Are you tired?" They hadn't walked all that far. Was Arianrod frail, or sick? She didn't look it.

"Just a little. It isn't bad. Let me just stop here." She indicated an intersection where the street ran perpendicular to a dead-end alley, and led Seren into the shadows at its mouth. "They shouldn't have noticed you're missing yet, so you should be able to get out of the city without any trouble. And then you can do whatever you'd like. You can try to be the strongest. Just remember what I told you, and be careful."

They let go of each other's hands, and Seren felt sorry. They'd probably never see each other again, would they? She stared at Arianrod, leaning against the alley wall, breathing a little fast. She wanted to remember the way she looked.

"Oh," she said. "I almost forgot. They said it's your birthday today, right? I meant to give you . . . my best wishes."

The words fell lamely in the air between them, but Arianrod didn't laugh again. She smiled a little, but mostly she looked thoughtful. "You're a strange girl."

"Yes," Seren said. "I've been told that."

"Have you? Well, don't let it worry you. They tell me that, too." She held out her hand again, and Seren was confused for a moment before she realized: a handshake, for farewell. Arianrod's grip was firm, even though she was still leaning against the wall. "Good luck," she said. "I hope you don't die."

"Thank you," Seren said. "No one's . . . ever said that to me before."

As she made her way down the street, she couldn't resist looking back, just once. From that distance, Arianrod had looked small, and very alone. It was an image Seren had remembered, every bit as vividly as that confident smile.

ARIANROD HAD NOT been on the throne two years when Seren returned to Stonespire, yet already the difference had been stark. Cleaner streets, fewer beggars— almost none of them children. When she passed by her old haunts, she saw teams of builders at work, knocking down the most squalid hovels and building anew. And Caius Margraine's headless law had been repealed. Stealing was no longer a death sentence.

But some things were still the same, or close enough that something more had to be done. Seren had been prepared for that, since before she ever left Sahai. She had three outstanding debts in Esthrades, she had decided. When they were all settled, one way or another . . . well, she'd see where that left her.

Malvan was easy to find, and might have been even without her skills. He had turned to legitimate enterprise in the face of more aggressive efforts by the city guardsmen, and was now styling himself a shopkeeper. She found him poring over a book of accounts like the miser he was, surrounded by gold-plated candlesticks and porcelain vases from Sahai. But she had not forgotten his former merchandise.

"Hello, Malvan," she said.

The man looked up at the sound of his name, but without any real interest. "What do you want?"

"Just several moments of your time."

He scowled. "My time isn't so cheap I care to waste it. Are you here on *business*?"

"I am, actually," Seren said. She did not smile; she had learned that refusing to do so unsettled people, which was just as well, because it had never come easily to her anyway. But she kept her tone polite. "I'm here to collect a debt."

His scowl hardened. "I don't owe *you* any debts. I've never seen you in my life."

Seren deigned not to answer that, instead pacing slowly around the room, drawing closer to him in a wide arc. "So many of your victims must be grown now, if they managed to survive. I wonder what their lives look like now—what was left to salvage after you were done with them. I suspect they know more of hunger than I do—perhaps even more than I ever did, though I once called myself an expert."

Malvan reached out with his left hand as if to push her aside, his right extending reflexively across the top of the table. "Listen here, you bitch, I don't know what—"

Seren drew the knife from her sleeve and pinned his wrist to the table, driving the point down so that it pierced the wood beneath his flesh. "I'm talking."

His screaming drew two men out from the back room: his associates, no doubt, though she couldn't say she recognized them. Perhaps they were new.

She let go of the knife that was currently stuck in Malvan's wrist and drew another one from her boot. "If you don't want to end up like him, go back in that room and stay there."

They nearly tripped over each other in their haste to do as she'd bid. So much for loyalty.

Malvan's lungs were finally starting to tire by that point—or at least she hoped they were. "If you don't stop screaming," she said, "I'll do the other one."

He struggled to obey her, clamping his jaw shut even as harsh noises of pain were trapped behind his clenched teeth. He shook with the strain of it, white-faced, sweating.

It was only fair. This was what his kind had forced her to do—her and so many others, who had died forgotten and destroyed. They had had to choke on their own suffering, the brutal unfairness of their lives, while he had stood above them, unmoved, *profiting*. This was only the smallest taste of what it had been like. And yet, looking at him, she could not truly feel a sense of peace at the thought of what she was about to do. Even more than his death, she wanted him to understand the vileness of what he had done. She wanted the knowledge of his crimes to fill him with horror and shame. But that power was beyond even the most talented assassin. A man might beg, weeping, for mercy, but if the knife were to fall into *his* hand instead, he'd wield it as cheerfully as if mercy were a word he'd never learned.

"If you'd threatened even one fewer child," she told him, "you might have lived past today. Let that be the last thing you think about as I slit your throat."

SEREN CAME UPON the old woman staggering down a side street, one hand braced along the row of buildings. She was much thinner than she had been, stooped, with dirt in her scraggly hair; as Seren drew closer, she realized the old woman was now shorter than she was. With her skills, she could have ended things in an instant, and perhaps she would have. But just as she came within arm's reach, the old woman looked up—and revealed two walls of white, both eyes completely webbed over with cataracts. "What is it?" she snapped, faint and wheezy. "Who's taken it into their fool head to trouble an old blind woman?"

They stood there facing each other, separated by impenetrable darkness. Seren had never planned for this. She had imagined the old woman might already be dead, to be sure. But although she had guessed—correctly, it seemed—that Malvan would not remember her, she had lived with the old woman for years. She had been bracing herself, this whole time, for the inevitability of being remembered.

But after the changes of adolescence, her voice sounded too different to recognize. If Seren did not choose to reveal herself, the old woman could not possibly guess who she was.

It was like that day with Arianrod all those years ago, the realization that she would pass unnoticed before everyone's eyes. It was the feeling of being safe behind invisibility—of having the freedom to do whatever she wished. She did not have to confront the old woman directly, or have the knowledge of who she once was thrown back in her face. Her past remained in her hands alone.

Still, part of her ached for vengeance, years of pent-up pain and anger screaming for release. But she had killed Malvan not one hour ago, and all the satisfaction she had felt had already faded, leaving her no less hollow than before. She did not regret what she had done—even if he no longer bought and sold children, it was not for lack of trying, and who knew when he would have happened upon some equally vile method of turning a profit? But the old woman was blind and decrepit—she would have been helpless against even the smallest child she had ever housed. She had harmed so many, but she could harm no one anymore.

Seren stood there, torn between rage and sorrow, for moments that felt like hours. But in the end, all her knives remained sheathed. "I mistook you for someone I had business with," she said. "Be on your way."

THAT WAS TWO down, and one to go—but the hardest of them all by far. After all, she had tried to repay Arianrod once already, and been refused. She was strong now, but did that truly mean she had something to offer?

Merely asking would be enough to put the past to rest, she told herself. If Arianrod released her, or else proved too hateful to abide, Seren need not pursue the matter further. And she had to know for sure—to be certain Arianrod wasn't ruined, broken, because of what she'd done to help Seren all those years ago. *Does she still smile the way she did that day? Or did he kill that confidence in her? Was he able to make her afraid?*

The line of the day's complainants stretched out the doors of Stonespire Hall, curling around the edge of the wall to keep out of the way. Seren waited quietly until she came near to the threshold, where there was a guard within speaking distance. "Excuse me," she said, unused to courtesies. "If I wished to hold my turn until there were fewer people present, would that be possible?"

The guard smiled at her, and Seren caught her breath. She knew him. He was no longer young, but she remembered the shape of his long face and the mildness of his expression. "You're far from the first person to ask that," he said. "I'll keep you to the side here, and let you know when we've finished for the day. I'm afraid I can't let you wait within the hall itself, for the sake of the marquise's safety."

Seren stood where he asked and waited, trying to ignore the increasing tension in her limbs. Eventually the guard cut the line off, telling the remainder to come back tomorrow, and when even the truncated line was completed, he motioned to Seren to go in.

She remembered how Caius Margraine had looked on that throne, as if it could barely contain him. But the figure upon it now wasn't so much sitting on it as draped over it, the very picture of idle relaxation after a day's work. Her pale hair fell freely to her back, and she swept it out of her face so she could see to the end of the hall. "One more, is it? Well, come forward. Unless you'd prefer to shout your problem at me?"

Seren looked up at her, and felt such a shock of recognition and relief that it was difficult to breathe.

She was just the same. Oh, her body had made all the typical transitions to adulthood, of course: her limbs had grown long, her face had matured, her figure had filled out. But essentially, in every way that mattered, she was just exactly the same. If anything, her grin had grown even sharper than Seren remembered—bolder, archer, more knowing. It reached to her bright, searching eyes, just as it always had. It seemed impossible to remove, impossible to ever threaten away.

Of course Caius Margraine could never have taken that from her. It seemed ridiculous, now, to even imagine it.

She'd gone over this so many times in her mind, but faced with the reality, she found all her prepared words slipping away. "My name is Seren Almasy," she began, and cursed herself immediately. Announcing herself was useless. Arianrod had never known her name. "I'm sure that means nothing to you, but . . . even if my name is unfamiliar, you and I are not strangers."

No one else had remembered her. Malvan, the old woman, even that guard at the door. It had been comforting, until now, to know how different she appeared from the pathetic orphan she once was. But seeing blankness in Arianrod's face was somehow painful. How much of what had happened between them did she even remember?

Then Arianrod's face changed, and she sat up straight, all her languidness gone. She abandoned her throne, descending the steps so they were face-to-face, and tilted her head, as if to bring Seren's face in line with the light, or see it from a different angle. And then Seren saw it: recognition, sudden and unmistakable.

Whatever shock Arianrod might have felt was gone in a moment, chased away by a bright and unaffected laugh. "Well!" she said. "After all this time! I'd hardly have known you. Have you only just returned?"

"To Esthrades? Yes, I've only been here a few days . . ." Seren mumbled, taken aback.

"You did end up leaving the country, then? Good for you. I don't think you'd ever have been found if you'd just gone as far as the forest, but I suppose this way you've gotten to see some of the world, eh?" She suddenly seemed to remember where they were. "Oh, bah, this is no place for that kind of conversation, is it? Come on, my judgments are through for the day. Let's rest ourselves, and you can tell me whatever it is you've come to tell me then."

The transition was a blur in Seren's memory, but somehow Arianrod managed to get her out to the blood apple orchard—the first time she had ever seen it, though she barely took notice of it. Arianrod leaned back against the trunk of a tree, and Seren stood across from her, still feeling stiff.

"I told myself so many stories over the years about what had happened to you," Arianrod said. "You went to so many places, and had all manner of trades: you were a poor fisherwoman in Lakeport, or else you apprenticed under a merchant in Eldren Cael and became fabulously wealthy. Or even that you had some ugly husband and a whole brood of children. But if I'm honest, I always thought it was most likely that you'd just gotten yourself killed. A cruel underestimation of your abilities, it seems, but you have to admit you were so hapless back then. I am glad to know you still live—that all I did back then wasn't for nothing."

Seren thought of how much her freedom had truly cost Arianrod, and bowed her head. "I . . . I would've come sooner, but I only recently learned that . . . that your father . . ."

"That he died?" Arianrod frowned. "That was more than a year ago. What rock were you hiding under that you did not hear of it?"

"I have been across the sea, in Sahai," Seren said. "They are not so fascinated by Lantian events there, so the news from the west is much reduced."

Arianrod's face froze, her shoulders stiffening. "You've been to Sahai?"

"Yes," Seren said. "I lived in the capital for . . . it's more than a decade now. Just shy of thirteen years, I think."

Arianrod was looking at her as if she'd suddenly sprouted wings. "It seems it was an error on my part not to ask you for your story immediately," she said. "What on earth have you really been doing all these years?"

So Seren told her. Someone else, who was skilled in making speeches, would doubtless have been able to infuse her tale with more glamor and intrigue than she managed, but still she tried her best to answer Arianrod's increasingly frequent questions. Many times, she saw a look of frustration cross Arianrod's face when she gave a particularly meager description of some place or event, as if she wished she could just grab Seren by the shoulders and shake the memories loose. But finally she finished, and waited for what Arianrod would say.

For a few moments, it actually seemed as if she'd rendered Arianrod speechless. "All those stories I told myself, and the truth turns out to be more interesting than any of them! I really did underestimate you, didn't I? Although . . . to think of it another way, if I truly thought nothing good would come of your escape, I wouldn't have assisted in it. But I assume the purpose of your visit was not simply to inform me of your doings. There was something you wanted to ask of me, yes?"

"No. I mean—yes, but . . ." Seren fumbled for the proper explanation. "You've given me enough already. I came because I wanted to give you something."

She'd been dreading the old answer: *What could you possibly do for me?* It didn't come, but there was no answer in its place, either. At last, Arianrod said, "I'm not sure I understand."

"You've heard what happened to me. You must know I am skilled—I would never have risen as far as I have in the Inxia Morain if I weren't. Surely you can think of some use for me?"

"Ah," Arianrod said. "And what price would you demand for these skills of yours?"

Seren hadn't given that a single thought. "Whatever you think is fair. Whatever would be customary."

Arianrod's eyebrows rose. "Yes, well, I'm afraid that *assassin* isn't a customary position within the Margraine household, so we don't have an established rate. I do know, however, that the price the Inxia Morain exact for even a single job is quite extraordinary, so I can't imagine what it would cost to employ one continuously."

"No," Seren said, "it isn't about—it has nothing to do with the price. I have all the coin I need already. I only offered because . . . because of what you did for me, and what you suffered for my sake. I can protect you, or strike down your enemies . . . whatever you require. To settle the debt between us."

She knew immediately that she'd said something wrong. The very air seemed to cool between them, and Arianrod drew herself up to every inch of her superior height. "What I *suffered*? What precisely is it that you think I suffered?"

Whatever irritation Seren had felt at the cheerful condescension of so many years ago, this coldness was far worse. "I'm . . . sorry if I've offended you. As far away as I was, I only recently happened to hear the full story of what took place after I left. How unjustly he treated you . . . it grieved me to know of it. I wish that it had not happened. That's all."

Arianrod hissed a deep breath out through her teeth, leaning her forehead against her hand. "Seren Almasy, wasn't it? It was a mistake not to ask you back then. Well, Miss Almasy, whatever I did back then, I did for my own sake, because it was what I wished. I thank you very much for your kind offer, but at this time I judge that it is not in my best interests to accept it."

Seren ought to have just let the matter drop. She had told herself she would, and at least this rejection was worlds more polite than the previous one. Still she heard herself ask, "Why? How is it that I am not of use to you?"

"I'm sure you'd be of great use to many people," Arianrod said. "But I don't know the measure of you, Almasy. I spent an afternoon with you once, more than ten years ago now, and of what happened to you afterward I have only a half-hour's summary. A retainer of your competence would no doubt be a great boon, but what is most important is that I surround myself with people I can trust."

Seren's heart sank. "And you can't trust me?"

"I can't," Arianrod said, "because you don't know the measure of me, either. I think you may harbor more than a few misconceptions about me. I might have helped you in the past, but I am not a person given to kindness, or who frets over a lack of it. And given how deadly I know you must be, I would prefer not to be near you when you are inevitably disillusioned with being in my service."

Seren shook her head. "No. If that's what it is, then you don't understand me, either."

Arianrod shrugged. "All the more reason."

"No, I mean . . . I do know you," Seren said. "The things that angered me when I lived here . . . I couldn't think further than wanting to destroy them, but you wanted to *change* them. To replace them with something better. You told me that, before. You told me that you would make everything work, and that if you didn't know how to fix it, you wouldn't rest until you did. Have you forgotten that? Or do you want something different now?"

"Of course not," Arianrod said. "What would be the point of ruling at all, if I weren't capable of fixing anything?"

"Then it's fine," Seren said. "Just let me help you fix things. And if someone tries to stop you, let me kill them. For my own satisfaction."

Arianrod didn't say no immediately, which meant she was considering it. She even looked a bit uncomfortable, which meant she was strongly considering it. Finally, she said, "I would never ask an assassin to swear vows, but even they must be able to obey contracts. If I allow you to stay here, the terms of our contract will be as follows. Should you ever wish to leave my service, I will let you do so in peace, with no questions or protestations. But should I ever wish to dismiss you, you will ask me no questions, either, but depart without violence or retribution."

"I would not have done that anyway," Seren said. "But it's a promise, if you like."

"Then I suppose I've run out of reasons to say no." She cast a contemplative look out at the orchard. "Given that we ought to celebrate such an auspicious bargain . . . it was an apple, wasn't it?"

"I beg your pardon?" Seren asked.

"The thing that started it all. It was an apple that you stole, was it not?"

Taken aback, Seren couldn't speak for a moment. "I'm . . . surprised that you remembered."

"I'm a genius, Almasy. I have an excellent memory."

"Seren," Seren insisted.

Arianrod shrugged. "As you prefer. I was thinking that my father still owes you for that day, but of course it's a debt he can hardly repay in his current position. Debts do generally pass from parents to their children, so . . ." Seren watched as she reached overhead, heard the soft snap as she plucked free a carefully chosen apple. She held it out, smiling that impenetrable smile. "Here—with more than a decade's interest. The rarest apple in the known world."

Seren froze. This must be a test, surely? But she didn't know what the correct answer was. If she reached for it, would Arianrod call her impertinent? Say she presumed beyond her place?

Arianrod waved the apple teasingly. "What's this? You're too afraid to take what you're owed? I know what tradition dictates, but I'm the only Margraine left to taste of these. It's not as if I don't have any to spare."

Seren had decided a long time ago that she wouldn't be afraid, especially over something as inconsequential as even the rarest apple. Before she could lose her nerve, she took it from Arianrod's hand, breaking its skin with a hearty bite.

She very nearly spat it out. It took all her self-control not to sputter or visibly choke it down, to force herself to chew it. Arianrod's smile broke open as she burst into laughter—not the condescending laughter Seren had hated, but the merry laugh of a child caught at a prank. She pulled the apple gently from Seren's unresisting fingers, biting into it with no discomfort at all. "I suppose I should beg your pardon," she said. "But I couldn't resist the look on your face!"

SOMETIME IN THE darkest part of the night, Almasy started shivering. She didn't wake up, or not precisely, just thrashed about and mumbled and shook, agitated beyond all their attempts to calm her. When Lucius brushed aside her sweat-soaked hair to touch her forehead, his face turned grim. "The fever's only gotten worse," he said to Deinol, the flickering of the firelight making his features seem unfamiliar. "But I suppose that must be evident enough."

"What should we do?" Deinol asked.

"Keep her warm through the night—we'll have to keep the fire going. Watch her carefully. Hope she wakes up. Get her to eat and drink something if she does. I would look at her wound again, but it's not as if I'd know what to do with it."

Deinol was silent for a moment longer. "I mean what should we do after? We aren't healers, and she must need one, if she's going to get through this. Right?"

"Right." He brushed his hair out of his eyes. "Bound to be one at Stonespire, though. A good one. Best in the area, if the Margraines employ them."

"Stonespire," Deinol repeated, in disbelief. "Our exile wasn't lifted just because she's sick, Lucius. You know any healer employed by the Margraines wouldn't tend to her anyway."

"We're so close," Lucius said quietly. "We can't let her fail when she's this close, Deinol."

"It's not about us letting her do anything. It's not in our hands. We're risking our necks if we go back there—ours, and whatever's left of hers. It's useless."

Lucius stared into the fire. "Even if it is, it's what she wants."

Deinol snorted. "Right, because she's only ever wanted sensible and reasonable things before."

"Has everything you've wanted always been sensible?" He fed a twig into the flames. "It's her last wish. Don't you think she was right, that last wishes should mean something?"

"Lucius, you can't really say that we owe her."

"Can't I? She interceded for us directly. We probably only survived that encounter with Ryker because of her."

"Aye, she's helped us, sure. But it's only ever been after she put us in danger in the first place."

"Not that night on the street. That was all us, and you know it." *That was all you,* he might have said, but didn't, because he was Lucius.

Deinol tore up the grass. "Gods, there's no reasoning with you when you're like this. *I'm* supposed to be the unreasonable one, you know."

Lucius smiled sadly. "You're right. I'm sorry about that. I'm sorry . . . for more than that. But I'm still going to go back to Stonespire, and do all I can to see that the names of the traitors reach the marquise—and that Seren reaches her as well, if she manages to live that long. It's . . . the right thing."

"Fuck," Deinol said, rubbing a hand across his face. "Fuck, it is, isn't it?" He looked over at Almasy's trembling form, so much smaller than it should have been. That was the problem, for her and Deinol both. It was what Seth would have wanted him to do. And Deinol couldn't ignore that any more than she had.

CHAPTER FIFTY

Valyanrend

SHE'D BEEN PLANNING to investigate Tethantys's tip for herself, and confront Roger later once she'd confirmed it was true. But that plan was ruined once Roger himself caught her coming around the corner to the dead-end alley she'd been told to check. There was no chance of slipping out of sight—she practically ran right into him. "What the hell are you doing?" he asked, making as if to grab her by the shoulders, though she darted out of the way before he could make contact. "We both know you're well enough acquainted with Sheath not to think there's anything for you here."

Marceline smiled sweetly. They *did* both know that, which meant they also both knew there was no reason for him to be here, either. He was doubtless scrambling for some way to get around that. Let him; she could use a bit of fun. "You look rather sweat-stained for someone normally so lazy. Up to a lot of work down that alley, were you?"

He scowled. "Don't be daft. What's that way that I could possibly be busy with?"

"You were the one who came from that way. You might as well be the one to tell me."

"You'd like that, wouldn't you? But I'll let you into my tricks as little as I ever have. If I want to have a think undisturbed, that's my business."

Marceline tilted her head. "Oh, undisturbed, is it? Now I understand. If you don't want to be disturbed, what's a better thinking place than a tunnel under the ground?"

That was another look she wanted to remember forever, that barely concealed panic as his face went ashen. He reached for her again, but she was ready for him, dancing back out of reach. "What, you're trying to threaten me now?"

He held his hands up, surrendering. "Nothing like it. Just trying to get you to listen to some sense before you dash off to run your mouth at anyone who'll listen. Monkey, the value of a place like that only goes down the less secret it—"

"Ugh, I know that! I'm not an idiot. Do you really think I'm in such a hurry to tell people, when nobody likes to brag more than you do?"

"You're going to tell Tom, at least."

"I'm not going to bloody tell anyone! That I've decided on. Yet. The only people who know about it besides us are that friend of yours and *his* friend, and it can stay that way as long as you—"

Roger cut her off. "What friend of mine? What friend of his?"

Marceline shrugged. "He called himself Tethantys. He said the two of you were intimately acquainted."

"Like hell we are. I've never so much as heard that name in my life."

"That's just what he said you'd say. And given that everything else he told me turned out to be true, I'm more inclined to believe him."

"Come on. What would be the point in insisting on that, when I've already admitted the most important bit?" He ran his hands through his hair, fingers grasping as if they could seize on his next move. "I'll allow it's possible he's changed his name. What exactly did he say to you?"

"Well . . . a lot of things. We talked for a while, and not everything he said made sense to me. But if you mean about the tunnels, he said that they went all over the city. And he said they contained some very valuable things, but you hadn't done anything with them."

"And you didn't find that odd? I'm not so arrogant as to say it's *impossible* that I've been spied on, but even if some fellow caught me going in or out of the tunnels, how the hell would he know what I have or haven't done there? He couldn't very well count the bloody books to see if I'd taken any of them, and unless he's watching me constantly—"

"Books?" Marceline interrupted. "What books?"

"That's what I found in there. Banned books, books the Ninists tried to burn. They must be worth a fortune or several now—many of them might be the only existing copies left. So he's right that they're valuable, but I'm not about to just sell them without making sure I know what's in them, am I?"

Marceline couldn't help but agree—you could always sell the books after you'd already read them, and have the knowledge and the coin together. "I didn't know what valuable things he was talking about, but if it's books . . . You're right, there's no way he could tell what you were doing with them. Even if he were the best spy the world had ever seen, I can't say how he could have done it." She hesitated, not wanting to hear Roger jeer at her, but without any other possible explanation. "When I met him . . . I thought he might be a ghost."

Roger laughed, of course, but for some reason it was weaker than she would've expected. "Why on earth would you say that?"

"Because he was there, but it was like his presence didn't have any . . . weight. Like he wasn't *really* there, the way a shadow has the outline of a real thing but isn't one. He had no smell, and when he whispered in my ear I couldn't feel his breath. I don't know about that friend of his, Asariel—she stayed too far back for me to be sure. But I suppose ghosts don't have—"

Roger blanched. "Did you say Asariel? That old crone was with him?"

"She wasn't *that* old," Marceline said. "Still pretty, I thought."

"Still *pretty*? She was as old as Gran if she was a day!"

"Oh," Marceline said. "Then it must have been someone else. Your Gran was past eighty when she died, right? The woman I saw was . . . maybe not even forty, or maybe just past it."

"Two different women with *that* name? Asariel? When have you ever heard that before?" He looked almost as troubled as when he'd first seen her, but she wasn't enjoying it half as much. "There wasn't another woman with them, was there? A younger one? Thin, sort of spindly, with red hair?"

Marceline shook her head. "No one like that. It was just the two of them. Why?"

He ignored that. "What did this Tethantys fellow look like?"

Marceline tried to think back to their meeting, to recall his face clearly. She knew what his face had *felt* like, the things it had made her think about him, but as to the actual features . . . "He had dark circles under his eyes. He was pale, rather thin . . . and there was something odd about his smile." But the instant she said it, with Roger's face right there across from her, she suddenly understood what it was. It wasn't the strangeness of seeing something wrong, or unfamiliar; it was the strangeness of seeing something familiar in an unfamiliar place.

Her expression must have changed, because Roger asked, "What is it?"

"It was you," she said. "When he smiled, he looked like you. I can't explain it, but he did."

To her surprise, Roger accepted that with only a grim nod. "The woman I told you about was the companion of the Asariel I saw—the crone. I don't know what *her* name was, but she reminded me of someone, too." He scuffed at the dirt of the alley with one boot. "I'll tell you what, monkey. I think there's something you and I need to look at. Together."

MARCELINE WAS FAR too cheerful for Roger's liking, following him through the tunnels without a shred of respect for the enormity of the discovery, or the mysteries it still contained. It was all right for *some,* he supposed, who apparently just got *told* things by dissembling strangers.

"Did you check if any of these connect to the lower aqueducts?" she asked, swinging her arms at her sides.

"Not so far. I doubt they do. Otherwise these tunnels would have been discovered a lot earlier. Plenty of thieves use the lower aqueducts to get around in a pinch."

Marceline wrinkled her nose. "Maybe they wanted to make sure these tunnels wouldn't flood."

"Or maybe it's just that the lower aqueducts were built to do one thing, and these were built for something else."

"Like what?" She darted slightly forward, so he could see her out of the corner of his eye. "Storing books? I want to see those, too, by the way."

"All in good time," Roger said, holding the candlestick higher. "There's something else I want to show you first."

She didn't protest, but she didn't stop asking questions, either, launching them one on the heels of another, almost quicker than Roger could make sense of them. No, it was Morgan who had stumbled on the tunnels first; no, she hadn't been hiding out in them all this time; no, he didn't know if they'd been built before or after the lower aqueducts. . . .

"Hush now," he said, as they entered the statue chamber. "This is it."

She didn't seem to feel the same sense of awe or strangeness that he had; she got so close to the statues that she could have brushed by them, scrunching up her face as if she were inspecting a loaf of bread for mold, or testing the firmness of a fruit. "They're not Ninist, are they?"

"No. I can't say what they could be, though, or if they were meant to be religious at all."

"They seem ceremonial enough to me. Religions love that." She kept making slow half-turns, scanning the faces from left to right and back again. "Funny about the details, though. With the Nine it makes sense, because they're supposed to be real people, but these . . ."

Roger knew what she was thinking, because the same thought had occurred to him. "Gods aren't supposed to look like people. If they even look human, it's usually a representation: a wise elder, a warrior, a mother." He drew close to the third statue. "This one isn't a warrior-goddess, leading soldiers into battle with a warhorn or a flaming weapon; she's just some woman with a broken sword. There's a mother over there, but she just looks like a mother, not like *the* Mother. I can't say why it makes me so uneasy."

Marceline laughed. "Neither can I. It's nothing to be anxious about."

But she'd stopped right in front of the statue that had so fascinated and unnerved Roger, the man with the crown clutched in his fist. She peered into his face, just as Roger had, but whatever she saw didn't seem to have any effect on her. Then she stood on the tips of her toes, and cupped the statue's cheek in her hand, heedless of how rough the stone must have felt against her palm.

"Don't do that!" Roger said, and realized he was whispering.

"Why? It's just stone. It's not going to hurt me."

"It's . . . probably blasphemous or something."

"Even if it is, it's not *my* religion." She leaned even closer, and spoke into the statue's ear. "I don't suppose you have anything you'd like to add to this discussion?" She tilted her head, leaning her ear against its mouth. "Not a word. Imagine that."

"Very funny." He paced along the half-circle again, examining them in the light of the candle to make sure nothing had changed.

"Hello," Marceline said, crouching down at the statue's feet. "What's this?"

"That strange writing? Aye, they all have that."

Marceline rubbed at it with the pad of her thumb. "I . . . think they might be runes."

"What are runes?"

"What, you don't know? Tom's been asked about them once or twice, by the odd scholar that's stumbled into Sheath. They're not really a *foreign* language, they're just very, very old. From so long ago that Lantian was spoken and written differently."

Roger rolled his eyes. "I know what Old Lantian is, monkey. But I thought . . ." He tried to remember the little Gran had said about it. "I thought their letters were basically the same as ours, even though their words were different."

Marceline nodded. "Aye, but runes are even older than that—sort of like our ancestors' first go at writing. They're like . . . a more complicated way of saying things, before we figured out how to simplify it."

"So what you're saying is, you can translate runes into Old Lantian, and Old Lantian into our Lantian?"

"Maybe Tom could. But I thought you didn't want to tell anyone else."

"Just tell him you and I found some writing we want to translate."

"And if he asks where?"

Roger threw up his hands. "You can't think of something to tell him?"

"I could, but I don't *like* to. Did you write down all the symbols on the statues already, or should we do it now?"

"No, I've done it. I'll give you the paper when we get back to the Dragon's Head."

Marceline stood up again, looking into the eyes of the man with the crown. "Roger, I was thinking . . . when Tethantys said you were in possession of valuable things you weren't using. What if he didn't mean the books?"

"And he meant these instead?" The thought had occurred to Roger, too, though he couldn't say he liked it. "How do you 'use' a statue, though? These are carved right into the ground. Even if we wanted to move them, and found enough people to help, I don't know that we could manage it without damaging them."

"Then maybe it's the runes themselves. Maybe they're some sort of puzzle, and solving it will lead to something valuable."

"Like following finger signs?" Roger groaned. "If that's all it turns out to be, I'll be grateful. But I'm afraid the real answer's going to be stranger than either of us can imagine."

CHAPTER FIFTY-ONE

Stonespire

THEIR FIRST STROKE of luck was that the guards on the Stonespire gate that morning had no idea who they were, but were entirely sympathetic to the story of a couple travelers who had helped their sick friend come this far in the hope of finding a healer. Their second stroke of luck was that there did seem to be some sort of famous healer currently in Stonespire, which both provided a potential opportunity and made their story seem more credible. The third stroke couldn't exactly be called good luck or bad, but fell somewhere in the gray middle: the comrade the gate guards summoned to help them to the healer was none other than Bridger, she of the terrifying stature and even more terrifying abilities with a sword.

Perhaps under any other circumstances, Bridger would have arrested them on sight; she'd certainly have been within her rights, after what the marquise had said. But she didn't, because those three strokes of luck were nothing compared to the brutal cut of the bad: for almost half a day, they hadn't been able to wake Almasy at all. What Bridger saw, carried in Lucius's arms, was a rapidly withering shell: covered in sweat, full of labored breathing and the occasional delirious jerk of limbs, but incapable of being roused to true consciousness or understanding. Instead of unsheathing her sword, or even just her anger, Bridger stood there staring, pressing her lips together. Then she said, "I believe Healer Shing is currently at the hall. If you don't mind, I will escort you."

They walked in silence for a while—Deinol certainly didn't know what to say. But then Bridger turned to Lucius. "When I apprehended the two of you in the city, you made sure he left me alive. Why?"

Lucius nodded at Almasy's still form. "She told me what you did for the children of this city. The life of such a person is more valuable than mine."

She turned her face forward again. "The man your friend wounded so badly . . . his name is Denton Halley. He is the one who found me, who trained me, who convinced those above him that I was needed in the guard. He was the favorite of the eleventh Daven, who gave all his trust even to one so young. Even when Lord Caius did all he could to put obstacles in his way, Dent still wanted to serve, and accepted every indignity thrown at him. And when our lord attacked his daughter and left her on the verge of death, it was Dent who pulled her away from him, who brought her to the healer, who did not leave her side till she was well and defended her from her father ever after, no matter the risk to himself. All the years of his life he has devoted to others. But I expect you did not know that."

Her words must have truly pained Lucius, if even a trace of it was visible in his face. To save him from having to respond, Deinol hastened to change the subject. "So, er, Bridger. What do you think our chances are of getting through this with our heads?"

"Your heads aren't at issue. What I'm worried about is whether you'll be let into the hall. Down in the city I command as much respect as anyone, but most of the hall guard are close to Captain Ingret. I believe I am acting in accordance with her ladyship's wishes, but that doesn't mean they'll let me flout her orders, and she ordered you and Miss Almasy gone."

"We have more than just Seren," Lucius said. "We have the conspirators' names."

Bridger turned sharply toward them. "What conspirators?"

"The rentholders who seek to overthrow her," Deinol said. "That's what we were doing all this time."

They were silent while she took that in. "In that case, I can guarantee your entry, though not how long it will take. Let's hope the current shift is a favorable one."

Climbing the steps to Stonespire Hall in the daytime was an entirely different experience. Everything was busy and complicated: horses were being hustled into the stables at the base of the hill, merchants and laborers were straining to carry supplies up the steep steps, and everyone else had to thread their way around hooves and past barrels and crates and one another. Strangely, Deinol didn't see any guards on the steps. "Isn't all this a nightmare for your people?" he asked Bridger.

She shook her head. "It's always been this way. The Margraines take pride in it. They want to show that they don't fear their own people."

Deinol squinted dubiously up at the hall. "And how has that worked out for them in practice?"

Bridger considered the question. "Well, the only Margraine who's ever been assassinated was the eighth Daven—probably. And the one who probably assassinated him was his brother. And it happened out in the forest, not in Stonespire at all. So . . . I'd say fairly well, on balance."

Valyanrend had seen one bloody shift of power after another for generations; it was all Deinol knew. How strange to think that a single family could hold confident sway over a place for hundreds of years.

No one tried to stop them from passing under the gate, but when they approached the double doors leading to the hall itself, Bridger pulled up short. The doors were open, but a guard stood on either side of them. With a wince, Deinol recognized one of them—the bandaged arm would have given him away, even if his face hadn't. "Guardsman Halley," Bridger hailed him, in obvious relief. "I know this is going to seem very odd, but—"

"Not at all," Halley said. "Given the obvious severity of the problem, I can wait to hear the full explanation. Healer Shing is within the hall, waiting to check the stitches she put in my arm. Fetch her and meet us in the orchard."

Bridger dashed through the double doors without another word. "This way," Halley said to Deinol and Lucius. "We can't let anyone in the hall see you." They climbed a narrow stone staircase onto the outer wall, and followed it until it met the outside of the hall, ducking through a low doorway. Halley made sure it was tightly shut behind them before continuing on, down a winding stair and through a narrow corridor into a brief stone passage. Then, finally, there was sunlight again, filtered through the branches of the trees.

"Don't move from this spot," Halley said. "I'll fetch the marquise."

He left them alone with a fortune in blood apples. Even with so much hanging in the balance, Deinol couldn't help thinking of Roger's story. A puzzle too great for any thief to solve, he had said. The orchard was beyond price, but a single apple was worthless. But the apples were so close, part of him wanted to just reach up and touch one—not to steal it, just to hold something so rare in the palm of his hand.

It could only have been a couple minutes, but already the sound of the marquise's voice pulled him out of his reverie. "Dent, you know I hold your opinion in high regard, but you must admit this is highly unusual. This had better be a true emergency."

"You can judge for yourself, my lady. I apologize for the abruptness, but I wished to allow you some measure of privacy, in case you became . . . alarmed."

"*Alarmed?* Please. What do you think—"

Suddenly, they were face-to-face. The marquise must have seen all three of them at once. She had been picking her way over the roots of one of the trees, and now she missed her footing. She stumbled a step back and sideways, the fingers of her left hand coming to rest against the trunk.

Deinol had been steeling himself for her anger, but it was as if he and Lucius were not even there. "Dent," she snapped, "why would you bring her to me instead of Zara? What do you think *I* can do for her?"

Halley relaxed, shrugging off her words. "Bridger has already gone to fetch the healer, my lady. I merely thought you would wish to be apprised of the situation as soon as possible."

"So far I have yet to be apprised of anything. What happened to her? Is she ill?"

"It's a fever," Deinol said, hoping he wouldn't regret drawing her attention, "but it came from the wound in her shoulder. You'd have to treat that first, perhaps. We'd never have come back here, if not to get her to the proper healer."

"And she wanted us to give you a list of names," Lucius said. "Of the other members of the little conspiracy among your rentholders. Cantor, Claremont, and Apglen. If you doubt us, we are prepared to tell you the full story of how we came by those names. We have no wish to plague you any further."

"She was certain of those three?" the marquise asked.

"She was. She insisted that we tell you if she could not." He hesitated, then plunged forward, with what was either bravery or the greatest foolishness. "Though we urged her to think of herself, all she cared about was making it to Stonespire. To help you, and . . . to see you again."

She did not answer, but closed her eyes, putting a hand to her forehead. "There's no need to keep her out here. We'll bring her to her rooms, so she'll be settled when Zara arrives. Dent, I must speak with Zara, so you'll have to either dismiss today's complainants until the morrow, or else take down their grievances as best you can in my absence." She opened her eyes again, finally fixing them fully on Lucius and Deinol. "You two. I take it you are not responsible for this?"

Deinol ducked his head. "Well, I suppose I am somewhat at fault, but I didn't mean to—"

"I wasn't talking about the intricacies of your conscience," the marquise interrupted. "All I want to know is how the hell this happened."

Lucius came to the rescue, of course. "She took an arrow in the shoulder—we had it treated to the best of our ability, but it still became infected or . . . something. She said it couldn't be poison. It was one of your rentholders who shot her. A Ryker . . . Andrew, I think?"

The marquise stared down at Almasy in disbelief. "Andrew Ryker? That overgrown pudding? Andrew *Ryker* did this to her?" She looked back up at Lucius. "Is he alive?"

"No longer."

"Pity." Somehow, Deinol didn't think it was a pity for Andrew Ryker. She sighed. "All right, listen. It would be clear even to a simpleton that you only defied my exile because you were trying to do the best thing for me and for her, so I can't very well punish you for it. But the two of you have been nothing but a massive nuisance since the moment I laid eyes on you, and I can only imagine you'll continue to be a disaster wherever you may go in the future. Can I please, for the love of the gods, induce you to leave my country in peace, before you ruin any more of it?"

Deinol would have been only too happy to agree, but before he or Lucius could say anything, Bridger returned with an old woman in tow, and the marquise was distracted by their arrival. "There she is. Bridger, take Seren to her rooms. Bring Zara with you. I'll be along in a moment." After taking Seren from Lucius, Bridger and the old woman hurried out, leaving Lucius and Deinol temporarily alone with the marquise.

"I promise we will leave," Lucius said. "You'll never see us again. But please, if you would listen for just a few moments . . . you should know what she spoke of, the last time she spoke to anyone."

"Did it pertain to this conspiracy?" she asked, as coldly as ever.

"No," Lucius said. "It was a personal—"

"Then leave it be." She was already moving away from him.

But Lucius would not. "She wanted to see you."

"You have *said* that," Lady Margraine snapped. But she had stopped moving. She studied Lucius's face, and finally said, "If it was personal, then I hardly need to hear about it from you. Let her tell me herself, in her own way."

"You must know that isn't possible," Lucius insisted, with far more courage in meeting that icy glare than Deinol could have summoned. "She won't recover from that wound. Even if your healer is the best in the country, you can't possibly—"

"Should I ever wish to inquire about what is and is not possible for ordinary people, I shall be sure to consult you," Lady Margraine said. "In the meantime, if you will excuse me."

IT WAS HARDLY pleasant for the captain of the guard to realize no one had felt it necessary to inform him of an unfolding crisis. By the time Gravis arrived at Almasy's sickroom, Zara and the marquise were already within, and a crowd of guards and servants swarmed outside. Gravis set them to flight with one harsh look and several harsher words, then shut the door behind him and approached the bed.

After a single glance at Almasy, he didn't need Zara to tell him the situation was grave. It seemed the marquise did, though, because the two of them were still arguing.

"It is late to call in a healer now," Zara was saying. "Too late, one might say. Even three days ago, there might have been much I could have done. Now . . . this is not how I would have had it."

Lady Margraine ground her teeth. "While many things might be laid at Seren's feet, she can hardly be blamed for not injuring herself at a time that was convenient for you. Many people have done all they could to bring her to you as quickly as possible."

"You are not listening to me," Zara said. "The wound is infected, do you understand? And here, in the shoulder . . . it's too high up. We can't cut it off, and even if we did, or attempted to purge the wound . . . the severity of her fever should tell you how far the infection has spread."

"Are you telling me you're just going to do nothing?"

"There are all manner of things I *can* do, your ladyship. I can clean and bandage the wound again; I know some herbalist remedies that may bring down her fever. I am telling you not to expect much to result from it. If you would prefer me to be less honest, I can do that as well, but that won't change anything. At this point, she is closer to death than she is to life."

When had that girl ever been told that she could not have her way? Lord Caius had said the words to her many a time, but as often she had found a way to circumvent him, whether through persuasion, trickery, or direct disobedience. And Lord Caius had been dead for three long years. Without him, who had been there to gainsay her?

For a moment, Gravis thought he really did see the anguish and understanding cross her face—that there were some things all her will and all her stubbornness could not turn aside. But then it was gone, and she turned to Zara again. "Very well," she said. "If this is how it must be, then I will take care of this part myself." She paused, gathering her thoughts. "Wait out here. When I've finished, I'll call you back in or . . . no. That might not be possible. Simply wait. One hour. One hour, and then return and help her."

"Have you heard a single word I have said?" Zara snapped. "Another hour isn't going to make any difference in—"

"Zara, will you stop your godsforsaken blabbering and for *once* follow an order that is given to you, or else so help me—" She broke off, curling one hand into a fist, but then she took a deep breath and let it go. "You will give me *one hour*. You will not come in here, send anyone else in here, or speak a single word to bother me until that time, and at that time you will return to this room and do whatever you can for her, heedless of any other concerns. I know I cannot command you to succeed; I am only commanding you to try. I have given you all you have ever demanded to heal my people, all at my expense, and never questioned you. What was the point of all of that, of your duty and my generosity, if you're simply going to fail me in a matter of this importance because you cannot trust me?" She shoved Zara bodily toward the door, throwing it open and almost carrying her across the threshold, as Gravis hurried to follow them. "One hour. You will do as I have said, or pray the gods come to your aid." She took three strides back across the threshold, and then the door slammed shut behind her. He would have said she slammed it, and perhaps she had, but he hadn't seen her touch it at all.

They went down to the kitchens. For matters of less import, sundials and rudimentary timepieces would have sufficed. But the heavy Sahaian clockwork was in the kitchens, merrily ticking away. Every several years, the artisans of Sahai claimed, with great fanfare, that they'd developed a way to make their timekeeping even *more* accurate than previous versions, and eventually the marquise had decided she wanted one. But the great clock had not sat for three days in her study before she ordered it removed, saying the constant ticking made it impossible for her to work. So they'd shoved it into a corner of the kitchens and left it there. As for Gravis, he felt certain no one had ever needed to count time by the second until the Sahaians proved it was possible, but one had to earn one's coin how one could.

The cook and her attendant servants gave him and Zara odd looks, but did not prevent them from pulling chairs up to the clock and waiting. "Do you think she's mad?" Zara asked calmly, without even an attempt to lower her voice. Well, leave it to her to get to the heart of a matter.

"No," Gravis said. "If she's mad, then she's been mad since the day she was born. But she hasn't changed."

Zara pondered that for a while, as Gravis watched that slender metal arm make its tireless circles. "I think she has changed somewhat," she said. "But you're right. Fundamentally, she has always been the same. But I wonder . . ." She pursed her lips. "Whatever it truly was that attacked her in the great hall, she did seek to protect me from it. And her concern over Seren is without ulterior motive, as far as I can see. I wonder when it was that she started to care about people?"

"Always," someone said—Dent, of course, leaning against the wall and absently stroking his injured arm. "For as long as I've known her, which is as long as she's been alive. She just isn't *nice* about it." He smiled. "Sorry, should I have announced myself?"

"You've always been one to test the boundaries of your luck, Denton," Zara said. "I don't see why you should stop now."

"Well, I didn't want to test it so far as to disturb her up there. I suppose I have no choice but to wait with the rest of you."

"The waiting is well enough," Zara said. "I just fear what will happen when we're done with it."

"You may fear, healer," Dent said. "I'm going to hope."

Gravis, who alone of the three of them knew the marquise's secret, felt fear and hope in equal measure. She had told him already she could not heal, when he'd asked about her father. Had her powers grown since then? Or what if she sought to make use of some forbidden method, which caused more problems than it solved?

They waited out the rest of the hour in silence. They all tried to eat, but only Dent managed more than a couple bites. But when the hour was up, he ran as fast as Gravis and Zara to the door. Gravis made sure he was in the lead, since he was best prepared for whatever they might face. And then he threw the door open.

The results were rather anticlimactic. Almasy was right where they'd left her, lying in the same position on the bed. Lady Margraine was sprawled out upon the floor, as if she'd tripped and just decided to take a nap right where she had fallen.

Their reactions were predictable: Zara ran to Almasy, and Gravis and Dent ran to the marquise. It was easy to see that she would be fine: she breathed steadily and without difficulty, her skin warm but not overheated. It was one of her childhood fainting spells come again, and this time he knew the cause as well as the effect. He put an arm around her back, shifting her to a sitting position on the floor, and looked back up at Zara.

She was staring at Almasy's shoulder, gently testing the area around the wound with her fingertips. "This isn't possible," she said.

At this point, there was literally nothing that could have surprised Gravis, or that he would have doubted, but he prepared himself to feign shock anyway. "What is it?"

"I'm *sure* this wound was infected," Zara said. "It's . . . the cut is the same, yet it's like I'm looking at a completely different injury. My eyes haven't deteriorated *that* much." She glared at him. "Something tells me you expected this, Captain."

"Ah, no, I just . . . I don't know about wounds the way you do, and I didn't get much of a look at it—"

"Never mind that for the present," Zara said, arranging her implements on the bedside table with impressive speed. "If this is all I have to deal with, I can have this wound dressed in a twinkling. But I have to work. There will be time to question you later." She spared a glance at Lady Margraine's still form. "You should proba-bly move her, lest I trip over her while I'm working. Though I don't expect she'll be pleased at the thought that you carried her about while she was unconscious."

She certainly wouldn't be. "I'd ask you to do it," Gravis said to Dent, with a dry laugh, "but you can't possibly manage it with your arm still healing. But perhaps you'll accompany me, and speak in my defense."

Halfway up the steps to her room, Lady Margraine did start to stir. That was good news—it usually took her much longer to awaken—but Gravis braced himself just in case. She did look startled to see him suddenly so close to her, but she didn't lash out, thank the gods. "Did it work?" she asked him. "What did Zara say?"

"Zara says Almasy will be fine," Gravis said, mindful of Dent's presence beside him. "So I suppose 'it' worked, whatever 'it' was."

He felt her relax. "How strange. At first I really thought . . . that I wasn't going to be able to do anything. But it was such a simple solution. I just had to . . . change . . . my way of thinking about things."

Gravis looked up for a moment, to make sure Dent had fully opened the door to her room before he passed through it. When he looked down at her again, she was already asleep.

CHAPTER FIFTY-TWO

Esthrades

THE FIRE CRACKLED softly, like a whisper, yet it was the loudest sound Deinol could hear. The forest loomed up beside them like a single solid creature, but even though he had wanted to camp near it rather than inside it, Deinol still feared it less than he once had. Perhaps some of that had to do with the space they'd carved out around the fire by instinct, that had been Almasy's place for all these past days. And he had buried Seth in the forest, on a hill with a single tree. He was part of the forest now, too.

They still had little money—even less now than when they'd attempted that godsforsaken robbery in Stonespire. It still wasn't enough to get them back to Valyanrend, and Deinol still didn't know what they were going to do about it. But those concerns were distant now, because first he had to wait for what Lucius was going to say.

There it was: "I have to tell you something."

I know what it is, Deinol thought. But he said, "Tell me."

Lucius stared into the fire. "I . . . I don't think I can do this anymore, Deinol."

Deinol leaned back on his hands. "It was those guards at Stonespire, wasn't it? They reminded you of something. Something you'd been taught? Something from your old life?"

Lucius shook his head. "It was more than that. I remembered . . . myself. After I abandoned Aurnis, I thought everything I'd wanted before that had no more place in my life. I thought if I was a coward it didn't matter if I was rotten—I'd be useless either way. So I didn't care who I was, or the kind of life I led. But it had never occurred to me that I might bring myself into conflict with people who had succeeded where I had failed—who had made vows, and kept them. Who protected people." He ran a hand through his long hair, smiling a sheepish smile. "So that's why it's no good anymore. I remember too much . . . about the person I tried to be."

"And so you can't steal anymore," Deinol said. "I understand."

Lucius raised his eyebrows. "That's it? It doesn't feel to you as if I'm . . . abandoning you? Abandoning everyone?"

Deinol laughed. "What, are you suggesting stealing's all I'm good for? You were the one who first suggested to me that we go into business together, remember? It's not like banditry was my life's dream—it was a way to put coin in our pockets. There'll be others. And as for abandoning everyone . . . hell, Morgan'll probably be relieved. Roger'll mock you to his dying breath, but I'm sure you can live with that."

"From Roger? I'll survive." A slight smile tugged at his lips for a moment, but then it faded again. "But what do you expect that we'll do?"

Deinol picked up his hands, holding them before the flames and examining the patterns the crushed grass had made on his palms. "I know you don't like to talk about your old life, but since it still obviously has such a hold on you, it would help me if you could answer at least one question. What did you *want* to do, back then?"

He could tell that Lucius's hesitation had nothing to do with being uncertain of his answer, only of whether he should speak it aloud. But it didn't last long. "I wanted to be a *kaishinrian*. I wanted to prove I was worthy of it—the highest honor for a warrior."

Deinol looked up in surprise, and had to catch himself before singeing his fingertips. "That was one of your lot's royal guards, wasn't it? So you would have served the . . . it was a queen you had, wasn't it? Before Elgar?"

"It was, but it wasn't her I wanted to serve. It was her son. Ryo. We were about the same age, and I . . ." He winced. "Gods, you're going to laugh at me."

Deinol grinned. "Can't promise otherwise. But you've been privy to all of my greatest foolishness, so it's only fair."

Lucius mumbled a few inaudible syllables before finally pulling himself together. "I . . . admired him. You can't compare him to someone like Elgar—I don't know if I can explain how different they were. Ryo was so brave—too brave for his own good, more often than not. And he cared about his people—about getting things right. The way Ryo treated his *kaishinrian,* they weren't just there to die for him, or to be ordered around. They were his friends—his greatest friends, who had sworn to uphold his honor and one another's. I wanted to be part of that."

"Oh," Deinol said. "Well, you see, I didn't think that was funny at all."

Lucius smiled sadly. "Thank you for saying that."

"But didn't you say they all died?"

"Ryo and his *kaishinrian*? Of course. He would never have surrendered, and they would never have let themselves outlive him." Lucius took a deep, trembling breath. "Taro Renne, Haken Gain, Gao Shrike, Rana Korinu, and Kaitan Enrei. Those were their names. Names everyone in Kaiferi knew—everyone in Aurnis, perhaps. Names I can only wish would never be forgotten."

Something nagged at his memory: a drunken evening and an overheard conversation, the man in the eyepatch who'd jostled him by accident. "You know, I think I met a fellow named Kaitan back in Stonespire."

"I wouldn't be surprised. It's a common enough name—I knew two or three of them when I lived in Kaiferi."

No, something still didn't seem right. Deinol put a hand to his forehead. "No, wait, it wasn't Kaitan. It was something like it. Kai-something." He tried to think back to that night. It had been the name of the shorter man, the one with the intense stare . . .

He snapped his fingers. "Kaihen! That was it. I'm sure of it."

He'd expected to be laughed at, for fussing over such a trivial detail. But Lucius's face changed as he'd never seen it before: beyond surprised, beyond aghast. "What?" he asked, in a choked whisper. "What did you say?"

Deinol searched his memories a second time, wondering if he could still have been mistaken. But no, he was certain of it now. "It was a fellow named Kaihen. At least, that was what his companions called him. Another man and a woman, all Aurnian, all with swords like yours. Does that mean something to you?"

Lucius wasn't even looking at him anymore; he fisted both hands in his hair and pulled, as if trying to yank it out. "How could that . . . how could it *be*? I *saw* him die!"

"Lucius, you have to talk to me." Truly frightened now, he put a hand on Lucius's arm, trying to steady him. "Who is this Kaihen fellow? Can you know so much just from a name?"

"It's not a name." Lucius was bent over, hunched in on himself as if he was in pain. "It's a title. *Kaihen* means . . . the *kai* part means 'royal,' or else it's used for something that belongs to the king or queen. Like *kaishinrian,* the royal swordsmen, or even Kaiferi, 'seat of the ruler.' So *kaihen* is 'royal one.' But no one should be called that anymore, because . . ."

Again Deinol struggled to picture that night. Could that man really have been the Aurnian prince? Could he possibly have survived?

But if Lucius believed that, he should have been overjoyed. Instead he looked worse than Deinol could ever remember seeing him. He'd shown less horror and anguish upon learning Seth was dead than upon learning this prince of his might be alive. And though Deinol hated to be suspicious of Lucius above all others, he couldn't help feeling that something wasn't right. "Lucius, what—"

But Lucius abruptly got to his feet, pacing around the fire. "Deinol, listen to me. If there's even a chance Ryo could still be alive . . . then I have no choice. I have to find him. I have to finish this."

"You have to finish what?"

"I have to . . ." His jaw clenched, cutting off his words. He ran a trembling hand through his hair. "You wouldn't understand. And even if you could, I can't explain. He was my prince. I just . . . I have to make things right. For the person I was, and for the person I wanted to be. But *you* don't have to do any of that. In fact, I think it would be better if you didn't."

"If I didn't go with you? Have you lost your wits? There's not a single damned chance I won't go with you." He grinned, trying to lighten the air between them. "Besides, I'm the one who knows where they were going."

"You do?" For a moment he thought Lucius was going to grab him by the collar and shake him. "Where is it?"

"Well, I can't say for sure they didn't change their plans, but I heard them talk about going to Araveil. There's some kind of movement stirring there, some unrest against Elgar that they wanted to inflame into something more." He shrugged. "And I can't help noticing that, while we don't have enough coin to get to Valyanrend, Araveil is much closer. And once we're in a big city it'll be easier to find ways to earn more. That don't involve stealing," he added. "I promise."

Lucius looked so pained, torn in two different directions. "Deinol, if you come with me . . . it's probably inevitable that you'll learn things. Things about me. Things that you're going to wish you didn't know."

"Probably," Deinol said. "If it were any simpler or easier than that, I doubt you'd be so upset. But even if I were willing to be completely selfish, what would you say my chances are of getting back to Valyanrend on my own? Realistically speaking."

The answer was written on Lucius's face before he ever said a word. "Too low. And I can't spend the time it would take to go with you." He covered his face, fingertips pressing against his closed eyelids. "Gods, perhaps it just has to be this way. I'm not going to run from it. I've done too much running already." He opened his eyes, tried to settle his face in his accustomed manner. It almost worked.

"So we're going to Araveil?" Deinol asked.

"We are."

"Then there's something we have to do first, Lucius." He looked again at the empty space around the fire. "It's clear you think this errand of yours will be dangerous. One or both of us might not ever make it back to Valyanrend, and even if we do, who knows how long we'll be away? We can't let Morgan and the others wait that long for the truth. I can't bear that they might never know, and Morgan be left wondering if Seth's alive somewhere she can't get to him, or dead in a ditch, or in some prison again. So we have to set that right, first. I know our coin is sparse, but we have to get a message to them. We have to let them know."

Lucius nodded firmly. "We'll do it, no matter how much coin it takes," he said. "We'll tell them everything."

CHAPTER FIFTY-THREE

Issamira

BRADDOCK WOKE UP first. Morgan struggled to follow him only reluctantly, the lack of his presence beside her the first indication that something was wrong. As she began to identify sounds, those indications multiplied: his hurried movements, and beyond that, beyond the walls of their shared tent, something more. Shouting.

Her eyes snapped open. Braddock had just jammed his second boot on, and was reaching for his ax instead of his shirt. That was bad. "What's happened?" Morgan asked.

"Can't say for sure. Some sort of attack. They're fighting out there." He hefted the ax. "You'll be safer hiding here than if you run. I'll keep them away until it's over. Be careful." With that, he was gone, running out of the tent and into the fight.

Morgan wasn't foolish enough to disregard him, but she stayed near the entrance of the tent, trying to get as much of a view as she could. They weren't being overrun, at least; given their apparent numbers, the attackers had probably hoped to rely on surprise to give them the upper hand, and that had already faded. Without it, they seemed to be losing ground. Lord Vespas's men were more disciplined, slowly closing in around the shrinking remainder of their enemy. She looked for Lord Vespas himself, but she didn't have to look long.

In peaceful conversation, Lord Vespas appeared capable, but languid, perhaps even a bit foppish. Morgan had guessed from their first meeting that this attitude was, to some extent, a pose. But it was one thing to know that was true, and another to see him with sword in hand; she could not completely dismiss the feeling that he was a different person. He stood at the center of a whirlwind of action and violence, but none of it touched him. He moved from one position of stillness to another, and every time he moved, someone died.

By that point, most of the attackers had been caught in the tightening semi-circle of Vespas's men, but a few slipped past, heading for the tents. Perhaps they sought to search them for hostages, but before they could get far, Braddock came charging after them. The wide swing of his ax cut one down, but in his hurry to block their path to the tents, he blundered too close to the remaining men. Before Morgan could so much as draw in a breath to shout, one of them was already lunging—but instead of going straight forward, he was shoved to the side by the force of an oncoming blow, sword tearing through his abdomen.

Somehow, Lord Vespas managed to remove his sword from the man's body with a motion that flung the new-made corpse cleanly to the ground. He did not pause for a moment, but immediately struck again, cutting down the last man before he even had time to face him. A quick glance around the area told him there were no foes left, and only then did he spare any time for Morgan and Braddock.

"Are you all right?" He was completely composed.

"Fine," Braddock said. "I appreciate the assistance. Morgan?"

"I'm unharmed. Did we . . . are there any of them left alive?"

"I'm afraid not," Lord Vespas said. "I'm surprised none of them attempted to surrender."

Braddock cast a grim look over the field. "I don't need to ask whose men these were, do I?"

"You don't?" Morgan examined the bodies. A few were clad in faded red and green, but there was nothing more distinctive about them than that.

Braddock answered her, but he was looking at Lord Vespas. "The noble that scout served—and he *was* a scout. These are hers, aren't they?"

A couple of Lord Vespas's retainers flinched at the audacity of that, but his lordship himself remained still. "You must think me a very foolish host."

"I don't. If you trusted too easily, Morgan and I wouldn't even be here. But I wouldn't want to be you right now, either. Even I know this is going to get complicated."

"Indeed. Dahren Selreshe is one of the foremost lords of Issamira. His wife, Amali, is a hero of the same war in which I distinguished myself—she fought at my side, and I at hers, more times than I can count. For even the queen's uncle to accuse such an important pair is no small thing."

"And that's why you trusted her men," Braddock said. "I can't truly find fault with you for that. Someone who's risked death together with you . . . it's hard to break that bond, even if you want to."

"I have yet to think it broken," Lord Vespas insisted. "These soldiers committed treason, but it need not be Amali's hand behind it. It is her husband who truly commands the forces under the Selreshe name; I would not have thought him capable of this, either, but if one of them *must* be a traitor, I would place him above her a hundred times over."

"What does that mean you're going to do?" Braddock asked. "Surely this has gotten too big to ignore?"

"Too big by half. I don't see how I have any choice but to go to their seat and demand an explanation. If none is forthcoming, I shall have to take them captive and bring them before my niece."

"Do you have enough men to accomplish such a thing?"

"Well, that depends. I certainly don't have enough men to besiege a castle, so if they deny me entry—which would surely be an admission of guilt—I will have to ask Adora to take a queen's actions against them. But I expect they'll let me in to parley, and then I won't have to involve her." He gave them a tight smile. "I know what you're going to say: you agreed to come with me to Shallowsend, not to risk your lives confronting a potential traitor. I won't drag you along. You can go ahead with a few of my men, and stay at Shallowsend at my expense until my business with the Selreshes is concluded."

Morgan's thoughts had been racing far ahead ever since Braddock had identified the attackers' origin; now, seeing him start to relax, she hurried to speak before he could. "My lord, I understand your offer is kindly meant, but we don't wish to be at your retainers' mercy indefinitely. Who knows how long this could take you, or whether you will even return from it? I do not trust others to judge us in your stead."

"But you do trust me to judge you?" He laughed. "You don't have to answer that. Since this situation is partly due to my incompetence, I won't make you suffer for it. My men will be given strict orders: if I do not return to Shallowsend within a fortnight of your arrival there, you will be released without any further inquiry. Will that satisfy?"

In a way, it did; Morgan doubted Vespas's servants were willing to disobey him by detaining her and Braddock longer than he'd commanded, or by treating them any less gently than he had. Even if they had to wait a full fortnight at Shallowsend, it might have taken just as long or longer to accompany him to the Selreshes' seat and back again. But even so, she found herself more than reluctant to let things end like this.

"My lord," she said, "would it be out of the question for the two of us to remain with you?"

Lord Vespas wasn't the only one to look at her with surprise, but Braddock made no objection in words. "I suppose it's possible, but why would you want to? You'll be much safer at Shallowsend."

"Perhaps," Morgan said, "but I'm uncomfortable with being left in the hands of your retainers, even if they are beholden to you. And surely you need as many soldiers as possible at your side? If you trust us enough to let us go home, surely you can trust us not to interfere as you complete this mission."

Lord Vespas cupped his chin in his hand. He must have known Morgan wasn't being entirely truthful about her reasons, but she could allow him that much. "I find it curious that this is what you want, Miss Imrick; it seems to help me at your own expense. But you can judge what is in your interests better than I can. I suppose you're both agreed on this?"

Morgan wouldn't have supposed that at all, but Braddock gave a stiff nod. Lord Vespas smiled. "How well you two communicate. I know more than one staid marriage whose members would deeply envy you."

Braddock held his tongue until they were back inside their tent. She wouldn't have blamed him for being angry with her, but all he said was, "Morgan, are you sure?"

"I can't truly say so," she admitted. "But you said it yourself: he trusts this woman too much. It's put him in danger once already. What do you think's going to happen once he gets to her seat?"

"Very possibly nothing good," Braddock said, "but even so, would that be any concern of ours?"

"I don't know," Morgan said. "But I don't . . . want him to die. Do you?"

"I suppose not. So long as he doesn't throw us into his dungeons the second we get to Shallowsend, that is."

"He won't do that," Morgan said; she was certain of it now. "If he were still suspicious of us at all, he'd never have allowed us to accompany him on a mission this delicate."

Braddock scoffed. "If he's no longer suspicious of us, why not just let us go?"

Morgan's instincts kept telling her the same strange thing: it wasn't that Lord Vespas was *no longer* suspicious of them, it was that he never had been. But weren't his suspicions what had gotten them into this in the first place? "If you think it's too dangerous, by all means let's just go to Shallowsend. It's not that I'm willing to die for him."

Braddock shook his head. "Did you see him fight? So long as he doesn't let his sympathies get in the way, I almost feel sorry for the Selreshes. And somehow I think he wouldn't, at a crucial moment. There's still a coldness in him. The war-time practicality of a former general, perhaps."

Morgan couldn't deny that; she had glimpsed it long before tonight. "So we'll go?"

"We'll go. After all the trouble these damned nobles have put us through, I'd like to hear their explanation myself."

CHAPTER FIFTY-FOUR

Stonespire

SEREN WAS MOVING even before she had fully awoken, but both her movement and her drowsiness were cut short by a stabbing pain in her shoulder. Waves of dizziness and fatigue overpowered her, forcing her to sink back down on the . . . pillows? She struggled to view her surroundings. Why were there pillows here?

Then she realized she knew where she was: this was Stonespire Hall. More than that, this was the room that had been hers, before Arianrod had expelled her. What on earth was she doing here?

She would've thought she was dreaming, that her wishes had taken control of her feverish mind. But her mind felt clear, and the pain in her shoulder was no hallucination, no more than the feel of the bedsheets against her skin. They had been pulled up to her chin, and Seren peeled them back with the hand that wasn't attached to her wounded shoulder. She was shirtless underneath, and it wasn't hard to see why: a mass of bandages dressed the wound, clean and neat, but unyielding in restricting her movements.

That wound should have been the death of her; she'd been certain of it. Could Zara or anyone else have found some way to scour it of infection? And if they had, did that mean Arianrod had ordered them to?

Though sitting up properly was a lost cause, she wriggled a bit until she could shift her position, propping up her back a bit more. She adjusted the bedsheets, too; if she wasn't strong enough to get up, and she wasn't, the least she could do was try to enjoy the rest that was her only real option.

She was just closing her eyes when she heard the door latch shift, and then the door creaked open. She kept her eyes closed, feeling more than hearing a presence come nearer to her side. And then familiar fingers tilted her chin just slightly, and Arianrod asked, "Seren?"

Seren opened her eyes. Perhaps, in that first moment, there was something like relief in Arianrod's face. But then again, perhaps Seren had only wanted to see it there.

She took Arianrod's hand, pressed the knuckles against her cheek. "My lady," she said, and was pleased to hear that her voice had scarcely a tremor in it, despite how long it must have gone unused.

Arianrod hesitated—if it had been anyone else, Seren would have thought they were at a loss. But then she frowned, and pulled her hand free, smoothing it absently along her side until it disappeared in the folds of her dress.

"I had not thought," she said slowly, "that such foolishness was possible from you. But it seems I have vastly overestimated your competence."

Seren tried to sit up. "If you'd let me explain—"

"*Don't* do that." Arianrod pressed a hand against Seren's forehead, keeping her down without aggravating her shoulder. "I understand more than you think. Your friends did quite a lot of talking when they brought you here. And don't worry, they're unharmed—I dismissed them, but I'm sure you can find them again with little trouble."

"I have no desire to find them," Seren said. "I don't care if I never see them again. What I want is—"

"Your life was mine," Arianrod said, as if Seren had not spoken. "That was what it gave you such pleasure to swear, over and over until I was sick of hearing it. I never demanded such a thing. I never *wanted* such a thing of you, or thought it possible that you could truly offer it. But you would go on about your debt and your obligation, for reasons I won't claim to understand. Perhaps you merely wanted to disguise that you only stayed with me because it suited you." The fingers of one hand clenched into a fist. "But even so, Seren, you forgot yourself. You played your own game too fully. Now I find that, denied my presence even for a handful of days, you have attempted to squander your life at the first opportunity, like a child refusing to eat out of temper. And you have left it to me to repair your mistakes, though I thought I made it clear I wanted nothing more to do with you."

Seren tried to gather her wits, to find the proper words to explain. "It was never my intention to make you do anything on my behalf. I didn't think you *could* do anything, not with my wound in such a state. All I wanted was to make sure the information about the conspirators reached you. And . . . to see you one last time, if I could. That part was selfish, I admit, but I didn't think you would begrudge—"

"Gods, I cannot believe what I am hearing," Arianrod said. "I thought you wanted to be stronger than anyone. Have you forgotten that already? It was such a near thing—if I had not happened to hit upon a spell that would do it—"

"A spell?" Seren repeated.

"Of course. Surely you must have guessed you were beyond all other help."

"Then . . . you really are the one who saved me." She forced herself to look up, at Arianrod's face. "Why would you do that?"

Arianrod stared at her in utter blankness. "What do you mean, why? Who else could have helped you, if I didn't?"

"Why did anyone need to help me?" Seren asked. "It's like you said: you'd washed your hands of me."

Arianrod was still giving her that look, not angry or disappointed, just entirely at a loss. And that had to be genuine: Arianrod would never pretend she didn't understand something. "Seren, I have absolutely no idea what you are trying to say. Someone had to help you because you were *dying*. Did you expect me to just drop you on the steps of Stonespire while I went about my day, knowing full well I could have saved you? What would be the point of such a waste?"

Seren's voice caught in her throat; some absurd, childish part of her wanted to weep. Once again, she had been rendered helpless, and once again Arianrod had saved her. And still there was nothing of equal value she could give Arianrod in return.

Arianrod took a deep breath, pressing her hand against the side of her face. "Seren, I . . . I have to admit I don't know what to do with you. I could try to dismiss you once more, but I suspect you would endanger yourself again as close to immediately as you could manage. If I keep you here instead, no doubt you will glut me on more useless protestations, pleading for my trust while denying me your own. Should I keep you shut up in this room forever, so you can neither embarrass me nor do yourself any further harm? That would be almost as great a waste as leaving you to die." She made as if to brush the hair out of her face, but then just let her hand fall. "If you have any more fruitful suggestions, by all means offer them. But it's clear that coming to see you was a mistake, so for the moment I shall leave you to your rest." She turned away, heading for the doorway without another word more.

"No," Seren said, stretching her good hand weakly toward her. "Please— please don't go. I'm not good at—talking, you know that, but please, just listen to what I have to say."

As nervous as she was, she never doubted what Arianrod would do. They called her cold, and proud—arrogant and heartless and unreasonable. They called her all those things, and pleased themselves to do it. But all the same, Seren knew what Arianrod would do—could imagine her, in the moments before it actually happened, turning from the door, seating herself primly, crossing one leg over the other. "All right," she said, with hardly even a sigh. "I'm listening."

That meant, of course, that Seren had to talk. *Come on,* she thought, *there's no sense in being cautious now. What are you afraid of ruining that you haven't ruined already?* "I don't think you understood me," she said. "When you dismissed me. You acted as if I had betrayed you. But I never would have done that. Why did you think I had?"

"Why?" Arianrod snapped. "How many times did I tell you I needed to be able to rely on you? And yet, without any explanation, you resisted my authority and attempted to refute my judgment, for the sake of a couple of criminals whose relation to you you would not disclose. In front of everyone in the godsdamned hall, no less! If I simply let such a thing pass with no consequence, how much faith would my people have in me *or* those I employ?" She scuffed one foot against the carpet. "And even before that night . . . it isn't as if I expect my retainers to have no secrets at all, but you would refuse to answer even the most basic questions, or else say things that could only be blatant lies—like that those men were nothing to you. If you were willing to sacrifice so much for them, why make such a fuss when I sentenced you to their company?"

"No," Seren said, "I didn't—they weren't—" Her shoulder throbbed, and she broke off, clutching it with her free hand. The words were all jumbled up inside her head, but Arianrod was the brightest person she had ever known. If anyone could make sense of all this, it would be her. "I didn't care about helping those men for their own sake. That much really is true. But they had a close companion—a young boy. He died, outside Saltmoor, that day Kern's ruse called me away. I was caught and outnumbered, and—he died trying to help me." She struggled to catch her breath. "That boy cared for those men so deeply . . . and they for him. And I felt I just *had* to do whatever I could to save them, for his sake. I surprised even myself, but . . . I just couldn't forget him."

In the space where she had been prepared to hear any number of reasonable rebukes—that she had been too sentimental, that she had been ridiculous, that she had accomplished nothing, that Seth was dead and could no longer be harmed by anything that might have happened to his friends—there was only silence. And then, finally, the last one: "Why did you not tell me this before?"

"At the time, because I thought that it had no place there. That it would be irrelevant to you, and certainly irrelevant to the law. You can't logically argue that someone should be spared because they possess noble friends. As to why I didn't tell you before all that . . . I should have. I should have told you many things that I didn't, but it was never because I didn't trust you. If anything, I didn't want to presume that you cared to know things about me that had nothing to do with you. But I need you to understand . . . though I felt I had to intercede for those men, I would never have put their safety and happiness, or anyone's, above your own. If you don't believe anything else I've said, or any promise I've ever made to you, please at least believe that I would never harm you, or allow you to come to harm if I could prevent it. I would do anything before that."

"I don't understand why," Arianrod said. "If this boy died for you and I didn't, don't you owe him more than you could ever owe me?"

"It's just as you thought, my lady. It's just as you always said." Again, she almost felt as if she could weep, but she closed her eyes, willing her face to stillness. "It pleased me to believe a debt between us existed. You guessed that much, but not the reason. So long as that debt remained—so long as it was more than I could ever repay—I had an excuse to remain at your side."

It had been something so tenuous at first; she had grown dissatisfied with her life in Sahai, all strength and no purpose, and had grasped at a scrap of unfinished business with a girl who had laughed at her more than ten years before. She had thought it would be so easy to walk away if she found nothing of value, and had never planned what she would do if she found too much.

Arianrod was quiet for a long time, hiding her mouth against her fist. "If you wish to remain here," she finally said, "then do so, for that reason alone. I would have preferred that from the beginning. If you wish to continue to *serve,* and are truly resolved not to hide things from me any longer . . . I will grant you that opportunity. Though once you're well enough to walk about, you may have to do a little public groveling—I can't let my people think I'm too forgiving, you know."

"Thank you," Seren said. "For . . . so much more than I can say. I'll do whatever I need to do, prostrations or otherwise."

Arianrod sighed. "Whatever you found here . . . I hope it's worth as much as you think."

"It's because you're here," Seren said.

"That's what I meant." She got to her feet. Seren thought she would just leave, but she lingered in the doorway. "Seren, I don't want there to be any misunderstandings between us. When you asked me, some time ago, about what happened when we were young—about whether I would have refused to help you, knowing what my father would do to me for it—I ought to have just given you a simple reply. It's true that I think such questions are pointless, when the past is unchangeable and so much has happened since. But more than that, I was angry. I was angry that you asked me that question—that you had ever once doubted the answer. I was angry that you thought me so weak, that I would give up anything just for the chance to spare myself a little pain. But now I understand; that wasn't it at all. That wasn't why you asked, or what you wanted to know."

She paused, tension drawing her features tight. "I cannot say the scars are nothing to me. I wish so much that I could. I wish I could either rid myself of them forever, or else that I could strengthen myself so that I no longer care about them. Even after so long, I have been able to do neither—a great embarrassment, and one that gnaws at me. But, Seren, no matter how much I may hate them, the truth is they're just . . . marks in flesh. They're not more important than your life."

There was so much Seren wanted to say, and not a single word in her head with which to say it. For some moments they just stared at each other helplessly, on either side of a gap that still wouldn't close.

In the end, Arianrod huffed out an impatient breath. "Look," she said, "I'm . . . sorry. I'm sorry that . . . all this happened to you."

"I'm not sorry," Seren said. Her throat felt rough, and she wasn't sure how her voice sounded, but she tried her best to make it clear. She wanted Arianrod to know how firmly she meant it.

Arianrod pressed her lips together, tossed her hair back from her face, and left.

CHAPTER FIFTY-FIVE

Valyanrend

SPEAKER'S SQUARE WAS so named for the purpose it had served in the days of Elesthene. From the perch above the square, the chief orator chosen by the Ninist hierarchy, the only one they called Speaker, used to address the people of the city. Roger doubted he'd have had any interest in the speeches of those days, all about how to live according to the will of the Ninists' Lord of Heaven, or this or that passage from the *Niniad*. Hell, he doubted he'd like anything he had to hear today much better, but here he was anyway. It was seldom that Elgar took to Speaker's Square to address his subjects in person, rather than simply disseminating his news through heralds and messengers. Whatever the topic, today's message must be truly important to him.

Marceline was fussing around him, ducking this way and that way, trying to peer over the heads of the crowd. He couldn't really blame her; he could see many full-grown adults more anxious than she was. If he remembered correctly, the last time Elgar had done this had been more than three and a half years ago, when he first announced the war against Lanvaldis. But this time Elgar had declared war on Reglay without feeling the need to tell his people with his own voice. Surely it couldn't be *another* war, with the first not even officially concluded?

"What do you think?" Marceline asked. "Is it because there's very good news, or very bad news?"

"I don't think it's a matter of the severity of the message, in either direction," Roger said. "I'd guess Elgar wants to communicate how serious he is about whatever he's going to say. And he wants to witness the way people react to it." A ripple of excitement passed through the crowd, and he looked up to the balcony of Speaker's Square. "Ah, here we are. It'll be a show of some sort, though I can't promise you'll like it."

He had seen Elgar twice or thrice—always from a distance, but it was enough that he was no longer surprised by what the man looked like. Lord Protector Norverian, who had come before him, had been impressively tall and boyishly handsome—he never would've risen so far under Gerde Selte if he hadn't been—but Roger wasn't naïve enough to judge a man by the skin he wore. Norverian had been an idiot, only able to attain his place after the grand duchess's death because there was no one else alive and willing. But Elgar, whatever he looked like, had much more underneath.

He'd been expecting Marceline to show some sort of derisiveness—*can't believe he's what all the fuss is about, can you?*—to prove to him she wasn't intimidated. But he never could have predicted the shock that crossed her face, as if she were looking at a man with three heads. "*That's* Elgar?"

"What, you never saw him before?" Now that he thought about it, he supposed she'd had no reason to. She would've been twelve the last time Elgar did this, and even if she'd been precocious enough to care about such things back then, he doubted Tom would have let her go.

Marceline brushed her hand against her hip, as if searching for something to hold onto. "Then that must mean . . ." But before she could say more, Elgar started speaking.

His voice was not deep or booming, but he could make it carry when he wished. "My people," he began, "I am only here to address you at all because of the courage our soldiers have shown in the Reglian campaign. According to the last message I have received from the front, only Mist's Edge still remains under siege, and its fall is inevitable. Indeed, I would have wished for nothing more than to celebrate that victory alongside my soldiers. But I cannot. I left for Reglay with them because I believed it was my duty to place myself where the danger was greatest. I tell you now that I have returned to Valyanrend for the very same reason."

"Put himself where the danger is greatest my ass," Roger muttered under his breath. But Marceline didn't look scornful; she was watching Elgar with huge, staring eyes.

"There is a threat," Elgar continued, "not only upon my life, but upon the safety and peace of this city. It grieves me to sow the seeds of suspicion—perhaps to turn brother against brother—but I can keep the secret from the populace no longer. There is a rebellion brewing in Valyanrend. Their bloody attacks on my guardsmen have grown bolder and bolder, and I have no way of knowing if or when they will start murdering civilians as well. But I am convinced, now, that they will not stop until they are destroyed."

He let that settle for a few moments: both the fear of whatever this rebellion might be, and the fear of what Elgar himself might do to suppress it. Then he spoke again, a slight smile upon his lips. "But it would be irresponsible and unkind of me to deliver only bad tidings. Here are the good: we believe we have discovered the larger aims behind this rebellion, and with it, the key to their future plans. So rather than bid you live in fear without recourse, I ask only that you remain strong for just a little longer. Soon, I promise you, you shall see these conspirators dragged into the light. Traitors will be punished, and tranquility restored to this city. Soon. Await it, but keep your wits and your good hearts about you."

That was all. He extended a hand—whether in some form of benediction, or simply in farewell, Roger did not know—and left the balcony. There were murmurs all around him—some anxious, some angry, some as unimpressed as Roger himself. What was the point of such a speech? Why give your enemy notice that you were onto him? If he'd asked the people to help him catch the rebels, that would be one thing, but to watch *him* catch them? *Do it or don't do it, but there's no need to talk about it.*

Roger rolled his eyes. "Gods, I can't believe I dragged myself out here just to listen to that drivel. *I'll destroy the lot of them, blah blah blah* . . . If we wanted to hear that, we could just . . . monkey?"

He looked around him in bewilderment, but Marceline had already disappeared.

THEY HADN'T BEEN debating the speech for five minutes before it devolved into shouting, though with Rask around that was never a surprise. What unnerved Naishe more was how difficult even she found it to remain calm. A sense of foreboding wrapped itself around her, and she couldn't tell whether that itself had been Elgar's aim, or whether what she felt was a warning of his true end.

Mouse alone stayed cheerful. "Now, now, Rask, there aren't any spies. No one's feeding Elgar anything. I expect that was one of the reasons he said what he did—to make us doubt our own when we're at the height of our strength."

"He said he knew all about our aims—our future plans! How else could that be possible?"

"Putting it like that only makes me more doubtful that it's true," Wren said. Thank the gods he was speaking up today. "*We* hardly know our future plans."

"No," Rask said—quietly, but with no less of his usual heat. "We can talk around it all we like, but we all know what we want to target next."

The rest of them were silent. So Naishe said it, because someone had to. "The warehouse in Silkspoint."

"The bloody warehouse!" Rask snapped. "That must be what he meant!"

"How could it be?" Naishe felt she had to say. "I'm the one who found that information, and I wasn't caught at it. How could they know for certain that we even know about the warehouse?"

"I did already mention the spies," Rask muttered.

"No, Mouse is right about that. If he'd infiltrated our ranks already, there'd be no need to announce anything; he'd know where we gather, and he could storm in, arrest and kill us at his leisure. This is a subtler game. We need to figure out what he expects us to do, and what he wants us to do. I'm not sure if those two things are the same."

Mouse shook his head. "We can't allow *him* to determine what we do."

"Of course we can," Naishe said. "It would be foolish *not* to."

Rask groaned. "I hate to say it, but . . . she is right about that, Mouse."

"All right, I take your point," Mouse said. "In that case, what do you make of the boldness of his predictions? He said we'd be destroyed, and soon. Two very confident words."

"It's a taunt," Rask said. "It has to be. The only other possibility is that it's a bluff, and a man with that much power doesn't *need* to bluff. If he wants to have enough men to stamp us out, they're already there at his fingertips."

"But he doesn't know where to point them," Mouse said.

Naishe held up a hand. "No, wait. A taunt . . . perhaps that's right."

"You two are agreeing again? Are you sure you're both feeling all right?"

Before either Naishe or Rask could answer, the door banged open, and everyone leaped to their feet. Even Naishe, who was certain any talk of spies was nonsense, felt her heart jump into her throat as she turned to face the doorway. And there, red-faced and out of breath, was the girl who called herself the monkey. She had a hand pressed to her chest, but it didn't dampen her imperious expression any. "I have to tell you something."

Rask had been on the point of drawing his sword. He sheathed it in disgust, threw up his hands, and gave Mouse an accusatory glare. "Do you see what a mistake this was?"

Mouse ignored him. "What is it, monkey?"

She was still breathing hard, but she couldn't have run here all the way from the speech, or she'd have gotten here before them. Had she gone someplace else first? "I saw him. Elgar. I didn't know it was him, but I was down by that warehouse in Silkspoint, and he was there. I spoke to him. Or he spoke to me, I suppose."

"Are you bloody joking? You *went* to the warehouse?" Rask looked about ready to shake the girl until her teeth rattled, and Naishe adjusted her position so she stood between them.

But the monkey looked as intimidated as she did repentant. "Oh, piss off. He couldn't even connect me to Sheath, let alone to you lot. But he told me I didn't want to go near that warehouse in the coming weeks, because there'd be more guards there, and I might get hurt by accident. So after I saw him at the speech, and realized it was him, I ran back down there to check. But there *aren't* more guards there. I didn't see a single one."

The rest of them were silent, pondering this news. Naishe wasn't troubled by the monkey's excursions, but she *was* troubled by the discrepancy between what Elgar had said and what seemed to be happening. Elgar might not have told some common girl the truth of his plans, but if he wanted to scare her away from the place, he must have had his reasons.

Rask, of course, couldn't resist a final barb. "And did you at least leave him alone, or did you try to work your little tricks on even him?"

She rolled her eyes. "I didn't *try,* I *did.* He'd already let me think he was rich, so it's his own fault, really. But I'm pretty sure the trinket I nabbed is worthless; I can't even say why he was carrying it." She reached into her pocket, and pulled out a little white stone.

Rask snatched it immediately, though she didn't resist. "He was carrying this? What the hell is it?"

"That's what I was hoping you lot could tell me. I thought it might be an arrowhead or something, but if it isn't, I don't know what else it could be."

All eyes turned reflexively to Wren, who was too intent on the little stone to duck his head the way he usually would. "May I?" he asked Rask, who grudgingly handed the stone over.

Wren held it close to his face, turned it over and over in his hands, rubbed it between his thumb and forefinger. "I doubt it," he said at last. "It's about the right size, and its bluntness doesn't really mean anything—it could be old, and worn away by time. But the stone's too soft—see how it's sort of chalky, the way it rubs off on my fingers? And there aren't any marks that would indicate tools were used to shape it. Still, my father's been in the business much longer than I have; if you all like, I can bring this home with me tonight and show it to him."

Mouse looked at the monkey. "If you won't accuse us of stealing it from you?"

She shrugged. "I stole it to begin with, and it doesn't look like it's valuable. He can borrow it if you like."

"All right," Rask said, as Wren pocketed the stone. "*Thank you,* monkey, for your impulsive, foolhardy, but ultimately useful efforts on our behalf. Now can we get you to show yourself out so we can have a proper discussion?"

"No," the monkey said. Her breathing had evened out by now, but she was still pink in the face. "I came to warn you. I came to *tell* you. Don't go to the warehouse in Silkspoint. That's just what he wants you to do."

She was but a child, and she almost certainly had no evidence for such a confident claim. Yet Naishe felt a chill, as if the words were the echo of something she herself believed. Did she?

"Monkey, you told us yourself that security in Silkspoint is supposed to increase, but that it hasn't yet," Mouse said gently. "If that's true, our best window of opportunity to search the warehouse is now—or as soon as possible."

"*No,*" she said. "Whatever security he wants, he's already put it in place. He wouldn't have made that speech if he wasn't already prepared."

"What makes you so sure of that?"

She balled her hands into frustrated fists. "I just *am*! If you'd seen him by the warehouse that day, you'd think the same thing! When he thought I was just some ordinary girl, he warned me to avoid even the street outside the warehouse, at all times. Something dangerous is meant to happen there, and I'm sure you're its target."

"Or your dissembling wasn't as flawless as you believe, and he suspected you, and he warned you away from the warehouse because he wanted you away," Mouse said. "I still think we have an opportunity."

"And I think," Naishe said, "you have nowhere near enough information to conclude that, Mouse."

"And I agree with her," said Rask. "Which makes three times, which no doubt means I'm about to turn to stone or something."

Mouse was silent, thinking. "We need to do two things," he finally decided. "One, we need eyes on that warehouse, night and day, so we can find out the truth of how many guards are or aren't stationed there. And two, we need to summon the rest of the group leaders and have a full debate. With a vote at the end. If the vote proves I'm being overeager, I'll abide by it. But not until then."

Wren was avoiding everyone's eyes again, so Naishe was forced to exchange a glance with Rask instead. And behind the irritation, his face showed a foreboding that uncomfortably mirrored her own.

CHAPTER FIFTY-SIX

Stonespire

THOUGH SHE'D BEEN granted several days of travel in which to compose what she was going to say, Adora didn't truly feel confident. She was going to convince Arianrod to help her, because she knew that it was possible and she knew that she had to do it. That didn't mean there wasn't an undercurrent of dread in the pit of her stomach as the three of them approached Stonespire Hall.

"Just . . . let me do the talking, all right?" she said to Cadfael and Voltest. She still had her ring with her, which meant this would be easy unless she had to deal with the Margraines' captain of the guard, who had disliked her since she was a child. She doubted it was personal—he seemed to distrust women in general—but she'd still prefer to avoid him if possible. As for her two companions, she had finally prevailed upon Voltest to wash the soot from his face before they entered the city. He'd looked as sullen as a cat after he first dunked his head in the river, but he did, as she'd promised, look much less like a risen corpse. Cadfael had confessed to having met Arianrod once before, when he was briefly employed by Kelken Rayl, of all people. "She and I hardly saw each other. I doubt she'll remember me," he'd said, but Adora knew better than anyone what a fearsome thing Arianrod's memory was.

The man at the gate was someone she didn't recognize, but at least he wasn't Captain Ingret. "Excuse me," she called to him. "I know it's a bit late, but could you pass a message to the marquise, please?" She knew what a bedraggled picture she made, and waved the ring at him before he could dismiss her for a beggar. "This is a royal seal, and will serve to confirm my identity until your mistress can remove all doubt. I'm afraid I must ask to speak with her immediately."

The guardsman turned the ring over carefully in his hands, staring from it to her and back again. "What, another one? It's been like weeds." He caught himself, embarrassed. "That is . . . there've been so many royals around here, Your Grace. Very unusual. But I meant no disrespect. If you'll just wait here, I'll fetch the marquise."

He was as good as his word, and returned with Arianrod in tow. Adora had been steeling herself for this meeting—for how much Arianrod would doubtless discern right away, and how unbearable she would be about it—but she couldn't stop a slight flinch when they finally came face-to-face.

She had been certain that Arianrod would laugh—laughter was the beginning of gloating, after all, and Arianrod was certainly going to gloat. But she didn't even smirk. She took in the entire scene—Adora in her dust-stained traveling clothes, Voltest with his long hair still slightly damp, Cadfael as stone-faced as ever—and let out a soft sigh. "Who is it, then? Who took the throne from you? Your uncle? Some talented player who's convinced the people he's Prince Landon? It can't possibly have been that buffoon Hephestion."

Adora opened her mouth, and hastily choked back the wrong words before she could utter them. However much she might want to, she couldn't afford to waste time defending her uncle and Hephestion. She had to remain focused on what was important. "Arianrod, I know this must be a terrible imposition, but it was the best course open to me. I've come seeking your help, because—"

"Because you've lost your damn throne, just like I told you you would. That much is clear. By all means, come in. I'm dying to hear the details."

"I've hardly traveled all this way just to give you the satisfaction of being right," Adora insisted. "I have come, first of all, to resume a debate you and I have been having for many years now, on the subject of magic. It has come to my attention that you have been intellectually dishonest with me—that all this time you have been concealing a most intriguing bit of information, which could have won you the argument instantly. How curious that you never mentioned it."

There was the smirk, though Adora didn't miss the instant of surprise it was summoned to mask. "I thought you'd never figure it out. How do you think I managed to scald your annoying brother's soup at every single supper he ate at the hall?"

"I *knew* that was y—" Not the time, Adora reminded herself. "I'm afraid my need is great, and time is precious. I have come here, in particular, because the woman styling herself queen of my kingdom has carried out her usurpation with the help of complex and powerful magic. And I can't imagine anyone knows more about complex and powerful magic than you—you certainly know much more than you ever told me."

Arianrod's eyes lit up with avid interest, just as Adora had known they would. "Magic? You're sure of this?"

"There can be no mistake," Adora said. "And if my word isn't enough for you, I have come with Voltest, here, who can use magic himself, though he is not a mage. He can tell you more about what this woman has done."

"Not a mage?" Arianrod repeated, examining Voltest closely. "A *wardrenfell*, perhaps?"

Voltest inclined his head reluctantly. "I see the queen did not overstate your knowledge of the arcane."

"It's rather difficult to overstate my knowledge of anything," Arianrod said, "but that in particular. And you've brought him, too—Cadfael, wasn't it? I see you still bear that sword." She grinned at Adora. "I'll give you this much: if you had to fail, at least you've failed incredibly usefully. I've been searching all over for two like this. To think that you of all people would bring them right to my doorstep!"

WHEN ADORA HAD been accustomed to visiting Stonespire Hall, the study at the back of the second floor, that beautiful, sunlight-filled room built of wood against the backbone of the stone tower, had nominally belonged to Arianrod's father. Throughout their long history, the Margraines had prided themselves on their learning, and it had been seen as a matter of course that the ruling marquis or marquise would wish for an expansive study. But Caius Margraine, who looked upon books as if they were enemies lying in wait, had seen little use for the room, and seldom occupied it, even to write a letter. In his absence, Arianrod had taken up her own residence there, filling the room with her own books and papers and letters. And though even Adora, who had spoken to him only seldom, knew he was a combative man, he had allowed his daughter to usurp this one place without a fight. Perhaps it was because he didn't want to bother arguing over a room he hated anyway. But Adora had always wondered if it had been intended, in his proud and unyielding way, as an unspoken salve against the great wrong he had done his daughter, to give her a refuge she loved where he would not venture to intrude.

It wasn't something she could ever ask, or even touch upon. Though she was one of very few people outside Stonespire who even knew the details of Arianrod's injury, that was due to an unfortunate accident, a diplomatic visit with her father and Hephestion that had occurred too soon after Arianrod's tenth birthday. Beyond that, they had never spoken of it.

As she settled into a chair beside Arianrod's desk, she felt her body start to relax out of habit, despite the challenge before her. This place was so familiar. They had whiled away whole afternoons here, playing three-hour games of sesquigon or engaged in some stubborn debate until the setting sun slanted through the windows and Arianrod declared herself too famished to continue without sustenance. But in truth, this situation was uncharted territory. Arianrod might seem just the same as she had three years ago, but she was the marquise of Esthrades now. They controlled the fate of nations between them, and if Adora could not win *this* argument, she dared not think what would happen to Issamira.

"I believe I understand your predicament," Arianrod said. "I thank you for such a thorough explanation. I suppose it's obvious at this point, but to be clear, you are formally requesting my help? Not simply supplies or other aid, but my *personal* help—my power against this Jocelyn Selreshe's?"

It was still so strange to think about, that two women she'd known for so long had borne such power within themselves all their lives, and Adora had never known. But to Arianrod it was a commonplace truth, and Adora endeavored to act that way as well. "That's correct."

"Then—and this is not an obvious question, and not rhetorical—do you understand what a weighty thing you ask of me? To leave my people undefended and leaderless for the gods know how long, to make a journey I have never made before across the Curse and to your capital, and to wager my own life and health in what may very well be open combat against another mage? I'm not above doing favors for you, Adora, but this is far beyond the loan of my copy of Gorrin."

"You refused me that, too," Adora couldn't help saying.

"And think what would have happened if I hadn't! This Jocelyn would be reading it as we speak!" Arianrod leaned back in her chair, implacably smiling as if she wasn't poised to crush Adora's hopes. "If you truly want my help, the burden is on you to convince me to give it to you, is it not?"

Adora had never intended to lose her temper. She knew Arianrod was good at making people angry, not always by design. But all of the people she cared about most were in Jocelyn's clutches, and Arianrod knew that full well and could just sit there, as self-satisfied as always. "No," she said. "I came prepared to treat with you, but not to play this game."

"What game?"

"It has always pleased you to feed your own vanity, even at my expense," Adora said. "I have never objected to it. I would not even mind it now, save that you know precisely how much hangs in the balance for me, and you *still* have the gall to waste my time. I don't *have* time, and especially not for this posturing. If you want to negotiate, or ask questions about the situation, or ensure that we're prepared to protect you as much as we can, by all means go ahead. If your pride or your practicality demand a price, merely name it and I will pay it. But don't pretend that this has nothing to do with you. Don't pretend you aren't ultimately going to help me, because we both know you will."

Arianrod's face was icy perfection, betraying not the tiniest twitch in response to Adora's words. "Oh?"

"Jocelyn is everything you care about," Adora said. "She's a mage, and she's clever, and she's just stolen herself an entire country. Magic, intelligence, and power—those are the things that mean the most to you, and if she isn't stopped, she'll get away with beating you at all of them. I don't know how her abilities compare to yours, but she's taken the magic of a *wardrenfell,* which means whatever her power was before, it is now far greater. In order to *get* that power, she had to exhibit extraordinary cleverness—for all the research I'm sure you've done on magic, I'd be willing to bet her trick was one you'd never thought of. And she used her new abilities to become the ruler of Issamira: a country more than thrice the size of your tiny Esthrades, and that could easily crush it, if she wished. I'm sure none of these things have escaped your notice, and I'm sure you don't intend to let any of them pass unanswered. I'm only wounded that you thought *I* wouldn't notice, or that I never knew you well enough to know that even if I didn't need your help—even if you weren't entirely necessary to my plan—you'd *still* want to be part of it, just for the chance to match yourself against her."

She had argued with Arianrod before, even said the odd harsh thing to her over the years, but she had never been quite *that* bold. Any nervousness proved unwarranted, however: Arianrod raised a hand to cover her mouth, but Adora could still see the smile in her eyes. "Well," she said, "it's good to know you're serious, at least. You only ever get angry when you're serious." She dropped her hand, tugging absently at her hair. "Magic, intelligence, and power, was it? After all this time, that's what you think of me?"

"Do you feel I've insulted you?" Adora asked.

Arianrod laughed. "No, that would merely be amusing. As it stands, you didn't strike nearly as close to the bone as you think you did, but I suppose I'm still impressed. That bit about her cleverness . . . yes, that was mostly true. I did assume, foolishly, that it was impossible to steal a *wardrenfell*'s power—there are ultimately no excuses that can counter that. And to have her prove me wrong is . . . more than a little irksome. But there is one thing you need to understand. I'm aware that you've had to learn a great deal about magic very quickly, and that must not have been easy. But you seem to believe that your Jocelyn has accomplished something I actually *envy*. Know this, Adora: even if I had been able to figure out a way to steal another's magic, I would *never* have attempted it. That would be even more foolish."

"Why?" Adora asked. "It worked, didn't it?"

Arianrod scowled. "In a manner of speaking. She has the power she wanted, but at what price?"

"I'll be the first to admit that I don't understand magic," Adora said. "I obviously don't have it, and I've never truly studied it—it seems that was part of *my* foolishness. So I don't understand why there must be a price for what Jocelyn has done."

"It isn't that there *must* be. Perhaps there will not be. But I would be very surprised—much more surprised than I was to learn that it was possible at all." She stretched out her arm, idly examining the tips of her fingers. "I do admire cleverness—my own, primarily, but occasionally other people's as well. And I have long coveted the secrets of magic, and all the knowledge and potential it contains. But I would never admire power. Loving power for its own sake is an empty and foolish thing to do."

"I—"

"No, don't apologize. You aren't truly sorry, and I don't need you to be. But I do need you to make one thing clear, before we begin any kind of negotiations. Who is it that sits before me now, and bargains for my aid?"

Adora would have accused her of making one of her jests, except that her face was so uncommonly serious. "Are you trying to say you don't know who I am?"

"I'm saying it has seemed to me, for quite some time now, that *you* don't truly know who you are, Adora," Arianrod said. "I know the title my family has claimed among our people, but I have the power and the duties of a queen, and have always known myself to be such. But what are you? A princess regent? What good is that to me? When you first made your request, I feared you had simply come to ask me to make decisions for you, as you might have asked Landon, or your father. It seems you are more determined than that, but it's still not enough. Not until I am convinced you truly speak for Issamira." She extended a hand, a bargain waiting to be sealed. "One queen to another, Adora, or not at all."

They had never been meant to be equals. Her father had only brought her and Hephestion to Esthrades to begin with as a subtle slight against its marquis, that Jotun Avestri did not think the place worthy of his heir, only of the children with far fewer responsibilities. "It will be good for you to know Arianrod well," he had said, many times. "There is reason to hope she will be more reasonable than Caius, but she's frightfully bright already. Landon will doubtless need your help in dealing with her. And if she grows to trust or like you even a little, so much the better." It was Landon who had always been meant to sit across from Arianrod, to take his place as her equal, while Adora was good for games of sesquigon and the exchange of books. But Adora had already sworn to take up her brother's charge—to him, and to Voltest, and to herself. She could hardly avoid making that promise to Arianrod, too.

She took the extended arm, and nodded as firmly as she could. "Let it be as you say, then. One queen to another."

She thought Arianrod relaxed, just slightly. That smirk definitely returned, though Adora was oddly comforted to see it. Arianrod just didn't seem like Arianrod after too long without that expression on her face.

"In that case," she said, "I have two conditions. First: I already know the plan this Voltest has devised is flawed in several respects. I am prepared to work with you and him to create an alternate strategy, but you must leave it to me to know my own limits, and determine what is and is not possible for me."

"Of course," Adora said. "That's only fair."

"The second condition is the matter of my recompense." Arianrod folded her hands. "Your need is undeniable, and the effort it would take to help you is not so great as what it would take to win the war against Elgar without Issamira's help. It makes sense for me to help you, so I will help you. But I *won't* do it for nothing, no matter what you may think. If you want me to solve the problem that you created, you'll have to do something for me in return."

She didn't have much of a choice, and Arianrod doubtlessly knew it. "What did you have in mind?"

"Dispense with this princess regent business for good. Once we've taken back Issamira, have yourself crowned immediately, and say nothing of holding the throne for Landon or of continuing to await his return—"

"That will not be a problem," Adora said. "I already had every intention of formally assuming the throne upon my return. And I will never wait for Landon again, or count on him for anything."

Arianrod tilted her head, eyebrows lifting. "I was under the impression that you held your brother as your exemplar in all things."

"I once thought magic didn't exist, and I was wrong then, too," Adora said. "It seems the world is both more than I believed, and less."

To her surprise, Arianrod somehow managed to dredge up some courtesy, and let the matter slide. "That may be, but I wasn't done. I want you to take the throne properly, and when you've done that, I want you to prepare your armies, and join the fight against Elgar."

It wasn't a surprising request, especially from someone in Arianrod's position. But still it unnerved Adora to think of it—that she could really do that, could send forth entire legions as her father once did, and that she'd be responsible for all their deaths.

But Elgar was Arianrod's enemy as surely as Jocelyn was Adora's. Arianrod would risk her own life to confront Jocelyn; Adora knew that all too well. And even beyond that . . . if he ever managed to defeat Arianrod, Elgar would come for Issamira and its people next. She could not pretend not to know that.

"It is a fair price to ask," she said. "I suppose . . . given what Elgar has already done, and what he seems poised to do, conflict between us would always have come to pass eventually."

"No doubt," Arianrod said. "But that is still not what I need to hear."

"I know. And I accept. As soon as my rightful powers are restored to me, I will declare war upon Hallarnon, or Elesthene, or whatever Elgar wishes to call his collection of trophies. I will defend Esthrades, so far as I am able. You and I both know Valyanrend has never been taken from the outside, but I believe we can drive him behind its walls, as our ancestors drove the agents of Ninism all those years ago."

Arianrod nodded. "You have the men and the resources for it. And if matters farther north go as I intend, Elgar's own resources will be stretched thin. But we cannot make decisions to that end until you have regained your seat in Eldren Cael." She smiled. "Let us make sure you do."

THE STUDY FELT quite different the following day, in the light of early morning with four people in it. It was not a very large room, and did not have enough chairs for Arianrod, Adora, Voltest, and Cadfael, so Cadfael spread himself out along the windowsill, and Voltest stood stiff and awkward in the corner, his back to the far wall. "It is necessary for us to form a tentative plan for handling Jocelyn," Arianrod said, "but in order for me to be of greatest use to you, I must first understand the nature of a *wardenfell*'s magic. I'm told that killing Jocelyn is not our primary goal?"

"That's right," Adora said. "As far as I'm concerned, she's already done more than enough to justify the charge of treason and her lawful execution, but Voltest worries about the ultimate fate of Lirien Arvel's magic. I don't suppose you can provide any insight on that subject?"

Arianrod grimaced. "I can tell you for certain that a mage's powers cannot be stolen—it would be like stealing the wetness from water. But Jocelyn has proven that a *wardrenfell can* be separated from their powers, and if that's true, I can't say for certain that Lirien's magic would return to her if we killed Jocelyn. I don't know if magic can . . . die? But I think it likely that we would not be able to recover it."

"That is my suspicion as well," Voltest said.

"Then I anticipate your cooperation in helping me to understand the difference between your abilities and my own. But there is something else I must investigate first." Without waiting for agreement, she turned to Cadfael. "I need to understand the properties of that sword. Unsheathe it, if you would, and set it down on the desk here."

When Cadfael hesitated, Adora said, "Please just do it, Cadfael. Whatever Arianrod intends, I know it's only to help us succeed."

"I'm not going to damage the sword, if that's what's stopping you," Arianrod said. "If anything, you should be concerned about the opposite."

Cadfael swung himself down from the windowsill, but before he could do anything else, he stopped, his eye caught by something by the door. Adora had not heard it open, nor any footsteps from beyond it, but a woman was standing on the threshold. She was dressed more like a guard than a chambermaid, but she was not carrying any weapons that Adora could see. Cadfael took a few steps toward her, and she inclined her head to him. Arianrod turned, too, and smiled. "Ah, there you are. Stay and watch, if you feel well enough. The day's experiments should certainly prove interesting."

Cadfael had waited politely for her to finish speaking, but as soon as it was clear she was done, he asked, "Were you injured?"

Adora had not noticed, but as the woman touched her shoulder lightly, she saw a scrap of white peeking out from under her shirt: the edge of a bandage. "It's healed . . . quite rapidly," the woman said. "I don't even need the sling anymore." Then, as if she were not used to the words, "I . . . appreciate your concern."

That seemed to satisfy him, though it did little to satisfy Adora's curiosity. "Cadfael, you know her?"

"Do you not know her?" he asked. "She is her ladyship's bodyguard."

Adora tried not to laugh, and was not entirely successful. "Her what? Arianrod, you used to scorn the very idea! Can it be you have grown cautious after all?"

Arianrod rolled her eyes. "Ugh, the title was *her* idea, not mine. She's too useful to quibble about it. Can we get back to the sword, please?"

Adora was still curious—anyone who had risen so high in Arianrod's confidence and esteem was a rare sight—but she knew there were more pressing concerns. She nodded to Cadfael, and he drew his sword, laying the naked blade on the desk and stepping away. Arianrod approached the desk as if facing off against a dangerous foe, but finally she wrapped her hand around the hilt, and lifted the sword several inches into the air. It hung there for an instant or two, the point trembling slightly, but no longer than that: Arianrod's hand opened as if against her will, and the sword clanged back down on the desk, making Cadfael wince.

Arianrod shook out her hand as if it had been injured. "Well, that's that. I didn't really think I'd be able to manage more." She turned to Voltest next. "Will you attempt to do what I just did—or more, if possible?"

Voltest reached out, but his fingers had no sooner brushed the hilt of the sword than he leaped back with a yelp, cradling his fingers. "What the hell? What *is* that?"

"It's vardrath steel," Arianrod said. "You'll be able to pick it up, of course, Adora, but just tell me what you feel."

As she'd said, Adora lifted the sword without issue. "It's cold," she said, "but that's all."

"Is the cold lingering?"

"No, I think it's warming up."

"Can you pass it to Seren?"

Adora was confused for only a moment before the woman's outstretched hand enlightened her. She wrapped one hand around the hilt and laid the other against the flat of the blade. "The blade is colder," she said, "but I can feel it in both places."

"That makes sense. The hilt seems to be forged from a different metal." To Cadfael, she said, "That's all I wanted to know. You can have it back now." As he took the sword from Seren, she added, "I wondered if anyone who wasn't a mage would be able to feel anything at all. I felt a coldness as well—so intense that it burned. And more than that. An . . . opposition. Something set against the very fabric of my being."

"But no outright pain?" Voltest asked. "I felt the coldness, but the pain was worse. And I . . ." He put a hand to his mouth. "There was . . . the taste of ash, the smell of something burning."

"No, I can't say what I felt was pain, exactly. That's an interesting result, though. I wasn't sure if it would be worse for a *wardrenfell* or better, and that's . . . certainly illuminating."

"But why can't we touch the steel?" Voltest insisted.

Arianrod grinned. "Even my two fellow scholars haven't come across this one, eh? My interest in vardrath steel was piqued at Mist's Edge, when I first saw a man I knew to be a mage fling himself violently away from the approach of this very blade. And my research bore great results. *Vardrath*, like so many of our words, is a corruption of a more complicated word in Old Lantian: *wardrenwrathe*."

Voltest caught his breath, and answered before Adora could. "Of course. *Spell-breaker*."

"An acceptable translation," Arianrod said. "So, of course, it does more than simply prevent those with magic from wielding it. Though I can't confirm this myself, I've read that wounds made with vardrath steel cannot be healed with magic. And it certainly helped you, didn't it?" she asked Cadfael. "Isn't the sword how you managed to dispel the enchantment that would've killed you?"

Cadfael clapped a hand to his forehead in surprise. "The sword? I . . ." He traced the line of his scar carefully. "Was *that* what did it? The day I returned home in a fever . . . I was half-delirious. My head felt so hot . . . and the sword was so . . . cold . . ." He frowned at it. "You're saying its presence would be painful to a *wardrenfell*?"

"Not if you simply carried it with you, no. As Voltest just proved, it's direct proximity that causes pain." As he finally sheathed it, she added, "It means you'll be a valuable ally in the fight against Jocelyn. According to Voltest, the power she stole tends toward healing magic, and Jocelyn herself is apparently skilled at affecting the minds of others. The sword should shield you from being so affected, and hopefully the wounds *you* inflict will remain."

"My sister has a sword forged from the exact same steel," Cadfael said. "Should we not seek that as well?"

Arianrod looked to Adora and Voltest. "Do we know where this sword is now?"

Voltest shook his head. "I cannot search for his sister directly, and at the times when I have seen her, she has been without any weapon."

"Then it's not something we can think about now. Perhaps when we reach the palace itself we'll learn more." She dusted off her hands. "Next, Voltest, I'd like to learn more about the differences between *wardrenfell* and mages. I *know* it's impossible to steal a true mage's magic the way that Jocelyn has done, so if there were some way for me to understand exactly what she did to Lirien . . ."

He still looked suspicious, but Adora doubted Voltest was ever truly without suspicion. "What would you need me to do?"

"When I cast, can you see the spell?" She glanced at a book on a nearby table, and it floated gently into the air. "Can you see that, for example?"

"I can see a floating book," Voltest said. "Is that not the spell?"

"That's all you can perceive?"

"What did you expect me to perceive?"

"It's not something I can really explain." She thought for a moment. "What about th—"

Voltest flung his hands up in front of his face, and Arianrod gave a slight flinch. "What was *that*?" he demanded, still shaking slightly.

She had already recovered. "It wouldn't have harmed you. But that's good to know. It seems you can see spells aimed at you directly, but nothing else."

He glared at her, but he seemed calmer. "And you can see . . . all spells?"

"I suppose *see* isn't the most strictly accurate word—it's more that I'm . . . aware of their presence. But we'll go with that, for simplicity's sake. The answer to your question is yes—theoretically speaking. I can certainly see all of *my* spells, and I know it's a gift mages possessed in the past, but I can't be entirely certain. Why don't you try casting a spell—not at me, just on yourself or anything in this room—and we'll see what I can perceive?"

Voltest nodded. "Well, it would be a shame to damage any of these books, so . . ." He raised a hand, and fire coated his arm, surrounding it from elbow to fingertips. It didn't so much as disturb a loose thread on his clothes, but Arianrod gave a start, her mouth dropping open in shock. She shut it again quickly, but the disquiet was plain on her face, and it gave even Voltest pause. "What is it? What did you see?"

She put one hand on the edge of the desk, gripping it tightly. "That does explain how Jocelyn could seize it so easily, but I never imagined it would be so bad as that."

"So bad as what?" Voltest asked again. "What on earth did you see?"

"It was a foolish assumption, I admit that," Arianrod said. "I thought that casting a spell was more or less the same from mage to *wardrenfell,* that your magic would flow through you in the same manner as mine. But however that power came to attach itself to your being, it never truly merged, did it? If anything, it's like a parasite. When you cast a spell, that power acts in accordance with your wish, but in return it entwines itself more deeply, like ivy growing up a tree. It's not inconceivable that, one day—"

"It might kill its host?" Voltest asked dryly, as if it was a possibility he had considered many times before.

"Perhaps," Arianrod said. "But magic is of the mind. I suspect your mind would be corrupted long before your physical body. Surely you've noticed that already?" She frowned. "But if I could see this, surely Jocelyn could as well. The chance that she would have corrupted her mind in stealing Lirien's power was astonishingly higher even than I believed. And yet she still attempted it. Was she truly so desperate, to take such a risk?"

Voltest shook his head. "Whatever this . . . corruption . . . is, it is far more advanced in me than in any of my companions, and Lirien has always borne it best. That is why I wish to do whatever we can to restore her powers to her, so she can continue to hold the rest of us in check. But the queen gave us to understand you found my plan infeasible. Can you truly not imitate what Jocelyn has done?"

Arianrod hesitated, overshadowed by solemnity the likes of which Adora had scarce seen from her before. "Let me be entirely clear. I am *capable* of doing what you want me to do. I can say that for certain now. When you cast, I can see the lines of your power clearly, the nature of the connection between you and the magic that has claimed you as its host. Were you to direct that power at me, I could take it. It would be like plucking off a leech, and attaching it to my own flesh instead, but I *could* do it. What I need you and Adora to understand is that I *will* not do it. Any attempt you make to persuade me will just be a waste of time." She sighed. "I don't truly expect that to stop either of you, but I had to try."

Adora's heart sank—that plan had truly seemed the simplest and best—but she fought against letting it show. "I would not try to convince you to do something you felt it unsafe to attempt. But perhaps, in light of my lack of understanding of magic, you might explain why you're so set against it?"

"I'm trying, believe me. What Jocelyn has done, it's . . . it's filling a container that's already full. It's forcing something where it oughtn't fit. It frankly shouldn't have worked as well as it seems to have done; I can't imagine the effort of will it must take to hold it all together. But it is *so* dangerous, and so unwise. And it's not at all safe to conclude that it won't have disastrous consequences for her in the future."

"So if Jocelyn can't keep holding herself together, the magic might kill her all on its own?"

Arianrod tapped her forehead. "Again, Adora, magic is of the *mind*. It's Jocelyn's mind that might crack under the strain—although I must admit, her moment of greatest danger was when she cast the spell itself. Somehow she weathered that— foolhardy, but commendable."

"But you don't think there's enough of a chance that you could weather it, too?"

"If you jumped out that window, Adora, there's a *chance* you wouldn't break your neck. If I told you someone else, once, had made the same jump and lived, how much more likely would that make you to attempt it? You seem to think that Jocelyn's ability to steal a *wardrenfell*'s magic without shattering the walls of her mind is due to some incredible skill on her part. And no doubt some manner of skill was involved in it. But it is one part skill to a hundred parts sheer luck." Again she pointed at her forehead. "If it were only a matter of risking my life, it would be different. But though I have to die someday, I *don't* have to live the rest of my life with a mind like a smashed eggshell. And I'm not going to risk it, thank you very much."

"That's fair," Adora had to admit. "You're wagering much in my cause already. It wouldn't be right for me to ask so much more of you, especially for something that is my fault."

Arianrod smirked at her, of course. "I'm glad to hear it, though you don't have to look so downcast. With that settled, it simply falls to us to figure out a way to stop Jocelyn without resorting to that step. And, luckily for you, I think I already have one. Voltest, what do you think would happen if, instead of removing the leech and attaching it to myself, I were to merely pluck it off and flick it away?"

"And what, release the magic into the world?" He scowled. "What would prevent Jocelyn from just scooping it up again?"

"I came to quite a different conclusion," Arianrod said. "What happened the last time that magic was loose in the world?"

"The last . . . ? Ah. It . . . chose Lirien, for whatever reason."

"Precisely. Set free, would it not choose Lirien again?"

Voltest's stiff posture finally relaxed as he contemplated it, so preoccupied with his thoughts that he forgot to be guarded. "I see what you're saying. But right now, Lirien has no power, and thus no way to voluntarily draw the magic to her, whereas Jocelyn is free to reach for it. To counteract that disadvantage, she'd have to be very close. As close as possible, but certainly in the same room. A matter of feet."

"We could achieve that," Arianrod said. "We know Lirien isn't dead."

"But she's certainly imprisoned. We'd have to release her and confront Jocelyn at the same time."

Arianrod shrugged. "Complicated, but possible. Adora, what do you think?"

"I'll leave the magical half of it to you and Voltest," Adora said, "but if it works as you say, I'm fairly confident about the nonmagical half. It's not as if I can't navigate my own palace. If Jocelyn tries to set my guards against me, I can't say for certain whether they'd *all* remain loyal, but they certainly wouldn't all betray me."

"Voltest believes your mother is still alive. She'll speak in your defense, as will Hephestion, as soon as he's free from Jocelyn's control. Your legitimacy can be reestablished easily enough." She looked around at the rest of them. "Well? Is this a plan we can all agree upon, or not?"

THE WIND FLOATED through the tower window, and the slight coolness made Seren perk up a little, brought some of the firmness back to her fingers as they tugged at Arianrod's laces. There was hardly even an ache from her shoulder anymore; Arianrod had been continuing to heal it—a little at a time, so as not to tire herself. But she refused to say how the spell worked, or why she was so certain it still could not erase her scars. And Seren knew better than to ask, though that did not mean she could stop wondering.

Arianrod's back felt stiff through the layers of cloth, as if she were holding herself too tightly. "Are you all right, my lady?" Seren asked, as she pulled the last lace free and held the dress upright.

"I'm fine." The expected answer. To get more information, she'd have to be cleverer.

"Did you find it tiring to spend all day at your plans and experimentations with the others?"

"On the contrary," Arianrod said, her voice muffled and then clear as she tugged a shift over her head, "I found it refreshing. Exhilarating, even. I haven't had to test my mind to such an extent in quite some time." But her posture hadn't relaxed, and she was barely smiling. This was not the attitude of one who felt pleasantly fulfilled.

"Then it must be that you've left something undone," Seren said. "Or else that there is something else you could do, and you're trying to decide whether to do it."

Arianrod sighed, but it was only performative; there was no release of tension there, either. "Damn. Am I that obvious?"

Seren leaned against the side of the bed. "To me. In that way."

"How encouraging."

"Do you want to tell me about it?"

Arianrod moved to sit beside her. "I would have to, I suppose, unless I abandoned the whole thing completely. A . . . thought occurred to me, in the midst of all our planning. Or perhaps I should say a thought had nagged at me from the beginning, and I finally thought of a possible solution to it."

She pulled a lock of hair free from where it had gotten stuck behind her ear, twirling it between her fingers. "Here's the central problem. In order for me to steal Lirien's magic from Jocelyn, I need her to direct that magic at me. She would never do such a thing if she knew I was also a mage—she would never be that stupid. She doesn't know I am a mage yet—or so we have every reason to believe."

"But if the whole enterprise revolves around that one point," Seren guessed, "then you could devise a thousand different plans, and it wouldn't matter. They would all be undone at the same time, by the same single thing. If Jocelyn finds out, then that's it."

"Precisely." Arianrod let her hair drop, and leaned back against her hands. "We're supposed to simply hope Jocelyn doesn't find out? Someone clever enough to do all the things that she has done? I have little practice with playacting—and of all the things I have difficulty feigning, ignorance is one of the greatest."

Seren wanted to reach out to her, even just to feel how fast her pulse beat or the tension with which she held herself, but she refrained. "I agree that's a problem. Even I can see that. It makes me uneasy." *But that's not what you're uneasy about,* she didn't say.

She didn't have to. "I held the question in the back of my mind for hours," Arianrod said. "If Jocelyn were ever to refuse to directly engage her magic with mine—to target me at all—how would I solve the problem? And it's not the question but the answer that bothers me. Because an answer did occur to me, but . . ."

Seren waited for more, but heard only silence, and tried to fill in the gaps herself. "It's not likely to work? It's an inelegant solution?"

Arianrod laughed, at some irony Seren didn't yet understand. "Oh, it's about as inelegant as can be. It's something I'd only ever want to try when all else had failed. But its chance of succeeding would be high, I believe."

"Then why hesitate?"

Arianrod leaned forward and tugged at her hair again—a much harsher and more restless movement than before. "The plan . . . would involve you. I suppose I could attempt it with one or more of the others, but I'm not confident in the results. To give us all our best chance . . . it would have to be you."

"Is that all?" Seren asked. "I'd much rather be able to help than the reverse."

"No, that's not all. I wasn't done." Again Seren waited, and again nothing came. But this time she did not guess, only let the silence stretch on until Arianrod herself chose to break it.

"Seren," she said, "what I am proposing, now, is a thing for which I would want to ask your permission. And I *would* ask for it, if asking would have any meaning. But in order to ask, I would have to explain, and I can't do that. Our opponent in this matter has a talent for manipulating the minds of others, and you are not protected from it as I am. So I simply cannot risk telling you any more of my plans than is strictly necessary, just in case the worst should happen. Even if she can't steal the knowledge from you directly, knowing too much might alter your behavior and raise her suspicions. Do you understand?"

"Of course. Completely." She still did not touch Arianrod, but leaned toward her, turning sideways to face her directly. "You don't need to tell me. I don't mind not knowing, if that'll make it easier. And if you need to involve me in something without my knowing, or put me in danger . . . we're all going to be in danger anyway. It's all right."

"It's more than that. I'm telling you as much as I can, but you need to listen to me. *Truly* listen, and think about what I might mean. The plan involves a spell that occurred to me. Another enchantment. Even if everything goes as I expect, that spell will still . . ." She ground her teeth in frustration. "If I say the spell will hurt you, you'll say that's of no consequence, because you'll be thinking only about the kind of pain you usually face—the kind of pain you can accept. But this is something different, and it's not something that can be avoided. No matter what you do before or after, if I have to use that spell, it *will* hurt you. It will hurt you in a way you cannot accept."

Seren remained silent, but she didn't look away from Arianrod's face. Arianrod was right: her instinct was simply to agree, to resolve to suffer whatever consequences came of it. But when had she ever seen Arianrod this grave? Seren owed her, at least, her best attempt at thinking this through.

Pain, then. What was the worst kind of pain she could imagine? "Will your spell kill me? Maim or cripple me, so that I can't fight anymore?"

Arianrod shook her head, but she did look relieved that Seren was actually asking questions. "Any one of us could be maimed or killed fighting Jocelyn, but the spell itself wouldn't have the power to do that, no."

She needed a better imagination. Magic could do *anything*. What were the worst things she could think of, whether or not she thought they were possible? "Would it take anything away from my mind? My memories of my training, my abilities? My memories of you?"

"No."

"And it wouldn't . . . separate us? Make it impossible for me to be near you again?"

Arianrod clicked her tongue. "No, but . . . you might not want to be near me, afterward."

"No. Never." She'd clenched her hands into fists without realizing it, and felt a sliver of embarrassment as she relaxed them again. "My lady, if it's as you've described, I still think you should cast your spell, and I'll handle whatever pain I have to. Whatever permission I can give, you have it."

She could tell Arianrod wasn't fully satisfied; her back and shoulders still rigid, she rubbed the bridge of her nose as she spoke. "If you're serious about helping me, you'll have to follow these instructions exactly. Choose one of your knives—any one you like, but only one—and give it to me. I'm going to enchant it. Probably not right away, so I'll have time to think about the best way to cast the spell, but sometime before we reach Eldren Cael. After I return it to you, you must wear it so that it is visible to all, not hidden away. And it must be the only weapon that you wield, until Jocelyn is defeated. You must put all your other blades aside, and refrain from picking up any stray weapons in the fighting. That is absolutely essential. Do you understand?"

Wordlessly, Seren got to her feet and began stripping herself of her knives. She made a pile of them on the little desk, and then she considered which one would be best to use. "Your spell won't ruin the knife?"

"No. And I can remove the enchantment when we're done."

"Then this one." The one she kept at her left forearm, the easiest and best. Arianrod didn't seem surprised at the choice. "Is there anything else?"

Arianrod took the knife, but she set it on the desk, too. "There is one thing. If I must rely on this plan, we'll almost certainly have to fight Jocelyn directly—subterfuge and manipulation will have failed. In that fight, defend yourself as you have to, but you must not attack Jocelyn until I order it. Remember, our primary goal isn't to kill her, it's to take back the power she stole."

"I'm not permitted to defend you?"

Arianrod shrugged. "By all means, defend me if you can, though I honestly think I'll be in better shape than you for that fight. But don't attack her directly. Not until I tell you. This won't work if you can't agree to that."

"I can. I will. I promise I will." Seren bowed her head. "You can trust me."

Finally, Arianrod's shoulders relaxed, though she did not smile. "Then I will do it. But let's leave it between us. It's not something the others need to know, or that I would want to explain."

"Of course." As if she'd ever want anyone to know that she'd stripped herself of her weapons! They were more than power and ability; for so many years they had been a comfort and support, a silent assurance that she was not helpless and never would be again. Moving without their weight and presence felt awful. Wrong. Far more vulnerable than nakedness could ever be. But she could not say that it hurt her. The hurt must be still to come, somewhere in the future beyond view.

She would endure it. Arianrod was risking so much to help the queen, and Seren would share as much of that burden as she could.

She supposed the conversation was over, but still she stared at Arianrod, the shape of her body clearly visible underneath that thin fabric. She was healthy, but she was not strong, not the way Seren or the rest of her guards were. It was an obvious, glaring weakness, that her body couldn't defend itself without resorting to the power that lay in her mind. Looking at her, Seren still felt that same contradictory fear. *What could you possibly do for me?* She was afraid of that, yes: that Arianrod was so strong that there was nothing Seren could give her. But at the same time, she feared that she couldn't do enough—that she would fail to provide something Arianrod needed. Gripped by that fear, she couldn't bring herself to leave, to return to her room alone.

"My lady."

Arianrod was fiddling with the knife on the desk. "What is it?"

She couldn't look up, but she forced the question out. "Can I . . . stay with you tonight?"

It wasn't something she had ever asked before; she had only ever waited for Arianrod to ask her. Under normal circumstances, she would never have dared. But it would be impossible once they left Stonespire; they'd be traveling, sleeping in tents at best, with other people in close proximity. And once they got to Eldren Cael . . . who could say what would happen to any of them then?

"I don't mind. The bed's big enough." She turned to look at Seren, and caught herself. "Oh. Or did you mean . . ." She put a hand to her mouth to catch her laughter, but when she let it fall again her smile remained. As it should be. It had been so strange to wait so long before seeing it. "Well, that's fine, too. Come here."

They were so close already that closing the distance was the work of an instant. Seren had thought it would be different somehow—more solemn or melancholy— but Arianrod kissed her as confidently as ever, without even a trace of hesitance. It was Seren who changed things, though she hadn't meant to do it: spurred on by an impulse she couldn't hold back, she flung her arms around Arianrod's neck and held her as tightly as she could, as if that alone could protect Arianrod from anything, or keep them together.

Arianrod pulled away only enough to free her hands. She put them on Seren's shoulders a little dubiously, as if uncertain whether that was the appropriate action, but her smile was undimmed. "Don't be concerned. I know what I'm doing." She ran her fingers through Seren's hair as she brushed it back from her forehead. "Have a little more confidence in me. You're usually good at that."

"I've always had confidence in you," Seren said.

"An excellent foundation! Now you just need to act on it."

There was nothing sharp or mocking in her tone. Seren remembered what Arianrod had said when they were reunited: *I don't want there to be any misunderstandings between us.* She had done Arianrod a disservice, to always be wondering if some word or gesture was a trick or a test, when Arianrod had tried to be more straightforward than she could ever have guessed. Sometimes a smile was just a smile.

She did one other thing, later, that she had never dared. She had thought they would simply drift off to sleep, but Arianrod got out of bed and walked over to the desk. She took Seren's discarded knives and set them carefully into the largest drawer—all but the knife that was to be enchanted. "They'll be safe in here," she said, as if in answer to a question. As she turned away and bent her knees to better see what she was doing, her long hair fell to one side, baring her back to full view. But Seren's first instinct this time wasn't to look away. And when Arianrod closed the drawer and sat back down on the bed, Seren reached over and brushed her hair aside again, running her hand gently down Arianrod's back.

Arianrod stiffened, moving just far enough away to separate Seren's hand from her skin. "Don't."

"Please." She knew she had no right to ask, and would not have asked again if Arianrod had refused her. But after a moment, Arianrod relaxed, leaning back against Seren's hand.

It was the longest she'd spent looking at the scars directly. Even the cuts that had been the deepest were now only slightly pink, and most had faded to a mottled silver. But their effect was in their multitude. They stretched from the base of her neck to the small of her back, a tangled web of lines and curves, wider rifts and thinner slivers weaving in and out. Too many strokes to count, and each stroke immortalized.

Of course it was painful to look at them; of course it filled her with guilt and regret and sorrow. But at the same time, she felt such tenderness; they were part of Arianrod, proof that Arianrod was real and here with her now.

She traced the lines with her fingertips, following them one by one. She kissed them, slowly, gently, taking her time. If she were never allowed to touch them again, she wanted to memorize them by more than just sight.

Arianrod didn't stiffen up again, and showed no other reaction for a long time. Finally, she said, "That's . . . that's enough." But she didn't pull away, so Seren didn't pull away, either, though she obediently left the scars alone. She was afraid to look at Arianrod's face, so she put her arms around her instead, pressing her cheek against Arianrod's back.

Somehow she felt certain that, if either of them spoke, Arianrod would move away. She knew this moment would have to end eventually, no matter what she did. But she wanted to hold onto it as long as she could, so she said nothing. She held Arianrod, and listened to their breathing, and felt the warmth of her skin. And the moments slipped slowly from her grasp, stretching into the night.

CHAPTER FIFTY-SEVEN

Valyanrend

"You're not even really looking," Roger said, standing on the tips of his toes to peer at the top shelf.

"I'm looking enough. You're the one with the bloody candlestick, and the light in here's rotten. And I'm not sure the book's really in here, anyway."

"It is, monkey, I remember it. I *know* I read that title. And since your old man can't do anything else for us without it, if we can't find it we're sunk."

Tom had looked at the runes from the statues, all right, with the help of a scholar's catalogue he'd pulled out of his stash. But fully half the runes had been "irregular," untranslatable with the catalogue alone. The scholar had listed a more detailed work that might help: *On the Flaws of Standard Runic Form,* which under normal circumstances sounded like the last thing Marceline or Roger would ever want to read.

Long lost to time—or it should have been. But Roger insisted otherwise. "I gave this room the most thorough looking-over the first time I entered it. I must've come across that title then."

"Along with who knows how many others? There must be hundreds of books here."

"As long as there's not an infinite number, we'll find it eventually."

Marceline ran her fingers along the next row of spines. It was hard not to be awed by the room—a trove of knowledge and wealth together, more at once than most thieves could hope to amass in their whole careers. And its last collector had just offered it up, free, to whoever might come sauntering by. She read the titles absentmindedly: *Historical Impossibilities in the* Niniad, *The Life and Crimes of Captain Aura Blackthorn, On the Rights of Natural Children* . . . Easy to see why these would've been banned, or burned. But nothing at all about runes.

Moving onto the next shelf, she paused. A fat tome bound in black leather caught her eye immediately: *A Short History of Valyanrend and Its Districts.* Hell, if that was the short version, she'd hate to see the long one.

As she eased it free of its fellows, a huge cloud of dust puffed up into her face, making her sneeze. Roger glanced down at her. "Did you find it?"

She waved away the dust. "Not yet."

"Come on, don't piss about."

"I'm *not.* There's a question of my own I want to answer." What used to be in Ashencourt? *What a good question,* the woman called Asariel had said. But if it was such a good question, why hadn't she answered it?

She cracked open the book and started reading, carefully turning the stiff, yellowed pages. *The city of Valyanrend, as it is now known, was almost certainly first called* Valyanrendir—*"World's Eye" in Old Lantian. Such a bold boast conveys the high hopes its builders must have had for the city—hopes that have been borne out in the power and influence Valyanrend has possessed over the centuries.* She flipped ahead, scanning the pages for the word *Ashencourt.* No luck yet, but it was a large book.

"*Hah!*" Roger yelled, and she almost dropped it. "What did I say?" He stabbed a finger into the middle of a shelf. "*On the Flaws of Standard Runic Form,* by Mr. Yonas Haas."

"Careful," Marceline said, as he pulled the slender book down—the binding was badly damaged. "That looks like it'll fall apart if you stare at it too hard."

"I've got it." As he started reading, his face resolved into a scowl. "Gods, scholars are difficult. His writing's so dry I could use it for kindling."

"Well, tell me if you find something, and I'll tell you the same."

The room fell silent as they read, with naught but the turn of a page to break it. Though Roger had a smaller book and a much closer light source, Marceline was the first to spy what she was looking for. "There it is. Ashencourt."

"Ashencourt? What do you want to know about that old place for?"

"Just listen." She pointed to the page. *"Though Ashencourt is today little more than a few dilapidated taverns down some back alleys, few places in all of Valyanrend can boast greater past importance. In the days when magic thrived in this land, the most talented alchemists and enchanters plied their trades there. Alchemists could brew concoctions that even the brightest of today's herbalists could never hope to equal—medicines to cure almost any ailment, or even, in rare cases, to restore the drinker from the very edge of life. What alchemists were to plants and growing things, enchanters were to objects: stone and metal and glass, linen and leather and silk, gold and silver and jewels. They could make stone that was harder than stone, glass that would never shatter, goblets that would change color if poison were poured into them. Indeed, it is the most magnificent and costly creation of Ashencourt's enchanters that gave the district its name: ashencast, once the most sought-after stone in the world."*

"Ashencast?" Roger frowned. "I'm a thief from a family of thieves stretching back for generations, and I've never heard a word about it."

"I doubt the book's lying, Roger." She kept reading. *"When anything was built of ashencast, objects or people within the resulting structure could be protected from all manner of unpleasant occurrences, though the specifics depended on the individual enchanter. Because ashencast was so expensive, and one would require a great deal of it to build anything substantial, we have few records of such structures, but there are three of great fame. The most recent is the library at Selindwyr's University, enchanted to protect the books housed within from fire, humidity, or other agents of deterioration."* She looked up. "What's a university?"

Roger shrugged. "Don't ask me."

"But the book makes it sound like a place anyone would know. Selindwyr is where Aurnis is now, right?"

"Aye, and a bit of northern Hallarnon and Lanvaldis. Might be this university went the way of Selindwyr itself. What's the rest of it say?"

Oh, so now he was interested, was he? *"Though most of Valyanrend is older than surviving written records of it, many enchanters believed the Arkhe Laeshet, the great aqueduct the common people have taken to calling the Precipitate, was built of a material similar to ashencast, that prevents the water from being poisoned or otherwise befouled. And then, of course, there are the great golden walls surrounding Valyanrend's . . . Citadel."*

She and Roger stared at each other in astonishment. "But the walls outside the Citadel are black," Marceline said, half afraid he would correct her, that she'd somehow been seeing them wrong all this time. "Have they ever . . . not been?"

"Black as pitch," Roger spat. "I never heard a soul say otherwise, not even

Gran. Perhaps the walls were destroyed and rebuilt? During the fall of Elesthene, perhaps—there were riots all over this city then."

"Doesn't say much about this ashencast, if that's the case."

"Aye, but it's the only explanation I can think of."

"Well, I don't like it," Marceline said. "Universities, golden walls, alchemists, enchanters . . . we've never heard about any of it. Who knows how much more we might have lost?" No wonder Asariel had seemed so sad, if she was mourning what had once been a street of marvels, now only a run-down back alley that everyone had forgotten. When had all the enchanters and alchemists left? Had they been killed, or had new people with the talent just stopped being born as magic died out? What had happened to the wares they sold? Was there any chance you might still find an enchanted goblet or a life-saving draft somewhere, locked in a cupboard or collecting dust in a far-off corner?

". . . Oh," she said. "I understand now."

Roger had gone back to his own book after she'd fallen silent, but now he looked up again. "You understand what?"

"*What a good question,* Asariel said, when I asked her about Ashencourt. I didn't know what she meant then, but I think it's because it's a question that gives rise to so many others."

Roger tapped the page he was currently reading. "Do you want to know about *our* question?"

"Of course. What did you find out?"

"I'll save you the specifics, but it seems like there were some runes that got wrongly classified as variants of other runes, rather than having their own separate meanings. So the translations would be slightly off, or you'd get certain words marked as 'corrupted,' untranslatable."

"Does that mean you can use that to translate the statues' runes or not?"

But Roger wasn't looking at her, all his attention suddenly focused on the book. "Oh, fuck."

"*What?*"

"It says . . ." He pointed an accusing finger at the page. "It says some of the most common mistranslations had to do with old religious traditions—with *the* oldest written religious tradition. And look what it uses as an example."

He turned the book around and held it out to her. The page was dense with words and runes, but one word in her own script jumped out at her immediately: *Tethantys.*

ROGER THREW THE book down at the statue's feet. "They're fucking identical! Gods damn me, this is . . . not what I wanted."

Marceline crouched at the feet of the man holding the crown, running her fingers over the runes carved into it. If the scholar who had written that book could be believed, those runes spelled out nothing more or less than Tethantys's name.

She picked the book up and closed it carefully. "So long ago, when written language was new, Tethantys was the name of a god of ambition. But over time, *tethantys* became a word for ambition itself, and the original meaning was lost."

"But just how the hell is this statue connected to that man you saw? You can't really think that he's . . ." He couldn't finish the sentence.

"A god," Marceline said, because one of them had to. "*This* god, to be exact."

Roger paced in front of the statues. "It can't be. Gods aren't real, and even if they were, they'd never bother with the two of us. They wouldn't have to be furtive about any of this—if they wanted this place discovered, why not announce it from on high? They'd never just have a stroll with you in the square. I can't even conceive of it."

"But I can't come up with another explanation, either," Marceline said. "I *know* he wasn't a real person, Roger. Not like you and me."

Roger strode right up to the statue, glaring into its eyes. "All right, then, you've had your fun. You've led us on a merry chase with all your talk of valuables down here, when I suppose what you were really after was recognition. Still just chasing your own significance after all these centuries, eh? Sounds like a god of thieves to me. So are you going to tell us the next step or aren't you? What is it you wanted us to do?"

Nothing. Marceline couldn't even have said if she was surprised or not, or what she'd been expecting.

"Pfft." Roger flicked the statue on the nose. "Can you imagine being the religious sort? I've talked to this bastard without an answer for half a minute and I already want to wring his bloody neck. But I wonder . . . in the days when the Ninists outlawed all other religions, I wonder if there were still any poor souls willing to risk it all, to pray to him." He scoffed at the statue. "And what did you give them? This same silence?"

CHAPTER FIFTY-EIGHT

Issamira

THEY ARRIVED BEFORE the castle as the day drew to a close, the light of sunset casting the old stones of the place in a forbidding shadow. It seemed built on the opposite premise of Raventower: squat and square, it must not have gone up more than three stories, save for a single tower at the rear that was dimly visible above the outer wall.

Though the walls themselves looked solid and well maintained, it was difficult to tell the state of things beyond them.

"This is already strange," Lord Vespas said. "There are no guards on the gate."

He was right, though Morgan herself could hardly have said what was or wasn't normal at a great lord's abode. The gates were of wood studded with iron, but there seemed to be nothing behind—no portcullis or other metal. That most likely meant the doors had to be pushed open, rather than operated by winch. But not only did no one stand before the gate, no one stood atop the wall to watch for visitors. "Do they close up for the night here?"

Lord Vespas shook his head. "Journeys are sacred in Issamira, remember? Any traveler who begged refuge would at least receive an audience. And I ever knew Dahren and Amali to be open-handed with their hospitality. It's true that it has been years since my last visit, and anyone can change with time. But to not even have a single man on the gate . . ."

Braddock spoke up. "So without a man on the gate, and without breaking the doors down, how are we going to get in?"

"That's a good question." Lord Vespas bowed his head, resigned. "First I shall try to take the most peaceful path, and only harm my dignity. I'm going to yell."

He was as good as his word, shouting and banging on the door with a louder commotion than Morgan would have believed possible from a single man. A couple of his soldiers soon stepped forward to help him, but for what seemed like a very long time, there was no response from within the castle. Then, just as Morgan was preparing to ask him how long he intended to continue this, a man's face appeared atop the wall. From such a height, it was difficult to make out his age or features, but his hair was wildly tousled, as if he'd just woken up. "Who goes down there?" he asked blearily. "What's all that racket?"

"My apologies," Lord Vespas called up to him, his composure immediately restored. "I am Lord Vespas Hahrenraith, former general in the Issamiri army and old friend of the lord and lady of this place. Are they at home?"

"'Course they are," the man said. "Where else would they be?"

"I . . . don't know. That was why I asked. But if they *are* here, I must speak with them, as soon as possible. I met with some trouble on the road, the full nature of which they need to hear."

The man shifted uneasily, and Morgan and Braddock exchanged a look. That was suspicious, wasn't it? "It's very delicate," he said. "In here." He jerked a thumb over his shoulder, as if they could possibly be confused about where he meant. "I don't want things to get upset. To get more upset. But if you're going to insist . . ."

He pulled back from the edge of the wall. What was he doing? Morgan didn't think he was conferring with another person; she couldn't see so much as a trace of anyone else. They were too far away to tell if he was making any noise. But whatever he did, he soon bent his head back toward them. "I'm sure it wouldn't be acceptable for me to turn away such important visitors. If you wait, I'll fetch others to help with the doors."

He didn't wait for a reply, just disappeared from the top of the wall again. Lord Vespas inched closer to Morgan and Braddock. "Do you wish to remain outside?" he asked, too quietly for his guards to overhear.

It was tempting, in a way; that encounter had been strange enough to put her on her highest guard. But she shook her head slightly, with a sidelong glance at Braddock to make sure he didn't feel differently. All he did was tighten his grip on his ax.

Lord Vespas nodded back at them, and soon after the heavy doors began to swing outward, pushed by several men. They all looked more or less like the first: disheveled and hazy, as if woken from sleep.

"You'll all follow me, please," the first man said. "I'll take you inside." Lord Vespas gestured to his guards, and the man stiffened. "No, that's far too many. You can come, and that woman if you like. But not more than a dozen soldiers with you. Our numbers are much depleted here, and my lord and lady may become alarmed at more than that." Morgan knew she must be *that woman,* as she was the only one of their party not carrying any weapons.

She and Braddock waited for Lord Vespas's decision. These men had already opened the gates to him, and did not seem prepared to come to blows; he could simply force his way in and take his questions to Lord and Lady Selreshe directly. But that was an almost warlike approach, and especially if these were his old friends, perhaps he preferred to handle things more subtly—and perhaps, even after all he had seen, he trusted them enough to believe this wasn't a trap.

He sighed. "All right. Let me see . . . you'll accompany Miss Imrick, I assume?" he asked Braddock. When Braddock nodded, he chose the remaining eleven out of his own retainers, and told the rest to remain until sunrise. As those who would venture inside approached the threshold, most lifted their hands, as Morgan had seen Hephestion and his men do at Ibb's Rest. She and Braddock politely did the same, though Morgan couldn't help noticing she was the only one of the lot who used both hands. After that, the strange manservant finally let them pass, though when his comrades helped him shut the doors behind them, Morgan prayed they hadn't all made a mistake.

The yard before the castle was ill-kept, strewn about with straw and rocks and the occasional horse apple. Torches were lit haphazardly, asymmetrically, not according to any possible pattern or line that she could determine. Morgan could not see anyone but the handful who had originally welcomed them; they had probably come from the small gatehouse leaning against the inside wall, but it now looked deserted. "Have you fallen on hard times of late?" Lord Vespas said. "I had not heard such a thing."

"Hard times, my lord?"

"I mean, do your masters not pay you or someone else to keep some cleanliness or order around here?"

"Ah." The man looked solemn. "As to cleanliness and order, my lord, it's the young mistress who is wont to direct such things, and she's been at Eldren Cael for . . . some great time, it must have been. Without her, things get . . . disordered."

"I never knew Amali to need anyone else to direct her own affairs," Lord Vespas said.

"And yet I don't remember seeing you here before, my lord. You can call me Rhys. This way, please."

He led them into the castle—which, if anything, was even worse. In the great hall, large candles in standing candelabra blazed cheerfully enough, but the stands and wicks looked like they hadn't been cleaned in weeks, the drippings of the present candles sitting atop the crusty mess of previous ones. Dust and cobwebs coated every corner, and Braddock kicked a nonchalant rat out of his way at the base of the stairs. On the second floor, more ill-maintained candles cast a fitful light on a narrow hallway. It ended in a row of doors, single and double, and had arms stretching off to either side. Rhys made a right and continued down the hallway, and Lord Vespas was close behind him. But then they stopped, and the rest of the group stopped with them—one of the doors was rattling in its frame, as if someone was throwing themselves against it.

Rhys glanced nervously at them, and then back at the door. Braddock drifted in front of Morgan, putting himself between her and that side of the hallway. Lord Vespas opened his mouth, but before he could say anything, the latest impact burst the door open, and people rushed through.

The door had struck Braddock in the head, and he staggered back, dazed, half-falling against two of Lord Vespas's guards. The newcomers surged past him. There were four of them, grimy, disheveled, shrieking as often as they drew breath. Morgan thought one of them might have been weeping, but before she had a chance to feel pity, she caught sight of the weapons they carried.

They didn't seem to be trained warriors; they were garbed like household servants. They carried a sword, a cleaver, a fireplace poker, and a broom. One of them was only wearing one shoe. What had happened to drive them to such a pitch of fury?

Lord Vespas's soldiers had their attackers outnumbered and outmatched, but the hallway was narrow, and they struggled to get past Braddock's still-reeling form. Rhys had shrunk back against the wall, but the others ignored him. Caught in front, Lord Vespas engaged the men with the sword and cleaver at once, and Morgan readied her fists to take down the fellow with the broom.

She soon faced a problem. In any other fight she'd ever had, her opponent had backed off once she'd hurt him enough, but pain seemed to have no meaning for this man. She knocked him down, broke his nose, struck a tooth loose, but still he kept coming toward her, screaming as shrilly as ever. Would she have to kill him to make him stop?

Lord Vespas seemed about to take that step; he'd sliced off the arm of the man with the sword, but had only slowed him down. Two of his soldiers finally forced their way forward, and bore the battered man with the broom to the ground; Braddock had recovered enough to engage the fellow with the cleaver. But as Morgan watched, the man with the poker dropped his weapon, sidled up to Lord Vespas, and pulled a stubby knife from his belt.

She only had a moment. She saw the man and the knife, and knew that either Lord Vespas couldn't see him or couldn't get out of the way in time. And she moved.

She caught him in the ribs with her elbow, pushing him out of arm's reach of Lord Vespas but missing the spot in the pit of his stomach that would have winded him. He recoiled only slightly, then lunged for her instead. Morgan had no idea what was wrong with this man, or any of them, but she knew every second he still had that knife and she didn't was a second she courted death, so she didn't have time to find out. She just managed to dodge the blade, and this time she hit him right where she wanted to, a fist square under his jaw. That sent him back for more than a moment, and she grabbed his still-outstretched arm and twisted it, unyielding until he yelled and released his grip. The knife dropped into her free hand. But as she tightened her fist around the hilt and drew it back to strike, someone shouted, "No!"

Lord Vespas drove his shoulder into her attacker's body, separating them. Before Morgan could say a word, he raised his sword and ran the man straight through.

There was stillness after that, full of the sound of labored breathing. Morgan looked around, but it seemed all their attackers were either dead, unconscious, or wounded and prostrate. Lord Vespas stalked over to Rhys and seized him by the collar, shaking him like a doll.

"What is the meaning of this?" he demanded. "What have you done to this household?"

The servant cringed away from him, squeezing his eyes shut. "Forgive me, my lord, forgive . . . the household is *like* this, I didn't—"

"What you've done is a crime! Every one of you could die for this! Do you understand me?"

"Forgive me, forgive me," Rhys wailed, almost in tears. "I've no malice in my heart, my lord, but it's so terrible when she's angry! She makes you so terrible when she's angry!"

Lord Vespas finally stopped shaking him. "When who is angry? Amali?"

Rhys shook his head firmly. "The young mistress, my lord. She's gone now, but she's so . . . particular . . . and she gets so angry . . ."

"Where is Amali, then?" Lord Vespas asked. "Where is your lord?"

Rhys pointed at the double doors in front of them, a mere handful of strides down the hall.

Lord Vespas released him immediately, bounding toward the doors. His soldiers hurried to follow them, and Morgan and Braddock moved, too, not wanting to be left behind. His lordship didn't even take a moment to prepare himself, just flung the doors wide and burst into the room.

By that time, Morgan had hardly any shock left to feel, and would not safely have deemed any horror too great to be beyond those doors. But instead of more screaming or more weaponry, the room contained two silent, unarmed people, one seated at the head of the long table and the other in a tangled heap in the corner. They looked to be about Lord Vespas's age, though strain and care had been far unkinder to their forms than to his. The one on the floor was shaking, and as he raised his head, Morgan realized that he was sobbing, that dry, almost soundless shudder you give when you have cried for too long and still cannot stop. The woman's face was still, and she trembled only a little. Both her hands were laid flat on the table in front of her, ten fingers carefully spread. She was staring at them as if she needed to make sure they were all there—or, perhaps, as if she feared what they might do if she took her eyes off them.

Lord Vespas approached the center of the table, keeping each of the two figures at an equal distance. "Amali. Dahren. It grieves me more than I can say to have to force my way into your home like this, but violent acts have been carried out in your name against me and mine. I am afraid I must ask you to deny knowledge of these acts, or else to explain them."

The man did not react, but the woman sagged into her chair. "Vespas. I'm . . . glad it's you. You will do what needs to be done, as you always have." Again she watched her fingers carefully as they moved across the table, reaching for a folded sheet of parchment and holding it out to him. "Dahren and I would like to confess. The specifics will be difficult to explain, but the charge is treason, and we neither ask nor expect leniency. I . . . made an attempt at a written confession."

Lord Vespas crossed to her and unfolded the paper, his frown deepening as he read. She watched his face, trying to read his expression. "What does it say?"

Something that might've been pain flickered in his eyes. "Amali, it is in your own hand."

"I know that, but . . . just tell me what it says, Vespas, please."

He sighed. "It is a confession of treason, as you said. Though as to what precisely you claim to have done, or how someone as true as I know you to be *could* ever have done such a thing . . . Amali, you must explain it to me. What you have done, and how, and *why*." He crossed the last bit of distance between them, and gripped both her hands tightly in his. "If someone has hurt you, if someone is threatening you . . . I will do all in my power to help you, but you must help me understand. What has brought you to this point? What on earth could do this to you?"

Lady Amali did not pull her hands from his; she just let them lie limply there. Perhaps it was a relief not to have to watch them anymore. "You mentioned . . . violent acts, committed in the Selreshe name? Were they acts against you in particular?"

"Yes." He relaxed slightly. "So you didn't know."

"Not specifically, but I am not surprised. I am sure it was . . ." She gritted her teeth. "That it was my daughter's hand behind it. Your reputation still runs so far before you, and my Jocelyn . . . once she has set her eyes upon a thing, she *will* have it. To be denied, for her, is . . . unthinkable. Impossible. So she is wary of anyone powerful and clever, anyone who could see through her or thwart her aims. When she left here, she wanted to marry your nephew—only Adora herself would be set above the woman who will be his wife. Perhaps she suspected you would interfere. But she has been in Eldren Cael for some time now, and her ambitions have ever led to bigger and bigger ones. By now, she may well want even more."

She bowed her head. "I knew this about her. I knew the sort of person she was, and what her plans were in going to Eldren Cael—I knew enough to suspect how much worse those plans might become. And I let her go anyway. This must surely be treason. I can hardly recall the precise letter of the law, if ever I knew it, but you, Vespas, you must surely be able to see that it was treason in deed."

"Not without knowing the reason why," Lord Vespas insisted. "Do you seek to shield your daughter? Are you offering yourself as a sacrifice out of love?"

That word seemed to cut her more deeply than any other. She laughed, a dry and bitter laugh. "Love? Love, you ask? Oh, I loved her when she was a child, Vespas—before I knew any reason not to. But now? I have felt, many times, that I love her. But I no longer know whether that feeling is real, or something that she put there. No. I did not stop her because I *couldn't*. Because I have never been able to refuse her anything."

She winced, leaning forward, gripping his hands so tightly her nails dug into them. "Don't misunderstand. I'm not talking about the sentimentality of a mother. I mean I *cannot* refuse her. Anything, no matter how wrong. No matter how horrifying. And it isn't just me and Dahren, Vespas. In all my years with her, I have never, never, seen her demand something and be refused."

Lord Vespas released her hands, and she stared at them fixedly as they dropped to the table. He tried to speak, but could not for several moments, and when his words did come they were as uncertain as Morgan had ever heard them. "Can such a thing be possible?"

Again Amali Selreshe laughed her grim laugh. "We are the proof, Vespas. Can you recognize us anymore? Either of us? And our servants . . . the things that happened to our servants over the years . . ." She put her face in her hands. "I'm sure that she . . . that she broke them, somehow. She was playing with them like toys, and she broke them. Some we had to dismiss—some took their own lives. And I have been powerless to stop it."

Lord Vespas leaned his forearms on the table so his face was level with hers. "Amali, listen to me. If all is as you say, then the fault is not your own—no more than if Jocelyn had overpowered you and Dahren with physical strength, and locked you in some dungeon. I know your wits must have been scattered by her, and I cannot imagine the effort it will take to gather them back again. But if you can believe anything I say, believe that this was not your fault." He hesitated. "I think it would be best for you to confess these things to Adora, if you can. Jocelyn must be stopped, and it is my duty to inform my queen of what has transpired here. Are you capable of making such a journey?"

"I believe so. Physically I am much less changed, though I wouldn't want to hold a bow again for a long time. It's strange, but ever since she left, I've started to feel . . . better, perhaps. More myself. And it has done me good to speak to you again, though it is bitter to have you see what I've become." She looked down at her husband's form. "I don't know what Dahren will do, though. He hasn't spoken to me in days, and he barely eats. He *can* walk, but I don't know if he will agree to leave here. I'll talk to him again, as soon as I . . . I just want to see the sun again."

"It's still dark outside," Lord Vespas said gently. "But the sun will return for you, if you're willing to wait."

An array of servants watched as he helped Lady Amali from the castle, but thankfully there were no more attempts at violence. She stood in the open, shaking off Lord Vespas's arm and remaining apart, gazing up into the starry sky. Lord Vespas left her to herself as he saw to the reopening of the gate. "It's all right. You can enter," he said, as soon as he was face-to-face with the guards he'd left outside.

Before any of them could say more, a shrill cry split the air, and Morgan looked up to see a bird circling high above, dark wings spread wide. Lord Vespas squinted into the sky and smiled. "Daya. Some good fortune at last." He tilted his head back and whistled, an inhuman, ghostly sound.

The bird made one last quarter-circle, couched its wings, and dropped like a stone. Morgan felt the rush of air as it pulled up just in time to glide over their heads, and then, nonchalant as you please, it helped itself to a perch on Lord Vespas's outstretched arm. He ruffled its feathers cheerfully. "You've arrived at a wonderful time, my girl. I don't remember the last time I needed to send a message so quickly. But I'll get to your business first, never fear." He gently pulled away the parchment tied around the bird's leg, and it immediately sprang into the air again. Morgan was afraid it would fly away, but it merely drifted in circles far above them. Its cries sounded oddly triumphant to her now, as if it were aware of a job well done.

Lord Vespas unfolded the parchment, and Morgan watched his face for any sign as to its contents. His frown deepened, his brows drawing together. "Well," he announced at last. "It seems I have been preempted. I had thought our next destination must needs be Eldren Cael, but my niece has forbidden me just such a course."

"Forbidden?" Morgan asked.

"Indeed, though she's as apologetic about it as only Adora could be. It seems there is some delicate plan of hers that I would ruin, were I to arrive in the capital now. And . . . reading this, I am certain she found out about Amali's daughter long before I did."

"Do you intend to do as it says?" Braddock asked. "Do you believe it?"

"After everything we saw in there?" He laughed bitterly. "I hardly know what to believe. If Amali could be reduced to this, what might Jocelyn have done to Adora, or any of my family? Yet this letter sounds like Adora in every particular. No one else could have faked her voice so well—and I doubt Jocelyn knows about my birds."

Morgan bit her lip. She remembered Hephestion's kindness well, and would have hated to see him in Lady Amali's state. "My lord, supposing your niece did write the letter, do you trust her judgment?"

"Will I avoid Eldren Cael as she asks, you mean?" He sighed. "Eldren Cael is where I most want to be right now, to see for myself what Jocelyn has wrought. But the trouble is, I *do* trust Adora's judgment. Worse, she is not simply my niece, Miss Imrick; she is my queen. I hate to say it, but I think my path is clear."

One of his soldiers asked, "My lord, if we do not go to Eldren Cael, what will we do instead? Should we remain to keep watch over those still living here?"

"Some of you must," Lord Vespas said. "They've already shown that they might harm themselves or each other at a moment's notice. But I must take Amali out of here—and Dahren as well, if he can consent to it. Away from this place of horrors, I hope she may regain more of her former self. So we shall finally head back home, to house Amali, replenish our forces, and give my two friends here the freedom I promised them."

Even after such a night, Morgan's spirits still rose to hear that. But she hadn't forgotten the question she had meant to ask his lordship, and if they were to part ways soon, she might not get another chance. So she waited until they had started marching, and took an opportune moment to walk at his side. "My lord," she said, "during the fight, you stopped me from attacking one of the men. But you killed him yourself, so I don't understand . . ."

"Ah, of course." He stroked his beard. "I'm fairly certain you only attacked that man at all in order to protect me."

"That's . . . true enough," Morgan admitted, "but I don't see what it has to do with anything."

"I saw you, before we passed through the gate. You put both hands together as you crossed the threshold." He smiled at her sadly. "Once forfeit, it can never be undone. I did not want you to suffer such a stain for my sake."

CHAPTER FIFTY-NINE

Lanvaldis

A PILE OF ash lay at the other end of the field, beside a small, lonely barn. A short expanse to cross—any one of their party but Kel could've sprinted the distance in a matter of seconds. But for all they knew, it might have been as out of reach as the moon.

"So they did burn it," Talis said. "Unfortunate, but not unexpected. It's what I'd have done."

"And it would've been just as useless," Laen snapped. Beside him, Hywel was quiet, winding and unwinding his braid around his hand. "It was never *in* the house. We can still recover it."

"The barn?" Hayne asked.

"Aye, and well hidden. Hywel or I'll have to be the one to go—even if we told you, I don't think you'd be able to find it."

"We haven't decided that anyone should go," Lord Ithan said, one hand resting against his sword. He had been a cheerful traveling companion, but it was clear the news they'd heard this morning had shaken him. "With the capital in such an uproar . . ."

"With Araveil in such an uproar, now's the best time to retrieve it," Laen insisted. "If the riots truly have lasted days already, it means Selwyn's forces there aren't sufficient. She'll have to pull them from other areas—this is the last place she'll want to keep even a few. She doesn't even have any reason to think I'm back from Esthrades."

"That's all true," Ithan said, "but there are still so many of our soldiers there—Eira's former men, who couldn't so easily forget the vows they swore. This wasn't supposed to happen yet. To think they've so lost control of the people . . ."

Kel stayed silent. Unbeknownst to the Lanvalds, the mission Arianrod had given him wasn't to see Laen safely to the throne; it was to cause enough chaos here that Elgar would be forced to send more of his people east. It seemed as if that was already happening, even without his involvement. Yet he couldn't shake a sense of unease. Lord Ithan was right; it was too soon. Without their king, the seasoned and organized fighters among Laen's supporters wouldn't involve themselves, and more of the rioters would be injured or killed, leaving that many fewer to fight when it counted.

They couldn't worry about Araveil before they'd solved the problem right in front of them, he supposed. "One thing's for certain—we shouldn't all go in there. Someone could be lying in wait for us. Talis, can your wind, ah, hear anything?"

She scowled at the building. "It's carrying sounds from farther off, in the village, but nothing from in there."

"We need that paper," Laen said. "We need proof. Without it, sooner or later, the support behind me will crumble. You must know that as well, Ithan."

Indeed, he didn't deny it. "At the very least, you must allow me to accompany you—to go ahead of you, in case there is some trap yet to be sprung."

Laen opened his mouth to argue, but Hywel said, "That much is just sensible, Laen. And . . . if you wanted me to go instead of you . . . as the younger born, I should perhaps take on more of the risk."

"Don't be a fool," Laen said. "Of course I'm going. Talis, you'll watch the door?"

"I'll watch more than that," she said. "If anyone tries to approach that barn, from any direction, I'll keep them away."

"Good. And . . ." He glanced at Hayne. "Might I have one of those? Just one. Just in case."

While the weapons Arianrod had provided would doubtless be invaluable if they had to stand and fight, right now they needed to move quickly, and it was difficult to do that while carrying bags of rocks. They'd left most of them hidden with the cart, but Hayne was carrying five over her shoulder—a last resort, if conflict should prove inevitable.

Kel leaned uneasily against his crutches. "Remember, Laen, once you throw it, you can't control it. If you aren't behind cover, you could end up hurting yourself just as easily."

"I know. I'll only use it if there's no other choice—you have my word."

His face was as solemn and earnest as Kel had ever seen it. He nodded to Hayne, and she passed Laen a single wrapped stone.

"Your Grace—" Ilyn started.

He shook his head. "Ilyn, if Lord Ithan's going to be protecting me, then it's only fair for you to stay with Hywel. Defend him as you would me."

She clearly wasn't happy about it, but she bowed her head. "As you command."

Kel watched as Laen and Ithan trudged across the field, making a cautious path for the barn. "Lessa," he said, "will you do something for me?"

She looked up in surprise. "Of course. What do you need?"

"We may have to get out of here quickly. It would help if the horses were already untied, and we had someone in the cart ready to spur them on at a moment's notice. Would you take care of that?"

"Would I go back to the cart?" She bit her lip. "But if we have to leave quickly, then how will you . . ."

"Your brother's right," Hywel said. "I'm sure Lord Ithan could carry him, if that truly became necessary."

Kel wasn't at all sure that Ithan could carry him and run at the same time, and he didn't think Hywel was sure, either. But he knew Hywel was trying to help him, so he said nothing. Alessa finally nodded. "All right. I'll be ready."

After she was gone, Kel turned back to see that Laen and Ithan had already disappeared into the barn. "How long do you think it will take him?"

"He's got to climb up to the rafters," Hywel said. "The panel is tightly lodged— he'll have to pry it up. He—"

"Quiet," Talis hissed, her head cocked. The wind around her was anything but, tugging anxiously at the trees. "There are people coming. A dozen or so. Moving quickly."

"Should we call Laen back?" Hywel asked. "Or—"

A loud crash stunned them all into silence. The wall of the barn shuddered and ripped open, planks of wood splintering and flying through the air. Another crack, and Lord Ithan came plunging through the hole right as another opened just above his head, his sword drawn and his clothes caked with dirt.

A behemoth lumbered out after him, a huge man with a horned helm and a gigantic metal warhammer. Oddly, his armor was all mismatched: the helm dark, the gauntlets gleaming, the breastplate dull. There wasn't enough to cover his massive form, and blood had seeped into the leather beneath where Lord Ithan must have cut him a few times, but it didn't seem to be slowing him any.

Hywel went pale, taking an involuntary step back. "Ghilan," he breathed.

Talis glared at the man. "Impossible. How did I not hear him? The others—"

Kel caught his first sight of the others, then: soldiers, or at least fighters, if the sheen off their weapons was any indication. He remembered those blue-black uniforms from Mist's Edge. No sigils, no other colors, just that same hue, over and over. These were Elgar's men.

Ithan was keeping the big man busy, dodging the swings of the hammer and darting in to sting whenever he could. But Laen must still be in the barn, and the soldiers were about to fill the space between it and the rest of them. He'd never get through. "Talis, you've got to help him!" Kel said.

"I'm trying!" she snapped. "Why isn't it—"

Laen finally appeared, dashing out of the hole in the wall at a breathless sprint, both fists clenched. But the closest soldiers broke into a run as well, and Kel doubted he would make it all the way to the treeline before they caught up to him. Ilyn stepped forward, but she could hardly disobey her liege in full view of him, so all she did was draw her sword and stay near Hywel, teeth gritting.

Talis finally released a gust of wind, but it curved oddly around Ghilan and Lord Ithan, missing the front of the column of Elgar's men but scattering the rest like dead leaves. Then, when Laen still had half the distance to go, he stopped.

He cocked his right arm back and threw, and for a moment Kel thought it was the rock hurtling toward them. But the object glinted in the light, and he caught a glimpse of sharp silver edges—

And then Hywel snatched it out of the air. It was a tiny metal box.

In real time, it could only have been a few moments. Kel saw the soldiers' heads snap back toward him and Hywel, and he knew they'd seen the throw. Now that they were certain the prize they'd sought was here, they'd never let it get away. They'd chase down Hywel, and kill Ilyn if she stood between them. Kel couldn't run, so he'd inevitably be captured, and against this many Hayne would only be cut down defending him. He'd thought Talis had enough power to protect them, but whatever was happening to her wind, it was clear he couldn't pin his hopes on her.

He'd lost so many already. Herren on the journey to Mist's Edge, and Dirk and who knew how many others in its destruction. All killed as a result of his plans, and for his sake. He couldn't keep doing this to the people he was meant to protect.

He couldn't save himself. But there were still things he *could* save.

Quick as a blink, he pulled the box from Hywel's fingers and opened the lid. It was so small that the parchment within had to be folded up many times to fit inside, but he could still feel the hardened wax of a royal seal. He snapped the box shut again, shoving it at Hywel. But the parchment he gave to Hayne.

"Hayne," he said, "run to the cart and leave with Lessa. If I live, and you believe there is something you can do for me, by all means attempt it. But above everything else, you must protect this paper with your life. That is an order from your king."

He'd thought there would be a moment of tension, of protest, as Hayne weighed his words against what she believed she had to do for him. But instead she met his eyes, and nodded. "Until we meet again, Your Grace." And then she was gone, running with the parchment and her small sack of stones, headed for Lessa and safety. Kel watched carefully, but none of the soldiers tried to go after her—they had been preoccupied with Talis's fitful winds, and likely thought the box Hywel held had not been robbed of its contents.

Talis kept throwing back the grasping arms reaching out for Laen, and managed to wound some soldiers severely enough that they could not get up again. But as the distance between her and Laen lessened, Elgar's men began to come dangerously close to her, too. "Ilyn," Kel said, "you could go with Hayne."

"You ought to," Hywel said, and Kel shot him a grateful look, relieved that the prince understood what he was trying to do. "I have to stay, to distract them with this"—he held up the box—"but you'd be better off with the others."

Ilyn shook her head. "My king bade me protect you, and that is what I mean to do."

Before Hywel could answer, a horrible scream split the air. The big man's warhammer had finally struck home, a direct hit to the leg that left Ithan helpless on the grass. Talis surged forward, perhaps hoping to drag Laen away from the soldiers, but quicker than Kel could have believed, Ghilan was there, too. But he did not swing the hammer again: he had dropped it entirely, and was instead reaching for something at his belt.

Kel heard what happened before he saw it, a second scream that was so much worse than the first, because it never ended. Ithan was groaning on the grass, clutching his broken leg as he struggled in vain to stand. But Talis just kept screaming, though when Kel finally understood what Ghilan had done, he didn't know why. There were manacles clamped around her wrists, the metal the same bright blaze as the big man's gauntlets. How were they hurting her?

"Ilyn, don't fight," Hywel said softly. "With Talis and Ithan both down, it's only a matter of time."

Laen must have seen the same thing: without Talis's wind to scatter them, the soldiers' hands would be on him in another instant. With a snarl, he drew back his arm again, and Kel saw the unwrapped stone. At such close range, Laen would surely rip himself apart along with his foes, but he didn't hesitate for a moment.

"Laen!" Kel screamed, but the rock had already left his hand. It sailed toward Ghilan's broad and armored chest . . .

. . . and came to an abrupt stop, snatched up by his mailed fist.

Metal or stone, Arianrod had said. But Ghilan's gauntlets were clearly touching the rock, and nothing had happened.

He tossed it into the air and caught it again, laughing as they all cringed away from it. He had a loud, hearty laugh that filled all the space around him, yet it somehow felt as unpleasantly intimate as the softest snicker. "Gods above, such carelessness! You've got to mind where you throw things, boy."

He watched their faces. "What, was something supposed to happen?" With no more hesitation than Laen had shown, he swung his powerful arm in an overhand throw. The rock bounced once on the grass before striking a stone, and then rolled to a stop, wholly intact.

The big man laughed again. "Forgive my little test. The administrator would have been curious." He looked them over with a wide smile, his greedy little eyes taking everything in. "But I've got to say, did ever a man catch such a haul of princes?"

Chapter Sixty

Near the Gods' Curse

"It's time," Cadfael said, with a solemn nod toward his skillet, now merrily sizzling with the mixture of eggs, cheese, sausage, and scraps of bread he'd thrown together. "Eat it while it's hot." He passed out the hollowed crusts of their morning loaves, letting everyone scoop up as much as they wanted—though Adora was happy to let Voltest go first, because he wouldn't get burned if it was too hot.

Cadfael had made a fuss wondering what magical fire was going to do to the cooking, but once created, the flames Voltest conjured seemed to behave just like ordinary ones. You just couldn't ask him to cook anything with them; no matter what you gave him, animal, vegetable, or mineral, he inevitably charred it to a perfect black. When Cadfael ventured to ask whether he was doing it by accident or on purpose, Voltest had answered, "I do it by accident, but the fire does it on purpose." Rather than try to untangle *that* knot, everyone agreed to simply let Cadfael prepare the food.

They weren't wholly alone—Arianrod had brought some of her guard along with her, and they would pick up some of Adora's after crossing the Curse, though far from an army's worth. Should the guardsmen of Eldren Cael become aware of a conflict in their city before the truth of what Jocelyn had done could be made clear, there was a danger that the situation might devolve into open fighting between Issamiri citizens. Adora wished to spare as many of her people's lives as she could— and, given their plans, it was possible to execute a scheme in which the only life lost was Jocelyn's. But in order for it to work, they could only move a limited number of people, and they had to move them very carefully.

Despite the added escort, however, the five of them often found themselves apart from the rest, even when they weren't going over their plans. Voltest seemed to find the company of other people odious at the best of times, and the unease he inspired in them only irritated him. Seren chose to remain as Arianrod's shadow, and Adora stuck close to her as well, eager in any spare moment to learn whatever she could about magic, the general and the specific.

"How has your practice been going?" Arianrod asked Cadfael.

He was still watching the food. "Well, I think."

"*He* thinks," Voltest said, mouth already full. "I still see much room for improvement. If I were really trying, I'd have burned him already."

"That's the point of practice, isn't it? If I couldn't improve, we might as well stop. But I have a much clearer idea of the range of the sword's effect."

"Do tell," Arianrod said.

"As long as I'm even carrying the sword, he can't cast spells on me at all," Cadfael said. "Even when it's sheathed. He can cast spells *at* me just fine—he did nearly hit me with more than one gout of flame. But he says he can normally set a person's body afire without having to touch them, and that hasn't worked at all. He tries, but I don't even feel warm." He reached up to trace his scar. "I think the same thing happened when I fought Talis three years ago—she didn't do this to me until I'd already thrown my sword away. At the time I thought she was toying with me, but I suppose it was just because she hadn't been able to before." He tapped the hilt of the sword. "Would you like to try as well, Lady Margraine? Three is a good number."

"That's a good idea," Arianrod said. "Set your hands in your lap. I'll see if I can lift them."

Cadfael did as she'd said, but it was clear after several moments that nothing was going to happen. "Can you feel anything?" Arianrod asked.

"Not even a tug."

"Interesting. I don't feel anything, either—none of the coldness from before. The spell leaves me easily enough, it just doesn't connect with anything. I suppose you felt no pain when he thwarted you earlier, Voltest?"

"None. It was just as you said."

Arianrod grinned. "Well, this is good news! If spells cast directly on Cadfael have no effect, Jocelyn really shouldn't be able to alter his mind—or freeze him solid, for that matter."

"If only the rest of us could practice," Voltest said. "I can hardly fight myself."

"*You* won't be fighting Jocelyn," Arianrod reminded him. "You only need to concern yourself with finding Lirien Arvel."

"If all goes well, you mean."

"It will," Arianrod said. "One way or another."

"Be honest with us," Voltest insisted. "The power of a mage and a *wardrenfell* together . . . for strength alone, you can't possibly hope to match her, can you?"

Arianrod licked a bit of egg off her fingers. "For strength alone? No, not at all."

"But Jocelyn doesn't know that," Adora said.

Arianrod frowned. "If she does not, we must make sure she becomes aware of it."

"What? But why?"

Arianrod spread her hands. "Bluffing, Adora, is a very risky strategy, and one I prefer not to employ if I can help it. Instead, I suggest that we try to outwit her the same way she outwitted you—by inducing her to underestimate us. She would understand, correctly, that her power outstrips mine by a considerable magnitude. The very deliciousness of that fact will make it compelling to her, and, hopefully, obscure that it is beside the point." She smiled. "Of course, it would be best if Jocelyn only learned of my magic at all once it was already too late. But one must plan for every eventuality."

She and Seren exchanged a quick glance as she said it. Adora was still finding it difficult to penetrate that dispassionate mask she liked to put on. It was clear enough that she was shy, and the great respect she had for Arianrod was never in doubt. Still, as supper ended and Cadfael and Voltest left to practice some more, Adora kept an eye on her. Seren remained where she was—waiting for a command, perhaps?—but Arianrod just said, "Go get some rest. I'll be fine out here."

Adora waited for her to slink away before speaking. "I know I was surprised at first, but I think it's a good thing. You ought to have someone at your side that you can trust."

"Well, I'll not dispute that," Arianrod said, though she looked as if she suspected something deeper in Adora's words. She stood up. "Shall we take a turn about the camp before bed? You can ask me whatever new questions you've thought up."

Adora followed her. "There is something that's been weighing on me. This . . . preference Jocelyn has, for using magic to manipulate people's minds. Could you use your magic to . . . negate hers, somehow? To release Hephestion from her grip?"

Arianrod sniffed. "Doubtful. She's an expert at that particular trick, while all I have is the theory. And she has all of Lirien's magic supporting her. Besides, I assume you, ah, want your brother returned to you in as close to his original condition as possible?"

Adora gave a start. "You mean there's a chance he won't be?"

Arianrod hesitated, which did not bode well. She was not as callous as most people believed; the idea of sparing the feelings of others simply never occurred to her, the vast majority of the time. If even she suspected this was a subject she should approach delicately, then whatever she had to say was . . . not going to be good.

"Think of it like this," she said at last. "When invaded by magic, the human mind *wants* to retain its natural shape, and wants to return to that shape if it is ever disrupted. That's a good thing, most of the time—it's why mages have always found controlling the minds of others so difficult, and it means that, once we've taken care of Jocelyn, Hephestion should go back to his own views and opinions without our having to laboriously correct every thought she inserted into his head. But that also means your brother's mind isn't some solid, inert thing, like a stone that can be picked up and moved and then moved back, with no change to it at all. It can be moved, but it may struggle, and left alone, it may very well wander off from where you've placed it and go somewhere else. What Jocelyn is doing is pulling at it, stretching it against its inclinations. There's bound to be a tremendous amount of strain."

"So what you're saying," Adora said, trying to keep her voice calm, "is that, once we defeat Jocelyn, Hephestion will go back to normal—*if* the strain of what she's doing hasn't torn his mind apart first."

Arianrod clicked her tongue. "Just so." But before Adora could say anything, she added, "I doubt she'll take any great risks with him, though. If Hephestion cracks up, it won't be subtle, and she needs him acting as much like himself as possible in order to avoid suspicion." Again she hesitated, her breath surprisingly heavy. "And then . . . you're intelligent enough to have guessed what her ultimate plan must be. They're not married yet, so she needs to be careful with him until then. Because—"

Adora finished it for her. "Because once she's carrying his legitimate heir, she'll no longer need him. And she would be willing to force him even to that."

Arianrod nodded. "I understand your concern, but it would be far better to simply take care of Jocelyn first than to fight her for control of Hephestion's mind. If I try to engage her in terms of brute force, I'm just going to lose."

"You mustn't underestimate her cunning, either," Adora said. "I'm afraid I made that mistake. I . . . I worry my own wits are no match for hers."

"It's rather too early to say that," Arianrod said. "Her maneuver was far bolder than it was clever. Like all bold moves, it leaves her open to reprisal."

Adora laughed. "Are you trying to make me feel better?"

"I'm trying to warn you against stepping back into the trap she used to ensnare you in the first place."

"I know," Adora said. "It's clear to me now: she always wanted me to doubt my own capabilities, so I'd stay hesitant. Not bold enough to dismiss her, reluctant to go against Mother—susceptible to being led away from my duties in a search for Landon, if that part was her doing as well. The soldiers who tried to kill me must have been, at least. Do you think she controlled them?"

"She couldn't have done it directly," Arianrod said. "Not over such a distance. But with powers like hers . . . you slip someone a bribe, you give them a little push to help them accept it, and even if they regret it afterward, what can they do? If they'd tried to tell you what she was planning, she would have just said they were part of it."

Adora shook her head. "Is there truly no limit to such power? Could she induce my guards to abandon the oaths they swore as easily as calling for more wine at dinner?"

"Well, not *quite*," Arianrod said. "Your resistance to the idea of doing something does matter, to some extent. In the absence of contrary inclinations, magical compulsion is the effort of an instant. But when you already believe you don't want to do something, a mage needs to exert more power. It can take more time, and cause more strain."

Adora bit her lip. "But what about something that's completely antithetical to who you are? Something you'd rather die than do. Can magic compel you to even that?"

Arianrod sighed. "That's a complicated question, and we don't have the leisure to explore its every facet. So I'll give you the simplified version: as long as a mage possesses sufficient skill and power, yes, magic can make you do anything."

The total lack of equivocation in her statement chilled Adora's blood. "You're . . . certain?"

Arianrod smiled grimly. "See, that's the mistake. If I used magic to drop a boulder on top of you, you wouldn't think that you could keep it from crushing you if you just *tried* hard enough. But when magic is inside your head, for some reason people think that makes it less real."

"So we have to fight Jocelyn, but she's going to be able to make any of us do *anything*?"

"Not any of us, no," Arianrod said. "She won't have any effect on Cadfael at all. You already know that I can perceive spells, and Voltest can at least perceive those that are directed at him, so we should be able to protect ourselves. But as for you, yes, you'll have to be prepared for Jocelyn to try to make you do something."

"And I won't be able to do anything to stop it."

"But I will be," Arianrod said. "If she tries to affect you, I'll sabotage the spell. Don't worry about that."

"That's easy for you to say," Adora muttered.

"No, it isn't. I'm going to have to work even harder than the rest of you if we're going to succeed. But you can't let yourself be distracted. To the extent that your mind is your own, when we confront her you'll need to stay as focused as you can on making her angry. We know from Voltest that these *wardrenfell* are susceptible to emotional outbursts, and I believe that's in the nature of the magic itself. Perhaps Jocelyn has a little more control over it, but she won't have more than that. Emotional people make mistakes, and you're the only one of us who knows her. Besides, you . . . understand people. I'm sure you can find her vulnerabilities. All right?"

Adora sighed. "All right." She knew Jocelyn bore her resentment, even anger, but she still didn't really know why. She sensed it ran deeper than Jocelyn's jealousy over the throne, but what else had Adora done except try to treat her with courtesy?

There was one more question she had to ask. "Are you truly certain you can convince Jocelyn to underestimate you? That that's the correct path to defeating her?"

"It's certainly not the *ideal* path," Arianrod said, "but things are already far from ideal, wouldn't you say? You remember when we used to play sesquigon. The board can be thrown into reverse at a moment's notice, or not. You need a strategy for both situations. The surest way I have to beat her is by knowing something she doesn't."

"And what's that?"

"That I'm a genius, Adora."

She would have expected a smirk with that remark, but there was none. "*That's* your sure way?"

"It is. I'd say you'll see it for yourself, but I hope you won't have to. It will mean things are about to get more troublesome for me." She tossed her hair back from her face. "But you'll listen to me?"

Adora couldn't resist a slight smile at that. "And not tell Jocelyn you're a genius? I suppose I'll have to resist the temptation somehow."

PERHAPS ARIANROD HAD slept poorly after staying up so late talking the night before, but they hadn't been riding three hours before she started lagging behind. That wasn't like her, so Adora altered her horse's pace to ride alongside her, waiting to see if she would say anything. When she remained steadfastly silent, Adora spoke up. "Are you all right?"

Arianrod frowned. "I've just been feeling a touch . . . unwell. Perhaps the climate disagrees with me."

"I don't blame you," Voltest called from ahead of them. "I've never felt well on the Curse."

Arianrod squinted into the distance. "But we aren't on the Curse yet. Are we?"

"No," Adora said, "but we're fast approaching it. The land is so flat here that it can be hard to tell." She smiled. "I can't exactly call it beautiful, but it is, as far as I know, the only landscape of its kind in the world. And we won't be needing a guide, of course; I already proved to Cadfael on the way north that my navigational skills are as strong as ever."

Arianrod smirked back at her, though it looked a little strained. "I've been looking forward to these skills of yours as much as to the Curse itself. We'll have to see if I can't figure out what tricks you're using."

Adora knew, perhaps better than anyone, how clever Arianrod truly was, but she was confident that this particular secret would be beyond her power to guess—especially since they didn't have time to dally on the Curse while she pondered it. But the closer they got, the less she thought about that, and the more she worried about Arianrod's health. She didn't go any slower, and she didn't look any more tired. But she looked troubled, and that expression was exceedingly rare to see on that face.

By the time they reached the Curse proper, Seren and Adora were both close by Arianrod's side. Horses tended to spook if they crossed the Curse in large groups, so their party spread out into several smaller divisions. It had the additional benefit of allowing Adora to spend some time with just those who knew the full details of their plan, without worrying that anyone would overhear some snatch of conversation not meant for their ears.

They hadn't been riding half a mile before Arianrod brought her horse to a complete stop. "Can someone hold the reins for me? I need to test something."

Adora dismounted, and held both her own horse and Arianrod's while the latter stood very still, one arm extended, fingers waving almost imperceptibly. It looked unnervingly as if she were testing the wind, even though Adora knew that couldn't be true. Surely she couldn't have figured it out so quickly?

Arianrod crouched on the ground, smoothing her hand over its surface. She grasped a handful of dust in one fist, then let it sit on her open palm as she sifted through it with one finger. Finally, she stood up, letting the dust float to the ground.

"This is quite alarming," she said.

Adora stared at her blankly. "But Arianrod, you already knew the Curse was blighted land. You know that nothing can grow here, that only dust storms can survive in such desolate air."

"It's far worse than that," Arianrod said. She called ahead of them. "Voltest. You said you've crossed this before?"

"Yes, several times. Why?"

"Try to cast something," Arianrod said. "Any spell at all, it doesn't matter which."

Voltest raised his hand as he had in the study at Stonespire, making sure to hold it out of his horse's line of sight. But instead of enveloping his arm, the flames flickered dimly around his fingers before sputtering out. He scowled and tried again, and then again, but the result was the same: the flames were snuffed out of existence almost before they had time to form. "What the—where is it going? What is this?"

"You've never cast on the Curse before?" Arianrod asked.

"I couldn't," he said. "I needed a guide to help me get across, and I could hardly reveal myself to them."

"You can't sense how to cross on your own?"

"Of course not. How do you expect me to do that?" But then he seemed to recall something. "Lirien was the same, but Talis once told me she could make it across alone. She said . . . what was it? That the wind was trying to escape, but couldn't."

If this Talis could control wind as easily as Voltest controlled fire, it was probably inevitable that she would have sensed the secret of the Curse. But Arianrod . . . "Are you saying you can sense it?" Adora asked. "You can sense the wind already?"

"The wind?" Arianrod said. "What are you talking about? I can sense the drain on my magic. As far as I can tell, it's pulling toward a central point—the center of the Curse, most likely. If I had to, I could navigate based on that premise." She brushed her hair back. "You weren't exaggerating when you said the Curse was inimical to all life—it's as if it even wants to kill magic. What about your sword, Cadfael? It kills magic too, in a way. Do you feel anything from it?"

Cadfael put a hand on the hilt of his sword, then shook his head. "Nothing. It's warm, in this weather, but not warmer than it should be. And not a trace of cold."

Arianrod turned back to Adora. "I suppose you did not know that it could do this."

"I don't believe even my father knew about this," Adora said. "Without a mage among us, how could we possibly have detected it?"

"That's true enough." She brushed her thumb against her fingertips, as if she could still feel some dirt there. "Adora, leave the horses and come walk with me for a while."

Just the two of them, she obviously meant—a conversation she wanted to keep secret even from Cadfael and Voltest, though perhaps she left Seren behind only out of courtesy to Adora. Given the Curse's importance to her people, Adora thought it best to agree. She was as careful as Arianrod in making sure they were far out of earshot before she asked, "What is it?"

"I wouldn't presume that you could or would tell me all of Issamira's secrets," Arianrod said. "But there was something else I sensed, or think I sensed. It's getting smaller, isn't it? It's retreating."

Adora was too shocked to answer, but she didn't have to—Arianrod simply looked at her face and smirked. "Ah. That, you knew."

"That could be measured without magic," Adora said. "But to answer your question properly, it is shrinking. Slowly, but unmistakably. Very few people know about this—my family, and those we trust to help with the measurements."

"Who was the first to discover it? Your father?"

"No, it goes back generations. There are those among my ancestors who believed that it started with Talia Avestri. That she did not merely halt the Curse's expansion, but reversed it."

"You say that like you have no information that could confirm or disprove it."

"That's because we don't," Adora said. "As far as we've been able to measure, as time has passed, the rate of shrinkage has accelerated. So when it first began—"

"It must have been so small and gradual as to be nigh-undetectable," Arianrod finished. "So it would have to have started sometime after Talia Avestri's vigil, but you can't precisely determine when?"

"Exactly. Is that a problem?"

Arianrod laughed. "For me or for you? At least as a mage, I'd probably call this whole revelation a good thing. And as the ruler of Esthrades, too, I suppose, not that I was planning on invading you in the near future. It'll certainly make travel into and out of Issamira much more pleasant as the years go by. But for you and your family . . . I imagine this has you very worried, doesn't it?"

"It would be difficult not to be," Adora admitted. "It's why we've endeavored to keep this information from the people, though I don't like doing so. They tend to view the Curse favorably, as protection against invaders, and I can't entirely say they're wrong. Then there's the reputation of the Avestri to uphold as well. What if we made it known that the Curse was growing smaller, and then one day the process reversed itself again? Would the people not claim that meant the influence of the Avestri was waning?" She sighed. "But if the Curse were to shrink even more dramatically, if it were to disappear entirely . . . I'm hopeful I could get my people to see the benefits as well as the drawbacks. If life returned to this blasted land, what could we not use it for? Would it not be better served, after all, as a place where plants can grow and people can live than as a desolate barrier between us and the north?"

"A fine point," Arianrod said, though the smile faded from her lips as she stared once more at the barren ground. "But the situation is more serious than that, Adora. Not in the distant future, but in the more immediate one."

"What do you mean?"

"I mean that I solved your people's great riddle, simply by being a mage. I wasn't trying to—I wasn't focusing on it especially. And I still couldn't help but notice, from the effect the land had on my magic. As you saw, it was different for Voltest, but I suspect any true mage, upon setting foot on this land, would come to the same conclusions I did. *Any* true mage. And you can believe what I have said about Elgar or not, but I am certain he is a true mage."

The realization made Adora tremble. *We would have thought we were safe.* Elgar *would* come to the Curse, if he lived long enough. His ambitions were unquenchable, and Issamira an essential part of them. Sooner or later, he had followed his armies to every land he meant to conquer. And the moment he did, the single greatest defensive advantage the Issamiri possessed would become useless.

Worse, even if they stopped Elgar, that wouldn't be the end. There would be other mages after him—Arianrod and Jocelyn were both proof of that. How many of those mages might yearn to be conquerors? How long until a mage stumbled across the secret and sought to sell it to rival powers, out of nothing more than opportunity and greed?

Adora could no longer be certain that the secret of the Curse would remain a secret for the Issamiri alone. Defeating Elgar would only be the beginning—she had to be able to lead her people into a world where the Curse would no longer protect them.

CHAPTER SIXTY-ONE

Valyanrend

FOG WAS NOT common to Valyanrend, and Marceline had caught more than one person standing in the doorway of their house, peering into it uneasily before stepping outside. She hadn't heard any rain overnight, and there was none after the sun rose, but that made it more unsettling—as if the fog had just drifted in, untethered, silent, and alone. The cobblestones were dry, but the air was damp, raising the hair on her arms. The chill seemed somehow old and stale, though it had been mild just the day before.

It was not a morning made for tarrying out of doors, so Marceline had set out to visit her sister in the Fades. But she wasn't even halfway there when the sun finally broke through, and it was then that she saw him, matching his stride so easily to hers.

He was young, in the first full bloom of life and strength. Lithe and fit and long of limb, he looked as if he could run a race or fight a battle on the instant, as easy as a smile. The sun glittered in his fiery hair, as if it had come out just for him, and his eyes . . . Before Marceline had ever met Mouse, she had heard that the girls who knew him sighed over his beautiful eyes, and never truly understood what that meant. But now, without a trace of doubt, she knew that this stranger's eyes were beautiful, the most perfect eyes she had ever seen.

She was instantly on her guard.

He smiled, warm as the sun on her skin. "Good morning, Marceline. How wonderful to speak to you face-to-face."

"I know who you are," Marceline said.

"Oh, of course," he replied, and she remembered Tethantys had told her he was vain. "Who wouldn't know *me*?"

"I know you're a liar," she insisted.

He shrugged. "Sometimes. At others, I reveal truths hidden so close to your heart that they might never see the light without me."

"Well, I don't need any of that, thank you," Marceline said. "So you can just be on your way."

"You're so certain? That's not what you said to Tethantys. You *are* one of his, though, so I suppose it can't be helped."

"I'm not one of anyone's," Marceline said.

"Yes, Tethantys's always say that." He beamed at her so innocently. "It's not something you accept or refuse, you understand? It's a path. For you not to walk it, you'd have to deny who you are."

Who she was, eh? That connection wasn't hard to make. "One who would be a thief can hardly give up ambition," she said. "Is that it?"

Amerei—for it could be no other—threw back his elegant head and laughed, clapping a hand to his forehead. "Ambition! Oh, poor Tethantys! Is that what these times have reduced him to? As if all that he is could be encompassed in that simple little word!" He brushed the hair out of his face, his features settling into seriousness. "Tethantys is every dream of something new, and the daring to pursue it, no matter the risk. He is the will to make the impossible possible. When the walls of this great city went up, do you think he could have been absent? Do you think he did not whisper in the ears of those builders, urging them to reach ever higher?"

Marceline looked around them, worried that someone might have heard him talking about such impossible things, but Amerei only laughed. "Oh, they can't see me. Tethantys only showed himself to you, so if I were to do more than that, *I'd* be the one dealing with the others' ire. But by all means, let's keep walking. You wouldn't want anyone to take notice of *you*."

Marceline trudged numbly in the direction of the Fades, though she could hardly bring him to Cerise's. "So . . . to live that long . . . you really do claim to be gods."

Amerei shrugged. "*God* is a mortal word. We have heard it before, but we don't truly understand what it means. We have never claimed to be anything but ourselves."

"But people worshipped you, once."

She'd thought that would spark his vanity again, but instead he looked wistful, almost sad. "We were so young then—how could we not be flattered by such attention? But in the end, great harm resulted from that worship. If you think we seek a return to those times, you're mistaken."

"Then what do you seek?"

He smiled. "A world that is better suited to us, of course. Isn't that what everyone seeks?"

Could she believe such an answer from a professed liar? "And how is talking to me going to help you achieve that?" she asked.

"Ah, of course! We were having such a lovely time that I strayed from the point. Tethantys told you something, you see—something he wasn't supposed to. So, to chastise him, I meant to tell you something, too."

"Tethantys gave me a choice," Marceline said.

"I can give you a choice as well, if you would prefer that. But I chose my subject so carefully. I confess, I sought to ingratiate myself to you by telling you about your friends."

"My friends?" Marceline did not know of a single person who had ever called her friend.

"Oh dear, are they not? Perhaps you won't care after all, then."

She was tired of his games. "Damn it, just tell me. I won't care about *what*?"

He smiled, golden in the sunlight. "You were right. About the reasons for Elgar's speech, and the reasons for his orders surrounding a particular warehouse in Silkspoint, and the reasons why he warned you away from that place when he thought you were just a poor little girl. Your friends should have listened to you, but I'm afraid they didn't. And they're dying. That's what I came to tell you."

In the next instant he was gone, but Marceline barely noticed. He was nothing but an empty space in the corner of her eye as she turned on her heel, dashing back west in the direction of Silkspoint.

BEFORE ANYTHING ELSE, she heard the shouting.

Five turns before the warehouse, a woman tried to snatch at her sleeve. "You mustn't go that way," she said. "Can't you hear there's trouble?" Marceline shook her off and kept running.

Two turns before the warehouse, the streets were already clogged with people, living and dead—dozens or more. They were shouting, bleeding, fighting, dying, throwing themselves at the soldiers or running, every one stumbling into the space of three others. It took a moment to focus her eyes, but then it was easy to spot the soldiers—she spied a glint or two of metal plate, but most of them just wore Elgar's blue-black. But there was no formation to them, no order or forethought whatsoever. Each soldier flung himself into the crowd as if he fought alone, carving through everyone he could reach without discipline or hesitation.

She'd run here without a plan—without even thinking at all, because if she *had* thought, she wouldn't have come. She was a thief, and a thief would never charge into a fight. But beyond reason, beyond practicality, she had needed to see if it was true. Somehow the only thing worse than their dying would be their dying where she couldn't see.

But all the people she could see around her now were strangers—strangers who were very much having the worst of it. Why did the soldiers not press them to surrender, take captives to interrogate about the location of their leaders? They were killing with an abandon she could never have imagined, as if every foe they'd ever have to fight were in the streets today.

Another moment of that, and she'd have run away. But then she spotted Naishe, struggling past the bodies pressing in on all sides, friend and foe alike. She had her quiver on her back, but could not have hoped to draw her bow in such close quarters. As the soldiers began to tighten around her and the last of her band, Naishe flickered in and out of view, dodging and stabbing and pushing back against the relentless tide. The distance between her and Marceline lessened, inch by inch. But there were too many focused on her, too many comrades who couldn't hold their own. And Marceline remembered the knife she carried.

She'd practiced it, hadn't she, on the back of the door at Tom's? She'd thrown the knife over and over, and now it stuck . . . most of the time. If it was all she could do for Naishe, shouldn't she at least do that much?

She drew the knife, and aimed it at the guard closest to her—with a prayer, just in case, to any gods who might exist, and be listening.

Perhaps the gods only half heard her: the knife flew straight and true, striking the soldier's face dead-on . . . hilt-first. She wasn't strong enough to break his nose, but the impact distracted him from Naishe. He turned and locked eyes with Marceline, and the look of utter fury on his face, as if he beheld his mortal enemy, made any possible defiance she could have felt wither and die. He didn't call out to her, even to threaten. He simply changed direction, and charged at her, sword drawn.

The distance between them was too small. It had helped her hit him with the knife, but it also helped him catch up to her, pinning her arm to the side of a building with his free hand. She didn't understand. *I should be just a child to them,* she thought. *Are they under orders to kill everyone in the area? What could possibly be the point of that?*

It was in the nature of a thief to be resourceful—to slip out of even the tightest snare. But with that blade closing in on her, with no escape in sight, all Marceline did was close her eyes, shrink in on herself, and wait.

There was a noise, but it didn't sound like a blade slicing into flesh, and she didn't feel anything but a spray of liquid across her face, like rain. It had sounded like something moving very fast, and then a slight choking noise, and then nothing.

Marceline forced her eyes open.

She was just in time to see the guard's body drop. There was an arrow in his throat.

Behind him was Naishe, the only one left standing from her knot of combatants, lowering her bow. Blood was streaming down her face from a wound on her temple. "Are you all right?" she asked.

Marceline walked toward her slowly, half uncertain she was real. She reached up to touch the side of Naishe's head, and sagged in relief. It was bleeding freely, but it wasn't deep. She would be fine.

"I thought they were going to kill you," she said.

Naishe shook her head. "It would take more than that to kill me." In anyone else that would've irritated her, but Naishe didn't say it like a boast, just a fact. She was already walking past Marceline, and beckoned for her to follow. "Come on. We can't waste time here."

Marceline hurried to her side. "Do you know where Mouse is?"

"No, but he isn't the priority now. I have to get you out of here. This isn't a battle we can win."

Marceline felt the stirrings of returning panic. She'd been so certain Naishe would be able to do something to stop this. "We can't just abandon him!"

"That's the only thing we can do," Naishe told her, as stoic as ever. "Perhaps we ought to have abandoned him when he first outlined his plan, when Rask and I both felt uneasy with it. But in the end we trusted his orders, and it's his orders that put us here. As leader, he should take responsibility for that. We shouldn't put his life higher than our own, or our other comrades'. And I don't believe he would want us to."

Her words did nothing to assuage Marceline's despair. "But if we don't even try—"

"I *have* tried," Naishe insisted. "He and his group were north of the warehouse; that area is swarming with guards right now. If you think this is bad . . ." She trailed off. "There are people much closer to us than he is—people we might be able to help. Or that *I* might be able to help. You should get yourself to safety."

"But—"

Naishe put a hand on her arm. "Please. Don't throw your life after his. Let me save at least one person."

Her untouchable mask had dropped; there was real pain in her eyes, horror and sorrow that ran as deep as Marceline's, and regret that ran much deeper. Marceline knew that she said none of this lightly—that no one would have given more to stop this, if stopping it were possible.

"I'm going to help you, at least," she said. "What should we do?"

"Stay close to me. We're going to keep moving, but we're going to rescue as many people as we can along our route. They aren't trying to capture, contain, or drive off anyone—they're just butchering them. It's obscene. We have to get to safety before we can be identified—so if guards do get a close look at our faces, we're going to have to kill them."

"Where is safety?" Marceline asked. "The meeting place?"

"No. Now that you say it, that's a good question." Naishe grimaced. "Rask and his people were the farthest to the warehouse, right behind Mouse and Wren and their number. He called the retreat first—I heard him. But he had some reason to think the meeting place had been discovered—he was telling his people to disperse. Let me think . . . do you know Ashencourt?"

"Aye—you'd be surprised how much I've heard about that place lately. What's there?"

"A long-abandoned shop—the sign's old and hard to read, but it's something about 'Reliable Remedies.' We only started using it recently. If we're separated, let's meet again there."

It was so strange: in their immediate vicinity, bodies littered the street, in numbers Marceline's mind struggled to comprehend. But as soon as she and Naishe turned back around another bend, putting the warehouse and all roads that led to it behind them, the carnage abruptly stopped. There were some living people, wounded or exhausted. But no soldiers, and no dead.

They didn't find many of their people alive—a couple already in full flight, a young woman with a wounded arm whom they warned from retreating to the meeting place. No one wanted to stay and help them, and Marceline couldn't blame them. She was surprised she herself hadn't run away—she'd be safe from the soldiers in Sheath, she was sure. No one would look for members of the resistance in Sheath.

Why was she still staying, then? There was a deep, relentless sadness in her when she thought of the others: Mouse, Wren, Talia. Perhaps she wanted to see with her own eyes what had become of them. Or perhaps there was something about having Naishe see her run away, after Naishe had saved her life, that made the thought of running seem too sour.

Then, as the two of them rounded a corner at top speed, Naishe stopped so abruptly that Marceline almost ran into her. Coming around from the other side, stopped just as completely and staring just as wide, was Wren Fletcher, sweat-soaked hair swept back from his mismatched eyes, a bloody sword hanging limply in his hand.

Even with all they had to do, with all the danger they were in, for a handful of moments those two just stared at each other, as if they were the only two people in the world. Wren recovered first—which was, honestly, stunning. "Naishe. I'm so . . . I wasn't sure . . ."

She cut him off, putting her hand over his wrist. "How bad is it by the warehouse?"

He shuddered. "Bad. I think some of ours got away, but the majority were cut down. Most of Zack's and mine, and about a third of Rask's—most of his retreated when he called, and he helped them fight back out. I managed to escape when there was no one left alive around me to fight for. I don't even know how I did it, to be honest. I feel like I shouldn't even be here."

Naishe pursed her lips, as if trying to force a bitter taste down her throat. "Mouse?"

Wren looked away. "Dead."

Marceline didn't trust herself to speak, but Naishe asked calmly, "Are you sure of that?"

"I saw it with my own eyes. He was my oldest friend, Naishe. I didn't want to die with him, but I wouldn't have abandoned him while he lived." He stared at his hands. "It was so strange. It was as if they knew which one he was. They charged right past me to get to him—like I wasn't even there. Even when I managed to kill a couple, I was of no consequence to them. And they were so many . . . they surrounded him and . . ." He squeezed his eyes shut. "I'm sure you can imagine."

Naishe still had her hand on his arm. "The monkey and I have been trying to pick up any stragglers. Do you know which way the guards were headed?"

Wren bit his lip. "They were vicious at first—terrifyingly focused, brutally effective. They just swept through us. But right at the end, they fell apart. Perhaps they no longer knew what to do after they'd broken us. Most of them either went north, where Zack's people were, or else fell back toward the warehouse. We should avoid that area."

"Well enough," Naishe said. "We'll go east and around. I think it would be best if we sheltered in Ashencourt."

"I'll follow you, then, if that's all right." When she nodded, he finally broke the contact between them, stepping around her to tap Marceline's shoulder gently. "I'm touched you came to help us, monkey. Though I can't help but wish you'd been spared all this."

They almost didn't find anyone else. At first the streets were deserted, and then more and more non-resistance people started filtering in, ordinary citizens who were confused and wary about what must have taken place. The three of them started moving faster—they didn't want anyone to get a good enough view of them to answer any guards' questions. It was Marceline who saw her, little more than a slim shadow at the corner of a building.

She grabbed Naishe's arm. "Wait!" she hissed. "Look!"

When they saw who she meant, they moved as fast as she did. Talia was leaning against the wall, sweat-streaked and panting for breath. One arm was pressed tightly against her heaving abdomen, as if forcing her upright, and the other was clenched into a shaking fist at her side. Though her feet looked about ready to give out, when she saw them a bright smile burst across her face. "Thank the . . . gods. I couldn't find anyone . . . the rest of us were . . . killed, and I thought . . ."

"It's all right," Wren said. "I saw Rask with most of your lot—they managed to get out. They aren't all—"

Talia shook her head fiercely. "You don't understand. I . . . stayed. We'd gotten closer than anyone . . . some of us . . . we couldn't bear to give up when we were so close. I told Rask we could make it, but he . . . he wouldn't listen."

"You ignored his orders?" Naishe's face was stern. "Talia, you shouldn't have—"

"I know . . . I know." She laughed weakly. "I'm not the fighter . . . that Rask is. I wasn't strong enough to save the rest of them, or . . . to make it all the way back. But I made it . . . that far. Like I told him I would."

Her fist unclenched, clawing at her side. "It's in . . . it's right here." Naishe gently brushed her fingers aside, reaching into her pocket and removing a bloodstained sheet of parchment crumpled around an object Marceline couldn't make out.

"That's it," Talia said. "That's what Elgar was protecting in there. That's what Mouse wanted."

Naishe didn't even try to unwrap it, still focused on Talia. "You truly found it? Gods, even Rask might have to forgive you for that."

Talia shook her head. "Always thought he was an ass, but . . . he was right. It was dangerous, too dangerous, but I had to try. Just hope it's worth it . . . just hope it . . . does some good . . ."

Then her other arm shifted, and the rest of them saw why it had been pressed against her stomach so tightly. There was a harsh noise as all three of them, even Naishe, felt their breath leave them in a horrified gasp.

Talia just laughed again. "Aye, it's . . . bad. I made it, but not . . . not clean."

Naishe shoved Elgar's prize into her pocket, with barely a glance at it, and gripped Talia's free arm. "Talia, listen. I can fix this. I know it's a ways off yet, but if you can just hold on until we get you to the Ashencourt house, I swear I know what to do. I've seen my mother—I've helped—you have to trust me. I can treat this wound, but you have to hold on until we reach Ashencourt."

Talia looked more troubled than relieved. "Naishe, I can barely walk. I'll slow you down so much . . . it isn't worth—"

"I said *listen* to me," Naishe snapped, with all the harshness she would use when arguing with Rask, or in the days when she'd first dismissed Marceline as a thief. "There's no reason for you to die of this. My mother fixed worse than this all the time. But if you tell yourself it's already lost, you'll never make it to Ashencourt. And I need you to make it. I won't get there a step ahead of you, you can be sure of that."

"And you know if she doesn't, I won't, either," Wren said.

Talia gritted her teeth, her face wracked with indecision. "The last time I tried to walk—"

"The last time you tried to walk you were alone. Come on, Wren." But as the two of them moved toward her, Naishe suddenly flinched. "Gods *damn* it."

"What?" Marceline asked.

"My supplies are all back at the bloody meeting place. The Ashencourt house is so new, I haven't stocked . . . there'll be bandages there, but . . ." She still kept moving, supporting Talia on one side, and Wren mirrored her on the other. "I know there isn't any rashenot. That's the most important thing—with a wound this severe I've got to stitch it, so it's not even just the wound itself. It's the needle, my hands . . ." She screwed her face up in frustration, her words trailing off.

"I think I understand," Marceline said, trying to summon the details of that conversation with Peck. "What is it you need? The complete list?"

"Besides the rashenot? Not much. My needle and thread would be ideal, but I could replace those easily if I had to; they're everywhere. There might even be spares in the other house, for all I know. It's the rashenot itself that's most difficult to come by."

Marceline slowed, taking stock of the situation. Physically, she was the weakest of the three of them, which was why Talia was giving each of her arms to the other two and there was no more room for Marceline to help. Naishe had to stay with Talia at all times, to do whatever could be done for her with what she had, and Wren didn't know what rashenot smelled like. Every line of thought led to the same conclusion.

"I can get it," she heard herself say.

Naishe turned to look at her. She didn't say that it was too dangerous, or that Marceline couldn't possibly manage it, or that she didn't trust Marceline to do it. She said, "Can you?"

Marceline knew what that question meant: both an opportunity to back out and a sober testing of her intentions. Her mind raced for a moment, almost panicking, but even through the uncertainty and fear, she couldn't see how she could give a different answer.

"I can," she said. "I will." She nodded at them. "I'll meet you there after."

Naishe nodded back. "Be safe."

Talia groaned, "Monkey . . ."

"It'll be fine," Marceline said. She didn't want to give herself too much time to think about it, to change her mind. "But you'd *better* make it there, Talia. If I stick my neck out like this for nothing, I'll never forgive you. Remember that."

She swallowed any additional words she might have spoken along with the lump in her throat, and ran back the way they had come.

She saw no more fighting. Soldiers still ran through the streets, but they glanced at Marceline without a trace of interest—many looked as confused and tentative as the civilians who were starting to approach them with questions. Where had all that rage and purpose gone? Did they believe they had eliminated the entire resistance at a stroke?

The meeting place looked the same as ever, which almost made her angry—as if it had the gall to pretend that everything was normal. But the important thing was that there were no soldiers near it—no one at all that she could see.

Her hand trembled on the latch. Could she really be the first one here? Had everyone else abandoned this place? Or, even worse, was there no one else left to make it back?

When she shut the door behind her, she drew the bolt on the inside—paltry protection against anyone armed and determined to get in, but it might buy her a little time. The first floor was deserted, but she knew Naishe kept her supplies in a small room adjoining the space where Mouse presided over his meetings. She corrected herself reflexively—where Mouse *had* presided over his meetings—and crept up the stairs, though even she couldn't prevent a board from squeaking here and there.

Again she paused when she reached the door, trying not to think about her first meeting with Mouse and the rest of them. When she heard the sound of rustling from inside, her heart sprang into her throat. She edged closer, trying to peer through the crack in the door, but it was suddenly flung open, a blade pointed at her neck.

Marceline yelped, but in the next instant she relaxed. So did Rask, and he withdrew his sword, sheathing it again and stepping away from her. "Monkey? What the hell do you want?"

"I'm getting something for Naishe. What are you doing?" There was a great pile in the room of books and loose papers, and Rask was rummaging around for even more, throwing it all together haphazardly.

"What I have to. What is it you need?"

Marceline scowled. "Give me a proper answer, and I'll give you the same."

His expression matched hers. "There's no point in continuing to fight out there. This building was our main meeting place—there are all kinds of records. I can't let them fall into Elgar's hands. Who knows how many of us he could identify?"

Well, Marceline had to admit that was smart, even if she also knew he might have been able to keep Talia from getting injured if he'd stayed to fight with her. "Are you going to be able to carry all that, though?"

He didn't answer. "What is it you need? If Elgar's guards know about this place—and I'd bet my last pair of breeches they do—they'll be here soon. I won't allow anything to be left for them."

"It's medicine." She stepped into the adjoining room, but he followed her. "I can find it on my own."

He ignored that. "We should probably destroy whatever of this you don't need, too. Throw it all together."

He reached for the jar of lesser anguis, and Marceline clamped her hand down on the lid. "Don't! That's dangerous!"

Rask didn't remove his hand. "Dangerous how?"

"It's lesser anguis. Naishe says it's highly flammable. The slightest spark could do it."

"It'll catch fire?" He wrested it from her, and she didn't have the strength to stop him. "So her little potions will come to some use after all. Thank you for that."

She bundled Naishe's needle and thread in a tiny ball of bandages, stuffing the lot of it into her pocket. "Rask, Naishe said—"

The sound of several shouts and many footsteps drew them both to the window. "Shit," Rask snapped, staring down at the group of guards outside the door. It was hard to tell with that blue-black color, but their clothes looked fresh and unstained. Was this a different group from the ones near the warehouse? "You won't be able to get out that way. Go out into the other room. Take the window at the very back. If you could climb the bloody Precipitate, a couple rooftops should be no trouble."

Marceline shook her head. "Not without the rashenot. Just give me a moment and I'll—"

"Monkey, there's no time! You've got to go!"

"It's for Talia," Marceline said. "Talia fought through them without you—she got it from them, but she's badly hurt."

His eyes widened, and he drove his fist into the wall in frustration. "I told that stupid girl to retreat!"

"Naishe can save her," Marceline insisted. "Naishe told us she can save her, or I wouldn't be here at all. I just have to get it to Ashencourt."

"The Ashencourt house? Is it safe?" There was the sound of feet stomping over the floorboards below, and he hissed in frustration. "Damn it, fine! Take the thing—wrap it up in one of those blankets like a sling, so you can still climb. You understand?"

"Aye, I know!" She lunged for the jars—she thought she remembered which one it was, but she had to be sure. A single sniff confirmed it: bitter enough to make her very nostrils cringe, but still it was sweet to her.

As she was wrapping it up as Rask had suggested, Rask himself was dripping the anguis everywhere he could, starting with the pile of papers and leading toward the door, where the footsteps were now on the stairs. When the guards flung open the door, Rask threw the jar and all its remaining contents into their faces. They recoiled as the glass shattered, several fragments cutting into the face and hands of the nearest one, and splattering the group of them with the last drops of the anguis.

Rask had already retreated to the pile, pulling out his flint and striker on the way. Marceline shrank back toward the far window as he struck the flint, coaxing a spark at the edge of the shallow puddle.

The anguis was as obliging as Naishe had said: in an instant the entire pile was awash with flame, a trail running faster than any mortal creature down the line of liquid Rask had set down and into the faces of the oncoming guardsmen. Those at the front screamed as the fire caught their clothes and spread. If this was what *lesser* anguis was like, Marceline didn't want to see what the greater version could do.

They hadn't won victory yet, though. The guards at the back, who hadn't been caught in the initial spray, still pressed forward around their screaming comrades, careful to avoid the line of flame. Then one of the injured ones stumbled, a knee going down right across the burning liquid, and the rest of them recoiled as his wailing became unbearable. Despite the chaos, Marceline tried to keep count: the one who'd just fallen wouldn't be getting up again, but there were two uninjured, two more that might manage to put the flames out, or charge at them anyway . . . still too many. "What now?" she asked Rask.

He scowled. "Now you go out the damned window, like I said."

"But you—"

"They've seen us. I have to make sure they burn along with this place. You run back to Naishe and Talia."

"You'll never fight them all," Marceline said. "You'll never get—"

"You haven't seen me fight." As the first soldier made his way around the flames, Rask drew his sword. "Monkey, if you don't go now, you won't be able to! I need to focus!"

The heat was already reddening her skin, the smoke stinging her eyes, and the window was right there. Marceline swung herself out and up, her last glimpse of the room's interior the sight of Rask closing with his foes.

THE WHOLE WAY to the Ashencourt house, Naishe prayed that she hadn't made a mistake. To have saved the monkey only to lose her for good by allowing her such a dangerous undertaking . . . she didn't want to think about it. The only way to remain calm was to keep her attention firmly focused on what she had to do, and that alone: one foot in front of the other. Keep Talia steady, and don't jostle her. Take enough of her weight, but keep moving, moving, moving. Just reach the house. Just reach the door.

Wren matched her step for step, Talia's free arm slung across his shoulders. They were close, Naishe knew. Just a little more . . .

Wren coughed as he tried to speak. "Isn't it . . . around that corner there?"

"That's right." She struggled forward. "Are you with us, Talia?"

"Barely." She was too weak even to laugh. From Talia, that was a bad sign. "Will I get . . . to lie down when we get there?"

"You'll have to." Anything to slow the bleeding. "And as soon as the monkey gets back with my rashenot, I'll take care of the rest."

That was what she had to say, and that was what had to be true. The monkey had to come back, and Naishe had to do a healer's work, had to remember, had to—

"Here," Wren said, reaching for the door.

They managed to get her inside, to drag a cot into the center of the room and lay her down on it. They used a torn-up blanket for a bandage—had to stem the bleeding until it was safe to stitch—and then they waited. But they couldn't wait long, Naishe knew.

"Naishe," Talia murmured, pallid and sweating, "I don't want the monkey . . . don't want her to . . . die for . . ."

"That's not going to happen," Wren said, and Naishe was grateful, because she didn't know how her voice would have sounded if she'd tried to force it out. She held Talia's hand, and squeezed her eyes shut. Gods, she had to find the strength for this somewhere. Her mother had all sorts of tricks for her stitching, ways to add stability and reduce scarring, but Naishe just needed to remember something, anything, that would work.

There was one other matter—something she dreaded, but that she might as well get over with while they were stuck waiting here and Talia was still conscious. "Talia," she said. "I have to explain something to you. It's going to be difficult."

Talia pointed feebly at her stomach. "Not as difficult as this accursed thing. Tell me."

"I don't have . . ." She choked on the words, and steadied herself before beginning again. "A proper healer would have various ways to numb the pain before treating a wound or setting a bone. Snow's down's easy to get, but you can't use it on open wounds; it can't get into the blood. Other methods are a bit rarer, but normally I could . . ." She was stalling. She just had to say it. "I don't have anything here, that I could safely use, that would dull your pain. But I have to stitch it anyway."

". . . Oh," Talia said.

She was quiet after that, which was awful. And then she said, with a fragile laugh, "If that's the case, it almost sounds like . . . dying would be simpler."

No, she couldn't die. Naishe wanted to tell her that, but she knew it would just be laying another burden on Talia's shoulders. She had done far too much already.

Wren said, "Talia, you can trust her. You know you can. At least let her try."

Talia sighed. "It's not as if it can get any worse, can it?"

The door banged open, and for a moment Naishe thought Talia's words had brought on some further doom, that somehow the soldiers had managed to follow them even here. But there, scratched up, wild-eyed, and wearing what looked like a blanket on her back, was the monkey. She was the most welcome sight Naishe could ever remember seeing.

Talia sagged into the cot, her relief palpable. The monkey was still moving: shutting the door, pulling something out of her pocket and shoving it at Naishe—her needle and thread—and unslinging the blanket from her back. She set the jar of rashenot carefully down on the floor. "You should know, the meeting house is burned. *And* the guards knew where it was, so don't try to go back there."

"Did the guards burn it?" Naishe asked, already cleaning her hands and instruments.

"No, it was Rask. To keep them from taking anything." She squinted at Talia. "Should I do anything? To help you with her?"

"Yes." Could she really do this? So many times she'd followed her mother, so many times, and she'd been resentful every time. She wanted to go outside, she wanted to practice her archery, she wanted to climb trees or ford rivers or sleep out under the stars. But still her mother had brought her. *Watch closely, Vanaishendi. You mustn't touch, but see and hear all you can. For a healer, every misfortune is a lesson, to be better prepared for those that follow.*

Gods, why hadn't she listened? What could have been more important than this?

Help me, she pleaded. *Mother, she's dying, you've got to help me.*

"Both of you," she said to Wren and the monkey. "There's nothing here I can tie her limbs to. You've got to hold her, so she doesn't thrash when I'm stitching." They both flinched, but they nodded. They must have known it was the only way. "Talia, can you hear me? I know it will hurt, but . . . it has to be this way. To help you. You understand that, right?"

Talia blinked at her, her eyes barely focusing. "I understand, but . . . I can't promise you I won't move. Just . . . get it over with. Don't mind whatever I do."

Naishe nodded, and they began.

After Talia lost consciousness, it became much easier. Before that, it was a nightmare. Talia could hardly help from crying out in pain, and the rest of them felt so guilty about it they couldn't meet one another's eyes while they did what they had to do. More than once, Naishe thought she wouldn't be able to go on. But she fixed a picture in her mind—the clearest picture she could recall of her mother's actions—and forced herself to follow it. It was just like bringing Talia here had been: one foot in front of the other.

And then she raised the needle to make another stitch, and realized she had to tie it off instead. It was done.

She thought Talia might wake again, after, but she didn't. The stitches Naishe had made were far from her mother's, far from that perfect image in her mind. And yet, perhaps, they were close enough after all.

Once they'd ensured Talia's breathing was steady, the three of them all but collapsed on the floor. Wren seemed calm, but after several moments of staring about her in a daze, Naishe realized that the monkey was shaking.

Of course. She was so young. A child, still, however she pretended otherwise. It was a child's right to be overwhelmed at horrors.

Naishe enfolded her in her arms, and pulled her close. The monkey made a little strangled sound, unable to force words out, or else keeping sobs in. Naishe stroked her matted hair, hummed a half-remembered tune from her childhood—a song from a time when someone stronger and wiser and older was always there to take care of things so she wouldn't have to.

She held the girl until she stopped shaking, until her body felt relaxed and still. Only then did she speak. "It's all right," she said. "You can leave. You can go home. No one could ask any more of you than you've already done."

For what felt like a long time, the girl stayed where she was. But Naishe did not press her, and did not speak again. Finally, she stirred, gently disentangling herself from Naishe's arms. "I will . . . I think . . . I will go home. But I'll come back. To see her."

"Monkey, wait." Wren dug in his pockets, then extended his open palm. On it lay the small white stone she had taken from Elgar. "I asked my father, but he didn't know any more about it than I did. We don't think it was ever meant to be an arrowhead. I meant to give it back to you before the battle, but I'm afraid it slipped my mind."

After she had gone, Naishe sat on the floor beside Talia, watching the fitful rise and fall of her breathing. She couldn't say whether she had done the right thing. She had felt that it was, but even more than that, she had felt that it was the only thing she could do.

Wren went to the back room to get more blankets, laying one gently over Talia and wrapping another around Naishe's shoulders. She took it gratefully, only then recognizing the chill that had surrounded her. "Wren, you should go, too. You'll be safest at home with your parents."

Wren didn't break eye contact—unusual for him. It was more unusual still to be able to look into both his eyes at once, but she felt better for it. "Do you want me to go?" he asked.

"You heard what happened to Rask at the safehouse. Anyone who stays here may be putting themselves in danger. And if we ever all meet again—if there's even a resistance left after this—these actions may be held against us. We know that we saved the ones we could, that we felt we had to prioritize Talia's life over anything else . . . but the others may not see it that way."

Wren nodded. "I know that. But Naishe, do you *want* me to leave?"

Perhaps it would've shown better leadership to say yes. There was nothing he could feasibly do to help her or Talia by remaining here, and he *would* be much safer with his family. But she knew Wren wasn't asking her for orders, or direction, or advice. He was asking her to tell him the truth.

"No," she said.

Wren folded another blanket, creating a makeshift cushion so he could sit beside her. His shoulder brushed against hers, though she could not truly say who was leaning against whom. "All right, then," he said.

CHAPTER SIXTY-TWO

Araveil

"DON'T DO THAT," Hywel said, and Kel couldn't help but be thankful; all that banging was grating on his ears. "You'll hurt yourself."

"What's the alternative?" Laen panted, contorting his body into heretofore unseen shapes, as if all the manacles around his wrists needed were the right angle at which to strike the stone before they would break. "Just lie back and accept it?"

"You can be chained up and accept it, or be chained up and pretend there's something you can do about it," his brother said. "There aren't any alternatives. It's the same either way."

Kel didn't think either of them was approaching this in precisely the right way, but as he was in a less painful position, he thought it wouldn't be fair to say anything.

The three of them—Kel, Laen, and Hywel—were kept in their own private cell, stone-walled and uniformly square. Laen and Hywel were chained hand and foot to the wall, but even though there was an extra set of chains hanging there, Kel was given quite different treatment. He hoped it was because someone understood about his legs, and was concerned about what might befall him if he were chained in a similar way—it implied they wished to keep him not just alive but in decent health. He had never been able to stand on his feet continuously, without crutches, for so much as half an hour before the pain became overwhelming, and no doubt if he *had* been chained his legs would simply have given out before too long. Then he would have been left hanging by the wrists, and he couldn't imagine that position would be very sustainable.

Instead, one of the soldiers had brought in a wooden chair—simply carved, but it had arms, which was what they required. Instead of being chained to a wall, Kel was bound hand and foot to the chair with ropes—not pleasant, but clearly the superior option.

The chair sat a couple feet away from the back wall—no doubt so Kel couldn't crack his head open if he knocked it over. From that vantage point, he could see most of the cell, but since Laen was chained in the middle of the wall and Hywel on his far side, Kel and Hywel had to crane their necks to look each other in the face, and Kel imagined most of him was cut off from Hywel's view by his brother's body.

Clang, clang, clang. At least Laen's strength was greater than Kel had thought, for him to still be at it after all this time. "We must still have supporters in Araveil," he said. "Do you think they'd be able to get us out of here?"

"I don't know," Hywel said. "How many of them are even alive? We don't even know if Ilyn and Ithan are alive."

"We know Lessa and Hayne are," Kel spoke up. "Talis probably is as well, given all the preparations they'd made to subdue her without killing her."

Laen scoffed. "Aye, such a great help she turned out to be."

"We couldn't have known they would be able to stop Talis's magic," Kel said. "Even the marquise didn't say anything about that."

"That doesn't mean she didn't know about it," Laen said. "Just that she didn't tell you."

Kel had to admit he didn't know for sure, so he let the rebuke pass. He wanted to save his strength, of mind and body both, to work out a way they could salvage this, but where could he begin? Even if they could break Talis free, what then?

The heavy door rattled in its frame as someone fumbled with their keys outside it. When a servant finally swung it wide, Kel held his breath. Standing in the doorway was one person he had seen before, and one he had only heard tales of, but he knew both were formidable.

The big man, Ghilan, looked much more relaxed when he wasn't dressed for battle, but he didn't look much less frightening. This close, his great height and breadth were even more apparent, the muscles in his huge arms clearly visible beneath the thin gray wool of his tunic. His bone-white smile reached all the way to his pale little eyes: no insincerity, but a great deal of hunger. Beside him, the woman who could only be Edith Selwyn looked slender and small, but not especially vulnerable. It wasn't the rapier she wore at her belt so much as the ease and confidence of her bearing that reinforced that impression; she knew she was in charge, down to the marrow of her bones. Perhaps there were those who found her beautiful: her golden hair was long and shining, and the shape and features of her face were soft, even if its expression wasn't. But her eyes, a more faded gray than her retainer's tunic, reminded Kel of the skin of a fish: slippery, and cold.

"Laen Markham," she said. "We meet again. I did warn you that this would be your fate, if you continued down such a grievous path."

"I always knew I'd have to fight you, Selwyn," Laen snapped. "Don't pretend you care for my well-being."

"I merely care for our province's well-being. It does not do for hot-blooded young boys to disturb the peace in such a manner."

"This is no peace." Laen probably would have spat in her face if he could have managed it, but she was standing too far away; he settled for hitting the stone floor at her feet. "If you have simply come to gloat, I'll have none of it."

"I have come, as ever, in search of information. You've a much more curious following this time. Reglay's king? The fascinating creature you brought to us? Wherever you picked them up, I'd wager that you returned to Araveil much more knowledgeable than when you left it."

"Talis is human," Kel said. "She's not a creature."

She turned those cold fish-eyes in his direction, and he had to suppress a shudder. "Human? Once, to be sure, but no longer. I have long awaited the chance to secure such a prize. Now if only I could find a true mage, I'd have everything I need."

"You'll learn nothing about that from us," Laen said.

"I'll learn at least something," she replied, and drew her rapier.

Kel could see Laen struggling not to flinch as she approached him, but she merely held the gleaming blade against his cheek. After several seconds passed, she did the same to Hywel, and then moved on to Kel. She angled the blade down so it could reach him, and he stayed very still. It didn't feel strange, though, just like any other bit of metal.

"Hmm," she said, finally sheathing the rapier. "Well, it isn't any of you three, at least." She stepped back toward Ghilan, and cleared her throat. "The imperator has sent one of his subordinates here. He is currently under my hospitality. I suspect that, when we next meet, we shall discuss any prisoners that may reside here, and what is to be done with them. If there is any way you can make yourselves useful to me, any illumination you can provide, it is in both our interests that you reveal it."

So they could live for as long as they talked, was that it? "I don't know what subjects are relevant to you," Kel said. There had to be something he could say that would be useless, or close enough—or else something she was destined to find out anyway.

Laen glared at him. "What are you doing?"

"Trying to find out more information," Kel said, but it was the administrator's cold eyes he looked at. "Just as you are. You can't begrudge me that much, can you?"

To his surprise, she could; her lips pressed together in a displeased little frown. "Knowledge is wasted on those who lack the talent to put it to use."

"I may not need to do that," Kel said, "but I need to understand what you want, or how would I be able to give it to you?"

She clicked her tongue. "Magic. The creature. The true nature of the stone Laen Markham attempted to use against my retainer. The whereabouts of any of your friends who may still be free."

"I don't know anything about the last one," Kel said. "But I know more about the stone than Laen and Hywel do, and they know more about Talis than I do. They traveled with her before I ever met them." If he divided the valuable information among the three of them, he made it less likely she'd decide to save one and kill the rest.

But Laen didn't understand, of course. "How dare you? You little coward!"

"Laen, stay calm," Kel said, trying his best to follow his own advice.

"He's right," Hywel said. "Let it go. Let it go, Laen."

His brother scoffed. "No matter what Kelken does, I won't give that traitor a single word that might help her. Do you hear me, Selwyn?"

She must have, though she didn't even shrug. "You may yet have time to change your mind, and leave off this childish petulance. I cannot say how *much* time, but I will do what I can to afford you the opportunity to—"

"Let me be clear," Laen said. "Selwyn, you are a grasping, coldhearted bitch who stole this country from your betters despite having not a drop of legitimacy or merit in your veins. You are a blight on the people of this land, who know and feel your unworthiness, and the doom you would lead Lanvaldis into. They will always fight you, no matter what you do to me. But I will not cooperate with you. I wouldn't so much as give you the location of a pile of dung I encountered on the road."

Hywel and Kel were holding their breath; Ghilan's anticipatory giggle could almost have been called childlike, were it not for the depth of its pitch. But Administrator Selwyn's face didn't change, and she didn't respond to Laen at all. Instead, she turned her head to the side, over her shoulder, and addressed her retainer. "Ghilan, Imperator Elgar has given us specific orders regarding the so-called heirs of King Eira, has he not?"

The big man looked surprised; no doubt he knew the administrator was fully aware of whatever those orders were. "He has, Administrator."

She raised an eyebrow, but otherwise kept herself perfectly still. "And you and I are nothing if not loyal servants to His Eminence, are we not?"

That made Ghilan's mouth stretch in a wide grin, a dry snicker escaping it like cracking wood. "Oh, aye, Administrator. For loyalty there's no one like the two of us, I'm sure."

"Well, then we'd best make entirely certain those orders are followed, no? It would not do to overlook some crucial detail. Please recite them for me again, if you would."

"Of course." He bowed. "His Eminence wished that the boy, the heir of King Eira, should . . . be kept alive." His grin broadened after that slight pause, and Kel suspected that he had realized whatever his mistress was planning to do. "But he said that the other members of the boy's party were expendable."

"Yes, that's what I thought I remembered as well," the administrator said. "We shall, of course, respect His Eminence's wishes in this, as in all things." She paced to the end of the row, and lowered her chin so she could lock eyes with Kel. "However, when obeying orders it is wise to consider the greater intent behind them, not only the specific words employed in their conveyance. The young king of Reglay, I think, should not be considered part of the boy's party, but his own separate actor."

"I agree," Ghilan said.

"And the creature, of course, is necessary to my research, so I can hardly dispense with her. But as for the rest . . . as for the rest, I suppose there is no one to speak for them."

"No one at all," the big man said.

Laen gritted his teeth. "If you think to threaten my brother, or any of my friends, know that once I escape these bonds I will *ensure*—"

Quick as a blink, Administrator Selwyn's rapier was drawn and in her hand. She held the point to Laen's throat, and then she pressed it in.

The blade sank in so quickly, as if Laen's skin were no barrier at all. His eyes bulged, and he made a dry choking sound; blood spurted from his neck when Selwyn pulled her sword back out. Hywel made a sound, too, like a cut-off gasp, and then he started to shake, as if he wanted to sob but couldn't. Laen's body was shaking, too, until it wasn't.

Administrator Selwyn cleaned her sword, and returned it to its sheath. Only then did she turn back to her retainer. "Ghilan," she said, "what do you see here?"

"Hmm," the big man mused, stepping in front of Hywel. "I see the boy, the heir of King Eira, who we've got to keep alive . . ." He glanced over at Kel. ". . . the king of Reglay . . ." Then he looked at Laen's body. "And a sack of spoiling meat, Administrator. I believe that's all."

A twitch ran across the administrator's mouth, one corner curling up ever so slightly. "Precisely so. If it's spoiled, probably best to dispose of it before the smell becomes too severe, wouldn't you say?"

Ghilan bowed. "I'll have someone see to it at once, Administrator."

He walked over to Hywel, who was still making that gasping noise, a sob or scream or retch that couldn't break free, and patted his cheek. "Cheer up, little bit," he said. "Just think, now you have a crown!"

FROM THE MOMENT they met, Edith Selwyn had regarded Varalen as one vulture regards another along the spine of a rotting corpse. He had never expected outright submission—Elgar had put her in charge of the whole province, after all—but surely just a smidge of gratitude wasn't unreasonable, given the great assistance he'd provided? Or so he had thought, but one look into that woman's eyes put all such thoughts to rest. Here was someone who had never felt gratitude a moment in her life—who felt herself entitled to any good fortune she had ever received, and guarded it as jealously as a dragon.

Varalen knew the nature of vultures and dragons too well not to be cautious. Even breaking his fast with her in her rooms, he was attended by three of his men. At her side she had only the big man with the warhammer, but Varalen didn't doubt he was sufficient. If she was a vulture, he was a hyena: just as hungry, but gleeful where she was grim, delighting in every scrap of flesh he could seize between his jaws.

Varalen cut into his hard-boiled eggs, trying not to grimace. He hated boiled eggs. "Do you feel you have been able to return this city to some semblance of proper order, Administrator?"

Though she had tied her hair back during the fighting, she had kept it loose ever since, a prop or curtain whenever she required one. "That was never in doubt. The chaos the pretender's misguided supporters created was dramatic, but it could never have sustained itself for long."

It certainly could have, absent the men I provided, Varalen thought. The rioters may have been mostly untrained, but they were numerous, and subduing them without a massacre had been no easy undertaking. "You must be pleased with the array of captives you've gathered."

The administrator allowed herself a small smile before tearing into a roll of bread with her teeth, and Varalen tried not to think of carrion birds. "Pleased indeed. The pretender, the king of Reglay . . . even the creature Eira sought to capture to no avail. Gerald Holm, more or less the leader of the rebels, was too wise to take part in the riot, but we took a relative of his—she was close to the pretender, so there may yet be a use for her. We even turned up the wayward scion of House Vandrith. I'm told he fought with formidable skill, but Ghilan took care of him."

"He's dead?" Varalen asked.

The big man shook his head. "Shattered his leg with my hammer, but he's alive. I figured he'd be too valuable to kill—give us a hostage with the rest of his kin. They can't rightly ask for him back any more than that sword of theirs."

Varalen cleared his throat. "Speaking of hostages, Administrator, were there not two pretenders to the throne of King Eira?"

"There were," she agreed, "but you needn't worry yourself about the other. He's dead."

"Killed in the fighting?"

She shrugged. "Or just afterward. Either way, I'm quite certain of it."

"And this . . . creature, as you call her. Is she some sort of mage?"

Selwyn's mouth pinched around her next bite; this "creature" was clearly a prized jewel atop her hoard. "Not precisely. The only word we have is *wardrenfell,* a rather clumsy and archaic term for one who possesses stray magic. The creatures are born human, but she is clearly other than that now."

"Did the imperator command you to capture her?"

Selwyn frowned, taking shelter behind her hair. "I only know of the creature's existence because my own research coincided with some correspondence of King Eira's I found upon taking up residence here. The imperator gave me leave to continue my research even after I became administrator, but I had no conclusive findings to report to him until now."

So whatever this was about, Selwyn possessed a passion for it that had lasted years. Varalen doubted it was a matter of some quaint little historical footnote; she didn't seem like *that* sort of scholar. "And now? What are these findings? You've been able to restrain her in some fashion?"

He knew that look: the disdainful glare of a studied expert who was positively incensed that a layman had dared attempt to comprehend her work. "*Restrain* hardly begins to describe it. We have rendered the creature not only powerless but practically insensate. She retains consciousness, but only barely; she seems blind and deaf to her surroundings. Unfortunately, I have not yet discovered a way to turn the creature's power toward our ends. Direct contact between vardrath steel and her skin appears to cause her tremendous pain, but I doubt this could be used as a persuasive tool. Perhaps if we could amass enough of the steel to build a chamber out of it . . ."

"Well, how much do you have?" Varalen asked, trying to bring her back to current realities.

"Nowhere near that much, I fear."

He wouldn't be put off that easily. "You have the manacles, and the big man's gauntlets . . ."

"And my rapier, and a handful of other ancient swords we were able to confiscate from the noble houses of Lanvaldis. Including the sword Ithan Vandrith and his family sought so desperately to keep from us."

Varalen frowned. "Why does the name *Vandrith* sound so familiar to me? I did spend quite a bit of time in southern Lanvaldis, helping King Eira's men fight off Caius Margraine, but I don't recall meeting anyone with that name."

"It's most likely his wife you're thinking of," Selwyn said. "Before she was Elin Margraine, she was Elin Vandrith. Twin sister to Lady Euvalie, the current head of their house."

"*Her* mother?" Varalen asked. "Arianrod Margraine's mother's family has a sword of vardrath steel?"

"Had," Selwyn said. "It is ours now."

Varalen had won an unquestionable victory in Araveil, and in another life he might have allowed himself a moment to breathe. But there was no time to waste. When *all* his enemies were defeated, Elgar had said. Only then would he take away Ryam's illness. And Elgar's greatest enemy was still free to do as she pleased.

The plan sprang into his mind fully formed. He knew exactly what he would do. "Administrator," he said, "I will need to take that sword with me when I go."

He'd known she would try to resist. Her displeasure was irrelevant. "You cannot order—"

"I can order such a thing, and whatever else I like," Varalen told her. "I speak with the imperator's voice. Unless he comes here himself, or sends word relieving me, I can command you as he could, in his interests."

In actuality, Elgar had given him no such authority, but he was confident Selwyn wouldn't call his bluff. He'd come into her city with an army, after all; why shouldn't she think he had the power to use it as he wished? "It is surely in His Eminence's best interests that I continue my research," she said instead.

Not so much as you might think, given his own magical proclivities. "With that in mind, Administrator, I believe my request is very reasonable," Varalen said. "I will not interfere with your research here; I will leave you to do with your creature as you see fit, and to play around with whatever other vardrath steel you may have or come to have. I merely require one sword's worth. You'll hardly miss it." His eyes drifted over her shoulder, coming to rest on the man beside her. "One sword, and him."

"Out of the question," Selwyn snapped. "If you want fighting men, you have plenty of your own."

"I don't have any as good as he is," Varalen said. "Not since Commander Shinsei was . . . injured at Mist's Edge. You can keep his gauntlets, but I'll need the man himself. Unless you'd rather explain your disobedience to the imperator."

He could feel her frustration, but she knew better than to fight back. Vultures were carrion birds; they loved the taste of flesh, but they were not true predators. "Are you prepared to go with him?" she asked Ghilan.

He shrugged. "Capable more than content, but orders are orders. My lord, I assume I'll be allowed to return to Araveil once your mission is complete?"

"I don't see why not," Varalen said.

"And what is this mission?" the administrator asked.

Varalen held back for the moment, sticking to generalities as she had. "With Lanvaldis calm again, I need to move on. It makes sense to pacify Esthrades next."

"Now that its marquise is gone, you mean?"

Varalen started. "Gone? Surely you can't mean she's dead?"

Ghilan laughed. "That'd be lucky, wouldn't it? But I imagine it'd take a lot to kill that one."

Administrator Selwyn gave her retainer a severe glance, and he quieted down, though not without a sly grin at the both of them. "Arianrod Margraine has once more left Esthrades in the hands of a quarter-court while she attends to matters elsewhere," she told Varalen. "It seems she has gone to Issamira, but the reports we have started to receive from thence have been confusing and contradictory. First there were rumors that Adora Avestri had been killed, but now there are many more reports that she is very much alive, and moving across the country in a flurry of activity. We've been hearing that her brother Hephestion usurped her throne, or that he only did so by mistake, fearing she was dead . . . that their uncle is dead, or that he is alive . . . it seems clear that *something* at the heart of that conflict has now come to the surface, but we may not know what precisely it is until the smoke clears."

And when the smoke clears, Varalen thought, *I'd be willing to bet Issamira will have a true ruler once more. And that means Elgar's time is running out.*

But he had to return to Elgar before they could do anything about Issamira, and Varalen had something he needed to accomplish first, while he remained in the east. "If Arianrod Margraine has abandoned her throne for the time being, that only makes my opportunity the richer, and my need greater and more urgent. I must have the sword, Administrator. The sword, and the loan of your man, to secure His Eminence's hold upon this continent."

"I cannot object to anything in His Eminence's interests," Selwyn said, though doubtless she wished she could. "But may I ask what you will be using such valuable assets for?"

Varalen grinned at her. "I'm going to use your vardrath steel for the same purpose you did. I'm going to catch myself a mage."

He'd expected that to put an end to all Selwyn's questions, but instead she only looked more concerned. "My lord, a *wardrenfell* and a mage are not the same thing. We have never tested the steel on a mage before. If you attempt to use it in that fashion, I will not bear responsibility if you are displeased with the result."

"Do you have reason to believe the steel will have no effect on a mage at all, Administrator?"

She allowed her hair to obscure her expression again, probably pondering whether she could risk lying to him. But in the end, she gritted her teeth and said, "No. I know for certain vardrath steel was used as a weapon against mages in the distant past. I have found many records to that effect. So whatever it does to them, it must be powerful enough to be useful. But that does not mean it will do the same thing to your prey that it did to my creature. The effect may be reduced, or greatly strengthened. It's even possible prolonged exposure to the steel might kill a mage outright. Would you be content with that?"

Elgar would no doubt prefer Arianrod Margraine alive if he could get her, but Varalen doubted he'd quibble with the precise outcome, so long as the mission was successful. As for Varalen himself? He gave Selwyn a patient smile. "Content? I'd be ecstatic."

"SHIT," DEINOL SAID. "What happened here?"

Coming to Araveil at all had been a sobering experience. It was as if a pall of dejection and fatigue had been thrown over the city and its people. Passersby walked with lowered heads and slumped shoulders, hardly stopping to exchange more than a few anxious words. Deinol saw no children playing in the street, and even the calls of shopkeeps and vendors seemed muted. But they saw an even harsher sight when they stumbled onto a wide square around a bell tower: the ruins of what must once have been a great market, now nearly deserted, still littered with smashed stalls and trampled produce.

"Did some drunken giant stumble through here?" Deinol asked a passing woman, hoping to get at least the hint of a smile.

Instead, he got a melancholy sigh. "You must have just arrived. A group of impatient fools, who struggled bravely but uselessly against the administrator's men. They thought they were fighting for King Eira's nephew, but while they were busy with their little riot, Selwyn's soldiers snapped him up. I hear he's in the dungeons now, or dead."

"Shit," Deinol said again. "If only we'd gotten here a couple days earlier."

"I'm not sure what you think you could have done, sir. The reinforcements from the west decided the matter beyond amendment. Some lord drove them hard all the way from Reglay to make it here, or so we're told. Oswhent, they call him. He's yet to show his face since the battle."

Deinol nearly staggered in shock. "*That* little ponce? He's commanding an army now?" He grinned at Lucius. "Guess Elgar was pretty forgiving about his failure with us, eh?"

Lucius didn't smile back. "Where is this army staying?"

The woman waved her arm vaguely. "In the west of the city, and some are in the palace with that Oswhent. I try not to go near them."

"A wise decision," Lucius said. *Then* he smiled. "Deinol, what say we go near them?"

"I was just about to suggest that." He winked at the woman. "Thanks for the advice."

They acted confident enough, but they both knew it was in jest. They'd gotten into enough scrapes to be cautious. They edged closer and closer to the palace until they started to see a preponderance of blue-black clothing, then moved west from there.

"They're remarkably spread out," Lucius said.

"I suppose they can afford to be. They crushed the rioters pretty decisively, and the prince is a hostage now."

"I wish I could stop *him* gloating about it," Lucius muttered.

"Who, Oswhent? Aye, me too. What a lickspittle he turned out to be." He stopped short, grabbing Lucius by the elbow. "Wait."

"What is it?" Lucius asked, following his line of sight. "Did that soldier look at us? He seems oblivious enough to me."

"No, it's not that, I . . . I know him. But he can't be a soldier, he's . . ." He'd only known the man for a short time, but he'd know that politely confused expression anywhere. "Look, trust me, all right?"

He barely waited for Lucius to nod before crossing the street, and put his hand on the young man's shoulder. "Ritsu? Is that you?"

Ritsu had been muttering something to himself—it sounded like "bandages"—but he looked up at Deinol's words. "What? . . . Oh. I know you, don't I?"

"It's Deinol. I'm glad you remember." He looked Ritsu over, but he wasn't injured anywhere, and he didn't look noticeably worse than when they'd parted. But the memory of that moment stung him with guilt. "Listen, I'm sorry about what happened before. What I did. Even though I was grieving, there's no excuse for it. I've felt so rotten about it since then—I've wished I could apologize."

Ritsu stared blankly. "Apologize . . . for what?"

Deinol could still remember precisely where he'd hit him, right between his ear and eye. He poked the spot with one finger. "It was right here, I think. I'm glad it's healed well, but it probably hurt for a while, eh?"

"Oh!" Finally some life came into his face. "Yes, of course. I remember. It was after your . . . oh. After what happened to your friend."

Deinol bowed his head. "Aye. A difficult time for us both, but I'm glad to find you well."

"Yes. So am I. I mean, I'm glad to find you well, too." He smiled. "It's good to see you again."

Deinol couldn't help but feel touched at that, after all the trouble he'd dragged Ritsu into. "I'd like you to meet another friend of mine," he said, stepping back and clapping Lucius on the shoulder. "This is Lucius Aquila. Lucius, Seth and I met Ritsu on the road. I know he must seem . . . odd, but he's a good man."

"Am I?" Ritsu asked. "Thank you. That's kind of you to say."

"Aye," Deinol said. "Odd just like that."

Lucius didn't spend even a moment at a loss, just held out his hand. "Well met."

But as Ritsu looked up and into Lucius's face, the dreamy confusion left him, replaced by something like awe. "Wait," he said. "I know you."

Lucius's outstretched hand dropped a couple inches. "I . . . don't think you do. I certainly don't know you. What did you say your name was?"

"It's Ritsu," Deinol said. "Ritsu Hanae."

Lucius shook his head. "I've never met anyone by that name. Not that I can recall, anyway."

Deinol remembered that Ritsu had wanted to find someone—some *tsunshin*-wielding swordsman who had bested him once—and for a moment he feared Lucius was that man after all. But instead, Ritsu said something he never would have expected. "Oh, no, I didn't mean . . . of course you never met me, sir. But I had the pleasure—the great honor—of watching many of your duels. My closest friend revered you since your first formal matches as a student of the second school. We even saw your last match with Rana Korinu—we ran away from practice to make it in time." He ducked his head, too excited and restless to make a formal bow. "We didn't know when we'd get to see it again! Sebastian said you two used to spar all the time in training, but since *kaishinrian* can duel only when their liege allows it . . ."

In the face of all this adulation, Lucius only looked wary. "Never mind that. Here's what I want to know: why is any Aurnian garbed in Elgar's color?"

Ritsu looked down at himself, as if stunned to find the clothes there—stunned, and horrified, and hurt. He opened and shut his mouth, tugging at the hem of his shirt, and Deinol put a hand on Lucius's arm.

"Listen," he said, "you can't speak to him like that. However it happened, I'm sure it isn't his fault. He's . . . overly tractable, and easily confused. I don't see your sword," he said to Ritsu, suddenly recognizing its absence. "Does that mean you haven't been doing any fighting?"

Ritsu stared down at the empty space at his hip. "No fighting," he agreed slowly. "Lord Oswhent said I wasn't to do any fighting. They gave me a list. I'm supposed to fetch . . ." He frowned. "Candles, bandages . . ."

"You see?" Deinol said to Lucius. "They've just made an errand boy of him. I don't think he has anywhere else to go."

Lucius didn't apologize, but he didn't say anything else against Ritsu. Given his friend's passionate hatred for Elgar and his men, Deinol doubted he'd get more than that.

"Why don't you come with us?" he asked Ritsu. "We're looking for more Aurnians, anyway. Wouldn't you rather reunite with them than be bossed around by this lot?"

"Don't tell him that," Lucius said. "Does he look like he can keep a secret?"

"Lucius, that isn't like you. I won't reveal anything you don't want me to, but have some pity on him, will you?"

"Is he right?" Lucius asked Ritsu. "Would you rather be with us?"

To Deinol's gratified surprise, Ritsu nodded immediately. "I'd be honored to accompany you, sir. And I'd rather be with Deinol. I like him."

Lucius sighed. "If we're going to be companions, you can't call me sir. Call me Lucius, or nothing."

"But . . . well, if that's what you wish."

"It is. Thank you." He smiled, his mild and enigmatic smile. "Now let's see what we can do about those clothes."

CHAPTER SIXTY-THREE

Eldren Cael

THERE WAS NO increased security at Eldren Cael's gates, but they hadn't truly been expecting any. Jocelyn most likely believed Adora was dead, but even if she hadn't, she would never have believed Adora would return to the capital without Uncle or an army. Adora wouldn't have believed it herself a few weeks ago.

They could probably have made it all the way to the palace without drawing notice if they had wished it. They were all wearing traveling clothes, not finery, and Adora's face and form were hardly well known among the people. But while they'd wanted secrecy and anonymity before arriving here, so as to keep Jocelyn ill prepared for their return, now it was time to reveal themselves. Jocelyn would feel more strongly disposed toward killing them immediately if there was no proof they had ever been present.

The only guards in the area were a woman about her age and a man about a decade older; they were muttering to each other when Adora approached them, biting back her instinctive *I beg your pardon* and replacing it with something more authoritative. "I understand this is unusual," she said, in a voice loud enough for every nearby civilian to hear her, "but I have been through quite the ordeal, and was left with no other choice." She extended her hand so that her ring was in full view. "It took longer than I would have liked, but I've returned. As you can see, I've picked up something of an escort between the Curse and the capital, but I'd like you to accompany me to the palace. Just *to* the palace, not within it, and then you may return to your posts."

The soldiers gaped at her, but she had expected that. "Is it her?" the woman hissed to her companion.

He peered at Adora's face. "I did see her a couple times, in processions and the like. With that resemblance, and that ring . . ." He caught himself, making a hasty bow, and the woman immediately followed suit. "Excuse us for the inspection, Your Grace. These past few weeks have just been so . . . strange."

The murmurs were already spreading through the crowd. *The queen . . . What did he say? The queen! The queen has returned!* Adora did her best to seem indifferent to them. "I understand, but I cannot afford to waste any more time. To the palace, if you would?"

"Of course, right away, but . . ."

The woman spoke up in his stead when he trailed off. "Your Grace, though we are sworn to your service, we are only two. I'm not sure how much you know of what has transpired in your absence, but if I may speak frankly . . . ?"

"By all means," Adora said.

"Then . . . your return will be . . . I mean no disrespect, but I doubt your brother's wife will—"

"She will never be my brother's wife," Adora said, not bothering to keep the anger from her voice.

The guards actually relaxed a little, as if they were relieved not to have to pretend politeness to Jocelyn. "Yes, well, if you feel that way . . . perhaps you know, or suspect . . ." The woman cleared her throat. "Lady Selreshe may resist your return, Your Grace. Indeed, I think the only question is how directly and how . . . violently she may resist it. I beg you not to disregard the possibility that she may try to kill you outright."

Jotun Avestri had never lost a single battle he commanded himself. Adora tried to smile at this woman the way her father must have, when one of his subjects asked him about the outcome of the morrow's fighting. "I'm counting on it. Jocelyn Selreshe's crimes are already severe enough to seal her fate. If she shows her true colors immediately, rather than hiding behind denials and false ignorance, we can have this resolved that much more quickly. There are far greater matters that command my attention."

And perhaps she hadn't entirely bungled it, for both the guards seemed to stand up straighter, to breathe more easily. "If you are confident of that, Your Grace," the man said, "then nothing could make me happier than to see you to the palace without delay."

As Adora had intended, word of her return spread through the city in every direction, and the crowd that massed around her as she walked grew greater with every step. Her own guards and Arianrod's made a protective circle around their group, so no stranger could get too close—they still didn't know what spies or other actors Jocelyn might have. But Adora smiled at those who came to see her, and pressed the hands of those who offered theirs. Her people needed to know they were not to blame for anything that had happened, and that if she had returned in vengeance, none of it would be directed at them.

When the smooth, familiar planes of the palace finally came into view, a sudden ache of longing warred with the surge of Adora's nerves. Things would only get more difficult from here, as they tried their best to prevent any deaths in their effort to separate Jocelyn and Feste. She'd been half afraid the palace doors would be barred to them, or that a wall of soldiers would be standing in front of it, but she saw no such thing. On the contrary, among the guards who were watching the approaching crowd warily, she saw a welcome sight.

"Mehrine!" she shouted, trying to catch the attention of the woman who had so often stood guard over her mother's chambers. "Don't be alarmed! These people merely celebrate my return."

The other guards relaxed when they saw Mehrine take her hand from the hilt of her sword and shove her way through the crowd to Adora's side. "Your Grace! So it is you! Thank the gods."

"Are you not attending my mother?"

She scoffed. "I'm no longer permitted to. If Jocelyn Selreshe imprisoned every royal guard who's been unnerved by her behavior, the damned palace would be empty. But it's been a tangled mess of reassignments, dismissals, secrets . . . I've been taking my post here and biding my time. Without you, I couldn't disobey the prince openly, but now . . ."

"We're taking her prisoner," Adora assured her, "but you'll have to listen to me very carefully. The situation is even more delicate than you've guessed." To the rest of the guards, she shouted, "Open the doors! Clear us a path!"

They stared uncertainly for a moment, but then Mehrine roared, "What are you waiting for, you idiots? Your queen has returned to you!" Between that, and the excited shouts of the crowd, they needed no further spur to action, and soon the way inside was clear.

But it was there that the ease of their journey ended. They left the civilians on the steps of the palace, and the rest of them poured inside. But they had no sooner passed the entryway and set foot into the long corridor before the great hall when *its* doors opened as well, admitting Jocelyn, Hephestion, and an array of guards.

This was the chaos Adora had feared, soldiers pointing weapons at soldiers, everyone screaming at once to know what was happening and proclaim that they were in the right. "Hold!" Adora screamed above the tumult, as loudly as she could. "Restrain yourselves! There is no need to come to blows here!"

"And how are you the judge of that, miss?" Jocelyn asked. She rounded on the soldiers. "What is the meaning of this intrusion? Why were Hephestion and I not notified of . . . whatever this is?"

Her playacting was serviceable, though Adora couldn't blame Arianrod for laughing at it. She herself couldn't summon quite so much levity, and she knew blind rage would weaken her position. So instead she reached within herself for all the disregard she felt, the conviction that Jocelyn was merely a vile blight temporarily standing in the way of her destiny, and distilled it into a single look. "What's this, Jocelyn? Have you taken advantage of our hospitality for so long that you have confused guests with hosts? Or if it's vengeful spirits you fear, I can assure you that I am quite alive—the assassins you sent were a great inconvenience, but ultimately no more than that."

She saw the tremor as Jocelyn's jaw clenched, but otherwise she ignored Adora, saving her words for Hephestion. "A truly heartless woman, or else a mad one, to come here with a ring she must have found or stolen. Perhaps she sought to take advantage of your grief."

To think *she* could talk about taking advantage! But Adora kept her tone calm. "I understand, Jocelyn. Your rebuke, as ever, is piercing and well-aimed. You do not recognize me because you were expecting—if indeed you expected anything at all—the timidity of a princess regent, come to bargain and plead with you. But all that is gone from me now. I am not offering you terms. I am telling you I will have everything you took from me. My brother, my mother, my guardsmen, the life of my poor captain . . . and my throne. None of them belong to you, nor do you deserve them."

"Gods' sakes," Jocelyn snapped at Hephestion, "tell her she's done enough! How much more of this do you need to hear?"

Feste raised a tentative hand. "We can't . . . we can't allow this to continue. Whoever this woman is, she isn't my sister."

"Not so fast, Hephestion," Arianrod spoke up. "You aren't the only one who can vouch for her identity." She smirked at the assembled crowd. "Arianrod Margraine, current marquise of Esthrades, and one who's played host to these two siblings since they were children. I know both of them well. And if my word isn't enough, perhaps Queen Maribel might break the stalemate? I am sure she can recognize her own daughter?"

"And I can't recognize my own sister?" Feste asked. "Listen, Arianrod—or whoever you are—"

Arianrod ignored him; her grin was all for Jocelyn. "Oh dear, how to spin your lies? Shall you have him claim that he and his sister never made such visits to me, and risk that some guards here might remember their departure and return? Or shall you try to say that I'm an imposter as well, and strain the bounds of common sense?"

Before Jocelyn could answer, one of the younger guardsmen stepped forward, tugging at his neighbor's arm. "Come on," he begged. "Come on, you know it's her. You've seen her. You *know* she's the queen! I don't know why he's lying, but he's lying! Don't defend him!"

"There can be no doubt of *his* identity," the older man said, not putting up his sword.

"Nor hers, either! You know that!" He bowed his head to Adora. "Azel, Your Grace. I want to save the prince, too, please believe me! That woman's done something to him! She made him lock the captain up—he'd never have done that, not without a trial or anything. He still can't tell us what she's done wrong—"

"That's enough," Hephestion said, pushing through the crowd to put a hand on the boy's arm. "Don't forget your—"

Before Adora could even think to give a command, Cadfael was already moving. He launched himself forward, using his shoulder to shove the older guardsman out of the way, and slipped between him and Feste. Their bodies crashed together, and Adora saw Cadfael's drawn sword press harmlessly against Feste's abdomen. Her brother clawed at it, fingers brushing the flat. And then he looked about him as if he did not know where he was. His eyes flickered from face to face, but when they landed on Jocelyn, his reaction was unmistakable: he shrank from her in fear, drawing as far away as he could get.

There could be no denying that. Every sword in the corridor suddenly knew where to aim, and Jocelyn found herself in the center of a forest of them. But Azel pushed all the way to the forefront. "I knew it!" he roared. "What did you do to him?"

Arianrod raised a hand. "No, don't—"

It was too late. Azel stared in horror as ice gripped the tip of his sword, crawling rapidly down the blade. Perhaps he couldn't drop it, or perhaps he was merely too mesmerized to remember that he could, but the ice crept toward the hilt—

And Cadfael's sword clanged across his, dashing all the ice into water instantly. "Bold, but too bold, boy," he said. "You must leave this one to us."

"He's right," Adora called to the rest of the guards. "No one pursues Jocelyn without my leave, or follows us if we engage with her. That's an order. If you want to help, keep my brother safe, and send someone to take this man to Lirien Arvel, immediately." She gestured at Voltest with one hand, never taking her eyes from Jocelyn.

"I can do it, sir," Azel said—quite the impressive recovery. "I know where she is! Follow me!"

As those two ran down the corridor, Cadfael lunged again, right at Jocelyn this time. For a moment Adora thought he'd forgotten the plan, that he simply meant to kill her—but the blade stopped short of Jocelyn's body, driving her back before it as if it were afire. She was hemmed in by the doorway to the great hall, and took another few strides backward to give herself some space. "Come on!" Arianrod shouted. "We can close ourselves off! Seren, with me!"

Adora wasn't entirely sure they wouldn't be safer without Seren, who was after all another person without protection against Jocelyn's spells, but she assumed Arianrod had some reason for it. Either way, there was no time to argue: the two of them, Adora, and Cadfael plunged into the great hall after her, and Seren and Cadfael immediately slammed the doors shut. It wouldn't keep anyone out who was determined to get in, but Adora hoped the guards would obey her command; they had to allow Voltest and Lirien a way to follow them, after all.

That was their next problem: they had to keep Jocelyn contained until Lirien drew near. Adora didn't know how long it would take, but probably no less than ten minutes, and perhaps more, depending on where Lirien was being kept. And Jocelyn only needed a matter of seconds to cast a spell.

"It would be best if you could corner her, Cadfael," Arianrod was saying. "With the sword against her flesh, she shouldn't be able to cast."

Jocelyn had already retreated past the rows of tables and benches on either side of the hall, inching toward the throne. *Tell me she's not actually going to sit on it,* Adora thought, but it seemed Jocelyn wanted the height of the steps leading to it. "You can surrender, Jocelyn," Adora said. "You must know that's the best choice open to you now. My people know what you've done. Even if you escape us, they'll try to capture you, or kill you outright."

Jocelyn bent down, and Adora heard something skitter across the floor: a small knife in a sheath. "That's the only weapon I'm carrying," Jocelyn said, with an ironic smile. "But I doubt that's enough to be considered surrender, is it? What do you expect me to do about my gifts?"

"It's my understanding that you have two 'gifts,' only one of which properly belongs to you," Arianrod said. "You could certainly start by giving the other one back."

Adora stepped forward and picked the knife up from the floor; even if it wasn't Jocelyn's primary weapon, it was still safest to keep it out of her hands. Beside and before her, she heard a thump, and looked up to see that Cadfael had slipped and fallen. He'd been trying to close in on Jocelyn, but she'd frozen the floor beneath his feet.

"She can still do that?" Adora hissed to Arianrod, who was holding a position near one of the tables.

"She can't cast *on* him, but she can cast *at* him; Voltest proved that. She can't turn his head into a block of ice, but she can certainly hurl a block of ice at his head. He's going to need to use his reflexes."

Adora unsheathed the knife, wondering if there was anything she could do with it. If Cadfael couldn't close the distance between himself and Jocelyn, she didn't know how she could do any better. And would any wounds she caused even remain, given the powers Jocelyn had stolen from Lirien? The more she thought about it, the more it seemed the best thing to do was—

"*Shit,*" Arianrod snapped, grabbing Adora's wrist and slamming her hand down against the table. Adora felt it, then, a double strike that left her breathless: first Jocelyn's magic, a creeping snake that suddenly pulled tight around her, choking her with the desire, the *need,* to plunge the knife into her own heart; then Arianrod's hot on its heels, full of fire and force, shoving the first intruder out of her mind with all the subtlety of a hurricane.

Arianrod's fingers still wrapped tight around her wrist, refusing to release their death grip until she was sure Adora no longer had any desire to move her hand. Adora herself was too busy gasping for breath to do much else, but even though Jocelyn's magic was gone from her now, she could still remember the horror of that thought that had masqueraded as her own, how completely she had surrendered to Jocelyn's wish for her.

Jocelyn smirked at both of them. "I thought so," she said. "We have not met before, my lady, but you have more of a reputation than you think. Did you assume I would not wonder why Adora brought you here? But perhaps henceforth you will see no more need to feign ignorance. You are not famous for it, and I think it a pity you should start now. Much more refreshing for the two of us to speak frankly, since it seems we truly understand each other so well."

Arianrod released her at last, returning Jocelyn's smile with one no less confident. "I confess I do find frankness refreshing, but you can hardly blame me for the subterfuge. Now I'm going to have to use so much more of my strength, and unlike you, I'm still capable of tiring. Favors for one's allies are all very well, but I have my own affairs to handle, and had wished to take care of Adora's as quickly as possible."

"You consider Adora your ally, then?" Jocelyn asked, and again Adora had to admit that Arianrod and Lirien had been right. Jocelyn's thoughts so obsessively returned to her that it was impossible to conclude there wasn't some deeper grievance there.

Arianrod balked in mock surprise. "Does that seem strange to you? How could the ruler of the largest and most powerful free country in Lantistyne *not* be of use to me?"

"But Adora is no longer the ruler of the largest and most powerful free country in Lantistyne," Jocelyn said. "I am."

Adora had never met anyone who could more easily infuriate others than Arianrod, and that condescending wave of her hand was a perfect example: *oh, all right,* it seemed to say, *you can have your little point.* "Well, shoving oneself into the position of future queen of Issamira, even for five minutes, is more than most people have ever accomplished, I suppose."

"I should think it would be wasteful for us to fight each other," Jocelyn said. "And I have no quarrel with you. Indeed, in some ways you might find me a more satisfactory ally than Adora. Unless you are bound by sentimentality for one you have known so long?"

Arianrod laughed. "No, no, it's much simpler than that. You're right: it *is* wasteful for us to fight each other. You clearly have a wealth of knowledge, and a wealth of skill. Under some other circumstances, I could actually have learned something from you, and it is no small feat to teach me something. But you have made that possibility impossible." She shook her head, and Adora thought she looked genuinely disappointed, even regretful. "How could someone with your skill make such a stupid mistake? You let your ambition lead you around by the nose, and it has tricked you into doing something that will destroy you. Whatever Adora may be—whatever disagreements we have had—I know that she would never misstep so gravely as you have done. And so she is the better ally, and the better queen, no matter what you might promise me. The more sober judgment she will exercise upon the throne is more than worth the effort it will take to place her there."

Adora could not say for certain whether Arianrod had spoken the unadorned truth, or simply what she thought would make Jocelyn angriest, but either way it had the desired effect. As Jocelyn gritted her teeth, water beaded into existence above their heads, freezing instantly and raining down on them in sharp points. Adora flinched, but Arianrod didn't, and the spikes of hail bounced away from them as if they'd struck a pane of glass. "Come on," Arianrod said. "Help me move this table. I don't think she intends to make this easy for us."

As Arianrod kept additional ice away from them, they flipped one table onto its side and moved another behind it, like a grim reenactment of the mock forts Adora had made with her brothers when they were children. "Is this really going to help?"

"Blocking her line of sight? Of course." Arianrod crouched behind the table. "Mages who aren't born blind find it much harder to hit targets they can't see. Like this, she has to imagine where we are—along with all the other things she has to imagine to bring the spell forth at all." She gave an ironic grin. "I normally wouldn't be telling you this, but that's how you fight a mage: attack their imagination, or else their concentration. Making her angry is going to do both, so you *could* help me with that a little more." She poked her head out, scanning the room. "Of course, that means I need an eyeline as well, to keep Seren and Cadfael safe. But you can stay here if you like. Until Lirien arrives, all we can do is try not to die."

Adora didn't want to be a coward, but she didn't want to be a fool, either, and she could still remember how it had felt to have Jocelyn's fingers in her mind. For a handful of minutes she stayed flush against the underside of the table, listening to the sounds of the fight, wondering what she could do.

But then there was a sudden creaking of wood as the table was ripped apart around her, and Adora stumbled backward onto the heels of her hands. Arianrod was no longer at her side, but she gave an almost careless glance backward, and

Adora felt a rush of hot air before the equivalent of a bucketful of water dropped directly over her head, making her cough and sputter.

"Sorry!" Arianrod called, laughing as if they were children playing a game. "I couldn't quite get it to disappear into steam, but at least melted it won't hurt you." She beckoned Adora forward. "Come on. Watch where I step."

Adora did, though she didn't know how Arianrod managed it; she was hardly in exceptionally strong or swift physical form, yet she managed to dodge falling ice and skid around frozen puddles with the skill of a master. "How are you doing that?"

"I can see it!" Arianrod shouted back, still with that same exuberance, as if she wasn't even aware her life was in danger. "I can see it as she casts!"

Though none of them were able to close in on Jocelyn, who indefatigably sent death their way from her position on the steps, still Arianrod shaped the oncoming chaos, diverting, directing, and canceling spells as if she'd been doing it all her life. She gave primacy to Adora and Seren, since Cadfael's sword gave him some protection; though he bore a few scratches from hailstones that had grazed him, he did not truly look any worse for wear.

"Are you sure you want Seren to stay with us?" Adora whispered, not wanting Jocelyn to overhear. "I don't know if there's anything she can do like this."

Arianrod shook her head. "There's something she can do. Just not yet. It isn't the right time."

She stepped away from Adora, and raised her voice. "You're disappointing me, Jocelyn," she taunted, kicking a splintered fragment of wood out of her way. "What possibilities we could have created! Two of our intellect? Two of our power? What a fight we could have had! Like the mages of old. And instead you give me *this*." She splashed the toe of her boot into a puddle. "Water, water, water—that's all that's in your head, isn't it? You devised such a daring plan, and now you're down to rain and icicles! You surrendered all the boundless creativity that is the birthright of a mage, all for the crudest form of power—for nothing more than a bigger *stick*. Surely you can do better than this?"

In the next instant, a freezing gale blew snow into their faces, and Adora involuntarily clutched herself against the chill. It was difficult not to marvel at it—a full blizzard indoors—but Arianrod gave a scornful laugh. "Can you even manage *hot* water? At this point I'd be surprised if you could boil one of these puddles."

But Adora saw that her breath was coming faster as her gait slowed, and most of the color had drained from her face. For all her bluster, she couldn't keep matching Jocelyn's pace like this.

A sudden impact against the closed doors to the hall made them all jump, and Adora feared the guards outside had run out of patience. But instead the doors gave way to reveal Voltest's red cloak, and Lirien close behind him. In the scramble to stay alive, Adora had almost forgotten what they were waiting for.

But just before the doors shut again, Jocelyn attacked once more with a hail of frozen points of every size, and this time Arianrod was not strong enough to cover them all. Adora was unharmed, but she heard Cadfael shout as an icicle the size of a spearhead plunged into his thigh. He dropped to his knees, bracing his sword against the floor.

She turned to Arianrod in a panic. "Seren's still unwounded. If there's something she can do, shouldn't she do it now?"

But still Arianrod shook her head. "Not yet," she repeated. "Not yet." She took a deep breath. "You should try now, Adora. Jocelyn's angry already. See if you can get her to focus on you."

"Adora!" She whirled at the sound of her name, to see Cadfael sprawled on the floor in a pool of water, blood spreading fitfully through it. He waved his right hand weakly, the one still clamped around the hilt of his sword. "Take it!" he called. "I can't stand up, I'm useless, take—"

Ice dropped out of the air again, falling in a jagged sheet between them and temporarily cutting Cadfael out of view. Adora moved back to avoid it, but slipped sideways on the slick floor, falling on her left side with a wrenching crack to her hip and elbow. She pinioned her body, trying to find the leverage to push herself upright, but all she did was slide. Still more ice fell, and she flung her arms over her head, but this time it bounced off the air before it could hit the floor, ricocheting to the far reaches of the room—Arianrod's work, no doubt, though Adora could not see her. One thing at a time. She needed to find Cadfael. She needed to take the sword.

From her position on the floor, the two of them were on the same level. Cadfael nodded when she caught his eye, and he swept his arm across the floor hard, sending the sword sliding at the jagged mass of ice between them.

The sword didn't shear through the ice; it melted it on contact, skating through the resulting puddle toward where Adora lay. She flung her arm out as far as she could, just managing to close her nearly numb fingers on the hilt.

The first thing she felt was a contradiction: though the sword was freezing in her hands, holding it made her body feel warmer, somehow. There was a sense of sharper clarity, as if the world had snapped back into focus. She staggered to her feet, and even that much flailing with the sword turned everything to water in a wide circle around her, the last errant snowflakes melting as they touched her skin.

The frigid air weighed down on her with every step, as if trying to solidify around her. She couldn't risk stepping on the ice, because if she lost her balance she'd either let go of the sword or cut herself with it. So she made sweeping strokes as she crossed the room, alternating between swiping the blade at her feet to melt the ice and keeping it held upright to warm the air in front of her face. It was slow progress, but she moved ever forward, keeping her eyes fixed on the woman standing in front of her throne.

"I finally understand, Jocelyn," she said. "Your anger has always puzzled me, because I believed I treated you with the same kindness I showed everyone. But you were right. All this time, you were right.

"You well knew my lack of confidence, my retreating nature—you used it against me with an expert's skill. And yet you always knew where I stood, didn't you? Whatever my mother may have thought—or, for all I know, whatever you may have helped her to think—I would never have allowed you to marry Hephestion, because I would never have let you so near to the throne. No matter what else I doubted, I was certain of that. What a sting, to have someone with so little confidence in herself think even less of you!" She took another step, and another. There was a mere handful of feet between them now, and she could look up right into Jocelyn's furious eyes. "I didn't realize it before, but you were right. I've always thought I was better than you."

She braced herself for whatever Jocelyn's retaliation would be, but it didn't come. The anger burned in her eyes, but it was only her eyes that moved, sliding to a point behind Adora's shoulder. She remembered, too late, what Arianrod had said about lines of sight.

Adora turned, but she could barely begin to shout a warning. Arianrod was behind her, and behind *her,* creeping forward on soundless feet, was Seren, her knife drawn and ready. But rather than turn it on herself as Adora had almost done, she lunged.

Arianrod finally saw her, but had no chance to move away, no chance to even raise a hand. And the knife bit into her flesh, driven hilt-deep into her belly before she could make a sound.

Chapter Sixty-four

Eldren Cael

ARIANROD STAGGERED, ALL the air leaving her body in a rush. She sagged against Seren's chest, gasping as she sought to catch her breath. The fingers of one hand trembled uselessly; the other, the one closer to Seren, wrapped around the hilt of the knife, but she did not pull it out, as if just holding it was all she could manage.

Seren wanted so desperately to help her, to carry her away from this fight, even just to hold her steady. But though her arm was right there, though it would take a movement of mere inches, she couldn't so much as twitch her fingers, any more than she'd been able to shout a warning before the knife pierced Arianrod's skin. Instead, she could feel the hateful intent coiling in her limbs, preparing to strike again, to finish the job. *No,* Seren thought, *no, not again, anything but that,* but it didn't matter any more than it had the first time. Still her arm moved against her wishes, trying to disentangle her hand from Arianrod's so she could pull the knife free.

Then something occurred to her, or occurred to the presence in her head: Arianrod shouldn't be able to hold on so tightly. Seren had far more muscle—she'd be significantly stronger even if Arianrod hadn't just been stabbed. And yet the fingers around her hand and the knife were tight as an iron cuff, not even weakening as she tugged her arm away. As she . . .

Seren watched, as if from outside herself, as her arm stopped moving. Her body was completely frozen in place, as if it were nothing more than a cage for her thoughts. But those thoughts were clear again, devoid of any hateful demands. Had something happened to Jocelyn? She could not turn her head to look; it was all she could do just to breathe, and only the knife filled her vision. The knife that Arianrod had enchanted—because Jocelyn would never have directed her stolen power at another mage, lest it be stolen from her in the same way.

Where was that power now? Directed at Seren, who was helpless to steal or redirect it. She had no magic of her own. But the knife . . .

It will hurt you in a way you cannot accept, Arianrod had said.

She had anticipated this. No—she had intended it.

FOR A MOMENT Adora wasn't able to do anything. She stood there, frozen, watching Arianrod struggle to breathe. Voltest and Lirien had stopped in place, too, as if waiting for a signal; Cadfael was still unable to stand. And Seren's face was flat and lifeless, which was somehow more horrible than if it had been contorted in rage.

But Jocelyn didn't look triumphant. In truth, she didn't look like much of anything, as if half her mind were somewhere else. Seren tried to tug her knife free of the wound, still with that lifeless face, but somehow Arianrod managed to hold on. Her breathing was dry and raspy, and her free hand trembled as she clutched Seren's shoulder.

"In a way, I'm relieved, Jocelyn," she said, her face twisting into the ghost of a smirk. "Despite everything you've done to yourself, you still remembered your favorite little trick. It speaks well . . . of your strength as a mage." She coughed, but it was the diversion of a moment, and when her smirk reformed, it was stronger. "More importantly, I was counting on it."

Jocelyn snapped out of her twilight state with a scream that nearly made Adora drop the sword. Still screaming, she fell to her knees, as if something impossibly heavy were bearing down on her. Arianrod said nothing more; she gripped the knife in one hand and Seren's shoulder in the other, her limbs trembling but her face intent. And Seren gasped as if she'd only just now been able to breathe, her formerly dull eyes wide with horror.

Before another moment could be wasted, Adora ran to Jocelyn, and held the blade of Cadfael's sword against the back of her neck. She couldn't afford to lose focus now; they had almost won, but she needed to be sure. "Lirien," she called, "where is your magic? Can you sense it?"

Adora herself hadn't sensed anything, not even the slightest stirring in the air. But Lirien raised one hand, and a single drop of water condensed on the tip of her finger. "Ah," she said, with unmistakable sadness. "There it is again after all."

"I do so hate to interrupt," Arianrod said, with enough dryness to blister bone, "but perhaps you've noticed the knife sticking out of my abdomen? I didn't go to all that trouble to restore your healing abilities so you could *not* use them."

"Oh—of course," Lirien said, jolted out of whatever melancholy had gripped her. She put one hand on Arianrod's stomach, and held the hilt of the knife firmly in the other. "This'll . . . hurt, still. I can't heal it until the knife is out."

"Even if I *were* in need of coddling, it hurts well enough already," Arianrod said. "Would you believe I've never been stabbed before? It's certainly an experience."

Lirien chuckled in spite of herself, but then was serious again, pulling the knife free in one swift and sudden motion. Arianrod hissed between her teeth, but then relaxed, and no blood spilled at all. Lirien made as if to hand the knife to Seren, but she cringed away from it, and Lirien held onto it helplessly.

"Well, thank the gods that's done," Arianrod said, rubbing her side as if making sure there weren't any cuts Lirien had missed. "Listen, Adora, there's no need to be alarmed, but I've never cast so many spells in succession before, and that last one in particular quite fatigued me. So don't be surprised if I . . . oh, drat."

She didn't faint or swoon, she *dropped*—like a puppet whose strings had been cut. She would have hit the floor quite painfully if Seren hadn't caught her first. The anguish had not faded from her face, and she tried to hold Arianrod's body as far away from her own as possible, as if fearful of touching her.

"It's all right," Adora said. "The wound is healed. What she needs most now is simply rest. You understand that, don't you?"

Seren struggled to speak, wetting her dry lips. "Yes. Could you . . . ?"

"I cannot at the moment," Adora said, keeping her eyes trained on Jocelyn's limp form. Though her eyes were open, she looked as exhausted as Arianrod; Adora wondered if she would be able to cast even without the sword at her neck. "There is something I must do here. Lirien, perhaps you would help get the marquise to a bed, and examine her once she arrives there?"

Lirien was tending to the wound in Cadfael's leg, but it, too, was the work of an instant. "I'll do what I can. I think I know enough of the palace by now to find an appropriate place for her." To Seren, she said, "I assume you can carry her?"

Seren hesitated, but then nodded, and they left.

And then there was only the last thing, the dreadful and necessary thing. Adora felt as if she were alone in the room with it, staring it down. But perhaps Cadfael felt it a little, too, for he came to stand by her side. He reached for the hilt of his sword, but did not quite touch it. "I can do it, Your Grace, if you wish," he said.

Tempting, but impossible. The very fact that it was tempting at all showed how far she still had to go. "Thank you, but no," she said. "This duty falls to me." And the duty and the stain of it would be hers, no matter whether he held the sword or she did. She had to remember that, too.

She took a deep breath. "Lady Jocelyn Selreshe, for conspiring to rape and murder, a plot of highest treason against your sovereign, the unconscionable torture of her loyal servant, and the cruel and horrific use of magic to compel the minds of multiple unwilling individuals, I sentence you to death at my hand." *Please,* she thought. *Please don't let her beg.*

Jocelyn did not seem to be in any pain, but she was clearly conscious, her head turned so she could see Adora out of one eye. Her breathing was shallow, and her eyes fluttered dazedly. "How you love your words, little queen. But I suppose the time for words has passed."

Adora raised Cadfael's sword high. She thought of all the suffering she had seen in Voltest's flames. She thought of how lost and vulnerable her brother had looked as Jocelyn forced falsehoods into his head, and of her mother's bitter tears. She remembered Rhia pierced and torn by that knife, the way her face twisted with pain as she still refused to yield. *For my sake. All for my sake. I have to protect them now. I have to be their queen. And that means I have to do this.*

"Jocelyn," she said, "if any actions of mine contributed to what transpired here, I deeply regret it. If there were any way to avoid all this death, I wish that I had found it. And I hope that your spirit may know peace in a world beyond this one."

I lost my right to pray two-handed long ago, she reminded herself, and swung the heavy sword down.

As EXHAUSTED AS they were, she and Cadfael raced down to the dungeons, pushing themselves to move ever faster. They took the stairs two at a time, and threw their shoulders against the door almost before they could turn the latch. But after everything, faced with the moment he must have long awaited, Cadfael grew suddenly shy, shrinking back from the doorway. "Perhaps you should go to her first," he said to Adora. "We know she has suffered much, and if she is truly convinced I am dead . . . with the evidence of Jocelyn's foul powers all around her, it may upset her to see me."

"As you wish," Adora said, since the most important thing was to get Rhia out of the dungeons immediately. She was easy to find, since Adora had seen the cell in Voltest's vision. Thank the gods, though she was chained, she did not look truly miserable: thinner than Adora remembered, but otherwise for all the world like someone enduring a minor inconvenience.

Her face lit up with such a guileless and hopeful expression that Adora's heart ached. "Your Grace," she croaked, and swallowed hard to drive the hoarseness from her voice. "I knew you would return. I knew even Jocelyn was uncertain of your death. Is . . . is it all right? Did we lose . . . ?"

"No one today, save Jocelyn herself," Adora told her. Everything was in disorder around the cells—scattered papers and overturned benches—though she could not tell whether this area had been recently abandoned or whether Jocelyn had driven everyone else out of it when she took power. "The rest of my family lives, and Lirien has reclaimed her magic. Have you any idea where the keys are?"

"I think they're hung up in the corner."

"Yes, of course." Adora snatched them down, fumbling eagerly until she found a key that could possibly be for the door. "When was the last time you ate?"

Rhia smiled weakly as Adora swung the door open and started trying different keys on the cuffs. "Oh, this morning, Your Grace. She wasn't trying to starve me to death. But I'll certainly be happy to go back to choosing my own food."

When Adora finally had all the manacles open, Rhia stepped forward, away from the wall—and almost immediately stumbled, her limbs weak from disuse. Adora caught her before she could fall, but the look Rhia gave her was full of worry and sadness. "Your Grace, in your absence . . . I mangled things horribly. I failed to protect your family, to stop Jocelyn . . . I was not worthy of the faith you placed in me."

It was a great effort for Adora to remain still. She wanted to burst into tears, to take Rhia's hands in hers and beg her forgiveness. But queens did not do that, either. She could not appear distraught in front of those who trusted her. She had to prove to them that she was strong enough to do what must be done.

Instead, she put her hands on Rhia's shoulders, lest she lose her footing again. "The greatest mistake was mine, Rhia. I should never have left the capital to begin with. I left you, Feste, Mother, all in the clutches of such a powerful foe, with no warning and no recourse. You have borne yourself with greater strength and honor than one twice your years and experience might have displayed. If you must blame someone, blame Jocelyn, or me." She stepped back just a little, testing Rhia's ability to take her own weight. "But even more important than this, Rhia . . . there is something I must explain to you. Something that will not seem possible, and yet has come to pass. On my way back here, it so happened that I . . ."

She trailed off. Rhia had gone oddly still, and when Adora followed her gaze, she saw that Cadfael had stepped into the room. Perhaps his eagerness had gotten the better of him after all, though his face was hard to read.

As soon as she saw that Rhia could walk without stumbling, Adora moved away to give her space. She closed the distance between her and her brother, but she did not speak, just looked him up and down as if ensuring all of him was still there. He watched her just as closely, but though his lips parted several times, he didn't say anything, either. Perhaps neither of them could.

Then Rhia lifted one hand, and rested the palm flat against Cadfael's forehead, covering the length of his scar. She had never seen it before, Adora realized. They both finally smiled, as if at some secret joke, though there were tears in their eyes.

Cadfael said, "You've grown so tall."

Rhia flung her arms around his neck, hiding her face against his shoulder as he held her steady. "Liar."

CHAPTER SIXTY-FIVE

Araveil

SILENCE.

Despite the height of the tower, the room in which they were held had no windows, and the sound of the wind could not cut through the thick stone. It could even be raining out there, pouring, water lashing the walls unceasingly, and they would never know. Though there was a corridor right outside, any bustle of activity failed to pass through the heavy wooden door; for all Kel knew, they had been abandoned, left to rot in an empty castle.

Yet Hywel was more silent than the room, more silent than the tower. For three days he had not spoken a word, and though his chest rose and fell, Kel could not hear him breathing. He had given not one single scream or sob; he had said nothing when his brother's body was dragged from the room. He had not opened his mouth even to eat or drink, and yesterday—Kel thought it was yesterday—they had finally taken him down from the wall and forced gruel down his throat. Now that they only had one heir of King Eira, Kel supposed they could not allow him to erase himself. Hywel, for his part, had not resisted when they took him down; when he realized they would make him eat no matter what, he had swallowed the thin soup of his own accord, and made not a sound. They did not bother to return him to the wall, just shackled his ankles so that he could not run, and a wrist to each ankle with a length of chain so his ability to move his arms was limited. Even that precaution hardly seemed necessary; when they returned at the next meal to make him eat again, they had to pick him up from precisely the same place they had dropped him. Even now he lay there on his back, limbs sprawled out as much as he could make them, eyes open but clouded, turned to the ceiling but too unfocused to see even that.

"Hywel," Kel said.

It was a powerful thing, to break such a silence. His voice had not been loud, yet still he felt it all around him, the stillness disturbed by his intent. "Hywel. Look at me."

Hywel did not. He moved only to breathe. Kel looked at his slack fingers, his expressionless mouth. "It's your brother who's dead, not you," he said. "You oughtn't act like it."

He saw it, then: a flinch that made the fingers of one hand twitch slightly. "If you were gone, and Laen were still here, you can be sure he wouldn't be lying on the floor like this. He'd already be making plans—he'd be determined to avenge you. You must know that."

For the first time in three days, he heard Hywel breathe. He drew a deep draft of air in, and expelled it in a rusty whisper. "Then perhaps I ought to've died, instead of him."

"We have no way of knowing that," Kel said. "And it doesn't matter. You're the one who's here. You're the king now."

Hywel still wouldn't look at him, but his eyes were clearer now, as if the anguish in them had bubbled to the surface. "I don't want to be the king."

"That doesn't matter, either."

Hywel said nothing. His chest rose and fell, his lips pressed together.

Kel took a deep breath. "Listen, Hywel. Here's what I know. There are people out there right now—right outside these walls, in the streets of this city—who are fighting for you. They're fighting for your name, for your birthright. If they die, they'll die on your behalf."

Hywel gritted his teeth. "I never asked them to."

"That doesn't *matter*!" Kel shouted. "They're *fighting* for you!"

Hywel shook his head. "For my brother," he said. "For Laen."

"Your brother's name is your name," Kel said. "By supporting him, you were making a promise to succeed him if you had to, whether you meant to make it or not. But what's happening out there is even more important than that."

He saw Hywel's eyes twitch and blink, but they didn't turn to look at him. "What do you mean?"

"I spoke to Arianrod Margraine before we left," Kel said. "Her plans are bigger than Lanvaldis, bigger than Reglay. If they hadn't been, I would never have agreed to leave Reglay behind." He leaned forward as much as he could, trying to bridge the distance between them in whatever way was open to him. "She needed us to stir up a rebellion, so that Elgar will send his troops here and leave Valyanrend open to attack. We don't have to *win* a rebellion, but we have to create one, and sustain it for long enough. If you give up here, and your people hear of it, they'll go back to how they were before. The rebellion will die, Elgar will keep his soldiers in Hallarnon, and all our plans will have been for nothing. Your brother's death will be for nothing."

"My brother's death," Hywel said hoarsely, "could never have been *for* anything."

"But your life can be! Was your brother the only thing you cared about in the whole world? What about Ilyn, who fought as hard for Laen as you did? Are you going to let them execute her, or imprison her forever? Talis is suffering who knows what torments at Selwyn's hands, all because she lent herself to your brother's cause! And . . ." The words felt bitter in his mouth, but damn it, if it was the only way . . . "My sister. She and Hayne are guarding your birthright with their lives, but perhaps that no longer matters to you, either?"

That provoked a stronger response, as he'd known it would. "I haven't forgotten any of them. Of course I want to help them, but what could I possibly do from here?"

"You still have to try! That's what being the king means!" Kel struggled with how to explain it to him. "If I know anything about being a king—if I truly believe in any part of it—it's that. You aren't allowed to stop trying. Your people give their lives for you, so you have to spend yours for them, until there's nothing left. That doesn't always mean dying in battle, but it isn't you lying here grieving yourself to death."

Hywel bit his lip so hard it was a wonder it didn't bleed. "What if it had been you in my place?" he whispered. "What if Alessa had been slain by Selwyn, and Laen and I were still here? Would you still have such strong words for me then?"

Kel knew he owed him a true answer, not just the one he thought would be likeliest to rouse him. He looked at his hands, bound to the arms of the chair. "If Lessa had died . . . that sadness would never leave me. It would make everything gray. It would keep me from smiling, from laughing, from joy and contentment and peace. But it wouldn't keep me from doing what I had to do. I would owe it to her, as much as to anyone else."

Hywel let out a deep sigh, squeezing his eyes shut. "How can you be so brave?"

"I'm not brave," Kel said. "I'm just more afraid of what will happen if I don't do what I need to do than I am of what will happen if I do."

For a moment, he almost thought Hywel smiled. But then he was silent again, a silence that filled the small room, his eyes closed all the while. He might almost have been asleep, save for the occasional restless movement that passed over his face. Kel was wondering what on earth he had left to say to convince him when Hywel finally spoke again. "Kelken," he said.

"What is it?"

"Make a promise with me."

Hywel still refused to open his eyes or look at him. But for the first time, his voice wasn't the least bit hoarse or raspy or weak. For the first time, it sounded like his true voice.

"All right," he said. "What promise?"

"Let me stay like this for five more minutes. After five minutes, I'll get up. And after I get up . . . after I get up I'll be the king. From that moment, for as long as I live, whether Selwyn kills me tomorrow or I end my days as an old man. I promise you that. I swear it by the brother I failed to save. I swear it by my mother, whose wisdom can't help me now, and by my father who loved her, without a crown or a name. And I swear it by our friends, and your sister—all of whom I *will* rescue, if they don't manage to rescue us first. So you see . . . then I'll be like you. Then I'll *have* to keep it, because I've sworn by everyone I love."

Kel didn't say anything. He didn't have to. It was to himself that Hywel had truly sworn, and it was up to the strength of his own will to keep the promise. And he didn't worry that he had no way to count the minutes in such an unchanging place: no matter how many minutes he lay there, Hywel had become the king already.

So he sat there in the quiet as the time passed, and eventually Hywel opened his eyes. He hoisted himself to a sitting position, rested his chained wrists on his knees, and looked over at Kel. His eyes were somber, but they were clear.

"All right," he said. "What are we going to do now?"

In Ritsu's memories of him, Deinol was almost always loud, but he and the swordsman who traveled with him had taken to speaking in hushed tones, so that Ritsu couldn't make out the words. Deinol would spare him the occasional apologetic look while they were speaking, or clap him on the shoulder afterward, so Ritsu knew the secrecy was what the swordsman wanted, not what Deinol did.

He wondered if there was more to the swordsman than he remembered. He had told Ritsu his name, Lucius Aquila, but the words kept sliding around inside his head, too slippery to fully grasp. He was much clearer in Ritsu's memories. He remembered the skill of Lucius's *tsunshin,* of course, but also his quiet and mild demeanor, the way he remained the most retreating and unnoticed of his fellows. Ritsu remembered how he had smiled when he lost to Rana Korinu that day— smiled, and bowed, and said that he would rather the chance to lose to her than to win against anyone else.

He sat on the riverbank and stared into the depths of the water. His reflection stared back at him, wavering and dark, but there. It both did and didn't look like his idea of himself, his face older and younger and thinner and softer than it should have been. He almost felt as if he himself were the same as that divided image—that he could only be half of himself at any one time, and that the other half lay trapped beneath the surface, everything reflected all the way down.

"Ritsu, what are you doing?" Deinol asked—in his normal voice, so he and Lucius must have finished talking.

Ritsu finally looked away from the river, over his shoulder at the two of them. "I'm trying to remember."

"Aye," Deinol said, scratching the back of his neck. "You don't seem to be very good at that."

"What exactly is it you can't remember?" Lucius asked, in that flat, removed voice.

"Come on," Deinol said. "If he could remember that, he wouldn't have forgotten in the first place, would he?"

Lucius relented slightly, walking a few steps closer to Ritsu. "What I meant was, you must be conscious of some kind of void, or gap, or else you'd never have noticed you'd forgotten anything at all. What part of your life can't you remember? Your childhood? Something that happened in the distant past, or recently?"

"I'm not sure when it happened," Ritsu said. "I only remember part of it, but I can't *stop* remembering. A large open space, damp and dark. It must have been underground. The rock was rough underneath me—natural rock, not blocks of stone. I think water was dripping from somewhere. From the walls? But only slightly."

Lucius ran a hand through his hair. "Wasn't it Serenin Palace?"

Ritsu started; the place had begun to seem like a vision, too insubstantial to be real. To hear it named so casually stunned him. "What?"

"You told me you saw my matches, so you must have lived in Kaiferi like I did," Lucius said. "Our people built Kaiferi from the bones of an old Selindwyri city the Elesthenians sacked and destroyed long before we ever arrived on these shores. The palace, too, was built upon the remains of an older one. The city lies atop a great river underground, and Serenin Palace goes deeper beneath the surface than any other building. Sometimes, at the very bottom level, especially if there's a great difference in temperature, the walls . . . sweat, so to speak. Water forces its way through cracks in the mortar, freezes and melts and freezes and melts . . ." He shook himself, as if departing a dream. "It's the only place in Kaiferi I know that's as you've described."

"But I've never been to Serenin Palace," Ritsu said.

"Are you sure? I can't imagine what you'd be doing in the lower levels, either. But if you don't remember everything, who's to say you haven't been there?"

Ritsu frowned, raising one hand to his face to feel it. "What would I have been there for?"

"You're asking me? I just hope it wasn't as a prisoner."

The words seemed to echo strangely inside his head, and Ritsu fell silent. *As a prisoner.* But he had never broken any laws. Had he?

Lucius turned to Deinol, but did not lower his voice again. "What do you think? Do you want to stay with him this time?"

The camp they'd set up was well outside Araveil; Lucius and Deinol said they couldn't afford to spend coin on anything but food, and they didn't want to risk Lord Oswhent or his men recognizing Ritsu. They made him stay out here while they ventured into the city for news. Sometimes Lucius went alone, and sometimes Deinol accompanied him. But Ritsu didn't mind either way; it was peaceful to sit out here by the slender little river, whether or not there was anyone else nearby.

"I suppose he's fine for the present," Deinol said. "Unless you'd like me to stay, Ritsu?"

"That isn't necessary," Ritsu said, only half thinking about the question. *As a prisoner.*

"Well, if you say so. We'll bring food when we come back. You know not to get yourself lost."

"I know," Ritsu said.

He waited for them to leave, and when he was sure he was alone, he resumed his vigil by the riverbank. He knew the river was a slight, shallow thing, without depths enough to cover him completely. But he spread his palms out above the surface, just shy of shattering his trembling reflection. And then he leaned out as far as he could, and submerged his face in the water, breaking through the barrier to the other side.

It was cold, and so dark. He pulled his head out again, gasping, but the darkness spread behind his eyelids anyway, and across the span of his mind.

It was so dark, in the cavernous underbelly of Serenin Palace. Of course that was where it had happened. All the way back in Kaiferi, in the days after the Hallern conquest, when Ritsu Hanae was still the only person he knew how to be. How could he have forgotten that?

Now it seemed seared into his memory, determined to unfurl itself across his mind whether he wished it or not. They had been dragged down here, Ritsu and Sebastian both. They and a couple hundred other men, and thirty or so women who had been soldiers or *shinrian* that had survived the fighting. The men were almost all young—some, like Ritsu and Sebastian, were hardly more than boys— and all were fit and able-bodied, either the picture of health or possessed of only minor wounds that would heal without permanent damage. They had been taken, clearly, according to some specific set of criteria, but the why had eluded them so far, and their captors were not forthcoming.

At first they'd just thought they were meant to be hostages, until the guards started dragging them into the far chamber, one by one by one. Ritsu didn't know what was in there—or rather, he knew now, only too well. But all he had known back then was that they were always taken in one at a time. There would be silence at first, and then something would happen. Sometimes it would be terrible screaming, as if from unimaginable pain. Sometimes it would be muted whimpering or sobbing. And sometimes there would never be anything but silence. But always, without fail, when it was over the soldiers would drag a corpse back out, and begin again.

Many of the captives had tried to escape, once they saw what was happening— against that fate, what did you really have to lose? But though the soldiers battered anyone who got too unruly, no one was killed, or even cut with a naked blade. Why? Ritsu had wondered. If they were just being killed in there anyway, why be so careful not to kill them beforehand?

He and Sebastian had not tried to escape. They weren't strong or brave; they were young, and clung to the belief that death couldn't possibly happen to them, that some other way would have to reveal itself. They had survived the fighting in the city because they hadn't properly been part of it. Ritsu's father had been, and had died out in the streets; his mother had been slain in the same raid that saw his capture. Sebastian's father had been cut down at his market stall, the undeserving target of rage from an army that had not wanted to wait so long to claim its prize.

At first, before the killings started, Sebastian had been silent and still, but with every corpse that was dragged out he grew more and more agitated, his hands shaking, knees knocking together. The guards started giving him wary looks, all too ready to lash out if he started to panic. Ritsu did not want his friend to be hit, so he tried to calm him any way he could: he put an arm around his shoulders, squeezed his hand tightly. "I'm scared, too," he whispered, "but you can't let them see."

"Do you think they're going to kill everyone?" Sebastian whispered back, voice trembling. "Will they not stop until they've slaughtered all of us?"

"I don't know," Ritsu had to admit. "I don't know what they're doing. But you've got to stay calm, or they'll hurt you. I'll . . . I'll think of something."

But he had not, by the time the guards came to take Sebastian away. Perhaps they had noticed his troubles, and wished to take him before he cracked any further. But when they seized his arms, Sebastian began to scream, *no no no no no,* an unending wail that felt like it was boring into Ritsu's skull. For a moment he had stayed where he was, because he was not a *shinrian* who could challenge an army to save his friend. But he didn't do nothing. In the end, he did the only thing an ordinary person could do.

"Wait!" he called to the guards. "Take me instead of him."

It wasn't that he didn't know what he was doing. He had known, all too well. But he had been so suffocated by despair that all he could think was, if he died, he wouldn't have to watch Sebastian die after him. He wouldn't have to see Sebastian's broken body dragged out like all the rest.

"You're going to take us all eventually, aren't you?" he asked them. "The order doesn't matter. Just give him a few more minutes."

The guards exchanged a look, and finally dropped Sebastian's arms. One of them nodded to Ritsu, and took his elbow lightly. Sebastian remained hunched over, averting his gaze, silent. Ritsu didn't blame him; he was probably ashamed to be letting Ritsu go through with his sacrifice. But still, he was sorry they wouldn't be able to say a proper good-bye to each other. He tried to think of something to call out to Sebastian over his shoulder, but his mind was blank, and then he was too far away.

The room they brought him to was small, and dimly lit. Ritsu looked all around it for whatever instruments of torture had dispatched all the rest, but he saw nothing. There was only a man in the room. A man who would be so many things to him, so many things against his will. But back then he had just looked like a man, thin and slightly pale, graying hair above his ears. Not a fighter, by the way he carried himself.

He didn't spare Ritsu a glance, locking eyes with one of the guards instead. "What was that commotion out there?"

The guard tugged on Ritsu's arm. "This one had a friend who panicked when we grabbed him. He offered to go in the other boy's stead. Should we not have listened?"

It was only then that the man looked into Ritsu's face, with perhaps a glint of curiosity. "No. This is fine." He placed his fingers against Ritsu's forehead, as if testing for weak points beneath the skin and bone. "What is your name, boy?"

"Ritsu," Ritsu said, because he couldn't think of a reason not to. "Ritsu Hanae."

That's why he asked, Ritsu thought now. *He wanted to know so he could take it away.*

He still wasn't sure what exactly the man had done. One moment they were standing face-to-face, then there was a whirlwind of pain and blindness, and then . . . he wasn't himself anymore. He'd been replaced with something else, something that was barely a person at all. That was where Shinsei had come from: someone who was strong, and trusted his master, and wanted to help him, and had nothing else.

But Elgar wasn't satisfied with just a handful of questions. He said to the guards, "Bring the other one in here. His friend."

Sebastian did not scream this time. When they brought him in, he looked tired and small, shoulders hunched and eyes cast down. But when he saw what he thought was his friend, he gasped. "Ritsu! I thought you'd already be . . ."

Shinsei ignored the boy, because he was not Ritsu, and he did not know or care who Ritsu was.

He shuddered to think what Sebastian must have seen in his face, but it was enough to let him know something was wrong. The boy who had been so meek a moment ago turned on Elgar in indignation. "What did you do to him?"

Elgar paid him no mind, other than to point a careless finger at him. "Kill him," he told Shinsei.

Gods, how bitter it was to remember the succession of emotions that passed across Sebastian's face. The confusion, the disbelief, and finally the realization. He tried to back away, but the guards held his arms, keeping him trapped in place. But even as Elgar handed Shinsei a sword, even as he took it up, still Sebastian's eyes never left his face. And instead of screaming like he had before, he spoke all in a rush, words coming as fast as he could make them. "Ritsu, listen to me. You have to remember, this isn't your fault. Please remember. It's not your fault, I don't blame you, it's not—"

That was all he had time to say. After that, Shinsei destroyed all he was, and felt nothing.

Back by the riverside, all alone with the truth, Ritsu screamed into the sky, sending a flock of birds into flight. He thrashed in the grass, tearing out great handfuls of it, beating his fists against the earth. He had done it. He had done it. The only way to escape from that knowledge was to become Shinsei, who did not know a Sebastian and could not care what happened to him. That was the other reason Elgar had done it, wasn't it? To make sure he wasn't Ritsu anymore, and then to make sure he never wanted to be Ritsu again.

But he didn't want to be Shinsei, either. Shinsei hurt people, and he didn't care, because his master was all that mattered to him. But Ritsu could remember what it felt like to have other things matter, all kinds of things all jumbled up in his head, and he didn't want to lose that, to clear it out and replace it with the clarity of emptiness. He wanted to remember: not Sebastian's death, but Sebastian himself. His parents. The sights and sounds and smells of Kaiferi, his home. The day he and Sebastian had snuck away from training to go see the *kaishinrian* spar—the awe and the bittersweet knowledge that they would never be that good, no matter how they tried. Even Ritsu Hanae's disappointment was precious, in a way, because it was his, and his alone.

But now Shinsei, that thing Elgar had put in here with him, was still there somewhere, lost for the moment in the shadows of his mind. What would happen when he found his way out, when he forgot how to be Ritsu again?

He touched his face, and found it wet with tears. The pain was still there, huge and horrifying, ready to overwhelm him, to turn him into a coward who could not face the truth.

"Forgive me," he wailed, covering his face. "Sebastian, forgive me, I didn't know, I didn't mean to, I'm so . . . so sorry . . ."

But that wasn't right, was it? Those were the wrong words. Sebastian's own words echoed in his mind, *not your fault, it's not your fault.* Sebastian had guessed that one day he'd remember, had given him those words as a gift against that day. He had known he was going to die, and still he had struggled to leave Ritsu with that, so he wouldn't be alone.

It would be wrong. It would be an unforgivable betrayal, to let himself forget how brave Sebastian had been for his sake.

He tried to burn that moment into his mind, into the very marrow of his bones—to keep it somewhere even Shinsei could not extinguish it. Remember Sebastian's bravery, if you remember nothing else. You have to remember him. Not the blood, not how he had looked as a lifeless body. Remember the young man with shaking hands, fighting down his fear so he could speak. The way he'd tried to smile.

Ritsu opened his eyes, and looked up at the gently swaying leaves. The sun was far away behind the clouds, and yet he still felt warm. "Thank you," he whispered. "Thank you, Sebastian."

CHAPTER SIXTY-SIX

Eldren Cael

THEY STILL STUCK to each other like shadows, though Rhia, at least, had long since left behind the fear that Cadfael might fade away if she took her eyes off him. Physically, her brother's face was much changed: in place of that delicate beauty the ladies of Araveil had so fawned over, the scar had created a more forbidding, unapproachable visage. But Rhia knew him, and in all the ways that mattered, down to the smallest glint in his eyes or quirk of his lips, he was so much like she remembered him.

Their days were full of questions, questions, questions. They tripped over each other's words, just barely managing to hold in their impatience enough to take turns. But whereas Rhia was torn between her desire to know everything about how Cadfael had spent their time apart and her desire to tell him all about hers, her brother seemed, as ever, more keen to ask than to explain, and she often had to drag his answers out of him. At least he was as grand a listener as she remembered, even if he never missed a chance to scold her for recklessness as she recounted her deeds and misadventures.

There was a subject they'd both been avoiding, however. In their first excited, half-confused burst of questions and answers, he had told her the rumors of his death were a lie—a lie he'd started himself. "I thought you wouldn't be returning to me," he had said. And she had realized they'd spent the last three years in the same grief—he must have thought she was dead all this time, just as she'd thought the same about him. It explained why he hadn't come looking for her, but it meant, she knew, that he'd ask her what really happened that night. She'd been rehearsing her answer ever since, but she didn't know how to begin the conversation. She would have to admit so many things to him—some that she'd long wanted to tell him, but others that still made her ashamed.

She walked the ramparts with him in the early morning, before the crushing heat of midday. She had earned enough trust among the guard that they left her and Cadfael to themselves, keeping a polite distance away. They were free to look out upon the city in peace, still reminiscing about the past. It was Rhia who broached the subject first, in order to give him permission. "Did Elgar truly tell you in person that Shinsei had killed me?"

"And smirked in the telling. I could never forget that. But Shinsei himself was not there, or else he did not reveal himself." He hesitated, but then asked, "Was it all a lie? Did you never encounter Shinsei at all?"

"I don't know," Rhia admitted. "That night, I fought . . . someone. But I never learned his name."

She leaned forward, and took his hand. Cadfael looked surprised, but he squeezed back, and Rhia took a deep breath, thinking back to that night. All the chaos in the city, and the snow falling as if trying to smother it. The snow twinkling in the young man's dark hair like little stars, but incapable of washing the blood off his hands.

"He was alone when I found him," she said. "I know I'd promised you I wouldn't stop until I got out of the city, and that I wouldn't fight anyone. But he had killed civilians. He said it was . . . faster. And I just got so angry . . ." She held his hand tightly. "I misjudged him. Badly. His opening strike . . . it was like nothing I had ever seen before. He shouldn't even have been able to move that fast, but somehow he did. I was so used to being the faster one; my mind was too slow to react. But my arm wasn't. It was like it moved on its own."

She watched his face, and saw the exact moment he realized what had happened. So many hours they had spent practicing, and he had been deaf to all her complaints. He couldn't speak at first, held captive by the conflicting emotions that passed across his face. But then he said, "You blocked it."

"It wasn't the most elegant maneuver I'd ever performed," Rhia said. "But I blocked it, Cadfael."

He laughed as if trying to dislodge a lump in his throat. "So it turns out my advice is actually wise, some of the time. Imagine that."

"That was the biggest surprise of the night," Rhia said, ducking in time to avoid a playful swat.

His laughter sounded freer that time, as if he'd finally remembered how it worked. "Well, go on. You can't just leave it there, not after all that."

"It was such a strange thing," she said. "It took all the speed and training and instinct I had to block that first strike, and I only just managed in time. But after that . . . I can't explain it, Cadfael. I don't know if his first strike was some lucky fluke, or whether I had rattled his confidence by turning it aside, or what it was, but after that it was as if I was fighting a different person. He was so much slower, so much sloppier; there was no trace of the unnatural agility that had frightened me before. I could see the confusion in his eyes, growing greater with each exchange of blows. And in the end, I was able to knock the sword from his hand. I would have killed him—I thought at first it would be right to kill him. But then he just collapsed in the snow. He squeezed his eyes shut, and put his hands over his face, and begged me not to kill him." She could still see him in her mind's eye, curled up into a quivering little ball—so far from the merciless invader who had struck such fear into her heart.

"I should have killed him, perhaps; the evidence of his murders lay all around me, and he would've killed me, too, if he could have. But I just . . . I couldn't. I don't know why. It didn't feel right to me, and you know it's always been hard for me to ignore my feelings. Perhaps, even though I knew, logically, what he had done, the sight of his misery and wretchedness spoke more clearly to my heart. Perhaps it was that I felt I didn't *need* to kill him, and if I could subdue him without any further death, why should I not do it? Or perhaps it was simply that I had never killed anyone before, and I was afraid."

"But you spared him," Cadfael said.

"I did. I know you'll be angry about it, but I did. Or . . . I tried to."

"What does that mean?"

"It was an even more frightening thing," Rhia said. "Even I wasn't naïve enough to let him go free just as he was; he'd just pick his sword back up and start fighting me again. So . . . perhaps it was a silly idea, but I thought I'd knock him out to buy myself some time to get away. But I'd never done anything like that before, and I'm sure it was clumsy. I tried to just hit him in the temple with the flat of my sword. There wasn't much strength behind the blow, but still, the moment the blade touched him, he just started *screaming*—at the top of his lungs, as if he were being torn apart. I . . ." She looked away. "I'm ashamed to say that's when I ran. I left him there on the ground, in the snow, screaming as if his heart would break. I have no idea what's happened to him since."

She gave him time to think about it, not pressing him for a reaction right away. She had no fear that he wouldn't believe her, but she wouldn't have blamed him for being at a loss. Instead, he reached for the hilt of his sword. "There's . . . something I have to tell you. Something about the swords. I can't say for sure, but it might help explain what happened that night."

"Something about our swords in particular?"

"Something about vardrath steel. I only found out recently—when I was in Stonespire, right before I came here." He ducked his head. "I asked the others not to mention it to you before I could. I wanted to be the one to explain. But it seems that vardrath steel . . . impedes magic, or undoes it. It's how I saved myself—in the delirium of a fever, I pressed the cold metal to my forehead, and it took away my curse. I have seen those who possess magic flinch from touching it—I've even seen them experience great pain. Could it not be possible that the man you fought had magic of his own, and that was why touching the sword to his flesh brought him pain?"

To think Rhia had believed she held the greater revelation to share! The first thought that crossed her mind was the memory of Jocelyn's frustration and puzzlement, and with it a chill as she realized: in that cell, without the sword to hand, she would have been fully affected by any of the horrible things Jocelyn had threatened, if only she'd actually attempted them. There had been nothing special about her *mind* after all. Then she thought about waking up on the lakeshore, and finding the sword kicked away from her body. *Lirien must not have been able to touch it with her hands, or to heal me while I held it.* Lirien must have known the whole time, but Rhia didn't blame her for keeping silent, even before her capture—it would require a great deal of trust to tell someone they held a weapon designed to make you powerless.

She tried to think back to that night. "I don't think so," she said. "The sword only touched him for a moment, but his screams continued long afterward."

Cadfael frowned. "That's different from what I observed with other users of magic. Perhaps there really was some other reason, though I can't think what it could be."

"But Cadfael, this is . . . this changes everything." Rhia drummed her fingers against the hilt of her sword. "With these gifts, we're so much more than just a couple of warriors. We could change so much—we could accomplish so much! If I had only known what the sword could do when Jocelyn took control of Prince Hephestion, perhaps I could have prevented it altogether! And in the future, if something like that should ever happen again—if a mage should ever attempt to terrorize the people—you and I could put a stop to it, when whole armies might be powerless. We could—"

Cadfael stabbed his fingers through the air. "No. Stop it. Not three days ago I pulled you out of a dungeon. I *know* how badly Jocelyn hurt you. But you're just the same as always. The first thing you want to do is run off and find some danger to stick your nose in—to risk your life for some cause you've just learned about that has nothing to do with you. This is why I didn't even want to tell you about the swords in the first place!"

"You didn't want to *tell* me?" That hurt all the more because she still remembered the last time he'd sought to avoid a problem by hiding its existence from her. "Cadfael, we both know we disagree about things, but you can't keep trying to prevent me from making decisions you don't like by preventing me from ever finding out that there's a decision to make! That isn't fair!"

"I know that!" He sighed, hanging his head. "I would never seriously have considered not telling you. I've learned my lesson, I swear it. And besides, the swords were Father's gift to us. We both ought to know what they can do."

"Do you . . . think he knew?" Rhia asked.

Cadfael shook his head decisively. "If he knew, I'm certain he would have told us. They were always going to be our birthright—they were meant to protect us. Why hide all the things they could protect us from?"

That sounded right. Father had never been one to keep secrets. He had answered every question they ever asked, no matter how painful those answers were. Someone who had confessed the truth about Mother's death would never have lied about a sword.

"I'm sorry for snapping at you," she said. "I know I've been reckless in the past, and I'll probably be reckless in the future. But the fate of the whole continent's on a knife's edge, and magic is an essential part of that. I just don't want to have something horrible happen to our world and think that we could have stopped it. We can't count on anyone else to do it for us." She gave him a sheepish smile. "It's like we have a destiny."

Cadfael had always scoffed at that word in the past, but now she saw dismay pass across his face. "What is it?" Rhia asked, when he stayed silent. "Did I say something wrong?"

"No, it's not that. It's . . . not something I can explain right now. I hope I'll be able to, someday." He finally returned her smile. "And it doesn't truly matter. You can talk about heroes and destiny as long as you like, but on the day I die, I'll meet my end knowing I've only ever done just what I wanted to do."

"Is that a promise?" Rhia asked, laughing.

He bowed. "A solemn oath. I will swear it to you, sister."

FOR TWO WHOLE days, Arianrod could not be wakened. She did not even stir or mumble like a dreamer; she just lay there, completely limp, breathing so shallowly you could barely notice it. Lirien insisted that there was nothing wrong with Arianrod that she could detect, but if this kept up much longer, they'd have to worry about her dying of thirst.

Adora sat by her bedside whenever she had a spare moment. Sometimes Seren joined her, standing awkwardly in the far corner of the room, but she never stayed for long. It was not for Adora to give her any instructions or commands, and left alone she skulked unhappily through the palace like a wandering shade, restless and taciturn. Adora knew she still blamed herself for Arianrod's injury, even though the wound itself had already disappeared as if it had never been. It was guilt that kept her away, when otherwise she would perhaps have stayed longer even than Adora herself.

Even though she'd been sitting at her bedside for the better part of an hour, when Arianrod finally opened her eyes, Adora still wasn't sure what to say. Arianrod didn't say anything, either, just blinked rapidly until she could focus, then turned to see Adora and met her gaze.

"Are you all right?" Adora asked, even knowing Arianrod would never have admitted to anything else. It just seemed like the appropriate thing to say.

Arianrod stretched. "Less sore than I expected, to be honest. Did you really have nothing better to do than watch me sleep?"

Adora hesitated. "I'm sure Seren would have done it instead, but she remains . . . conflicted about being near you. Lingering guilt, however undeserved."

"Ugh, I knew this would happen. Don't worry, I'll sort her out." But she didn't move to get up, just lay there propped on one elbow, watching Adora's face. She must have known Adora had something to say.

"Listen," Adora said, finally. "You . . . you saved my life back there. Probably more than once, I think."

Arianrod just stared at her, waiting for more. When she realized it would not be forthcoming, she said, "Yes, and what of it?"

"And I . . . I owe you an apology. All those things I said back at Stonespire . . . that you were vain and envious and difficult, that you put power above everything else, when throughout this endeavor you've been so . . . brave and noble and—"

Arianrod made a choking noise, flailing both arms as if to use them as leverage to swing herself upright. But her lower body barely moved, and all she managed to do was flop sideways on the bed. "No—*no*. I may have to lie here until I recover, but I do *not* have to lie here and listen to this nonsense. Please, Adora, if I saved your life, it was a practical decision. If you died, they'd have no choice but to crown Hephestion in your stead. Do you really think I wanted to treat with Hephestion for the rest of my life?"

In spite of herself, Adora laughed. And then she kept laughing, because it felt . . . right, somehow. It felt like a relief.

But when she had finished, she said, "You were right, you know."

And Arianrod didn't say *Of course I was* or *Aren't I always?* She stayed silent, and waited for the rest.

Adora took a deep breath. "When you first called me a coward, I was so angry, because I thought you didn't understand. I thought that you accused me of avoiding the throne out of fear for my own life, of prizing myself over my people. But that wasn't what you thought, or what I was.

"I was a coward, just in a different way. I said I didn't take the throne because of Landon, and that wasn't *wrong,* but really . . . really I was just so afraid of failing, of not being good enough. I was so afraid of making a mistake that I refused to try, and that was the greatest mistake of all. And that was what you meant all along. So what I wanted to say was . . . was that you were right, and I should have listened to you."

Arianrod's face stayed very still—not smirking, but in that old expression Adora had almost liked, that meant she was thinking about something. "How many disagreements have we had, over all these years? You could hardly expect to win them all. Besides, this way I have you in my debt already, and I won't have to waste further time convincing you of the next step."

Adora bowed her head. "I know our work isn't done. In truth, it's only just beginning. I want you to know I won't neglect my promise to you. I'm holding my coronation within the week, and I've already summoned my uncle to Eldren Cael. I'm sure he will agree to lead my armies—like you, he's been saying this war was inevitable for a long time. And I'll announce my decision to my people as soon as I'm crowned."

"And you'll be miserable about all of it," Arianrod said. "That much is clear from your face."

"I'm not unhappy to accept the duties of a queen," Adora said. "And I'm not going to shrink from hard decisions anymore. But when you're the aggressor in a war, it's hard to believe you're in the right. If Elgar had attacked us, I wouldn't feel conflicted about fighting back. And I know in my heart that, left unchecked, he will attack us eventually, and by then our best chance will already have passed. I know my people's history, and I would never want to be the Avestri that allowed us to be conquered and ruled by northerners again, after all my ancestors have done. But the common people, the ones fighting this war . . . will any of that truly matter to them? I'm condemning them to misery, for however long it takes us to win. Are we truly sure that our cause is just?"

She knew that justice wasn't something Arianrod spent any time thinking about. But she also knew that Arianrod had never mocked her for genuinely wanting to know something, no matter what that something was.

"Here's what perplexes me, Adora," Arianrod said. "You spend so much time with those war epics of yours, yet when it comes to war in your own time, war in which you may be called upon to play a part, you seem ill at the very idea. And then, on the *other* hand, none of this heartsickness seems to dampen your appetite for the glistening spears and heaven-shouted war cries, the blood-blossoming earth of your beloved Lisianthus." She subtly shifted the position of her legs, and almost succeeded in hiding her wince behind a raised eyebrow. "Why is it, I wonder, that you love war so much, but only in books?"

A question that was more than fair, and that she could not run away from. But the answer was buried so close to the heart of her that it took effort, and pain, to dig it out. "There are plenty of other war epics, by other poets, that do not move me. But Lisianthus uses such a setting to prove that, even in such a forsaken and hopeless situation, people could still be . . . human."

Arianrod leaned her chin against her knuckles. "And what do you think a human is, Adora?"

"I couldn't even begin to say," Adora said. "But when I read Lisianthus, I feel as if I know. I feel as if, despite all the sins of the past and present, there's something in humanity worth taking pride in. That even after the most hopeless chaos we can imagine, there's still the chance of finding a proper order."

Arianrod did her best to sit up straight, drawing her hand through her hair once and then letting it fall to her side. "Chaos, Adora, belongs most properly in the mind. It is there that it does its best work—it produces inspiration itself. Even every invention meant to create order must first have been conceived by a chaotic mind. Because chaos is *change,* and how can you have anything new without change?

"But they say a ruler's task is to maintain order. Not to make people *happy,* because people, in the main, are idiots, and do not know what they truly want, or even want the same things one hour to the next. So we give them the order that they need, which is never an order of the mind. We give them roads that run sensibly from one point to the next; we ensure their food and water will not poison them; we protect them from invaders, and even sometimes from one another. We give them a world they can comprehend, and we leave their minds alone.

"But what did Jocelyn want? What does Elgar want? Do you think they envisioned a world designed for anyone but themselves? They stampeded through everything, breaking things and killing people so they could seize control. And in order to consolidate that control, what they need most of all is for their people to be obedient. Not to dream or create, but to do as they're told. That's what order and chaos look like when they're turned around from how they should be: a nation full of dolls, stuffed with identical thoughts, and a world going to rot around them.

"That's why we can't just give up, Adora. That's why you can't surrender to Elgar tomorrow because you want to spare your people further bloodshed. Your people, or mine, or anyone's, could never thrive in the world he wants to create. Instead you need to win, and try to offer them something that Elgar can't." She gave a slow, heavy shrug, catching her breath. "That's what I have. That's all that I can give you."

"ADORA FINALLY TRACKED you down, did she?" Arianrod said. "I'll admit I'm grateful, just now, to be spared the walk."

Seren doubted Arianrod *could* walk as yet; though she was sitting up, she would almost certainly have left the bed behind already if she could have. As guilty as she still felt, it did her good to see Arianrod awake again, grinning just like her usual self.

"I'm sorry," she said. She didn't want to talk about it, but she owed Arianrod that much.

"No," Arianrod said firmly. "It isn't for you to apologize. You have nothing to apologize for."

"I let Jocelyn—"

"You didn't *let* Jocelyn do anything. You couldn't possibly have stopped her. More than that, it was all according to my plan anyway. It was a clever plan, and it obviously worked, but . . . it wouldn't be unreasonable of you to be angry with me, for having pushed you into playing such a . . . difficult role."

Seren shook her head. "You were right, I could never have been allowed to know what the knife was for. You even tried to warn me, as much as you could— that the pain I could not accept would be the pain of hurting you. It's only that . . . I wish it could all have happened the same way, except that I could have resisted her. I promised you that I would never harm you—that I would let anything come to pass before that. After failing to keep my last promise to you—after making you promises that you hated, or that you could never trust—I had truly believed I would be able to keep that one. That one day you would believe it, too. I know *I* wasn't truly the one who hurt you. But I can't help but feel that Jocelyn made a mockery of my promise, all the same."

Arianrod smoothed the bedsheets under her hands. "I understand your thinking," she said, "but you've come to entirely the wrong conclusion. About Jocelyn, and . . . about me. If anything, Jocelyn's magic helped prove the truth of your words. But I already believed you, even without that."

Seren started, torn between shock and sudden hope. "You believed me? Since when?"

"Since you said those words to me."

"But—"

Arianrod held up a hand. "When Jocelyn reached out with her magic to control your mind, the knife's enchantment would allow that magic to flow through to me, and I would reach back with my own to pull hers out, just like she did to Lirien. I suspected she would only control you in order to kill me, but I doubted

I could successfully dodge an attack from you, even if I knew it was coming. The only thing I absolutely needed was for you to inflict an initial wound that wasn't *immediately* fatal. I was counting on the presence of an exceptional healer whose powers I would imminently restore, but none of that would have been any use to me if you slashed my throat open—I'd simply die too quickly. So I—" She stopped, and smiled, but it wasn't quite a smirk. It was more like the expression she made after Seren had just made her laugh when she hadn't been expecting to. "See, you did it again. You must've cut hundreds of throats, yet you flinch from just the idea of cutting mine. Do you remember when you first brought the *ward-renholt* back to Stonespire, and I asked you to cut my arm? And you couldn't do it. When Jocelyn took hold of your mind . . . did you feel that you wanted to stab me, or that you had no choice?"

"The second one." She shuddered. "It was like I couldn't stop myself."

"Jocelyn was short on time," Arianrod said. "No one can resist magical compulsion forever, but strong contrary inclinations can delay it. Yours were *so* strong that, rather than take the time to wear them down, Jocelyn controlled you much more crudely, like a puppet. That doubtless robbed you of some of the skill you'd have possessed if she'd convinced you to attack me on your own, but even then . . . you exceeded my expectations. It would have been fine if the wound you'd inflicted had been *eventually* fatal—honestly, given Lirien's presence, anything that allowed me five minutes or more would have sufficed. But this wound . . ." She touched her abdomen, where it had been. "The healing process wouldn't have been pleasant, but I doubt it would have killed me, even without magic. The movements you'd have to make to kill someone must be second nature to you, so that you could perform them almost without thinking. Yet the wound you gave me was one that old teacher of yours would have called an embarrassment. So I wish . . . I wish you wouldn't grieve over it. You did as much as you could have done. And I . . . was right to believe in you."

Seren was bad with words at the best of times; as the shame that had gripped her for two days finally lifted, at first she felt nothing but an absence. But there was peace beyond it—a small, delicate, but undeniable sense of peace. She hadn't made a mistake. She had done precisely what she ought to have done.

"Well," she said. "I suppose you really are right about everything."

Arianrod laughed. "I'll have to remember you admitted it. Who knows when it might be useful?"

Chapter Sixty-seven

Issamira

THEY DIDN'T KNOW the full story of what had happened yet, but finally the news coming from the south was favorable enough to let the inhabitants of Shallowsend relax. Lord Vespas's niece had reclaimed her throne—from what or whom, precisely, she had reclaimed it, was not yet agreed upon, but Morgan would have confidently wagered Lady Amali's daughter was at the heart of the whole affair. And with the crisis finally resolved, Morgan and Braddock had not only to depart for home at last, but to rather uneasily take stock of the part they had played.

"Look at it this way," Braddock said, running his hand along the windowsill of their shared room: large, sunny, and fiendishly comfortable. "We've still got the money—every copper of the lot Hephestion promised us. It's a *lot* of money. And we'd never have gotten it if we hadn't gotten mixed up with these Avestri-and-Hahrenraith types. Whatever else happened, we're coming out of it richer, wiser, and unharmed. Isn't that the most important thing?"

"Aye, we kept our heads, and we acquitted ourselves well," Morgan agreed. "I just wish I knew the truth behind it all."

"What truth? Vespas's intentions?"

"Exactly. Whatever this journey with him was, it's not as he intended—or else not as he *pretended*. Spies? When, for a single instant, were we treated like spies? We were practically his confidants for the latter half of it! Even here, we've been treated as honored guests . . . yet he delays our departure."

"Well," Braddock said, scratching at his stubble, "some of that was us. We haven't exactly *insisted* upon leaving."

At that, Morgan couldn't help feeling sheepish, too. "If we wanted to make sure everything would be all right here . . . it's not truly our business, but I'll feel better now that we know Vespas and his family survived."

Braddock laughed. "It's strange to say. But I feel relieved, too."

They were interrupted by a knock at the door, and they both jumped slightly, rearranging their positions to hide it. "Come in," Morgan said, hoping they hadn't been overheard.

Their visitor was Lord Vespas himself, in quite the cheerful humor. "Good afternoon, my friends. I hope I'm not intruding. I merely came to inform you that my niece has summoned me to Eldren Cael in all haste, so I will be leaving at first light on the morrow. I thought you might wish to start your journey home at the same time."

Morgan and Braddock exchanged a look. "We would indeed, my lord," she said. "We've certainly been away long enough."

"Then you shall go with my blessing," Lord Vespas said. "But as that leaves us a few more waking hours together, I wonder if I might ask one last favor of you, Miss Imrick."

The twist in her stomach was instinctual, but Morgan was truly more curious than apprehensive. "What might that be, my lord?"

He smiled. "Just your company. It won't be an interrogation, I promise you that. There were simply a few matters I felt were left unresolved between us, and I do so hate it when that happens."

Morgan hesitated. He had called only her by name, but just to be sure, she asked, "You want to speak to just me?"

He inclined his head. "It's ultimately up to the two of you. But I think what I wish to say to you—the business I wish to conclude—would be more easily and expediently accomplished if we spoke alone."

Morgan looked at Braddock, whose affront at the suggestion was plain. But he didn't immediately insist on accompanying her, which meant he was waiting to see what she would say.

She considered Lord Vespas. It would be ridiculous to say she didn't fear him—he was a powerful and damnably clever individual who had killed many and was prepared to kill many more. But she did not fear him in a common, simplistic way, as one might fear an armed drunk or a bandit. She did not fear that he would harm her if they were alone together, because she knew if he truly wished to harm her he would not need to be alone with her to do it.

"It's all right," she said to Braddock. "If it'll be quicker this way, I'll do it."

"We shall simply climb one of the towers," Lord Vespas said. "If you fail to come down, Braddock will be the first to know."

The climb was so long she was short of breath by the end of it. The small room at the top was a study, though it did not look like his lordship's—it had the feel of a place left ritually untouched, like an altar or a grave. She thought she saw dust resting atop some of the books and stacks of parchment.

"My sister's favorite room in the castle," Lord Vespas said. "The very top of the tallest tower, you see. It remains for her use, whenever she deigns to visit me."

"That was kind of you," Morgan said.

He smiled. "Merely practical, Miss Imrick! Who on earth would want to climb all those stairs every time they had to write a letter?" He gestured to the far door-way, where a spacious balcony ended at a comfortably high stone wall. Morgan stepped out after him, only a little nervous. But once there, she couldn't help her breath from catching slightly.

Lord Vespas noticed, of course. "Are you all right?"

"Entirely," Morgan said. "I've just never been up this high before. I didn't know what things looked like from this far away."

"Ah, of course. I suppose I shouldn't take it for granted." He was silent for a time, letting her drink in the sight. The sun was lowering, but had not yet struck the clouds with the colors of sunset. The plains stretched impossibly far on every side, broken only by the glistening trail of the river, curving back and forth like the long body of a snake.

"It's possible," Morgan said, "that I agree with your sister. If I had a view like this, I'd want to keep it close by."

"I understand only too well. I am no sober ascetic, to be unmoved by such a sight. But . . . how shall I put it? I fear that, when one grows accustomed to looking at the world from such a vantage . . . things of vital importance slip from view." He nodded at the ground so far below. "From here it all looks so uniform, doesn't it? Serene. Removed. When it isn't any of those things. I have long wanted to comprehend things, to control them. How can I, if I can't even see that they're there?"

Morgan ran her hand along the balcony's stone ledge. "You may be accomplished with words, my lord, but you have not the soul of a poet. The metaphor is clever, and true, and I believe I take it as you intended. But where do you seek to lead me from there? Are you going to tell me that I am truly the more fortunate one, to see so much more of the world from my tavern windows?"

Lord Vespas shook his head. "I would not so insult you. I only mean to say that there are things you know that . . . that I covet."

"What things could those possibly be?"

He regarded her, for a rare moment, without even the faintest trace of humor. "If you were truly prepared to share with me, I suspect you would learn very quickly just how much of what you know is valuable to me."

Morgan tensed warily, on the brink of understanding but falling just short. "You can't possibly be saying that you still suspect us of spying, can you?"

"Gods, no! Surely, after all we have been through, we can at least leave that much behind." The humor returned as he laughed, but the intensity of his expression did not fade a hair. "I'm not asking you whether you are a spy. I know quite well you aren't. What I am asking is whether you would like to be one."

Morgan caught her breath again, though this time she'd all but forgotten the view. Finally it all made sense. Lord Vespas had been so keen to travel with them, to watch them closely, yet his apparent lack of suspicion once his wish had been granted had been so puzzling. What was it he had said the day they met? *All I know of you now is that you are clever and perceptive, you hail from the city of Valyanrend, and you travel with a strong protector.* The ingredients, in his mind, of a potential spy—for either side.

"It was never an interrogation," she said. "Not even at the very beginning. It was an audition."

Lord Vespas laughed again. "You see, when you say things like that it only makes me more convinced that you would be a good choice."

Morgan shook her head. "Your wit is truly formidable, my lord. You planned all this just on the basis of our meeting at Raventower?"

"Oh, not at all. I could hardly have known how eventful these past weeks would come to be. I merely seized on a bit of potential, the shred of an idea. I thought at first that it would be just as likely a waste of time, and that I would end up telling you I was satisfied and sending you on your way. But instead I found something truly remarkable. Something I had never expected to find. And I'm not talking about whatever foul magic has ensnared Amali's family. The two of you put your lives in danger to follow me into that castle, and you must have known it beforehand. Could you tell me, Miss Imrick, what made you do such a thing?"

Morgan gave a deep sigh. "I don't know that I can. I don't know that I can explain it even to myself. Braddock, at least, could say that he did it to protect me. But as for me . . . I suppose I wanted to know something, too. I wanted to know what forces are truly at work in this land." She hesitated, trying to choose her words so that she wouldn't betray anything about her friends or how deeply she had been involved. "There was a matter I got wind of, back home in Valyanrend. That Elgar was desperate to acquire some sort of magic stone. But in the end the thing was stolen, and he was never able to retrieve it. We thought he was foolish, crazy, but now . . . I wonder if it wasn't some great stroke of fortune that his plan never succeeded." She raised her hands helplessly, then let them fall. "I don't know for sure. But I *want* to know. For once in my life, I want to know. So it was that, and . . . I suppose . . . I knew you were going to go no matter what, and . . ."

"And you wished to ensure that nothing would happen to me?"

She nodded. "You may find it strange, but I don't wish to make an enemy of you, or feel that it is our destiny to be so."

"An uncommon viewpoint, in these times of strife, but one that speaks well of you."

"I don't think it's as uncommon as you do. Perhaps that's one of the things you can't see clearly from up here." She fidgeted awkwardly against the stone railing. How to get out of this situation? "My lord, such an arrangement between us must nearly be as dangerous for you as for me. Once back in Valyanrend, I could play you false in all sorts of ways. How can you be sure—"

"That you won't betray me to Elgar? That's the one thing I am sure of. I can't be sure how skilled you will prove to be at the task, or if you will even accept it. But you don't hate me, and so can hardly be expected to give me over to a man you do hate. You see, Miss Imrick, one of the first and most important things I determined about you was that you are conscious of the injustice of your situation, and that it burns you. The wit, perceptiveness, and discretion you have shown are merely the how. Your anger is the why."

Morgan opened her mouth to tell him he was mistaken. While others she knew had railed against injustice, she had always had as much as she could take just to manage the tavern. It was best not to worry about things above your head, things that had nothing to do with you—things you couldn't change. But the words stuck in her throat. How could she know what she knew, and not be angry? Didn't any-one, no matter how powerless or overlooked, at least have the ability to be angry in the privacy of her own mind?

"I do hate him. I've always hated him," she said. "But I love Valyanrend. I have never thought of myself as one who loved easily or well, but if I love anything at all, I love that city. I was born within it; I learned it; it grew into a part of me. I don't think you understand what that is like."

"True enough. I love a country, but that is an idea, not a place."

"So you see . . . however I may feel about him, it's his hostage," Morgan said. "He owns my city."

"He owns it," Lord Vespas agreed solemnly. "Until he does not."

Morgan's hand clenched into a fist before she could stop it. "If it were that easy, I would've already—"

What? She would've already what? Overthrown Elgar herself? What business did she have with that?

Lord Vespas could have pressed the point, but he did not, just gave her a mel-ancholy smile. "I would prefer if you gave me an answer before your departure tomorrow. If you wish to negotiate terms, we ought to do that before you leave as well. And though I'd hope I shouldn't have to say this after all our time together, the choice *is* truly yours to make. I won't penalize you for refusing."

Morgan looked down at the distant plains, waiting for her contradictory feel-ings to subside and leave her with whatever desire outweighed all the others. A man who manipulated others with lies was easy enough to dispatch; all you had to do was see through them. But a man who manipulated with the truth . . . what could be done against him?

WHEN SHE FINISHED recounting the exchange to Braddock, she could tell he was more surprised than she had been. But he struggled to hide it, and she didn't say anything, waiting for him to speak. "What did you tell him?" he asked.

"I told him I wanted to speak with you."

"But not to ask for my advice, clearly," Braddock said. "For one thing, you haven't asked for it, and for the other . . . you look like you came here wanting to convince me, not the other way around."

She couldn't deny it. "Does that make you angry?"

"Why would it? I can't promise I'll agree with whatever conclusions you've come to, but I can hear you out well enough."

"When he asked me," she said, "this is what I thought about. What did we really mean in accompanying him—in saving him? Wasn't it, more than anything, because we thought he was a good man?" Her mind had already done it—had made that leap from premise to premise to the unavoidable, inarguable conclusion, forever known and nevermore unknowable. But she needed to be able to take him there, too. She needed to, if she were ever to have any hope at this at all. "And if he is, how is that fair? How is it that in this country, people like him have the highest forms of power—a lordship, a generalship, the queen's own ear? And what he thinks of the queen, and what he says of her—if she were made even partially after his own mold . . . How is it that the Issamiri get to have him and his niece set over them, while in Valyanrend we have to have Elgar?"

Braddock was careful with his answer; perhaps he was beginning to make those leaps, too. "It isn't that we *have to*, Morgan. It isn't . . . preordained. It's just that that's how it happened. It's just that that's how things are right now."

And that was it. That was the crux of the whole thing.

"If it doesn't have to be this way," Morgan said, "then I don't want it to be this way. If it doesn't have to be this way, then it isn't all right that it is." She took a breath, keeping her tone level so he wouldn't think she was getting carried away. "Braddock, I can't stand to have him up there. Behind his walls, in his tower, controlling everything. I want him down from there, and if I have to pull him down myself, I don't care. I think . . . I think I want him gone more than I want anything. And I don't think there's anything I'd have to risk that could make me stop."

He had stood by her side through so many stubborn and dangerous decisions. He had languished with her in Elgar's dungeons, ventured into the Selreshes' hellish household . . . but this was different. This wasn't something you ventured once and then stopped. This was something you risked and kept risking until it was completed, or you lost everything—and either way, your whole world would change.

She wouldn't have blamed him for trying to talk her out of it. But instead he asked, "And this is the way to do that? Being Vespas's spy is going to turn Valyanrend into the place you want it to be?"

"Not in itself. Of course not. *He* doesn't care what Valyanrend becomes, so long as it no longer threatens Issamira. But he wants to destroy Elgar. He has more power than we do. And he would give me some of that power, to accomplish our goal. What I would do, Braddock . . . I would take what I can from him, and use it for *our* ends. And if he gets his own ends furthered through me, I can accept that." She smiled weakly. "Now you can feel free to tell me I'm mad, if you like."

"Oh, come on," Braddock said. "Mad? I'm hardly as flighty as that. What's mad about it?"

"Well," Morgan said, "there's the fact that it'll probably get us killed, to start with."

Braddock scoffed. "I might've been killed when I ran away from the army all those years ago, but I did it anyway. Nasser and Vash and I might've been killed for standing up to the rest of our party, and we still did it. If there's one thing I can say for myself, it's that I've never let the risk of death stop me from doing something I felt I should do."

"But do you feel you should do this?" Morgan asked. "Don't say yes just to comfort me, or because you feel like you have to. Please."

Braddock shrugged helplessly, but he was smiling—a kind, open smile, unclouded by anything gruff or guarded. "I don't know what you want me to say, Morgan. I tied myself to you a long time ago. Didn't you already know that?"

They weren't accustomed to being sentimental with each other, much less anybody else, and Morgan was struck speechless for a moment. She supposed she had known it, in a general sort of way, but that didn't lessen the impact of hearing it spoken.

Braddock wasn't finished. "When I first came to Sheath, I hadn't a blessed idea what to do with myself. I'd run away from plenty of things I didn't like; I was good at it by then. But I'd never known where I wanted to end up. I asked someone where to get a drink, and figured I'd go from there. But I never expected what he'd say to me. 'Morgan Imrick at the Dragon's Head'll give you what you ask for at a fair price, but you'll never want to run afoul of her fists.' I'm no thief or drunkard, so I thought I'd be safe. And, I admit, I was a little curious.

"I've made my share of mistakes in my life, but that was the best decision I ever made. I've never regretted it, and I don't intend to start now. So if you say you want to risk it all, let's risk it. It's not like we're getting any younger. And besides, a free Valyanrend . . . maybe that's something I'd like to see before I die, too."

CHAPTER SIXTY-EIGHT

Valyanrend

IN THE DAYS after the slaughter, there was a kind of peace. It was a wounded, mourning kind of peace, but the absence of bitterness or recriminations gave everyone room to breathe. Marceline had been convinced that that glimpse of Rask she'd had through the window would be the last anyone would ever see of him, but she was checking on Talia when he burst through the door of the Ashencourt house a day later, *still* smelling of smoke. Her astonishment must have shown on her face, for he'd managed a wry grin. "Told you, didn't I? I said you'd never seen me fight."

His cocky attitude belied a wound that made Marceline cringe: his right hand was burned past the wrist, the red and ruined skin peeling away. But Naishe hardly blinked. By then they had a much better stock of medical supplies, chief among them an Akozuchen concoction that was meant to lessen Talia's pain. Naishe had a salve for Rask's hand, and for his part, he meekly held still while she applied it and a great deal of bandages. She was very stern with him about returning so she could change the dressing, but he let out not a squeak of protest.

Even then Talia's condition had been hopeful, and she'd shown improvement every time Marceline visited her. She had gotten so used to calm and healing that she was actually surprised, one day, to find Naishe and Wren and Rask all there and fighting, as if that weren't their usual state.

"What on earth are you lot doing?" she asked, when she opened the door to the chaos of raised voices. "Can't you at least let Talia rest?"

They did look chastised at that, even Rask. But Talia herself was sitting on the edge of her cot, and she gave Marceline a cheerful wave. "Not to worry, monkey. They're not even really fighting. Rask is just sour because he lost the vote."

That wasn't at all illuminating. "What vote?" she asked. "Rask, don't—"

Rask was accustomed to beat his fist against tables, walls, or his other hand when he sought attention for a particular point, but with his burns still healing, even making a fist was painful for him. Luckily, he relaxed his hand at her warning, smoothing it down his side to disguise the motion. "It was a vote I ought to've won," he said. "If I'd been trounced, that'd be one thing. But to be passed over by so small a margin, and all on account of sentiment—"

"*What vote?*" Marceline asked again, louder.

It was Wren who answered. "Though Zack is gone, it seems there are still people who wish to be part of his resistance, and so we need a leader. He'd appointed some of us to lead individual groups, as he may or may not have told you. Those people voted for his successor today—the three of us among them."

"Zack," Marceline repeated, venturing a question she'd been wanting to ask for some time. "Is that . . . his name?"

"Yes," Wren said, even more quietly than usual. "Zackary Smith. That was his real name, though he was hardly much of a smith. I never liked the name he chose—it was the one all the boys in our neighborhood had used to bully him with. But I tried to use it in front of his resistance, because that was who he needed to be for them. Now that he doesn't need to be anything for anyone . . . I'd rather call him by the name I know."

Marceline hadn't yet been able to truly comprehend his death. She knew, of course, what it was like to know someone well and have them die, but the last time had been her mother, and she had been so young then. Cerise's father had hated her anyway, so she hadn't bothered grieving for him, and anyone else had just been chance acquaintances, met once or twice. But to think that she would never get to ask Mouse another question, never hear another of his plans . . . she'd understand that someday. But not yet. "So who won?" she asked. "Not Rask, it seems."

"I lost by one vote only," Rask snapped, pointing one bandaged finger at Wren. "*His* vote. You must not need to ask who he spent it on."

She didn't. "Naishe, are you . . . did you expect that? Are you prepared for it?"

"I must be, so I will be," Naishe said, as stoically as ever. "But I did not quite expect it, no."

"Rask, there's no point in blustering when the thing's been decided," Wren said. "If you could look at it calmly—"

"Are you going to ask me to be reasonable?" Rask asked. "You, of all people? I know you gave your vote to Naishe because you're infatuated with her, but I don't ask you to be *calmer*. Don't criticize others' decisions when your own are built on the head of your cock."

Wren balled both hands into fists, glaring at Rask. "Could you really be so stupid as to think that?"

Rask laughed. "Come on. Are you going to deny—"

"Of course I love her!" The words were so forceful even Rask fell silent. "I could never deny it. But love makes you want to *protect* people, not endanger them. If I were thinking with my heart, do you think I'd choose Naishe to lead us, when I just saw my dearest friend hacked to pieces for holding the same position? If I were thinking with my heart, I'd try to take it all on myself. But that would be a fool's errand." He brushed the hair out of his eyes. "I want Naishe to lead us because she should lead us. Because she is the best of us, and if I am to protect her, I know I can only do so from her side. Even if it pains me that I can't do more."

He bent his head, his fists uncurling. "I'm sorry. It seems that I'm a distraction here, so I'm going to leave. I'll return whenever I'm needed."

No one tried to stop him, not even Naishe. If she was rattled, or if she wanted to go after him, she gave no sign of it. Instead, once he was gone, she turned to Rask. "However you feel about it, the votes have been cast. Will you concede to my majority or not?"

Rask pulled his hand back with a wince, the result of another thoughtless fist he'd tried to make. "I'm irritated, but you don't have to worry about me. The important thing is that the resistance doesn't fall apart. We have to set that above our own pride, or our individual grievances. So I'll follow you the way I followed Mouse—disagreeably at times, but always within the bounds of what is due you."

"Then I need nothing else from you," Naishe said.

"Do you have a plan?" he asked. "You know you're going to need one."

Naishe took only a moment to consider it. "From today forward, grandiose missions, assassinations, and efforts at recruiting are secondary. If our failure at the warehouse taught us anything, it was that the time is not yet upon us for bold action. We protect ourselves, we rebuild, and above all, we gather the knowledge we need before we dare so far again. Starting with this." She set it firmly down on the table between them: a sheet of bloodstained parchment, and a black stone.

"What is that?" Rask asked.

"It's what Talia stole from the warehouse. What Elgar was keeping there."

Rask squinted at the parchment. "It's still mostly legible. 'By the order of the imperator.' It says . . . huh. It says no one's supposed to close the box, except on Elgar's orders or those of . . . a couple other names, most likely captains of his. Was there a box in the warehouse?"

Naishe took the parchment and read it over. "Talia? Are you well enough to answer?"

"Aye." She held her stomach as she spoke. "It's where the stone was. In the center of the warehouse, on a table. The box was the only thing there. That's why I went for it, because it looked so strange."

"And was the box closed or open?" Naishe asked.

Talia furrowed her brow. "Closed. I had to open it to get at the contents. That's all of it, too. I barely looked at it, just grabbed it and started trying to fight my way back out."

Marceline gave the stone a tentative poke. "So either someone ordered the box closed, or someone made a mistake."

"But the whole premise is ridiculous!" Rask said. "Who cares if a box is open or closed?"

"All I can think is that it changes the nature of this," Naishe said, picking up the stone and turning it over in her hand. Its surface was shiny and smooth, reflecting the light.

"From what? To what?"

Naishe threw the stone up in the air and caught it, but there was no playfulness in her face. "As I said, we don't know nearly enough. But this is the path to follow. And follow it we must."

WREN TOOK LONGER than usual to come down from the shop, but when he did he didn't look like anything momentous had happened. He was just the same Wren as ever, cautiously falling into step with her. But that made it harder for Naishe to say what she had to say, not easier.

She'd accomplished all she could for the resistance today, without losing focus.

But now that was done, there was one more thing she needed to do—not as the new leader of the resistance, but simply as herself.

"You've got amazing control over your face," Wren said, with a tentative laugh. "I can't even tell how you left things with Rask, and I'm half afraid to ask."

"He agreed to submit to my leadership," Naishe said. "That's as much as I could have asked for. I don't think for a moment that he'll never question it again, but perhaps that's as it should be. I wonder if we should have questioned Mouse more."

"We did question him," Wren pointed out. "We just didn't have enough support to overrule him. And maybe . . . maybe Elgar was always going to find a way to strike at us like this, no matter what Zack did. It's clear that, even though events at the warehouse must not have unfolded precisely as Elgar intended, he'd been plotting it for some time. He may have even more schemes lying in wait."

It was a sobering thought. She had even more people to protect now, and no one to look up to. But it was a sobering thought that would still be there tomorrow, and today she still had to find the right words. She owed it to both of them, to Wren and to herself.

"Wren," she started, "I . . . wanted to talk to you about what happened. What Rask said about you. I . . . know what you think of me."

Wren's laugh was short, self-deprecating. "I'd like to deny it, but after that whole display . . . I guess I haven't left much to the imagination, have I?" He dropped his gaze. "I wish I could've said it better. I was always trying to say it better. To say it the right way. I guess that doesn't matter now."

Naishe shook her head. "No, that's not what I mean. You think you know . . . how I see you. You think you know what you are to me. But you can't know that, Wren, because whenever I try to put it into words, even to myself . . ."

She stopped there, stuck, more anxious about looking at his face than she'd ever been. Wren was no longer turned away from her, but something in his expression seemed so delicate, as if a single misplaced word would shatter him into a million pieces.

But Naishe still understood so little about these kinds of words, and finally she took his hand in hers and leaned her cheek against his—as if she could help prop him up like that, could strengthen him somehow. She reached up and brushed the hair out of his face, so she could look into both of his eyes—the same fragile hope filtered through their different colors. And then she kissed him, because that seemed like the most succinct way to say what needed to be said.

MARCELINE BARRELED INTO the Dragon's Head with the force of a miniature tempest, then spun herself out halfway to the bar when she realized Roger wasn't alone. "Roger, you could've warned me! I meant to talk about . . . you should've *said* something!" She scowled at his guest. "Who's this?"

"I can introduce myself," Nasser said, extending a hand to her. He smiled his well-worn smile, eyes crinkling at the corners. "Nasser Kadife. I wonder, young lady, that you are so shocked to find lodgers at a tavern."

Marceline ignored him. "Roger, you said you weren't allowed to take lodgers until Morgan returns! How long has he been here?"

"No, I said the tavern would be too much trouble for me to manage by myself. And I'm letting Nasser stay because he's a friend of hers, so you can settle yourself down." He didn't have much of an opinion of Nasser either way; it was clear the man enjoyed a good conversation, but just as clear that something pressing had preoccupied him for the entire duration of his stay.

"I have been in this city . . . it must be a fortnight or more," Nasser said. "I regret we did not cross paths sooner, but I have not often been in Sheath. What I seek is not to be found here."

That drew the monkey's attention. "What is it you're looking for?"

"He doesn't like to say," Roger said. "I've gathered it's a person, or people, but he's not trusted me beyond that."

"It's not that," Nasser said. "I seek one who, I suspect, does not want me to find her. The more people who know I am looking, the greater the chance she will hear of it, and hide herself away more carefully." His shoulders slumped, a tense, sad expression passing over his face. "Though I am beginning to wonder if it is not already too late."

Marceline sat down beside him at the bar. "Why would it be too late?"

"Surely even one so young has heard of the massacre at Silkspoint by now," Nasser said. "The resistance stamped out, or so they say. I have no proof that she was ever there, but she did sympathize with them—even fancied herself part of them, though I cannot say for certain how true that ever was."

Roger laughed. "She's got something in common with the monkey, then. She ran afoul of a handful of resistance members some time ago, and has been trumping up her connection to them ever since."

He'd said it to needle her, but he was utterly disappointed; Marceline gave only the tiniest shrug. "It's true I was questioned by some of their leaders for a time, but it turned out to be a misunderstanding. I wouldn't know much about the bulk of their members, but I'd definitely keep looking, if I were you. What happened at Silkspoint was horrible, but it hardly destroyed the resistance. Even Elgar must not truly think that; I'm certain he announced it only to calm people who were unsettled by the attack—to assure them it accomplished something good."

"And how would you know this?" Nasser asked.

"I can't give you any proof," Marceline said. "I'm just trying to help. You can believe me or not."

When had she gotten so composed? And unless Roger missed his guess, she was underselling what she knew of the resistance, not the reverse. Nasser mulled over her words, but she didn't stay for further questioning. "I'm off then, Roger. If you want to speak in private, you know where I'll be."

"A charming girl," Nasser said.

Roger snorted. "You're the first person to call her that in her life."

The door swung open again so quickly he assumed she'd forgotten something, but no: it was a young man he'd never seen before, with the nervous expression of a first-timer in Sheath. "I . . . beg your pardon," he said. "This is the Dragon's Head, right? Is there a Roger Halfen here?"

Roger leaned over the bar. "Who wants to know?"

"I do. I just said that. Um. I was given this letter by some people who said they're friends of yours. They said if I brought it to Roger Halfen at the Dragon's Head, he'd give me three silvers extra for a safe and intact delivery."

It must have been from Braddock and Morgan. Roger swore under his breath. "Does she think I'm made of money?"

But when he paid the man and unfolded the letter, he realized it wasn't from Morgan and Braddock after all. He recognized Lucius's thin, looping handwriting, though he'd received far fewer letters from him than from the other two, and none for a long time. As he skimmed down the page, eager for news, he saw writing in a second hand, Deinol's slanted and slightly smudged scrawl. So Lucius *had* found them, then!

But as Roger read further, the grin disappeared from his face. Rather than excitedly reading ahead, he stood in half a stupor as the words revealed their meaning to his unwilling eyes. "Are you all right?" Nasser asked, and Roger only then remembered that he was there.

"Yes," he said. *No*, he thought. *No, no, no.*

I buried him with my own hands, Deinol had written. *I buried him in the forest, on a hill beneath a single tree.*

"I'm sorry," Roger said to Nasser. "I need to read the rest of this . . . upstairs."

But he didn't read any more of it. He shut the door to Morgan's room behind him and leaned against it, and threw the letter to the floor. Of course he'd considered the possibility, especially when he went so long without hearing from the three of them. But it was one thing to consider something in your head, and another to know it in your heart.

He stood beneath the roof where the six of them had met so many times, whiling away an evening with laughter against the rain. No matter what else happened, what empires rose or fell, the six of them would never spend another evening together. And Roger couldn't even remember when the last one had been, because it had never occurred to him, on whatever night that was, that he was bidding farewell to something he would never have again.

Chapter Sixty-nine

Araveil and Eldren Cael

THE CLIFFTOP WAS cold and still, not the ghost of a breeze to disturb the pine needles scattered at Talis's feet. No matter how many times she tried to fill her lungs with air, that smell choked her, sharper than the cold. Smoke was wafting up from the village, but on such a windless day it had yet to reach her. The men were much faster, their boots crunching through the dirt.

Some small, weak part of her knew this wasn't real, that it had all happened years ago. But that part was smothered by the scents, by the cold, by the sight and sounds of her pursuers. Faced with an identical scene, how could she not feel an identical despair?

No, she reminded herself. No matter where she was, or what she saw, that despair had never truly left her. It had been a chain around her neck long before those metal cuffs.

On that day, long ago, she had known what torture would befall her if those men caught her. She had known that, even with no other choices left to her, she could at least choose not to endure that. And then the wind had caught her, and filled her, and she had risen up to destroy them. But that wasn't what happened now. Now she fell and fell and fell, but she was always standing on that cliff, with them coming for her and nowhere to run. She was trapped in this nightmare as she had never been in life, and though she would have done anything to leave it, even that choice had been closed to her.

She didn't realize she was screaming until she heard the cuffs snap open.

As the metal pulled away from her skin, Talis finally caught her breath, and the mist lifted from her vision. This was not the clifftop above her village, but a large, windowless cell. And though she knew she'd just been freed, there were chains all over her body, three sets of cuffs locked around her arms and legs and connected to steel rings in the floor.

The woman facing her had eyes the color of her own, but with an expression in them Talis hoped hers had never held. On her left hand she wore an almost comically large gauntlet, and in her right she held the manacles she'd just removed from Talis's wrists. She was armed, but the sword remained sheathed at her side.

"I apologize for the length of time we left you in such a state," she said. "It was far longer than necessary for any fruitful observation or research, but we had to ensure you would not be able to escape first. Especially given the absence of my most capable retainer, I wished to leave no precaution undone."

Her tone wasn't smug or mocking, just blandly emotionless. Talis didn't feel the need to reply in words, and simply attempted to cut her into pieces. But though a wind picked up, she couldn't seem to pierce the woman's skin. It was like fighting Cadfael had been at first—any magic directed at her seemed to just disappear into some invisible gulf between them.

The woman raised her gauntleted hand. "That won't be effective. I would never have come down here without enough of the steel to ensure my own safety."

It *was* the metal that did it, then—it must have been the same as Cadfael's sword. "What the hell do you want with me?" Talis asked, and winced at how feeble her voice sounded.

The woman seemed to have expected the question. "Though it is my pleasure and privilege to govern this area in accordance with the imperator's wishes, I am first and foremost a scholar. I say this so that you will not misunderstand the motives behind my actions. It has been easy to observe that exposure to the steel causes you pain, but the *point* of the practice has not been the pain, merely the observation. I am driven by the pursuit of knowledge, not some base love of another's suffering. Indeed, in your case pain has been as much a hindrance as a help in my work. Screaming is inarticulate."

There was only one item in that speech that held any value or interest to Talis. "So you're her," she croaked. "Edith Selwyn."

"Administrator Edith Selwyn, though I don't expect you to take note of the title." She walked closer to Talis, who struggled in vain to rise higher than her knees. Even that was just barely possible; the chains were too short. Miken could've simply gotten the stone to release the chains from its grip, but that was not her gift. Her wind could cut through flesh, but not metal and rock.

Selwyn crouched before her, touching Talis's forehead with her bare hand, and Talis angled her body backward as much as she could so the cuffs wouldn't touch her skin. "You don't feel feverish," Selwyn said. "Do you think you are feverish?"

"How the hell should I know?"

"I should think it is not *that* complex a question," Selwyn said—with a hint of reproach, but no irony whatsoever. "Surely you've been ill before. Do you believe the steel is making you ill?"

"I believe it's fucking killing me!" Talis roared, straining against the chains with all the force of her anger—to miserable effect. "I believe it's tearing me to pieces!"

Selwyn hadn't taken a single step back—hadn't even flinched. "Mm, an interesting hypothesis. But no. See how quickly you have regained your voice and strength, even after only a couple of minutes? And the marks on your wrists where the cuffs were are no more severe than those we might find on any ordinary prisoner." She walked a circle around Talis, examining her from all angles. "Wherever you came from, I doubt you were much for study, so perhaps you are not aware. Pain, you see, always occurs in response to something. Pain is the body's awareness of a threat, of *damage*. Your pain is clear, but I am trying to move from the pain to the threat it signifies. The steel is not degrading your body, and it is not making you sick. But it must be doing *something* to you, or you wouldn't feel anything." She frowned. "Could it be that the magic within you wishes to express itself, and rails at being suppressed?"

"It *isn't* being suppressed," Talis said. "If anything, it's being . . . stolen."

"No," Selwyn said again. "The steel cannot hold any magic within itself. That would be antithetical to its purpose."

Talis coughed. "What's the damn point of asking me if you're not going to listen to my answers? It's not that I can't cast, it's that the magic doesn't go anywhere."

"Then what is *your* theory behind your own pain?"

"Do you think I know? I told you, it's like it's . . . ripping pieces out of me. It's unendurable."

There wasn't a trace of pity in Selwyn's expression. "And it strips you of your senses as well, does it not? You cannot see or hear?"

"I can, just . . . not what's really going on."

For the first time, she looked truly intrigued. "What do you see instead?"

"Memories."

"Of what?"

How was Talis supposed to explain that day to this horrible woman, when she hadn't even been able to tell Cadfael the whole truth? "The past," she growled. "Past suffering. The worst day of my life."

Selwyn tapped her chin. "*Memories* of pain? But even that should only be a signifier. And why would the steel show you that? Gods know painful memories do not preclude magical ability, or prevent its exercise."

She sighed. "I still don't know enough yet. I shall have to see if additional observation and reporting uncovers anything more valuable. Now that you have been appropriately secured, I need not wait so long before listening to your findings."

The cuffs descended, but even if Talis had known to expect it, there was nowhere for her to go. There was no time for her to scream a refusal, and even if she had, what would it have done?

"BREAKFAST, YOUR LADYSHIP," Cadfael said, knocking politely on the doorframe. The door was open, and the marquise already engaged with the queen; they both turned from the heavy book on the desk to look at him, and he lifted the tray high. "The cook says she hopes you eat more of this one."

"I hope the same," Lady Margraine said. "My appetite has been . . . slow to return. A pity, as the food is so interesting here. You've developed twice as many ways to prepare bashi as we have fish," she said to the queen.

"Three times, I don't doubt," Adora said, and she did not even seem to be joking. "Thank you again, Cadfael."

Though he was not a servant, Cadfael was grateful to the queen for allowing him and Rhia to remain in the palace, even though Cadfael was not officially her retainer and Rhia had not, and most likely would not, return to her position as captain of the guard. So he hadn't objected to running errands here and there, delivering messages or carrying food into and out of the marquise's chambers. She had left bed rest behind days ago, but perhaps she was not yet fully recovered—Seren, seated cross-legged on the windowsill, had not taken her eyes off her ladyship for a moment, a worried frown on her face.

The marquise and the queen went back to whatever they'd been arguing over, Adora jabbing a finger at the page of the open book. "There, you see? A causal translation is absolutely not supported by the text. It's not that he knows he won't fail because of any one quality, it's that he's . . . it's a plea. He's *asking* not to fail, it's uncertain, he's directly exhorting—"

"Direct address? Really?" the marquise said, as Cadfael gingerly set the tray down. "How would you even convey that in modern speech? *Oh, bravery, make sure I don't fuck up?* What kind of formulation is that? It only makes the barest kind of sense." She paused, grinning. "Wait, that was ten syllables, wasn't it? Hah! There, I translated it for you."

"*Bravery,*" Adora said primly, "does *not* have three syllables."

"Really? *That's* what you found most objectionable in that phrase?"

"Besides," the queen continued, determinedly ignoring that, "*bravery* isn't even a truly defensible translation of *yaelor.* It would be much more apt to use a specialized word, one whose use you limited in the rest of the text, and one which denoted—"

Even Cadfael didn't know why he felt not just recognition but dread at the word, a coldness at the base of his spine and in the pit of his stomach. "What? Did you say Yaelor?"

The queen had clearly forgotten he was there, and tore her focus away from Arianrod Margraine in confusion. "Oh . . . well, yes, I did say that. I'm surprised you've heard of it."

"It?" Cadfael asked. "I thought it was a person—that is, a name. I met . . . a man . . . who called himself that."

Adora's face relaxed. "I see. Perhaps his parents were scholars? Or else they heard it from one."

"But what is it?"

The queen looked to Lady Margraine, but she was unusually silent, with a slight shrug that implied she'd leave it to Adora to explain. The queen considered the question. "It's an Old Lantian word with something of a . . . complex evolution. Eventually it did just come to mean *valor* or *bravery,* as Arianrod said, but in ancient poetry it retained the sense of a kind of . . . spirit, or quality . . . an essence of virtue that was not to be invoked lightly. Even just to speak the word aloud held meaning—which is why I was surprised to hear it used as a name."

What had he said, that first time? *That is the who, as well as the what. I can answer no more clearly than that.*

Cadfael asked, "Are there other—"

A shout cut him off. Lirien Arvel ran panting into the center of the room, her hair unbraided and in disarray, a hand pressed to her forehead as if she was trying to drive out pain. Right on her heels, some poor maidservant was frantically saying, "Forgive me, Your Grace, I tried to stop her, but—"

"It's all right," Adora said. "Lirien, what is amiss?"

Lirien kept her hand pressed to her head, though she tried to straighten her hair with the other. "I need to know if anyone has seen Voltest. So far, no one I've asked knows anything about him, and the rooms where he's been staying are empty. I know as well as anyone how reclusive he is, but I feel that he's gone from the castle—that he's heading north. And I don't think he's coming back. If anyone saw him leave, we could figure out when precisely his departure took place."

"And what would that tell you?" the marquise asked.

Lirien winced. "It would . . . confirm something. A feeling I had, not quite an hour ago—it woke me up, and I sought to confer with Voltest about it, but I couldn't find him. I think that might be why he left."

"You three are always aware of one another, aren't you?" Cadfael asked. "Talis told me that. Is that what you felt?"

Lirien stared at him more closely, as if paying attention to him for the first time. "That's right, though I certainly don't relish it. Talis had been . . . muted, for a while, like she was very far away. But for a small period of time, I felt like she was angry, and very hurt. The echoes of the pain haven't truly left me yet. There was fear, too. Whatever is happening to her, it isn't pleasant."

Cadfael felt afraid to hear of it, but his dread caused him to lose the next question to Adora. "Do you really think Voltest would just leave without telling you?"

Lirien snorted. "Voltest? He'd do anything in the world without telling me, or anyone else. You have to understand, I've been estranged from the two of them. I'm sure Voltest helped me more for his own good than for mine. And he would presumably have been able to use his flames to locate her precisely. The feeling I had was less exact, but I believe she is in the northeast. Somewhere in Lanvaldis, most likely."

"This companion of yours is suffering?" the marquise asked. "Being tormented?"

Lirien gave a stiff nod. "Yes, I would certainly say that."

"And is it true that the three of you . . . that your mental states are not as sound as you could wish to begin with?"

It was clear the question made Lirien uncomfortable, but she answered it.

"That's . . . unfortunately true, although Voltest has it worst. But even Talis is more affected by it than I am."

Cadfael finally managed to get a word in, although by now his question was for Lady Margraine. "What are you implying? Do you think that Talis is mad, or that she will become so?"

"It's a graver problem even than that," the marquise said. "The three of them are connected—they have admitted as much. Should one of them go mad, it's not impossible that they might drag the others down into that pit along with them. You've seen their power for yourself. If even one of them were to lose control of themselves, the results would be horrific. But all three?"

Lirien bowed her head. "I . . . can't promise that wouldn't happen. They have influenced me before, sometimes greatly. I can't say . . . I can't be sure . . ."

"I need to find Rhia," Cadfael interrupted. "She should be a part of this."

"Of course," Adora said. "Should I go with you?"

"No, I'll be faster on my own. You lot learn what you can from one another while I fetch her—you can summarize anything useful for us when I return."

He left the room, but he didn't immediately do as he'd said. Rhia *did* need to be located, but he had to do something else first. He fled to the room where he'd been staying, shut the door firmly behind him, and made sure there were no stray servants around. Once he was confident he was alone, he drew in a deep breath. This was probably a bad idea. If Yaelor could see everything, he most likely knew that Cadfael had need of him, and had already chosen not to appear. But on the other hand, Yaelor did owe him a favor, since the plot against Adora was now as unquestionably dead as Jocelyn Selreshe. Wasn't now a fine time to collect it?

He gathered himself, and said, "Y—"

"You were correct, boy," came a booming voice from right beside him. "That would have been a terrible idea. Did I not tell you from the first that I am no dog, to be summoned by the sound of my name?"

By now, Cadfael was well used to how difficult he was, and hardly even felt irritated at it. "I meant no offense. But you and I have business to conclude."

"We have business to *continue*," Yaelor said. "But I expect you have sought me out in order to claim the reward I promised you. So be it. I never break my word."

His correction made Cadfael uneasy. "Does this mean you're going to ask me to do something else after this?"

Yaelor shook his head. "I would not make a servant of you, whatever you may think. From now on, you must determine for yourself what you ought to do." He raised one eyebrow, a mild challenge. "Go on, ask. I assume you no longer care to know the whereabouts of the one called Shinsei?"

"Definitely not." He was still angry about all the time Elgar had made him waste in that useless search. "This isn't the answer you owe me," he said, mindful of many a fireside story he had heard from his father as a boy, "but I'm simply curious: why did you not tell me from the beginning that Rhia was alive? You must have known that would get me to do whatever you wished."

Yaelor hesitated. "It was permitted to me to ask you to complete a task for me—not to attempt to compel you, but simply to offer you a choice you were free to accept or refuse. Telling you about her would have gone beyond that—I would have been aiding you directly, giving you valuable information. That is more than I am allowed." He smirked. "And I did tell you I know you well. Had I told you that your sister lived, who's to say you would not have left the queen to her fate, and merely tried to rescue Rhia from the palace on your own?"

Even Cadfael was not entirely sure of the answer to that. Before he had ever met Adora, would he have cared if she died? "I suppose," he admitted, "that it was for the best that we all made the choices we did. Strange as it is to say, this outcome is probably among the best we could have hoped for."

"But you hardly wish to end things here, boy," Yaelor said. "Perhaps your sister's safety might once have been enough for you. But things have changed, else you would not be standing before me now."

If Yaelor knew so much, he must have known there were two things Cadfael wanted to ask him. Perhaps he even knew that it was no true struggle to choose between them.

"Talis," he said. "Where is she now? Is she in danger? Is she truly the reason Voltest left us?"

"She is," Yaelor said. "In danger, and also the reason the one possessed of fire abandoned you. As to where, she is in the city of your childhood, within the palace of your former king."

"Captured? Imprisoned?"

"Indeed."

"How can I free her?"

Yaelor sighed. "You know I cannot answer such a question. There are many things you might do, that may succeed or fail. But that is in the future, and beyond my knowledge." He folded his arms. "The one possessed of fire seeks to free her as well, but he will have difficulty. The one who holds her captive is Edith Selwyn, the so-called administrator of Lanvaldis, and she possesses the same weapon your father left you."

"Vardrath steel?" He remembered Voltest's cry of pain at just a moment's contact with the sword. What might Selwyn be doing to Talis with it? "Is she in pain? Is Talis in pain?"

"Yes," Yaelor said.

"Will she be all right?"

"I do not know."

"Is she dying? Will she die before I can make it there?"

"All manner of things may happen to her before you can return to Araveil," Yaelor said. "But the *wardrenwrathe* itself will not kill her. The wound it inflicts upon her kind is not a pain of the body, but a pain of the soul."

"What does that mean? What will it do to her?"

"There is no certain answer to that. Given enough time, and skillful application, there is a chance it could tear the magic from her, but that is unlikely. Far likelier that she would go mad first, but even that is not a necessity. It is still possible that she could survive this ordeal with merely the memory of its unpleasantness."

Cadfael worded his next question carefully. "When you first appeared to me, you told me that I couldn't help Talis. If I were to attempt to save her now . . . do you think I would succeed? Or should I not even try?"

"I cannot tell you the outcome of a thing before it has even begun," Yaelor said. "Your cause would not be doomed from the start, but beyond that . . . things should not be attempted because of how likely they are to succeed. They should be attempted because of their innate worth, regardless of outcome."

"That sounds like a more pretentious version of something my sister would say," Cadfael said. "I wonder you have not shown yourself to her yet."

To his surprise, Yaelor looked . . . if he didn't know better, he would have called it longing. "The time is not right. Perhaps, in the future, it might yet be possible."

That reminded Cadfael of the other question he had wanted to ask—the thing, save Talis's whereabouts, he had wanted to know most. But still he dreaded asking it, because part of him already felt certain he would not like the answer. "Why is it that you had to ask me to save the queen for you? You said you were only permitted to ask me, and no one else. What makes me different?"

Yaelor bowed his head, a stormy look descending upon his proud face. "I answered your question. I answered many of your questions, as was fair and not miserly of me, because they were all about the same subject. But this is a different subject, and not within the boundaries of the pact we struck."

"I know that. I know your honor doesn't compel you to tell me. But why don't you want to tell me? Or is that something else that's not allowed?"

Yaelor closed his eyes. Cadfael could hear the deep and heavy breaths, the sound of air being forced in and out of that enormous body, and yet he could feel no disturbance in the wind at all. "It is not strictly forbidden. I could tell you, if I truly wished to, without upsetting the balance."

"Then why don't you?"

"Because I know you too well." He opened his eyes again, and they looked more like Cadfael's father's than they ever had before; there was softness within them, just the slightest bit. "If I were to tell you the truth, it would cause you grief. I will ask no more tasks of you, but as you are now, there is still much you might do. If you wish to save the one possessed of the wind, I wish you well. If you wish to protect your sister, I give you my blessing. But I believe that, were you to know the truth, you would become locked inside your own pain. You would be too pre-occupied with yourself to help anyone. That is not what I desire."

So he was right, then. He was more than right: it seemed the truth was even more terrible than he had believed. "But how can you just leave it there forever?" he asked. "Don't I deserve to know?"

Yaelor raised his chin imperiously. "Deserve? Many in your position have lived their whole lives without knowing, and been none the worse for it."

Well, that was comforting, in a way. "How about this, then? I won't bind you with a promise. But if I succeed in saving Talis, come to me again. Decide for your-self, at that point, if I'm worthy of the truth."

Yaelor lowered his chin again—a concession, perhaps? And then he laughed. "How strange," he said. "That you of all people should surprise me."

"I'm comforted to know that's still possible," Cadfael said.

"I suppose . . . I am as well." The sternness returned to his face. "Your sister. You must know that, if you leave for Araveil, she will wish to go with you."

"Of course," Cadfael said. "And I don't intend to stop her. Did you think I went through so much to find her only to be separated from her again? Besides, she wouldn't be *safer* if I left her alone; she'd just find some different danger to get involved in. Better for her to face danger with me at her side."

"I see," Yaelor said. "I know well how much you would do for her. But remem-ber that threats can oft come from unusual places. If she travels with you, protect her well."

Cadfael scoffed. "I would have done that anyway. If you have any more advice, I hope it's more useful."

"You may find it so," Yaelor said. "It is simply this: be wary of the one possessed of water. And remember, too, that Amerei remains, and she has not forgotten you."

"DO YOU UNDERSTAND everything I've said? Was I talking too fast?"

"No," Rhia said, "though I'm surprised to find you this agitated. Could it have something to do with the reason why you're explaining this to me now, while we're alone, instead of getting us back to the others first? Do you know something about Talis or Voltest or Lirien that you don't want them to know?"

Everybody else was one thing, but he did not like to lie to Rhia if he could help it. Though it had been more than three years ago, the memory of their last argument still pained him. And just because he couldn't tell her about Yaelor, that didn't mean he couldn't tell her the truth. "It's about Edith Selwyn. I heard that she had gotten her hands on vardrath steel—that she knows its secret. If that's true, I suspect she is the one tormenting Talis in Lanvaldis—and she may be able to defeat Voltest, or capture him as well."

Rhia accepted that without question. How had she survived all this time while remaining so trusting? "I wish we could have told him that before he left. But are you saying you have a different plan? That you know something that could aid in Talis's rescue?"

"Not exactly," Cadfael said. He took a deep breath, steeling himself to make the decision. "I hope this won't cause more trouble for you, but . . . I want to go back to Araveil. I want to save Talis from Selwyn."

Rhia looked shocked, but quickly recovered, and gave him a firm nod. "Voltest will need all the help he can get—especially from those who don't only rely on magic." She smiled her guileless smile. "You've changed so much more than I thought! To think you'd be so eager to do the right thing!"

Cadfael laughed. "I don't care in the slightest whether it's the right thing. In that respect, I'm afraid you'll find I haven't changed at all. I'm doing it because I want to, and for no other reason."

Rhia shook her head. "When I found out you were alive, I worried that you had done nothing but close your heart for all those years we were separated, and let yourself grow cold. But I see now I underestimated you. To think you made so many friends! Not just Talis, but Seren as well, and the king of Reglay and his sister . . . and the way you protected Her Grace . . ."

Cadfael ducked his head, embarrassed. "No, you don't understand. They're not my friends, not any of them. I *did* close my heart, I just . . . I thought that someone should do the things you would have done." He smiled weakly. "If I'd known you were alive the whole time, I'm sure I wouldn't have bothered with it. It was very troublesome."

"But it's because of all that that we're together again now."

Cadfael sighed. "No, Rhia, I know you love to believe things like that, but . . . ugh, I suppose it's not worth arguing over. However it happened, we *are* together again. And I promise I'll protect you, even if we do this."

"And *I'll* protect *you*," Rhia said. "You haven't seen me fight in three years. I'm so much better than I was back then—you'll hardly be able to believe it. I'm probably as good as you are by now."

Cadfael tousled her hair. "And do you think I haven't improved a whit in three whole years? We'll see."

He'd wanted to tell her about his plans beforehand, so that when they returned to the others they would already be united in their decision. He'd expected their surprise—even Seren's, who had remained quiet as a shadow throughout the discussion, forgotten by everyone save him and the marquise. Only Lirien did not look surprised, and that bothered him—she knew him the least of anyone there. Did it have something to do with the fact that he was Rhia's brother?

"I can't say it's a terrible idea," the queen said at last. "I'll miss having you both here, but Arianrod is right: we have to regard the safety of the *wardrenfell* as a matter of the highest importance. And since Arianrod and I have to make preparations for the war with Hallarnon . . ."

"It makes the most sense for us to go," Cadfael finished. "We know what we'd be up against—at least more than anyone else you might send. And Lanvaldis is our home, after all."

"As far as that goes, I must have traveled around Lanvaldis at least as much as you two," Lirien said. She rolled her shoulders, as if physically shaking off a twinge of reluctance or resignation. "I suppose I should go with you. I've had my share of disagreements with those two, and I can't say I really like either of them as they are now, but if anything happens to them, I expect it'll go the worse for me. Unless you two take some issue with that plan?"

"With your accompanying us?" Rhia asked. "Not at all. Your help would be most welcome."

"I don't know how much I'll be able to provide," Lirien said, "but I'll do what I can."

But would she provide help in truth, or the harm Yaelor feared? Part of Cadfael wished he could tell her not to come with them, but he knew it was impossible. Rhia would never stand for such rudeness without a reason, and he couldn't give her one she could believe. He knew that Lirien had protected Rhia while she was Jocelyn's captive, but still. . . . Capricious as water, Talis had said. Was that the kind of person he could trust?

He reminded himself that he bore the most effective weapon against her at his fingertips. Rhia did as well, but the gods only knew if she would use it. As for the rest, it would not do to allow prejudice to cloud his judgment. But he intended to treat Lirien Arvel with the utmost caution, all the same.

CHAPTER SEVENTY

Eldren Cael

THE CROWN LAY between them on the table, newly polished, its golden points reaching upward like tongues of bright flame. Below that, it was set all around with gems of every color: ruby, emerald, sapphire, amethyst, topaz . . . and an opal in the front, where it would rest above the center of her forehead. "Will it serve?" her mother asked.

Adora fought the urge to duck her head, to lower her eyes. "Gods, it's the crown Talia Avestri herself wore. I could hardly ask for more."

She didn't miss the irony in her mother's smile. "No, but I expect you could ask for less, if it's too unwieldy. Even your father didn't put *that* on every morning."

"I can't imagine Talia Avestri did, either. A warrior who rose up from nothing? It would've only slowed her down."

"It would slow anyone down, if they let it. She didn't, nor did your father." That smile wasn't ironic at all. "Nor will you. I know that."

"Mother—"

She held up a hand. "Let me say this first. Adora, did you think . . . that I did not wish for you to be queen? That I thought you were not equal to it?"

She wanted to open this wound again now? Now, when everything was finally going as it ought? "If you did," Adora said, choosing her words carefully, "it was not wholly without cause. And there is also Jocelyn's presence to consider. We'll never know what thoughts or what decisions might not truly have been our own, so I believe we should not blame ourselves or each other too harshly for anything that transpired while she was with us."

"That is a fair and reasoned point," her mother said, "but it isn't an answer to my question. Did you think I saw you as unworthy?"

Adora sighed, running her hand along the edge of the table. "I suppose. At times."

Her mother did not rebuke her for that answer, nor did she look wounded by it. She reached out to brush her fingertips against the golden points of the crown. "Ever since you were a child, you've been so . . . quiet. You shunned social gatherings, or any large group of people; your own chambers seemed to be your favorite place in the world. But you weren't a sad child; you just always knew very clearly what you wanted to do and what you didn't. Reading your epics, playing sesquigon with my brother, telling us stories about the history of this land and its heroes . . . you were happy, at least to my eyes. I worried that, if we dragged you from your tower and forced you into that crown, it would only make you miserable. That you would be crushed by the weight of an obligation you hated but couldn't escape. But that wasn't true." She met Adora's eyes. "Your duty made you solemn, but not truly sad—it was your sense of the weight lying behind all your actions that had never been there before. The rest was something that I put there, because I feared . . . because I feared too much. You were prepared to accept your role long before I was. And I am guilty of having treated you like a child for far too long."

Adora took her mother's hand in hers. She had not cried at their first meeting, when she had found her mother after Jocelyn's death and told her everything would be all right. Her mother had wept, and fallen into her arms, but Adora had stood strong. And so she was not in danger of crying now. But that didn't mean she felt nothing, or that she needed to feel nothing. A queen must project strength, but every person is allowed to feel.

"There's something I have to tell you," she said. "Just you, and no one else. And you must never breathe a word of it to anyone, not even Feste."

She had turned the matter over in her mind, wondering if it were not better to simply keep the truth from every other soul. But though Landon had never been very close to Feste, he was her mother's firstborn. She had birthed him, and raised him, and Adora knew she still grieved for him. She did not deserve to die never knowing what had happened to him.

So she leaned over and whispered in her mother's ear: the secret that she would never tell another person again, not as long as she lived.

Her mother swallowed hard, but otherwise did not break composure. "You did well to handle it as you have. We could not ever allow this to become known, for the stability of the kingdom. And Hephestion is . . . not discreet." A pause. "Thank you for telling me. I will pray for his happiness."

Adora nodded, forcing down the ache that still wanted to rise in her chest. "As will I."

THOUGH THE GUESTS it had held had only filled a tiny portion of its vastness, the palace still felt emptier after their departure. Adora had purposely held back from everything she wished to say, to Rhia and Cadfael both, because she refused to believe that they would not meet again. She had wished them well, and thanked them for everything—all the courtesies and gratitude a queen could bestow. And she had apologized to Lirien, who, however Adora felt about her personally, had suffered much from becoming entangled with the royal family.

But at least all her guests had not left: though Arianrod was by now completely recovered, she said she would stay through Adora's coronation. Perhaps she simply wanted to make sure Adora would keep her word, and declare war on Hallarnon once the throne was officially hers. If so, she would not be disappointed.

"All right, tell me what you think of this," Arianrod was saying to Seren as Adora entered the room. "Killing Claremonts would be frowned upon—they do have a drop of Margraine blood in them, so they are my kin. The old man's about to die anyway, so we leave him to fate; the daughter spilled everything to Gravis, so she gets a pardon. Then we just disinherit and exile the sons, and that's that. The Rykers are much easier: you already took care of Andrew, and his only heir's a distant cousin—"

"What are you doing?" Adora asked.

Arianrod waved an unrolled length of parchment in the air. "We had a bit of a conspiracy at home right before I left, but my guards have finally rounded up every last one of its members. Which means I have to decide who lives, who dies, and who gets to keep the property."

"Will that occupy you for the day?"

"It should barely occupy me another half-hour. Why, did you want me for something?"

"I could ask your opinion on half a hundred things," Adora said, "but just now I was wondering if you'd had a chance to observe Feste's progress."

Her brother's first few days after Jocelyn's death had been frightening: he had screamed if anyone came near him, and had eventually barricaded himself in his room. He had accepted trays of food, and eventually warmed up to the servants who brought them. But the sight of Adora still terrified him.

Arianrod thought it was because Jocelyn had forcibly convinced him Adora was dead—so now, seeing her alive, he was faced with how unreliable his thoughts could be. There was no longer anyone there to manipulate them, but he didn't know that—and Arianrod had refused Adora's suggestion that they try to explain it to him, claiming that would put too much strain on his recovering mind. Though Adora longed to look him in the face, she had thought it best not to argue.

"I saw him just this morning," Arianrod said. "There's nothing for you to worry about—he's making fine progress. I'm sure he'll ask to see you himself soon enough."

"Does that mean you're pleased with this . . . method of yours? When Uncle arrives, he'll be bringing at least one of Jocelyn's other victims, so if we could do the same thing in that case . . ."

"Oh, it's terribly simple," Arianrod said. "You just ask them things, instead of telling them things—even things that seem impossibly obvious. It's like I said: magic affects the surface of the mind. Everything he knows to be true is still undisturbed in the depths—it's just that *he* doesn't know that. The more he's able to figure out for himself, the more he'll realize he understands. And I believe that eventually he will trust himself again. These other victims . . . I haven't seen them. It may be that some of them are too warped ever to recover. But even a shred of their original selves may be enough to bring them back, given time and rest."

"I'm sure Uncle will be relieved to hear that." She hesitated. "You should also know that he is bringing every weapon forged of vardrath steel from his armory. He does not have many, but he has a few."

Arianrod gave no visible reaction. "To do anything else would be foolish, knowing what you now know."

"But you . . . will be saddened by that, perhaps. That such weapons will become more and more commonplace as people learn of magic's return. I know that you were forced to sacrifice that secret in order to help me as you have."

"It's the thought of their fear that disappoints me most," Arianrod said. "Using that steel to smoke mages out, like snakes in the grass. It's how the Ninists were able to persecute us in the first place—by exploiting that fear."

"An unfortunate truth," Adora agreed. "But I promise you, no such fear will ever be encouraged in Issamira so long as I rule."

She had hoped she might steal a spare hour with Arianrod to keep debating about her translation of Lisianthus, but it was not to be. Adora's mother soon strode through the doorway, a rolled-up sheet of parchment in her hand. "I intercepted an Esthradian messenger in the great hall," she said to Arianrod. "It seems he brings you news from home."

"So soon after the last message? That's rather strange." As she read it, though her face changed only slightly, Adora felt some shift in the air, from contentment to foreboding. Seren slipped soundlessly closer to Arianrod's side, and even her mother looked troubled, staring at the back of the parchment as if she could see through it.

Finally, Arianrod looked up, meeting each of their eyes in turn. "It's a message from Gravis," she said. "Elgar's armies have come to Esthrades."

CHAPTER SEVENTY-ONE

Valyanrend

THEIR ARRIVAL, SO soon after Roger had learned of Seth's death, seemed like a dream at first. Morgan opened the tavern door with only her usual amount of care, gently enough to ensure it did not bang against the wall; fast on her heels, Braddock caught and shut it. And then there they were, standing in the middle of the room, dusty and sun-darkened, but otherwise the same.

"Well," Morgan said. "So you have been looking after the place. I don't know whether to be surprised or not." She set her pack down on the bar. "You're probably thinking this is a bit abrupt. But we figured any message we might send wouldn't arrive much faster than we would ourselves."

Roger finally found his voice. "Did you only just . . . what even *happened* to you?"

"More than you'll probably believe, swindler," Braddock said, lurching into a seat—not his usual one by the window, but a stool at the bar. "We'll tell you, but not without ale."

"I have my own stories to tell, and I'll wager they're harder to swallow than yours," Roger said. He reached for a couple of tankards, but Morgan stopped him with a hand on his arm.

"I'm back for good," she said. "That means I'm the only one allowed behind the bar again."

She really was back, wasn't she? Of all of the six of them, she and Roger had known each other the longest, since they were children in Sheath together. He had felt her absence the most keenly, yet now, in her presence, he half felt as if she'd never been gone at all.

Though neither of them was the sentimental sort, still he risked throwing an arm around her shoulders, pulling her against his side in a loose embrace. "It's good to see you."

She patted his back awkwardly. "It's *very* good to be back, though we have much to do. I suppose it was too much to hope for that the others would've beaten us here?"

The others. Roger's blood immediately chilled, and he knew Morgan must have felt him stiffen. "About that. There's . . . something you need to know. I have a letter, and you can . . . read it, or I can just tell you."

Morgan pulled back, studying his face. "It's nothing good, clearly. If you still have the letter, just give it to me. That might be easier for both of us."

She read it in silence. Roger could not have said if she made it all the way through, but at some point she must have learned all she needed to know, for she slammed it down on the bar and turned away, walking quickly across the room. From his stool, Braddock reached gingerly for the letter, handling it like a dead rat.

Roger had thought she simply needed space, but then he realized where she had gone: she was staring at the mantel, where Seth's old collection of trinkets still lay gathering dust. She ran shaking fingers over them: the colored glass, the oddly shaped stones, that fragment of expensive porcelain. The tears streaked down her face so silently Roger was shocked when he noticed them.

Braddock came up beside her, and gently placed his hands on her shoulders. She pulled him closer, burying her face in his chest, though she still made no sound louder than breathing. And Braddock held her not the way Roger had, but with no trace of awkwardness, stroking her hair as her body relaxed.

Roger felt like a fool for his obliviousness. "The two of you, eh? I suppose I ought to have seen that much earlier."

Braddock's only answer was a derisive snort, but Morgan looked up, wiping her face with the back of one hand. "Yes, you really ought to have. Now let me finish getting that ale. We still have much to speak about, but we can drink to Seth tonight, at least."

IT WAS THE same room, but it felt entirely different from the last time Marceline had been in it. There was no heaviness in the air, no longer even a lingering scent of medicine. Talia lay dozing on her cot, her face smooth and flushed with color. Her eyes fluttered lazily open as Marceline drew near. "You have good timing, monkey. Now that my stitches are out, I'm hopeful Naishe will finally ease her grip on me."

She was still careful when sitting up and swinging her legs over the side of the bed, but she lifted the edge of her shirt cheerfully, giving Marceline a full view of the scar. It looked clean and solid, but it was hardly subtle, a mottled red gash surrounded by some lesser scarring where the stitches had been.

Naishe patted it with the lightest of touches, testing the skin and watching Talia's face closely for any flinching. "I'm sorry," she said. "If my mother had been here, or I'd shown more responsibility in learning what she had to teach . . ."

"Naishe, don't be silly. If you only knew how happy I am to be alive! I feel as if I could run the length of the city."

"But you won't," Naishe said, with not the barest twitch of her lips to betray that she took it as a joke.

"Aye, healer. You're my leader now, too. I'm doubly bound to obey your orders."

Marceline hovered by Naishe's side, hefting the black stone in her hand. "I have to thank you, too, Naishe. I know it's no small thing for you to lend me this, even for a brief time."

"With all you've done for us, I can give you at least that much." She smiled. "All the same, let's keep it between us until you return it. Wouldn't want someone like Rask to say you can't be trusted."

Marceline rolled her eyes. "Does Rask still not trust me?"

"I said someone *like* Rask. I think Rask himself has spent enough time with you to know what you can and can't be trusted with."

"And what can't I be trusted with?" Marceline asked.

"Other people's pockets."

Well, that was true. "So what's causing him more pain, that hand of his or having to answer to you?"

Naishe laughed. "He's enduring both with surprising grace. His hand's never going to be beautiful, but the permanent damage should stay limited to just the look of it. His swordplay won't suffer, and that's what he cares about most."

Marceline tucked the stone into the crook of her left elbow, holding it tight against her side. "Well, he's one of yours now. They all are. You've got to take care of them, even the ones you don't like. Even the ones who don't like you."

"So I do," Naishe said. "So I will." She barely hesitated. "And you. You're one of mine, too."

Marceline made a sort of sputtering laugh. "What? Come on. You know what I am. There's no way you would have a thief for one of your own."

"It doesn't matter," Naishe said. "I've decided, and that's the end of it."

"Don't I get a say in this?"

"You don't." But then she seemed to relent. "You know I'm not saying you have to do anything. You don't have to join up with us, or help any more than you have already. Even if we never see each other again, we'll still be connected." She gave a little laugh, as sheepish as Marceline had ever seen her. "I suppose that's a long-winded way of saying something simple. Thank you, monkey."

She didn't even have to think about it. "Marceline."

"What?"

"That's my name. My real name. What, had you forgotten I had one?"

"Very nearly. The other suits you so well." She clasped Marceline's hand firmly. "Vanaishendi Kadife. A name for a name. Well met, at long last."

It was more formal than Marceline would have liked, but for Naishe it seemed exactly right. So she didn't fight it, just shook Naishe's hand and looked her in the eye—until she remembered something that nearly made her drop the stone. "Wait. Did you say *Kadife*?"

SHE APPROACHED THE Dragon's Head at precisely the same time as a stranger, a slender man in travel-stained clothes. He inclined his head politely and let her pass ahead of him, which meant he definitely wasn't from Sheath. Marceline went inside, but she kept one eye trained on him over her shoulder, and saw him pause in the doorway and make a quick hand gesture she didn't understand.

Morgan was behind the bar, Roger was sitting in front of it, and Braddock was back at his usual seat by the window, though it was still early. She was relieved that Nasser wasn't with them: she wanted a bit of time to practice pretending she didn't know exactly where his daughter was, or how grievously he'd underestimated her involvement with the resistance. Better to leave that problem for another day.

The stranger walked right up to the bar, with none of the nervousness of a newcomer. "Morgan Imrick, I believe?"

"Yes? You're looking for me in particular?"

"Indeed." He set a lacquered box, about the size of a loaf of bread, down on the bar between them. "This is for you. From our mutual friend, in recognition of your help."

Morgan ran a hand along the edge of the box, but didn't open it. "I can only think of one person you must mean, and it would be . . . surely impossible for him to deliver this so fast? I've only been home for a day."

The man smiled. "It is my duty to deliver things as quickly as the best horses can take me. He will be pleased to hear I have done so well. If that is your only objection, I cannot tarry here any further. Good day, Miss Imrick."

"And there's nothing I can get you before you leave?"

He bowed his head. "I appreciate the offer, but there is simply too much to do. I expect you will find the same."

As soon as the door shut behind him, the four of them clustered around the box, and Morgan took hold of the lid. "Let's see what he has for me this time."

There were only two items in the box, one far more interesting than the other: a sheet of parchment, and an ornate, slightly curved dagger in a black sheath with a golden hilt. Marceline was itching to touch it, but Morgan went for the parchment first, leaning over the box while she read so no one could touch the dagger without her leave.

"He sounds in good spirits, at least. His niece has appointed him the head of her army—and there *will* be war, he is certain of that. But he sends a warning . . ." She looked down at the dagger, and frowned deeply. *"We have both seen how catastrophically evil magic can be when used improperly, and I have dire news to that end. Your Elgar is a mage as well, of no less ability than Amali's daughter. We count a mage among our allies, and she assures me there is no doubt of it. She encountered his magic herself: a black stone, bearing a terrible curse.*

"There is no telling what Elgar may be capable of, so I give you the only protection I can. This dagger is forged of vardrath steel. When in close proximity to magic, or one who possesses it, the blade will feel cold. It will destroy any spell it touches, and while you bear it, you cannot be afflicted by magic directly. I know it is small, but it is all I could spare. May it aid you in the dangerous but necessary work you do."

Marceline knew, more or less, what had befallen Morgan and Braddock on their journey, because Roger had asked for assistance when explaining their own discoveries to his newly returned friends. But even if she had not, the news about Elgar would not have surprised her. She had already guessed—if she hadn't, she wouldn't be here now.

Morgan set the parchment down, and drew the dagger from its sheath. It glinted bright as mirrorglass, without a single scratch or flaw. Roger whistled. "The price you could get for that."

"It's far too valuable to sell," Morgan said. "If what he says is true, I'll be wearing it at all times."

Marceline cleared her throat. "There's something I need to talk to you about. Just Roger, I thought, but if you have that knife, you should be part of it, too."

Roger laughed. "That sounds ominous."

"It is. And we shouldn't talk about it here." She nodded at him. "You know where I want to go."

"I don't mind, if Morgan's all right with leaving the tavern for a bit. She can even test out that knife."

But the test did not go as they'd planned. She and Roger led Morgan and

Braddock down the tunnels to the statue chamber, but in response to Roger's repeated inquiries, Morgan only shook her head. "There's no coldness. The blade feels just the same."

Roger paced around the statues. "That can't be. I told you about that jewel I carried, the ruby. There was something in these tunnels that made it react so violently it shattered, and you're telling me there's *no* magic here?"

"I'm telling you the knife isn't cold," Morgan said. "How would I know any more than that?"

"Try this." Marceline reached into her pocket, and tossed the stone to Morgan. She held it in her left hand, and the knife in her right, slowly moving the blade closer to the stone. Finally, they touched, and Morgan flinched.

She didn't have to say anything: the cold air wafting off the blade showed white in the candlelight. It dissipated slowly, curling away like smoke.

"Huh," Morgan said. "Now it's starting to warm up again."

"Because you killed the magic inside the stone," Marceline said. "There's nothing there anymore."

"And how would you know that?" Roger demanded. "Where did you even get that stone, monkey?"

"The resistance stole it. Elgar was keeping it in a warehouse, within a wooden box. The warehouse was packed with soldiers—soldiers who tried to kill anyone who so much as got near the building. I saw that much with my own eyes. I nearly died myself, just for trying to watch what was happening." She pointed at it. "A black stone, with a terrible curse. That was Elgar's work, I'm sure of it. And Amerei said—" She broke off, giving in to a stab of self-consciousness, and addressed her next words to Morgan and Braddock. "Do you believe me about Amerei? Roger saw Tethantys and Asariel once, too, although they looked different to him. But I'm the only one who spoke to Amerei."

"I believe you," Morgan said, with a glance at the statues. "I thought Braddock and I were going to be the ones with the more unbelievable story, this time."

"Amerei said that I was right about Elgar's plans for the warehouse, that it was a trap," Marceline said. "And now I've finally figured out how he did it. The soldiers at the warehouse were so . . . bloodthirsty. They attacked everyone in the area, everyone they could see. I told you how they attacked me. Only one person said something different: Wren told me the soldiers went right past him. *Like I wasn't even there,* he said. It's the only reason he survived. Because he was carrying *this.*"

She reached into her pocket again, and brandished the little white stone. "I stole this off Elgar himself. It's white, like a flag of parley. And that's what it means. That's how it works."

The three of them just stared at her. "I'm not sure I understand," Morgan said.

"*You* don't? After everything you saw in Issamira? If magic can make people do things, surely it can make them kill. Single-mindedly, without fear or conscience. I don't know why it only affected Elgar's soldiers, but that's why he placed it in the warehouse, in a place he wanted the resistance to strike, with orders not to close it in the box until the right time. The soldiers were under its control from the moment the box was closed until Talia opened it again to steal the stone." She tossed the white stone into the air and caught it. "Of course he'd need to make sure he was protected. After I stole this, I'm sure he made himself another one, but he couldn't do anything about the one I'd taken. Thank the gods Wren forgot to give it back to me."

She took a deep breath; this was the most important part. "The resistance knew Elgar was running short on men. They figured he'd have to institute a draft, so they searched for evidence of it, to show the people what he planned. But they were never going to find it, because he doesn't *need* a draft. All he needs are live bodies, and that magic of his, and he'll have the army of his dreams. That means he doesn't have to care where he takes them from—whether they're loyal, whether they can be trusted. He can take them from the countries he's conquered—he can take them from—"

"Sheath," Roger said. "He'd be stupid not to. Clear his city of its undesirables and swell the ranks of his army at a stroke."

"Aye," Marceline said. "That's why I needed to tell you. That's what you have to understand. This is *our* fight now, because we don't have a choice. We have to help the resistance, or the Issamiri, or *anyone* else. We have to kill him. Because if we don't . . ."

She trailed off. Roger looked thunderstruck, but Morgan was perfectly calm. "I suppose this raises the stakes," she said, "but in a way it also makes things simpler. I was already determined to overthrow him, before I ever came back here. Honestly, I was hoping to secure your help, Roger, but I hadn't the faintest idea how to convince you. Now I find the monkey's done all the work for me."

"It wasn't just me," Marceline said. "It's what *they* want." She pointed at the statues. "Tethantys and Amerei spoke as if they were . . . rivals, of a sort, and perhaps that's true. But they both pushed me in the same direction. Amerei guided me to the attack—perhaps he even knew Talia would need my help, and without Talia we'd never have recovered the stone. And I solved Tethantys's riddle, too. The valuable thing Roger's not using—it isn't the books or the statues. It's the tunnels themselves. We could use them to get in or out of any place in the city, undetected."

"I see what you're saying," Roger said. "They've been pointing us toward figuring out Elgar's plans *and* a potential means of fighting back."

"Exactly. The four of us must be the only people who know enough to put this all together—the only ones in all of Lantistyne, probably, save Elgar himself. Even those nobles in Issamira can't have figured it out yet. Tethantys and Amerei must have wanted to make sure we'd piece it together. And it's possible they're not done with us yet."

Roger glared at the statue of Tethantys. "So they've taken a side, eh?"

"*Anyone* would side against Elgar if they knew the truth of what he was planning—even those who are loyal to him now." She sighed. "Though I doubt it'll be easy to convince them of what we know without exposing ourselves, and it's too risky to do that right away. We need a plan."

"Aye, we do," Morgan said. "But first we need to be sure we're all in agreement." She held out the knife. "I already had every intention of staking my life on this, but I'll swear it now, in front of all of you. I'll see Elgar dead, or die myself in the attempt."

"And I'll do no less," Braddock said, putting his hand over hers.

"I swear." Marceline slapped her hand down on the pile. "To protect Sheath. To protect everyone from him."

As one, they looked to Roger. He heaved a deep sigh, shoving his hands in his pockets. "You don't have to worry about me. I understand the stakes here. This isn't something I can talk my way out of. I can either stand . . . or fall."

"You might be able to run, if you left now," Braddock said, with a little smirk. "Across the sea might be far enough."

Roger snorted. "Fuck that. You think I'm going to let him steal a whole city from me? A whole continent? We don't know enough to say whether there's a limit to the number of people he can control, but we ought to assume there isn't. To go that far . . . to rob so many people of their very selves . . . You're right, Marceline. Even if I were a god, I'd still be furious with him."

"So we can count on you?" Morgan asked.

"Aye, under one condition. I'm the best schemer of the four of us, so leave that part to me. We're in a better position than you might think. We have the ability to get anywhere we need to be unseen, and the ability to destroy anything he uses magic to build. I'm sure Marceline's resistance friends will want to help, and your nobleman. And Elgar doesn't know that we know, so we've got to be careful about when and how we let him find out." Marceline knew that look; his mind had already leaped ahead, building one of those elegant plans that were the envy of every swindler in Sheath. He touched his hand to theirs, on top of the dagger. "All right. Let's kill the bastard."

About the Author

ISABELLE STEIGER was born in the city and grew up in the woods. She received her first notebook when she was eight, and she's been filling them up ever since. She lives in New York.